I0819901

The Arthuriad

Volumes 1-3

Zane Newitt

This title is intended for the enjoyment of adults, and is not recommended for children due to the mature content it contains. This book is intended to entertain the reader, and not to offend or upset in any way whatsoever. The reader should be aware that this book contains adult content.

This book is meant to be educational, informative and entertaining. Although the author and publisher have made every effort to ensure that the information in this book was correct at the time of publication, the author and publisher do not assume and hereby disclaim any liability to any party for loss, damage or disruption caused by errors or omissions, whether such errors or omissions result from negligence, accident or any other cause.

First published 2020
by Rowanvale Books Ltd
The Gate
Keppoch Street
Roath
Cardiff
CF24 3JW
www.rowanvalebooks.com

A CIP catalogue record for this book is available from the British Library.
ISBN: 978-1-912655-56-4

THE ARTHURIAD VOLUME ONE

THE MYSTERY OF

Merlin

At the end
Priests and Druids
alike wanted him dead

Find out why...

ZANE NEWITT

Morgana, Morgana, M… … …

'The shiny silver of armor. The errand of mounted knights. The mysteries of Britain. The famous Wizard and the Boy-King. The Sword and the Cup. The romance and ideal of Camelot. The betrayal of a friend. The Grail Quest... All seduction veiled in grandeur – if not grounded in the word of truth. History and lore's most powerful lure to drag some, unwitting, into an old heresy dedicated to the premise that Jesus Christ is not God and in its aim the preparation of a watered down and inclusive world for a Second Messiah which is called Anti-Christ.'

Dr. Zane Newitt
Winter, 2016

PROLOGUE I
68 AD

Paul, the prisoner of the Lord and the apostle to whom was committed the simple good news of Christ and the dispensing of the Grace of God, desired greatly to journey to Britain: to preach unto the heathen and to the dispersed children of Israel who rejected the message of Peter during his administration (for, by divine accord and binding agreement, Paul could go to unbelieving Jews who were uncircumcised in heart and mind as well as to the Gentiles).

While yet under house arrest in the regal Palace Britannia, the Apostle grew to greatly love the Silures, the royal clan of the Britons who were fellow political prisoners of Rome.

King Caradoc, comely Eurgain, pious Linus and other Britons had become his dear brothers and sisters in the Lord; their conversation so Godly, in nationalism zealous, in wit fiery, and in kindness, of no equal. Paul yearned to see their homeland for reasons both emotional and theological, wanting to see the mettle of the nation who had whipped Caesar and who would not yield to the imperialism of Rome.

The bloodlines that constitute the Britons,

specifically the great Royal Clans of the Cymru and Lloegyr, are the resultant mixture of two major migrations; firstly, of Albyne, the daughter of Diocletian, from the Near East; and secondly of Brutus of Troy, after whom the Isles are most commonly named.

Add a sprinkling of Hebrews fleeing to both the Continent and the Islands during the second dispersion, and also as a result of Paul's terror upon the Messianic followers when he was yet Saul, and indeed the stock of Britain was a unique assortment.

A visit was important to him beyond cultural curiosity (for Paul was a man of letters and of culture, knowing how he ought to interact with Men from all parts of the known world). The divergent origins had produced dangerous doctrinal predispositions that greatly worried Paul.

The original Jewish immigrants did not bring the truth of the God of Abraham, Isaac and Jacob. Instead they were idolaters and progenitors of dark doctrines passed infectiously from their Babylonian and Assyrian captors. For their part, the British Isles became awash with the errors of dualism, relic worship, veneration of tradition, emanationism, angel worship and Gnosticism. The Jewish colonies had much stained their spiritual identity with devilish compromise and deep betrayal of their Most High God through the blending of truth and error, which is iniquity. They intermarried with the local tribes and, through intrigue and political maneuvering, became, over time, the wise men. In dress, identical to the native druids; in manner of life, foreign to all that is called good.

Paul had dealt with the Traditions of the

Fathers and their corrupt priesthood structure. He oft battled and overcame the tendencies towards legalism and reversion to the Law by his own countrymen. James, the brother of the Lord, had ever been his adversary, calling Paul a liar, and wicked, at every turn.

Moreover, Paul had masterfully deconstructed the empty conclusions of fatalism and nihilism, the folly of philosophers, effectually presenting the hope of the resurrection to atheists, Neo-Platonists and the pantheists of Greece. He possessed the ability to meet foe and friend alike on a common ground from which to share the truth of God's existence, power and love, even to those who exalted human intellect above all and who worshipped and adored the creature in the stead of the Creator.

To the aged Apostle, those campaigns seemed – at this he both laughed and sighed within – immeasurably less taxing than overcoming the superstition, idolatry, sincere confusion (for Peter's message was ministered to remnants of his little flock in the Isles in the Sea during Boadicea's war. Thus, Paul would take great caution to only visit those for purposes of fellowship, refusing to build upon another's foundation lest the saints increase in disappointment and confusion about the delay of their promised Kingdom), and sacred wisdom possessed by the Britons.

When thinking of the task at hand, Paul quickly reminded himself that it was the word of truth that did the saving – that he didn't need to help the Gospel, only to boldly preach it.

Years before his imprisonment and long before he had written to those in Rome, he had deployed his friend Aristobulus to the British Isles to teach the Pauline Mysteries. Now, at last, during his final season of liberty, Paul himself went to the British Isles.

Landing first upon the Isle of Wight, he then made the mainland, receiving great reception at the hill which is called Ludgate (each gate of the small port city of Londinium bore the name of a warrior, king or hero of great fame).

The Tribes of Lloegyr met and hosted Paul for a space of three months until, finally, thirty-five years after the Passion of the Lord Jesus Christ, Paul ventured to Cymru. There he found, amongst wondrous valleys, rolling hills and shades of green his eyes had never seen, the kingdom of his friends, the Silures.

Paul would even half-jest that Cymru was more beautiful than the third heaven, and Paul had now seen both.

Assembled within the crowded boat-shaped circle hewn into the earth, roofed only by the stars of heaven, at the place called Llaniltud, Paul preached unto the druids (of which there are two primary and several minor divergent sects), and unto the Kingdom Saints taught by Peter.

Mary, the Mother of the Lord, with her company, had reportedly stayed in Gaul for a time, then exiled herself on a tiny island to the west of the Northern Isle called Ynys Mon, fearing that men would swear by her. However, Anna and many who had been with the man who provided his tomb for the Savior were amongst those who came to hear Paul.

Doing all in his might, he labored to fill up that which they were lacking.

Paul preached Jesus Christ according to the revelation of the Mystery which was hidden in God since before the foundation of the world. Within its tenets were divided out those things which belonged to Israel versus those unique blessings and positions belonging to the heavenly body; under grace Christ became Man's sin and imputed His righteousness unto all Men, especially to those that believed, through the Cross. Man's flesh, being dead, therefore, could do nothing to please God. Thus was vanished the necessity of works. There was no tithing system for profiting, no ritual to be administered by priests, no levers of guilt and reward, only the simplicity of Christ reconciling the world unto Himself and the free offer of salvation on the merits of His shed blood.

Those with a Jewish ancestry rejected him with audible and violent rumblings, each and every one. The druids listened with respectful contemplation as they do to all men, and then informed Paul: "Little Pause," as the druids translated his Greek name, "we know already the secrets of the One True God."

To conclude his preaching, Paul warned against misappropriating the kingdom promises and principles that belonged to Israel (to her times past and to a time yet to come), and against reading Paul's good news back into the message of Peter and the Eleven. Paul focused on the 'but now' of human history where God was erecting a heavenly body with spiritual blessings.

Other than the kinsmen of the Silure and Princess Eurgain (who was also present), the Apostle's message was rejected by all save one druid, a prince from the area of what history would call later call the Vale of Glamorgan.

Adjusting his white robe to cover the midnight-blue enamel-scaled breastplate so that it wouldn't bruise the old Apostle, he embraced Paul heartedly. The trees surrounding the circle funneled and intensified the clamor and debate, the wrangling. Saying nothing (for the embrace said what was required) save "so, then, faith cometh by hearing", the druid hooded his robe, attempting to leave the starlit assembly.

Victory is not measured by numbers of converts, but by the quality of each convert and Paul knew that just one man could turn the world upside down – for good, or for ill. Paul used elbows and dodges to stop the druid ere he was fully outside the Cor.

Thanking the armored warrior-priest, Paul gifted him fourteen single-page letters, rolled and bound beautifully with camel leather and metallic buckles. The 'book', Paul fastened on the druid's body using the straps of his own robe. With only minor protestations at the intrusion the druid began to query Paul, but the Apostle placed a finger to his lips, staying his voice.

"In these letters are words that bring eternal life. Thirteen are to you and one is for you. Study." And now it was Paul who quickly left the druid's side and returned to the center of the wooded meeting place.

Understanding the great potential for good, and for evil, of these coveted Isles just beyond the outstretched fingertips of Rome, as his last act before leaving Britain, Paul reached out to Anna, cousin of Mary, and begged the Cup that she bore.

Paul sized up the man who was of Anna's company: a kinsman of the Lord who bore a resemblance to the Savior, yet with dishonest eyes. Paul did not like this man. Returning to Anna, he looked up at her, imploring: "They will worship the Grail at the expense of the One whose blood it bore. And there is no salvation in it to save them in their day of trouble."

The Jewess declined. "We will see that it remains guarded and, if meet, we shall hide it as we have the Lady and the coffin of the Law of Moses."

"Nay. Give me the Cup that I might destroy it."

"Nay," said Anna.

Eurgain raised her voice in an effort to support and help Paul but was put down swiftly.

"Nay," said Anna.

PROLOGUE II
484 AD

Regal, red and raging, the seven-tailed dragon orbited over the Blessed Isles, announcing his dominion o'er the white heaven above and the green earth below.

The head of the winged serpent was constant in flight, position unchanging. His seven tails, or rather one tail with seven spikes, moved in a chaotic dance, dragging behind and beneath the head, crackling in and out of the low cloud cover and making Christ-Mass morning a flash of yellows and reds, creating brightness as if there were two suns.

Merlin knew the stars, the luminaries, and their courses of traffic. His own little dwelling place, near a chapel outside the great mountain fortress of Caer Caradoc, provided a special high place for observation. Merlin cared for his ailing, elderly mother, with whom he dwelled, and had made haste early in the morning to ensure that she was well so he could spend the sum of the day posted near a large standing stone, just up the mountain from their home, and study the red serpent's path.

Leaning back, arms folded, head cocked to

the right, the robed druid said within himself: *A vision of perfection save the tail, which doth worry me.*

Meanwhile, another wonderful dragon was far too busy looking down to look up.

King Meurig, who was the Senior King, the Uther Pendragon, Protector of the Tribes and Royal Clans of the Cymru, and his young bride, Queen Onbrawst (a powerful woman, always of a soft and temperate disposition but one not to be crossed by scheming or dishonesty), were about to be delivered of a precious gift: their first son.

Kings held several plenary courts, manors and fortresses from which they managed their administrative, military, legal and residential responsibilities of governance. Often their queens would live only in the residential manors, and sometimes alone, receiving their husbands to bed but periodically. However, this was at the discretion of the couple and there was no law or custom demanding the same.

With relative quiet (for Saxon invasions were rare in winter), other than the shared trauma and turmoil of a first pregnancy, they had spent most of the winter in their residential mansion in the South East of Cymru. The men of the Cymru loved their wives and, from beggar of lowest station to king of the purest royal lineage, the great majority of couples were friends, partners and protectors of their spouses; the union was considered sacred.

The couple mutually enjoyed the manor, as it had family ties for Onbrawst and was very near to where Meurig had received his schooling as a boy.

The mansion home was near the coast but securely surrounded by a small ring of fortress watchtowers that could, through the sparking of a simple fire, send an alarm through a spiderweb of interlocking towers in a matter of seconds. Merlin had designed this and many other ringed fortress 'webs' that, like interlocking wheels, provided maximum protection with minimum investment of the Cymry's most valuable resource: its men.

From the most ancient times the place had been called Caer Bovum, which is "the Fortress of the Bull". The palace's position and name, like many of the mysteries of the druids, had multiple meanings. Looking down from the ceiling of heaven, Caer Bovum aligned identically with the most prominent star within the constellation Taurus.

Unfamiliar or apathetic to this fact, to King Meurig and Queen Onbrawst it was simply their favorite place of dwelling; romantic, near the sea, full of memories and love.

"What troubles you, my son?"

***

Even with Merlin sitting poorly postured against the monolith, he towered above his mother, standing before him, offering him a cider and a concerned, maternal reckoning.

"You should be resting." Merlin's smile blended great respect with a little grumble of interruption. But he welcomed the scrumpy sup. "I can follow its course, can tell with great certainty that this great portent will traverse far to the East, turn on itself and return once more to our land. I believe I can even predict the timing of its return."

"One more time we shall have such a visitor, brighter than the noonday sun! That is joyous, my jeweled prince! Why such pause?"

"In the dragon's grandeur, dancing along

heavenly skies, no looking-glass known to man, nor any means of divination, of science or observation, can know the detailed form of his ethereal body. We can see it flying far, far up there." Merlin drew its path with his left hand upon a firmament canvas of nothing. "Especially on clear winter nights and on mornings when the mists recoil. But now that it is within the heavens where the birds fly, this dragon's tail has at least one broken spike and should it prick the earth below, I know not what it would do to creaturekind and land alike; nor can I allow myself to imagine thusly. The position of the dragon's head is perfect and will herald the birth of our future High King. Pray that the tail touches not the earth."

Merlin was a man who taught and spake mostly by riddles, and his candor and plainness of speech worried his mother. Due to his sober expression, she too now hoped that Merlin's foretold dragon would light up the Christ-Mass sky, but then be quickly away safely to its starry home.

Morning became midday and the comet passed safely over the kingdoms of Western Britain, to great celebration of Merlin's prophecy. However, tragically, one small splinter of the comet's tail did fall out of formation and touch down just to the east of the center of the Isle in the kingdom called Lloegyr (tribes and clans who were of the same blood as the Cymry).

Where the comet touched, men melted within themselves and all life died, the land becoming at once a great wasteland. Only a small share of the Island was affected. The spike of the dragon's tail singed a border between east and west. For tribes and small kingdoms within the shadow of the tail's touch, a pestilence and disease took first the virility of the men and livestock, followed by their lives.

Merlin saw only a small mushroom of dust and yellow-hued clouding far to the east. Far and away from the kingdom he served, he hoped against hope that none perished. When the pomp of Meurig's firstborn's entrance into the world of Men had abated, Merlin would go and investigate and warn his people of what might happen if the tail of the dragon made direct impact with the kingdom of the Silures on its next visitation, which Merlin knew to be fifty and three years from the day of his first visit.

And thus, on the day of the Christ-Mass, under the banner of a Red Dragon, under the Sign of the Bull, was born King Arthur, the Bear of Britain.

PROLOGUE III
An Ancient Rite

"My cock works fine, My Heart, I just can't fight anymore." Meurig, trying to suppress panic, eyes begging for confirmation of worth, clasped Queen Onbrawst's fingers.

It is a timeless tactic, primal and dark, practiced by all nations and tribes save the Cymry: to pierce the king or an important chieftain through his loins with a spear, arrow or sword poisoned with a special concoction that destroys his virility; with his virility the perceived fertility of the land; and with the perceived fertility of the land, his crown. And, should a drought follow, even his life.

Even with the Saviour come four hundred and ninety-eight years ago now, the Tribes and Clans held fast to this custom, fully believing that yield and harvest were connected to he who was head of the Dragons (High King). The same practice applied for he who held the Spear of Lugh in Eire.

A raid near the Northern borderlands in Gwynedd (far from the king's palace in Gwent) had escalated the need for Meurig's personal presence. It was alleged that one of the Sons of Cunedda (the Royal Clans of the North of Cymru) was under suspicion for treacherously giving the Saxon raiders passage, in exchange for future conquered land in the South. The metallic anxiety of civil war was in the air, heightened by burgeoning raids.

Whether by chance or by design, a young Saxon found the king's thigh before any investigation amongst his own countrymen could occur.

A Saxon chief and Witan (member of the loose Germanic Confederation's High Council) called Hortwulf had slain Meurig's father, King Tewdrig, also during a raid, with a fortuitous spear. Now the horde seemed on the verge of celebrating the killing of a second Pendragon.

It was not to be so; Meurig lived.

Bloodied and soiled as if he were a spring lamb baptized in shepherd's dye, the midnight-blue under-tunic of the proud king was now black and thick with his own blood.

Returning to Caer Bovum at last, to his great bed with Onbrawst kneeling by and cradling his head with her shoulders while giving him both hands, the king managed to cough up familiar words often heard when emergencies and distresses were escalated.

"Bring me the Merlin."

Merlin, with two healers, began to address the poisoned wound.

"You are not here for nursing."

"No?" The towering druid stood and yielded, yet motioned for the women to continue their work.

"No, not for nursing, for politics." The king coughed a broken expulsion from the deepest part of his lungs. "It is early spring and I am felled. The people will want a sacral, but the young Bear is only fourteen. He is too young."

"Do you think the crops rise and fall with your loins, my lord?"

Meurig mustered a laugh, always puzzled at Merlin's moments of sacrilege against any and all faiths (but 'twas the humor that accompanies respect, not disdain).

"I don't know, but the people believe so."

"Too long have we labored to unite the south with you two," Merlin started, winking at Onbrawst. Their marriage was strategically ingenious. It enjoined the kingdom of Gwent with the lands of Gwrgan Fawr, the lord of Ergyn. This fused together the great Royal Clans of the Silures, the Island's most powerful tribe.

One people under one future king under one purpose.

Kingdom matchmaking aside, Meurig and Onbrawst were no political pawns. Rather, the people enjoyed the glow and shine of living in a country where their leaders were actually and passionately in love.

"Your son has experienced a season of fostering in the North with Cai, has had three winters here in Llaniltud and has already forged key relationships in Nevern in the West, in Powys and in the Midlands. At this moment, he is dazzling friend and foe on the field of battle in Little Britain, aiding our kin and becoming a young man of renown. He is well embraced by all of the Britons. The spark in that boy is brighter than the comet that hailed his birth! The crown must not pass to an uncle, nephew or cousin. Nor can we split the High Kingship into king and wledig. No. The wave of war coming to these Isles demands a Pendragon, even if he is but fourteen, to lift and engage the spirit of the nation."

Merlin sent the healers away and drew closer.

"As you are Christian, you may consider retirement as did your father Tewdrig, in the stead of the Sacral Rites." Merlin was a hard man in matters of military strategy, soft and conciliatory as a friend. "I am so sorry that you will not officially wield sword and spear again, my friend. But we need you. We need your wisdom and your council and your love. Retirement, and not sacrifice, my lord."

Meurig now felt the rush of an involuntary stream of tears run at once from his left eye. He blinked repeatedly. He preferred death in battle to the hermitage he faced; but in the end he concurred with the druid's words.

Three days later King Meurig, under his own power, was able to stand a little and move around of his own accord. The high thigh wound had severed many nerves where the leg attached to his pubis bone. This caused his weight to shift to his knee and calf on the wounded side, resulting in a low, awkward limp.

Clumsily, he made his way to a dining hall where he sat for a cider with Merlin.

The conversation regarding his office and successor resumed, less emotional and more head-driven after three days of rest and healing.

"He is so young. How will they accept him?"

"It is spring." Merlin paused and posited his face for an uncomfortably intrusive query. "Did your boy's eyes and heart fall upon any damsel whilst at school?"

"Would a teenaged boy tell his parents of schoolyard love, Lord Merlin?" Onbrawst was always inserting wisdom and wit - a truly timeless queen, and mother.

"He is a virgin then?" Merlin's cheeks crimsoned at the asking.

"What does that have to do with a young man's eyes or heart?" Meurig bellowed with laughter. "Rather to worry about his loins!"

That Meurig could muse about what was now an unmentionable subject informed the druid that either the poison in the king's male parts had failed or that he had come to terms with it. Either way, Merlin reckoned Meurig to be a remarkable man.

"Stop, you. And he is surely pure, but don't speak of it again!" scolded Onbrawst. Upon further contemplation, she added: "Well, he had puppy-eyes over some dark little thing for a while. He and that treetop-tall whelp from Gwynedd whispered about her more than a few times." Onbrawst's humor, which matched her husband's, returned. "Meurig and I used to think it odd that he doted on one that looked so much like his sister."

Merlin consumed that information. He then repeated, "It is spring. And this is my recommendation." The druid requested more drink, which he consumed in two swallows. "There will be no sacral rites. You will offer your sword to the Llyn Fawr, and your kingship will die."

Words hard to utter.

"But the young Bear will rise in your death of retirement. He will be the primary actor in the spring rites, he will hunt the White Stag to show his virility and strength, and then he will join his spirit with the land through the Sacred Rite." Merlin paused to interpret the expressions of the boy's parents.

Queen Onbrawst's visage was as that of any parent confronted with the thought of their child having intercourse. That it would be in a ritualistic context layered shame atop shock. Merlin wanted to provide words of comfort, but Meurig's unspoken gestures made it clear that the effort would be vain and that he should just press on with the information. "Get on with it, wizard" might have been said, or at least heard, by the Merlin.

"The rites will appease our countrymen, who yet cleave to the old gods while we continue our gestation as a Christian nation. If Arthur returns from Brittany now, this can all be done in perfect coordination with both the rites of spring and with the Pentecost celebrations, letting him come onto the scene with pomp and ceremony to bring joy to men of both faiths.

"That your boy, the Bear, was born on Christmas day and announced by a heavenly messenger will satisfy the sign of his coming. Add to it the timing of his ascent and they will in no way refuse him on account of his youth."

Meurig agreed, but still doubted. "Will this ritual alone convince men that they should have a boy-king, Merlin?"

"It will go far, but not of itself."

"What more?" asked Onbrawst.

Merlin's thoughts again returned to the sad deeds soon at hand relative to his friend's abdication of crown and glory. He placed a comforting hand upon the king's forearm.

"What more? A sword. You have a sword to return to the waters and I have a sword to go and raise from the same, my lord," said Merlin.

***

Meurig first went up to Llyn Fawr. He wore simple beige clothing with just two or three golden torques looped round his arms and a tight leather band about his neck. Scarred but handsome; humble.

The injured Pendragon struggled to maneuver around but managed at last several paces into the lake. The cold still waters were now disturbed, splashing upon his wool tunic in protest.

Meurig winced when the short waves lapped over his injury; the war wound was ablaze in returned protest. The water and the wound worked in concert to afflict the day, but he appreciated the pain as it reminded him of the validity of his purpose. He could not defeat the coming horde; the people could not place their trust in a lame king. Focusing hard, he prepared himself.

Then he saw her.

A nearby swan-shaped barge undulated gently, docile and lazy upon the lake. Next to it was a platform that led deep down to a mysterious cavern beneath the water. Turtles circled the barge and diverse birds made symphony above.

Accompanied by percussion and strings played not by the hands of men, the Lady of the Lake rose from the waters.

Hair as late summer straw, bound with golden crown plated with hundreds of diamond-beaded threads. In blinding brilliance, she shone from the diamonds kissing the face of the water and the diamonds glistening in alternating notes within her headpiece. Add to this the rays of sun drawn to her dress and the Lady was as a luminary being, a star resting upon the center of the lake.

Through the light, the drawn-back locks revealed a long neck, freckled cheeks and a pointed, simple nose resting upon thin upper and thicker lower lips. Her eyes were soft, light blue, and sparkling.

She wore white-scaled armor made of a light, unknown material that seemed like leather but with some metal composition. Around the armor flowed a silky white garment with pillowed sleeves and hand-pieces of samite.

Her declaration was as though the waters themselves were sing-speaking, projected towards the king by the acutely directed winds.

"Paramount King Meurig. Greeting. You are a great king, a dear friend, an encouraging and selfless father and, above all things, you love your wife as you love yourself. The Clans, Tribes, Cantrefs, Kingdoms and Nation of Cymru give you our deepest thanksgiving.

"I accept your return of the agency of your power and throne to the source of all life under God's creation. From the waters first He called forth life and to the waters your life now returns. This in an honorable rite. May the Lord of heaven and our great goddess guide and succor your next life cycle. Meurig, cast me your sword."

Meurig's sword was resting upon both palms. He looked at the shaft that had been his ever companion throughout a generation of war and unavoidable bloodshed. It was not customary for him to speak during this ceremony, for the dead ought not to speak. The hilt he clasped hard with his left hand and he slung the blade high, arcing end over end.

The Lady of Llyn Fawr the sword did catch, and she retreated into the lake, seamlessly, leaving only the barge, and silence.

Meurig was officially abdicated, retired as High King of the Britons.

Next, a short time later, the Merlin of Britain

visited the same location. While he was at Llyn Fawr seeking a far more unique weapon from the one who possessed the authority to give and to repossess it, he was wholly unaware of the details and arrangement for the spring rites. And, most acutely, who would be selected to represent the Land and the Moon as Arthur's counterpart in the ceremony.

A sixteen-year-old, petite, with raven's hair and the eyes of a Persian cat, was chosen. Local whispers declared her possessed at times or rather having some mysterious accord with a goddess, or even with the primal witch. Though promised to Llew son of Cynfarch, she was in her office for this deed anon and she was indeed a virgin. And that innocence she would give as a willing actor in the theatre of sacred fornication to validate a too-young king; for she, though yet sixteen, was a radical patriot.

And, though of royal blood, never at any of the three courts but ever at Llyn Fawr, elsewise on Ynys Mon, or tending the orchards in the Isle of Apples.

Some say she was only fostered by mortals.

Some say she was of the Fae...

CHAPTER 1
A Typical Raid

The brave warriors of the Trinovates were in pursuit of German raiders, following them from the eastern shores north into Iceni territory.

It was the Lord's Day and the village was unprepared, caught unawares. Though they did give chase well, the lay army forgot to leave a rear-guard band in position for a second wave. The Saxon diversion worked and the village was left defenseless.

A woman's station in military matters was as diverse and numbered as the Tribes. In several Tribes they were raised to fight alongside the men and were equally lethal in combat. In others, they assumed more domestic roles. In all Tribes, women owned property, enjoyed rights of inheritance and were active in commerce and trade.

In this particular Tribe, the men were giving chase and the women were very brave but simply were not fighters; neither were the elderly, nor the children.

A flat platform boat kissed and hissed and crackled against the pebbly shore.

And then another; a third and a fourth.

A girl of twelve, holding a straw-made doll

wrapped in green plaid wool of remarkable skill and craftsmanship, didn't want to look up at the pungent heap of tar- and dung-smeared muscles with hair arching over her. The Saxon's double-headed ax beneath her chin forced their eyes to meet.

His dirty fingernails raked flesh with garment as he tore her clothes, and then tore her. Blood and innocence were spilled right there on the pebbles, with only seagulls to scream protest. Her brother came sprinting to her aid, ghostly white, now the witness of things none so young, or old, or any person at all, ought to see.

That invaders take time mid-battle to rape and violate is but befuddling on the surface. In truth, it makes every sense. For what is invasion but the imposition of will?

Invasion is rape, in every way.

To mock the boy's horror the Saxon twisted the boy's arm, turned him over a felled dead tree along the beach, yanked his trousers about his ankles, bent him over, and punished him without mercy from behind. The boy screamed a deathly rattle, but the scream only encouraged more. And yet his young sister, during her identical torture, had given not a sound. That the boy rewarded the villain with his screams whilst the girl had not infuriated him.

She just lay upon an elbow on her side, with a glazed, dead look in eyes that should have been alight with life.

Seeing the object of her torture, covered with blood (while two hundred more invaders were sprinting and many others engaged in like deviancy), at her eye-level, the distant eyes at once regenerated. With the bravery of her glorious ancestor Buddug, or Boudica, the freshly violated twelve-year-old girl swung at it with a large branch. The blow to his groin dropped the Saxon; the siblings stood and rallied, sprinting for the village.

But too soon, the Saxon rallied also.

Much faster than the children, he caught their stride quickly and shoved them both down violently, but three feet from the village chapel door. A simple circular structure with a modest cruciform hewn through the eastern wall, the humble wooden building was warm, friendly, welcoming and nearly salvation for the ruined children.

Locked in their own private war, the freckled siblings did not notice that the chapel was ablaze from the hinder side and that women and old men were being butchered sloppily. There was no precision in the killings, only malice and barbarism.

The brave girl stood again, blood and urine glazing and painting her naked thighs.

"You cannot kill us!" She screamed with authority at the Saxon until her voice was nearly gone.

He understood none of these things. Her Brythonic language was an affront, profane ringing in his Germanic ears.

"You cannot kill us," she rasped. "We are not soldiers. Our elders teach that soldiers only kill other soldiers. You cannot kill us."

Whether he deduced some of her meaning, and her impugnation of his cowardice, or whether he simply grew tired of her screaming, he thought to stop her tongue by removing her brother's.

The grimy man with poorly-made black leather armor jerked the wailing boy up by his hair and clasped his jaw so tightly that the lad had no other choice but to open it; teeth were cracking and falling from the side of his mouth, causing the tortured boy to bleed, now from both ends. Gasping, his tongue waggled out.

The Saxon swiftly dropped his axe and drew a dagger and cut, nay, sawed the boy's tongue off; then he made a mechanical turn down and to the left, showing the trophy to the resilient heroine. Now tears came as she looked upon her brother, but she remained brave to the end. She arched her back and found the black eyes of the Boar, whispering with the residue of her voice.

"In the West Country, far from here, lives a great king. Some day, be it today or ten years from today, he will send all of you bad men home, or into the ground. He will avenge us. He will save our people!" She found one more scream within her mighty and shattered soul. *"King Arthur!"*

The Saxon knew this name, as did any living at the time, in any language. The double-headed axe cleaved her forehead, leaving a red-haired and green-ribboned scalp upon the ground. The brute yanked the green ribbon from the lifeless locks it complemented, a trophy of his conquest and power-mad perversion.

In addition to murder of the defenseless, the Saxons raped old women and children, and committed sins against nature with horses and sheep.

The party of male warriors later returned from what they believed to be a successful expulsion and small skirmish to a village charred black, bodies stacked and burned. Some had been burned alive and then thrown into a nearby pond, for the invaders to watch the screams of "hot then cold". Those bodies floated, bubbled skin and eyeballs separating from the corpses.

To be raided on the eastern shores of Britain, even now giving way to the phrase "Saxon Shores", was not a light matter, nor a political matter, nor a controversy. It was cancer, an open and overt cancer seeking to devour and remove the existence of a People Group from the earth, forever.

And although it was only in the early years of the Saxon Wars, it was already moving west.

CHAPTER 2
The Battle of Mynydd Baedan and Waiting

Several years, eleven major battles and over sixty minor clashes later, a brisk December dusk found the Round Table Knight selected by lot for the aridity of waiting alongside his king.

And waiting yet more.

The strategy demanded waiting.

Finally breaking the long silence, seeking to ease the moment with his best friend, he said: "What chance has a boar versus a bloodhound and a bear made of iron?"

Arthur gave no answer.

The Iron Bear above, the Bloodhound Prince below.

Merlin was right; even the ignorant heart of the Saxon can be crippled through the use of terror. Merlin was also absent.

The mighty King Arthur's horse, a mare called Llamrei, jostled restlessly beneath him, sensing the uneasy rhythm of her master unsuccessfully laboring to stare stoically at the mound called Baedan.

Arthur's thoughts flinched, even if his face did not betray it. The terror inflicted, the thrashing of enemies along trails and in gullies in the valley of Maesteg that opened up below Baedan hill, the escalating brass of screams as hungry men with foreign tongues died within earshot did not give the just king pleasure. But he yearned for when it was finished; it would give the nation peace.

The three nations of Germania were finally come, setting aside intrigue, false witness and the cowardice of raiding to face him in his very own lands as upright men, as an upright army. Should these three hundred thousand invaders have calculated that he Ravens from the North would flank and funnel them through a field of slaughter… That Maelgwn and his famous blood-soaked Hosts would use unconventional tactics to establish a rear-guard position that forced the invader to either ascend Baedan Hill on foot to face a heavily clad, well-fed, professional equestrian army led by Arthur, or instead face the Bloodhound Prince in the valley below, or lastly, hold their ground and starve… Should they have known of this triad of doom masked as choice, they would have greatly preferred the death of the cruel winter and famine plaguing their homeland and simply stayed home.

The Western Sea feeds the heads of three great rivers that converge near the battle site. The winds press upon the confluence, regularly producing a thick and ethereal mist, as it did this day, creating a shadowy canopy over the whole of the valley. Arthur and his knights had to peer down the slope, and could see only shadows, and glimpses of blackened snow below.

The screams of the Saxons made many of the mounted cavalry atop the hill retch. Others were moved to forget the discipline of a Cymry warrior. Bloodlust overcame them, and these abandoned the ranks and joined the battle below.

As Merlin had mentored Arthur on the power of both words and song, the king countered the influence of the death cries with melodic bardic songs and hymns of victory, attempting, through polarity, to neutralize the field. Moreover, the leadership of Ammwn Ddu, Owain the Raven, and Arthur's young son, Llacheu, held tight the line of restless warriors.

The strategy required that they remain still, and still they remained.

This was no easy feat. The full complement of the British confederacy numbered twenty-four groups of three thousand. They were positioned throughout the interlocking wheels of fortresses that sprawled like a great tent over the whole of the seven cantrefs of Glamorgan and several thousand warriors lined the top of Baedan in groups three lines deep.

"Hold!" was bellowed through the mist. Horses expelled their breath in concert, and here and there one complained with a whinny. If a Saxon raised his dreary eyes above the shelf of mist, he would see a quilt of wonderfully colored killing instruments, each defined first by their royal clan and secondly their tribe.

The Silures, the Royal Clan of the South East, maintained with careful and studious pride the traditions of their ancestors and donned an efficient armor, gilded in midnight-blue enamel, designed for speed, defense, and killing while mounted. Upon their shields were the double chevrons. The Northern tribes wore black like ravens, or black and red, had a single chevron and were less armored than their kinsmen from the South.

A marriage by Queen Marchel, aunt to Arthur,

to an Irish king called Coronac had ended Irish raiding and produced a sub-kingdom in the South through Marchel's son, Brychan. This brought Arthur's Irish allies to Baedan, whose warriors dressed in speckled green.

King Hoel from Brittany, familial allies with the Silures for generations, carried a brilliant blue plaid, honoring their heritage from the Silures.

Banners, flags, plaids and colors of many other tribes from the remnants of Lloegyr to the Midlands were also present.

Each warrior attached a small, dark blue shield to the left shoulder; engraved upon the shield was the image of the Woman, sometimes called "The Compromise of Arthur". Although she was the Mother of the Lord, the artistry and style of the image left her identity vague. Though he revered her greatly, the king left her identity to the individual's perception and perspective and beyond that, spake of it not.

Trumpet, drum and stringed instrument continued and singing was perpetual. The Saxons battling below were at all times surrounded by sounds of triumph and power in a language they knew not but understood nevertheless.

The tongue of the Cymru; the language of heaven.

"Hold now!"

"Steady, brethren!"

Had Merlin calculated the taxation of waiting? King Arthur peered left, then right, surveying his men.

"Have you found him, Urien?"

"I find him not." Urien had been charged to abandon the battle and to find Merlin who, as one of Arthur's three principal counselors (and the young king's closest friend save Bedwyr), would not be truant for the sentinel event of his people's history, lest it be by some as yet unknown treachery.

Urien, younger than Arthur but already with two strong teenaged warriors dominating the fields, was in a foul mood as his oldest, Prince Owain, would bathe in much killing while he was out hunting for an old wizard.

"Then again to it," said Arthur, who now fiddled with the hilt of his legendary sword.

Excalibur would saturate the soil with Saxon blood soon enough. The strategy was to wait. The young king, not yet thirty and three, and (were it not for retirement caused by injury) not even the most senior king in his own household, used the pains of pause to reflect on the strategy.

The strategy…

CHAPTER 3
The Strategy

Across the stone bridge o'er the Usk River, a short ride northeast leads to the walled megalopolis that includes Caerwent and Caerleon.

Protected by the hilltop fortress called Lodge Hill (the ingenious design of which made it so that just two watchmen could survey the whole of Gwent. Also, the place most frequented by Arthur himself when he desired solitude), in the heart of the city, surrounded by springs and natural baths, assembled all the great companions of Arthur's Britain in a great circular amphitheater.

They were come to his court for official discourse, debate and preparation for the battle of Baedan, only two night's winks hence.

It being a bitter December night, the hard cider, drink of the Cymry Warrior, was replaced with spiced wine that was prepared in large iron casks and stirred slowly, producing a pop, sizzle and hiss that contributed to the symphony of bardic song, loud clamorous debate, a dash of laughter and not a few of the lewd words that are precursor to pugilism.

The great Royal Clans sat in a circle within the amphitheater, no one tribe greater than the next.

The kings and princes, with their bishops, druids and women of renown, formed the second ring. Each king had twelve bards (Maelgwn brought twenty-four) forming the third ring. Behind them, and arranged by rank or by role, were the warriors. Some clans and tribes had professional warriors and others served both as farmers and spearmen. Depending upon the local tribe, the landowners who were not warriors formed the outmost ring.

There were no slaves amongst the Britons. All men were deemed of royal descent as sons of Brutus, and the purpose of a king was to administrate, not dominate, the people. To this all kingdoms, to include Powys, Morgannwg, Dyfed, Gwynedd and Deheuarth, agreed in each of their several customs and ancient laws.

The kingdoms in Eastern Britain, collectively called Lloegyr, depleted in times past by Roman treachery and recently by key losses during the Saxon Wars, also sent what remained of their armies and joined the rings of attendees arranged by their customs.

There were no Picts present at Baedan or the preceding councils, for Maelgwn Gwynedd trusted them not (though they would have him to be king over them).

Lastly, at the very center, there was one circle, inside even the ring of the kings and bishops (although this circle could, from time to time, include both).

The circle was a great stone table with golden and brass rivets, a set of six interlocking rings crewed by four knights apiece that formed one large round circle with a small circle of one with two seats in the very center. And each of the locking rings or circles could both rotate, and orbit. Thus, twenty-four knights plus Arthur and Maelgwn were seated at the Round Table (a table of the same design was found in a place called Cwbbor at Caermelyn, Arthur's legislative court). The knights had arranged their seating to show the people that how they met privately matched the manner in which they spoke openly: nothing was held back from the armies, or from the public.

As dusk gave way to nightfall and all guests were assembled, Arthur's father, the Uther Pendragon, stilled the fighting, fellowship and song, bringing the conference to order.

With a booming, deep and paternal projection that filled the whole of the amphitheater, he said: "Blessings and welcome, kinsmen."

As Uther addressed the assembly, King Arthur, a young man with a sense of his own place in history, stepped outside of himself. He looked upon the special collection of thousands of Britons and considered, *There are not enough bards, books or scribes to record the deeds and constitution of the heroes, and perhaps villains, who stand here.*

In this time, this perilous time, this special dispensation of radical change and radical courage, he thought, *I am not great. Rather, I am surrounded by the convergence of greatness.*

Pious bishops such as Bedwini, Illtud and Dyfrig (who would pray over the armies), mystical women with the power to command men's hearts, minds and loins, sat or stood side by side with the men; Onbrawst, Marchel and Vivien were amongst them.

Catching a glimpse of his father, Arthur stood and then reseated and swiveled back towards the center of the Round Table to hear the Uther Pendragon articulate the agenda to the gathered stadium of Britons.

Meurig, the "Wonderful Head of the Dragons", wore brilliant blue enamel armor and held his helmet (blue and silver with red horsehair, similar to the Roman style but closer in fit and shape to a Corinthian helmet; molded and tightly formed to the face of the warrior) securely beneath his left shoulder. Though retired for a decade and eight years, this red-caped Silure Warrior was yet fierce to look upon and few would desire to combat him, wounded or whole.

"Three are the topics for homily tonight, kinsmen and allies.

"Merlin has crafted a battle strategy that differs from our campaigns in the North. Never before has the Long Knife" (the term, in addition to "The Boar", most ascribed to the invaders) "consolidated for a singular assault so near our capital and strongholds. As Merlin will explain, we have let them come this far west with minimal resistance by design.

"Second: we will discuss a policy for Saxon residency after our victory with options ranging from expatriation to annihilation. Or, for those with merciful disposition, grants of citizenship after the ninth generation may be considered."

Any notion of quarter resulted in expected grumbles. However, Saxon settlements had already been long established in the East and no Briton would uproot and kill innocent children now born in Britain (albeit with foreign blood), without first exhausting all other considerations.

"And lastly, after military and political discussion, my oldest companion and advisor Dyfrig will look to the care of our souls, praying for the armies, the families and our nation. Then, when finished, shall the bishops discuss the mode of baptism and the Saxon policy for worship and congregational membership."

All of a spiritual ilk knew that the mode of baptism for Saxons that survived Baedan was just another thorn to prick the ceaseless quarrel between the new Religion of Romanism, which was gaining some following, and the long established British Primitive Church. The doctrinal differences were minor, save one, the ceremonial differences vast (and the disputes and fighting over them, vicious and often violent).

The one doctrine that could be taken advantage of, could undo a nation, was the belief and practice that kings give great portions of land to the Church of the Britons near retirement or death (or after some great sin). As only the royalty were allowed to be clergy, this maneuver was a shell game; a means of doing penance whilst securing land influenced by a patriotic bishop's family or tribe, forever.

The Catholics had no such demand for gifts of land or property, no need for a "mansion given here or a mansion given up there". Rather, and more overarchingly, they interpreted that the True Church possessed temporal power to occupy all land it touched anyhow, until the Lord came again. Thus they made treaties, behaving more like a government than an ecclesiastical body, whereby converted church land would be absorbed and owned by Rome, whilst private holdings would be left to sovereignty of the land holders.

Because the British Church held such large and strategically located tracts and grants of land, conversion to the popular Roman Religion was, to some, the equivalent of giving away Britain to Rome.

Meanwhile, the druids, Gnostics and those who followed the paths of old gods also had a place at the 'round table' to discuss their concerns and the survival of their faiths, waxing old like a garment thrown to the rear of a closet, well in the shadow of rising Christendom.

After three songs moved the assembly into an animated spirit, it was time for Merlin to speak.

Gwenhwyfar ferch Cwyrd of Gwent strode awkward with a bobble and a hobble. No longer upright with shoulders down and bosom proud, she held her left elbow fixed and her head tilted, a woman whose very body bore the outworking of the grief within her broken spirit. With a morose tug to the king's elbow, Gwenhwyfar took her seat next to Arthur. Though garlanded in an emerald dress to match her foresty eyes, she may as well have worn the widow's black at all times. Truly the queen was a crimson-haired white phantom.

"How many will come home, Bear?" spake a wife and mother, dead though she lived and beyond consolation. No soft oratory by husband, priest, kin or king could comfort the shattered and shadowed heart of a widow, yet worse than the widow, for she had not been robbed of a husband before his season; rather, taken from her were sons.

"Only Llacheu will fight at Baedan, Gwen. Amr has already been sent north, part of the ancillary units to prevent scatter raiding. He is with his cousin at Ynys Mon and not called to the fight." Arthur was a soft and sensitive man. Gentle. His voice broke twice as he tried to say, "If I could do more—"

The queen, who possessed no other natural station than to be a mother, stayed his speech and tried to be understanding whilst the madness continued to rise in the tide of her eyes. "Our nation sends boys to war at fourteen and princes must be willing to do that which they expect of their men." The response was cold, but the soft kiss upon Arthur's brow warm. "I cannot endure talk of war and religion this night, sweetheart. I have greeted those whose pride needed greeting and the requirements of hospitality are met. I am leaving now."

Gwenhwyfar departed from Arthur.

In her crippled walk, long ceasing to be regal, she found Merlin ten or twelve rows up from Arthur. She pulled him into an arched corridor.

"I am a Christian Lady, Lord Merlin. Two of my boys sleep in the ground at the Long Knife's hand. I am a Christian Lady, Lord Merlin." The queen was several spans under Merlin's great height yet somehow, in this moment, with eyes on the same level, she peered into the old wizard's face. "Whatever dark arts will protect my boys – do them."

Merlin gave a strange answer that none heard save Queen Gwenhwyfar, only it seemed her countenance fell yet further.

Whispers rumored of Merlin acting most peculiar of late.

Arthur gave a last look upon Gwenhwyfar as she evaporated in a sea of kinsmen.

The inner rings within a ring rotated outward from the center to the north, south, east and west, creating a singular point within the circle from which Merlin could address all seated in the amphitheater.

Starting from the corridor where he had conversed with the queen down to the center, two rows formed, making an archway of men; one side with sword, one with flame. To onlookers it appeared that, from any vantage or position, the hooded druid walked beneath an escort of flaming scepters, making his way with supernatural authority to the center of the Round Table.

"The old man gets more pomp than I do!" Old Meurig was famous for his humor and mused privately with a poke to his wife, the great Queen Onbrawst. "I brought the lad into the world, not Mer—"

"You paced around, stumbling over oak barrels, half drunken on cider; I brought the boy into the world of men, my love. Your work to beget Arthur was much shorter in duration than mine." Onbrawst was always equal to the task when a verbal joust was at hand, and she kissed her husband hard upon the lips. The retired monarch's warmth could thaw the most frigid of winters. "Now listen to the Merlin, love," she concluded.

"What is greater than eleven?" Merlin opened.

None of the several thousand attendees knew how they ought to answer a man wiser than Solomon and endowed with a wit and propensity for riddle. Even young Taliesin the bard opened his mouth to speak, cocked his head and shut it once more, declining response.

King Arthur felt no intimidation, for he knew well that when Merlin appeared to say something complicated, his aim was, in reality, simplicity.

"What is greater than eleven, Lord Merlin, is –" Arthur counted his fingers with a grin "– twelve."

A smile, revealing he was pleased, curled. Merlin became a pointed nose with a grin and no eyes, like a wrinkled squash. "And the Iron Bear is…" The pregnancy of Merlin's pause caused all to lean forward, whether seated or afoot. "Correct!"

Merlin looked up at the assembly with a laugh, chased soon by a scold. "Now don't go a-roaring with mindless yawps yet, Britons. You know not why he answered as he did." Merlin smiled once more and then changed temperament to a serious and proud tone.

"Eleven times we have met the Long Knife in battle. With apologies and grace to those honorable progeny who remain and are amongst us, Vortigern the traitor brought the Boar here. He slew our Northern princes through intrigue. He was hunted down and butchered by the great Wledig, Ambrosious…" Ambrosious and Merlin had been friends, closer than brothers, and when the great battle leader died he bade Merlin move north to Dinas Emrys to manage his own estates. Upon the death of Merlin's mother, this he did. "…And by Uther Pendragon, with the allied support and skill of the spear of Budic and Hoel, our kinsmen across the sea in Little Britain.

"Eleven times we have soaked our native land in the Boar's blood. The Long Knife has crept in unawares through the Northern Kingdoms. They have slashed through the forests of Caledonia, have met us on water and in marsh.

"Three campaigns spanning twenty years, eleven major battles and countless minor raids. Eleven!" Now Merlin raised the clenched fist of victory, his robe falling down his arm but a little, revealing two very old blue serpents, painted forever into his skin. At the erection of his victorious arm, the assembled royal clans of the Britons broke into a deafening cheer that could be heard two cantrefs away.

"Eleven!" Merlin returned his clenched fist to join his right hand upon his staff and the crowd's roar ceased.

"A War King was needed to guide you, proud heroes, to corral your interests of Self and put our survival above ambition. Ambitions of cloth and o'er men's souls. Ambition of lands and of quests. We live in an Age of Saints, of gilded warriors. It was imperative that we not fall in upon ourselves with the weight of our own greatness, for as it is written, Pride goeth before Destruction."

Merlin looked directly at Maelgwn, the greatest of all warriors since Achilles who, for now, had given up crown and conquest to serve Arthur, with a special measure of gratitude. Upon Maelgwn's spear rested the unity and hope of the entire Island Kingdom.

"Whatever Providence each of you worship, give praise, for a War King was needed and the War King was given. Praise God for King Arthur, the possessor of the two swords, and by the authority of the three swords! Praise the one who will overcome the Dragon whose sigil is that Dragon. Praise the one who unites our land. Praise the Bear Exalted! Praise for Arthur and for eleven, but—"

It was more difficult to gain the praises of Merlin than for Arthur to push a boulder up Mynydd Snowdonia with a dry piece of straw. The young sandy-haired king was ready for the "but" and braced for further expectations, corrections and improvements demanded by his Merlin.

Instead, the wordplay ensued.

"Eleven is great, but alas, one more time, boy, we need one more, we need TWELVE! What is greater than eleven?" Now the crowd followed, chanting "twelve" with the rhythmic harmony of Illtud's famous choirs.

Next the cheers and chants shifted to "one more, one more" in that special and heavenly tongue of the Cymry. It is said that angels joined in the singing and chanting (for they spake the same tongue) and that the Constellations grew jealous and, for just one evening, altered their circuits to get closer and listen.

This time it was more difficult for Merlin to quell the noise he had created. When at last it relented, he continued.

"But how will we defeat them? How will we give our whelps and babes a chance to grow up in a Summer Kingdom of peace?"

The assembly quieted. Still. Ready to hear "the how".

Merlin in an instant transitioned from riddles to direct, patient teaching. He wanted the men who would die over the ensuing days to understand why, and he wanted this for their wives and mothers as well.

"A fortnight ago," he began, "the Saxon kings sued us for peace and we conferenced with them at great length. Our emissaries in Little Britain and on the Continent informed us three weeks ago that a fleet of ships such as never was assembled had already left Germania ere the conference began.

"Moreover, separate Saxon tribes and princes who could not be under the same tent together without putting knife to gullet had demoted their sigils and flew one united battle banner. Remarkably, if only temporarily, the Germanic peoples are coming, united."

The Merlin cleared his throat.

"We have learned that only the Vandals held

out, and why would they not? Africa is under their dominion and the Black Boar is at present content to leave our Islands alone. But not so for the Angles, the Saxons, the Jutes and the tribes of Dan.

"Thus, the invitation to discuss peace was a delay tactic and one well-known. We played the part, courteous and firm, and soundly rejected the Long Knife's empty terms of eastern homesteading and harmonious integration. As if a Fox would integrate with a Hen!"

Merlin continued. "We gave safe conduct to the Saxon princes and intentionally gave appearance of weakened defenses all along both the old roads east, and the outlying trade and watchtower villages. Although raiding occurs under every moon and season, there is an unspoken agreement amongst all kindreds that no battle campaigns occur during winter. For this cause, the Long Knife sought further to deceive us, making their winter visit falsely appear all the more benign. We countered by making our defenses look equally benign.

"The nature, my beloved kinsmen, of their assault is a 'one-time', sentinel event with all lots cast. They are invading in winter, they are united, and they think that we are being true to our character of war-time honor and wholly unprepared. They will annihilate us, or they will be lost for a generation, as every boy who can carry a stick is with them."

Merlin's tone made the imminent danger grave. Then his disposition lifted.

"As always, the Saxon is a dullard, a dribbler and a *fool!*" screamed the old wizard excitedly under the starry winter night at the table round in Caerleon. "The strategy." Merlin's head tilted here, then there. "The strategy, my brothers and sisters, is to simply let the Boar in" – Merlin here began talking with his hands, shrugging his shoulders, and lightening his tone as a confident child does when at play – "let him starve, then make him climb."

Merlin went on to say how the Saxon horde would receive little interference in landing, making ready and then marching west from Lloegyr all the way into the Vale of Glamorgan (this they had already begun to do).

The Saxons would come as far as the Maesteg Valley, with her gulches, winding paths and open, hilly fields. Then the real differentiator of the strategy would activate.

In most cultures, the rulers build defensive structures that remove them from the masses and afford maximum protection with minimum effort. The Cymry did not view the king above the pig farmer and thus mitigation of loss of life and property for the common man was, to princes, paramount. To this end, from ancient times, fortresses were built high atop mountains, near caves where feasible escape routes for children, women and creaturekind were well-known, exercised and rehearsed.

When attacked, the armies would descend from the fortress hilltop, escort the people to safety, lob preliminary volleys, and meet the enemy in open combat, typically and with hope that the open warfare would occur ere they reached even the outskirts of the tribe's lands and homes.

The technique of scorching the harvest, killing the livestock and starting over anew if the battle was won was not an option in the mind of the Briton.

This time, the strategy was very different.

"Let the Boar in, starve him, make him climb." Merlin's words would be immortal.

The people would be long retreated to the hill fortresses atop and around Baedan hill, far away from the thousands of marching soldiers come to destroy them. The exodus would be intentionally slovenly; some livestock would be left, hearths still aflame and a general illusion of a hasty departure projected.

The three kings of the Saxon armies would undoubtedly call for the slaughter and immediate consumption of the livestock and the burning of any habitable living structures along the roads, knowing that more bounty would be available upon victory in an open battle.

Instead of the descent of an entire army and a massive conflict where the Royal Tribes would be outnumbered, the Britons would instead surprise and harass the Saxons from the sides of the valley and ultimately trap them at the foot of Baedan Hill.

Instead of Arthur's remaining troops descending upon the plain, they would simply wait atop the hill in frightening and disciplined formation and then, when starving and desperate, the Saxons would climb to their deaths from an untenable low-ground position.

CHAPTER 4
The Policy

After Merlin had articulated his brilliant strategy for triumphing in the sentinel event to come, the congress of Britons shifted to how they might manage the surviving Saxon populations in Lloegyr.

This level of planning was not one of arrogance or assumption, but rather of necessity.

There were well over twenty diverse tribes of unwelcome Germanic invaders and many of them had inhabited hides of land, illegally and immorally, on the Blessed Isles. Most of the men occupying these lands would take up arms and drive westward, right into Merlin's trap. If the magnitude of victory matched Merlin's predictions, that would mean thousands of Saxon children, women and aged to deal with, in just a few days.

A reasonable person would think that this topic would ignite grand debates of every philosophical persuasion.

But Religion is a far heavier stone than Reason.

Quickly local chieftains, major cattle owners, clergy and all of the Cymry agreed that Saxon women and children would be treated with mercy and respect; that deportation back to the

Continent would be safely conducted, sanitary, well-planned and with protection. Those born on Britain's soil could stay but not own land for nine generations; and only those political prisoners who were of the most extreme danger would be executed.

"Well, that was easy," said Cai.

"Of course it was; all the more time to argue about Religion," mused a metallic and vibratory voice that belonged to Maelgwn Gwynedd. He gave his foster-mother, Vivien, a comforting look of support, knowing he could leave and enjoy mead and meal but that she would suffer sitting through the entire session of old men about to argue about how to save souls, or rather, increase their power and position over them.

Determining the policy of water baptism for the new Germans would not be so easy!

The primitive British Church predated Rome, significantly. When synods or councils were gathered, the seating was based upon primacy. The clergy of Cymru and Eire were seated first. The beliefs of the native church eschewed Statism on a centralized or federal level (although a local bishop had come to supplant the place of a druid in many cases, settling minor disputes, and adjudicating land grants along with other small scale administrative functions). By contrast, the Roman Church declared itself the Pillar and Ground of Truth for obedience by the Nations. The Britons were finding themselves increasingly overwhelmed.

And the Roman Church had gold. Excessive, immeasurable amounts of it.

Because of this, they could plant priests amongst the Britons, influence major farmers, cattlemen and landowners and lob volleys of pressure over to the Isles all the way from Rome.

Some of the influence was finding fertile soil. During the Saxon Wars, for example, the Church at home attempted to levy a tax for protection of chapels and relics and was beginning, like those in Rome, to make tithing compulsory.

Arthur refused to levy this toll on an already distressed people, instead insisting that giving be voluntary and that the ecclesiastical organism make use of its existing revenues.

He would say, "A man who own cows must defend his herd; why should a bishop be any different with his flock?"

The controversy became so inflamed with a bishop called Padarn that Arthur stripped the vestments from the saint's back and banished him from his assembly. Bishop Bedwini took his bishopric.

Other principal Saints and Patrons of Cymru such as Dyfrig, Illtud and young Dewi appreciated Arthur's position and respect was reciprocal in times of both agreement and discord. The Roman Church (ever positioning for a cut of the collection plate) did not. For Rome fancied itself the Seat of the Universal Church. And the Catholics were positioning for the Bishop of Rome to be officially designated as the all-father, or Pope.

This greatly concerned the old British church (and ancient assemblies in other nations), pagans and heathens alike.

For his part, Merlin could see that Imperial Rome was slowly and methodically giving way to Holy Rome. In his travels, the Merlin witnessed intimidation, absorption of pagan belief into the burgeoning traditions of the Church, and ever-increasing forced adoption of Latin at the expense of the native written language of the Britons and the script of the Irish.

A man dedicated to pursuit of spiritual truth and societal justice, the Merlin never hated Christianity. He did recognize, however, the dangerous blend of Church and State, having seen a measure of corruption and imposition by his own druids when given similar opportunities. "Power corrupts whether you follow Christ or Rhiannon," he had said.

The Romans never took by sword what they would now take by crucifix. Left alone, Britain would inevitably follow Jesus anyhow; 'twas the method more than the outcome that concerned the druid. And the extinction of free thought and critical thinking skills.

In the Isles, the common man could read, he could look at nature and make a personal decision regarding his beliefs. Literacy was strong with regard to the native language, and the 'Latin game' bothered Merlin immensely.

"It's easy to render a country ignorant when their official language is officially foreign," he would often protest. The imposition of an official language and other such presuppositions, in the Merlin's view, were not for the Pulpit to determine.

The Lady of Llyn Fawr, a Breton called Vivien, had waning and vague influence in political matters. Christians still viewed her as having some ancient magick as old and as cherished as the Island itself. In some Christian sects, her veneration gave way to that of the Virgin Mary.

None knew her age (and not even a fool would inquire) but she had fostered Maelgwn, and he was two winters older than Arthur. Her blonde hair now shared space with some silver locks but it still featured indescribable entrancements and fell well beneath her thighs. Her garb was silver and white and even the most pious Christian opened themselves to the notion of a real-life goddess standing amongst them when they looked upon her.

She compressed authoritative thin red lips. *I am called the Virgin as well, married to the god. Indeed, when recognized as King of Glamorgan and Gwent, Arthur honored the king-making rites, but he did so in a private grove, his Apostolic and Catholic coronations carried out in public splendor,* she thought, listening to the bishops and priests beginning their rant about how to cleanse the souls of the invaders.

Of those rites, she recalled how, just two months later, she had visited court and witnessed the Church's perversion of a festival dedicated to the Babylonian goddess Astarte, now repurposed for their goddess, Mary.

She had lashed out openly at the bishops. "You have your risen king, he was made so at the rites! And his name is Arthur!" Too popular to kill at present, Vivien was tolerated at the table of political Britain.

And besides, 'twas Vivien who had taught Maelgwn his martial arts and, by extension, the whole of the army that had also adopted it. The Lady ever featured armor as part of her ornate and creative attire and gently reminded the males that she could kill most of them with ease, via technique in combat or enchantment, upon her whim.

Outside of fear, the bishops were simply too busy to deal with the Lady of the Lake. They had the Catholics to contend with and the Catholics with them. Yet, her friend – her lover, as the rites made requisite – Merlin, the man she respected above all others, had sought her counsel and presence. He felt she was greatly needed in light of the great changes coming in the 'Summer Kingdom' of peace that would now be an imminent reality, should Arthur and his Companions adjudicate Merlin's strategy at Baedan Hill.

Truth is not afraid to compete. Truth is not afraid to tolerate. Factions were healthy, checking their rivals and rendering taut the sinews of public discourse.

Factionism was deadly, Merlin and Vivien postulated. Diverse beliefs and gods were safe; a diversity of common law was deadly.

Rome's hatred of the competing Christian and Gnostic groups concerned them. The Church tried to convert the pagans. All faiths evangelize. But the greater concern was that they had aggressively begun to cannibalize their own dissidents, though they claimed the same Christ.

Such was the concern for the remnant of influential pagans that they worked extensively with the local Apostolic Britons, who had roots in the Isles dating back to the thirty-fifth year of the first century, and other Christians of local influence (such as the followers of Pelagius), constantly gauging the strengthening political power of Rome.

Borrowing in part from the height of successful republics of antiquity, the Merlin and the Lady of the Lake favored a nation where freedom of religion flourished. The young King Arthur agreed. And he was politically brilliant in this arena. Where the old wizard mentored the Bear of Glamorgan on many matters, the sandy-haired young king both agreed with and perfected their stance on this most defining topic with an intangible gift that could be cultivated but never taught.

Vivien remembered one rainy day before an overtly tense tussle between twenty Roman Catholic priests, a hundred and seventy Apostolic presbyters, the British Church's Great Bishop, Dubricius (who was also called Dyfrig in the language of heaven) and not a few influential pagans. Arthur had interrupted with boldness and grace.

"Merlin–" he looked up at the towering druid "–I think you are trying to say this." Merlin, taller than any Briton save Maelgwn but Briton to his core, sat down, smiling at his young liege. Old Meurig smiled too.

"No society can operate when divorced from a common set of norms. From a single moral fabric. To this end, Britain should be a Christian nation in principle, namely that we should, by enforcement of the common law, and executed amongst the Confederacy and in every Cantref: not kill, nor breach a covenant, nor defraud a neighbor, nor rape. Neither shall we steal, neither shall any principality or power do any of these against any citizen, and of the rights that are their obverse, from encroachment refrain. For without its counterpart in responsibility, no liberty can long sustain.

"And this shall be the end of the law, that men may worship what gods they will, only that they do not kill their neighbor for it."

In a few words, Arthur both enforced the Christian foundation of his realm and protected the liberties of all men, even those who disagreed with it.

Facing the real peril of a theocracy, Vivien

and Merlin could both acquiesce to and support Arthur's vision of a Christian government.

But now there were to be new subjects and, with them, a renewed effort for the policies of Rome to yet again bleed and burrow into the policies of the local ecclesiastical structures. Vivien, Merlin and anyone with a salt's pinch of common sense knew that any policy made for Saxon citizens could be used as license for later use against the Britons. Forced baptism per the sacerdotal system of the Catholics for them could be forced baptism per the sacerdotal system for all. Land ceded to Rome in Lloegyr today would be land ceded to Rome in Cymru tomorrow.

And so the debates and clamor droned and droned.

The Briton bishops were adamant that a man should be baptized after conversion to the Faith and then again, for kings, before death. And the mode of this baptism should be by immersion.

The Catholics viewed this method as 'incomplete' and insisted that an infant be ceremonially washed to remit Adam's Original Sin. Subsequently the individual would do works, affirmations and confirmations. The baptism, for the Catholic, or those of Catholic leanings, was an ordinance in replacement of Abraham's circumcision. The mode was sprinkling.

"They fight like this over which day to observe Easter too," heckled Meurig. Onbrawst laughed aloud.

The arguing was intense and the hour growing late.

The assembly began to disband and revelry turned to fatigue. A full stadium empties slowly, and warriors and women alike sought slumber.

"We have a battle to rest for and many, many Clans to organize down at Ogmore. This goes too long," Arthur protested.

The Lady of Llan Fawr interjected, "And if a Saxon sees not the Light of your Christ and His Church and prefers Odin and Loki or other deities of their fathers, what then?"

"We honor the diverse beliefs of those born here, Lady," said a saint of extreme influence. "But," he continued, "the Saxon is come to annihilate us, to remove our lamp and to stamp out our people, forever!"

He had a point and Vivien absorbed the words.

"Thus, for those children who are allowed to settle here, they must be Christian of some denomination or sect, they must be baptized, and if their parents allow this not" – the saint paused – "this will be rare, I assure you, for most of the Germanic horde dies in two days!"

"Not if we're still here talking about this!" Meurig delivered more well-placed levity, bringing interruption.

"I shall cut to the quick, my lord."

"Please do."

"We will baptize the children and execute the non-consenting parent. That will be the policy."

That the non-consenting parent would be removed from his head met no opposition. After all, these were the invaders who would rape, kill and assimilate every Briton, were they able. But the response gave Vivien great pause.

The arguing about 'mode and timing' kicked right back up again.

King Arthur rose.

"Retire from the amphitheater and continue this back at our great hall or your privy chambers. All of Caerleon has had enough debate tonight over sprinkling versus dunking. It is the same God we serve, after all."

An irritated king gave a polite nod and exited the Round Table.

The arguing continued for a short space even after their dismissal, as emotions were running hot and the embers were still red and orange. Suddenly Merlin, acting very passionately about some matter, with great conviction seemed to command the paused awe of every clergyman. And of Vivien.

Arthur had already paced out some distance between himself and those still engaged. He could see something different about Merlin's disposition, but of the nature of the post-conference bantering, he knew not. His mind had returned solely to the war strategy and all that must happen next. His confederacy assembled, the strategy articulated, it was time for history's greatest king to lead a war to end all wars; at least for a generation. A generation of peace.

And yet, that something strange had just happened with Merlin twanged his ribs twice or thrice, and then was dismissed.

To himself, he said, "I need a cider," and he sought out Bedwyr for the same.

CHAPTER 5
The Victory at Hand

"Hold!" Cai yelled, breaking Arthur's contemplation.

"You steady that horse, boy!" Cadoc hollered.

The Battle of Baedan started at the noon hour and lasted but three days.

Exhausted by Maelgwn and his bloodthirsty Hosts at once striking and withdrawing, and three days bereft of food, drink or sleep, at last the Saxons, who knew not how to make war upon steed, began to climb the mountain as their final, fatal recourse.

Like a statue come randomly to life, "Let the Boar in," said Arthur, and his head snapped sideways at Bedwyr.

Finally breaking his stoic silence, he said: "Starve him."

"Make him climb!" Bedwyr stole the king's line and, remarkably, spotted a smile from his Sovereign. Spotting a light moment that would soon be gone, Arthur's First Knight continued. "To what do we set the trump, my lord? We dare not issue an attack, what shall we signal?" Bedwyr laughed aloud. "Is there a trump for 'here they come, look down at your feet, go to it?'"

Excalibur was already swinging high above

and picking up the last shards of light breaking through dusk-shadowed trees. "Kill will suffice, Bedwyr. *Kill!*"

With their black leather lacquered armor and wooden shields, the swarm of climbing Saxons looked like cockroaches swarming a dead tree trunk. Their numbers were as the sands of the shore. No horse flinched; no Briton gave ground and the downward slashing from atop their war horses was organized, swift and without error.

No volleys could be lobbed lest the Ravens be shot by their own kinsmen, so archery was used near range and with less volume.

When a Saxon would slay a Briton with stone or fortuitous strike, both rider and horse would topple down the mountain, creating a boulder of flesh, killing as it rolled. The death of one Briton above oft resulted in the loss of three Saxons below. When a Briton felled the Saxon with long weapons, a spear, arrow or from mounted position, it was easier. To kill a man whose eyes are through the helm opposite your own is a far more difficult proposition. And some simply could not do it, could not kill.

To take the life essence of another man, to see the light leave his eyes by your hand, to be around the body of death: this changes and in many ways ruins a man. Nightmares, barriers to intimacy, drunkenness, loss of virility and suicide were the real ongoing disease of war.

Many thought that Merlin and Illtud should counsel and train the young warriors to objectivize the deed; to step outside of themselves and kill for the cause. This, the two men knew, was folly, so both they and other mentors, counselors and strategists trained the young warriors to do just the opposite.

"For politicians it must needs be strategic and cold. For warriors, it must needs be personal," said Merlin on many occasions. "The Saxon is not invading to take soil. He is invading to take *your* soil. The Saxon is not here to take a Cymry woman to wife; he is here for *your* wife, your schoolyard fancy, your sister! The Saxon is not here to be your neighbor. He is here to remove *you* personally, and your sons, from history itself, to take your poems, your ballads, all that is *you* and exterminate it." Then the old wizard would draw up his authority, usually gazing up and then snapping back down, chin to chest. "It is personal, young men. When you are engaged in close combat you must heed these instructions. Do this and you will both live to see one more tomorrow and mitigate the madness of the kill."

Merlin would then brandish his short leaf, dangerously sharp and knotted with engraved entwined ravens and bears. The top of the hilt featured three lines that looked like an inverted arrow or the rays of the sun. Emulating the lethal maneuver, he would say, "Find the short rib here on the enemy's left, lest he be left-handed, then use diagonal slide step and come to his right." Merlin sounded like his lifelong friend Vivien, the soft-spoken warrior who could have been the resurrection of Buddug, had her people needed her in that capacity. But the people had Arthur (of this she was most glad). "The blade must go through the armor at the rib like this–" Merlin drew a great breath "–and then, without reservation or hesitation, do and say the following."

Merlin's next motion and scripted words were portrayed so frighteningly that the young warriors, professional soldiers all, recoiled in fear.

Merlin looked deep into a phantom Saxon's

eyes and growled, breathing inward deeply, "We are not Walles" (which by interpretation means 'foreigner'), "you are! We do this for defense! We *live here*! WE LIVE HERE!" At conclusion of the final syllable and while demonstrating an upward stab from short rib through top clavicle (this path severing the heart and producing a fount of blood and instant death), he breathed outward in thrice measure of the intake of breath and screamed, spending the entire volume of his lungs. And then, in an instant, ceased.

The combination of the stab with the scream resulted in a Saxon's last experience ere he entered Hell being one of utter and complete terror; but the ritual was not for him, but rather for the Cymry warrior. By bawling aloud, the honorable nature of the deed, a legitimate and audible justification was spoken into existence. The sheer violence of delivery helped the Cymry warrior spill the negative energy as one spills their seed, releases and then sleeps. In this way, Merlin was helping them find a killing ritual to "do it and then let go". The routine had many favorable results amongst young warriors, sent to go and defend their country, sometimes as young as fourteen or fifteen years old.

The Saxons also started picking up some of the phrase in the singing, angelic and authoritative Brythonic tongue of their enemy. Thus, when engaged closely and nearing the moment of the stroke, pre-screams filled the fields and crags of battle.

And so it was at Baedan Hill. The layering of sounds: harp and horn and stringed instruments, choirs of men singing hymns under streamers, fiery female singers blasting imprecatory prose and curses into the sky o'er the enemy, battle drums, the protest of steed and the undisciplined screaming of soldiers in broken Latin, in Gaelic, in thirteen dialects of Jutish, Angle-land and Saesneg. In Cymraeg could be heard in strict and disciplined performance, well-timed through the night, blended with the sound of snow and the soundlessness of snow, with the wind and against the wintery wind, above all and through all, the ritual Merlin had taught the young men: "WE LIVE HERE!"

But Merlin was not there.

Arthur scrambled away from the direct action a few times to scout. He identified his son, safe. Llacheu was ascending a ridge well clustered by armed knights. Gwenhwyfar would be pleased.

Arthur scanned the Vale for Maelgwn and found him not, but given the numbers in mortal clutch, the mist, and the fading light, he was not surprised at his inability to see the great soldier.

The Britons began rotating the front-line cavalry and had developed a strategy for fighting in the wintery cold: water.

Merlin and Illtud, masters of aquatics, had developed wooden tributaries that caused great amounts of water to be redirected down the mountain, like three well-organized girthy waterfalls made by men. The water itself was a cold and unyielding adversary and the Saxons found themselves dying in freezing mud.

Meanwhile, skins were thrown upon the warriors who were out of rotation. They were warmed, given hot drink, recomposed and then rotated back into the alignment.

The song and music now increased so that it became one with the rushing winds, masking the screaming. It had become so deafening that time seemed to stop and then alter the speed at which men moved, rendering them participants watching a drama, watching their own theatre.

The panic of the terrorized invader grew and grew as there was no place of retreat: Arthur's sword at the throat and Maelgwn's spear at the heel.

Finally, freezing in mud, blinded by mist, surrounded by death, the Germanic kings – the loose confederation famous for sacking Rome, conquering Northern Africa and much of the known world through numbers and ferocity – realized that they would not have this special and coveted Isle, not today, and not for many days.

Osla I was slain; Cedric the Gewessi hacked his way out of death's pursuit, retreating to the east of the fighting. Aelle, the third king, possessor of the largest divisions, screamed in a Latin tongue (for no Cymry would learn the sounds of the Long Knife) for quarter, crudely offering himself as prisoner to Arthur. Owain ap Urien granted King Aelle's request for mercy but not before he struck him hard with the hilt of his sword, taking the unconscious and defeated king and battle lord into custody.

The Boar. Let him in, starve him, make him climb. Kill the Boar.

Cleaving the head of the adder did not immediately stop the flailing of its tail. The Saxons' panic made them at once easy to kill and hard to compel to simply lay down arms and live. Even as the Britons sought to explain that it was over, the Saxons climbed upwards to their awaiting death.

"They cease not. Will we have to slay all of them?" screeched Bedwyr, heavy breath forming clouds in the cold.

"Aelle cannot signal their surrender." Owain

surveyed the bound Germanic king for alert eyes, but he was yet unresponsive.

At the base of the Baedan, Maelgwn's men had harassed and attacked from behind and funneled the Saxons to either 'climb or die' so effectively that they could now see more Cymry warriors than Saxon.

Like a fist slowly clenching, the invaders were now far fewer than the Island's defenders, and when the fist fully closed, there would be scant few left.

The small plain and three ridges leading up the hill where piles of Saxons went to their god or on to Hell would one day be called 'The Bridge of Slaughter' and 'The Place of the Soldiers' in Cymraeg.

Finally, with the wine press virtually closed and the Ravens now indeed climbing the mountain on the heels of upward fleeing Saxons, the German attack's back broke. They started to drop arms, fall to knees and cry for mercy in their barbaric tongues.

King Arthur, ever 'in office' (as Vivien taught him), tried to be balanced. He was not a cold stoic, neither a jesting fool. When others wept, he wept. When they rejoiced, he was glad-hearted with them. One of the king's greatest attributes was his sense of timing and ability to meet people upon their level and in their context rather than always his own. Balance was slipping and Arthur just wanted to hug his men, to yell joyously.

Nearly twenty years of the Saxon Wars were nigh to a climatic and unanimous victory. In these moments, men hug. Men embrace. Jumping around like boys in the schoolyard kicking a ball, the great companions of Arthur shoulder-checked one, and then the other, frantically looking for the next man to congratulate.

Midnight Blues hugged Black. Black embraced Speckled Green. Blue Plaid mauled Yellow. All the Royal Clans and Tribes and kinsmen rejoiced!

Bringing this confederacy together had not been easy. Although the Round Table Fellowship formed a unique principality (especially when they met at Caermelyn and were under a specific code; a peculiar nation of twenty-four and two within a larger nation of several million), beyond its hallowed halls there was ongoing need for vigilance and discipline in keeping the nation from crackling and splintering into Civil War. Even before the battle had commenced, this was freshly evident.

The collective armies had had to ride directly west from Caerleon to the beach-head at Ogmore, where they organized and finalized tactical aspects of the strategy. From Ogmore to the base of Mynydd Baedan was only two hours, directly north, by horseback.

As Merlin had never arrived at Ogmore, there were some minor delays and, with the wait, came the tribal skirmishes. Urien was dispatched to find Merlin and much of the management of the Northern Tribes fell to his son Owain (for Maelgwn left in the night for his unit's part in the Strategy).

The Tribes had grown so restless that Owain and Arthur tried to calm all by playing an ancient board game called gwyddbwyll. It did not work. Report followed report to both Arthur and Owain of one tribe harassing, fighting and hacking at the other.

Owain, in an error of youth, even threatened to kill some of the men of the South (Arthur's very own Silure tribe). Arthur said nothing at first in response to the threat, but simply crushed a clay game piece. Letting the bits fall to the gwyddbwyll board, the eyes of the Pendragon found Owain's soul.

"Your move."

Owain had settled his Ravens.

Arthur also got his first look at Maelgwn's youngest son, adorned in golden armor (Arthur's own fetching lad Llacheu also favored shimmering in gold armor), and the Pendragon very much enjoyed seeing the future of Britain strolling about the tents together.

All strife was now gone and all the Tribes were, at least for this rare, unspeakable savored moment, together.

Still looking for more men to shoulder check, pump fists with, shout to the heavens with and embrace, Arthur found Cai. He hugged him tightly. This was not easy given the height and thickness of the man with whom Arthur had spent two years as foster brother and two decades more as friend. Twenty years of fighting by boat, in forest, on sand and in crags. So much loss of life for love of hope. Cymru would survive, led by history's greatest king, and into the bosom of his steward he could finally breathe.

"We did it, Brother."

Releasing Cai, Arthur clasped Bedwyr's left hand.

Arthur smiled.

Arthur wept.

CHAPTER 6
On Fostering

King Arthur and Cai ap Cynfarch were foster brothers. The practice of fostering in Cymru had a very specific, very well intended purpose.

Well before Arthur and most of his famous Companions were born, a great treachery was visited upon most of the nobility of the Britons. Although the cowardly sin against warfare and honor occurred at the mountain fortress of Caer Caradoc in the southeast, it, in dark and far-reaching irony, forever impacted the kings and princes of Northern Cymru.

A treacherous king called Vortigern had conscripted the Saxons and made them hirelings to ward off raiding from the tribes from the Emerald Isles. The hirelings soon began to devour the flock and would not go home to Germania when finished with their employ.

A conciliatory council was called. The Britons and Saxons agreed to discuss possible co-habitation, a peace accord for slow and regulated migration to the eastern parts of the Isles. This was before the Saxons were exposed as wholly untrustworthy demoniacs.

Instead of honor and reciprocal diplomacy, the Boar waited until the Britons were drunken or retired and then ambushed them with blades concealed. Caer Caradoc was so full of butchery that its beautiful dykes and waterfalls ran red with the foamy life essence of innocent men and women. A fortress celebrating the son of Bran the Blessed now became a place of cursing, the place of mourning. Many royals were laid to rest in glorious burial mounds right where they fell and many Wells (where it was believed that a man's soul could traverse through the Deep, back to its source) were erected.

The incident became known as the Night of Long Knives and, in earnest, launched the Saxon Wars.

Over four hundred princes, chieftains both major and minor, bishops and druids perished that night due to the treachery of the Boar; the cowardice of the Long Knife. Perhaps the greater loss was the women, who were murdered as well without regard or honor. This left an enormous void of those vessels of honor to give future sons to the Ravens of the North.

What the Saxons meant for evil, however, God wrought for good. By chance, against hope, two rulers from the South East were away in Brittany, missing the conference entirely. And so, by horrific murder of so many princes, the Saxons created the stage that would be filled by the one who would come to destroy them.

The Pendragon, Tewdrig, and his battle commander Ambrosious survived the ambush by their absence. Later in life Tewdrig begat Meurig, and Meurig begat King Arthur.

The resulting void of rulers for the North of Britain resulted in Arthur and the Silures having to establish kings with wives and provide stability. For example, the dismal King Cynfarch survived the Night of Long Knives. The Silures gave him to wife Nyfain, daughter of Brychan. This union gave the world Urien and Llew and Arawan who, downstream, gave the world some of Arthur's greatest allies such as Owain and Gwalchmai.

These remnant Sons of Cunedda, the most powerful senior bloodline in the North, both appreciated and resented the South. Only a handful of chiefs survived and as these married and gave Cymru new sons, and with great sacrifice and efforts from the South, the North loosely began to restabilize.

Feeling like they no longer needed "help", the Northern indigenous kings like Cynfarch and Cadwallon Lahir increasingly fomented and flowered the seeds of resentment, and raiding of the South became frequent. And the Bishops of the North were slowly giving way to Catholic leanings as well.

To combat this dilemma, as ongoing acts of grace, friendship and hope, fosterage became formalized and frequent.

Sons and daughters of the South would spend two summers reared by the North (and not just a "nobility for nobility swap"; often a prince would learn to tend sheep, a princess to work the plow) and the children of the North would do the same, living at the hearth of the Clans in the South.

This forged friendships, reduced frictions, sowed seeds of youthful romance (and thus future political marriages), and greatly aided in fusing together one united Cymru.

Sometimes.

Though a noble pursuit that bore much good fruit, such as the bond unbreakable between Arthur and Cai, there were times where the fosterage had the opposite result. In these cases, a prince from the South would be turned against his own family and become a dormant pawn, just waiting to strike or to betray. The host family would corrupt the heart of their foster child, creating assassins and killers and traitors, leaders of cowardly raids to steal cattle, sheep, precious resources and people.

The national character of the Britons was strong, gilded. They were a moral people. But when the exceptions arose, they arose, sharp as long thorns hiding in plain sight in the rose garden, the tare in the wheat.

For Arthur's part, he enjoyed many adventures with Cai in the North and his love for Cai well exceeded the love of a brother. They were together, and inseparable, from Arthur's twelfth unto fourteenth year prior to joining Hoel on the Continent; then Arthur returned to school near Caer Bovum at an old college that would one day be known as Llaniltud Fawr.

Cai accepted the office of steward during that tender age and it was an office that he manned with zeal and fervor, as if he had been born for the very purpose. Just minutes after introductions made when just a boy, Cai fondly remembered King Meurig dismounting his horse, kneeling down gracefully to meet eyes with the lad.

Meurig's words were soft in tone but grave in nature.

Noticing a special, loyal light in the boy, the king said, "I give you the greatest tasks of all men, young Sir Cai. It will not earn you much public glory but the Lord God and I, Uther Pendragon, will be watching, and we will be very thankful and very proud." Meurig lightly pushed Arthur away at this point, encouraging him to go play with other boys. The opening remarks of the charge had Cai brimming with excitement and expectation of what would come next.

"At your service, my lord?" His voice begged Meurig to continue.

"Protect Arthur at all times. This is the sole purpose of your occupation for the next two years. And when I come and visit, I will monitor the execution of your stewardship privily, to see that you give me neither eye nor lip service. Your sole purpose." Meurig increased the gravity of his tone, garnished with the reward offered for the thankless and private employ. "Do this for just two years and you and whatever lass you wed will live in riches at Caerleon all of your years. You shall never want."

The two years were over too soon and Cai petitioned Uther Pendragon to be the steward of Arthur, not for just two years, but forever. Meurig happily accepted. Cai would do anything to protect his friend and king. His foster-brother.

CHAPTER 7
The Absent Sister

The Princess Gwyar ferch Onbrawst was also fostered.

She was noticeably, yet not unusually, absent at the gathering of the Tribes in Caerleon before the battle of Baedan.

Either the Long Knife will have the day and a dark age of rape, tyranny and annihilation will befall us all, she accurately surmised, *or we will win and our own Religionists will bite, devour and consume each other and then turn to us and do the same thing.*

Fondling the pretty purple floral head o'er the toxic monkshood plant and then jerking it cleanly from the soil, root and all, she said: "Kill me swiftly or kill me slow. In the end, I'm no less dead." Gwyar made an angry smirk, gazing upon the limp stem. "I'm still dead, yes?"

Seagulls cried an ugly song of agreement with the princess's appraisal, swooping in to feed upon the offerings of the island's coastal shore.

"Why waste time with meetings?" she finished her thought.

As Arthur, Cai, Urien, Bedwyr, Hoel ap Budic, Cadog, mighty Mofran and the rest of Arthur's glorious twenty-four were presently engaged, leading thousands of their kinsmen in the most important battle in her people's (and perhaps any people's) history, Gwyar was pleasantly enjoying the magical little intersection, found on many of the Isles, where the forest lies behind and the beach lies ahead. A gateway between two worlds; from ocean to greenery within seven paces, truly the Isles testified to the artistry of the Creator.

Britain itself was this gateway.

More special perhaps than the rest was Ynys Enlli, the Island of the Currents. The island of treacherous currents. A remnant dot of now long-sunken earth between herself and the long land-end arm of the Llyn Peninsula, Ynys Enlli at once felt like it was at the end of the world, and the center of it.

Unreachable because of undercurrents and tides that ran to and fro in defiance of the observable laws of nature and guarded by a citadel of dolphins, Ynys Enlli could be accessed by neither barge nor boat nor swim from October through springtime. It was December and yet Gwyar traveled here as she pleased and personally stewarded all the permanent residents, providing supplies, wines and foodstuffs during the harsh winter.

Although but a two-mile journey, it was hopelessly impossible; yet she frequented the Island often, and none dared to asked how.

Following a short hike, beach became forest, and forest became a steep sloped mountain. To the west and nearly atop Mynydd Enlli's peak was found a large structure that housed a striking garden and the oldest apple orchard in the world; local legend recorded that a great dragon had brought the first seeds there following a clash involving the Sons of Brutus and a Giant whose son was Gogmagog. Additionally, the unique edifice accommodated living quarters for twenty and four souls and ten guardians.

A stone round table, similar to those found at Caermelyn and at Caerleon, dominated the hall. Differing from those palaces and forts, this table rested upon a floor made entirely of dark blue glass. Wondrous fish and other illuminated swimmers and sea horses spiraled in ethereal dance through what appeared to be a great natural aquarium that spanned the breadth of the hall.

Sometimes the mist enveloped the whole of the dwelling, as if to guard it. Sometimes the Dragon's Breath escorted but shards, strings and beads of sun through the archer's slits in the towers and, on rare occasions, the breath recoiled entirely, showing off the top of the great tower to an unbelieving and skeptical world.

And while the mist guarded this Castle of Glass, the Castle of Glass guarded the Isle of Apples, and the Isle of Apples guarded many mysteries and the treasures of Britain.

Sitting at a grey table in a circular room prominently featuring a curious mirror and two dark-stoned indoor wells, Gwyar put fists under chin and rested atop her elbows. There alone in the Isles in the Sea, she harbored and again and again quelled resentments which were meet and just. Gwyar's thoughts now turned and rested upon her son, who could well be sword to sword with a Saxon at that very moment, far far away in the South.

Gwalchmai, the Hawk of May, son of Gwyar and the Lion (who was Cynfarch's son), was said to bring sunshine wheresoever he trod. It was told that days of incessant downpour would at once open to clouds of happy blue the moment his feet touched the ground of this village or that village.

Gwalchmai's hair was reddish blonde; he favored two slightly curved leaf swords that complemented his motions and could be sheathed efficiently on his back. He, of course, fought in the style of the Bretons. A student of philosophy and the sciences, he respected all Faiths and Religions though himself was a Christian, probably from spending two summers with Arthur, Gwenhwyfar and Saint Illtud down in Glamorgan.

Larger than Arthur and of a gentle disposition, many thought Gwalchmai would make a fine king and, although not near the skill of Maelgwn with sword or shaft, he possessed and excelled in all the intangibles of leadership, critical thinking skills and wisdom, similarly to the great Pendragon himself.

Princess Gwyar desperately hoped he was safe and would return from Baedan with his usual vigor, bringing Sun and Summer to a dark world.

Yet Gwyar too was dark.

The stock of Onbrawst and Meurig gave the world King Arthur, the sandy blond-haired (though most Silures had dark hair and brown eyes with olive-colored skin) and blue-eyed King of Kings. The boy-king was now a man who could conquer the world and make himself Emperor but who, against the nature of Men, found no drunkenness of power and sought no kingdom beyond the protection of the sovereignty of his own.

Indeed, Arthur put himself under the very laws that he adjudicated and had, by his own imposition, less local power than a chieftain, and a chieftain less power under the roof of a citizen than the citizen. Thus, on a daily basis and in a very real way the common man was, logically, more powerful than the High King, and this by the insistent design of Arthur and the Silure kings before him.

The Law ruled from the Yellow Fortress of Caermelyn. The Law and not Men.

This was the uniqueness of Arthur's Cymru. *But what happens when one faction or denomination homogenizes with the Law?* Gwyar pondered. The threat of Romanism and the invasion of the Long Knife ever threatened what Arthur and Merlin had exhaustively labored for twenty years to build.

Yes, Arthur was a light, but Gwyar was a shadow.

Without controversy Onbrawst and the wondrous Meurig gave the world not only Arthur, but his infamous sister too. And in an age of heroes and villains so plentiful that their legends cannot a hundred libraries nor ten thousand scrolls contain, she was indeed most mysterious, most fascinating, and most to be feared.

Like Arthur, Gwyar too was fostered.

CHAPTER 8
What Is Wrong with Gwyar?

Three alone have knowledge of Gwyar's origin tale, and it is at that speculation. And these three are the Merlin, and King Meurig and Queen Onbrawst.

On a rainy and desperately dark day two years ere Arthur was born, the stately Queen Obrawst, newly delivered of a baby girl, was visiting the Lady of Llyn Fawr. The queen favored the romance of rain and, to resume health and form after months of pregnancy and the travail of childbirth, she took a walk near the lake. Alone.

Guards for the queen were quite close and the area was safe. Safe enough… to any foe of mortal coil.

The Isles in the Sea were at one time overrun with creaturekind trapped betwixt this world and the next - the next world for them being the Underworld; and without hope for any alternative destiny, as they were from a time when all flesh was corrupted by Fallen Ones, and abominable spirits begotten. Though often shining and brilliant in appearance and possessing unnatural long days in the here and now, they could not escape their dark nature or their fiery end. As happens by misfortune in the Isles, Onbrawst had wandered into the wrong ring of stones at just the wrong time.

"Dance!" boomed the Twlyth Teg's king. "You are in our circle and yet will not dance?" The Fae lord's eyes were all red with no pupil, and his head inclined with inquisitiveness as he towered over the Cymry queen (for this race of Fae were very tall, and not tiny as are other races, forms and kinds).

Onbrawst was a pious, yet neither haughty nor arrogant, Christian lady. Disoriented by an encircling funnel of darkness and billows of smoke crackling with spires that enveloped and smudged yet burned not the flesh, she was miserably enchanted, confused and out of place. Her disposition pushed her to a reactive, rude and out-of-character response.

A brief error with just cause, fated to life-long effects.

Looking up at the ivy-crowned Being requesting she spin and spiral with his untoward mates, she spake before thinking. "Thou offspring of the Devil! I would not justify you by my dance!"

The Fae abhor rudeness from the Sons of Adam. He looked up to the heavens as if the stars too shared his gaping offense. His knuckles met hard upon the queen's same cheek. There was a hollow thump and a rattle. The blow rolled her eyes and split her face. Flaccid, she swooned into his cradled upper arm; her head fell back like that of a child's doll. The Fae King opened her green gown and cupped her left breast, enjoying the full shape of it (for she was newly nursing her babe).

In one movement he spun her round, reviving her, and his right hand quickly un-hooded the entrance between her legs. He made sure the queen's bloodied eyes met his own. Though violating a lady touched only by her husband, loved only by her husband, somehow the Fae made both Onbrawst and the Fair Folk watching feel like *he* was the one offended by her outrageous refusal.

Following one more uninvited painful fumbling, and a pat on her flank as if she were livestock and no woman, the red-eyed creature's voice rose deep from the Underworld. Metallically he spoke.

"Cursings and Blessings from the line of Uther Pendragon."

***

Onbrawst stirred amongst shallow reeds near the shore of Llyn Fawr. With unfocused vision, she glimpsed a silver swan arching its proud neck. The swan's head plunged and disappeared, reappeared and then plunged again to fish when Vivien suddenly, no less blurry, replaced the bird before Onbrawst.

"My heart, you have fainted!" Vivien rushed to the queen's side.

"Where is my baby?" Onbrawst didn't acknowledge Vivien's concerned greeting, a feeling of dread dominating her.

"Oh, the babe does well, Dear Heart; you've been gone but twenty minutes."

"But it was night and now day—" Onbrawst captured and held her tongue before tripping on more confusion. She lightly applied fingertips, as if they were feathers, to her broken face. No wound. Her garment was perfect with no tear and no part of her felt molested.

Was it a dream? she thought.

"You are not a fortnight removed from giving birth." Vivien could assume all of life's most important offices in an instant. At present, she was Maternal Nurse. "You need rest and tea, not walking."

"I'll forgo the tea and accept the cider drink." The endless humor of Onbrawst resurrected. "I thought a walk and some air would help. Baby Gwyar decided to come violently into the world of Men."

"A cloudy cider from the apples of Ynys Enlli it is!" If Vivien knew at the time that Onbrawst had befallen some peril in the Faerie Realm, she concealed it brilliantly, or she simply didn't know.

A young priestess in a lakeside home that would later be repurposed as a chapel watched o'er the babe.

"There, there she is," said Vivien. "Ready for mama to hold her."

Cursings and Blessings from the line of Uther Pendragon. The words at once flooded back at the very instant Onbrawst picked up the dark-haired little bundle.

"Look at those bright eyes!" Vivien was crowding over Onbrawst's shoulders, anxious to take in as much new baby as possible. Then she saw the eyes, which most certainly had been grey-blue upon birth.

Onbrawst saw what Vivien saw. She interpreted Vivien's pause – for she shared it as well.

The baby's eyes had changed to a soft golden color with dark speckles in the gold and hues of bronze around the pupil.

The touch of the baby was different, and not. The scent of the baby was new, yet still Onbrawst's very own. The baby had changed but was yet hers.

Queen Onbrawst, a warm and sweet woman who greeted more oft with hug and kiss than bow and handshake, had felt, against all her might, the seeping loss of natural affection toward the child from that day forward.

Difficulties compounded over the years to follow and, when any person would pose a question to the effect of "What is wrong with her?", Onbrawst would give a public answer to quickly defend the lass; but the deepest secret caverns of her soul gave another.

To herself, she said: "She was changed, if she is my baby girl at all."

Onbrawst did all to love her, even by rote, but was filled with a shameful relief when Vivien agreed to foster Gwyar when she turned eight.

CHAPTER 9
The Watchful Steward

The tears that accompany rejoicing contain extra salt, and find a way into every wrinkle fashioned by so many smiles over the years. Salty tears and blue woad paint rendered the noble king's face a mess.

The Tribes rarely wore facial dyes. They did so for ceremonial reasons, or periodically to honor their ancestors. The bishops constantly lobbed critical quips about body markings, whether under or upon the skin, as 'heathen barbarism', and the practice was diminishing. Arthur favored a handful of different uniforms, armor and appearances and did, to manifest extra ferocity, don the paint from time to time.

On his right cheek was an image like an inverted arrow-head or three rays of light. The image was called *the Awen* and represented divine inspiration. To a Christian, the image was viewed as a beautiful picture of the Trinity, depicting light that can be felt but not seen, light that can be seen but not felt and, lastly, light that can be both felt and seen. To the druids and other sects, it had diverse meanings. Upon his left cheek was a perfectly rendered bear claw; the sigil of the Silures. And so, the decorated story upon his face rendered 'Arthur, the Iron Bear, is divinely inspired to vanquish the invader and save his people'.

This imagery borne upon his visage was messianic and menacing.

Less menacing was his handsome face, now just a smear of blue with a touch of frost and smudges of mud. Some of what was now a distasteful blue paste crept into the corner of his mouth.

"Victory is brackish and makes me look ugly!" Arthur jested aloud, laughing and laughing. Certainly, this was the zenith of his military career and he was filled with elation. He could not possibly feel better.

Optimism flooded over the king. Merlin would be found (probably not in attendance deliberately to teach another of his obscure and treasured, but hard to receive, lessons - this one maybe about learning to rely on others more than the aging wizard), and he was about to be home for an extended spell after three separate war campaigns. The coldness between he and Gwenhwyfar surely would thaw.

All would be well at this, the dawn of the Summer Kingdom.

Arthur gave Excalibur one final loop into the sky, stars kissing the blade, then sheathed it gracefully. His red cape whirled around, and his blue helmet was cradled beneath his left arm. The night was dark, grimy and filled with death and fright but, in spite of this, the Round Table Fellows, archers, and soldiers looked upon their king, inhaling pride at how regal he looked.

Many fires were blazing atop Baedan. There was a sloped plain where pavilions and well-organized stations of munitions, food and provisions were positioned. A short walk up and leftward of the plain revealed a thick, frightful forest. A rear-guard assault through the forest was impossible, due to the lack of entry points and the natural positioning of the hill. The enemy would have to go through the plain if they desired to hide in the forest.

Or be smuggled in unawares.

So many torches contrasting against the white of the tents rendered it almost as if it were yet day and not well after midnight. The fighting had stopped below but there was a brief frenzy of disorganization due to the euphoria of victory: a moment of chaos for an always well-ordered army. The king scanned scores of faces amongst the tents until he spotted Llacheu's likeness, several hundred feet away.

Arthur hollered after his son.

"Llacheu! My son, my son, we did it!"

The shimmering knight, yet at a distance, did not acknowledge his father's spirited yell. Rather, he continued to make his way outside the torch-lit boundaries, now very near the forest. The prince walked with a small company of young men and the behavior was not suspicious, given the noise and circumstance. Arthur continued to swim as a salmon, muscling upstream through friends, warriors, choir singers, noblewomen and physicians, trying to get one hug from his son ere he considered respite for what remained of 'victory day'.

After four minutes more of trailing after the boy, Arthur finally caught stride with the small troop encircling Prince Llacheu. They were in the forest, but not the thick. Owls and an adder made protest at the crackling caused by the boots of men. The Pendragon softly clasped the boy's shoulders and gave a fatherly tug, whirling the lad around and finding the eyes of his child.

His boy was still wearing his helmet. It was ornate and the envy of the army: golden with a simple groove inlaid for a crown and dragon wings adorning the sides like fins. Llacheu's chin and eyes alone were exposed.

At the instant the king opened his mouth to proudly greet the prince, Arthur saw, or perhaps rather felt, Cai's battle club find the back of Llacheu's helmet. A clangor of metal, then dull resonation, long lasting. The blow dropped the recipient's chin down hard against his own chest plate. Head springing back up, likely as reflex only, he managed to turn towards his assailant.

This was Cai's aim. The next swing separated helmet from head, cracking the top of Llacheu's skull. The fatal blow spilled the prince's brains all over his father. Arthur's face was now tears of two kinds: blue paint, and his own son's grey matter, splattered and smeared.

Llacheu's blue eyes now white-grey, he crashed hard and stiff to both knees, then rolled left to wintery, muddy ground; dead. The dagger meant for his father twitched along with nerves still active in a dead left hand.

Horns were sounding above, but Arthur heard them not. Others had seen the action developing and were already furiously sprinting into defensive positions at the edge of the wood. 'Twas not a small circle of youthful soldiers carrying on outside the battle camp that Arthur had happened upon. It was ambush. It was treachery.

Approximately nine hundred Saxons had been carefully and meticulously placed into the woods by twenty villainous Britons from the North. Thanks to his treacherous son, they were positioned within striking distance to ambush the king.

The tactic was obvious when later analyzed.

Nine hundred loosely disciplined infantry could not overcome the thousands of Cymry led by professional equestrian soldiers. Nor was that their aim. Rather, the dodge was to lure Arthur away, slay the king and a small number of key leaders. The traitors commanding the scheme would do this in the forest and then pretend to vanquish or capture the very Saxons with whom they were in league. Arthur would be dead and Llacheu crowned a puppet king.

But Cai, the steward of King Arthur, had sniffed out the ruse. It was his appointment to watch everything.

At the moment the boy's shattered head met earth, it was three hours past midnight and a mist suddenly filled the forest, as if some great dragon had set his nostrils to cinder the entire wood, joined in outraged accord with the Britons. Arthur had not a moment to consider his own despair. Bedwyr had rapidly readied Arthur's steed and the Pendragon was at an instant mounted, with his spear unharnessed and ready, a long black weapon called Rhongomyniad. He engaged in killing the immediate near threat, the young warriors who were with the bloody corpse that had once been his son. When these were all slain, by the king's own hand, the Round Table Companions paused.

"How will we identify friend from foe in the mist? Even in daylight, some are our own kinsmen," said a mounted knight, dejected and anxious.

"Hawk of May." The call of the king was stone, bereft of emotion.

"Yes, my lord." Gwalchmai step-jumped forward, ready to receive instruction from the great War King.

"Where your feet tread, the Sun shines." Arthur surveyed his options rapidly and continued. "In the mist, fifty men will seem as five hundred. Bring but fifty and gather all white battle standards." Here, Arthur's natural leadership attributes exceeded those of all men, even the Merlin. At key moments, champions make key decisions.

"The white standard will cast shadow against the dragon's white breath. At the same time, burn the top of the standard, creating bright oranges and yellows. As one banner burns out, have your men rapidly set another alight." As Arthur spoke, Gwalchmai was absorbing the plan swiftly. The hearers marveled at the brilliance of using white against white to produce contrasting shadow. The Hawk of May had the scene mapped in his mind and was ready to act.

"If a cluster of men are not under the Sun you've created," Arthur continued, "then they are not of us. End them." Arthur looked to the lump that was his son, the fostered traitor.

"Know this, friends. We will probably not discover the leader of this plot out here in the cold tonight. Kill without discernment or investigation. We cannot negotiate with treachery. The truth will out in the fullness of its time."

"We are to it!" said several Round Table Companions.

Bedwyr was friend first, Round Table Companion second. Having grown up with both Arthur and Gwenhwyfar, he looked at the king for a fleeting moment, knowing the heartbreak that would rush in when the thrush and thrust of the battle was over. Llacheu's death (compounded by the manner thereof) would ruin Gwenhwyfar beyond redemption. Only one of her sons now lived and he was far to the North sweeping for tertiary raids, significantly removed from the fight, safe amongst monks, priests and druids up in Ynys Mons.

Would it ruin Arthur too?

Arthur had sent Llacheu for his fosterage to the steady thorn, the cantankerous rebel Caw. He did this as a demonstration of the king's grace and endless selfless and creative approaches for peace. Caw concocted endless superfluous land disputes in all directions, ever hassling Maelgwn, Urien and even suing for tracts as far south as Erging. Although incorrigible, Caw was reputed to be a good father of several sons and daughters, many of whom were radically loyal to Arthur. The Pendragon had visited Llacheu oft during his two summers and both Arthur and the Golden Prince had enjoyed holding Caw's newborn son, Gildas, earlier that very year.

The disputes had not seemed murderous. Neither treacherous. Yet, apparently, they were both. If, Bedwyr speculated, Caw sought to use the confusion at the conclusion of Baedan to assassinate the king, if he had turned Llacheu indeed against his own father, then what of the other son? What of Amr? Amr was under the roof of Caw as well, the two brothers having been sent North together.

Bedwyr paused his speculation. He, Owain, Cadwr and Gwalchmai took ten and fell in behind Arthur and his ten. Into the thick of the wood they went.

At just after three in the morning the

Pendragon gave a softly spoken order, carried out uniformly, with discipline and fearsome perfection.

"Blaze them."

Instantly banners of white became crackling orange, yellow, blue and red. The knights were thigh-high in mist and vaulted by banner and flame. The sight was so menacing that even the forest ghosts feared these men and not the reverse. The tactic illuminated the woods and at once differentiated friend from foe. Scores of the black lacquered leather chest armor were made manifest as expected, and not a few of the Ravens from the North.

Arthur opted for Excalibur, putting away his renowned spear, and brandished the Sword of Power, personally leading the advance.

The Britons that practiced Vivien and Maelgwn's methods were not hackers, not undisciplined, not aggressive. Their method was driven by counter-fighting. A diagonal position was ever maintained, except at the moment of the counter maneuver, away from the opponent's strong hand. When, on rare occasion, the Briton would need to strike first, a 'goad' was required, provoking the enemy to move, and to err. The goad took many forms, from a shifting step towards the opponent, to an intentional lazy jab, a head feint or an intentionally weak sword thrust to the foot of the opponent, enticing a drop of high guard or other ill-planned reaction.

With mist confusing belt-line-level maneuvers and the burning fabrics above creating disorientation, Arthur wheeled Excalibur around high, twice, three, now four times. He then waved down in the mist, well below the belt-line.

The 'up, up, up, then down' goad inevitably

caused the Saxon's eyes to search for the steel downward below the mist line. Upon their low aggressive strikes, Arthur would move but slightly to the side yet simultaneously forward through the plane of the blow, maintaining his diagonal line, and put Excalibur to the rib cage of the opponent. The union of Excalibur's sharpness and Arthur's technique rendered this a *one move kill shot*.

Up, up, up, then down, slide on the diagonal, kill through the ribs.

Although Owain, Bedwyr, Cadwr and the Hawk of May picked off sundry Saxons, Arthur himself was well ahead of them, tilling his enemy as a plow through soft soil.

There was no mania or screaming, neither was Arthur outside of himself. Methodically and stately, the Pendragon wedged through and annihilated the enemy. It is not known if even one Saxon or traitor escaped the slaughter within the ghostly and frightful wood north of the tabletop-shaped plane at the peak of Mynydd Baedan.

Bedwyr's eyes compassed the high willow and black poplar trees glaring down hard upon him.

"Now there be hundreds more fellows to haunt these woods," said Bedwyr to the trees.

***

The sun rose on day three after the battle had ensued and King Arthur was finally in his tent for the elusive sleep. The nation had been saved, but Arthur had nearly been felled by his own son. The sum of the matter being too much for even Arthur's balanced disposition, he politely asked Cai to remain awake and guard the tent (yet from afar, so that not even Cai would hear the king).

This Cai did.

Certainly, this was the abyss of Arthur's parenting career. Yet his mind went to Amr and his heart told him the abyss was yet bottomless. He could not feel worse.

Arthur wept.

CHAPTER 10
To Broceliande

A dark messenger clad head to foot in black had bidden Merlin go to the mysterious forests of Broceliande in the land of the Bretons. And Merlin was required to hearken to the call, dreadfully ill timing notwithstanding.

It grieved Merlin mercilessly to miss the Battle of Mynydd Baedan.

The days and events leading up to the epic - and where the Saxons were concerned, final - confrontation of his generation were a swirl of intrigue and change. In addition to being summonsed to this covert congress in Brittany, Merlin's acute, if not supernatural, discernment alerted him that the altercation with the bishops at Caerleon might result in them putting him in the dirt, permanently.

Pious men become corrupt with anger and corrupt men plunge into villainy. Hatred and misunderstanding (or understanding all the more) leads to a path of darkness and evil. Merlin felt he was at dire risk to be thrust into the Deep by the religious and atop this he had to make his mind ready, along with many arrangements, to go before the Brotherhood that had guided his spiritual journey for countless moons.

There were preparations ere he met with them that were not optional.

The dark messenger communicated to Merlin that it was time for him to complete the circle and to compass the square, to learn the Secret Rite. The pinnacle and crown of all esoteric wisdom; the final step in the spiral staircase of becoming. Because Merlin now knew in his heart that he would attend the meeting to learn *about* this mystery but not partake *in* it, he fully recognized that his travels to Brittany might be a one-way journey.

This Brotherhood was not the local orders of druids, but rather a more enlightened guild several rungs above his local colleagues (whose most sacred mysteries did but approach the outer porches of the Sacred Wisdom possessed by the Brotherhood). They were a Principality not to be trifled with.

The native faith was waxing like a moth-eaten old garment. Beautiful and vibrant in parts, elsewise steadily diminishing. And in no way dangerous.

Merlin had ever been a free-thinker. He naturally eschewed anything overly organized or official when it came to the governance of men's souls. And this extended to men and women of cloth, rank and diadem without respect of persons. From his earliest memories Merlin had intensely hated centralized power and corruption. This, he and Arthur shared with uncannily identical fervor.

There were, at Merlin's time, only a few strongholds of the old druidic orders (notwithstanding the utter norths of Albion where the Picts ruled). Ynys Mons, where a remnant remained of that fateful Roman purge so long ago, and Lough Derg in Eire. This was the sacred inland island where Patrick did not quite exterminate all of the 'snakes', as is commonly reported. A revival led by the daughter of Gebhan had flowered. Ironically, the very places that tyrants sought to annihilate from history protested violently by and through their obstinacy and existence.

These two locations wielded some influence that could even match and apply leverage with the Christian politicians.

Aside from these, each royal court had twelve bards (but this was an office and not a religion) and a few tribes still featured two small, local councils, the druids and the Dynion Hysbys. The druids were at all times confused with and blamed for the deeds of the Dynion Hysbys.

In Brittany and Cerne, Christ and His bishops ruled but followers of the old gods – sacred Tree and Water cults – persisted, and Vivien was their queen.

Although formally attached to none, the wizard was somehow viewed as Arch-Druid over all. The Dynion Hysbys especially hated Merlin because he had made an open show of their corruption and folly when he was yet a boy during that incident when the coward Vortigern was building a fortress near the town that now bears the wizard's name.

Yet they too, when confronted, would acquiesce to the Merlin.

Not so for the Brotherhood that had summonsed him.

Truly Merlin coveted the knowledge of the other Adepts, but now he was intent upon communicating to them a secret; a Hidden Thing of his own. The Catholic priests surely now officially loathed him and the Cymry bishops were in angry contemplation, brooding and stewing about his words. Thus, Merlin faced perils behind him and soon, perils from his own.

It was three days after the beginning of the battle. Merlin's strategy allowed him to make a reasonable calculation that the enemy was now starving and thirsty and had probably made their terminal decision to fight their way up the hill. If the Tribes of the Britons had been patient and carried out their part, victory was at hand, if not already won.

Merlin was long past exhaustion from traversing up north of Maesteg first, then through the city of his birth and then winding north yet further again, up past Gwynedd, to his initial destination. Afterwards, he had cut back across the midlands and down south to the port where he would travel by barge to Brittany. Ten youthful warriors could not match the druid's verve but, on this day, he was sore tired.

A man of great years, he had seen a span of events equal to several lifetimes. Merlin had been eyewitness to the cowardice of Vortigern, hiring and transplanting Saxons to Cymru's shores. He had seen Northern Britain crippled after the Night of Long Knives, had guided difficult and sometimes contradictory policies to help the mighty men of Ynys Mons and Gwynedd in the Old North not pass into extinction (as was the ever-encroaching reality for the Tribes of Lloegyr in the East). And now many of those same mighty men resented the Silures, and were leaning religiously towards Rome.

He had marveled in his long years at too many examples of vanity and greed in the form of endless raids and land skirmishes; witness to the utter foolishness of men that culminated in the Scots and the Gaels swapping great swathes of each other's countries.

Merlin had been present when a holy well sprang at the passing of one Pendragon, and he had personally consoled a second when his career was cut short by yet more cowardice by the Germanic maniacs.

Merlin enjoyed wine and hard drink, cider and ale; the best in the world, by his unbiased estimation. He lived hard, laughed often and drew upon mysterious authority as and when needed.

Merlin loved his mother and had never known his father.

He had been married once to a wife lost, Gwendoloena, and had lusted for but one woman since her passing: Nimue.

Merlin saw things in the Isles that he loved so dear, and things terrifying. The wizard witnessed things that challenge, alter and disrupt every man's worldview, regardless of his gods. These were the Blessed Isles and Merlin understood many of their secrets and why they were coveted. *The Coveted Isles.*

And he was blessed enough to see the rise of King Arthur, the Iron Bear and savior of his people.

Through the myriad failures in every person's life, of enterprise and relationship, of family quarrels and failed crops, of mentorships gone afoul, once in a lifetime chance happens and a person gets it right. And Merlin had got it right when it came to Arthur.

Thinking of the thirty-three-year-old sovereign gave Merlin a grin that produced happy, permanent smile-wrinkles.

Arthur was a ready pupil, a focused, accountable and competitive student, and above all attributes, was aware of the burden of his own place in history. Arthur was a living legend and, up to now, with no sign of wavering, had managed it to perfection. When he needed to be warm, he was warm. When he needed to be aloof, withdrawn. When anger was called for, wrathful. When forgiveness the needful thing, gracious and friendly.

Moreover, Arthur was a warm, jovial, attentive and wonderful father. Attributes oft not reciprocated by his sons, Merlin time and time again observed. Arthur selflessly handled this sad situation as well, empathizing with and regretful for the long shadow he cast over their lives.

The young king's love-life was a tightly guarded vault that not even Merlin could breach. The true love modeled daily by his parents did not translate to Arthur, as if some great fracture lay upon his heart. The king did not walk around gloomy or defeated by this, but his relationship with Gwenhwyfar seemed more of office than romance. Yet the Merlin doubted not that he loved her.

Great was Merlin's regret at missing his pupil and friend's moment of glory and the more Merlin immersed himself in regret, the more he determined to finish his course, and return to his king, alive. To this end, before leaving in the middle of the night at the conference in Caerleon, the Merlin secured the greatest surety of survival that any person living in that legendary and perilous time could. The druid swayed Maelgwn to leave Baedan early (and that only if victory was at hand) and to accompany him to and, by the Grace of God, from Broceliande.

They met at a port in Glamorgan later named after Arthur and it was a direct route south into Brittany. Ironically, the Merlin had traveled far from Baedan and then stealthily traversed back near the battle area to leave by boat for Broceliande.

Thus, Maelgwn, the Bloodhound Prince, upon abandoning Baedan near its conclusion, did not travel far.

One never knew the reception they would receive from the warrior greater than Achilles.

Though three hundred orderly vessels stacked the shores and many boatmen bustled about, these two stood out like cedar trees amongst mulberry bushes, two or more heads taller than any of their kinsmen.

For this reason, the salutations were brief to mitigate being seen. Merlin was nearly as tall as Maelgwn, and their moment of recognition created one of those instances where history pauses, and remembers. Two titans, ever used to condescending, exchanged a wordless greeting; eye to eye.

Breaking the silence, Merlin but said: "Lancelot."

Two perfect light blue crystals where eyes should dwell were looking back. A deep mannish voice that shook the leaves yet was somehow soft: "Merlin. To Little Britain then?"

Maelgwn was famous for cutting to the quick and these few words allowed Merlin to fully trust that he would have his shield of protection, his escort.

"To Broceliande."

CHAPTER 11
Follow the Gold

"Bedwyr. Where is he?"

Arthur's face now was clean. His short beard, at this season of life still full of the sandy colors of youth, was groomed and he was as presentable as a man operating on four hours of sleep, after three days of glory matched in equal measure with hell, could be.

A windy winter drizzle had brought back the mists but now there was a morning respite from ill weather. A sunny rainbow had formed, seemingly resting directly upon the Pendragon's tent.

Bedwyr's disposition did not match the break in the weather. His face was ashen; his eyes scanned the frozen snowy greens below.

"Which he?" Bedwyr gazed to the blue winter skies. "Merlin not found. Maelgwn…" No words, or angels from the sky, cascaded down to help the great knight. "Maelgwn now added to the missing."

No response was made (or needed), beyond the king encouraging Bedwyr to join him for the first meal of the day.

Shortly after, he went down and reposed with his men, who had also built a valley of white tents beneath the shadow of Baedan. As mid-morning progressed, he found himself losing the great optimism he had enjoyed from the night before. The king was now sensing that a great wrong had befallen his counselor, his friend. The Merlin possessed unparalleled strategic and tactical warfare skills, yet he had been absent to see Arthur carry out his strategy with absolute perfection. Arthur wished he could repeat the moment of victory for the Merlin in the same way that a son wishes he could recapture a great fish when his father is away from camp and, by misfortune, misses his boy's great conquest.

Arthur now had his first few real moments to contemplate, consider and begin to investigate.

After the amphitheater assembly in Caerleon, Merlin and the bishops had exchanged words. This was not uncommon and, with the ruckus the Counselor of Britain had created with his speech, it would have been impossible for Arthur to hear a horn blown from his lap, let alone Merlin who, at that time, was far away from the king.

Perhaps the discord had been more than the standard rhetoric and rancor of priests and their competing gods. That was Arthur's only lead, and thin at that. Church offerings and tithes, land deeds, water baptism and Sunday attendance, matters of soul and entry into the next world were not the only 'fork in the road' quandaries now faced by a free nation. *For the first time, truly free.* Unfortunately, matters of sword and tax prevailed as well.

The Pendragon did not possess the largest army in the known world but it had no peer for skill, vigor, loyalty, will and strategy. But would it continue to exist under its current construct? And should it? Arthur would soon have to congress with his twenty-four Round Table Companions (Arthur, the king, and the Champion Lancelot summing twenty-six) and then send the armies home for the winter - or longer.

The twenty-four Round Table Fellows, princes, kings and mighty men of Arthur's Britain, met on military matters alone. Arthur was the only connection between this fellowship of wartime companions and policy-making for the several kingdoms of Britannia. Each local *Rix* or chieftain served as a type of senator and, along with other representatives, formed a republican monarchy. The local tribal leaders made policy in their own lands. If tyranny arose at the local level and the natural rights of man were infringed, a petition could be made of the king, or, in some parts, of the druids or of the Church. The Round Table Fellowship was committed to the protection of the borders of Britain and Brittany and to carrying out the wishes of the local tribes. National versus local. Never, declared the Bear of Glamorgan, would the twain mix.

Should the unified army disband, reduce or remain? What was their role in a dawning era of peace? Should Arthur take Rome as his great-grandfather had? The proper course of action in imminent peace is as dangerous as when faced with imminent war.

Merlin would certainly know. But he was gone.

Urien, still smarting from scouting whilst his brothers had got to slay the Long Knife, brought a good tiding for his king.

"The Boar is awake," he grumbled.

Instead of fretting about what he could not control (Merlin's whereabouts), the great king attended to that which he could (deposing Aelle).

"We shall congress with our companions tomorrow, Bedwyr. I go now to see my enemy, alas, eye to eye, held this hour in the camp of King Urien."

"Will you run him through?" Bedwyr asked.

The Pendragon's answer surprised Bedwyr. "Have you not seen enough of it, companion?" His eyes guided them both to pools of blood mixed with snowy, muddy hoo-prints littered all around the pavilions.

"Cut the root, that it cease to bring forth bad fruit, my lord."

"You have the wisdom of the bards, my friend," Arthur responded. "And to that subject, we must swiftly get word to the queen before she hears it as a bardic ballad first. Will you please personally go and give her the report? That our lands and her father's lands are safe. Safe. Safe from all save the cost paid to earn it."

"To that task I shall presently attend." Bedwyr departed from the presence of Arthur, full of dread for the questions that would ensue about the queen's son on the immediate other side of rejoicing over the victory. And he wagered the sorrow would outweigh the elation. Greatly.

"There is much merit to Bedwyr's sentiment," said King Urien. Arthur and the powerful young king of the Old North paced thrice round the tent wherein Aelle was bound.

Urien's closest men had fought against him personally during the battle. Their report, sure to be a bard's song, revealed that the aging king of the South Saxons was swift as Lancelot with a sword but forgot himself with rage, resulting in clumsy unbalance, and that Lancelot himself had been needed to undo him.

Aelle had slain ten Britons but moved ahead

of his left rear flank in the course of action. Isolated and then cut off from his men, Aelle was defenseless as Lancelot clipped his left knee and right hand with one action. The Champion of Britain did this intentionally when he desired a prisoner instead of a corpse. The motion was effortless, fluid and looked more a short dance than a sword fight. Stunned and wounded, the Saxon warrior was easily subdued after that.

Prisoner of a tree stump within the tent, Aelle saw the flap ripple open. The sunlight kissed the ground and splintered shards of light through the white fabric. The Saxon heard, either in earnest or in his head, the melody of bardic ballads. A god greater than Odin entered the tent, clothed in the sun, compassed in all glory. Nothing better reflects the measure of a man than how he is seen in the mind's eye of his most hated enemies.

Arthur had no such gilded imagery for the foe before him.

Aelle. Pretender ruler of a sliver of the Isle, earned illegitimately. He had secured the Insula Vectis, a small but important daughter island off the mainland in Lloegyr. This fiend had sacked twenty small towns over many years of raiding and conquest, including an infamous and despicable tale of sore treatment of an entire river village near a place called Adeferas. The village had been abandoned but for an afternoon as its warriors went north in chase instead of staying put. What happened to the women, the children, and the elderly had haunted bedtime warnings and ruined mealtime reflections for two decades now.

Aelle had led them.

Aelle had been first man off the raiders' boat, boasting of this always.

All leaders of merit are first historians, and Arthur knew the history of this man.

The greying leader of the greatest foreign invasion against the Tribes of the Britons since before the days of Magnus Maximus was a full head taller than Arthur and half again his mass in muscle (the Bear of Glamorgan himself no small man), yet Aelle was ashamed that he had fought against this man and would have bowed before Arthur save for the bindings that prevented him.

Instead he gazed upon Arthur with defeated eyes.

King Arthur was wearing a simple blue tunic, trousers, with black belt and boots. Crimson caped with a large embroidered ensign aligned atop his left breast. A small silver shield was clasped to the great sovereign's right shoulder, itself covered with an additional sigil. The Saxon beheld the *Walles* warrior, wearing simple cuffs and thin silver breastplate; minimal armor for speed, coverage only upon mortal parts, in design superior to Roman armor, in appearance beautiful like unto their ancestors from Troy.

Aelle's eyes moved now to the king's helmet, tucked snugly in his left arm. Stories had spread amongst the Saxon tribes that Arthur's Champion was engineer of the *Walles* armor, that he found no function in Roman helmets that covered a man's nose at the expense of his vision, that he had fitted the helmet more closely to conform to the face of the wearer, removing any extra weight or distraction beyond that which was necessary to save a man's life from arrow, axe, sword or spear. The German marveled at the Briton. Lacking plume or horn, the simple helmet was fitted roundly to a man's head. Arthur's bore two draconian or serpentine fins above the ear and a special groove whereby he could wear, when the occasion was meet, a simple circlet of gold.

Sandy hair and blue eyes revealed a brain that was always busy. A king of Glamorgan and Gwent at fourteen and surely but a fortnight from being crowned Emperor of the World should he covet such. Aelle beheld a man who was a legend.

Even my people call their children Arthur! he cried within. His eyes panned down to the brand sheathed in the king's belt. *But not known for legendary mercy!*

Excalibur remained yet in scabbard, for now. Arthur knew not if the old Saxon spoke the Cymry tongue. Some of his forebears had been conscripts of Rome and thus, by deduction, Arthur tried Latin.

"This is a time of war and this is no mean country. However, it is not requisite that you be judged under the laws extended to a citizen of Glamorgan, or of the Confederacy of Britons," he began.

"Dragon." Aelle's Latin was broken but functional. "I know no law but death, no mandate but to wipe the *Walles* from OUR land. If you slay me bound like an animal, then like your enemy you will become. Wherewith then would we be different?"

The Saxon King did fear Arthur. The fear was a poison that oscillated between worshipful reverence and overt hatred, making Aelle double-minded, and very dangerous. Fear was the prevailing mechanism and its agency at last gave way fully to his hatred of the Britons. Moreover, by provoking this god-like king, Aelle might be slain, but not deposed.

Arthur, though anxious, even hungry, to rid the world of Aelle, was not to spring the trap, not soon to let hunger take the bait. And then, a random glance passed upon Aelle's scrip, a simple leather purse. It was worn and soft, revealing a bulge of gold coins.

Illtud had required that Arthur study the economy of gold and, when war campaigns interrupted the course of schooling, Merlin took up the slack and made Arthur do the same.

In times past it had been used as means for exchange on the Isles. At other times, gold was only used for trade and purchasing power at the ports. Presently, the currency of the Cymry was land deeds, livestock, property and rights of inheritance. A complex system which intended to give every man, low- or high-born, the same opportunity, was not without error or corruption. It led fallen men to manipulate laws and lent itself to raiding (indeed, the theft of another man's horse was a capital offense throughout the Isles) but it spared them from being poisoned with lust for gold.

During one of many discussions considering a policy change, Merlin had taught Arthur about value-based currency founded upon precious metals. But he had also made a warning. A warning turned memory that flew now as a fiery dart into Arthur's recollection.

"Remember this." The old druid had paused so that Arthur would mark him. "When pursuing the source of a conflict, follow the gold."

In the Mystery Schools, Merlin had been made to learn some legends about men of great wealth, without respect to nation, kindred or culture. These bowed not to any god save themselves, and loaned gold to both sides of a conflict to ensure, regardless of outcome, the wielding of power greater in might than ten Excaliburs: debt. Merlin could see hints and shadows of this practice staining the variant Christian churches, but knew not its source.

Arthur began to deconstruct the situation as if the Merlin were at his side, lecturing, quizzing and provoking. *Who would Aelle be indebted to if today had been his victory at Baedan? Who is he indebted to now?*

"There were legions of Saxons, Angles, Jutes, Picts and some Ravens from the north of my own blood in league with you. Now they lie, fodder for vultures." Arthur evoked the authority of words just as Merlin had trained him. "How did you feed, arm and transport them?"

"Victory fed them, bravery armed them and they were borne here by truth."

"What is truth?" posed Arthur.

Aelle's disposition shifted in the twinkle of an eye to that of a man who wanted to remove the stones of burden from his chest, for he knew he would not be spared. In these cases, talking can prolong the blade, provided that the talking is profitable. "This Island is the germinating seed of something more terrible than you or your cursed wizard have foreseen; nay, *can* foresee. Though you were victorious today, you have lost. And would you have lost, you would have won."

"Riddles must come with age," sighed Arthur, now looking deep through the shutters that housed the soul of the aging king of the South Saxons. "You have not my Merlin's wit, however. How now, Aelle, would a defeated chieftain in any wise be rendered a victor?"

Knowing some of the truth of the matter, Aelle conjured a veil and lied overtly. "You would have been co-emperor of the world with my three sons. Only a fool would rid the world of the great King Arthur. The *Walles* would be subjugated under the thumb of the house of South Saxons, your warriors conscripts, your women planted with the seed of Saxon. Your people who have no value to lift sword or push plow or spread legs - swept aside like mayflies. But you, young king, would live, though your people be enslaved or perish."

Again, violence was tempered with the Pendragon's unwavering self-control.

"Postulate with all fantasy. The 'ifs' of the future are made irrelevant by the 'ares' of the present. For you, Saxon raider, have lost." Arthur, not deterred, returned to the paramount issue. "This catalyst for evil, who gave it to you?" The Bear of Glamorgan made an aerial show of the contents of the scrip. The tent rained, for a moment, with Roman gold.

Aelle answered him not.

CHAPTER 12
The Bishops' Adjudication of Merlin

Now, the prominent bishops and elders of the Church of the Britons were these:

Dyfrig (who was also called Dubricious), the Bishop of Llandaff, a See founded by King Meurig.

Bishop Teilo, Dyfrig's chief disciple.

Illtud the Wise, teacher, preacher and philosopher from Caer Bovum, near the palace of Meurig and Queen Onbrawst.

Aidan, disciple of Dyfrig.

Bishop Comereg.

Meirchion, a very old man born at Glywysing in Arthur's kingdom of Glamorgan. He made residence in a palace near Illtud's school. Although from the South, his line hailed from the house Coel Hen, giving him deeply imbedded allies and affinity to the Old North. He was naturally amongst the southern kings placed in authority in the North to help fill the vacuum from the Night of Long Knives. Meirchion, who is also called Mark I, converted wholly to Catholicism and became something unique to the Isles; a sort of Roman Catholic priest-king.

(Being of royal pedigree as qualification for

service in the clergy was not uncommon to the Isles. They, too, believed they were a nation of priests and kings. However, they maintained a strict segregation of power and function. Often, a king would retire and become an elder, or a solitary saint. Sometimes a bishop would retire young and become a knight. That Mark did both was abhorrent, and bothered Illtud, above the others, to no end.)

Bishop Cadfan, son of Eneas and Gwen Teirbron from Brittany, but schooled under Illtud.

Bedwini, Bishop of Caerleon and Arthur's great friend.

Not present was David son of Non. He was but sixteen and sent home to Mynyw in the far south west of Cymru.

And so it was that these seven bishops, plus the priest-king Meirchion, remained long after the armies started their war march to Ogmore to prepare for Baedan. *The bishops and elders were preparing for a battle of their own.*

They met in a small, comely timber home in Gelliwig, which is in Gwent. Queen Gwenhwyfar was lodging in a stately white house nearby.

There was an ancient custom amongst the Britons that required secrecy and safety regarding anything shared privily amongst the clergy (and the bards and druids before them). *Secrecy unto the grave.* This custom created comfort and confidence, allowing the elders to speak their minds without fear of gossip, as gossip on spiritual matters could directly result in the separation of one's head from their body.

Knowing this custom, Meirchion, a hideous hybrid of a crone and stork, save with great swine ears, arrogantly spoke first.

"He must die. A dangerous heretic with the

High King's ear is a danger to the safety of the Nation, and her soul." Meirchion slumped down on a lounging couch, hungrily and rudely pushing around a charger filled with meats and cheeses.

"You would place the Bishop of Rome at the king's ear in the place of his druid." Dyfrig was not only bishop of the See located closest to that golden fortress of such fame where met the Table Round Fellowship in Caermelyn; he was also the unofficial leader of the primitive Church of the Britons, and commanded much respect from these men. "And that is your purpose here, Mark the Mad."

"See my sword?" Meirchion unsheathed his leaf blade, showing but a hint of steel above hilt, and then re-sheathed it. "Many have seen the rest of it for calling me that. And it was the last thing they saw. Shall I show you my madness?"

"We've suffered the fullness of violence on our Islands. For a thousand generations. Forever. If we yet have a nation when our boys return home, let us have an end of it. Let us rather endeavor always for peace. And a just peace indeed, not in word only." Bedwini was Arthur's personal bishop and ever spoke with a pleasant voice.

"Blessed is the peacemaker," Meirchion mocked Bedwini, and continued eating.

Dyfrig didn't flinch at the Crone-Stork's boorish threats. Utterly ignoring them, he gracefully took command of the discourse. "I do not like you, King Mark, but I concur on this. He does have our High King's ear. And not his alone. Merlin might be the most influential man in these Isles. His prophecies are honored by men of all religions. His riddles ever create awe and men dedicate whole days to gleeful analysis of them. He dazzles children; he brings joy and then, at an instant, fear and mystery. I cannot find the word." The bishop looked through a window at the heavenly hosts observing them, twinkling with their diverse glories and curiosity. "Merlin is a star.

"Morever," said Dyfrig, "his battle strategies have directly put us at the precipice of winning this war. The brains behind our army's bulk. This is as much Merlin's Britannia as it is our Arthur's."

All nodded at this truth. The men paused for some dining and then Dyfrig resumed.

"Let me tell of you briefly of another man. His name was Marcion and he lived about four hundred years ago. From Pontus, he was once succored by the Church in Rome, but then in the process of time he..." Dyfrig again searched for careful words, "...saw Scriptures and practices differently. He, like the Merlin, changed."

Dyfrig's face crinkled here with serious consternation. "He professed words similar to what fall from the Merlin's lips, and men heard him and believed. A sect formed around Marcion, a sect based upon no sect. An organization based upon no organization. His cult came to detest all of the institutions and ordinances that have been the center, guidestone and devotion of our heavenly calling. These Marcionites threatened all established religion, rejected any priesthood or ecclesiastical authority, and radically encouraged individual study and an obsession that would have no man in church on Sunday yet all paying lip-service to loving the Lord. All centered on this notion, this *easy believism* they called *GRACE*."

The learned men were well-read and had studied Marcion and his heresies, but none had connected them to the druid's disposition until Dyfrig illuminated the situation.

"Men will hear Merlin and should they swear by him or adopt his revelations, we will no longer have to worry about fighting Rome for paramount authority, nor for Land Grants or territories. Neither will Rome concern herself with making us drink of her cup." He looked sharply at the Catholic ruler, and his eyes met Cadfan's as well. "Why?" He asked the assembly and then answered his own question. "Because Merlin will have all men everywhere end all Religion. Theirs and Ours." He pointed at Meirchion and then to himself and Illtud.

"Surely you would not have us slay Merlin?" Saint Illtud the Wise at last spoke up.

Dyfrig clasped bony fingers together, rendering the tips red, and the knuckles white. "No, we shall not."

Meirchion rose in anger.

"Sit down." Dyfrig and Illtud were in unison, crisp and direct.

"As a druid, Merlin never evangelized Arthur to be a druid. As a... whatever he has become, he would not evangelize our king to be as he. Imposition is not part of his anti-establishment composition."

"However..." Dyfrig's hands motioned Meirchion back down yet again. "The ancient ideas and customs of the druids are part of our heritage and diminishing. The very mention of Merlin's new beliefs may sow seeds that we cannot accept."

"Wherefore," the bishop's words were careful, "I propose exile and strong encouragement for retirement. Let him share with Arthur over ciders and strong wine what he will, but let us greatly reduce audience time with the king. Let us forcefully encourage Arthur to name another bard to balance representation at Court."

"Retirement, not tyrannical murder." Bedwini the Peaceful was happy. "This is a balanced and just move."

All of the other bishops agreed to this, unanimously overwhelming the hard position of Meirchion (and the soft acquiescence towards him of Cadfan). Merlin's mysterious new beliefs, shared so brazenly at Caerleon, warranted censorship and control, but not death.

At last Meirchion's manners, subtle and serpentine, changed. "Very well. Control the rebel pagan and isolate him in his age." He finished with an empty sneering: "Please."

The assembly agreed to retire and discuss recommendations for the baptism of Saxon converts, along with attendance and worship requirements, in a fortnight (if victory was nigh) and to fast and pray until they heard of the final disposition of the Battle of Mynydd Baedan.

As they exited the house, Meirchion caught Cadfan clean at the elbow, jerking him close. Grave whispers ensued.

"Son of Brittany, Son of Llyn. You connect the Blessed Isles to the Continent."

"I'm just a student of Scripture who finds merit in the Sacraments of Rome," Cadfan said, humbly.

"You have lands of immeasurable importance. Doubt it not." Meirchion was yet slithery. "Now listen. Retirement is fine for the Merlin."

"Oh?" said Cadfan.

"Men travel in retirement. They visit loved ones. They repose in the serenity of silent contemplation on any number of our daughter islands, mountaintops or caves. And *sometimes*," a near hiss could be heard now, "sometimes misfortune befalls someone not often expected or missed at Court."

A low growl answered him. "And if long time unnoticed, sometimes they are simply forgotten altogether."

Meirchion unclamped Cadfan, allowing him to leave.

Next the old Crone-Stork validated that Vivien was lodging in Gwenhwyfar's white house, resting for the night after the meetings in Caerleon.

Boldly, and with poorly feigned manners, he encroached upon the door of her chamber.

"A few words, Lady?"

CHAPTER 13
Will I Now Lose My Final Son, Too?

Returning straightway from the battle, Bedwyr was met with warm reception as he politely petitioned the butler upon arriving at the residence of Queen Gwenhwyfar ferch Cywyrd. Known as the white house of Gelliwig, it was immaculate from vault to floorboard. Of all the palatial abodes and small lodges where the queen now had 'homes', this great and safe place was in earnest her only 'home'. Securely nestled under the best vantage point from Lodge Hill, she truly loved the serenity, safety and familiarity of this place. It was, after all, her father's home and she desired never to live outside the cantref where she had been born, although she had used to enjoy travel.

At thirty and five, grievous sorrow had doubled her years. The queen was a woman with passion and expertise in the advanced arts and toil of the world's most difficult occupation: motherhood. It was what she had been born for, what she excelled at; she was mother first, queen second, and tertiary wife.

And this 'mother of mothers' had, in just the

past three seasons, lost two young sons in the Saxon Wars. Presently she worried to distraction about the remaining two. As soldiers bask in the glory of battle campaigns, boasting boldly of scars, touting questing tales of damsels fair and dragons felled, there is but brokenness back at hearth and home. Brokenness of mothers and wives. Brokenness that exceeds the capacity of the spirit, leaving shards where verve once flourished.

Hour over hour, there is despair in the place of daily functioning.

To see one's babe grow to fourteen and then go off to war, and this without exception, without respect of station or privilege, engendered all the more hatred towards the Germanic horde – the invaders. The Cymry possessed respect for all children and mothers under heaven. For this cause, they never invaded anyone, save (with the hypocrisy not lost on the common person) their own rival clans.

The queen, like any other parent, was numbered amongst the broken.

Struggling to flicker somewhere well beneath the surface of her ghostly shell, Gwenhwyfar still possessed great beauty and authority. Her hair was long and red, full of curls that were corralled, braided and plaited. Her torques were petite, but ornate. Her long neck flattered and displayed her hair, ending in perfect soft 'Ls', curving over soft, round, feminine shoulders. Firm breasts supported her beloved green gowns and the freckles upon her chest and shoulders were an alluring, speckled and adorable garnish. Her cheeks were a bit larger than her chin, her nose was turned up just so; her face was symmetrical, proportioned, winsome and commanding, a striking Cymry woman.

The beauty was still there, except for the eyes. These were sunken into pits, always purple around the soft fleshy area as if she had been struck daily upon the nose.

Already fair-skinned, her depression took her pale but healthy complexion and made it look as spilled milk. Her face and neck were almost translucid. She ever chewed upon her fingernails and her promenade was not quite right.

And she loathed company.

The butler knocked softly at the door of her massive chamber, a 'house within a house', and then Bedwyr, her childhood friend, the one she had known seasons before she met Arthur and the man with whom the couple supped most often (especially before and between the Three War Campaigns), entered.

Bedwyr did not speak first.

"So." The dark-circled emerald eyes opened wide, causing the red lashes that were their canopy to almost disappear entirely within the folds of sad and swollen skin. "Merlin's magick could not save him. He told me as much."

Bedwyr opened his mouth. Some sound and throat-clearing ensued, some hand motion that should accompany speech, but words, the great knight could form not.

Only just inside the bedchamber doorway, a calming hand appeared upon the knight's shoulder.

"It was wrong to ask you to deliver news to my wife, our queen."

"Arthur!" Tears sprinted down his cheeks. "But how?"

"I finished with Aelle with as much haste as I could and am here to be my own messenger to our Lady. I will apprise you on Aelle later. Please,"

Arthur hugged Bedwyr hard, "go now and rest."

Bedwyr looked briefly upon the *Corpse Queen*. He exited.

The simple blue tunic of the king then embraced the ornate green gown. Gwenhwyfar accepted the hug, as it kept her failing body together.

Arthur Pendragon, the great king of the Britons, began to explain the death of Gwenhwyfar's third son with brave and rehearsed words, making every effort to bring a peace that passes understanding. Knowing that rumor and whisper would deliver the dark tiding of the treachery of Llacheu to the queen's ears, Arthur could not but tell her the truth. From the gore and detail he spared her, even upon her wail and request.

They cried.

They reminisced.

Gwenhwyfar spoke loud words most foul.

They napped.

They kissed hard.

She screamed while he held her.

For two days they ate not and drank but a little water. Over and over again, questions were posed, the open wound, the needing to know.

The never seeing their boy again.

The toll of three distinct war campaigns.

Screaming at God.

Cursing the Devil.

Bargaining for a return that would not be. That could not be.

The weeping.

Throughout the wrathful grieving that immediately follows loss, the king did all he could for the Queen of the Britons, but felt as if he was failing to serve her.

King Arthur had learned love, and loved outwardly, as modeled by his father. Meurig exhibited a true and rare adoration towards his spouse and constant companion, which included: gentleness, compromise, leadership, sacrifice, humor, affection and recognition of a woman's soft wisdom. The more senior Pendragon's only error was in not emphasizing to Arthur that such a love occurs next to never in this fallen world. In the spiraling dance of romance entwining men and women throughout the dispensations of time, real love is rare. When it is present in the home, when you see it all the time growing up as a lad, the expectation may develop that *what mother and father have must needs be for everyone, and certainly for me*. But this is rarely so.

Arthur came to love *Love* itself and the art of it more than he did the actual women in his life. A connection to the person was lost, obfuscated or long ago given away to someone else somewhere in the king's distant past and, though never cold, he had not yet found the deeper links with his wife that he saw daily between Onbrawst and Meurig.

As a result, when Arthur opened a door, he did it for the Office of Love, not necessarily for his woman. When he rubbed her feet and served her mead or cider, 'twas for some unknown, immeasurable standard of Love, and not as the relaxed and natural extension of time spent with his mate. When he complimented her for her excellence in ever mastering the difficulties of governing the home, three plenary courts, and a myriad of administrative functions, the words of high praise were a performance to Love, and not a pouring out upon her. And when he ensured she was pleasured (even if he could barely walk from the fatigue or pains of war), it was 'for Love'.

Moreover, when Arthur spoke poetically and

deeply of handholds hewn in heavenly molds wherein one would know their true love at finger's first clasp, it was for the Office of Love. It was, ultimately, not for the woman whose hand he held.

None of this did the young king do with intention to hurt Gwenhwyfar or any damsel, nor was he even aware of the fracture. Love itself had entered in and become a surreptitious idol to the king. His parents' unattainable, perfect relationship, along with an incident during the spring king-making rites, had created of Arthur a complex and, in many ways, abnormal man in matters of the heart.

Though given the choice and accepted without dissimulation, the marriage with Gwenhwyfar was political. By rote, Arthur was a wonderful husband, lover and partner. Tragedy unearths pre-existing cracks within, exposing them. And then it fissures the crust of the soul. Warm and friendly, Arthur, at the time when consolation and warmth was most needed, found himself just a little cold towards Gwenhwyfar, distant.

And there was more.

Arthur, when not on the field of battle or dominated by moments of war and defense, was lately of a truth thinking about another.

A painted and dark someone else.

Even with his son dead and extant blood yet to let in order to root out the treachery from within. Even with mountains more of private anxieties and discreet pressures yet to shoulder. Even with major policies and so many sleepless (and perhaps sleepless and *alone*) nights ahead before his Summer Kingdom could in earnest dawn, his thoughts ran not to these things but instead to a delicious and shadowy distraction;

to taboo acts, spiritual, fleshly and wrong.

A princess and daughter of a Giant, dark, painted, tiny. They had met while schooling at Llantwit Major. And she and the queen shared the same forename.

However, Arthur would not empower his lust to long burn, taking his thoughts captive no sooner than they formed; for no man that has ever lived, save Jesus of Nazareth, was honorable as Arthur the Silure.

He held his wife day after day during the tempest of dread.

On day three the queen began to consider matters outside the immediate sphere of her grief. She queried the king, "How did Merlin not see this? Was this part of his losing the Sight?"

Arthur knew not of what she meant.

"Can we please speak to him now?" she asked, with soft urgency.

"I don't know where he is," Arthur said.

"I see. Then let's decide what to do about our son." Gwenhwyfar made a sharp-turning subject change.

"Of our Llacheu? Gwen, as I've said, we—"

"Nay," Gwenhwyfar interrupted. Staring out of a window, she surveyed a blanket of January snow lightly layered with mist about the courtyard, covering it as a white cloth pressed hard against one's face after a warm bath. "Of Amr, our sole remaining son, heir to Glamorgan and Gwent, the Edling, and future of Britain." Her voice broke because it was filled heavily with obvious sarcasm. Obvious futility. She pivoted around slowly and said: "He is part of the plot too, is he not, husband?"

"The conspiracy to plunge our country deep into official Civil War goes above Caw and above religious disputes." Arthur joined her at the window. "Caw and the Saxons," and now he referred to what had been discovered when deposing Aelle, "are controlled by the same forces. By some Shadow Enemy I know not.

"Llacheu," Arthur continued, "Llacheu was meant to take my head or, alternatively, both he and I were to perish in the intrigue of contrived skirmish, and then…"

Queen Gwenhwyfar braced for the next sentence. There is no capacity for the tears of a grieving mother and now, after three days of weeping, more gestated, and streamed.

"Our inquiry confirmed that Amr was then to take the throne as a secondary plot, should Llacheu fall."

"You are sure of this?" screamed the queen. Stopping herself swiftly, she paused and answered her own question. "Yes, you are sure. Heirs to the Summer Kingdom when you and I go and sleep in the Lord, and for treachery they would have the crown now. Oh, the evil of power meets youth!"

"The sons of Maelgwn love me and the sons of Arthur hate me." The politics of North versus South were venomously worming into the sinews of the royal family.

Gwenhwyfar began to tremble, twitch and seize. "The Round Table Fellowship will not abide this treachery. They, or some of their own companies, will hunt down and kill our son as a Judas, a coward, a demoniac in league with the Long Knife." Taking both of Arthur's hands, she fell to the bed, screaming and screeching as a great owl. "Will I now lose my final son?"

The thunderous pain of the question rattled Arthur, yet he but looked at her, listening, temperate and warm, attempting not to break. Exerting force to peel back the vice that were her fingers in his, the Pendragon cupped his wife's cheeks. "We must save our people, though we lose ourselves."

"Let then it not be a bard's song or the subject of boasting in some tavern, months or years hence. Do all to quietly remove him, that men may not curse him save by rumor in his passing."

"What do you ask of me?" said Arthur.

"Go swiftly, Lord Arthur." Ice replaced sorrow, but for a moment. "And quietly." Gwenhwyfar's upper lip bit down hard upon the right side of the lower. "Take Excalibur and kill our son. Yourself."

Arthur was agape.

"And then never speak of it before gods or men," she concluded.

A thousand thousand scenarios were weighed and considered, filtered, mashed and reconfigured in Arthur's mind.

Merlin would know what to do. But Merlin was not there, causing the king to, in the corridors of his mind, launch a great counsel and debate with himself. In the end, he concluded that the queen's course was correct. Arthur shifted in countenance from grieving father and supportive husband to his office as king.

He rose.

"Amr was patrolling Ynys Mons with my nephew, Mordred, as of three days and more ago. I assume he remains in the North. I will go as a shadow and resolve this – in the shadows."

Arthur was a master of disguise. These arts he had learned from the Merlin. In an instant, he could transform from regal symbol of grace and splendor to black-cloaked night rider. He was adept at this and, under lighter or humorous circumstances, enjoyed putting a mask o'er the pressures of being history's most famous king. Indeed, he would often fool his mates and subtly attend a meal as a beggar or bard, only to reveal that they had hosted an angel unawares the entire time.

This journey from Gelliwig up to Gwynedd would not be filled with physical danger. The Saxons had been vanquished. The challenge would be traveling near roads and villages where great celebrations of liberty and hope were breaking out, and ongoing. It was his adoring and happy citizens that presented danger of discovery for the king.

"Would you have me do anything else, my queen?" It struck Arthur as he posed the query that Gwenhwyfar now looked as if she were no longer there at all. Indeed, she was a shell and not there.

"Yes, please," she responded. "Immediately and with great haste, please have your sister sent to me."

"Anna?"

"Gwyar."

The request was greatly peculiar, for this sister and the king's wife were as oil and water.

However, he thought, *What has remained straight and logical during the crisis, here at the end of the Saxon Wars?* King Arthur opted not to ask why and gave his queen an affirming look.

"The Mistress of the Isle of Apples to your court I shall summon, with haste."

He then embraced the shell of the queen, feeling the madness absorbing its host. King Arthur knew this would be the last time he would interact with this honorable and good woman as husband and wife.

He would go do right, but his wife could never look upon the executioner of her sons again. The marriage was surely now over; she already saw dead sons when she looked upon him.

Arthur fought back a rapid involuntary fantasy: *Now I can be with the painted woman who tries to rule my heart when my head turns to lust.* Killing the thought, he sorrowed for the queen, for himself, and for his traitor sons.

The king, after three days of intense time with Gwenhwyfar, departed her side. Forever.

CHAPTER 14
The Loose Ends Ere the Dawn of Day

Before departing to execute his son, Arthur convened with Bedwyr as promised.

They would speak of many things. But the plan regarding Amr, he would conceal. This was his accord with Gwenhwyfar, and they would do all to make their son a missing person instead of a publicly slain traitor.

The two friends hiked up the trail, not far from Gwen's white house, to their favorite fort, Lodge Hill. From there, they could signal to any of the wheel of fortresses protecting the kingdoms. Within twenty minutes the citizens and livestock could flee danger through trails and well-designed pathways out of the valleys and up into Lodge Hill for safety.

Its military value notwithstanding, the hill fort also provided spectacular views. The River Usk could be seen in all her green pomp and glory, cutting through breathtaking Caerleon, pouring gracefully into the Severn Sea. Nearly the whole of the Vale of Glamorgan, with its hills and valleys, its sheep and song, its forests and ancient slopes, could be ingested and enjoyed.

There was a great sloping field just below the fortress where wild horses sprinted and toiled playfully for territory. Sheep grazed freely. The hill and fortress were all the diverse splendors of Cymru consolidated into one place.

Arthur truly loved Lodge Hill.

He inhaled, gulping thirstily a few draughts of the cool January air, and then began to recount for Bedwyr what had occurred shortly after the knight had left the battle camp.

King Arthur's personal physicians had attended to Aelle's minor wounds immediately after Arthur had removed himself from their initial brief exchange. The king deliberated most cautiously with his cousin, and in the stead of Merlin, primary counselor, Illtud. He had made haste to the battle site after the discourse with the other bishops and shared Arthur's worry and surprise that Merlin had been gone since the eve of Baedan.

Not willing to rule out foul and murderous deeds by Meirchion, Illtud broke the tradition of secrecy amongst clergy and shared some of the late-night discourse amongst the seven elders. They didn't dismiss the likelihood Meirchion had been personally involved, but he was accounted for before and after they had all seen the wizard. However, he could have launched or coordinated a murderous plot with Caw. This all seemed most unlikely.

Or so Illtud hoped.

A cleric groomed for the Bishopric of Glamorgan and Gwent, Illtud was patient, humble, a devout student of Dyfrig, and no novice of matters political, philosophical and spiritual. Illtud and Merlin debated for hours, concluding always with a hearty hug and no mutual conciliation. Neither Merlin nor Illtud hated Rome or her Catholicism, as both saw great beauty amongst her traditions, and faithfulness and grace amongst her converts. However, they were in one accord regarding the Roman Church's ongoing tendencies towards statism. Both hoped to repel this peacefully.

Where Dyfrig had no stomach for pagans or Catholics and spent his time in ongoing communal contemplation with Meurig, Illtud was very active, ensuring that his cousin the king, now thirty and three, had what every king needs from his counselors - balance and perspective.

Now Merlin was missing.

Arthur had desired advice and to garner support for his desire to send a strong message back to all of Germania. But Aelle was a large bullish man, an old and very skilled fighter. Thus, there was direct and real risk in Arthur's proposition.

Urien, Gwalchmai, Cuneglasas, Cai and many others were against it. Illtud was in agreement so long as the crown would revert back to Meurig (for Llacheu currently lay upon sawdust and ice awaiting burial while Amr, although seventeen and older than his father had been when made ruler over his Tribes, was no Arthur and would be considered too young by the Cymry). With significant reservation and much protest, the Round Table Companions yielded to the king's proposed course.

Arthur would engage Aelle in combat himself, sovereign versus sovereign, thus officially ending the Battle of Mynydd Baedan and quelling the Saxon threat forever.

As Arthur was unscathed, Bedwyr knew the outcome was favorable and continued to listen, captivated. The king continued to describe what had unfolded next.

As noon had arrived that day the sun had dispensed its shards of glory upon Excalibur, unsheathed above the bent elbows of the stoic king of the Britons. Aelle was freed of his bonds and his battle gear fully restored. Armed with a number of diverse killing devices, he favored the short gladius: borrowed from Rome but modified, thinner, and curved. Aelle also used a great club, with hopes of countering the reach of Excalibur.

A hundred or more fighting men, not a few bards and all the Round Table Companions, save Maelgwn, formed a great circle. In the circle, the two kings engaged.

King Arthur, as with all of his men, had adopted the fighting style of Maelgwn. With an angular discipline that would cause Pythagoras to marvel, the Arthurian warrior was never fully exposed; it was more a dance than a fighting style, a true martial art. The Lady of the Lake, who was Vivien the Breton, had learned and perfected this way from her ancestor Vercingetorix, the great Gallic opponent of Julius Caesar.

The Saxon, clumsy but swift, swung low. Arthur opted not to block the blow of Aelle's club. The Cymry warrior's mind was trained to act contrarily to emotion or instinct; to move left when the mind begged to go right, to go towards a blow when the untrained emotion said to flee. Sliding towards his opponent whilst the club was midflight with two aggressive inside shuffle-steps positioned Arthur to run Excalibur through the Boar's ribcage, below his left shoulder, and circle away, out of range.

The crowd gasped at the speed with which the Long Knife had been defeated. As soon as they gasped, however, there was collective repentance of the same. Arthur was the second greatest warrior in all the land (and maybe the known world), so now many men looked up at each other and laughed at the notion that they had gasped in surprise in the first place.

"It is mortal." Arthur looked round the camp, seeing again the remains of the greatest loss of life in a generation. "The money, the numbers, the magnitude! Tell me how you brought so many thousand thousands of men here and I give you my word that those of your kind settled on our coasts will be given mercy. Who funded you? *Who?*"

He moved close to the enemy, and by good fortune the words uttered were heard only by Arthur. "You will spare not your own sons. But you will spare mine?" Air pushed awkwardly out of the Saxon as he spoke. There was a fixed supply of it that would not be replenished.

Sons? Arthur noted that his adversary had used the clear plural. Even with poor Latin, the meaning was clear. The communication, both spoken and by gesture of face and tone, was clear. Arthur's sons were treacherous and the plot was not confined to an internal struggle of North versus South amongst the Tribes. It extended to the commanders and elite within the invading horde as well. A conspiracy that transcended the war, and national borders.

(As Arthur shared these things with Bedwyr, he did not indicate that both sons were involved. Letting Bedwyr deduce this or not, Arthur was very selective with his words, providing the information whilst keeping the promise to his wife to kill Amr discreetly.)

Dark blood painted the Saxon's side black.

And then he screamed, this utterance heard by all. "Heed me, Head of the Dragon. You and I are the same! Empty carcass used by greater powers! Empty carcass, empty carcass!"

Aelle made a desperate, manic lunge for Arthur. Excalibur halved the club, blocking the overhand strike. Moving to the left, the Iron Bear opened the Boar's throat. "Who?" he screamed one final time, grabbing the larger man by the nape of the neck, very close to the gash.

A shriek of proud agony ensued. Aelle let loose the words "Ask", then "Priest", and finally "Meirchion".

Arthur, circling once more to the right, flashed Excalibur, removing the head.

Reflexively, the Pendragon knelt to the ground quickly and grasped his opponent's sword to cast it away, as if his headless foe could still somehow do him harm with the blade. As he was about to fling it hard against the trees, King Arthur noticed a green plaid ribbon woven around the hilt, and from age, pressure and oil, now part of it. His thumb found an edge of thread and unwound the ribbon. A glare and grimace, paired with rage, rushed through his ferocious visage. *This is one of ours!*

And though the High King was emboldened in his righteous anger, the earth, filled with so much innocent blood, and especially of the children of simple coastal villages, roared in victorious thanksgiving, justice having at last been delivered by the Sword of Power and the Just King!

Recomposing himself, but still riled as a great bear, Arthur declared: "We will send it to his sons, with our ordinances, written in Latin, for West Saxons."

The princes and mighty men of the Britons, of

Powys, of Dyfed, of Gwynedd, Cernwy, the Old North, Albion, Glamorgan and Gwent, the great men of the remnants of Lloegyr, the Irish and the Bretons all exhaled a unified and full exhalation of victory, knowing they were about to enjoy the first afternoon's rest in three generations.

Gwalchmai was first to respond. "We have no policy, lord."

"Not yet. And to that matter we must assemble soon, Hawk of May." King Arthur held his prize by the locks. "I must make haste to speak with my wife, then we will finalize those matters. We will decide on baptism and census and governance and all else quickly."

The eyes in the lifeless head blinked, now all nerves and no brain.

Arthur was eager for the children of the invaders to see the trophy, fresh and pitiful, and know that the Pendragon himself had finally removed the Boar's head from its thorny, black body.

"Too much deliberation and indecisiveness will render our message–" Arthur paused, as one does when attempting to avoid the impropriety of laughing at their own jest "–unrecognizable, from decay, to its recipients."

The men laughed.

And so it was that King Arthur felled King Aelle with his own hand, thus formally concluding the Battle of Mynydd Baedan.

The Round Table Companions had broken camp to rest, and then soon to deliberate on the Matter of Britain: to find Merlin. To find Maelgwn.

After hearing all these things, Bedwyr asked, still considering Arthur's report, "What will you do with the day?"

"I need three days more to mourn the loss of my son." A vague yet not untrue statement by the king. "Please rest fully today, Bedwyr," Arthur continued. "Illtud and Bedwini would have us go the New Troy as soon as we are able."

"To Londinium? But why?"

Arthur actually blushed for the former part of the answer he made and then rallied with confidence for the latter: "There will be another crowning," he chuckled, "this time to include attendees from Loegria, some Pictish tribes and even men of other nations. Additionally, we will be strategically close to West Saxons to both communicate and implement our intentions with the remnants of the invaders."

"Makes sense, Emperor Arthur." Bedwyr placed a humorous jab into the rib of his friend.

Arthur laughed aloud.

"Please help with any preparations you see fit over the next few days, but insulate me from visitors. I require solitude."

"Even from Cai? He will not like not knowing exactly what you are about."

"Assure him I will be safe and, for once, desire and insist upon no company," replied Arthur, "even from my steward."

The light mood was temporary as Arthur asked one more question of his most loyal knight.

"Merlin and Maelgwn?"

"Found them we have not, my lord."

Arthur had no choice save to compartmentalize his proliferating woe and worry for the two. Presently, his sole focus was serving his wife, now well sunken into madness and despair, and to rid the land of an eighteen-year-old assassin wrought from the king's very own loins.

At this, Bedwyr and Arthur hiked down from Lodge Hill.

The Pendragon then enjoyed an overly long

soak in the natural spring bathhouses of Caerleon. While the sulfuric, healing waters soothed many hurts, creating deep temporal relaxation, his mind wandered to the dark female image and fascination of his youth.

Back to when he was fourteen…

Arthur killed the thoughts, arose and robed. Then he made ready his disguise.

He preferred to be cleanly shaven but did wear a short, stubbly beard during war campaigns. He kept the scruff. However, he darkened it and his wavy hair with a coal-based dye, some of which he added around his eyes.

Trading his beloved dark blues and reds for nightshade black, to include long leather gloves and a doubly hooded rider's robe layered over an also black tunic, the young king was seemingly transformed into night itself.

Like a raven flying at midnight, a black-on-black shadow, knowing every hidden and short path, he rode until dawn. He passed through the forests of the Cornovii and then made hard north before sleeping, discreetly, in the woods, near the fortress of a chieftain called Ogyrfan Gawr.

That such a giant man had produced an equally petite girl-child was astonishing, yet on account of her power, she was no less giant than her father.

Ogyrfan Gawr was the father of Gwenhwyfar. The *other Gwenhwyfar.*

Arthur felt great guilt for sleeping under the shadow of the one who sometimes dominated his thoughts (and of late, increasingly so) while his Gwenhwyfar was surely playing out concurrent nightmarish thoughts, fighting impossible demons of dread. Yet, he wanted to be near the Gwen who was not his.

Was she making residence in her father's home this very night?

Against reason, was she thinking of the glorious king at that moment whilst he was but a stroll and staircase's climb away, sleeping sooty and destitute as a hermit in the wood?

A sleety, miserable winter rain had fallen and the night was frigid but Arthur managed to make a well-concealed fire and ate a few of the kind of mushroom that appears in an instant after the rain. He shut his eyes, thinking about her, enjoying the two to three hours of distraction that began as delightful visions and passed happily into sleep.

From Ogyrfan's fortress, the dark rider would continue north and then bank left, arriving unseen at last in Ynys Mon. At the northernmost tip lay Amlwch. Invasions were sometimes attempted through a port there that, if achieved, would grant wide open and easy admission to the Blessed Isles.

To protect this nook of vulnerability, by and through arts of engineering and architecture that could only have come from ancient, wiser times, or else by otherworldly helpers, the Cymry had been able to construct a port that could be reached with the greatest ease, but yet seen with the greatest difficulty. The location of the markers and use of angled embankments made navigation and landing at the place called Porth Amlwch easy if the routine of sea twists and turns was known, perilous if not.

Truly the harbor was at once inviting and lethally hidden.

Many souls littered the seas above Porth Amlwch, having known not how to make land. For this cause, young men could patrol the area with relative safety, as encroaches were rare. The northern patrol near the Caledonian Forrest was the most dangerous; the northern patrol near Porth Amlwch, the least.

The Prince Amr, under the guidance of Gwyar's oldest son, Mordred, could train and ride leisurely and lightly around the port area, enjoying strong drink, fair damsels and the infrequent and entertaining apprehension of thieves and rogues leaving the Isle.

Finding them was not difficult.

Arthur spotted the two, bundled in heavy, hooded cloaks but without armor, riding along a thin shoreline.

As was reported, the two were inseparable mates and Arthur, looking the part of a thief, of a dirty wretch or rogue, would need some fortune to separate Amr from Mordred. At a midrange distance, there was no chance the king would be identified, so, in the place of stealth, Arthur opted for an overtly obnoxious approach.

He dismounted and, with altered voice, began screaming profanities and goading words at the two boys.

"Drunkard." Amr tugged at the shoulder of Mordred.

The two made after the soot-smudged black-clad drunkard.

At that moment, Arthur heard, were it trick of wind or by some mysterious phantom emanation, Merlin's voice upon his ear. "*Patience, Bear.*"

The teenage warriors were at full gallop now.

"*Patience, Bear.*"

Arthur heeded but dismissed the origin of the spectral voice. At just the right time he mounted up and ran hard upon Mordred's side, causing Amr to bank hard that way as well. Rapidly, the elite equestrian zagged back in the opposite direction, causing his pursuers to crash their steeds hard, shoulder to shoulder.

Mordred fell violently from his white horse, which stumbled heavily but stayed aright. Rolling twice he landed, flat-backed and staring at the heavens. Flipping his wolfskin garment out of his face and thumbing off the fresh, sticky blood on his upper and lower lip, he coughed twice and then released a bellowing jackal's laugh, screaming:

"Amr! Get him!"

The king galloped with urgent haste, as he had to create distance between himself and Mordred. But he also had to keep Amr close enough to make the pursuit worthwhile and not cause the boy to give up on the fleet-horsed fleeing vagrant. Arthur balanced the pace just so and Amr nearly met stride with him o'er a short ridge away from Mordred.

The king, in his guise still shadowy though it was day, did not unleash Excalibur as the two men rapidly dismounted. Amr, smaller than his father but sculpted, young and very strong, attempted to wrestle his foe to the ground.

Eyes met during the brief struggle.

"Father?"

Instead of an oratory of surprise, bewilderment or excitement following the identification, Amr, knowing the matter, unhanded the king and drew his sword.

There was no confession, no manipulation of words or effort of evasion. No adolescent lies. No plea. Rather, hubris filled the traitorous boy's overly confident head, as Mordred was surely riding or running in lagging pursuit behind his friend.

Arthur drew his dagger, which was called

Carnwennan. Its short hilt was white as the foam atop the Irish Sea, its blade dark, dark grey. As the wintry light of day touched upon the blade, somehow it cast a shadow upon Arthur larger than the breadth and width of what it ought to have done.

Nearly as sharp as Excalibur (which could cut steel), Carnwennan threaded Amr's winter layers as if a seamstress were carefully cutting and resizing the material. Cloak and coat were naught, and neither was flesh or sternum. Through the breastbone the heart was cleaved, and in one motion the dagger reappeared near the apple of the Son of Pendragon's throat.

Arthur was atop the horse and vanished so quickly that he was gone and out of sight before the body fell to the winter's ground, welcoming one more treacherous Briton into her callous and cold embrace.

As he rode, the scream of one word from Mordred was heard -

"Brother!"

CHAPTER 15
We Both Know He Loves You Most

Women know things.

Women have an intuition that men will never possess. In several stations of the human experience, they are simply wiser, smarter.

How they know what they know, in what corridors they glean and what circles they gather, and of their innate ability to read the motives, circumstances and the real story behind any matter (and especially where relationships are involved) is a mystery that engenders awe and can never be comprehended by men.

And of the mysteries, motivations and true constitution of the Pendragon, as a man, as a friend, as lord and husband, Gwenhwyfar knew. For women know things.

A person being insane in general removes in no way their accuracy or credibility on a specific matter. Even one who is lunatic can sum one and one.

"Please, you are most welcome. Sit." The whole of the kingdom knew there was something different about Gwyar. Despite Gwenhwyfar possessing less fear than most for the king's sister and being brave (and mad), there was still a slight tremor in her salutation, though she was Queen and Sovereign and thus of the greater authority.

"How does your husband, Llew, sister-in-law?"

Princess Gwyar traced the rim of her teacup thrice clockwise, then paused.

Thrice clockwise once more. Gwenhwyfar wondered if this were some spell or enchantment being cast upon the room, but dismissed the thought as superstition.

Gwyar's hair, which was as black as a crow, was pulled back tightly, fastened flat to her head, and braided from forehead to end. She was wearing a knotted necklace made of black leather woven through three grey stones, two of which had a small engraving of the three rays, or Awen, and the third a beautiful etching of the four bear claws, the ensign of her Silure tribe. The necklace had no slack and Gwenhwyfar noted that it must ever choke its wearer.

In fact, all of Gwyar's attire was close-fitting. Her dark blue and grey dress, intricately laced along the ribs and at the bosom, seemed as if it were her skin and no garment. Although a mother many times over, she was youthful in form, a tiny hourglass like a faerie. Gwenhwyfar was bewildered at how beautiful she looked at certain angles and yet from other prisms, uncomely. She also seemed 'there and not there' when flashing a passing glance toward her, or away.

Lastly, to demonstrate respect and match the formality of the summons, the princess had one gold torque orbiting her left arm and wore the simple silver circlet crown, humble yet powerful; a popular fashion piece amongst her tribe.

By contrast and irony, Queen Gwenhwyfar

was in the same white gown in which she had slept and spent her days, certainly several times over. Her red hair was everywhere and nowhere close to regal in presentation. And she was pungent from a failure to bathe or pay regard to her hygiene.

In spite of this, Gwyar offered no return assessment and judged not the mad queen, but rather tried to respond with simplicity and grace. However, whenever Gwyar spoke it was with a quiet power, like a boiling kettle pot. Because of this she was often misunderstood.

"My husband, when not on the war campaign, is busy prattling about with the priests and bishops. Methinks he does flirt with becoming a Catholic. 'Tis rare we share a bed, my lady."

"Oh, dear," Gwenhwyfar began. "If men on this Island weren't so addicted to the goings-on of the next world, perhaps they would focus more on making the present one less of a shit pile."

"Well. We are an island obsessed with the Spirit," Gwyar offered.

A curling smile formed about the queen's face. Her green eyes flickered and flashed as she relished the segue, allowing her to cut to the quick.

"So valid a point. So, so valid. To my own spirit I must attend, and the burden of Arthur's I now transfer. To you." Gwenhwyfar said these things matter-of-factly, a communication flowing in one direction like a decree, no longer a conversation. "Monasticism is no longer just for men. To a nearby cell I go to be with God and my own spirit, not to return."

Gwyar loathed everything about life at court, about formalism, structure and authorities man-made. This was not an indictment of her brother, as

Arthur himself was like-minded. She could avoid most of her duties; he could avoid next to none. He ever sought to keep government small, non-intrusive and mindful that its function, under God, was to protect rights, not usurp them. However, Arthur did enjoy romantic ceremony, parades and promenades combined with great music and bardic tales, much more than did his sister.

Although, she admitted, she had her rituals as well. And she had other reasons for her monasticism and needful solitude with her goddess.

That Gwenhwyfar was on the verge of disappearing into the mist was clearly about to change two lives, and not hers alone.

"Before you protest and beg me to repent of this charge, I shall defend it preemptively," Gwenhwyfar began. "I love my husband. I made covenant between he and my God to be faithful, to honor him, to be his support and his friend."

The queen's face looked left of and over Gwyar, through a window that was in reality not there - a window to the past.

"He has vanquished the Saxon enemies but not those in his own house. He has proclaimed liberty throughout the land, but we all sense the grip of Rome is slowly closing. We stand at the door of an Age Golden but know such things are wrought through the personal destruction of those who wrought them."

Back to looking upon Gwyar, she went on: "He has your father, Meurig, still feisty, full of verve, limping about Caerleon bringing smiles and joy as he goes. But there are, sister-in-law, things a boy can't say to his father, a separation on private things that is natural, even for those as close as they.

"He has heroes, and mates and special men and true friends; knights for whom the bards will sing for ages."

Gwyar carefully interrupted.

"And he has the Merlin."

"Merlin has been missing nigh unto a week and, if he returns, he is not the same." This the queen said on the basis of her interaction with the druid at the conference preceding the great battle, and on her intuition. For women know these things. "He has changed."

"Missing?" Gwyar startled at this, for she had just seen Merlin on Ynys Enlli; he had come to visit her right before the great battle.

Did he not return? she thought. Making an attempt to go on further about this was pointless, as the queen was in full oratory stride, disregarding Gwyar's interruptions and listening to her not.

Gwenhwyfar made a great orbiting motion with both hands. "He has all things. But what he lacks is the very fuel that could keep the dream of the Summer Kingdom aflame, the glue to bind the dream, a flickering of hope for Cymru."

Gwenhwyfar now drew close to Gwyar.

"For all the needs and wants of men, one is greatest. One paramount." And now Wisdom of the Ages came forth from the Mad Queen. "A man must have a woman that he loves beside and behind him. For the woman is the glory of the man."

Gwenhwyfar now grew bold, imposing years of observation, intuition, whispers, half-truths and blunt facts upon the Lady of the Isle of Apples. Without anger but with seething conviction she pronounced, "And we both know he loves YOU most!"

The enchantress's neck erected, as an adder's. She rose without speaking, intending to leave the queen and her outlandish statement without retort.

"You will not make your leave," ordered Gwenhwyfar. Her eyes now blazed, the green somehow brighter after releasing such a long-held suppression. "Sometimes, he describes you in his sleep and knows not that I know."

"It is not me." Gwyar, just above a whisper.

"You were both so young. Barely children."

"It is not me." A note louder.

"Merlin and the Lady of the Lake were managing King Meurig's abdication and attaining the glorious, gilded blade for Arthur. They made it back to the ritual late. They didn't know."

"It. Is. Not. Me." Teacups began to shake and two candlesticks buckled, and fell. The room grew callous; wind blew, of a source and force unnatural.

Gwenhwyfar marveled not at the otherworldly manifestation (but no longer had to wonder whether her speculation about the room being under the sorceress's enchantment was unfounded), and proceeded. "The bishops couldn't care less about the spring rites, and demonstrations of virility or compatibility with the crops. They are clean of this as well."

CHAPTER 16
Not So. There Is One He Loves Even More

"Clean of what? It is not me." Gwyar's disingenuous response fell to a whisper as Gwenhwyfar's missives drew her mind back to the incident that had shaped the future of all Britons, *nay, all men*, forever.

The Dynion Hysbys had made selection of a sixteen-year-old virgin for the rites.

There were local tribes that held to old ways, and even older gods. They would not accept a young king who did not pass the rites and demonstrate to them that the harvest would be ever reliable.

The king was one with the land, and the land one with the king.

Although elements of this worldview had been modified or rejected, trickles of it remained, adopted even amongst the bishops. Indeed, a king wounded in battle or unreliable in bedroom would die (often to mean retirement, abdication, selling or gifting of lands, or living in a cell or cave for a period of time) and a young heir would rise in his place.

The term 'death' meant many things to the Cymry.

As for the bishops, the right of kingship was based upon the royal bloodline, balanced with the consent of the people. A horrible, tyrannical or unjust man of high birth might be displaced by an honorable man of lower estate. On this topic, the bishops had a more reasonable approach than their pagan kinsmen.

Most of the ruling families or Royal Clans had adopted some form of Christianity, and even though Christ was proclaimed publicly and with liberty and comfort first in the Blessed Isles, the common man was slower to adopt the faith. Those who had not adopted the Christian faith (whether of the sect of Pelagius, or of the Primitive Church of the Britons, or of Romanism) still fought Cymru's battles, still mined her tin, still developed her coal, still tended and raised her sheep and cattle.

Their influence was yet a part of the fabric of the Isles. Rituals of season and harvest, of death and life and love, and of war and kingship were required to maintain their support, to mitigate skirmishes, raids, and rebellion and, moreover, to show respect for a policy of religious and spiritual liberty.

And, although the bards held sway and authority in the plenary courts and palatial circuits, the cruel and nasty devising Dynion Hysbys lorded over the minds and souls of the middle and lower classes, often through dark arts and sinister black magick.

Raging with jealousy over the Merlin and his softer and more enlightened approach to managing the transition from the old gods to the One True God and His Son, the Dynion Hysbys pumped chest where they could, asserted authority where they might.

Gwyar remembered well that her brother had been in Brittany when she received the visit from the Dynion Hysbys. He had been pulled away, yet again, from school and was already earning a name on the battlefield, aiding King Budic II and his son Hoel Mawr in their fight against insurgents on the Continent.

The first sowing of spring was nigh and it was made clear to the sect of druid priestesses on Ynys Mon that they would need to be in Gwent for the arrival of the prince.

Gwyar was away from her foster-mother, who was busy loaning Merlin the Sword of Power to give to the soon-to-be boy-king.

She was unusual amongst the young ladies and girls. Ever preoccupied by darker paths and arcane studies, she quickly mastered the spectrum of divergent druidic theologies, and although she did not oppose them, she transcended them. Men feared Gwyar because she, like no other, seemed to be the same sort of creature as the Merlin. Outside of religion or sect, beyond classification, she was friendly to all gods but bowed to no God.

Command of herbs, poisons and the produce of nature she possessed. The mysteries seemed to flow through her and she was, by a very young age, viewed as one who hearkened back to those veiled times on either side of the Flood; those visitors to the Isles from the sides of the North, or else from the sky.

That her parentage was well-known didn't quell the speculation, though Onbrawst and Meurig were a picture of fidelity and loyalty.

When the Dynion Hysbys had visited the young priestesses, Gwyar recalled that she had been playing with other, younger girls, upon the pebbly strait of Afon Menai. They were near the very spot where the Romans had come and butchered her spiritual and blood ancestors; their blood still cried for revenge from the soils of Ynys Mon.

Ironically, only certain sects of Christians and druids had fallen to the sword of Roman persecution, which usually and almost unanimously left their conquered realms to their native gods.

There had been a time, five hundred years or more ago, when the connection between simple Christians and druids was clear. This fact was, to most, now murky or lost, as if some dispute divided two old friends and now, many years hence, the cause of the dispute was forgotten but the chasm too deep to heal.

Conversely, the Dynion Hysbys hated anything that resembled the name of Christ. Nor did they venerate the elemental spirits of earth or water, of air or fire. Neither did they seek union with the divine inspiration, or Awen, that connected all Britons. Rather, they claimed to appease powerful fertility gods and a great cloven-hoofed, bovine deity whom they called Arddu. According to them, the horned (although he manifested oft as a winged serpent as well) Arddu was chief of the gods.

It was said that the whole of the pantheon of deities such as Rhiannon, Arianrhod, Arawn and the Mighty Ones of the Cymry loathed Arddu and would neither acknowledge nor receive tribute or sacrifice from his Wise Men, though they hid amongst those who adored the gods and goddesses of Eire and Cymru.

Usually a druid or small collective of bards would accompany some of the Dynion Hysbys, but on the day they came to select a damsel for the rites, only they were present.

And they were accompanied by one man besides: a shadowy man who seemed to lead them. One whom Gwyar did not know.

He donned a many-layered black robe with underlying tunic of the same shade. Beads dangled and an inverted cruciform rattled, clacking against his sides as he walked, or rather glided.

Though his face was recessed too deeply into an overly large hood, and a black mask further made the actual features of his face unknowable, it was readily deduced that he was old, and not from the Isles.

Of Greece, or Italy, Gwyar assumed.

His fingers were plated with armor whose ends were metallic, pointy talons and his staff was not for walking, for it cast forth a vibratory hum that forced a bubble of separation between him and any who might approach him.

He and his dark companions made the pebbled strait a tessellated game board when standing amongst the druid priestesses, all in dresses of pure white.

"A young prince will slay the White Stag and then become one with the land and you will be the vessel; the cup of that union." His voice was confident, but broke and scratched every few words. That Gwyar was the object of his pronouncement was clear as a single talon pointed directly upon her bosom, nearly meeting the skin.

"Do you fear me?" he asked.

"I do not," she responded.

"Of course not; you were before I am." The hooded shadow man was still addressing Gwyar, but was now speaking to someone or something standing behind her as well. "Some of you, at least, was." His look fell back upon her.

Gwyar did not see the red-eyed Lord of the Tylwyth Teg towering behind her.

"I am but sixteen and you are at least a hundred," came her youthfully rebellious bite-back.

"At least a hundred, little crow." Some teeth showed briefly as the hood shifted in the wind bellowing off the strait. "See to it that she serves as actress in the rites."

He spoke but once more unto Princess Gwyar.

"In the rites, you are moon and the cup, the goddess. But this you already are, yes?"

She made no response as every tiny hair upon her arms, neck and shoulders stood and an icy wind moved about the whole of her body; at that instant she turned round rapidly.

Nothing.

The Man of the Fair Folk, the Fae King, was gone, or never there.

***

Gwenhwyfar reappeared in an instant. "Those nasty heathens and their godless ritual caused this; you are innocent."

The words refocused Gwyar's mind back to the present conversation (though Gwenhwyfar knew that further discourse may yet bring the entire palace crashing down).

Instead, and finally, a concession exhaled from the princess's throat, for she knew more than most that *women just know things*. And Gwenhwyfar knew, or partially knew, something more than any other woman had over the course of Gwyar's thirty and five years.

"Not even the Lady of the Lake knows that it was me at the Rites." Tears formed.

"Of course not. Merlin and Vivien would've never allowed such perversion." Gwenhwyfar was Christian; conservative and rigid. But she greatly regarded them as two honorable, special people, the last of a fading kind. Fading into the shadow of the Church.

"How did you know?" The confessing query finally came, and the shaking room settled.

Gwenhwyfar made a long, thoughtful response.

"It's remarkable how many years are uneventful or irrelevant, yet one year, or one moment, can change us forever. Though twenty years ago, that year of life, that one set of moons has impacted him, haunted him to this day.

"From the day he and I were wed, Arthur was very loyal, very faithful. Never did I worry about him wandering off to lay with damsels, dames or debased seductresses. His fidelity was a point of honor amongst gossiping women and pious bishops alike. But, from the beginning, even in our teens when you visited court, I noticed looks, moods, temperature shifts, that flame of discomfort that must look and yet cannot look but will not look away.

"That a man would lust after his sister was unthinkable, unnatural.

"That the most honorable man that ever lived would, or could do so, demanded investigation.

"And investigate I did."

The queen rubbed her face hard with cupped hands, the crust of tears and sleeplessness crumbling and tumbling from her cheeks.

She continued.

"It was impossible to trace the exact identity

of the priestess who had served as the Cup to Arthur's Sword in that ritual. Even upon aggressive, privy threats I could only gather that the participant portraying the goddess was young and dark."

Here Gwenhwyfar flirted with the sorceress's hair, as a foolish drunkard makes for a wasp's nest with a stick or intentionally steps upon an asp, caring not for her own life.

"As the priestess is dark, and you are dark. And as he has but this heel of Achilles, this one weakness, that he calls out to one not there on some nights, that he looks upon some astral projection crawling along our ceiling of YOU and then ravages ME." Now anger and jealousy crept in again and the accusations resumed, more forceful than before. "It is you he was with, you he obsesses over and YOU who will serve him at this court lest our Kingdom fall!"

The Mad Queen raged on, unable to cease from visiting the matter, again and again assaulting Gwyar verbally, now accusing her of being Otherworldly to her face. "He thinks on a dark Fae that visits his sleep and seduces him. He plays again the ordeal and, at the moment of climax, confuses our names. He calls to—"

Suddenly, a raised hand stayed the queen's mouth effortlessly, Gwyar using her craft and power. "He calls to the Morgaine and he calls to Gwen," she said.

"Yes."

At this moment Gwyar could spare the queen, whose mind as well as heart (and soul besides) was as a broken looking-glass, a clay pot dropped that could not be mended; or she could make an end of her with truth.

Knowing that Gwenhwyfar would have

her will enforced by sword and permanent custodians if it came to it, and that her husband and Gwyar's brother would have no leverage to adjudicate an appeal, that Gwyar would now be away from her Isle of Apples and imprisoned to life at court, resentment overruled grace as the Sorceress opted for cold truth in the stead of soft lies.

"You know much, yet not all, queen." Gwyar's eyes, massive and bronze-gold, opened extra wide to deliver this message. "At fourteen he did fall in love–" wailing now began, but Gwyar continued cold and unmoving, "–and he was poisoned by lust from what happened between us. However, lady, you have conflated two events into one. At fourteen he fell BOTH in love and in lust and those two names he entwines, commingles, blends and emotes in the shadows, and at night."

"But he did not know me until *after* it happened. I knew him not until he was fifteen, for we married the following spring," Gwenhwyfar argued.

"He calls out to the Morgaine, and I am she." She pointed and rested her forefinger upon her chest, and at the saying of the name *Morgaine* a shadow of Gwyar, yet seven times her size, blossomed slowly and then overtook the greater part of the chamber. Real fear, and ancient power, blossomed along with the Shadow. "And he calls out to Gwen." The same finger started to point at the queen, then reversed its course, tauntingly. "But that Gwen is *not* you. In your queries and investigations and hunts, you should have started by seeking to find the object of his love, or lust, before the event, not *at* the event. You should have simply asked Illtud about Arthur's days in school."

Gwenhwyfar seemed lost and shocked at these words. So Morgaine made all as clear as the mirror of a still lake on a summer day.

"I will stay at court, as you will terrorize me to do otherwise, until he remarries. There is *another* Gwenhwyfar coming to Caermelyn, mark this. And it is *she* whom he loves more! As I told you afore, it is not me! Or not me alone." A sinister stoicism now accompanied the verbal daggers.

The queen crumbled within herself, not having known that there was yet another rung left on her endless descent into living damnation. Had the king really been in love with another woman bearing her name? And before her? What of their two decades together?

Insult was her only recourse.

"You are a cruel witch, Gwyar. You would break me with these words, knowing I have lost my sons." The queen stood and gathered herself again, and again was fearless. Her gestures indicated plainly that tiny Gwyar and the tall darkened spirit with her should leave. "May you never know the hurt of losing a child. For I have lost all, and one at the hand of Arthur himself. May you never know this. Take care of the king. Now leave this place."

CHAPTER 17
When It Comes Time to Do That

Merlin did not hire a ship, as it would have brought too much attention upon the covert travelers. Arthur's younger brother, Prince Madoc, was a master at sea and ever stationed at, or patrolling near, the ports. His skills with sword and fist were wanting, but his ability to scout, to chart, to organize and to know every detail associated with the vessels that both entered and left the Isles more than compensated for those deficiencies. Either by direct report, else by some seemingly organized orchestra of whispers, Madoc ever knew any matter of interest pertaining to the sea. And Britannia's most famous druid and advisor to the king making off under cloak of night on hired boat would certainly meet the criteria for a 'matter of interest'.

And so, instead, Merlin and his travel companion paid for, boarded, and blended in upon one of the supply ships, which sailed their routes late at night from Cymru to their cousins in Brittany.

Small iron cauldrons were aflame throughout the concave hull of the vessel, allowing men to cluster round them on benches for warmth in the bitter cold. The seamen were ever scurrying to and fro, working. The passengers concentrated on not freezing to death; thus, the privacy was adequate.

As many of the battles of the Saxon War had been contested on wide rivers, great lakes and slivers of the sea, all Britons were well suited to harsh conditions on the water. Nevertheless, it was especially cold.

Maelgwn sat directly next to the Merlin, shoulder to shoulder, looking more a cuddling couple than two men of grit and war. A deliberate turn of the head was required in order to speak.

Ere Maelgwn initiated obviously forthcoming queries, Merlin took a moment to behold him.

Maelgwn.

The Lancelot.

The Bloodhound Prince.

The singular sentiment that coursed through Merlin every time he looked upon Maelgwn was *gratitude.*

Maelgwn, grandson of the mighty Cunedda. The strongest line of the remnant of Northern kings that survived the treacherous Night of the Long Knives. Maelgwn and his Hosts, the most feared and elite cell amongst all the armies, could have overpowered and harassed Arthur to such an extent that they would have been a divided nation, an easy harvest for the Saxon sickle. Some reasonably speculated that he could have even defeated Arthur outright and installed himself as the Head of the Dragons (a position historically reserved for the Royal Clan of the Silures - never a Northman - but Maelgwn seemed to be the exception to all norms and customs). Instead, Maelgwn had been introduced at age sixteen to

Arthur, who was fourteen at the time, and in the twinkling of an eye, loved him deeply.

They were both pupils, schoolyard friends at Illtud's.

From the beginning, Maelgwn plainly declared that Cymru would be united: under Arthur as head. This news met with pricks and thorns from the other kings and lords in the Old North and such was the discord that Maelgwn left his lands, at first for fosterage, and then over the process of time permanently, to reside with King Budic II, who was sometimes called Ban, and his sister Vivien, over in Brittany.

His fame grew over on the Continent, where he became known as the Lancelot, which is by interpretation, *the greater who serves the lesser.*

But zealous devotion to his native lands in Gwynedd deeply tormented Maelgwn and the course he set for himself troubled him often, so much so that he would periodically break from the Round Table Fellowship (though he was their Champion) and go back home, intermittently reclaiming his lands.

He especially enjoyed a small farm set against the River Camlan near Dollglau. There was a great allure to the place that was at once sad and magnetic. In addition to the serenity of dark greens and blues that sat upon the river as a perfectly layered sweet cake, the surrounding slopes formed nearly a perfectly shaped 'V', creating Leonidas's Thermopylae effect; the Thermopylae of Britannia. Massive armies would be neutralized by the narrow valley, meaning those that had expertise of the terrain could defend against very many with very few. Maelgwn had rehearsed with his men how to take flight through rehearsed routes from a pursuing enemy and then slaughter them as they funneled into the field near the river, called Maes Camlan.

Serenity matched with remarkable natural defenses rendered this tiny spot in North Cymru precious to Maelgwn.

Soon after resettling and enjoying Camlan or any of the other countless majestic and romantic creeks, mountains, waterfalls, ancient lakes and beautiful estates and fortresses of Gwynedd, like some recurring cycle of cursed moons, inevitably the conduct and flirtations with treachery by other Northern leaders, namely Caw and Meirchion, would wax great. Having no stomach to be around this, Maelgwn would go back to Arthur, or to Brittany, or to one of Vivien's Sacred Lakes in the south.

And then the sorrowful yearning for return to Gwynedd would return again.

Gratitude. Merlin had great empathy towards the displaced hero and marveled once more at the man comely as Adonis and skilled as Achilles, then readied himself to answer questions about the purpose of their secret engagement.

"Your strategy will live on through a thousand generations in epic poetry and bardic ballads. My Hosts salute you and I thank you. The Blessed Isles are free." Thus the conversation of two men, tall as trees but snuggled as children near the hearth, began with kind words from the Lancelot to the Merlin.

The congeniality was short-lived.

"Why am I here?" Maelgwn's directness returned.

Some frost and icicles formed and dangled from the old wizard's beard, framing his mouth and making his speech look mechanical. It was very cold and the channel between Glamorgan and Brittany was troubling its seafaring passengers; at first gently, now with harassing force.

Considering his words carefully, Merlin opted for direct words that would both liberate the burden from their concealment in his bosom and impress the urgent necessity for his extreme mandate upon Maelgwn.

Though direct and calculated, Merlin ought to have begun with, "I genuinely feared that the Iron Bear's life was in danger." Instead he took the longer path, and tried to build the foundation first.

"I belong to a Secret Society." Merlin paused, continuing with simplicity rather than deep explanation. "Our Order is governed by another Secret Society, and that Order by yet another. At the very zenith of this... *pyramid*... is an assembly called the Counsel of Nine."

Maelgwn was always fascinated by religion and spirituality (as are all Britons), having the broadest possible exposure to variant Christian sects and of course having seen fascinating and arcane things with his foster-mother, the Lady of the Lake, that would challenge any worldview. Therefore, Merlin's comments intrigued the impatient warrior.

"Are these men *like you,* Lord Merlin?" he asked.

Had he been with sharp-witted Bedwyr or enjoying ale with sunshiny Gwalchmai, Merlin would have countered with levity, "There is NO ONE like Me," and enjoyed a hearty laugh. Instead he provided a mundane and standard description. "From the infancy of man there has always been a guild of the special, the learned, the good, and the wise devoted to liberty, fraternity and equality," Merlin answered. "And to unlocking the Sacred Sciences or secrets of the Cosmos."

Lancelot frowned, his lips pressed tight together ensued straightway by his perfect eyes and brow following suit; the protesting expression of disinterest.

"I know." Merlin gave an agreeing jest in response to the warrior's expression. "Sounds like the crafty, overweight and crooked sorts that sell old cows as studs to fools or the potion peddlers at the markets." Here the druid humbled himself, his sigh of regret making a great cloud under the cold, evaporating and pushed up and outward into the sea by the fire cauldron. "And I bought the old cow. Drank the potion; a potion of lies."

Maelgwn at once re-engaged. "How do you know that what they teach is lies?"

"For many reasons now."

"Give me one."

"If the foundation be flawed then the building will fall. There are no *good men,*" said Merlin with conviction. "Aside from any stated purpose, the Brotherhood convened magi and wizards and diverse priests from religions the world over to learn the Higher Mysteries through a series of initiations, rites and courses that have spanned decades and decades.

"Some of these Mysteries we would take home and blend into or use to enhance our native beliefs; others were considered secrets to fall under the moral and spiritual jurisdiction of the Society and our governing principalities alone."

Here Maelgwn interrupted. "Decades? Sounds worse than the memorization work demanded of our bards. What mysteries could be beyond the grasp of men similar to you? What transition from milk to meat takes so long?"

"It's a ruse. The duration of learning the Higher Mysteries and the Seven Sacred Sciences makes the Teachers seem all the more impressive, and the students all the more filled with—"

"Pride." Maelgwn finished the wizard's sentence.

"Aye." Another great sigh ascended through the flame and into the night. "We have been ever learning but never coming to the knowledge of the truth. Now, as my days are shorter and the setting sun of retirement draws near, it was communicated to me that it was my time to learn the final secrets and to graduate; to promote to the Counsel of Nine." Merlin was hoping to get quickly to the core of his purpose for bringing Maelgwn on this perilous and secret journey and at this critical moment he feared his audience was losing patience.

And that he was.

The towering warrior flung the coats and skins that had a moment ago been layered upon him, as effortlessly as a child flings sticks into a pond. As he rose, the flames illuminated his perfect form; harder than the statues of the Greeks and nearly as pale, this chiseled killing machine could pulsate his lean brawn in a way to intimidate men and wild beast alike. A living grey statue. An invincible man. One did not want to find himself on the wrong side of Maelgwn's disposition, lest he also find himself on the wrong side of his spear.

And yet it was rumored, and held true here, that Maelgwn never raised his voice. Some yelling is healthy: '*tis the quiet ones to mark and fear*. In a low, low voice just above a whisper, his frightful protest came down heavy on Merlin, who was still hunkered over the cauldron. "You left our most important battle, your country, my men and OUR Arthur for some pagan pride parade? For some ceremony to tickle your conceit!"

A form, rustle and disruption was seen and felt behind Maelgwn, then a shadow.

The two famous travelers were no longer alone. Merlin would give his answer to two inquisitors now, not just one.

Maelgwn's favorite weapon was instantly in hand and ready to dispatch any thief, pirate or unwelcome guest. A unique killing instrument, the Lancelot's armament of choice was neither sword nor spear and yet both. Having no hilt or handle, it was a double-ended battle spike, the length of a sword, much shorter than a spear, and having one single crescent moon-shaped blade forming a hook to both guard one hand and serve as an extra killing option. Many Saxon and not a few Briton souls went on into hell on the other end of this famous killing instrument and the man who wielded it.

"Oh, put it away, Lord of Gwynedd." A familiar, pesky and irritating voice floated through the night, punching Maelgwn at once in both ears.

A figure stepped from behind several large barrels housed on the hull and strolled right into the midst of Merlin and Lancelot as if he owned not just that spot on the vessel but perhaps the entire boat - or an entire fleet. A short, crook-backed man with knobbly walking stick, of small stature and great confidence. Precisely half the height of the other two, the hooded man, obviously a druid, hugged Merlin hard, at his waist.

"Taliesin!" Merlin's great smile crackled, crushing and discarding the remaining ice chips around his moustache and corners of his mouth;

and the joy of seeing his great friend and pupil (and teacher) caused Merlin to forget, but for a moment, the dire nature of his discovery by one who had obviously followed Maelgwn to the port. The bitter cold and sway of the boat impacted Merlin's brain, first with too many delays articulating the present distress to Lancelot, second in not immediately protesting Taliesin's presence.

"But wait. You cannot be here!" The wizard recovered himself. "The entire nation save Maelgwn Gwynedd knows not my whereabouts, yet here stands the famous son of Ceridwen before me. I am breached!"

Unmoved by Merlin's concern, Taliesin responded: "King Arthur Pendragon has his Merlin; King Maelgwn has his."

"Whether I want one or not, so it seems," Maelgwn snarled.

Taliesin and Maelgwn shared a special history. Born in Glamorgan, Taliesin had been assigned to Maelgwn's courts in the North. Whilst all men greatly feared the tall king of the North, little Taliesin ever, instead, counseled, chastised, pestered and advised him. Merlin seemed to *see* that something tense, tempestuous and special would develop between the two and made use of Taliesin as an extension of his very own eyes upon the unpredictable warrior.

And Maelgwn secretly liked Taliesin *because* the little druid feared him not.

He also, unknowingly, had the somber distinction of being the last person to ever see Merlin and Taliesin together, dialoguing, matching wit and enjoying each other's company, this side of the Afterlife.

"You followed Maelgwn here?"

"I did, and two of my men besides. We saw him break hard from the trails at Maesteg and, in light of *our* recent discourse, thought a connection plausible, if not probable. I thought you said you were done with the Nine, having no desire to have fellowship with the unfruitful works of darkness, knowing it is a shame to even speak of what they do in secret." A finger like a long, knotted branch from a birch tree pointed up, up towards Maelgwn. "I agree with Goliath here; what matter have you with the naughty secrets of the religious elite? What have they to do with the Matter of Britain?"

"As I shared with you, I had no intention of completing the Sacred Rites, or learning the *Secret Teaching of the Ages,* as I too now find it to be folly. However…" Instantly, the conversation shifted from humorous barbs and sarcastic positioning to gravity unparalleled. Merlin, now fully warmed in brain and body, reassumed command of his surroundings and pronounced: "The messenger from the Nine indicated that King Arthur *was* the object of the final initiation and the *Secret Teaching of the Ages*. Not in allegory, not as a type, but that he personally was the subject and aim of prophecies and mysteries as old as the times of the gods."

Both listeners were silent.

Merlin continued. "As I continued to listen to the messenger, his aim was clear; the Nine's secret teachings had something to do with Arthur, and it was not safe, not positive and not good. There was malevolence in his voice that I have never associated with or heard from the supposed benevolent college of Seers."

Maelgwn's worldly wisdom about the nature of men and power resulted in thoughtful and true interjection. "They are about to initiate you into the highest levels of their Order, so their outward masks of White Magick and herbs and brotherly love is coming off. True power is what men of that ilk covet. They sound more like the dark Fae than men."

"Aye. Well said, Maelgwn. Discerning the change and potentially ill motive, combined with a recent conversion of–" Merlin looked at Taliesin, who smiled "–perspective in my own beliefs, I fear for our friend's life." The sadness of missing the great battle returned to Merlin at that moment. "And so, to reject the offer to join the Counsel of Nine, but to first learn, by guile, by magick or by sword, the meaning of the messenger's mystery, I hastened away from Caerleon, away from Baedan."

"And you summonsed the great Maelgwn as surety that your head would be attached to your neck long enough to do something with the information you will acquire." Taliesin confirmed the legitimacy of the Merlin's actions.

Maelgwn's angry disposition eased. "I now understand why we are here," he said, looking at Merlin.

Merlin then finished the warrior's sentence on his behalf: "But we don't understand why *you* are here." The focus shifted back to the one uninvited guest, warming hands and feet near the cauldron.

"As I said, I followed you here," he replied.

"Yes. And who in turn may have followed you?" Merlin continued to be haunted by an overwhelming feeling that, though Maelgwn was with him, he might not return from his dealings with the Counsel. "You are Taliesin and men will call you Merlin. This quest is not yours; my office you must soon take. You and your two men at the first port will disembark; Maelgwn Gwynedd and I to Broceliande will continue."

And then Merlin, feeling bereft of supernatural powers, still fully possessing the dominion of words and pitch, delivered a prophetic command upon Maelgwn, which at the time puzzled both hearers, being out of place.

"Lancelot. When it comes to the time to do that which you would do, for the sake of all free men, I beg you, do it not."

Merlin left no room for debate or further discussion regarding his utterance or the present quest, and limited the discourse to the pleasant conversation amongst warriors, men and friends. Taliesin and Maelgwn chose to accept and honor the old man's authority, although Maelgwn discerned that some great mystery was revealed from student to teacher and that Taliesin had said or done something to Merlin prior to the present distress. But sufficient unto the night was the peril of the dawn, and Maelgwn let the mystery remain such as they bade Taliesin farewell, making ground upon the Continent.

CHAPTER 18
The Present Sister

After delivering sorrowful justice to his son, King Arthur did not return to Caerleon. Instead, he and the twenty-six Round Table Companions, less Maelgwn, convened and lodged at Caermelyn, that famous yellow fortress woven forever into the Great Conversation through bards' songs in epic poetry and prose and celebrated the world over, from queens in Africa to artists in Rome.

The shining city on a hill that could not, and cannot, be hidden.

Near the ancient city of Caerdydd and within the commote of Ceiwbr, within the cantref of Breinyawl, within the kingdom of Glamorgan, was the magnificent fortress found. The gilded warriors held court at a nearby small castle which was upon a meadowy flat land under the shadow of the fortress.

The castle's great hall housed the Round Table, with its set of circles within circles and pivots and rivets. A sacred dwelling set aside for the twenty-six to congress around legislative affairs, celebrate quests or debate matters of national interest.

In the Round Table hall in Ceibwr were great scrolls affixed to ornate walls. They recorded the genealogies of the Cymry kings and chieftains from the present era back to Brutus, and upon some, back to Aedd Mawr who had lived thirteen hundred years before the advent of the Lord. The scrolls were scribed in three languages; Latin, Ogham, and lastly, the native alphabet of the Britons, which shared similarities with the scripts of the Near East. Additionally, elaborate stone cruciforms and memorials served the same purpose. The bards would compete one with another; the selected player placed with back to the scrolls and reciting the lines by memory. The other bards could randomly demand a 'switch' from paternal to maternal heredity and use other maneuvers of distraction and gamesmanship. Great laughter, greater concentration and, greatest above that, celebration of a special and unique people resulted from these and like games.

Harps and horns melodically filled the air, complemented by Illtud's perpetual choirs, constituted wholly of men rotating in shifts, ensuring songs and praises from eveningtide to first light.

Ever jubilant, the fortress Caermelyn, along with its satellite castles, chapels and estates, shone this day brighter than ten suns, a beacon of liberty to the whole of the world. For this was the first convening of the Round Table Fellowship since vanquishing the Saxons for good at the battle of Mynydd Baedan. The first convening of a liberated and free nation.

Old men were as young children, frolicking and hugging and wrestling about.

Young children were as old men, cheerfully speculating about the future, talking for the first time of a bright tomorrow where the hope of *anything* was attainable.

Catholic priests embraced the Briton bishops,

druids hugged hard anyone who would receive their noble embraces and even the Dynion Hysbys were affable.

Men of the North supped with the Silures and the western tribes danced and jostled with the chieftains of Powys.

Arthur, flanked by Gwalchmai and Bedwyr (with Cai three paces behind, vigilant), entered the Hall.

Eighteen years and twelve major battles (when accounting for smaller skirmishes, successful defense of raids and minor battles the number was sixty and four) and so much burden, terror and sacrifice had forged this happy moment in shimmering Caermelyn. And not just in Glamorgan was this disposition present. Everywhere, the Blessed Isles were singing a collective song; one unified chorus at all hours and at all times for the past seven days: "Victory and Freedom, Victory and Freedom, Victory and Freedom!"

King Arthur was undefeated, save in his heart and in the corridors of his own house.

Queen Gwenhwyfar's seat was empty. All knew and none asked.

Amr was not amongst the young men who returned from the northern patrols. None knew and none asked.

So much external frenzied joy did not fool the wise king. He wondered how many of those singing and laughing and celebrating with such exuberance that their voices betrayed and abandoned them were like him… broken.

How many widows bottled, buried and died slowly from inside out from the pains of war? How many dashed souls locked away the caverns and cankers of loneliness? How many couples allowed distance to injure what Saxon blade could not? Eighteen years of parting kisses and too-short returns. How many writs of divorcement could have been prevented simply through that which was more valuable than lands or gold? Time. Family time. Couples' time. The Saxons had lost the war but drawn so many Britons into despair. How many were like Arthur and Gwenhwyfar in this very room, at this very moment? Real smiles and real joy lacquered o'er a cracked mirror.

Arthur was broken.

As the Sovereign's eyes were descending towards his feet, they fell upon a young child. The young girl was vigorously and victoriously waving a smaller version of a great war banner. A faithful and well-crafted replica of those used in battle. A child's plaything. Arthur saw her smile as she whirled the red dragon in circles dozens of times in but a few seconds. *And that smile!*

Arthur was unbreakable.

The child at once reminded him that the Isles had no more choice to sacrifice the current generation than a baker has choice to fling his eggs upon an invading thief. *The eggs are broken, but the kitchen lives on.*

Winning the Saxon Wars had been for this child. For all children. She would spend the next generation as a free woman, able to study and learn and pursue arts or commerce or become a great physician. Devoting her focus to herself, her God, her family, her passions and occupations. And all without endless raids, invasions and repetitive, perpetual loss.

Art, science, spirituality, freedom of mobility. All the natural rights of man fastened strong by a grip called Hope to a torch called Liberty. Arthur and his knights, his wizard, his bishops and famous women of renown had given the world a Kingdom of Summer birthed, like the king himself, in the coldest days of winter.

King Arthur professed and practiced transparency, often inviting and encouraging any citizen to listen to Round Table proceedings. However, he balanced this by making it clear that the Hall was not a public square for debate and continuously reinforced the law. Namely that chieftains, councils or kings ruled over cantrefs, not this centralized republican body.

On this day, with the buzz and frolic of celebration, Cai the steward struggled to calm the crowds who were seated upon couches and rectangular tables positioned along beehive-styled stories running from floor to roof, allowing hundreds to see the noble assembly and hear firsthand of deeds fair, quests conquered and policies that might impact every hearth and home.

The assembly started with tidings that brought such a cheer and roar that Arthur forgot himself and joined the masses, fist pumping and feet jumping two and possibly three times, as a child leaps at the prospect of cake or confections.

"Maelgwn is found! The Lady of Llyn Fawr sends message that her foster-son has suffered a minor injury and convalesces under her care in Broceliande."

The herald, a druid sent by Vivien, possessed no additional details and none pressed for them. How the Bloodhound Prince had been leading his Hosts in delivering the final meticulous death strokes upon the enemy at Baedan and now, less than a fortnight later, was lain up wounded upon the Continent was, for now, irrelevant. He was alive and well.

Nor did any of the twenty-five use occasion of the good news as a platform to make inquiries about the bad. They would attend to the mystery of Merlin's disappearance at the right time and in the appropriate forum. Besides, the bishops and priests were already informed that Arthur would meet with them directly.

After several minutes of rapture, the Hall quieted and the Round Table Fellowship entered into great discourse as continuation of making the final determination about governing the remnant of Saxons, Angles, Jutes and many other fatherless and brotherless disparate Germanic tribes, surely starving and frightened to fits along the Saxon shores of Lloegyr.

An enduring principle of the Round Table Fellowship was that 'all elbows are equal when resting on this table', and meant that much of the policy discussions and decisions were led by the great knights themselves, not Arthur, who respected and obeyed delegated powers. He participated as a peer (as did Maelgwn when present) and did not lord his office as Pendragon over any of his fellows.

Cador, Urien and other brilliant and heroic men, each deserving of tomes and poems for their mighty and good deeds, described how living Germanic males would be allowed to stay but would live under leasehold contracts, not being allowed ownership of Briton soil for nine generations.

Women, children and the elderly or infirm would be treated with mercy and kindness, and the local chieftains were charged with all the moral authority the Round Table could muster not to become the very monsters they had just vanquished. The Round Table could make no local laws forbidding the violation or abuse of women, especially for non-citizens. However, they did remind the chieftains and lords that they would periodically give ear to appeals where severe violations of the natural laws of man occurred and hoped greatly that they would never have to side with a Saxon bringing accusation of tyranny against a Briton; for they would side with right, regardless of race.

Moreover, the great sailor Prince Madoc would arrange a fleet of ships and repatriate survivors back to their native lands. This would be a perilous journey but, for the sake of right and good, one that the Cymry would sponsor.

As for those who remained, they could be freely pursued by any Christian sect but had to forsake their old gods and be baptized (in spite of what Merlin had pronounced upon the bishops, as he was not there to further formalize his protests), else be executed per the agreements of both the Romanist and Cymry elders. As these newly baptized Germans could not own land, the Religious Leaders shifted attention to placing lessors over them that could, seeking a double advantage of land grants and human capital.

Next, great announcements about the dissolution of the professional and full-time army and naval forces were delivered. Over four hundred thousand men had been succored by the people to fight the invaders for the past eighteen years. Four hundred thousand men would have to integrate back into the communities they had protected and bled for. Where lands had been lost during skirmishes, raids or fraud (for in the chaos of war, many professional criminals and baser sorts did harm to the soldiers, taking advantage of them), they would be restored and debts cancelled.

Men who had held sword longer than plow

would now sow and reap, and the transition would not be easy.

Bishop Bedwini, whose speech never ceased to be soothing and seasoned with salt (a man who could deliver difficult truths with grace but conviction), made a formal oratory as to the *why* the military would be dissolved.

Using history to inform the present, professional soldiers were, as an organism, injurious to the liberty and often invented reasons to remain necessary, starting pretender wars. Or turning on the people. When being invaded, or for common defense, a terrifying military frightens the enemy. When at peace, it tends to terrify the people.

The Round Table Fellowship reduced the full-time army to one tenth of its size and dramatically reduced part-time or reserve forces as well. What remained of the armies under the direct control of the Pendragon would continue to secure borderlands and retain continuity of training, in the event that some unknown invader dared light upon Britannia's shores. In the Summer Kingdom, this was most unlikely.

Arthur personally asked for a full appraisal from his leaders and counselors relative to extant external threats within the borders of Cymru. The scope of his questions did not address internal conflicts, squabbles or rivalries with his countrymen such as Caw (who remained in the North, celebrating with King Llew) and Meirchion (who, along with his young child Mark, was present), but rather to pockets of Saxons, Picts or other threats that would require military action.

The Picts, an ancient people second only to the Cymry as settlers to the Isles amongst the Sons of Adam, continued to desire a marital alliance with the Northern Tribes and were a disruption, but no menace.

The puzzling West Saxons' king with a Briton's name, Cedric, had survived and escaped Mynydd Baedan. He led a peculiar band of Saxon, Briton and Irish rebels called the Gewisse. A persistent and valiant young king of similar age and disposition to Arthur, Cedric was formidable but had no strength of number or manpower (for most of his subjects lay in the field of slaughter or feeding carrion upon the slopes and crags of Baedan). He would need to be contained, monitored and ultimately killed or deported, but posed no real threat to the Summer Kingdom.

Prince Madoc's port guards indicated that Cedric had fled Cymru and was rumored as fugitive in the Emerald Isle. At the hearing of this, King Arthur turned towards the stories, seeking his Aunt Marchel. Married to King Anlach and critical participant in forging peace between the Silures and Irish, she could quickly wield her influence to flush out the fleeing invader.

Satisfied with Saxon policies of land ownership, deportation, massive reduction of the standing military forces and, hopefully, having struck a common-ground position to appease the grumbling factions within the church, the Round Table Fellowship shifted to discussions about what would become – *of themselves.*

The governance structure of local chieftains and their druids or bishops ruling in diverse ways over local cantrefs (being approximately one hundred villages or large farms) worked as the best hope to check tyranny and preserve liberty and had long endured, through both the Roman and Saxon Wars. A Pendragon or High King protected the borders and solved major disputes and, if the Silure man was ineligible or infirm, he could appoint an Wledig or Battle Commander to serve along his side, or in his stead.

The notion of two sets of twelve knights and nobles in a type of 'government within the government' was a foreign concept but Merlin had forged it nevertheless, the extremity of the Saxon Wars demanding such a group be instituted.

With but a few detractors from the North, the consensus of the people was to retain the Round Table Fellowship. They would be greatly needed to stabilize and reconstruct a nation whose fathers and grandfathers and grandfather's fathers had only ever known perpetual raiding and then, all-out perpetual war.

Their ongoing existence delivered a message to future invaders and to the evils that still dwelled within the land (or any land): that Arthur and Lancelot and their mighty men could and would quickly activate when the cause was meet.

Questions of 'What will we do now?' frequented the gathering, and King Arthur helped create a vision for them on how they would fill the void of war.

"Quest." Arthur let the powerful word rest upon its own pillars for a few minutes. "Without a quest, what purpose has a knight? And when all quests are fulfilled, what becomes of him?"

The twenty-four knights were enthralled at this saying. One of Maelgwn's sons, a young warrior not seated yet at the Table, was especially touched by Pendragon's words and committed, at that very moment, to one day being the greatest of the Questing Knights of the Round Table.

As for the types of quests relevant to a sitting body of heroes without a war to fight, Arthur gave examples.

"There are missing persons to find," (he spake of Merlin) "and there is much we don't know about the other creaturekind that shares habitation in this land. There are treasures, there are riddles, there are worthy commissions from bishops and druids alike. We shall not serve vanity, but we shall find questing for good quests."

The king went on to say that the Round Table Fellowship would also be dismissed to spend more time with wives, children and friends, joining at Caermelyn only one time per new moon. And, as knights might be about a worthy quest, the number for a quorum was reduced from twenty and one to fifteen.

Having all these matters pronounced with careful communication, edification and education, the audience in the small castle under the shadow of the great yellow fortress began to see Arthur's vision for the Summer Kingdom; *a unified Cymru with local leadership and small government. Of knights questing and seeking great and glorious things. An age of enterprise and freedom.*

As there was ongoing revelry and feasting to be had, the twenty-six save Maelgwn adjourned, but not before Arthur charged one of his own with his first quest.

"Hawk of May." Arthur warmly saluted Gwalchmai.

Gwyar, in accord with her dictate from the High Queen, was at court but in a high balcony, not yet reacquainted with her brother. Dressed in simple black garb, she was as a ghost during the revelries and proceedings. Although passionate about sovereignty, she was for the greater part ambivalent towards the banter about internal policies and certainly had no patience to suffer grown boys speaking of quests. But the mention of her son's name roused her from boredom. Alert, she listened hard.

"You will go to Broceliande and bring Maelgwn back to the Island." There was no option to decline, based upon the tone of the king. Joyful but direct, he continued. "Whatever evil befell him there, beware of and defeat. Go then unto the fortress of Ogyrfan. The two of you will personally escort his daughter, Gwenhwyfar."

Gwalchmai, not understanding the full wishes of the king, posed the question: "Escort her to where?"

"New Troy," the king responded.

Gwyar screamed "No!" as her own prophecies crashed upon her heart as great stones hurled by some giant down a slope. With the noise of the crowd she was heard not, but the Round Table vibrated and creaked. Few noticed and fewer cared, given the great happy frenzy of the day.

"If Maelgwn needs extra time to rest, give him some leave, but please ensure that you make as much haste as you are able. In a fortnight less a day you must have Gwenhwyfar ferch Ogyrfan to me. We meet at Ludgate." The king finished his charges.

***

Later that night the Pendragon struggled to find sleep. His heart seemed to desire to jump right out of his chest, pounding like a great battle drum. His shoulder muscles were stuck in a permanent 'shrugging' posture and he reassembled his pillows at least thirty-nine times.

Somewhere between wakefulness and slumber, with his senses compromised, she came.

Arthur's hands felt fastened, as it were by

large iron nails, to the bed and he watched, or dreamt, as the shadow woman enveloped the vaulted ceiling of his bedroom and then slowly transformed, shrinking down to human size, hovering atop him. This he saw every detail of, yet he knew his eyes were closed.

The entity's eyes flashed gold mixed with bronze. King Arthur was aroused. Deep in the paralysis of the encumbered sleep, he relived the king-making rites; the lust, the power, the communion with the heaven and earth through forces that paradoxically were in no way part of either heaven or earth. The aromas and lights in the cave. The masks. The location along a river and yet in a forest. The Stag. The memory of being presented proudly by Meurig like some newborn lion cub to the several tribes gathered in Gwent straightway after.

Now his mind's eye took him to Saint Illtud's, to school. "I saw her first," he declared, only half-musing, "I saw her first." Lancelot grimaced and his young sister Gwyar, in the anteroom and back of the chapel, cringed.

Reaching the pinnacle and release of his arousal, the Iron Bear's hands suddenly unhinged from their invisible nails and he reached for the feminine spectre haunting him. "Morgana! Morgana!" he screamed. A grave sense of danger prevented him from uttering the name thrice, just as always. His third and final nocturnal chant cried "Gwen!" at the precise second that the encounter *finished.*

Cai, stationed upon simple stool outside the room, heard some indiscernible disruption. A moment later he carefully and quietly entered the room and looked upon the king. All was in order, and the king soundly sleeping.

***

The following morning Arthur and Cai were enjoying a cold but sunny winter's morn, strolling through the market. It was busy with the enterprises of livestock, provisions and artisans. Hundreds bustled in the square. Peradventure chance brought them upon Princess Gwyar, doing the same.

"Sister!" Arthur, face to face with a sibling he had not seen in the flesh in a great while. "It has been so long!"

"Seems as if it has been but an evening ago, brother." Face to face with Morgaine of the Faeries.

CHAPTER 19
All Things Are Lawful Unto Me, But Not All Things…

"Nimue. Use the Sight. Find the Merlin," directed Vivien, who had had a large basin placed in an anteroom where she was lodging, four days removed from Merlin's tangle with the priests and bishops at the amphitheater, and the morning following her hosting the repulsive priest, Meirchion.

"I don't know if there is enough of him still upon me to accurately locate him, mistress." Merlin had given the young enchantress a soft, affectionate but appropriate kiss before he had stolen away in the night before the troops assembled at Ogmore.

Desperate to find him, for diverse reasons, Vivien had ordered her apprentice, the young priestess Nimue, to use the arcane art of scrying to locate the wandering wizard.

Scrying is a form of divination whereby something attached to the subject is placed upon a clear pool of water filled *just so* in a special basin, pool or cauldron. By stirring the water thrice clockwise whilst saying the incantation, then placing the attachment (in this case the slightest remains of Merlin's kiss upon a handkerchief), then stirring the waters thrice clockwise again, the basin when at last still would form a window, or one-way mirror, between the diviner and the subject.

Per Nimue's worldview, that was supposedly how the process worked.

In reality, a familiar spirit must follow the attachment and, making sport of the enchantress, only respond if the words and rituals were followed. If the familiar spirit, a finite being with no powers of omnipresence, was not present then no reading would be had, forcing the diviner to suffer great embarrassment, speculate or guess. For this cause many enchanters and fortune tellers were reproved as pretenders and deceivers.

The waters stilled; the image of a man appeared! Nimue peered hard, hopeful. Looking and looking harder, she hoped to discover the subject, but - alas - raised her head from the Seeing Pool, dejected.

"He is…" Nimue did not quite know how to describe it.

"Describe," said Vivien.

"Shielded in white light. Yes, that is it. *Shielded.* I do not see Merlin; only the form of a man clothed in white light. I am sorry, mistress."

The Lady of Llyn Fawr forcefully, for haste and not anger, pushed young Nimue aside, wanting a closer look at the basin. As her head drew close, a necklace given her by her foster-son inadvertently breached the waters. Vivien saw even less than Nimue, finding only her goddess-like visage scowling back at her through the water. "My brother Budic is right. I am getting old." Laughter broke the intense and seemingly futile exercise.

Vivien paced away, mulling the words of Meirchion the priest-king, considering her course. A few paces more and she flopped down upon a slanted writing desk, made of oak and stained white; the kind used by monks and scribes. She mimicked them for a moment, drafting letters with her long fingers upon the desktop, distracted and thinking.

Then. Startled!

"My lady. I find not the Lord Merlin but I see—" Nimue triple-checked the looking pool for absolute verification. "Your foster-son, the great hero Lancelot. He just boarded a shipping vessel and sits next to the shielded figure."

"Nimue, you've done it!" Vivien stood, slow and authoritatively. "They are together. Has the Sight revealed unto you their destination?"

"The shipping vessel makes for…" Nimue became irony personified and her face a great beaming smile. "Broceliande. They are going to *your* forest, my Lady. Shipping vessels are slow and unwieldy, and make many stops. We can advance their arrival should we make our leave, right now."

"You must go alone, Nimue," and the Lady of the Lake delivered unto the girl her charges.

***

Broceliande was a magical forest, gargantuan in size, which covered the whole of central Brittany. Entire villages and minor cities resided within its protective oaks, so tall that they blocked out direct sunlight, allowing only brilliant shards of light to enter in.

Its most efficacious point of entry for Merlin and Maelgwn was to trek through the ancient city of Rhoazon, and then bear southeast where old paths and star routes guided those who knew the coordinates to the Fount of the Lady. And near to that, the estate of Vivien, the Lady of Llyn Fawr. Legends and whispers held that she could pass effortlessly through underwater or otherworldly passages from her sacred lakes in Glamorgan to her estate in Little Britain. Water spirits were venerated above all other deities amongst the Bretons who, like their cousins in Cymru, were Christian amongst the royalty and heathen amongst the farmers and cattlemen.

Merlin knew the paths, as did Maelgwn, who loved Vivien as a mother.

Alternatively, a stranger to the forest would surely find himself prisoner to a labyrinth of trees and stone, an abyss of creeks and fissures, from which he would become disoriented and lost, and die. Or bewitched and misplaced by the Fair Folk without hope of retrieval.

Intending to lodge at the Lady's estate as two lonely questers, Merlin was astounded to see the small turret alight and a familiar shape waiting, leaning casually against the stone walls within the archway. Ivy had invaded and supplanted most of the stone and the scene of the exotic maiden against the beauty of the archway seemed as a painting to the wizard.

He approached the painting, and the painting kissed him.

This time the kiss was beyond neighborly embrace, hard and wet upon the mouth. During the delivery she intentionally applied the lightest touch upon his fingertips and then clasped his free hand, the other dropping his walking staff at the gleeful shock of the exchange.

Knowing not how to evaluate the matter, all

the wisest man in the world could do was toss forward a clumsy greeting.

"Oh, the folly of trying to sneak away, knowing you and the Lady can *see* me anywhere, anyhow!"

"But I did not see you, lord," responded the innocent, mousey voice, its owner looking up at the tall Briton. "You cannot be *seen*, Lord Merlin." The smallest tone of accusation, and perhaps anger ever so slight, snuck into her tone. "But I did see *him*." A casual look at the other tall Briton.

"I thirst," was Maelgwn's only speech towards Nimue. By interpretation, it meant 'you two clearly need some time alone'. And into the home where he had spent so much of his youth training and playing and learning he entered.

Nimue reclaimed the hand she clasped and marched Merlin towards a secondary structure, a stunning little two-room cabin, used for highly-regarded servants or guests requiring privacy.

Every man has a woman before whom he will crumble. Even unto every god or angel. Mighty Zeus had Danaë, David swooned at the bathing beauty Bathsheba and Merlin, an immovable man of principle and duty and unwavering focus on the mission at hand, melted o'er Nimue.

Reason knows not Love. You love who you love.

Nimue immediately disrobed with one hand, still holding Merlin's with the other.

Markings covered the young priestess. An owl interwoven in perpetual knots was centered on her back and Silure bear claws were spaced out all over her thighs and hinderside. Her arms were a sleeve of moons and black branches that brought out little alluring patches of her snowy skin. Like her mistress, golden hair, everywhere.

Nimue granted no mercy in mixing religious interrogation with lovemaking.

"Why could I see you not in my scrying basin, *cariad*?" Another hard kiss.

She allowed no space for response.

"Covered by your new God, Lord Merlin." A harder, nearly violent, kiss followed.

"Yes." Merlin drew upon a failing reserve of self-control, momentarily. "I am dead, and my life is hidden in Christ, in God. I am saved now," he testified.

Nimue: a creature seemingly created to seduce and manipulate men. A radical loyalist to the goddess Modron, channel of the familiar spirit of Queen Achtland (who could be pleasured by no man) and the water god Nodens, she typically felt numb when snaring men in their folly and cared not for their politics or religion. They were targets. Subjects. Victims. Yet at Merlin's words, Nimue was not numb. His words, his manner of speaking, were different. She was disgusted. Hate replaced apathy and vile enmity replaced the small measure of fondness she had always possessed for the wizard, now turned Nazarene.

Though reviled, the seduction continued. Now as means of examination for purpose of gathering information. *Vivien and the Old Nasty Priest were right. He must not be allowed to live.* She convicted him in her mind.

She tempted and mocked Merlin's infant faith with questions of lust and sin, attempting to snare him in hypocrisy. And although Merlin did not ravage her and was fighting his flesh and seeking to suspend his burning towards her, he finally brought himself to simply state: "The flesh is dead anyhow. Don't you see, my love? All the land grants, the selling of this and the doing of that, the taste-not, touch-not rules of men cannot please a Holy God, else Christ suffered in vain."

"Then *do as thou wilt* is the whole of your law?" she asked.

"That is almost true, and yet a subtle perversion. I am not under law, but under grace," Merlin stated, as she now had him upon his back on the bed. Speaking through her skillful strokes and pets, he went on, "All things are lawful unto me, but not all things edify. All things are lawful unto me but not all things glorify God. All things are lawful unto me but I shall not be brought under the power of any. Do you understand?"

Nimue, a swarm of kissing bees hived around the wizard's neck, popped up to reply. "Because you can do a thing does not mean that you ought to do a thing?"

"Exactly, *cariad*! What we do or do not do is a function of love, not debt, guilt and reward."

"I see why the Catholics want you dead, Lord Merlin. Will you teach these things to Arthur?" Nimue asked, then resumed her swarm of kisses and caresses.

"There is yet beauty in Rome. And not all Catholic people are bad. We must always be careful to distinguish the people from their leaders. I long to see Rome. Paul was there."

"I hate Paul!" A visceral, loud objection. "He hates women and would subjugate us under the thumb of men as dogs or mules!"

"A common misconception by those who never read the man," answered Merlin, authoritatively. "Paul's letters must be read as such and he restricted the abuse of transitory signature gifts by women in a local assembly. Context drives meaning. After all, Paul had many women succor his ministry and it was he who pronounced words that would cost him his head, including the pronouncement that there is neither male nor female, as we are all one in Christ!" Merlin's words were masterful, given that he had not known a woman in years and that the very object of many nights of mortal self-indulgent thoughts was grinding upon his loins at the time.

But the words were lost on Nimue; she naturally could not receive them.

"Tell me that one part again, please," she requested, with an intentional erotic pant.

Merlin asked about which part, excited to share how Christ had died for her and reconciled with her personally five hundred years ago, and how the organized Church was the Devil's plaything. Playing a guessing game for a few more pets and grinds and jostles, she finally removed the last of the old man's clothing.

"Nay. The part about all things being powerful and such." She bungled his words with a purpose, begging his correction.

"No, lover." He tried to focus as she was on the verge of forcing him inside of her. "All things are lawful unto me, but I shall not be brought under the power of any."

But you are under my power now. And Nimue seduced Merlin.

Many enchantments are made the moment a man's life-making essence is spilled, for several reasons. Principle among these is the fact that, more powerful than any intoxicant, a man goes into the nether world for a few short seconds; open, susceptible and vulnerable to other worlds, deception and manipulation.

As Merlin lay panting, happy, the portal for betrayal open but for a few seconds, Nimue rapidly handed him a chalice. A post-lovemaking beverage. Truly not able to think in his ecstasy, he received her cup, questioning not. In addition to unleashing malicious and murderous spells upon Merlin using ancient and dark carnal magick (she doubted in her mind that they would take effect, given Merlin's apparent special relationship with the Saviour Himself), Nimue served him a lethal dose of mandrake mixed with mercury and finished with purple monkshood. She masked the poison, rendering it as a gentle cup of tea tasting somehow precisely as the tea his mother used to serve.

Nimue had enchanted the famous and wondrous Merlin of Britain, and poisoned him that he might die.

CHAPTER 20
And What Did Paul Say to You?

Two sons feeding the worms. Newly single. Estranged queen in self-imposed exile. The Bloodhound found and soon to join the Bear at Ludgate in New Troy. Army practically dissolved. Knights excited to see their wives and move on from wars to noble quests. Saxon policies in order and insufferable denominations appeased. Country celebrating the birth of their Golden Age.

It was time to resume the matter of greatest severity.

It was time to find his Merlin.

Feigning a gentle knock upon Meirchion's door, coupled with a soft "Priest, a word with you?" No sooner did the door crack open than Arthur shouldered in with force and righteous anger and grace. Grasping the priest by the collar of his robe as one gathers and yanks the scruff of a cat, King Arthur suspended the scrawny, contemptible rogue three inches from the floorboard. "You urged for his death in your privy council."

"Apparently not so privy," Meirchion whined.

"Illtud violated two hundred years of tradition gossiping with you as he did."

Arthur lowered his captive, glaring. "Tradition be damned when truth is at stake. Or my friend! Did you kill him? Kidnap him? Hear the severity and verity of my words and toy not. What hand had you in it?" The old Catholic was now witness to the ferocity of the king and the same look hundreds of Saxons had received, over the past two decades, immediately preceding imminent demise.

Meirchion calculated carefully his response. That he wanted the druid dead could no longer be concealed. The precise nature, or the *why,* had to be distorted. Sharing that Merlin professed an end to water baptism, tithes and land grants, a reconciliation between druid and the Briton's apostolic church and an unwavering conviction that Christ was all an individual needed and, topping all, that Merlin in his influence and brilliance as a speaker and leader would evangelize this 'good news' throughout the land, was unthinkable. For in sharing it, Arthur might find interest in the topic and his wanton neutrality over religion sway to this 'grace message' that would bankrupt Romanism's enterprise. Death threat from the High King or no, Meirchion offered half-truths to Arthur.

"In a moment of anger," he trembled, "I, amongst seven other aggravated saints, advocated for his death. It's true." At this saying, Meirchion thought he heard an actual lion's roar and hastened to continue his false account. "The wizard had gone mad and, though confessing some heretical form of Christianity, sought to subvert all and slander the Church. We had been fighting long through the night about baptism and doctrinal authority over the Saxon remnants in the east and I forgot myself. I am old, young king." The tone shifted to contrived self-pity dashed with piety. "I know not where Merlin went; only that the heathen witch-queen had some notion of his goings." At this, Meirchion betrayed Vivien, with whom he had just freshly made an accord.

***

"I cannot stay, my lord, forgive me." Nimue greeted Merlin as he woke from his night in heaven; his one opportunity to have her. "My charges were to make sure you were well and report back to the Lady of the Lake."

Merlin stretched and yawned and laughed, and his joints and muscles reminded him that lovers were meant to be young. "But you didn't even ask me why am I here," he mused. Neither Nimue nor Vivien knew of Merlin's secret affiliations with the Brotherhood. Nimue had simply come to seduce and then kill Merlin and thus was caught in a brief tangle, failing to ask conjured questions about his mission.

Women know things.

A man freshly waking from passionate lovemaking is a fool, even one wise as Solomon, or the Merlin.

"I was so raptured in seeing you, having long suppressed these feelings, that I simply failed to ask. And now I am curious. Why are you and the tall killing device here in the land of the Bretons?" (She spake of Maelgwn, refusing subtly to even speak his name or acknowledge his personhood. Clearly, she was not fond of him for some unknown past wrong. Given his history and volume of women, surely there was a tale there Merlin had no desire to speak, nay even think, of.)

Her tactic assuaged any suspicion and now it was Merlin's turn to lie.

"The - uh - tall killing device over there and I had great cause to think that spies would grant the Long Knife access to our ports. From this very forest. The sensitive information warranted grave and urgent investigation. Better that the assembled armies fret about one old wizard than a surprise threat to the entire campaign."

"Our victory suggests you quelled the threat, then?" she asked, half believing.

"The information provided was false." Merlin left it at that. "I am sorry my new faith troubles you, beautiful Nimue."

"It's as Arthur says, Merlin." Again, hatred had to be channeled into cunning words. "Let men worship what gods they will, *only that they don't kill their neighbors for it.*"

"I hope to see you again soon," said Merlin.

"I should like that, my lord." A parting kiss was exchanged.

Maelgwn presented himself, his mannerisms encouraging the two to leave. January rains are bitterly cold, even in a magical forest. Validating that Merlin knew where the Council had stood up their portable tabernacle, they moved on from the Fount and the Castle of the Lady, deeper into the unforgiving, alluring heart of the Broceliande wood.

As the famous travelers progressed deeper and deeper into the wood, Maelgwn felt as if they were rather in a boat, floating towards the very heart of darkness. He also noticed that the old druid's countenance had clearly changed. Merlin had hidden himself under the canopy of his grey hood for the sum of the day's ride, and a guttural cough had developed.

Maelgwn speculated that the wintry rain or nerves about confronting his former *Brothers and Elders* was causing Merlin to feel ill.

In reality, Nimue's poison was slowly taking effect.

***

At eventide, at the very moment they felt as if they could travel no more, they finally arrived at the temporary abode of the Council of Nine. As Maelgwn was the surety of Merlin's safety, he assessed the area and posed several questions before allowing Merlin to enter the edifice.

"If there is incident, how many men should I be prepared for?" he asked, rolling his shoulders and limbering for a fight after the stiffness of the cold ride. His unique battle spike made its first appearance.

Merlin turned to him, his wit, wisdom and humor overpowering the poison killing him from within. "Well, Lancelot, they are called the Council of NINE, so I suppose there are NINE of them."

They both laughed aloud. Merlin entered two folded curtains, each thirty and three feet in height. The entrance to the tabernacle of the Nine.

A stoic voice said: "Merlin. Enter. We are living in legendary and perilous times."

"Aye, of Biblical measure, yes?" contributed another. This one was less stoic and more mocking in tone and pitch.

Merlin made no response and continued to walk in, very slowly.

There he saw the civilized world's most powerful men sitting at a table within a trapezoidal hall fixed between two great obelisks. Dark without ceiling; ornate. Egyptian. The use of torches and great lanterns revealed the genius of the tabernacle's design, illuminating parts of the wooden, fabric and stone structure, veiling others.

The capstone was a glass pyramid, its masonry giving the illusion of suspension. Great lights descended on rods in six places, cascading independent streams of dusk's final light through the mist and clouds upon a great circular table, affixed in the easternmost chamber of the hall.

Many deities of Egypt presided over the hall in both paintings and stonework. *The Eye of Horus* was, of all the relics and idols, most prominent. It sprawled across the span of the western wall in dazzling dyes contrasted against the sandy-colored interior. The place was as splendid as it was dark.

Two hundred girthy men could congress in comfort at the great table. It had a circular top fastened to a square foundation. Onyx busts served as lifeless but menacing watchmen at each of the four corners of the table. Their likeness was that of a man, an ox, an eagle, and a lion. Lastly, a winged serpent was suspended directly over the table. The design of the artwork made it look as if the winged serpent was chief over the other watchers.

Rattle and tap. Rattle and tap. Fingers plated with steel talons became a hand, became a wrist, became arms that disappeared up a black robe donned by he who wore a black mask and was clearly known to Merlin as the lead spokesman of the Nine (although on prior visits he had worn white or benevolent garbs and diverse face coverings). "I think you have something to say to us, maybe to show us?" the thick accent of Italy began. "Or shall we go first? You may choose, my student."

Though powerful men engender fear, often terror, Merlin too was a foe worthy of respect; one to be reckoned with cautiously. He was Fear and Awe in the form of a man. Advanced in years, mighty. Taller than the Britons but Briton through and through. His face was two ridges and an authoritative chin. His hooded garb revealed only the bottom crescents of his eyes. The oscillating flicker of light provided only a hint of the faded but proud serpent enjoining its own tail, tattooed on the druid's long forearm. And he could answer menace with menace as needed. Instead, he chose respect. Respect and caution.

When given the option to speak or to listen, Merlin ever taught Arthur to start by listening, and to his own advice he here harkened. This would give him the advantage of considering, and then countering, their words.

Disquieted that the Merlin was outwitting them from the start, and knowing that the Briton was the paramount debater and disputer in the world, the leader reversed courses, recanting his courtesy, replacing it with disingenuity. "Rather, you are the guest; pupil, we insist that you begin. I know there is something you want to show us. Show it."

Merlin measured every word and action. Although the sum of all the wisdom of men is counted dung compared to the excellence of God's good news through Christ, a lifetime of learning was about to be aborted. Should he offend them (and they kill him), he would never learn their secrets. And right or wrong, Merlin wanted their gnosis; not for ill, but rather to help reconcile his mind on the purpose of a life filled with lies. *And their initiations and secrets might reveal much about Merlin himself.*

But what choice remained? Somehow they already knew he had changed. And that the nature of the visit was not to become one of them. The tension and tones confirmed this. Respectful, firm truth seemed the wizard's best, nay only, recourse.

From the folds of his grey robe Merlin produced a book; camel leather with metallic buckles. The cover was still decorated with a few specks of ink where once had been links in an ornate entrelacement of knot-work art that, in its original condition, had bedazzled any reader. Now only outlines of former art and thumb-worn smooth patches remained.

The words inside, however, were perfectly preserved. The vellum proudly declared its timelessness and resiliency to the reader. Such was the magnificence of the book that it seemed to be *alive.*

One of the Nine gently relieved it of Merlin's hands, covetously. He looked at it, agape, for what seemed forever, and then handed it to the Leader.

"Anything else in that robe?" Clearly the lump of a purse, holding cup or horn (or perhaps a weapon), lay across Merlin's chest, covered. After he declined to answer, the Leader of the Nine opened the book. The inscription on the sole blank sheet inside the cover he read aloud: "*In these letters are words that bring eternal life. Thirteen are to you and one is for you. Study. Pass forward. I love you, my son.*"

The design of the mask failed to cover the lower lip and most of his chin. A smile – a *concerned* smile - was evident. "It's part of a Bible," he said bluntly.

"To you versus for you; oh, the magnitude of distinction in those two words!" responded Merlin with passion. "Luke is written *for* us but these other thirteen are written *to* us." And now the unavoidable righteous indignation of any who is shown truth after being intentionally duped by systematized lies for years and years rose within the druid, overcoming him. "We have studied all the great religions and given hundreds of hours to learning of the sects of Christendom. And in all those years, never once was there mention of *HOW* to study the Bible. How to note and apply its divisions. By what sorcery beyond mine was this simple truth hidden?!" Merlin found himself unintentionally yelling. He calmed himself. "Luke and his Acts of the Apostles are written for us but Paul, Paul is writing to us. The inscription to this blessed scroll contains more truth than the libraries of a thousand scholars."

"This book is over five hundred years old." The Leader of the Nine was gliding around Merlin now, analyzing and date-setting the small tome while the wizard was preaching at them. "Where did you get it?"

The truth was that Taliesin, the Chief bard, the future Merlin of Britain, had given it to the current office holder, and to Taliesin from his father and from his father his father, back to its original gifting. Without hesitation, to ensure Taliesin's head remained attached to his shoulders, and with unshrinking confidence and calm, Merlin lied.

"Mad Meirchion set ablaze a rival chapel in the South of Cymru. Most of the library was destroyed, yet I found this." A lie spoken. A seed planted.

The book was being passed around the Council of Nine. Many had never seen the letter to the Ephesians at all and fewer still a complete set of Paul.

After circling the room and coming back to the spokesman of the Nine, the book was shoved back into Merlin's hands, causing five hundred years of careful preservation to crumple and bend unwillingly. Merlin, a man of letters, cringed as if harming the book was as the injury or murder of a friend or parent.

"And what did Paul say TO YOU?"

Merlin gave a direct and thorough answer, telling the truth in love, flavored with salt.

CHAPTER 21
The Secret Teaching of the Ages Pertaining to the Souls of Men

"There is much to consider. The old wizard... well," a shadowy figure released a bewildered laugh, "brought our wisdom to foolishness. And we are the illuminated ones!"

Another of the Brotherhood angrily turned his throne chair about, glaring at the three clergy sitting on a slab, palms in their hands. "Even our apostate theologians who have handled the Writ for a lifetime couldn't open up the Scriptures for us the way the druid did!"

"Former druid!" chided another. "What would he say to them?" Recalling the terminology the wizard just used, "What did he say to us?"

"He said that the gospel is hid to those who are lost, that we are blinded by the god of this world," contributed another.

"Blind me with that *Light*." This speaker seemed to imbibe some invisible devilish milk, slurping it as he spoke. "But these clergy were supposed to have, well, aided us."

Though intelligent without equal amongst

men (save, apparently, for Merlin), the Council of Nine placed in their employ fallen Christian scholars and scribes. Men of reprobate consciences who had forgotten their first love, they assisted the Council in understanding how Christians thought and the depths of Christian doctrine. Though the principalities that the Nine served guided them, there were things that they peered into and could not see. Through this combination of congress with Devils and false teachers, the Nine could quell and defeat any Christian teaching, save the one promoted by Merlin.

The leader notwithstanding, precisely four of the Nine knew some of what Merlin shared and four of the Nine knew none of it. The only man in the room not fully surprised nor confounded was the masked leader. The Adept of the adepts.

"Merlin's Mystery is not new to the enemies of the Cross of Christ. The Lord Arddu hates it above all doctrines and thus has worked hard to kill it in the womb, even from the Apostolic era. He conceals it from men and angels as he can. Our Lord is very devoted to keeping the Mystery of Merlin just that: a Mystery," said the leader. Four of the Brothers voiced agreement.

As the leader made manifest that he knew of the religion-destroying message, that God had already paid for the sins of all men living from Paul's day until the end of the age and that dead religion was of the Devil (immediately placing the Church in league with the aims of the Nine), some of his Brothers rose in anger. Clamor and yelling ensued.

Clearly compartmentalization existed, as it did for all Mystery Religions and most sects, pagan or Christian, even at the very top.

Meanwhile, Merlin was standing there fighting the pangs of poison, having emptied himself emotionally, sharing his testimony and plans with dark, dark souls. *Men he had used to view as ministers of Light.* Nimue's tea was assaulting the base of his brain and pain, wrenching and writhing pain, was firing in each and every nerve in his head. Theology becomes irrelevant when a man is at death's door.

Hypocritically, Merlin had just professed Christ with his mouth (and with sincerity), but his flesh reverted to Merlin's otherworldly powers, trying to heal himself that he might live long enough to hear of their designs on Arthur. Additionally, Merlin hoped that the wisdom of the Ancients now verbally abusing each other in his midst could share some insight or information about what Merlin really was.

To Merlin's knowledge, the Nine were mighty *men* but, save perhaps the Leader, lacked the Sight, or shapeshifting, or elemental or any supernatural abilities. Over the decades, they had clearly been dependent upon Ascended Masters from some other world that provided them information. Their power was gnosis, not magick. That Merlin possessed both always made him their prized possession.

The Leader pounded fist against one of the obelisks, causing his beads and the inverted cross that dangled at their ends to rattle, clank and fall to the floor.

"Brothers!" He commanded silence. "I will tell you *why* some know of this and some know not in due time. But now…" He turned to the fading Merlin, whose magick was not working. "Let us give the Merlin what *he* wants."

Merlin continued to wonder how the Leader

knew that he was there to disengage from the Nine but still coveted their knowledge. However discovered, the man was right, for these were Merlin's precise objectives.

The masked man changed countenance and asked Merlin to sit comfortably. This the masked man did as well.

Against reason, he gave the Merlin his wish.

"The Secret Teaching of the Ages has three spheres, student." The man motioned for water to be brought to the old wizard, then listed the spheres:

"The Secret Doctrine of the Ages pertaining to men's souls."

"The Secret Doctrine of the Ages pertaining to the eschaton, or end of all things."

"The Secret Doctrine of the Ages pertaining to the nature of Otherworldly beings, of Fae and Watcher, of Star and Dragon."

Additionally, he said, "And beside these are the *Seven Sacred Sciences,* many of which you have already mastered and know; but the Secret Doctrine of the Ages will clarify their import in the generations of man, or the *Great Conversation* as well."

"When you required I leave my king ere the battle for our liberation you said that the Secret Doctrine of the Ages involved him personally. Elsewise I would not have come. Was this a ruse?" The Merlin of Britain was bold.

"The Iron Bear born under the sign of the Red Dragon." The masked man mocked Merlin for his boldness. "This is the problem with obsessively reading Paul; you need to keep reading through to the back of the Writ as well, yes?"

Some laughed.

"Your famous King Arthur is part of the

doctrine." The man resumed a teacher's tone. "Patience. Listen."

At this point, although he did not unmask himself, the spokesman did remove his hooded robe along with his terrifying and foreign armor, which covered not just his hands but arms and chest as well, filled with serpentine fins and frightening spikes and hooks. Replacing these with simple tunic and trouser, he began to comfortably reveal the truth behind years of lies to Merlin. He began to teach the *real* Secret Doctrine of the Ages.

"I think I should introduce myself before I begin. Although we Brotherhood of Nine direct the Royal Bloodlines on behalf of our Ascended Masters and are pledged to a life of study and confinement to our mystical colleges, I will make an exception. After all, you've been with us for so long." A few protesting grumbles followed. Disregarding them, he said, "I am Simon Magus. Let us begin."

Without riddle or enigma, Simon Magus began to teach Merlin the Nine's doctrines pertaining to salvation. The lesson began with a declaration of a premise opposing the relativism taught at every other level of the secret societies, sects, neophytes and cults. An immediate validation that the top of the pyramid held far different doctrines than the 'regular folk' along the bottom and middle rungs.

"Every word of the Bible is true. Absolute truth."

Simon Magus paused. An impossibly long pause.

At last, he resumed. "Except for the ending of the tale. That God is assured victory is a lie. *We* will prevail. Elsewise it is all true."

Obviously Merlin could form no words in response to this. The same teachers who had taught that 'all the gods are one god', that 'man finds his own truth' and many other kindred worldviews was telling him that the group they mocked and derided the most in fact possessed the most truth! The Merlin vowed to just listen and not respond, doing nothing to endanger his quest to hear their aims on Arthur.

And continue Simon did, joyfully sharing the Brotherhood's fivefold plan to keep mankind lost and without God, without hope. He called it 'keeping the gate shut to the soul's salvation'. He went so far as to call most cults 'gatekeepers'. This involved, through false teaching, confusion and deception, finding just the right chapter of *The Great Conversation* in which to freeze a person, allowing them to proceed no further unto coming to the knowledge of the truth. Which gate kept a man locked unto damnation varied according to the individual.

The first gate of the lie program was polytheism, the belief in many gods. Many, many men would never see the real God whilst they worshipped the many gods of tribe, of stone, of stream, of season and circumstance. However, as men didn't see gods of rock and stone and merriment and season, they made idols. And idols didn't hug you, speak with you, or love you. You could neither be loved nor hated by a chunk of silver-decked wood. Moreover, the gods were cruel, contradictory, and often more of lower constitution of character than the men supposedly designed to worship them. Thus, men who seek truth sometimes conclude that polytheism is simply mythology; they open the first gate, searching for something more.

Convictions of silence gave way. Merlin had to

interrupt. "That is not so! I personally HAVE seen gods and spirits aplenty, not just idols made by hands. What about the Fae?"

"The Isles, and this vast forest, are an exception," Simon Magus laughed heartily. "Ye know not what ye worship. Neither what you see. In any event, that will be covered in section three." Another chuckle, and emphatic request that Merlin hold questions until the teacher had concluded his presentation. He even said "Patience," speaking to Merlin as if he were a child.

Simon Magus explained that the second tier of deception was pantheism. The belief that God is *IN* everything. Those who rejected actual gods separate from the creation but who sought something spiritual gravitated towards pantheism. This form of worship resulted in either lasciviousness, where there is no accountability from man to something tangibly greater than he, or in fatalism, where man abdicates personal responsibility and effort, as the 'force' of which we are all part will be as it will be.

Those thinking and considering pantheism carefully found that: "Man is God. Dirt is God. Man is–"

"Dirt." Merlin completed the line of thinking at this point in the initiation. "Man is both nothing and everything under that system, and a meaninglessness ensues. The prison of reincarnation to return in a different form of the same 'force' is the only hope, but to what end? 'Tis a belief in absolute nothingness. It is not peace. It is prison."

"Yes!" Simon was as a proud father of a son who had just caught his first fish or hunted his first hare. Beaming, he said, "Yet we keep ten thousand times ten thousand and ten thousand times that under this system in the East." The lesson continued.

From this gate, Simon explained, some found the emptiness and went into dejection and rejection of the spiritual. To them, there was not a god behind every stone, neither was the tree itself God; having no introduction to monotheism, they tripped into the pit of atheism.

As an aside, Simon Magus also explained that abuse by the Church under the name of God was organized and carried out to drive men to atheism, rebelling from God and anything remotely attached to religion. As this practice was only a few hundred years old, it had not formalized as part of the mysteries taught by the Nine, but was well on its way to becoming an additional gate.

"The fool hath said in his own heart, there is no God." Merlin again found himself speaking at the hearing of these intentional misdirections.

"Aye, in his heart, not in his head," Magus agreed. "Men in this gate look at the creation, the stars, the circuits of the sun. They behold the miracle of childbirth and they know in their heads that we are not here as a result of chance or random natural processes. They eschew accountability but they know that there is a God to whom they will answer."

"In this regard, there are no actual atheists," contributed Merlin.

"Again, you are correct, my student. Men toil behind this gate over anger, ill experiences and rejection of observable science, and replace it with a science of their own. A science falsely so called."

"What is the next gate?" Merlin was threading their strategy together and, although evil, it was fascinating and effective.

The initiator provided a brief summary, weaving it together again and again along the way. "There are many gods. No. God is in everything. This is not so. Fine. There is no God. That is not reasonable. From here…"

Magus paused again and Merlin could hardly contain himself. Again, he seduced his hearer with summary. "Many gods, God in all, no God, transitions to *I am God.*"

The structure and sensibility of this continuum of deception made absolute strategic sense to Merlin, the great strategist. When man knows that there is a spiritual reality but rejects or graduates from systems that do not hold under the light of scrutiny, what is left but to venerate himself? Especially for the atheist. If man graduated from primordial simple components to his present condition, why would he not then progress unto deity?

One of the Nine actually mocked this concept (perhaps he was the very one in charge of seeing its growth and popularity) and chimed, "From goo to you, through the zoo! From slime to divine!" The entire council laughed and even Merlin found himself amused at the ridiculous emptiness of atheistic naturalism.

The leader, Simon, brought the Brotherhood and their 'once gilded pledge and most promising student, turned grace believer' Merlin back to order. He reminded the assembly that, although naturalism and atheism would be mocked on the Blessed Isles where obsession with the spirit and the afterlife was paramount, it was vastly popular amongst the Greeks and other cultures and had kept many souls gated from pursuing a relationship with the One True God.

Merlin again, feeling somewhat more

comfortable during the discourse, inquired. "So, the Secret Doctrine of the Ages for men is that you know the truth, but lie anyhow?"

Simon Magus confirmed, even his laughter thick with the accent of magnificent Italy. "Yes." Asking all to resume sitting, he concluded the first of the three great spheres of the Nine's quest. Again, he opted for summary as a powerful preaching conduit of his false gospel:

Many gods.
All is God.
No gods.
I am God.

A person of intellectual honesty, he postulated, could no more think himself a god than a cat could think itself a hummingbird. Each star had its own glory, each element differed from another. Those who thought themselves a god did oppose themselves. A man was a man and a god was a god. And thus, after a season toiling under the weight of self-deception that they, a finite being full of flaws and scars and sickness and infirmity, were likened unto Zeus or Poseidon, they faced the fact. There was a God. And they were not Him.

"And what becomes of these?" asked the Merlin.

"They make it to the final gate. That Satan is God."

This booming statement shocked and confirmed what Merlin already knew. The Council of Nine formally and officially were in league with the Prince of Darkness.

Simon smiled. "When you reject Christ and determine that all the false doors are that, what door remains? These set aside the followings of polytheism, pantheism, atheism, self-deification and any other 'ism' I have forgotten besides and choose rather to follow the one god that makes sense; the god of this world."

"How much do you really control this journey into finding your Lord?" asked Merlin. "And why do you care if men choose Christ or Rhiannon or Bel or your god Arddu? What matters it to you?"

"Excellent questions! The right questions!" Simon Magus always and ever marveled at the genius of Cymru's greatest mind. "Men are blinded by unbelief by nature, but by nature seek the true God. Because of this paradox, all we do is give them a nudge in the wrong direction. We plant certain thoughts in leaders in cults and churches and sects. We publish certain writings and we watch and influence 'big issues', but the greater sum is just enjoying man doing what he does best; rebel."

"And the why?" the druid pressed.

"As to 'THE WHY' we seek to keep men lost, it has everything to do with the *End of Days*. And much to do with your King Arthur. Are you ready for the second sphere of the Secret Doctrine?"

CHAPTER 22
The Other Antichrist

In the days when Saul of Tarsus (who would later convert to the Faith and become the Apostle Paul) persecuted the Messianic assemblies, causing them to scatter abroad, Mary the Mother of the Lord and Mary of Magdala came, along with other noteworthy followers of the Lord, into Gaul.

Magdalene took a husband, one of Jesus's brothers, and bore him a child. A contention over certain sacred relics arose between the two Marys. So severe was the dispute that they parted, unreconciled: Magdalene unto the caves of what later became southern Little Britain, and Mary the Mother of the Lord unto the Isles, where she tangled with Anna, also over the matter of certain relics. By the time, three decades and more later, Paul finally visited the Isles, Mary was long since retired to the Isle of Apples, under the care of her guardians, the druids.

After learning the Brotherhood's first great secret, how they intentionally developed false doctrines to doom and blind men when they in fact knew the truth but hated God too much to accept it, the Merlin girded himself to hear about the second sphere of the Secret Doctrine of the Ages. Based upon the allusions provided and from what Merlin had begun to comprehend from rightly dividing the Scriptures, he was fairly certain that the subject would shift towards politics.

Night had fallen and, outside the massive curtain doors, the blackness of night was thick. 'Twas the type of night where one couldn't see their fingers, though they wiggled them two inches in front of their face. Yet, within the great temporary structure, strange and awesome blue and green lights filled the chamber. The illumination of the all-seeing eye was beautiful art made ugly to Merlin for what it stood for.

Although he was certain there were servants or soldiers (or both), Merlin had only seen the Nine, robed and hooded, save Magus, who was still in his leisurely attire and serving his brethren tea.

Merlin felt better when standing as the poison navigated his veins, destroying them as it traversed. He was content that his curiosity and academic need for their final set of secrets was more than satisfied and, were it not for the bait they had dangled before him regarding Arthur, he would have fled the place at once, having no need of further lessons. Instead, exercising the haste of a dying man, Merlin vowed to himself that he would just stand there and listen, saying nothing, arguing about nothing.

Simon Magus rose, speaking dramatically with his hands and head, deeply enjoying his own lecture. Although Merlin had been lured away from the most important military conflict of the age by a grave beseechment about the end of the world, his *teacher* rather started, to the dying man's chagrin, at its beginning. Before its beginning.

Magus spoke of God's eternal purpose for

the Ages. Again, he bluntly proclaimed his unwavering loyalty to his god, the angel Arddu, and his plan and program for thwarting the Creator. However, he had so mastered the truth, and was so articulate in explaining it, that any hearer would become captivated and bewitched, slipping into moments of confusion, thinking the man was Moses or the Apostle Paul, and not the Devil's most important human agent.

In the most unadorned declaration, he stated that God's eternal purpose was to glorify His son Jesus Christ, the possessor of heaven and earth. It was noteworthy that there were no hisses or protests at the mention of Christ, or of God's eternal purpose concerning Him. Nor were there jeers or curses when Magus confirmed plainly that Jesus was Himself God; distinct in personhood, but equal to and one with God the father (Merlin had no need for explanation of this, for the druids had well understood the triune name of the Hebrew God for generations).

The protest, the vitriolic fang-baring, claw-scraping hatred came when the Leader began to teach on how man, originally created in the triune image of the Creator, had been chosen to be God's agency to rule and reign over these spheres. Yes, Satan had wanted to be like the Most High, but that was in his connection to be promoted over man, not serving him. Yes, he had coveted a throne above the Lord's, but this only at hearing that he would bow down to Adam. Satan was man's adversary, not God's. As if God could have a rival. That man was the heir of salvation, that man would inherit everything good and wonderful in creation, that man was in a special relationship with the Sovereign ignited Arddu's rage, causing iniquity to form within him.

When Adam was about one hundred and thirty years, the great cherub could no longer contain and rebelled. Since that very day Arddu had ever sought to dispossess man from his place as agency for Christ, from his dominion. If man was disqualified, ineffective and lost then God's purpose would be thwarted and God, a relational being by nature, would have no choice but to turn to the angelic hosts to replace those roles.

God had greatly duped Arddu by concealing a great secret for four thousand years. It was ever known that Christ would rule earth through men. God would outmaneuver His enemy's aims on Adam, and then (after Arddu did his greatest work on the other side of the Flood), Noah, the Patriarchs and ultimately Israel, with whom He made His covenants concerning the Land. That Israel would inherit the kingdom was no secret (though Satan believed thoroughly he would still win in the end), but no mention was made of the other half of the Cosmos – heaven.

Though expelled from the upper heavens and though engaged in perpetual war with God's faithful angels, heaven belonged to the hosts. The luminaries declared God's message night over night, the Moon gave her glory over the night as the Sun his during the day. Heavenly thrones, powers and principalities held control over the governance of heaven. Satan had access to the Heavenly Father, even after the Fall. Satan was the prince of the power of the air, even after the Fall. Satan's legions controlled the nations through influencing corrupt men from their territorial domains which remained unchanged, even after the Fall.

In the heavenlies, the war was as it had been from the foundation of the world. Angel versus angel. Man, that worm and ape, toiled on the earth and Satan had many, many strategies for foiling man down there.

Again, as Simon Magus told the story of the generations of men (and angels) he would oscillate in tone and pitch and emotion and at times it seemed that he sincerely championed God's cause. At other times there seemed to be pity for the Devil. *Because truth engenders passion, those who have rejected it can still be convicted and tormented by its fire*; this was Merlin's only conclusion as he listed to the Sermon unfold. Simon had sold himself to the Devil but could preach and teach the truth.

And because of the little book and *how* the simplicity of Christ and what He was doing in the dispensation of grace was shared with Merlin, he knew the next part of the glorious story and eagerly wanted to join in telling it.

Simon continued. When studying the Scriptures, he shared, the theme was the same from beginning to end:

From Adam to Noah is about dominion over the earth.
From Noah to Abraham is about dominion over the earth.
From Abraham to Moses is about dominion over the earth.
From Moses to David is about dominion over the earth.
All the Prophets are about dominion over the earth.

All of these, he explained, spoke of a coming King, a Wonderful Counselor, a Mighty God. And surely this King was from heaven but the theme of the Scriptures was the earth.

Merlin fully agreed. Merlin could have given this presentation and thus far, beyond the pure demonic hubris of intentional aims against truth, was learning nothing new. The old wizard now wondered if Simon Magus may have been educating his brothers, countering the Merlin's testimony, which already had covered these grounds. *No, he is leading me somewhere with this; keep listening*, Merlin concluded.

Then Simon Magus transitioned to the four gospels. For in these four books and their correlative Hebrew Epistles do both Rome and the Britons draw their doctrine and enslave men. The great themes of the gospels are the deity, humanity, kingship and servant aspects of offices of the Lord Jesus Christ. However, the theme never changes where God's purposes are concerned. They still deal exclusively with Israel, from whom the kingdom is taken and given to Peter and the Eleven, who then take the name of the Little Flock or the Israel of God. To them is given a special inheritance, a great city that comes down from heaven. From this city, the twelve will reign over the twelve Tribes of Israel, who will in turn reign over the Gentile kings and by extension *the earth. Still the focus on earthly.*

"All the teachings about cutting out one's eye, or selling all possessions, or being water-baptized as ceremonial washing for priesthood functions. All the rules and regulations were given to the Jew. Yet your priest and bishops appropriate them and Jesus wouldn't have even spoken to a Gentile in His earthly ministry!" Simon was disgusted at the ignorance of the professing Church.

And on this point, Merlin agreed with the Devil worshipper.

The Brotherhood's masked master concluded the summary with doctrinal precision and accuracy.

"The earth. The earth. All the way through the 'Book' 'tis about the earth." He then looked up through the pyramidal glass ceiling. The wintry night in Brittany was still of the darkest pitch. And then, the thick overcast parted and a few stars emerged, then a few more, then the clouds at once dissolved and hosts and hosts of luminaries could be seen, orbiting around the still earth. "What about them?" he asked, still star-gazing. "What about heaven?" And now his look fell back upon the dying wizard. "The Creator reveals His twofold purpose, of possessing earth and *HEAVEN*, right from the first Book of Moses, but then fades to overwhelming silence on the one half of the cosmos. Why?"

Merlin, newly immersed in rightly dividing the word and understanding God's diverse programs and strategies, was full of the hunger and zeal of a newborn and could not contain himself. He had the answer, and *made* the answer.

"God did not want the Devil to know that it was always His intent to fill the heavens, demoting the angels and having Men be his agency there as well. Thus, he kept the battle focused on earth until the fullness of time, when the Lord Jesus did something unique on that Cross, allowing for the making of a New Creature; men who would fill up a Body in heaven and displace Satan there too, making his demise and defeat complete."

Here at death's door, Merlin, the most legendary of all save King Arthur Pendragon himself, the legend amongst legends, he who had fulfilled quests, conquered foes, explained dragons to architects, mapped the heavens, performed signs and wonders, seen things with Vivien that were unlawful to utter and, above all, raised, mentored and advised the Once and Future King of the Britons, had saved his best words for his final breaths.

His conclusion was equally astute. "Because God's heavenly program was a secret, there is very little information, as the Devil knows the Scripture better than slovenly and lazy man, who does not study. For this cause, we only know that entrance into the heavenly body is wholly based upon grace and that heaven will be filled with low-down Gentile dogs like us, with no preference for Israel, or rich, or poor, or man or woman. God picked the murderer Saul, the chief of the rebellion against God, and saved him for this heavenly calling. No religion, no works, all focused on the Cross!"

"Yes, we have heard this before ten times tonight!" one of the Nine rebuked Merlin. At the hearing of the name 'Paul', the disposition of the room became an anger, thick and foul.

"So, you know God's Mystery. Are you ready for ours?" Simon was smiling, little drops of perspiration forming where mask met skin.

"Yes." The dying man's insistence and confidence was waxing whilst his life essence waned. "What does all of this theological diatribe have to do with *my* king?"

"There are nine of us on this council." Simon's hand made a sweeping, circular motion, passing by each Brother seated. "Why nine?"

Merlin, an adept at the meaning of sacred geometry and the mystical association of numbers, answered immediately. "'Tis the number of wisdom and initiation."

"Very good!" The Italian accent was thick when Simon was excited or happy with Merlin's answer. "However, there is more. We are, in reality, two groups of four, with me as a sort of mediator or facilitator." An arrogant smile pushed the mask up nearly to his nose. He enjoyed being the leader of the world's most dangerous cult. "And the number four, Merlin?"

"It speaks to completing a path or to being comprehensive," he responded.

"So wise, druid!"

"*Former* druid." The agitation towards Merlin had not abated since the mention of Paul and the Cross and grace.

Simon resumed teaching.

Merlin's numerological deduction was precise. Simon began to explain that the Council was divided into two factions with paradoxically contradictory objectives. He called them *Immanentizers and Delayers.*

Finally, he began to speak of the end of all things, and how the Nine might fulfill their purpose: how they might immanentize it.

First he provided instruction about how Christian leaders must never read Paul and be thoroughly confused about the End of Days. Using as a pattern that contemporary eschatological doctrine espoused by Augustine of Hippo and earlier *Church Fathers,* they used their influence to ensure that the influential believed that the Resurrection would be preceded by a Golden Age lasting, figuratively, a thousand years – really, an unknown amount of time. Some Christian sects would be instructed to teach that only in this reign of the saints Christ would return; still others held that Christ would return in the heart of the believer and no more. The orthodoxy of the day rendered prophecy fulfilled in AD 70 and the Church as the New Israel.

On the basis on these teachings, the Council of Nine labored to build an anti-Golden Age. Looking like the real millennial reign, and duping souls until the prophesied One would yield up to Lucifer and his consort all things that he might be all in all at the end of the aeon. Where this translated into politics, the Immanentizers ever sought to build a world government by goading nation states into conflict. Through loans and debt-slavery they would create a drunken and power-mad leadership with one hand and deceive the world into thinking they were living in the Millennium with the other.

After a world leader would rise, convinced that he was the long-promised Messiah, the Church would be discarded as a harlot is beaten and thrown to the streets when her use is completed. The holy land and Israel would be restored and the world leader would run the world from that coveted city on seven hills.

The Immanentizers, every day and night, labored only to bring about world government, to foment war and peace, and to create every criterium requisite for the Apocalypse.

"And yet…" Simon noted Merlin was in shock at what he had once been a part of, once very nearly joined. "Why would we want the End of Days?"

"You already told me; because you believe Satan will win. That the whole of the Book is true save the end," Merlin answered.

"The Book says that when such things come to pass our Master will be filled with great wrath," and now in a whisper, "knowing that his time is short."

"You know he will lose, hence the whisper!"

Simon Magus struck the tall Briton square upon the nose, splattering famous blood everywhere.

In an instant, the greatest wizard and advisor to ever live was joined by the greatest warrior. Lancelot appeared, watching all somehow (but hearing none due to his vantage outside the great folds of the tabernacle). Of equal surprise, thirty heavily armored guardians appeared in an instant.

Sopping blood with the sleeve of his grey cloak, the Merlin followed a frequent custom: using jest instead of panic. "Sorry, Lancelot. I undercounted."

"Yes, you said nine!"

Merlin believed the Round Table Companion's return volley also full of humor. The guards chased Lancelot out of the Tabernacle into Broceliande's haunted and enchanted night.

Physically, Merlin could slay the Italian with no effort. Merlin was not some passive advisor; he was a Cymry warrior in his own right and many had fallen to his blade and staff. However, if Merlin was to die of poison, he would know of the plans for Arthur first. And, through whatever means necessary, keep his heart beating long enough to warn his beloved friend. And so he stopped the blood, pressing thumbs hard into nostrils, and sat down, calmly.

"Because the Lord Arddu is not here I will tell you that, though you blaspheme, you may be right. We believe he will win but our preference is not to immanentize." Simon now looked upon the four who served the obverse purpose. "Our preference is to delay."

The lesson continued.

As both Merlin and Magus had shared in their exchange, God was filling up a heavenly body with (primarily) Gentile believers to reign in the heavenly places. This meant that the Powers, Principalities, Thrones and Dominions currently running heaven (the Fallen Ones) would be expelled, dispossessed, and replaced with New Creatures from amongst the saved of the sons of Adam. This reconciliation of heaven could not be achieved until the Body of Christ was full. Thus, the plan was to keep men lost and blind. At first it had been thought that this would only last a few years, but the Church had fallen asleep after Paul. "Let them sleep while we feast on their immaturity!" Simon cried.

Working in concert with the Immanentizers, Magus explained: "Our Dark Lord wants man dedicated to kingdom building. A kingdom without a king. He has already defeated Christendom in the same way he has since the Mystery was gradually revealed - with works-based institutionalism."

Although always having to deal with a small group of the faithful, an endless kingdom where the Adversary was god of this world and prince of the power of the air would suit both he and the Nine well. Driven by a never-ending lust and covetousness for more, Satan would one day be compelled to battle for complete control; but he relished the great measure of control he already possessed.

Compelled by the dual command to convince man to 'put off' salvation whilst always having an Antichrist candidate ready was life's mandate for the Secret Societies.

"The second Secret Doctrine of the Ages is that you are both working to bring about the end of the world *AND* prevent it?"

"Aye," laughed Magus.

And then the part that was not humorous ensued.

"We have two candidates for the Antichrist, should your Lord tarry. Childebert, son of Clovis, who ever fights with your friends Howel and Budic, is one candidate. He is of the Merovingian line and his lineage runs all the way back to the brother of the Lord. The one who looked just like Jesus. The one who had lain with Mary the Magdalene. He will be passed off as a child of the Christ; the people will devour the lie! And," Simon again performed his unnaturally long pause, inhaling through his nose and exhaling dramatically, "your king Arthur Pendragon is our other candidate for Antichrist."

Simon let the plan settle. "Born on the Mass of the Christ, under the Sign of the Dragon, named after the Bear. Don't just read Paul, dear Merlin, read John the Revelator. Arthur *is* Antichrist! The world already loves him."

"The Merovingian or the Pendragon. Why else would we visit this damnable freezing forest in January?" one of the Nine grumbled.

"Arthur will never follow you. Never. Never!" The Merlin seethed with energy meet for defending his king, his friend.

"He doesn't have to," said Simon, sighing at the Merlin's ignorance of the matter. "If he has some secret sins, we will extort them. If he has loved ones, we will threaten him."

"He had sons, and we turned them against the famous king without complication," contributed another.

"Moreover," and now Simon revealed highly guarded secrets, "all he must do is suffer a grievous head wound, then will we be able to insert the spirit of Judas Iscariot, who is in his place in the Underworld awaiting that day, into him. You know we are in league with entities that can do this."

"The Dynion Hysbys." Merlin's face was as a ghost.

"Aye." Simon was gleeful at this point. "When your king was a boy I personally selected his first mate. Let us describe it thusly: we found one who opened a channel in Arthur for us to work with."

Neither Merlin nor Simon Magus, there representing God and the Devil, knew that it was Arthur's very own sister selected for him at the rites. Merlin, however, again felt the unknown pains of deep regret about those events, nearly two decades ago. That the Dynion Hysbys had aided this collected assembly of the world's most influential villains whilst Vivien and Merlin were busy preparing Excalibur to gift to the young prince vexed him thrice over the poison in his veins.

"And if he will not be your King of Kings, what then?" asked Merlin.

"As we said, we have the son of Merovech. But we prefer Arthur. He will join us, or we will wipe his lineage from every history book and every poem. He will be a myth. A children's nighttime story until, at some later time, should we delay and not immanentize, we will resurrect him for some future generation."

Merlin found himself looking at the author of the Saxon Wars, the puppet-masters of generations of distress, destruction and devastation upon enchanted Cymru. These men had worked out not only a well-constructed plan but a secondary plan, a tertiary plan and a fourth and fifth plan besides. Despair was swallowing Merlin; he was drowning, and his hope in peril.

However, he still managed a "You will fail—"

Before the sentence finished, Simon interrupted. "There is still the third sphere to cover, Merlin. You came here for the Secret Teaching of the Ages. Your despair for your friend is boiling on the kettle of the despair for your own soul; we've not even poured into the pot. It is time for you to know *what* you are, Merlin."

CHAPTER 23
The Lady of the Lake's Fateful Alliance

The Lady of Llyn Fawr galloped through the mists, weeping.

Dignity. Majesty. Self-control. These were the attributes to which she anchored a life of service to her deities, to her people. Spanning from Albion in the North, Lloegyr in the East, her cousins from the great kingdoms in the West Country to those who lived in the horn of Britain in the South and, of course, her own kinsmen in Little Britain, Vivien loved her people.

For them, the preservation of their customs and ways, for their heritage and the very survival of her great goddess, she had authorized a diabolical plot. Her anchors now jerked violently from the seabed of conscience.

Dignity in murder?

Majesty in seduction?

Self-control in enraged political posturing?

That which serves the people is moral. Murdering served the people; therefore, murder is moral.

The dangerous and faulty sophistry of her thoughts was swept quickly away along with the tears, streaming along the windblown slopes of her perfect face. Returning her hand to the harness she galloped, harder now.

The shoreline wound round a beach from which Britain could be seen. She turned south and rode hard into Broceliande, stopping at a great freshwater pool, seemingly placed by the gods themselves for private reflection, intimacy or mourning.

Would she make it in time to stop Nimue?

Fae of an outwardly benevolent but somber disposition scurried throughout the trees, gazing upon the solitary Lady. Tiny beings whose stars covered their little bodies, they were as fireflies gazed upon round a fire. They loved the Lady for her kindness and they swarmed near, concerned greatly for her overwhelming distress.

She was Lancelot's mother in every way save blood. A pillar of invincibility. Powerful beyond measure, yet feminine and soft. Vivien, the Lady of Lake, the most beautiful of all the Britons. It was a comeliness from within and external. Clad in her elegant garb, the flowing white dress, pillowed sleeves and hooded cloak, she was invisible against the snow save the golden glisten of her legendary hair. But the Fae were able to see her. Eyes elliptical and emerald, skin transparent, Vivien was the vicar of the goddess on Earth.

"To defeat the enemy from without," soggy twigs and snowy brush shifted audibly beneath her as she approached the Lady of the Lake, still atop her mount, "we must first defeat the enemy from within."

Vivien gathered herself in an instant. "And who is the enemy from within?"

"My Lady. We heard what was said at Caerleon ere the battle of Mount Baedan." There was no mercy in the words from Nimue, who had clearly completed her mission. The little faeries recoiled, scattering at her appearance. "The druid turned Christian who would betray our sacred knowledge, even the Mystery!" Escalating, her voice was venomous, metallic. "Because of your bravery and decisive action, we will never bow down to the Bishop of Rome and our mysteries will never be shared or defiled. Never!

"And what's more," she continued, "his recent conversation constitutes a dereliction of office. Not only was he distracted so close to receiving his final initiation, he had become – dangerous. I, like you, loved Merlin, but he has," she searched for the word, "changed."

Vivien considered her response. For the first time since living the legend, a legend that for her had begun with giving Merlin the Sword, she saw something hitherto undetected in the young enchantress. Hate. Nimue now, perhaps had always, shared the same flaw as her enemy. Similarity breeds contempt.

Vivien could not punish or rebuke Nimue for carrying out the very direction given to her by the Lady herself. But the joy with which she had performed the dark task gave Vivien great pause.

After Merlin had brought to ruin the hierarchical Sects of Christ with his words at Caerleon, Vivien had felt betrayed. Merlin had spoken of a Mystery and of an end of all the devices of man-made religion. In her hurt she had become selfish. With Merlin's fame and popularity, his turning to the Christ would result in the same for what remained of the small numbers of druids left on the Isles. The common man would trust Merlin where they distrusted and despised the priests and bishops, and the whole of the Island, save the nasty Dynion Hysbys, would turn to Christ.

Merlin, when passionate about any matter, was the Great Strategist, the Great Orator, the Great Evangelist.

The night he had said these things, in her hurt she had mourned and pondered in her chambers… and then the knock on the door.

An unwelcome guest.

On her worst day Vivien had tenfold the wit and one hundredfold the wisdom of Mad Meirchion. But that night had not been her worst day. It had been worse than her worst day. Merlin's salvation was Vivien's death. Death of relevance, death of influence, and perhaps death of liberty. On this day and this day alone, the Majestic Lady had allowed herself to be duped.

Meirchion had pointed out that the Church of Rome was much kinder towards the indigenous faiths of her vassal kingdoms. The shrines of Ephesus, the pagan faiths of North Africa and even the tolerance of Mithraism near to the Holy See in Rome were used as examples.

By contrast, the Cymry bishops were antagonistic towards other paths, often deliberating on diverse ways to separate the Lady's head from her shoulders. They planned a kingdom of priests and kings where the entire nobility would rule using Christian precepts with an iron fist. Catholicism, by contrast, was open to plurality and freedom under the wing and protection of Mother Rome.

Moreover, there was a great gulf of animosity between the druids and the Church of the Britons. It did not manifest often and many bards were Christian. Surface-level handshakes and embraces abounded at festivals and meals but, amongst the higher ranks and at sundry times, a great anger existed over some wrong perceived to have been done unto the Christian sect. Knowing this secret was part of Vivien's rearing in her own mysteries. Yet, in the process of time, of fighting the Saxon Wars, of exhausting endeavors to temper Northern versus Southern conflicts, she had forgotten all about the origin of their old hurts. *Had she remembered, Merlin might not be lying dead or dying presently.*

Merlin was becoming one of them, though different, and they hated her. Moreover, when Merlin shared that he would openly tell Arthur of the 'mystery', Vivien the Wise became a Fool: committing the sin of assumption.

However, even in her compromised condition that fateful night, she still clung to what all Britons cleaved unto; the threat of Rome upon Cymru's national sovereignty. Historically, the Romans and Silures fought to a draw many times and Cymru was ever a rival and equal of Rome, never bowing a knee; even whilst they paraded the great Caradoc captive around her capital, the Sword of Caesar plucked right from his very hands was on display in Lloegyr.

Meirchion, freshly come from a privy council with the bishops, had openly called for Merlin's head and was desperate for an ally in hopes of retaining his own. Thus, to quell the concerns of the Lady, he used the very name of the king he loathed to comfort her. Indicating that neither King Arthur nor the Round Table Companions would ever yield the sovereignty of a nation to a foreign king or potentate after fighting for so many years to win and protect it, he offered Vivien the illusion of a perfect picture of her future. The future of her kind. Her help in assassinating the Merlin in exchange for an alliance against the bishops, and a vow that her goddess and the old gods would be protected as the country continued its transition to the Christian Religion.

And so. Here she was. The plot activated.

Nimue had a few days' lead time on Vivien. Her repentance had been too slow. Her arrival to arrest the scheme too late. Her coming to her senses delinquent.

Meirchion officially had the Lady in a vice. If she honored the deal, what surety was there of Rome's help for her people, and at what cost? If she confessed to the Round Table that she was in league with him, even if pleading that she had taken leave of her senses due to grief, she would die the *Triple Death* reserved for traitors (a complete or threefold death required for complete justice of the condemned). Her only escape, her only recourse, was to ensure that Merlin *did not die.*

If he yet lived then there was no murder to confess, no collusion with the Swine Priest. Merlin *must live.*

"Nimue, we have violated the very thing that our High King champions. That men serve what gods they will, only that they don't kill their neighbors for it."

"He was a traitor. He was to reveal our mysteries."

"A mystery," Vivien interrupted. "There are many mysteries. I agree that Merlin has turned from our goddess, but we are wrong here."

"You have become weak and sentimental, Lady." Hate had fully consumed the young priestess.

Vivien looked to the snowy forest and a swarm of the celestial little beings at once enveloped Nimue, poking, pinching and stabbing her, causing her to flail arms in the air and run blindly.

There were so many of them that she was as a torch, an aimless whirling torch.

The Lady of the Lake uttered ancient words to a nearby stream. The waters immediately organized themselves into a well. The faeries manipulated the panicking Nimue's course, causing her to stumble and fall, head-first, down into the infant well, born for her death.

"The goddess will not receive one so full of hate and murder as you. She demands works. May Merlin's new God accept you by the grace Merlin is now so fond of." Vivien spoke again her ancient incantations; the well at once become a fount, and Nimue's tomb.

Vivien hastened into vast Broceliande, hoping to find and save the friend whom she had betrayed.

CHAPTER 24
A Good Secret to Replace a Bad Secret

While the merriment of free Cymru continued, the Pendragon labored to find his old mentor and friend. He honored the bishops and priest Meirchion by allowing them to convene amongst the wild horses and majesty of Lodge Hill.

Cai joined them.

"We are now ten days since seeing Merlin. Ten days! Maelgwn and Gwalchmai will return soon from Brittany and then we are all traveling to New Troy. When standing upon the platform under banners and trumpets, MY wizard had better be standing next to me." The Bear of Glamorgan's patience over the matter was officially spent.

The clergy, all grown soft and given to pampering, stamped their feet under massive coats, attempting to stay warm; the Usk river's frigid waters, paired with gusting winds, created a freeze that climbed all the way up the hill.

"Oh, Cai, please help me build these delicate souls a fire." Arthur was never too proud to aid in that which he requested of others, always showing hospitality (even when full of anger and dismay). As the king knelt to gather sticks, he noticed that one was missing amongst the shivering bishops.

"Where is Cadfan?" he asked, disappointed at their failure to meet his expectation that *all* present at the privy council meet him.

Arthur stood ere they answered, dropping the sticks.

"One who should be here is not and one not expected here is," he said.

Gwyar presented herself, emerging from one of the mid-level ridge trails in the fort; clearly on a morning walk. Mutually startled, they both laughed.

"The children of Meurig love this hill!" they cried in unison.

She was clearly upset over being displaced from Ynys Enlli and he was on the brink of unraveling at not knowing what had become of his friend. When not at war, Arthur loved the solace of the fort. When visiting family, or trading in Caerleon, Gwyar would leave the markets and come to this very spot. No matter what perils, quests, marriages or adventures separated them by distance or years, *Caerleon was still their home and this was their hill.*

"Are we so predictable, sister?" Arthur and she laughed again. They shared a light moment.

Illtud was intrigued by Gwyar, the rest feared her and Aiden, whose intolerance was burgeoning, loathed her.

"One witch is absent from court," (he spoke of Vivien, reportedly caring for Maelgwn and yet in Brittany) "and another appears. You know what the Writ says about their kind, my Lord?"

"*Suffer not a witch to live,*" Gwyar responded for her brother. She twisted hard upon her forearm and spoke an imprecation. Where she twisted and torqued corresponded to the spiraling crackle of bones seen and heard at the very same location upon Aiden's forearm. The pious preacher crumped in agony, crying curses at the king's sister, before shock caused him to pale and swoon. "Should any of you desire to enforce that part of your Book, here I am."

Frightened and powerless, they all spoke of Jesus's love under the new covenant; tolerance was restored.

Arthur clasped his face with both hands and exhaled, frustrated. "Cai, take the bishop down the hill. Sister, control your gifts. And *someone* tell me where Cadfan is immediately!"

Gwyar, moderately embarrassed, lowered her eyes, but her smile she retained. A smile soon to vanish, visage to become cold as the Usk's winds.

Meirchion stated, "Cadfan is in the North. He is blessing the foundation and flooring for a new chapel there."

"We were aware of no such chapel scheduled for erection," Dyfrig said, puzzled, Illtud's comments matching those of the more senior bishop.

"It's a little endeavor; 'tis nothing." The scheming Meirchion was enjoying the enigmatic discord. "It was fully authorized by Einion, the chieftain of Llyn, the son of Owain Ddantgwyn, an upright man who reveres the Bishop of Rome."

The Llyn Peninsula formed the northwest 'arm' of Cymru. And beyond the fingertip of the peninsula lay the Isle of Apples, the abode of treasures and secrets and Gwyar's orchards contained in the castle made of glass.

"Where in the cantref is the church to be built?" A pit of betrayal was sinking within Arthur's sister.

"The Bishop of Rome says Enlli is a Holy Place,

visited by many renowned saints and champions of the faith. Cadfan will be instated as Bishop of Ynys Enlli."

If words could be sharper than Excalibur, these were. Inside of a fortnight drawn away from her Isle, shackled at court per the dictate of a mad and broken queen, the Church had pierced its talons into the heart of Gwyar's world, changing it forever.

The princess could not act upon her desires to kill Meirchion. In so doing, her husband Llew and Einion ap Owain would surely put her to death and the Silure bishops would be gleeful to see them do it. Traversing from powerful sorceress to begging relative, her voice became as a whimpering puppy as she appealed to Arthur.

"I cannot interfere with this, sister. I'm sorry. Llyn is in Gwynedd and the local chieftain makes such designations for places of worship. It is not my place and would be an abuse of my power. The Summer Kingdom must not suffer corruption so soon after it has been born. Yes?"

Gwyar felt helpless and drew Arthur away from the gathered bishops, yet complaining and railing about the cold. Walking a short distance into the wood, with the fortress just overhead, the two spoke. For the first time in many years, really spoke.

"Bear." An affectionate opening. "You remember what is on the Isle of Apples, the secret I told you. The good secret we shared to replace the bad secret we conceal?"

"Of course." Arthur embraced Gwyar as if he were his namesake, a great bear. "I have been fond of Mary since I was fifteen because you shared this secret with me. Look," Arthur reached into his satchel, producing one of his favorite shoulder-fitted sigils, "she was with us at Baedan."

Gwyar smiled.

The druids and primitive Christians had once been great friends. From the very beginning, however, the Jewish Little Flock of Peter gave themselves over to idolatry. They boasted of their position and inheritance and, when the world did not end, began to assert their claims by venerating relics associated with their firsthand time spent with the Lord. And they began to worship and elevate people too.

After the Apostle Paul's visit, the druids came to the aid of the mother of Jesus (who had seen the corruption) and hid her, and the ark, and the cup. As the Jewish assembly died off, their doctrines and ways survived in the form of the Apostolic Church of the Britons. Try as they might, they could not discover the relics or the tomb of Mary, and they hated the druids for it. This conflict became a whisper with a fissure, a rarely discussed point of contention that floated like lake moss, ever just beneath the surface.

"They must never find Mary, Arthur. They will desecrate the grave, raise a shrine and make her a goddess, thus blaspheming everything the Blessed Lady stood for. She only ever wanted to live out her life with her foster-son, John."

There upon Lodge Hill, two famed heroes shared why the pagans and druids and heathen sects hated the Church. It was because that institution, in all its forms, was an insult to Jesus and those who really loved him. Gwyar did not hate the Christ; one of her many sacred and secret obligations was to forever hide the tomb of his mother. She hated the men who were *fake* Christians.

"Even if they put a chapel on the Island, I trust

that your magick will conceal the Lady and keep our good secret intact. Leave Gwent and return to the place you love." Arthur was an exceptional brother.

"I cannot," Gwyar wept. "I am bound here to support you behind the throne."

"Bound by?"

"Your queen."

"But why?"

"She thinks she knows that you love me."

"Well, I am glad you are here. Just no more arm-breaking whilst you stay." Arthur tried to solicit a smile from his distraught sister. Then he offered some help whilst adhering to his own laws. "I cannot stop a local chieftain from building a church. But I can intervene if any of our national treasures are in peril. I will need cause. Then the Round Table Fellowship will respond."

"That form of justice is reactive, and will be too late. They must not intrude upon the Isle of Apples!" Gwyar was not angered with Arthur. She gave him another tight, tight embrace and ran from the scene. She paused and turned back to the king.

"Do not marry the other Gwenhwyfar! And please stop ever putting Gwalchmai in danger!"

These were the types of requests said with a smile that overlay a warning, even a threat.

Gwyar vanished.

Arthur resumed his interrogation of the remaining bishops. They were most offended that Merlin had declared that one did not have to give land to the church; neither was baptism required, for the soul's salvation. His words were dangerous in their ability to control the nobility through land grants and the purchasing of heaven. The Pendragon cared not to delve into the merits of the theology from either faction, or from the secondhand account of Merlin's words. Rather, he wanted facts.

Shattering the tradition of the secret conferences amongst bishops and elders, the truth surfaced that the Britons favored asking Merlin to retire and that Meirchion had threatened his life.

Meirchion immediately provided an alibi for his comings and goings, before and after the great conference before Baedan, and made it clear that he had been arguing religion with Vivien late into the night and had no window of opportunity for a plot.

That Vivien knew he had spoken only in the anger of the moment and could testify of this satisfied Arthur to an extent. "I will have to validate this with the Lady of Llyn Fawr," he proclaimed.

"Upon her return, of course," responded Meirchion with feigned respect.

"Still, you threatened the life of one of three Chief Counselors to the Pendragon. There will be consequences for this." Arthur chose irony. Fed up with talks of gifts of land and tithes and gold for clergy, he decreed the following. "You are expelled from Glamorgan, forever. Your lands will be gifted in penance to your rival Illtud and, as he sees fit to appropriate, to the See of Llandaff." Arthur loved Illtud and Dyfrig but was fatigued over their constant wrangling for possession and material comforts, or gold. Here he chastised them as well. "That should be enough spoil and expansion to satisfy your greedy guts for a while, yes?"

Meirchion left Lodge Hill without lands or

a home. Arthur left Lodge Hill still without his Merlin.

Gwyar purchased the fastest steed in Caerleon, plus the employ of a servant. She clung on to the servant and slept as he rode without resting, making their way to the highest point in Glamorgan: Craig Y Llyn. When exhaustion took him she flung him from the mount and took the reins, then climbed on foot to the zenith. Peaking higher than even Caer Caradoc (where the nobles had been slain at the hand of the Long Knives so many years ago), she felt as if she looked down upon all the kingdoms of the world.

Below Craig Y Llyn was Llyn Y Fawr, where Vivien resided when not in Brittany.

Gwyar had not come for the scenic appeal. She had come for the power of the high mount and the lake. The moon cast her light upon Gwyar, whose arms were extended slowly and then clasped above her head. Calling upon elemental spirits from an older Age she commanded them, along with the spirits of the waters of the lake. At the same time, she called unto the dragon who ruled the high Mount.

The holy mountain and the lake. The mountain was heaven and the lake the primal earth covered in water. The mountain was Ynys Enlli and the lake was the ocean surrounding its shores. Gwyar was transformed into the great goddess of destruction, ready to deliver death from above.

"Morgana!" Once, at a whisper.

"Morgana!" Once more, louder.

When she finished the summonsing, the thing that the King of the Fae had put in her, nay, made part of her, took form in the sister of Arthur as never before, causing thunderbolts and visible, glowing red illumination to outline her tiny form.

The next morning two supply ships and her passengers made a watery grave of the short channel between the tip of Llyn and Ynys Enlli. The dolphins swam against the current, seals protested loudly and birds were everywhere out of season. The whole of the Island was covered in mist and an unnatural force surrounded the place.

Intruding upon the place that the bards called Avalon would not come without much peril to Cadfan and his Catholic pilgrims.

CHAPTER 25
I Will Go All the Way to The Bishop of Rome With My Mystery

Although the thirty guards were chasing Maelgwn, he was, in reality, in total control and may as well have been chasing them. When finding the clearing he desired, the Bloodhound Prince engaged.

The battle spike quickly felled two who rushed foolishly head-on at the knees, and a third who attempted a cowardly rear attack position. Maelgwn was said to be able to see in all directions at once. He was a poetic killing instrument, moving with great haste for concern over the old wizard whom the masked man had smitten upon the face.

As he would run one guard through the chest, two or three would attempt to tackle the Cymry warrior. Thus, he had to remove the battle spike quickly, avoiding any scenario where two men could bring him to the ground and, because of numbers, smother and slay him. Rather, he would kill and then run a short space, kill and run some more.

By twos and threes, and no more, he created killing spaces in which to engage them. Soon fear found fertile ground and the remaining guards fled. Maelgwn had ended above twenty men in half an hour. But, he felt, one moment was too long.

He raced back for the tabernacle.

***

"I know you are going to try and make a monster of my beloved king; what needs have I to hear more of your lies?" Merlin surveyed for more guards, looking for a window of escape. Of hope.

"Most appropriate that you choose the word monster." The Italian accent relished the unwanted invitation to share more. "And you know the information I have given you is truth. We use it for deception, for the Lord Arddu, but no lies have been told this night, Merlin, save for the one you have shared about your salvation."

Seeing no escape and knowing his travel companion would soon return, soaked in victorious blood and ready for more, Merlin had little choice but to indulge him. "The third sphere of the Secret Teaching of the Ages it is then." A dramatic exhale pushed out as the wizard sat.

Simon Magus went to it directly, giving his third sermon. This time the subject was an exposé on the reality of otherworldly beings. Merlin had admitted that he did not know where the gods came from save from 'the true North' or from the sky and Simon confirmed this, stating that it was presumptuous to think that many of the gods even knew of their own origins.

As with his instruction regarding the salvation of men's souls and the end of all things, he asserted the truth of God's word. Then he told the tale of Azazel and two hundred angels that had been charged with teaching, enlightening and watching over men.

This they did, but soon became corrupt and entered into a pact to go down amongst the daughters of men and take them for wives. The incursion began in the generation of Jared about four generations before the days of Noah. The first prophecy in Scripture, he explained, said that the seed of the woman would bruise the head of the Serpent. For this cause, the Jews reckoned their genealogies through maternal lines, but the blood came from the Father. Thus, the Devil launched a plot to fully pollute the seed of the woman, defiling all flesh, leaving nothing but corruption and abomination upon the face of earth.

With all of mankind corrupted, there would be no possibility of a Saviour to come through the seed of the woman, and nothing left to save.

"Beyond this, the Watchers simply lusted after the daughters of Adam. They looked upon them, filled with lust and envy, and had to have them." Magus here emphasized that often the Dark Lord used everyday motives like lust to slowly guide his larger agenda, keeping it from his very inner circle.

Magus taught Merlin how the sons of God had entered into the daughters of Men, resulting in demigods, Giants and other monstrosities. The act of procreation furthered the Watchers' desires to be like the Creator, so they brought forth all manner of abominable hybrids. Where the Lord God made a horse, they added wings to the horse. Where the Lord God made a leopard, they added bear claws to the leopard.

What Merlin was hearing was the explanation

for every ancient religion from Babylon to Egypt and from Germania to Africa. The ancients were worshipping these angels, or gods, and their progeny.

But there was more. Many of these angels had repented, but God had spared them not. The first few generations of these fallen ones were good, save their desire for worship. As their blood mixed with sinful man, the creatures became monstrously corrupt. Often demigods would kill the more foul or bloodthirsty beasts, becoming the heroes of legends of old.

When the corruption reached its climax, God's long suffering had come to an end; He flooded the whole world. In creative cruelty, He made the Watchers observe their offspring's destruction first-hand. Azazel was made the Scapegoat and fastened to the luminary hunter, Orion. The others were bound in the Underworld until the end of days.

As these Giants and monsters perished, their animating principles became known as *evil spirits*. Most were tossed into the Deep that surrounds the world (which was why all demons hated water, save the elemental water spirits who were commissioned to help manage the currents and sciences of water), but the Creator left one tenth of these to roam the earth.

"Why?" Merlin inquired.

"The Seed of the Woman had to come, or God's plans for restoring heaven and earth through the worm that is man could never be. So much did He love His son, and so much glory did He desire for Him, that He left these unclean spirits and let them manifest powerfully when He was come into the world: as a sign of His coming so that He could defeat and make a showing of them.

"They," Simon continued, "of course gathered round Israel, concentrating their power on foiling and disrupting the Covenant People and the Promised Land." Now Magus returned to an earlier discussion about polytheism. "So, yes, Merlin. Zeus, Poseidon, all your pantheon of gods and Fae have their origin on the other side of the Flood."

"If God destroyed them all, then besides these ghosts that He left to be made an example of, how do all these beings exist now *after* the Flood?"

"Merlin, ye know not the Scriptures; for does it not say that in the first Book of Moses there were Giants in those days, *and also after that,* and does not your Paul tell the women of Corinth to cover themselves *because of the angels*?"

"So the Watchers came back?"

"Nay," Simon patiently answered. "Those original two hundred are still bound. Other fallen ones made a similar attempt in Sodom and the displaced spirits found a way, through divine fornication, to bring their essence through the seed of men. Occasionally you will see a star fall from heaven, and isolated cases of rape occur where a fatherless child is born. Thus, it still happens, rarely, in diverse ways."

Simon directed one of the scribes to hand him a large Bible written in Latin. His mood shifted from educational to sinister again. He explained that life was in the blood and that the blood was passed from the father, not the mother. This was how Jesus had been able to come into the world, fully God, yet take on Mary's humanity. He had the mother's traits and the father's blood. It was the same for these gods and their offspring. As they continued to procreate and cross-pollinate, only those whose total paternal lineage was of the Fallen Ones were beyond redemption. If mother was the child of a Fallen One and father was mortal, the child would have supernatural powers but be yet human. If father was the child of a fallen one and mother was mortal, then the child was *a child of the damned.*

"The great tragedy is that, with whole races of Giants and faeries and elves created and crossbred along with other angelic activity, it is often nearly impossible to know if one, even one ten generations removed and with very diluted devil traits, is damned or not.

"Many races of otherworldly beings do not know this history but some do. And imagine their toil, their dread! They love Jesus more than you do. Devout, tirelessly charitable, not knowing, not knowing."

Merlin could not believe this. "More lies, Illuminated One."

"Let me read it to you." Magus went to the place in Isaiah and read the words that damned these woeful creatures regardless of their deeds, or their faith.

"O Lord our God, other lords beside thee have had dominion over us: but by thee only will we make mention of thy name.

"They are dead, they shall not live; they are deceased, they shall not rise: therefore hast thou visited and destroyed them, and made all their memory to perish."

The 'they' in the Latin text was clearly the Raphaim, a race of Nephilim or Fallen Ones. Giants who ruled as gods.

"They are not men," said Magus, "and they are not angels. Where have they to go? They will live an unnatural long life and good or bad, ill or grand, go into an abyss of nothingness. Outside the saving blood of your Lord Jesus Christ. The woeful and sorry damned. No more redeemable than the waste of a dung heap… no matter how beautiful your Lady of the Lake is."

"No! The Lady's father lay with a Fae, so her blood is mortal; you do lie again, deceiver."

"Very well," dismissively. "Perhaps you are right about her, Merlin. But I ask you…" Simon now stood (causing Merlin to do the same) and encroached upon Merlin, drawing nigh. "Who is your father?"

Merlin's long years flashed before him in an instant. *Is it true?* The priests called him 'Child of the Devil'. *Were they right for once?* His mother had overcompensated with a guilty love over Merlin his entire childhood and adult life. She had lain with a Devil, had been seduced mayhaps. Merlin didn't know and yet knew it to be true.

"Your grand journey to understanding God's plan for the Ages and the simplicity of salvation, and it's not for you. You are just another god, who will die like a man! A man with a soul beyond redemption."

Another of the Nine stood and reminded the Merlin that he had betrayed the Brotherhood, and all secret societies, by profaning their Secret Doctrines with his promotion of the false god Jesus Christ. At this moment a group of monks entered the Tabernacle. And Maelgwn had not yet returned.

Clearly Roman Catholics who had been turned and corrupted by the Brotherhood, Merlin ignored the hideous truths hurled at him by Simon Magus and the Nine.

"Brethren, forget not the beauty of Rome. The greatest and most lovely of all Christians come from there and the inspired letters that save men today were written from her palace and prisons." It then dawned upon the Merlin that, if he were a child of the woeful damned, his mind was simply under the power of suggestion and his magick was fully intact, just under self-imposed dormancy.

He was compelled to try.

Soon a vapor filled the large Tabernacle hall, making possible an escape in the misty confusion. Through the haze, determined to live, determined to defend the gospel of grace, he cried out: "I am the Merlin of Britain. I will take my truth, my mystery, to the Bishop of Rome; a great and honorable man by reputation. He will hear me, and the world will change."

The metallic glove with talons startled Merlin, clutching the tall Briton's throat. The masked face appeared, and the grip was sure.

"You will go to the Bishop of Rome?" He turned his masked face sideways, like a stalking predator playing with its prey.

With his empty hand, Simon Magus removed his mask.

"I AM the Bishop of Rome."

Maelgwn finally rushed in, screaming for the Merlin to identify himself. Magus's final words to the Merlin (accompanied by a chorus of accusations of being a traitor to everyone on all sides) were, "You are John the Baptist. You pointed the way to the Messiah, who is Arthur. You must decrease and the Pendragon must increase. I feel the poison in you. One third of the traitor's death is already upon you. In you. Today. You die."

Maelgwn's battle spike came down hard, cracking through the armored glove, spraying the Pope's blood onto Merlin's beard and face. Magus recoiled in pain, relinquishing his grip.

Maelgwn grasped the poisoned old man by his robe and ran the two out of the Tabernacle, into the forest.

The monks and guardians gave chase and Maelgwn fled, at times nearly carrying Merlin, an awkwardly tall load.

***

Dawn approached. The snow was lightly kissing the treetops and the heads of weary fugitives. At last they came to Vivien's estate. The small guest house was nearest and easiest to defend, so Maelgwn carried the Merlin inside, laying him upon the bed. They could *feel* their pursuers close by.

As they neared the guest house, Maelgwn could identify some of the monks as his own kinsmen, Ravens from the North. And many of them were soldiers. The Roman faith was encroaching steadily there and clearly they had been involved in the plot to lure Merlin to this fateful initiation. Maelgwn knew not the greater portions of what had been shared, but he knew it to be pure evil. Broceliande itself was rejecting them and moaning that such vile men trod on its paths and drank from its streams.

Maelgwn confirmed the count of the swiftest of the manhunters: three. "Easy enough; they should've brought more."

"Lancelot. Please come close." Nimue's concoction was about to render Merlin unconscious. "Thank you so much for being here."

"I have my Merlin, Taliesin, and Arthur needs his; happy to do it. I will defeat them and then we will find help for you. This forest has healers in many forms, Lord Merlin."

Merlin was not consoled by the glad tidings, but he appreciated the softness of the oft cold and unpredictable warrior. The old druid politely disregarded him and continued with a final admonition. "Lancelot, your son is what is best in all men. Protect him at all costs."

"Yes, Lord Merlin."

"Lancelot, when it comes time to do that which you would do, for Arthur's sake, do it not."

"Yes, Lord Merlin." Lancelot now had to hold the head of the wizard, who was quickly fading.

"Lancelot. The Wars are not over. Tell Arthur—" Merlin coughed violently. "Lancelot, tell Arthur to kill the Giants! Every Giant. Kill them!"

Merlin passed into unconsciousness.

Maelgwn turned quickly to the door as the enemy fast approached.

Then it happened.

The undefeated warrior, who was unscarred (save a scar he had earned fighting Arthur himself) and had suffered barely a scratch over twenty years of war. A man who was invincible, who danced and flew when he fought and who escaped any predicament with calm followed by athletic ferocity. The best of all fighters by chance stumbled upon a shoe left behind by Nimue. The fall was hard as he was caught unawares, failing to brace for the impact with his hands. The knight's beautiful face struck violently against the baseboard of the door frame, rendering him, like the wizard he had joined a few nights earlier on that cold boat, unconscious.

"Wake him up for this," Magus, now fully armored, masked and full of self-righteous victory, commanded.

They shook Merlin awake. As soon as half

an eyelid was opened the noose was around the neck, placed by one of the monks. A sloppy noose, one designed to strangle, not break bones for a mercifully swift death. Dangling from a tree, he was stripped naked to shame. The guards carelessly cast his garments and satchel into the wood, not seeing the cup he bore. They mocked him. "Poisoned to death. Strangled to death. That's two, and one remains."

They beat his lifeless body, and his form was more red than flesh-colored, stained with blood.

They spat upon him and plucked at his beard.

"To this Fount bring *The Wizard Turned Grace Believer*," Magus ordered, hissing, laughing and cajoling.

"Hear me, Merlin; for I know you live."

Merlin was unresponsive.

Simon Magus plunged Merlin's head into the Fount. He felt several nervous jerks, complaints and twitches, and then nothing. Magus continued his overkill, shoving a short blade into Merlin's kidneys, continuing to drown him.

The Fount became all blood.

"Merlin the Magician. Poisoned, I assume by one of your druids; Hung by priests; Drowned by the Rulers of the World. O, how you would have been the greatest amongst us… but you would not."

During the head Devil worshipper's oratory, the Fae concealed Lancelot, wanting no more legends and heroes to fall this day.

Simon at last pulled the Merlin's head up out of the water.

The Merlin was as dead…

EPILOGUE I
The Golden Age Begins Evil Present from the Beginning

Vivien arrived at her Castle several hours later.

Her foster-son's head wound was already bandaged and hot tea simmering at a low boil, filling the room with aromas of healing and love. He slept, breathing patterns normal. She thanked the Fair Folk, but saw them not.

Soon thereafter she found the Merlin. Weeping, she held him for but a few moments. Then as women, who are stronger than men, do when mourning or crisis is upon them, she took care of the necessities. She cleaned and dressed his wounds and found his clothing with the contents of his satchel, covering his nakedness, providing her friend with dignity. Much of his blood was on her hands. *Figuratively and literally.*

His life essence touching her enlightened a partial vision, for she loved him so and possessed the Sight. "You are still covered in light; I can barely see you, love." To herself she said, *I am a sorrowful child of the damned.*

Vivien took Merlin's body to an oak tree older than the Flood and used a wand to burn a door into the tree, and to hollow its center. She placed the Merlin in the Oak and then shut the door. And sealed it.

***

Retired King Meurig, the Pendragon before Arthur, was the type of father who ever had his arm around his son's far shoulder when talking to him. A perpetual hug, and perpetual lecture.

"I'm not like you," Arthur protested, unable to escape the paternal grasp. "You found your one true love as a young man and are blessed. Things have been…" the younger Pendragon, ever seeking to be respectful of women, was no less so regarding his estranged former wife "… less successful for me in this category."

"But we are but a month from Baedan. You just put your wife away and now are to court with the intentions of marrying a new wife. A new Gwenhwyfar, no less!"

"I am about to be handed the second of the Three Swords of Britain. There are tributaries and clerics and tribal leaders from the whole of the Island, other nations, and even Cedric has agreed to terms. Having a betrothed by my side will show strength." Arthur now didn't mind the hug and nudged into it, hoping his father would accept the rationale of his response.

Meurig was not to be fooled by the lad. He could outwit the Boar and command the Tribes, but he could not dupe his da. "So, it's a political arrangement then? You know what they say about her?"

"Father, I don't care. No, it is not political. I love her."

"You've not known her since you were both fourteen! How say you that you love her?"

"How old were you when you loved Mam?"

Meurig put both hands hard upon his son's shoulders. "Fourteen." The Uther Pendragon was a wonderful father. He had made his protest known, had heard his son's heart and now it was time for him to support the one who had brought peace to the Isles and joy unto his people. The War King was about to be made Emperor. An Emperor with a policy of no Empire. *Merlin would love that!* Meurig thought.

***

The Sword of Caesar, called Angau Coch, or *Red Death,* impaled an archaic anvil used by blacksmiths. *Excalibur could cut right through this,* Arthur mused. This special blade had been stuck in the shield of a prince called Nennius when he engaged Julius Caesar in combat. The Briton had never relinquished the sword and it had become a symbol of the Briton's resilience against all invaders.

Old Dyfrig was there in the courtyard of Saint Paul's church at Ludgate, in New Troy, which is Londinium. The aged bishop had crowned Arthur in the forests of Gwent at fourteen and was pink for laughing and smiling at the honor of crowning him at thirty and three; this time not as King of Glamorgan and Gwent, but as Emperor.

Arthur clasped Angau Coch's hilt with both hands and freed her from the stone, waving the sword high. Rays of sun fractured and showered the myriad of guests with light.

Gwalchmai held Excalibur as unspoken signal that he was to be Arthur's heir, and Bedwyr held Arthur's spear.

The sea of people parted, making a pathway.

Marching regally through an archway of countless swords, then torches, and then birch branches came Maelgwn, tall as a mountain, shimmering armor glossed and clean as it had been in the days ere the Saxon Wars. At his elbow was a woman of identical height to Gwyar and of similar form and presentation. She differed in overt seductive appeal and she was painted, bearing tribal marks upon her neck that disappeared into her dress, causing all men to chase the designs' origins and twists and turns about her body. *She liked to be looked at in this way.*

Maelgwn presented Gwenhwyfar to Arthur, and the crowds exploded in cheer and jubilation.

The Lancelot's eyes never met Arthur's. As he placed her little hand upon the palm of the Iron Bear his low, mannish voice spake but four words: "You saw her first."

Gwenhwyfar's father, Ogyrfan the Giant, looked on, enjoying the ceremony.

The Arthuriad Volume Two

The Madness of Maelgwn

...Seven Seeds Sowed the Soil for Civil War

Zane Newitt

'In the son alone rested salvation for the father. Lancelot. A beautiful, brutish beast, whose eyes, though oft he plucked them out, only returned again and again, filled with adultery. Whose spirit warred in losing toil with his flesh; who could not cease from sinning.

When good, the good that was Lancelot was real. The burning in his lusts, the insatiable, satisfied like the kettle's bubble, relieved only briefly and so quickly renewed again. When evil, the evil that was Lancelot was real. So, like antiquity's David, Lancelot was a fragmented man of dual natures.

The dichotomy did not pass; the son did not bear sin of his father. Rather, his fruit was the healing balm. The Galahad. All the angels of Lancelot's virtue present; all the devils of Lancelot's failings not found. Galahad was the perfect knight, the best ingredients of angels and of men. When he was translated for the sake of the Cup, sacrificed for Arthur, the King's salvation was sure; as surely was Lancelot's damnation wrought.

And what brokenness was already present, now unmasked when Galahad died, madness became.'

Dr. Zane Newitt
Autumn, 2018

The three wives of Arthur, who were his chief three ladies: that is to say, Gwenhwyfar, daughter of Gawrwyd Ceint; and Gwenhwyfar, daughter of Ogyrfan Gawr...

PROLOGUE
Brutus versus Gogmagog

King Brutus, whose forebears had escaped the fated fall of fabled Troy, that glorious city that lost its candlestick - due not to defeat of arms but rather to treachery, adultery and the justified madness of an elite warrior - now had a Giant problem... literally.

For when his fleets came ashore *the Blessed Isles in the Sea,* they found the lands overrun by wild beasts and strange, mystical creatures.

Worse, governing all life were gargantuan Giants.

A Giant is neither fully human, being some part angel, nor divine, being some part man. The angelic parents of these Giants took the spirit form of great Dragons who circumambulated the heavens in fixed courses, covered by their stars. These were sinister, ancient and wise. And the greatest amongst them was Y Ddraig Du, *the Black Dragon.*

Brutus and his armies made war with the Giants, as they held all men in subjugation. Like Caleb and Joshua of the Hebrews, Brutus and his generals had to clear their own promised land of milk and honey of the monstrous occupants. The number of the dead mounted, becoming great losses for both Man and Titan. Brutus and the king of the Giants, Gogmagog ap Ddraig Du, parlayed to decide rule of the Isles through trial by combat.

Against hope, the champion of Brutus prevailed, hurling Gogmagog from a high hilltop. Violently, he plunged atop a great apple orchard, nestled in the shadows of the mount near the mouth of an enchanted lake below. The liquescent press of the fall ran into the Lake.

The orchard was tended by powerful water faeries, called the Korrigan, and their renowned queen, who bore only a title: *The Lady of the Lake.*

A faerie is neither fully human, being some part angel, nor divine, being some part man. Whereas Giants came from the male progeny of angels, the faeries came from the female line. And though the Fae distrust men, by ancient rivalry, they loathe Giants.

The contention grew to enmity on this day, as Gogmagog's massive carcass had compassed and compressed the whole of the orchard, producing a mashy elixir comprised of the pressed apple juices, oaky sap and the Giant's demigod essence.

The Korrigan, though jubilant over the fallen rival king, hastened, worried and enraged, to examine what was salvageable of their orchard, an unfortunate casualty of the war. Seeing the faeries celebrate, the spectral Black Dragon descended from the heavens as a bird of prey, diving in a rush upon the watery spirits.

Tribes on the Continent as far as Gaul saw the calamity, recording it in their histories and remembering it in their oral traditions as *a comet striking down from heaven, the fire of angry gods.* Their assessment was not wrong.

Brutus and his men, overcome, or bewitched,

by mortal curiosity, looked on from the hilltop, awe-stricken at the otherworldly battle.

A great cosmic fire came forth from the Black Dragon, making smoky cinders of the orchard trees, creating a protective ring about the Giant and killing a great company of faeries in the process. A dead faerie's animating principle hath nowhere to rest and, displaced, haunts the area where it was slain, becoming almost always a dark thing.

The barrage of brimstone and death activated the Lady of the Lake, who called upon a dragon of her own. Using enchanted words in the Language of Heaven, made she her imprecatory prayer. Soon the Y Ddraig Hanner Nos, the Dragon of Midnight Blue, appeared in the firmament, just above where the birds fly.

With increasingly velocity, he dove and dove until in range of the Black Dragon. The serpentine spirits clashed, ethereal fire setting alight apple, wood, faerie and lake alike.

Such was the illumination of the struggle that the mortals were temporarily blinded and scattered. Striving against the chaos, Brutus dispensed a small troop of men to cautiously descend the hilltop.

Upon reaching the base of the mount, the troop found that Gogmagog had vanished, and the Korrigan too gone as vapor. Signs of fire, smoke, or bloodshed were not found.

Beginning to feel that they were indeed bewitched, or perhaps under a temporary madness from too many days at sea, they began to turn and climb back whence they had come. Suddenly appeared but one great tree standing, and a white-clad, hooded damsel holding its produce: a large, seven-seeded apple.

At her feet were several flagons; the sole remnants of the epic encounter.

"Drink," said the damsel, her seductive arm sleeved in white samite.

The scrumpy sup was unlike to anything the Sons of Adam had ever consumed. The spirit brought health and danger, purity and darkness as it refreshed, captivated and captured them, causing them to call for Brutus himself to partake of the elixir. This pleased the damsel, whose eyes gleamed to hear that the king himself would come.

But such was the power of it that the men were taken by madness. However, it was not yet upon them ere Brutus arrived.

"Drink," said the damsel.

"Drink not, Brutus!" The Lady of the Lake appeared, hovering upon the waters, with crystal-blue eyes whose centers were ablaze with a little red flame, filled with vengeful sorrow over the countless dead faeries, her people.

Plucking an apple from the tree (for there was now but one), she explained to Brutus, "No man can manage this enchantment. This apple is now filled with the strength of Giants, the ancient knowledge of Dragons, the cunning of faeries and the mortality of men.

"To drink it," she continued, "is to be at once full of a false strength, a boastful knowledge, a cunning tongue, and the woes of men. Such a combination would render you like unto" – she pointed at the king's men and their sorry state – "*them.*"

"But I must have it," said Brutus.

"You may not," rebuked the Lady.

Calling the Midnight Blue Dragon once more, she cleaved an apple into equal portions, taking a seed from each.

"You may enjoy any of the six seeds, in any combination, and in extreme moderation. But never at once." Now her voice was grave. "And never with the seventh seed."

Her serpentine protector clutched up the tree at the root and took flight, taking each apple and apportioning the seeds, spreading them to seven locations amongst the Blessed Isles and Brittany, desperately hoping that they would never be combined again.

"In moderation, and never seek the seventh." Brutus the Prudent brought captive his reason, and agreed. He and the Lady of the Lake sought to query the damsel whose offering had rendered the men with madness. But, like the Giant, and Y Ddraig Ddu, and the faeries before her, she had vanished.

And this was how Brutus, by right of combat of champions, earned the right to colonize the Isles with the sons of Troy. Through the uncanny and accidental confluence of gods and monsters, the national drink of the Isles was born as well, along with one of the earliest mysteries and quests (for the Isles were a place of treasure, of quest and of the Spirit).

Men lacked the temperance of Brutus, ever questing to find and combine the forbidden *Seventh Seed.*

It was rumored that centuries hence, the druids found each of the seeds and planted an orchard that grew in spite of impossible conditions, against contrary winds and treacherous currents pounding and undoing the soils. The place came to be known as the Isle of Apples.

CHAPTER 1
The First Lie, but Not the Last

Seed 2 – "You know I love her, and didn't even ask me how I would feel."

Merlin often taught that a partial truth equates a full lie.

At the king's very first moment of reprieve from the revelry and pomp of his crowning, Arthur took his champion aside and bade him convey all that had befallen the Merlin during their absence from Mynydd Baedan.

Vivien and Maelgwn had rehearsed the conversation, and all that remained was for him to perform. Twenty years of friendship, of brotherhood, some spent at school, the greater part on the war campaigns; the mightiest of bonds forged. Distrust or misuse was beyond contemplation.

There was little to lie about, save the main thing.

That a secret society had guided events that could render Arthur their puppet king might be beyond the grasp of the plausible, but necessitated no veil in the sharing. That these men's efforts could turn to the Merovingians and be atop Howel's doorstop *ought* to be shared.

That Merlin had experienced a conversion of faith and sought the Christian God likewise needed no cover, though the nature of his doctrine peculiar. Arthur's neutrality over the gods and radical defense of personal choice would surely extend unto his once druidic counselor.

That Roman soldiers had given chase and that Maelgwn had suffered injury need not be some secret.

But…

That Vivien had formed a regretful alliance with the vile old priest-king, Meirchion the Mad, that had contributed to Merlin's demise could never be shared.

Not for so long as the old crone drew breath.

Its discovery would result in execution for the Lady of the Lake, and provoke the Tribes to revolt in favor of their patroness and goddess. Moreover, Meirchion's part in the plot could spark a civil war against the North with potential help from abroad.

The perception of a poisoned beginning for the fresh-born Summer Kingdom could not be, must not be. Instead, it must grow and flourish; the age of peace and freedom. A rest from the era of death, so needed by Cymru. Respite from a greater menace, an enemy she knew not was coming.

For his part, Meirchion must never be able to confirm whether Merlin be alive or perished, lest he take occasion to double-cross Vivien. Vivien must in turn never overly oppose the Roman Church, lest the dispossessed and desperate king give Emperor Arthur just enough information to reopen the wound and destroy all. Thus, the deceit a taut line must hold. And Maelgwn must ever provide hints and whispers of hope that Merlin yet lived.

And so, full truth save the Lady's involvement, along with Merlin's final fate (which Maelgwn assumed was the grave, and durst not ask his foster-mother detailed questions of for the sake of her fractured and broken heart), was his course.

The only course?

Or I could take his head and lop off the need for a lie, the Bloodhound Prince thought. *I am meet to be Pendragon as well.*

In the maze of complexity that ran its woven courses through Maelgwn's brain, burrowed into the heart, and stained his soul, murder was situationally acceptable, but for untrue words to leave the knight's lips - unacceptable.

Had not Arthur's fathers persecuted the Old North? Had not they made full advantage of the *Night of Long Knives,* later causing the Sons of Cunnedda to make more sons, yet from their own daughters of the Silures in the south?

Maelgwn was master of lust unmatched and bereft of love, excepting his foster-mother.

And he loved Arthur.

And he loved Gwenhywfar.

And was not the one love now betrothed by imposition to the other?

The winds picked up in the courtyard, the Londinium air filled with a confused aroma, combing the stench of commerce with the sweet savors of cakes and flowers. A gust lifted Maelgwn's curly black locks up and off his brow, fully revealing eyes as a skulking predator upon the king.

The aroma without, a mirror of the confused shards of mind and spirit within.

Maelgwn's thoughts were both stench and beauty.

He could not pause long as Arthur, full of

perception on loan from the Merlin himself, would soon note the rehearsal of speech. For this cause, and for love, Maelgwn followed a pattern wrought of thirty and five years of chaos and pain. He put away all and, speaking in his mechanical tenor that was a numbness confused for strength or intimidation, communicated that which had been agreed by he and the Lady of the Lake.

"Unbelievable tales are often those most true." King Arthur comforted his champion after carefully hearing all, having listened actively without interruption.

Then the statements and queries followed.

"If Merlin weighed the threat heavy enough to miss Baedan, then we must give it equal measure." Arthur rubbed his forehead hard for a moment and continued, "We have had peace for but one moon. Are we to make war with Rome?"

The Roman Empire was an empire no more. No longer a shadow of the shadow of her former glory, the Cymry would put her to waste quickly.

Arthur continued to work out his thoughts while Maelgwn stole a glance at Gwenhwyfar, now waving at throngs of people from a tapered balcony. Such was his height that there was no risk the shorter sovereign would see his wandering eyes.

"Our nation has never invaded another. We defend our soil; we do not take to the dirt of others. Moreover, this seems to be a powerful cabal within the State, and not the State herself. We cannot kill Italians to avenge the loss of our friend." Here the careful prudence and longsuffering of Arthur won out.

But his tenacity lessened not.

"When next we convene at Caermelyn, embracing peacetime quests and sports, I shall declare this: that the twenty-four divide into troops of threes, and that they perpetually quest for Merlin. Those not on assigned rotation may quest whatever questing they will, at the pleasure of the knight and the Fellowship."

This verdict at once multiplied the risk of investigative knights, sharpened by recent war and fearing the impending dulling of tending to farm and wife, finding out the plot between Vivien and Mad Mark to murder the wizard.

Maelgwn gave a counterproposal.

"Send only two, and when I am not attending to my lands, I swear to always be the third. Only that they report to me for continuity of purpose."

For Maelgwn, this ensured that the quest would never be fulfilled; a quest for a concealed corpse, led by the son of the very woman who had concealed it. With complete trust, Arthur's tone was thankful, and edifying.

"Your plan is even better than mine, friend. Thank you." At that moment they both looked upon Gwenhwyfar's balcony, gesturing that they should return to the celebratory crowds.

Arthur made a final, friendly clutch upon Maelgwn's arm, asking a conclusive question.

"Have you told me everything, Maelgwn?"

Maelgwn looked upon Gwen II yet again. A seed of offense here planted as Arthur asked only after his lost friend and made no mention of the *other business between the two great friends.* The prerogative belonged to the High King, but that not a sentence was uttered showing a kernel of wheat's measure over Maelgwn's feelings hurt the Round Table Knight. Oh, the simple recognition he coveted and received not!

"Yes, Lord Arthur." A forced, anguished response; his first, but not last, lie to the king.

Just then a voice, a desperate phantom, was upon the Northern prince's shoulders, howling its cry directly into his right ear (yet was heard by no other man).

"Lancelot. When it comes time to do that which you would do, for the sake of all free men, I beg you, do it not."

Arthur had outpaced the towering warrior, making his way back to the throngs.

Recovering from his lie and eschewing the voice upon his shoulder: "Iron Bear—"

Arthur stopped and turned, familiar with the gravity of tone. "Yes, friend."

"Before Merlin and I were separated by fog and by ambush, he beseeched me to give you a directive. There was no riddle in it, no enigmatic lesson. Just a directive. A desperate directive." Maelgwn's palms faced the firmament, shoulders giving a confused but sincere shrug, passing along the order. "Kill the Giants," he said. "Kill every one."

CHAPTER 2
The Merovingian

"Locate, awaken and unleash the Giants on the Isles in the Sea," Simon Magus bade the Wise Man of the Dynion Hysbys, a sort of dark anti-druid whose actual name was not known. Whispers and rumors amongst the Tribes, and especially the noble, harmless and friendly druids, rendered him simply *the Adder*. "See it done."

"After such a long time dormant, hiding or, where not extreme in appearance, innocuously blended amongst men, will the Nephilim really bring the Sons of Brutus to anger again?" the Wise Man asked, challenging the head of the octopus, whose Roman arms controlled all secret societies upon the earth.

Simon always preferred education over empty dictates. His lessons were honest and sincere, to a point. Where misdirection and fabrication was needed to manipulate and control, even his own truth would be slightly blended and blurred. This was how the Mystery Schools were able to reign over the very many with the very few. Thus, calmly, he condescended: "If we are to create an apocalypse to either delay" - he now looked upon a faction of his fellows - "or bring about" - they nodded - "the Apocalypse, we will need to bring about hell on earth." His tone now scratchy and blistering with coughing, he continued, "Fire and brimstone from above, signs and wonders from the heavens, mayhem and mayhem upon the earth. Let her be again a den of dragons and abominations walking about in the open light of the day, as it was in the Days of Noah."

The Wise Man bowed, and vowed, "I will obey, find and resurrect that old hatred amongst the Giants in the Blessed Isles, my lord."

"And Arddu bless thy effort." Simon took the man by the hand, shaking it in sincerity. His voice now eased to a whisper in Italian. "It will take you some time to find many of them, and more time to cause them to do their Great Work. Know that you are setting out on a long quest; be patient, and mind well the timing."

"What is my mark, lord?"

The answer, blunt and no less educational than the former discourse, gave the Adder great pause.

"Twenty years."

The Wise Man fell open at the mouth as he suddenly saw the final two decades of his dark path filled hourly, risking his life rousing monsters below the earth in hollow hills, marshy rushes and foul caves.

Simon Magus proactively stayed response. "Ensure that there are minor slayings as soon as you are able. Create whispers of *the Round Table Knights*" (here his tone mocked the honorable and just men) "themselves being defeated or even disappearing, along with petty kings and well-known Churchmen, meeting untimely ends in caves and crooks in the North. Create a little fear so that they appreciate all the more the safety of their great Pendragon. But it must be but minor complaints; it must be a whisper, not an urgent crisis." The education continued. "For twenty years the Briton's famed War King must reign, and peace and safety reign with him. After that we will find for him another great war and declare, if he be the One, Britannia as the New Jerusalem.

"For three years, merriment and more peace unfettered.

"Then we will draw down a great dragon and make calamity, fire and disease from heaven that will cause men's eyes to melt within the socket. A slow death, a death that is certain but delays, that will not come. Hell on the earth where the worm dieth not, and the fire shall not be quenched. And war. So much more war. At the median of the third year, all the kings round him must fall." Simon Magus paused, then delivered some humor to lighten the burden. "Be thankful, Cymry, that you are on Giant and not Dragon detail; we have the more miserable task."

Simon Magus breathed in the winter air of Broceliande, deeply inhaling the forest's enchantments, secrets and good wonder into his chest. The little Fae found it blasphemy that one such as he would take their air, spoiling this special place by his very presence. Oblivious to the protest of his hidden watchers, he continued. "And now we seek out our alternative actor. Now we leave the forest to look in upon Childebert." Making motions for the tabernacle in the wood to be broken down and packed, he concluded, "From the Sons of Troy to the city of Troy's most tragic son." Simon Magus loved irony. "To Paris."

The Italian called after the Wise Man. "Wait. I

cannot believe, Arddu help me, that I forgot."

Dreading the additional edict from the Bishop of Rome, the Dynion Hysbys sighed, audibly. "Yes, Simon Magus?"

"The contents of Merlin's robe. Go back to the site where the traitor met his just end and retrieve them."

"Surely the Lancelot or some other friend has already discovered and buried the body. Three days have now passed!"

"Then find a merchant and purchase thyself a shovel!" Simon Magus was not accustomed to disobedience. *These Cymry, even the traitors, have too much freedom coursing through their blood. Would that the Caesars had removed their candle forever from the earth, like so many other petty tribes.*

Through his uncanny switches, corners and turns in his mannerisms, Magus traded hubris for manipulative dramatist. "My friend, I am sorry." The armored finger-claws now grasped the cloak of the Briton, pulling him to an embrace. "If the body has been removed or the contents sealed, then you will be the first to embark on a great quest – not just for Giants or treasure," and now the fullness of satanic revelation illuminated the Leader of the Council of Nine, "but the first to set out to recover the Cup of Christ. The quest for the Holy Grail." The Bishop of Rome gave the Wise Man an unholy kiss upon his neck, then returned his face to shadow, adjusting his mask.

"And now I say" – the thick accent was most profound when jesting – "and this time I mean it" – followed by a great singular chortle – "to Paris!"

***

Childebert, the Merovingian King of Paris, was

an ideal candidate for the Antichrist.

A heresy, that the Lord Himself had continued His generations through a marriage with Mary the Magdalene, had taken root among many sects. The Bishop of Rome had denounced it publicly and supported it financially and evangelically from the shadows.

Here again, the laity of the Catholic church were biblical in their understanding. The Scriptures were clear that Israel's long-prophesied Messiah would have no continuing generation (for the prophet Isaiah had said as much in plain words), and they were victims, dupes of poor leadership. That their tithes unknowingly were apportioned to fund devilish schemes was a great sin against these hard-working, gentle and romantic people.

Nevertheless, like other heresies manifesting in the dawn of the burgeoning Church, this one had its actors: the long-haired Merovingians.

Esteeming themselves direct descendants of Jesus Christ, and lingering in ambience until the *times of restitution of all things,* they were simply waiting for the right time to wage holy war, with or without the aid of Rome, in the region, and then the world.

Crowned King of Paris five hundred and eleven years from the year of the Lord's passion, Childebert possessed unmatched charisma and reigned well. He now sought to conjure cause to take Orleans next. The kinsmen of the Cymry, the *Bretons,* had long established their kingdoms and sister-cities on the Continent, and a collision was far off… yet inevitable. Lancelot had warned Arthur of the Italian Band's potential collusion with the House of Merovee in some plot, and Arthur remained vigilant of the same. But without evidence, he would let the matter lie dormant.

Magus had placed a subversive within the House of Merovee and seen to it that the king's own sister diverged from the family way, converting her to the orthodox Romanist faith. Chrotilda was radically devout to the Church of Rome, and she became the eyes and ears of Magus. She guided and supported and necessarily hassled Childebert in the like manner that Gwyar did for Arthur.

In addition to continued assessment of the liege who wore his hair in uncut locks as Sampson or John the Baptist, Simon sought ways in which the Merovingian's desire for expansion over the Franks could be leveraged to make alliances with a foe that could actually defeat the Tribes of the Cymry. *And that was not Rome.*

Magus believed that a confederacy of Teutonic tribes, known as the *Visigoths*, could be his unwilling agent to do as the Saxons, Angles and Jutes had done for the Council of Nine for the generations before Arthur had spoiled them. Once again, Magus would raise up an invader, slowly, methodically.

That a Germanic people would covet and attack the Isles in the Sea was an old, tired story. But this time the differences were substantial.

Merlin was gone. Though Cymru was filled with heroes and living legends, he was the strategic difference in war strategy and policy-making.

The armies would grow fat and stale from peace. This was man's nature.

The Council determined it would take twenty years to weaken the Round Table from within. Or to let the process of time, and the flesh of man, do this for and with them.

The Saxon kings had not the pedigree to rival the Pendragon or the kings of the Old North. Childebert, if viewed as a Messiah, and with an army equal to the

Cymry under his standard, could undo and supplant King Arthur.

If Childebert the Christ-child possessed the Cup of Christ, would not even Rome accept him?

Indeed! Magus was convinced that this generation would yield a different outcome. Either Childebert would be the Antichrist and fall to the Messiah Arthur, or Arthur would be Antichrist and fall to Childebert. *And thus the Mystery of Iniquity continued its dark work.*

The Visigoths were called *The Wild Boar*, and their theology was Arianism. The Christology of this religion demoted Jesus to possessing the blood of God, but being a separate and subordinate being to God the Father. Moreover, it held that Christ did not exist prior to His incarnation, bastardizing the Scripture that reads *"for there be gods many"*. This doctrine fit as a glove with the notion of the Nazarene's children being enlightened beings, even demigods, not equal in rank, but sharing direct substance with God, ruling and reigning over the whole of mankind on the merits of their divine blood.

Simon would make his visit under the guise of an emissary expelled from Rome for rejecting the Trinity, finding safety in North Africa where the Visigoths ruled. He would further his shadowy work of seducing the king. *And hope that his anti-druid would soon secure the Cup.*

CHAPTER 3
Four Cords and a Princess Broken

Seed 1: "I saw her first."

The whole of the kingdom, from beggar to king, from youth to aged, from city-center merchant to remote Northern village fisherman, all men, and especially all women (for women possess natural intuition about these things) in all places, knew that Gwen ferch Ogyrfan Gawr was a whore. A harlot of the highest estate.

Everyone… except for her betrothed, the discerning, wise and just king, Arthur Pendragon of Glamorgan. The blindness wrought by blood is cruel, and no respecter of persons.

He floated on clouds of happiness when around her, and a man with thirty-and-four winters was again as the year he had met her, again as a fourteen-year-old boy. Full of verve, unstoppable, ever jesting with, embracing, and actively seeking to serve and help his people with immeasurable resources powered by love.

A War King who had outsmarted, outlasted and out-willed the Saxon invaders for two decades was at once made captive to her will.

In spite of this, he was not rumored or mocked as a fool. For the people perceived rightly that Arthur and his former queen might have been great friends, might have known love, but never *in love* was Arthur. Never like his parents, Queen Onbrawst and King Meurig.

Thus, a thankful people durst not snicker and prattle about so great a ruler. Rather, a quiet respect short of an endorsement was the national mood since the pronouncement of their engagement. He had given them their liberty. He had forged for them their Golden Age. He was the Sun that had risen and illuminated their Summer Kingdom.

We are so grateful. Let him alone. Let him have his whore. This was the public sentiment.

As a lad, Arthur had actually known his new queen-intended before he had known his first spouse, the honorable and stunning, redheaded Queen Gwenhwyfar ferch Cwyrd, his neighbor in Gwent.

O, but 'twas the Gwen of the raven's hair that forged him.

***

Their paths had met in the grey time betwixt and between boyhood and manhood, lass and woman. And not theirs alone.

Arthur and Gwen ferch Ogyrfan, along with Maelgwn Hir of Gwynedd and Gwyar ferch Meurig, were inseparable schoolmates. Three months of joy uninterrupted can be as a hundred years to the young.

For these are the sticky years.

Two boys, two girls, a foursome fierce. The most popular, revered and feared troop, dominating and conquering all that they surveyed at the chapel college named after Illtud. Brilliant and fiery. Cymry royals at play, defending the southern beaches against imagined Saxons, frolicking in forests green and valleys grim, filling their time with song and food and daily enacting theatre; portraying the far-off dream of the Summer Kingdom.

Then the four cords were untwined, torn asunder most unwillingly.

Gwyar, older than the others, was first to leave.

Vivien had privily observed the lass's gaze upon her foster-son, seen her innocent adorations mixed with the flowering of unbridled love. Unbridled lust.

Knowing, even then, the shattered multiplicity within Maelgwn (for, after becoming well-drunken on cider he consumed during a revelry on Ynys Enlli, he had slain his very own uncle and lain with the dead man's wife), Vivien aborted the schoolyard love, painfully quieted in one direction (for as Gwyar looked upon Maelgwn, so did Maelgwn look upon another), promised the young priestess to a Northern prince, and promptly returned her to her druidic training at Ynys Mon.

The political marriage worked as designed, resulting in the birth of Gwalchmai, the Hawk of May, whose birth was a blessing to both the North and the South. The cost of leaving school was Gwyar's heart. And more.

A week after she left, Maelgwn too was called away. He went to a campaign on the Continent, where his legend as a warrior burgeoned. Around this time, Maelgwn entered into fosterage under Vivien. And thus, from time to time after this, Gwyar, at function, holy day or feast, would now layer unlawful lust atop indifferent rejection, being married and yet in love with her foster-brother.

Then King Meurig suffered a grievous wound, driving him into early abdication, and his heir, the would-be sandy-haired boy-king, was pried from school, and from Gwen ferch Ogyrfan, to participate in the king-making rites of spring and wield Excalibur as Pendragon.

The band of four broken.

This left only the little princess; *small as a faerie, but daughter of a Giant.*

Back then, Gwen was known by her three ever-companions as charitable, kind, full of dash and spirit, of good report - her only vice being that she toyed overly with the boys. A lustful look seemed ever carved into her visage. She was a poor student and sought nothing of the knowledge of books and scrolls, but was thrice smarter than the three when it came to life's classroom - the real world. She cared not for Gwyar's goddesses, and even less for Arthur's bishops and Hebrew God. Her father had taught her that there were no gods and that man was a cosmic mistake, a thing of nature, a thing of flesh alone.

And fleshly she was.

Gwen II fancied fashion and commerce over religion, and held no particular spirituality. And no youthful love captured this future queen.

As Gwyar looked upon Maelgwn did Maelgwn to Gwen.

As Arthur looked upon Gwen did Gwen look upon no one.

Thus, two loved Gwen and one loved Maelgwn, while none loved the seed of the Pendragon beyond the love of a brother, sister or great friend.

That the boys fancied her, she was aware. That Arthur would anger and cry "I saw her first" she heard of many times. But such troubles are supposed to fade as the season and dissolve as adulthood ensues. Not so here. The depth and intoxicating nature of the matter, none knew. For this claim to love based upon the primacy of *seeing* by the boy-king placed a seed of discord in Maelgwn; a seed that would, when watered with other violations, grow and blossom, to the ruin of many.

Nay, none saw these things, for the lives of children are as a sealed vault, withheld from parents and all elders. None saw.

Save perhaps the Fae.

Small as the Fae…

Daughter of a Giant.

And one dark day, visited by the Fae.

An overgrown oak tree, whose roots were already old before the Flood, encroached on the northwest side of the chapel. This was a stone structure in the stead of timber, due to its proximity to the wetter climate of the shore (in a country already doubly wet) breaching through windows, creating the need for a side door to access, trim and maintain its active and intrusive arms, some of which scraped the tessellated paving of the floor, near the altar.

One evening, wearied and alone, her bishops and schoolmasters at supper, Gwen exited the chapel through the 'tree door', hoping the burgeoning sunset mist would cease her weary melancholy.

The mist came, and she began to dance.

It was here that Gwen met him. Where he sought the child.

And so, not ten paces from the right hand of God (as was known the place of the bishop next to the altar in the church), did Gwen, the daughter of the Giant, meet the son of the Devil.

For she had been dancing round the Oak.

Once.

Twice.

Stopping short of the third circle with a terminating thud at his thighs, the top of her head jolted backwards, not reaching even unto his navel. Suddenly the silence was uncanny.

And there he towered.

Crowned with a circlet of ivory. Blood-red skin and eyes to match, save the sockets, which were black as pitch. Brutish and lean, and clearly a great lord or sovereign. A thousand thousand pairs of eyes suddenly accompanied them, behind, above, below and beside.

These were the Tylwyth Teg, an ancient and dangerous progeny of the damned. Often feigning allegiance to the most of corrupt men on the Blessed Isles, the Dynious Hysbys, their true loyalty was to ancient gods, or alternatively to Arddu (who is the Devil), or elsewise to none but themselves.

An unknown force of conduct compelled them inexplicably, and rarely, also to do good. Ever changing and spiraling in mysterious motives, they maneuvered and manipulated the Isles that had once been theirs.

"We like the way you dance."

Gwen recovered from the collision but could conjure no response outside of, "My thanks to you, lord."

"Will you dance with us?" the king of the Tylwyth Teg inquired.

"Dance with you?" The Fair Folk raised a buzzing cheer of encouragement. "Yes, I will," said the princess.

The company of Fair Folk turned the Giant's daughter to exhaustion until at last she swooned, falling as doth a baby bird from its nest. Light as air, right into the mouth of a hungry barn cat waiting agape.

Holding her snug, the king of the Tylwyth Teg's true motive was unwrapped, along with his trouser. Dividing her soul asunder with his dark arts, he knew at once that her mother had died, bringing her forth as a babe into the world of men. This occurred more than not when the sire was a Giant. Having none but a father, she ever sought to please and manipulate men in order to feel the security denied her by her mam.

And beauty.

Such, such beauty.

"I bless you to have dominion with all men, using but these." His black nails, gentle on the lids of her eyes, which at once were changed from dark but common brown to large, bronze and golden-speckled spheroids, great lights of lust for any man. Next his hand found her youthful garden. "And this." Upon touching the flower of her young womanhood, markings of colored ink began to dry themselves on her skin; from mound to crown, a canvas of flesh, filled with lustful patterns.

He also rendered Gwenhwyfar barren.

Next, the Fae King decided to taste for himself the instrument of carnality and lust he had rendered.

After having her, the Lord of the Fair Folk was filled with dismay and anger that his creation had already known a man, and was no virgin.

CHAPTER 4
The Queen, the Witch and the Stable Boy

From that very day, Gwen II began to use and discard men. Sometimes strategically, oft just for its own sake; never carelessly.

Arthur only saw her in person at times random and passing during the Saxon Wars. Married away at fifteen, leading three endless campaigns in the North (and when not on campaign, engaged in battles on the Continent), one year became twenty. The Pendragon noted her markings, but felt that her melting eyes were just as they always had been. He loved their friendship, his very soul driven always and always to honor and protect her. But a romantic love he contained as the Deep under the Great Stone, withholding it for the sake of honor, and for his wife, Gwen I.

All encounters were innocent, but not within his heart, where he betrayed not Gwen I by loving Gwen II, but rather betrayed Gwen II by marrying Gwen I in the first place.

But Gwen II cared for none of these things.

With Llacheu buried and Amr reckoned dead by all, and with Queen Gwenhwyfar self-exiled to her own place, a too-soon rumbling for Arthur to get heirs rattled and drummed low beneath the celebrating shouts and merriment of the people. Arthur wanted Gwen II, and the people wanted Silure babies of the houses of Glamorgan and Gwent.

Meurig liked none of it.

But he relented, and met his obligation as king (and more, as father).

At the behest of King Meurig, Gwen II and her father, the chieftain Ogyrfan of Croesoswallt, were summonsed to Caer Bovum to be queried on the matter of an arranged marriage. Meurig's great manor was but a short walk from Illtud's school – *and the oak tree where she had congressed with the Faerie King.*

After that, Meurig departed to join with Arthur and his Round Table Companions for the second crowning (for Arthur had vanquished fully the Saxon hordes and was made *Emperor* over Cymru, Alba, Lloegyr, Little Britain and sundry smaller vassal kingdoms. The republican monarch wanted none of this, and passionately advocated, with immovable conviction, local rule. But he enjoyed the celebration and joy of the Clans, Tribes and Nations nonetheless. They could have their great emperor, who would build no empire but rather straightway return home to Caerleon or to Caermelyn, never to encroach or infringe on other kingdoms and to raise an army only at their request when in dire need of defense) in Londoninium, and Gwenhwyfar was asked to wait.

To wait for the Lancelot.

For Maelgwn.

The journey from Croesoswallt to Londoninium required travel south through the Cymry kingdom of Powys, with a planned stop for repose at Amwythig, then west through the Midlands, with a turn southeast to the great port city of Lludgate, where Saint Paul had preached to the heathen above four hundred and fifty years earlier, a gilded place of worship erected to celebrate the same.

The Battle of Mynydd Baedan had been less than a moon ago, and the policies of expulsion and resettling not yet implemented. The threat of scattered survivors or opportunists remained in the shadow of a rejoicing nation. Robbers and villains of Cymry blood might turn opportunist in the distraction of celebration as well.

For this cause, the Champion of the Round Table Fellowship was bidden to personally see the princess safely to her husband-to-be. It was the logical choice. Maelgwn could see from all directions; he could sense and flush out attackers in the fog, or at night. He was a manslayer unmatched and never required much sleep. The report alone of his being with her would greatly discourage would-be malefactors.

Arthur placed reason and fevered focus on Gwen's safety above even an eye's twinkling moment of consideration over Lancelot's feelings. Arthur had seen her first at school; he declared this and, contrary to every other decision and manner of life, that was that. She was Arthur's noonday sun, and the light of it blinded him to Maelgwn Gwynedd, hurting in the shadows.

Gwenhwyfar's servants traveled separately. She and Maelgwn shared a steed. The sum of the trip was two nights and three days.

"Have you a wife?"

Gwenhwyfar was very forward. Her head was pressed into the rippling sea of muscles that was Maelgwn's back as she held tight, and rested upon, the warrior as he managed the bridle and harness.

Blissfully comfortable, her only complaint was that she could not see his face blush.

"I've had many wives, but when betwixt their legs I am at rehearsal but for one."

If Gwenhwyfar's soul were not black as her hair, she here would have blushed as well. Instead, her lips, thick and lush, pressed into a comfortable, flattered grin. She let her hair fall without pin or plait, ensuring that aromatic strands would badger her travel companion, and slept until they arrived at the chapel and small lodgings provided by a young saint called Tydecho, who was Arthur's nephew.

The circular timber home had a hearth that formed the center (and singular) beam of the dwelling. There were two beds on opposing sides, and a tiny common area. The fire blazed, and the desire within Maelgwn was fanned as well.

A great battle raged within him, as it had when he was sixteen. A battle he had lost when he put the sword to his uncle and ravaged his wife, who had begged for the ravaging. This was before Vivien had taught Maelgwn the form of martial art she had inherited from Buddug, then adapted and perfected for the Bretons and Britons. Thus, the kill had been sloppy; a crime of passion by a boy who was a bundle of nerve-endings with no brain. He had lost the battle; the battle of appetite, of self above others, of entitlement and hubris, of lust unrivaled. He had lost it with his uncle, *and one other time,* and then, as she had done with unwanted Morgaine, the Lady of the Lake had saved him.

Ironically, Vivien had directed Maelgwn towards the will-worship and temperance of the

Christian faith in an effort to help him control what she and he called "*the bubble*". She did not abuse or elevate guilt as a force when weaving in Christian mechanisms of morality with the young man. Instead, she taught Maelgwn to focus on the great focus of the spirit at the expense of the flesh, the distraction of prayer and outwardly directed vitality. Where her worldview encouraged enjoyment of the flesh to access the spirit, where it viewed carnal relations as enjoyable and, under love, without restriction or regulation, she discerned correctly that Christian temperance and not pagan excess might save Maelgwn from his torment - from the lust that 'bubbled' and, when burst, would at once release him, only to bubble at some unknown and random time again and again.

Here in Tydecho's quaint hut, where Gwenhwyfar ferch Ogyrfan Gawr, full of seductive pout and overtly contrived reluctance, took *the other bed* but disrobed slowly, letting the fire light all the comely and privy parts that should have been committed only to the future of Arthur's eyes, sleeping spread and without skin or blanket, the bubble appeared.

Now, Gwen did not try and seduce Maelgwn. For her part, she had simply been transported back to the times at Illtud's, where an extreme comfort had existed amongst the band of four. The ride had been difficult, and her clammed disposition against Maelgwn's torso had rendered her a sweaty woman without a bath. Nakedness was natural for Gwenhwyfar, modesty robbed so long ago by the encroaches of the Tylwyth Teg and his otherworldly companions, who had watched.

But all she did was seductive. Usually knowingly, sometimes not.

Maelgwn, privily, was praying the words the Apostle Paul had given to the preacher-boy Timotheus. "Flee, youthful lusts." And again. "Flee, youthful lusts."

It was not until he left the roundhouse the third time in an effort to outrun the bubble that Gwenhwyfar realized her nudity was maddening the stoic warrior.

She covered herself.

That which conceals is more appealing than that which reveals, so the problem was made rather worse.

Maelgwn was evaluating all whom he would have to murder, should he take her here and now. In all the wandering of a temporarily corrupted mind, simply killing her was not an option.

Nor, he rightly reckoned, was gossip or chatter.

He had no gift for conversation. He was a lover, and a killer, not a bard. *Let Taliesin to the poetry, and let me to the ladies who moisten at his words.*

Gwenhwyfar was to be betrothed and then marry the Pendragon, the king of kings and lord of lords. From this position, provided she was calculated and eschewed carelessness, she could do *anything* she wanted. For the rest of her life. She could not endanger that here over a sticky fumbling with the lust-mad Lancelot.

He left. He walked. He returned.

He had two ciders.

He lay down.

He read Scripture.

As the bubble expanded in the rear lobe of his head, the pressure became excruciating. This, and no Saxon or Pict, was his only equal. Only Lancelot could defeat Lancelot.

And Lancelot was winning.

He rose, also naked.

Lancelot was nearly ten spans tall, with a member as that of a great tannish stallion. His hair was curly, short, and black as Gwen's. Though he had a neck, it was abridged by muscles that sat atop muscles, connecting shoulder to neck, neck to head. Where most men had one small ridge of muscles here, Lancelot had two. His forearms were immense, but the rest of his build lean.

He was naked.

And coming for her.

Memories of youth rushed upon Gwen as she looked at the Bloodhound Prince. She forgot her future and leapt from the small bed to meet him.

Two of history's most famous Britons, alone and naked after midnight in a tiny roundhouse in Powys.

Just two paces from taking her tiny hand in his great paw, the two were suddenly three.

Yet only he saw the wizard.

Face to face was Maelgwn with the Merlin.

"You died." Maelgwn's erection shriveled, crinkling to match his brow as he questioned the phantom intruder.

"When it comes time to do that which you would do, do it not."

Beyond the understanding of this world, the Merlin had slammed the hilt of a dagger into Lancelot's hand, but spoke no further.

"I love Arthur. And I love Cymru," he said.

"Is there anyone, anything, else you love, Lancelot?" At this point, Gwen's arousal was as nearly dangerous as his own.

"You," he responded directly. "I shall ever revere you as my one true love, and whilst I live, I shall love no other. I shall love you as the queen.

I shall love you as the wife of the friend whom I love." As he finished this speech, he ran from the hut and plunged the dagger deep into the fleshy part of his thigh.

Merlin's dagger had burst the bubble, sending it back to its dark abode.

The journey continued. Maelgwn with bandaged, self-inflicted wound, Gwen burning between her legs, both legends rubbing each other, passionately repelling desire as they rode, speaking very little, focused solely on combating the lust that was consuming them.

But know each other, they did not.

Maelgwn delivered the Princess Gwen II unto Londoninium, and after the crowning, he made leave for repose in Camlan.

His bubble returned ferociously, and no ghost appeared to deter him. He privately forced his son, Rhun Hir, to bring him the wife of a man called Elphin, whose comely spouse roughly resembled Gwenhwyfar. Taliesin, the new Merlin, knew of the deed, and would discern the time to condemn Maelgwn.

Gwenhwyfar's burning continued as well.

On the very first night upon arriving to her new estates in Caerleon, she strolled through the stables, privily (for King Arthur had put her in her own apartment and, respectfully, sought not to bed her so soon in the courtship). Perchance, she found an attractive stable worker who was ensuring that the stables were warm and the horses, who were one half of the union of the equestrian contrivance that had been the decisive factor in defeating foot soldier invaders and winning the Saxon Wars, were spoiled, doted upon and of happy disposition. Indeed, many Cymry women jested, with no small measure of annoyance, that the horses were doted upon more than the wives.

Gwen II had no use for his name, and didn't bother with the asking.

She turned him around where he stood and whispered, with enlarged eyes, "Do you know who I am?"

Less than twenty winters had not given the young man the confidence to engage a painted goddess. *A painted devil.*

He stammered, but he managed a choppy, "Yes, my lady."

"I command you to *serve* your future queen."

She had his trousers untied and his cock in hand before he could muster the word "Arthur" in protest.

The events of the past few weeks were gestating in Princess Gwyar, as she surveyed the stables on a walk, taking the longer route to Lodge Hill, where she would make a small fire and commune with her goddess (and cider) under a clear winter night. The Usk River would be her choir and the diverse birds her chorus.

A walk at night in the south east of Cymru opens the door to the mind. The angels, adored in their stars, sing jealous praises towards the land, the view of them better in Cymru than in any other place on earth.

The clear Cymru night, the heavenly hosts dancing, the calm. It also had the effect of bringing down the guarding gates of one's mind, letting too many unfiltered contemplations bounce to and fro, loose and untamed.

How will I keep Gwalchmai safe? Why does my brother ever put him in harm's way in one moment, and imply him heir in the next? How do I keep my vow to the put-away queen? When will I return to

Ynys Enlli? Have Cadfan and his pilgrims found any of the Treasures? Have they found Her? How will I manage to serve my brother with that other Gwenhwyfar here? I don't want to see her. When will I see her?

Just then, she saw her.

Or, rather, heard her.

Gwenhwyfar was finishing her adulterous session with the stable boy, and Gwyar, sister to the Pendragon, both heard and then witnessed her; but she herself was, by Gwenhwyfar, unseen.

Gwyar repositioned herself three stalls over and let the boy, probably now empty of pride and full of shame (and now officially a traitor to the Silure Royal Clan), finish, dress and scurry away, as a small dog does when it thinks none saw it take the table scraps.

Then she made her move to intercept Gwen's path.

"How long has it been, my mate from school, my friend!" Gwyar feigned friendship, long having known what Gwen was, trying to determine how to best protect her lovesick brother, falling short of any immediate answers.

If she told Arthur this very night, who would he believe? How would it affect his rule? Would Gwyar be bound to him forever if he fell into heartbreak, and the Tribe's god-king diminished and sad? Gwenhwyfar was hell to Gwyar, a canker with no cure.

Gwenhwyfar felt no compulsion to return fettered words, and openly adjusted her undergarments. "Far from your Isle of Apples and Merlin's trinkets, are you not, Lady?"

"I am, tonight, just where and when I was supposed to be," countered Gwyar. Remembering the worldly smarts of her opponent, she opted for brevity. "I hope you found what you needed in our stables tonight, and that you look forward to being a chaste, loyal and good queen to my brother." At this, Gwyar hastened away from Gwen II.

"Witch," Gwen hissed after her, unheard.

Gwyar, once achieving her destination, screamed a terrific scream; a frustrated scream, such that lightning flashed and crackled from Lodge Hill.

Gwenhwyfar angrily slammed the door of her chamber, causing her to send away inquisitive servants and even spend above half of an hour convincing vigilant Cai that there was no matter.

Her anger was self-directed. She had been clumsy in using the boy. The king's very own sister might have stumbled upon them. If her, then anyone. If her, then the king himself!

She had been half disciplined with Lancelot (and this was simply her release, a fantasizing of that incident) and would not soon repeat the same.

Never again will I be careless.

The next morning she traded her body (and enjoyed the act, as it was well-organized with no fear, this time, of discovery) for an assassin to contrive a hanging. A false suicide by the stable boy.

Two days later, she poisoned the assassin, clipping frayed ends that the garment of her rule would not run and unravel. With a clean slate in the perversity of her mind, she set about to rule and reign as the replacement queen to Arthur Pendragon.

CHAPTER 5
The Field of Malevolence

It is a curious thing how one year can be as a hundred, bursting with adventure, intrigue, peril, and change, but how other years pass as leaves upon a stream, peaceful and of no repute or distinction. Taliesin spake an adage that was true. *Not all years are special.*

And so it was that time gave green and gilded Cymru three such years.

Arthur Pendragon would court and marry Gwenhwyfar ferch Ogyrfan. And although he woefully missed his wizard, never ceasing the search, the king's heart was finally happy.

The Round Table Knights quested.

Arthur was true to his word. There would be no overreaching, tyrannical central government. Freedom prospered. Local chieftains governed justly, and when they did not, the appeal and escalation to Caermelyn was careful and deliberate.

The Lady of Lake continued quietly in exile, remaining in Broceliande over on the Continent in the safety and solitude of her magical forest. Its founts and streams and ancient oaks and elemental water spirits her ever companions in the self-imposed imprisonment.

The bishops and the priests enjoyed relatively few conflicts in executing their policy of baptism and church membership for the remnants of the Angles, Saxons and Jutes (and the several divergent sub-groups of each, as there were over twenty and seven tribes still extant in the east of Lloegyr and the Midlands). No Germanic parent claimed fidelity to Odin or Thor, knowing they must declare for Christ. Their children were baptized by water into whatever sect of the faith the parent preferred. The bishops continued to favor the *believer's baptism,* but struggled with evangelism, as they would not sup, bathe or engage in sport or play with any Saxon. Some Saxons joined the Apostolic Britons' Church, as a result of hearing the good news preached in the streets and markets.

The Catholics, be they native-born or immigrants from Rome, Greece or Eire, fared better. Not above getting their hands dirty to help the common man, they established schools amongst the Germans, rebuilt houses and stables, provided supplies and used charity to earn converts; then implemented their sacerdotal policies of infant baptism as new Saxons were born upon Britannia's soil.

At this quiet time, there was no perceived extension of the policy of compulsory Church membership and baptism inward to the cantrefs and tribes in Cymru. This made the heathen and local Christian alike very happy, and a general spiritual liberty and contentment prevailed.

Arthur's principle rival, Caw, was also peaceful during these, the early years of the Summer Kingdom. Many of his sons favored the Silure king over their own father philosophically, working under Arthur's employ where scout work was available, and even came to own small farms in the South. Other sons held their tongues or grumbled within themselves. King Urien Rheged and his powerful son, Owain, were Arthur's constant eyes but had little to report on the Northern rebels save Hueil ap Caw, who continued to be a thorn.

As for Caw, his affections were drawn away from land disputes, vain genealogies and generational complaints, falling upon his youngest son. The infant Aneurin (who is also called Gildas) had given the aging Son of Cunedda pride and vigor. There was something special about the lad, and liberty and peace afforded Caw the time he had never enjoyed with his other sons and daughters; time to parent.

The political marriages seemed to be working for the Silure's other enemy (or at best, lukewarm and risky supporters) - the house of Meirchion. The radical Catholic had been evicted from his lands for his probable involvement in Merlin's vanishing. However, he was father to Cynfarch Oer, who was father to Llew, who was estranged husband to Gwyar, who was sister to King Arthur Pendragon. This made Gwyar's sons beloved by both North and South. Just as her aunt Marchell had mitigated war with the Emerald Isle, the daughters of Meurig gave their wombs to Cymru, doing much to keep the sons of Meurig off the battlefield against the other tribes. The women sacrificed personal happiness (for the local laws and customs, though diverse, all extended to women the right to marry whom they would, to divorce, to own land and trade) to prevent an undercurrent of civil war that had been brewing since so many Northern sons had been lost at the Night of Long Knives.

As for Meirchion himself, there was neither corpse nor grave marker to prove or disprove that Merlin had perished. Exposing Vivien would do nothing, yet she dared not reveal his plot either. And Meirchion the Mad was old. Very old, and nigh death. His efforts turned to his son Mark, whom he would rear on the southeastern-most horn of the Isles. He would establish Mark slowly there, and in Eire, and on the Continent, creating a future triangle in which to trap and slay the Pendragon. One day, many years hence. But at this time, it was enough for Meirchion to have food and lodging and live out his purgatory, all the while knowing Illtud was enjoying his hearths, his halls, his possessions of art and scrolls, and his sheep and cattle.

In Alba, the precocious painted Picts along the borderlands in the Old North behaved, abstaining from raiding, provided that King Maelgwn Gwynedd would periodically bed their queens and grant them permission to nominate him their king. He enjoyed the distraction some, the women more, and the title amused him.

Marital alliances through the line of Arthur's aunt Marchell and her progeny kept the raiders of Eire in check. In the east of the Isles, Cedric was peaceful, cultivating the small kingdom in Lloegyr that the Britons had allotted him.

For all of the Blessed Isles in the Sea, art and trade thrived. Many sons were begotten, such that newborn children began to match in proportion to lambs and calves. All of Britannia, including creaturekind, was in season, indulging in happy peacetime procreation.

During the Summer Kingdom, the bards were able to transition from perpetual war planning to formalizing and advancing their system of spirituality. As a result, the *Barddas* reached the zenith of its development. The twenty and four forms and meters of Cymry poetry were established, and the language of Heaven was codified in written form and etchings as never before, resulting in countless stones containing parallel cyphers that included the trade languages amongst the nations, Latin, the Ogham of the Emerald Isle, alongside the Cymraeg.

Personal wealth swelled, as treasure and savings were laid up through frugality.

Bishop Cadfan did found his small chapel on Ynys Enlli, yet not without ongoing travail, shipwreck and sacrifice. Gwyar did her privy dark work, protesting, and working magick from afar to ensure the secrets of the Isle of Apples remained concealed. However, she was not ignorant of the winds of change, nor of the fact that winds and currents and fogs would not deter the devout forever. After all, the island was very small. Soon, someone was bound to discover something.

And she honored the decree of the High Queen, the *first Gwenhwyfar.* Gwyar succored the king from the shadows, gave him confidence, advice and encouragement where a door of utterance manifested. Many times, the royal siblings retreated from court to Lodge Hill, where real decisions could be made far from priest and bishop, landlord, merchant or bard.

But Arthur's seeking of Gwyar for stately matters, family matters or any matters began to wane like the moon, becoming a sliver and then - gone. For so deeply in love with the *new Gwenhwyfar* was the great king that the importance of "older sister" was fading as the dusk. Even his nocturnal haunts ceased during these three years.

Gwyar had vowed to remain at Caerleon

only until another woman came into Arthur's life to give him the support arrested by the first Gwenhwyfar's abdication. The circumstance now allowed the king's sister to soon make her leave, whether in return to her husband in the North or to her Glass Castle and apple orchards on Ynys Enlli.

What circumstance allowed, conscience forbade. She felt bound to stay. To combat the malaise of her plight, Gwyar invited her son, the Northern prince Mordred ap Llew ap Cynfarch Oer, to live at court with her in Caerleon for a summer.

The loss of Amr ap Arthur ap Meurig to a murderous, filth-covered wretch deeply grieved Mordred. *A prince should have perished upon the sword of another prince or chieftain.* It was Mordred's twenty-and-first year, and he was still young enough to prefer *mother over father* when stricken with a broken heart.

His time here will be good for both of us, Gwyar surmised.

Mordred and his Hosts arrived at the entrance into Caerleon on the Summer Solstice, three and a half years after victory at Mynydd Baedan. His attire differed greatly from the skins and furs donned when patrolling the coasts on Ynys Mon. Though young, there was a grit and hardness about him, perhaps a contrived persona for would-be invaders from the sea.

But here he was, covered in gold, seemingly from head to boot.

Arthur's deceased son Llacheu had also favored gold armor, whether as rivets or grout lines in his breastplate, or in cuffs and gauntlets of shimmering gold over soft copper. Llacheu's golden ensembles had been shiny, whimsical, and perceived as adorable by the maidens and light-hearted by the men. It had suited the shimmering son of the Pendragon. Mordred, it suited not, and shouted and screeched arrogance to onlookers on him.

His headdress was molded to look like the deity Mab, the Divine Child. No detail was spared. This was not a functional helmet, but rather a wearable piece of self-promoting pride-art; a hollow and tightly-fitted head of Zeus or a mask of Ares, including golden hair and cheekbones with finite precision. The message was not lost on even the most casual observer: the boy counted himself entitled to be viewed and treated as a god.

And there was more.

His crown was distastefully hefty, a major departure from the simple circlets of the kings, princes and chieftains of the Royal Clans. The forearm pieces, gold and black, were dramatically oversized, forming a winged look that extended from wrist well past his elbows. Mail was not worn by Cyrmu warriors, but the under-armor featured some metal. It was master-crafted black leather, with concentric and interlaced gold-covered steel knots and tiny spikes spanning his torso, back and shoulders.

Mordred's jeweled cape represented the Ravens of the North, but its design featured neither the Awen to honor the divine inspiration that spirited the land, a cruciform to give glory to the Christian God, nor the double chevron of his mother's people, the mighty Silures.

His mount was equally gilded; a massive stallion, black as night, heavily armored, heavily decorated.

The son of Llew was a spectacle, come to stay with his mother, accompanied by twelve men.

"His own Round Table Fellowship," mocked an innkeeper, who resided on the port side of the bridge near a place later called Casnewydd, as he was sweeping his storefront.

"Nay, his own company of bards!" added a patron.

Mutterings aside, and in spite of the prince's excesses, the ancient codes of the Cymry demanded compulsory hospitality. Thus there were cheers and gifts, wine and water, as well as flattering salutations, as the golden knight crossed the bridge over the Usk River. A small parade developed and pressed upon him as he navigated the narrow streets, until at last he rode past the public bathhouses and finally came to the great amphitheater, the epicenter of the city.

Gwalchmai and Gwyar hid in the archways of the prodigious circular stadium, concealing themselves for the purpose of surprising Mordred at just the right moment.

Gwalchmai was younger than Mordred by eighteen full months, yet the elder nephew of Arthur was never rumored Edling, or *heir,* whilst the younger was – even before the death of Arthur's sons.

This was for no other cause than Gwalchmai's fosterage in the South and the quantity of his time with the Pendragon. The red-haired Gwalchmai possessed otherworldly charms, appeared to command the weather, warmed any room he entered and brought entire halls to laughter. He was the 'people's heir', whilst Mordred, for reasons not quite so clear, was subtly kept away from the Gelliwig, Caerleon and Caermelyn, having very little time with Arthur at any of these courts.

Gwyar wanted Mordred at court for

reconnection, for redeeming the time, and for love. Mordred, as was abundantly clear by the pomp of his entry and grandeur of his armor, cared for none of these things.

He was at Caerleon to assert his claims before King Arthur. His opportunity was now.

Arthur had younger brothers who were, for diverse reasons, ineligible for the throne, and Mordred, with Arthur's sons dead, was the hereditary heir. However, clear descent was subject to being negated by the people, whose rulers only governed by the consent of the governed. By voicing their will through the local bards, major landowners, bishops and priests, many kings had been passed over for lesser royalties on the basis of character and competence.

Now was Mordred's time. *Does Arthur even know me? Would he know me to look upon me? No matter; he shall know me. My will shall bring me all I desire. And I desire the Summer Kingdom.*

Mordred dismounted the stallion, and gave half-friendly embraces to the residents who had come to welcome him. Illtud's choirs introduced wondrous melodies into the summer air as tapestries danced in the breeze, seemingly to the singing. Harps and deep drums joined, and the smell of smoked beef caused a happy hunger for the hundreds of people reveling in and around the coliseum.

Yet Mordred saw none of his kin, least of all the High King.

He spun around a few times, sweating in his heavy, pretentious skeleton of gold, and began to grumpily inquire about the whereabouts of his mother. Just at the right time, *Morgaine appeared.*

"Looking for someone, Raven?" Even a powerful sorceress is capable of humor.

"Mother!" Mordred suspended political ambition as the moment broke his sourness; a sincerity of giddy reminiscence ensued. Gwyar was disconnected from the world of men save her sons, for whom she was as a lass with a new puppy - warm, doting, with smothers of love.

Tiny, Gwyar had to 'hug up', and in so doing pulled at the back of Mordred's mask-helmet, revealing his face, which was cleanly shaven, youthful and strikingly fair. He was of average height, a little shorter than his uncle Arthur, and of leaner build. He was of authoritative and mean-spirited disposition, and carried himself taller than he was.

The Hawk of May mauled him as well. "It's been three years!"

"You are - well - huge, Gwalchmai!" Prince Mordred awed at the burl and mass and bulk of his brother, who had let his red hair grow well beneath the shoulders and left it to run its own wild and curly course.

"It's been *three years*!" chuckled Gwalchmai.

The reunion continued for several minutes, and then Mordred returned to his aim - the wooing of the king. Or assertively demanding. *Whatever sophistry works, so long as the end is the crown.*

"Oh, my dear, my brother is, alas, not at Caerleon." Gwyar delivered the disappointment.

Mordred was not overly troubled. It was peacetime, and Arthur was sure to be at one of his three plenary courts and not far from the realm of his beloved Glamorgan and Gwent.

"Ah, off resolving a cattle dispute in Ergyng, or helping to thatch a roof for a cleric in Llandaff?" Here Mordred mocked that the king was a neighbor first and a sovereign second, ever helping his neighbor.

"Would that were so." Now Gwyar's tone was grave. "He has traveled north, near your father's lands. To the highlands of Eryri."

Mordred wished his helm was still covering his face so that he didn't have to hide his overt anger.

"Why to the mountains?!" he emoted, then endeavored to calm himself.

Gwalchmai answered carefully. "I do not know why word did not reach Ynys Mon, brother. But an urgent call for the Round Table Fellowship, the first of its kind in more than three years, has come forth, on account of reports that" – a cheerful man struggles to deliver morose tidings – "a Giant has emerged, slaying chieftains and warriors, killing without cause."

"A Giant?"

"Not a tall man, or a figure or type to describe a large man. An actual, otherworldly beast of intelligence and rage. A six-fingered colossus, with multiple rows of teeth and bright, carroty hair."

Mordred interrupted Gwyar's description. "Kings, chieftains? Father?"

"We know not who has fallen. Arthur himself has gone to scout and gather information on the matter." Gwyar offered a hopeful tone.

Mordred queried Gwalchmai as to why he hadn't joined the other knights.

"I appealed strenuously."

"Why?"

"I have not seen my brother in three years." Gwalchmai hugged Mordred tight.

"My husband, your uncle, will be back before you know. Welcome. Rest with us, Prince Mordred." Enter Gwenhwyfar ferch Ogyrfan. "In his stead, I offer myself." False humility. "Come, eat some dinner with us."

Gwen had manifested from thin air, and Gwyar was actually thankful that she broke the tension as surely, elsewise, Mordred would have remounted and raced back north to the mountains Eryri (which would later be called Snowdonia).

The new queen had mastered covering her ceaseless infidelity over the past three years, never again coming near to being discovered.

But Gwyar knew.

And it drove her to hatred.

She often wondered if she was hurting Arthur more by concealing versus revealing the matter.

The four, Gwyar, Mordred, Gwalchmai, and Gwen II, parted for a time, and then assembled for an evening meal.

'Twas here that the course of history changed.

There are no 'types' where love is concerned, no compatibility measures, no guarantees of 'like things with like things', no requisite mutual interests, no builds or equity of shapes and forms.

Indeed, *you love who you love, and that is that.*

And for the first time in her life, the one who had been abused by the Fae and in turn had abused men, hundreds of times, felt love. Real and actual love. *Love in the fashion of Meurig and Onbrawst.*

It happened over one meal.

And Mordred, though married to Kwyllog ferch Caw, instantly, fully and equally reciprocated. *And this is the only time love works, when it is requited equally.*

What Arthur had wanted for the sum of his life, Gwenhwyfar freely gifted to Mordred in their first moment. Her whole heart was given, spoken for, and taken.

Gwyar had become blinded by Gwen's constant playing of the harlot. Though gods and men alike feared her power and perception and *Sight*, she couldn't see this: Gwen was changed.

The following morning, Gwen II rose early, Prince Mordred the preoccupation of her dawn, and glided about the city, repenting openly with great contrition to the many whom she had wronged. She was careful, however, to have no direct interaction with past lovers (those who had not met *accidental* deaths and still drew breath to speak of it) who could reveal *that part* of her iniquity. She stooped to gather up spilled baskets of eggs at the market, she played with children, dancing round the poles, actually holding children!

Mordred had made the monster into a woman. A soft, kind, powerful woman.

Gwen had made the monster into a man. A soft, kind, powerful man.

Battling nerves, they stole a 'hand-hold' the following day. The innocent intertwine was alone more pleasing than a life of carnal pleasures and material goods, which before had been constantly fed into a bottomless well of the soul.

And oh, the first kiss!

She delivered a peck on his cheek, just below the eye. He absorbed it as a sponge absorbs vinegar, and when he could contain no further, turned inward and brought her lips to his. All time seemed to stop, and the two villains were born again as saints, not to God, but to love itself. They knew that somehow, in the end, they would be together.

They must be together.

Over the following days (with reports that Arthur would soon return with his report), the leaven leavened the lump, and the two sought where they could make love.

When Gwenhwyfar and Arthur had been betrothed, he had placed her in a well-appointed apartment within a small but luxurious farm home. Near the farm resided a storehouse; beside that, a small cell for chieftains or princes who retired unto monasticism. Arthur had visited the woman he loved with such frequency that the small estate came to be called Llanilltern, or *the place of the king.*

Gwen II loved this place, especially the nearby grove. Its form and features were an impassable blockade to the outside world. To be in this little grove was to be in a Cymru within Cymru. The diversity of flora and fauna, the goliath trees, the accompaniment of legions of birds and friendly fowl singing at all times. *For even the birds are Cymreig in Cymru. And the Cymry are a people who sing.* The place itself hummed notes of innocence, romance, virtue and love.

Ironic and fitting that it was the spot of Gwenhywfar ferch Ogyrfan's liaisons with Mordred ap Llew.

The spot of forbidden love.

And many times a day they knew each other upon its ferns and soft brush, its heather finding its way into every part of their inseparable forms.

Arthur was delinquent in his return to Caerleon. Messengers indicated that there was now twofold the trouble, as another abominable creature had delayed the king's homecoming. This beast presided in South Cymru, magnifying the fears of those in the cantrefs.

Mordred's mother sat at tea, listening to reports that both Giants lived, and that Arthur would need to reassemble some portion of the army from the Saxon Wars.

Insultingly, the messenger indicated that

Arthur wanted Gwen II, and not Gwyar, to organize this with the counselors, advisors and bishops in his stead. (The new Merlin, Taliesin, was away, chastising Maelgwn at this time).

"Fine." Mature Gwyar gave a childish snort, causing recall of like memories of the four at school. "Where is she?" she asked plainly.

None knew.

Gwyar thrice drew her forefinger round the teacup and, barely in a whisper, uttered, "*Morgana.*" Her eyes found her attendants and she said, quietly and authoritatively, "Leave." And the teatime acquaintances and envoys left, an immediate shadow filling the hall just as rapidly as they scurried away.

The thing that was in Gwyar or part of Gwyar or *was Gwyar* now manifested, and as her *Sight* focused, a most surprising voice was heard, in the shadows, there but not there, yet so clear.

"The field of malevolence in the thicket beyond Llanilltern."

A rush of unstoppable tears had their way with Morgaine's face and hands, and then her hair as she pushed it off her forehead, hoping better to see what wasn't there.

"Merlin!" Her voiced cracked nine times to finish the two-syllable word.

Alas, there were none but she in the great hall where tea was enjoyed in the Silure capital of Caerleon.

Immediately to her horse she sprang, the journey not far, the place concealed but well-known.

Arriving quickly, she yanked up by his robe a cleric, peacefully studying Scripture outside the cell on a warm yet windswept summer's day. Placing the reins in his hand, she commanded him: "Watch her." Not waiting for a response, she was off into the grove, swiftly, but now silent.

A manifold trauma blasted the sorceress at the privy viewing of the intercourse between her very own son and the harlot queen:

Mine son will die a traitor under our laws, in any cantref or realm.

Arthur's heart will burst asunder at being cuckolded by his own kin.

Another betrayal by his own house.

If I kill Gwen, will it break him more or less?

If only Merlin were here.

WHY MUST MEN AND WOMEN, PAGANS AND SAINTS, RICH AND POOR, BONDED AND FREE, BETRAY LOVE IN FAVOUR OF LUST? IS THERE NOT EVEN ONE WHO IS TRUE?

The terminal thought was pointed at herself as well as the wide-reaching audience that neither saw nor heard her. She had performed fertility and sacerdotal rites that involved union, or sacred fornication, with men portraying gods, with women portraying goddesses. *That it was religious made it no less adulterous.*

Morgaine of the Faeries was not high-minded; a moment of burden and sorrowful guilt for her husband, loveless marriage begotten of Statecraft or not – *how would he feel if I was in some field making love to another man? How would any spouse feel?*

Seeing the tryst crushed Gwyar, altering her. At utter loss for reason, and sickened to vomit by the relentless repetition in her busy mind of *what she had seen,* the subject overcame her. She took only one item from her chamber – a tattered, worn brown pouch – and fled Caerleon straight away, wanting greatly to unsee it, wanting greatly to know how best to serve Arthur and her son, knowing that to do one would be death to the other. In pain and distress that caused her eyes and left shoulder to twitch and her circulation to run unnatural courses, resulting in a hammering chest-pounding, she sought out herbs, and rest.

The Field of Malevolence. The wood which would come to be called *Mordred's Thicket,* the pitch branded *The Field of Melwas.* It was right here, in this very moment, that the Isles were lost to the Saxons. Not to Aelle, nor to Hengest or Horsa or Octa. And not to the villains who had orchestrated waves of destruction that slayed hundreds of thousands of Cymry, hundreds of chieftains, adding even a Pendragon to their murderous account. Rather, 'twas lost to young Saxons yet suckling, not yet having seen enough winters to lift an axe or wield the infamous *Long Knife*. Cymru was lost. Only, none knew of it.

Full of rage, and blinded by a multitude of unsolvable problems, Morgaine of the Faeries exiled herself to Broceliande, exorcising her condition by becoming a powerful enchantress in the forest, luring and punishing lovers unfaithful and untrue.

CHAPTER 6

King Arthur versus Itto Gawr

Seed 3 – "This was my chance to be Champion before my Tribes."

Centuries before the time of Arthur, the king of the Tylwyth Teg seduced and lay with a damsel that he mistook for a daughter of Adam.

Unbeknownst to him, she was a second-generation Nephilim. Her father was a Giant, and his father a Fallen One.

So few were these incursions in the present dispensation, on account of the protective and ongoing war in heavenly places, that the Fair Folk paid little heed to the possibility.

The accidental offspring of the Nephilim woman and the Fae king wrought a type of double abomination, for the babe was a crossbreed of not just one but two atrocities against God and nature, leaving very little remnant of the substance of man within it.

From the darkest and most fantastic, far-fetched yet true ancient history, this type of incident was the source and explanation for monsters and indescribably strange flesh (including when Fallen Ones would go after creaturekind).

In this peculiar case, the babe's eyes were

crimson-filled like unto his father, massive and perfectly round instead of elliptical, with no pupils. Yet he could see, and was able to change forms and walk secretly between the world of men and the realms of the Fae.

The unnatural mutation was elsewise like unto the Giants. Three times the height of a man, sulfuric skin, contorted vertebrae protruding and curving as the horns of a ram all atop his upper back, in tattered rags, the red-eyed monster operated without brain, without mercy. Dormant for long consecutive years, he would wake, eat a grotesque number of stags and fowl, and then return to a stench-filled cave, undisturbed and unknown.

Because of his lustful indiscretion, the master of the Fair Folk replaced all food consumed by the beast three-fold to the village in Cernyw (which is Gwent) where dwelt the Red-Eyed Giant. Barns were swept clean, and charms and delights often found upon entries to homes and halls. Moreover, lost wanderers were protected by the otherworldly creatures of the forest, guiding and directing them through enchantments to safer paths.

Many treasures and not a few monsters are hidden in comely, mystical Cymru. And this monster was hidden and sleeping.

Until the Dynion Hysbys found and woke him.

Whereas some Giants were far superior to men in knowledge, in the Sacred Sciences, in masonry and smithing skills, in remembering and recording histories, in theology and many other diverse and sundry spheres of the life-experience, others were more akin to wild beasts or carnivorous fish; constant in hunger and thirst, ever at the hunt for blood and flesh. So dramatic was the spectrum of acumen and disposition amongst these otherworldly beings that men venerated some of them as highly enlightened gods, whilst others they reckoned lower than dogs; a thing to be killed upon encounter, destroyed upon discovery.

The Red-Eyed Giant was of the latter kind.

By contrast, the Giant who had nominated himself the upstart *King of Gwynedd* and set up a court in the high peaks of Eryri was of the former. His name was Itto Mawr. In outward appearance he was in every particular as a man, save his size. His six fingers were the only outward anomaly, his extra rows of teeth subtle and concealed. He was well-groomed, with a comely long, grey beard that was braided and beaded, falling well below his waistline. Handsome to scale, this self-proclaimed ruler was charismatic, with kind eyes, rosy, high-sitting cheeks and a snub, upturned nose. Itto also had an eccentric mania for collecting the beards of his foes.

While Lancelot was frolicking in distracted and blissful fornication, leaping from bed to bed, losing himself inside painted Pictish princesses way up in the highlands of Alba, this Giant had usurped and taken over swaths of his kingdom.

Thus, in the space of but a few weeks, King Arthur had seen two very, very different co-inhabitants of his Isles. The one a mighty man of the mountains, the other a wretched monster from a heretofore unknown rank, putrid-smelling cave too near to Arthur's own cantref in Glamorgan.

Arthur did not openly engage Itto. The objective of his mission was to scout and to study. Horrifically, Arthur and his company saw

Itto kill twenty Ravens with no more effort than a milking cow swats the flies from her tail on a sticky summer day. Utilizing his advanced arts of disguise, the High King became as a rank and file Raven; a soldier amongst those assembled under Maelgwn and Caw's sons to fell this mighty usurper.

For above the space of a week, Arthur studied the Giant.

He primarily killed through lowering his left shoulder and trampling a man, or several men at a time. Once they were knocked flat and unconscious, he would snap the neck and then, with the speed of an adder, shear the beard and tuck it away into a bulging satchel stuffed with the hair and blood of fallen men of the North. The maneuvers were as the reaction of a loosed bull, yet more fluid. A creature ten times the size of a bull and as many times as quick with fist, hammer or club. Arthur judged that the top of his helm reached the kneecap of Itto, and that the Giant's hand could crush a head as effortlessly as squishing a plump grape.

The assembled warriors would attack Itto in groups of six or eight, or in singular combat. The nature of the opponent made it difficult for *many to attack one*. Arrows did not penetrate Itto's skin, the constitution of which, although in appearance as a mortal, was, at least in part, of some other substance; swords produced scratches and scrapes (and bellowing laughter) in the stead of gashes and gapes.

During one frantic flurry, Arthur stealthily unsheathed Carnwennan (the last time the Pendragon had used the enchanted blade was three and a half years earlier, also in the North, in execution of a traitor. The punch of the memory in

Arthur's bowels was more grievous than a direct strike by Itto Mawr could ever be). The ensuing shadow caused by the legendary dagger enabled Arthur to engage Itto at the back of the ankle, wholly unseen.

A cut! A real cut!

Itto cried out and swung violently at the disguised king. Arthur ducked the cedar tree whipping towards his head and sprinted towards the safety of the encampment.

It takes otherworldly weaponry to slay an otherworldly enemy, Arthur had learned on his perilous and privy experiment.

Privy to Men; not so for wise and brave Itto Mawr.

"Arthur ap Meurig ap Tewdrig ap Teithfalt! I thought you more brave, whelp!" The voice alone could shake one's bones and shatter marble.

Stunned at his discovery, Arthur removed the helm of the Ravens of the Old North and tore off his black cloak, revealing the dark blues and reds of the Silure tribe. Bowing his chest, having his feet shod with bravery, the Iron Bear said a rapid prayer and whipped around.

The eruption of cheers that the sandy-haired, blue-eyed king was amongst the Ordivices, his Cymreig kinsmen in the North, was deafening. Their savior had come, and the plague would be handled swiftly.

Arthur's prudence intended elsewise.

"I am he," he said, and stood stoic. Then he walked right up to the Pretender King of Gwynedd and withstood him, face to face – or rather, *face to knee.*

"A little far from the golden fortress of Caerleon and the spoiled fatness of Cybbor, eh?" Itto goaded him. Itto rubbed at his ankle, the wound now angry. "Bring me your army or your beard, or I will make of your absent friend's kingdom a wasteland." His snub nose turned further upward as he delivered the deeply ugly words with deeply kind eyes.

Merlin's greatest achievement in his young pupil was that Arthur always filtered; *think before you do, in haste act not.*

"I will make my leave and return unto you. Until then, I beseech you to leave the people of Gwynedd alone, troubling neither bishop nor farmer nor artisan."

The bravery of the piece of iron dressed as a man impressed upon Itto that he wanted to befriend, and neither eat nor clip, the thirty-and-six-year-old War King. But some force was *causing* the Giant to lust for nothing else save to destroy and disrupt. "Hurry back, son of Meurig," was all he could muster.

Arthur and his companions had to consider many issues as he traveled south towards home. Raising an army and marching into Gwynedd, even with cause, might have negative perceptions, on account of old hurts. Even in the Summer Kingdom, currents of *South versus North* ran and raged as veins of discord beneath the crystal sea of peace.

Arthur's next necessary step was assembling the Round Table, all twenty-six of them, seeking counsel from Bishop Bedwini in order to hear the Church's perspective; finding his new Merlin, the bard Taliesin, who was ever at some quarrel or rivalry with Maelgwn; and finding Maelgwn.

To this end, Arthur directed the youngest son of the *King of the Picts and the rightful King of Gwynedd* (Arthur laughed at this, as his Champion, who preferred no titles, now had seemingly doubled his collection of kingdoms on account of the peculiar fascination the Picts held for the beautiful grandson of Cunedda). "Rhyvn, please do all to bring Maelgwn to Caermelyn. Seven nights or sooner, but no more." No compromise or latitude was present in Arthur's tone. Rhyvn, the ever companion of Arthur's deceased son Llacheau, was ready to the task, hugging his hero tightly (for Maelgwn's sons adored the Silure king).

Arthur, the Iron Bear, desired to make haste homeward.

The Red-Eyed Giant had other notions.

Cai, at the king's side since the days of his fosterage, and Bedwyr were chief amongst Arthur's company. The latter saw the thing appear first, in full sprint at the horses on the byway but a few hours north of Caerleon near the Cwmbran, which is by interpretation *the valley of Bran* (who was also a Giant).

Throwing itself into ten warriors and bouncing through and ultimately off a cluster of horses as a wildcat bounces amongst a herd of stags, it came again and again, clawing, biting and visiting much damage onto the Cymry host.

Then, through a fakery of retreat, it hastened away, its stench leading Cai, Bedwyr and the king to its cave.

"What sorcery is upon us?" Cai, ever grave.

"Well, you don't see that every day." Bedwyr was ever ready to calm with jest and lightheartedness. "Let me at him first." His humor followed always with whole commitment unto the good.

Upon seeing a second otherworldly being, the king instantly wondered at and began attempting to piece together the connections. The Red-Eyed Devil gave the Pendragon no luxury of contemplation, appearing again in an instant from his cave and attacking Bedwyr.

Now, Bedwyr was Arthur's best friend. Above Cai. Above Urien. Above Gwalchmai, his heir. Above even Maelgwn, whom he loved.

And his best friend was in the dire.

Excalibur, that blade forged on Ynys Enlli using steely shavings of a cherubic flaming sword, first wielded at a time when Lions *did* lay down with Lambs. Excalibur, *the Sword of Power*. Arthur looked at that power seething in his protective palms and gripped the hilt harder than at any time before. Excalibur, *The Giant Slayer,* he thought as he plunged into the fray but two seconds late.

Bedwyr ducked, he dodged, he rolled. Ranked just below Gwalchmai and Maelgwn (and his sons) for skill, Bedwyr was amongst the elite ranks of swordsman living at the time. *Or any time*. He had dealt several blows to the monster but, in a slight sliver of a moment, separated his hands. The left hand held the sword low and swung to shoulder height; torqueing his mid-section and pivoting hard to generate momentum, the blade circled to above his head, where his second hand was intended to clasp the first, delivering a fatal downward overhand strike.

The second hand never made it.

Now agape, the monster's mouth revealed an extra rung of teeth set within a pink, mucusy second jaw that dislocated from the first and could distend out past the external mouth and then expand. A second mouth. The teeth were flat and level and would be regarded as 'perfect', if within the handsome mouth of a comely lad. Uniform. Shiny. But sharp as shears, as twenty-four little Excaliburs filed flat and designed for making effortless and surgical chops of flesh and bone.

The Red-Eyed Giant clamped down, cleanly severing Bedwyr's right hand well below the wrist. The twisted mixed offspring of Fae and Giant and angel and animal, and whatever else the Prince of Darkness had placed into its composition, this sin against nature most foul had swallowed the hand, glove, gauntlet and all, with satisfied eyes popping as a frog gulping a mosquito.

Then straightway his brawny, deformed neck came round to see the Pendragon rushing upon him.

Arthur, an elite counter-fighter, was in this instance on the offense. Excalibur cleaved three fingers quickly, exacting some recompense for loss of limb and appendage. The Red-Eyed Giant answered with a clumsy lunge that Arthur easily avoided. Then the king shuffled back out of range of four, then five, and soon, nine attempted strikes.

As the monster inhaled to recover and have another go, the Iron Bear now returned to form, making his countermoves, slashing hard at the thigh and then piercing Excalibur through the thing's throat from under the chin. The skull was so monstrously elongated that the legendary sword was absorbed to its cross-guard. A pungent, bloody, black brain matter flowed, covering the hilt's infamous elvish inscription, and down Arthur's arms.

Giving no thought to his stuck sword, nor the disgusting, viscous material glazed all over him, he kicked the beast to the ground. Dead. Immediately, he knelt to tend upon Bedwyr.

"If I had an enchanted faerie druid sword from the Garden of Eden, I could've done the same thing." The good-spirited Bedwyr did all he could to lessen the trauma of his friend, though he was the one maimed. He made the jest, smiled warmly, then passed hard into unconsciousness.

Twelve battles; never so much blood from one man!
Sixty raids, never so much!
So much blood!
So, so much!

The serrated line's placement was not accidental. The beast instinctively knew how to kill in a myriad of ways, and here it had sought to create a dramatic fount of spraying blood that would soak Arthur's friend and ensure that he would die in a crimson pool of his own life essence.

And spray it did. Men had passed away from much less blood than Bedwyr had already let.

"We have to get him to Gwyar," the king exclaimed, tearing his shirt sleeve into strips, doing all to slow the spraying blood.

Cai rushed ahead, and was already circling back to meet the king and his company as they approached the bridge into Caerleon.

"She is not here." Cai flung despairing and helpless hands towards the heavens.

"Gwyar gone. Vivien gone. Taliesin far, far away. I need a healer; I need a healer now," hollered Arthur, not at the men, but at the dismal situation.

Suddenly a hooded man of similar stature to the king manifested. Adorned in the sigils of the Ravens, but now abjured of the gold and pomp from his entry some days ago, the young man extended the right hand of fellowship to Arthur, unveiling his head from under hood with the left in one smooth and regal motion.

"My mother taught me several of her healing

arts, and I have received training on the Isle of Apples."

"Your mother?"

"Yes, uncle."

Though a stranger, Arthur saw familiar eyes looking back at him.

"Nephew." He took the offered hand warmly, yet with heightened angst and haste. Arthur then placed his dying friend in the hands of the young stallion who had, without reservation or guilt, been bedding his wife the queen for a fortnight.

Mordred had no special regard for Bedwyr, nor any of his neighbors, for he was by nature devoid of natural affection. But by nursing the Round Table Knight, he had cause; cause to remain at Caerleon, and with Gwenhwyfar.

Bedwyr lived.

Arthur departed immediately for the short ride over to Caermelyn, where the Round Table Companions were already assembling to consider their course against Itto Mawr.

With her husband gone, Gwen redeemed the time with Mordred, and savored it. She did things for him she had done for no man.

She cooked.

He helped her.

She sang.

He strummed the harp, providing tune and melody to harmonize with her suddenly soft and nurturing voice.

They read and held hands at tea.

They sculpted.

They talked. *Men and women never truly talk, but these did.*

The jubilance brought up from the grave long-dead memories of youth, from before she had been ruined by the Fae. There had been one other time, as a lass, that she had felt a similitude of this happiness, this thankful joy. *It had been with Lancelot at school. Was that a memory, or a dream?*

Arthur gave space of a few days for the Five Royal Tribes to assemble. Usually Gwyar or Gwenhwyfar took charge of the hospitality, being far superior in organization and style to the brawny gender, but Gwyar had vanished and Gwen had remained in Caerleon to host the nephew of the king and continue to look upon the convalescing knight, Bedwyr.

None found this curious, save Gwalchmai, who observed an extended glance between queen and nephew and liked it not.

Cobbling together meat and Illtud's choirs for but a few songs, Bedwini prayed for the assembly and the retired king, and Meurig opened the discussions.

As a constant, immutable principle, all Round Table assemblies were open; a clear looking-glass to the public. Nothing was done under a bushel, nothing in the closet. Murky politics are part of the fallen condition of man, and still ran their course amongst bishops, affluent landowners and local chieftains. But Arthur did all to combat this through his policies, hoping for, but never forcing, emulation.

The Round Table Companions met infrequently, save for sport or for quest, and the congregational spirit took every man, woman and child emotionally to a place of trauma and dread, reminding them too much of the Saxon Wars.

When the Saxons' presence had become a validated threat to the existence of the Cymry, Merlin had recommended the architecture of their defeat begin with study.

"Know your enemy first, and once you know

him, then will you know how to destroy him," the wizard would say.

Meurig reminded the assembly of this, and credited the quote to Merlin.

"I have another citation from the Merlin to share."

That familiar, feared yet coveted, low, metallic and mannish whispery voice, the one that paralyzed friend and foe, suddenly filled every story of the little castle that housed the Round Table.

"Maelgwn!" Arthur sprang from his seat, knocking his simple wooden throne (for all chairs at the round table were without respect of persons with one exception, and that not Arthur's) to the white marble floor, creating an irritating scratch and *skik*. He delivered a running hug upon the tall Briton.

"It has been too long since the best of us has been in these special halls. Suffer us to cheer and shout, for the Lancelot is come!"

Maelgwn disliked accolade and doting before men. But he had missed Arthur deeply as well, and thus suffered the shouts and songs of praise.

Finding a natural pause opened amongst the cheers, the hall teeming with renewed hope and vigor, the Bloodhound continued.

"When ambushed by the Italian Band, Merlin bade me pass along a request." Maelgwn looked upon Arthur, and Arthur's face acknowledged and remembered. "Nay, a command."

"Give us the Counselor of Britannia's words, Lancelot," beseeched Arthur's father.

"'Kill the Giants! Kill them all.'"

Though the words had been uttered years ago, that there was some connection was clear to all.

"With respect..." Maelgwn's posture further

commanded the ear of the room, his battle spike shimmering in dramatic symphony with his speech. "We have no time to figure out what these brutes are, neither have three months of theological committees to determine their origin." He looked at the bishops, and a few blushed at the imprecatory verbal arrow. "He has made his encampment at the base of Mallwyd in the shadow of Dinas Mawddwy. That means he is positioned to detain, to cut off, and to devastate from the very gateway into Gwynedd."

Opinions and worried grumblings here naturally flared. Maelgwn spoke authoritatively through the noise.

"Raise the armies, and by force of number, let us quickly remove this menace. I request of you," he said.

For King Arthur's part, he was still of a sore and vengeful disposition over Bedwyr's wicked wound, and wanted immediate and decisive action as well. Arthur added to Maelgwn's plea, and the Royal Tribes, Clans and Chieftains, already squabbling about feeding the confederacy and 'who would do what', gave a hasty consent.

The uplifting wave of Lancelot's entry had waned. Three years of peace were not enough; the collective soul of the Nation was yet war-torn, yet war-fatigued.

"We will resolve this quickly, kinsmen." The High King sought to comfort the people.

The twenty-six, less Bedwyr, plus forty thousand professional equestrian warriors, along with bards, choirs, carts of goods and every type of employ to the administering of war, hastened to Gwynedd.

***

A summer fog filled the field, yet the otherworldly being could apparently count swiftly and see all. Surveying the ranks, he mocked the Cymry.

"I see you are missing one."

Lancelot did not stand idle for pre-battle, verbal member-measuring matches. Already dismounted, and knowing that armor would be of no effect, he ran ahead of the army, shirtless with no helm and no covering save a small shield that was designed only to protect the hand and forearm. Besides this he had only his unique battle spike. Death was available from either end of it. It had the benefits of a spear with the length and ease of use of a sword, with a curved third blade as a fin, sheltering the leather-wrapped area where it was held.

Itto had gathered some followers of the sons of Adam, but they were servants (or slaves) and no warriors. Instead of giving cry for them to intercept the living instrument running upon them, the mighty man made a motion, pointing to where the wood opened at the base of the mount.

Another Giant appeared.

This one also had the features and appearance of a man, and was much shorter than Itto. Whether it was offspring or kin was unknown. The mortal mothers rarely survived giving birth to the gargantuan babes, who tore the womb apart and serrated the insides, culminating in unspeakable and horrific death.

The smaller Giant met Lancelot, and it did not fare well for the former.

Seeing the head of his own kind rolling as a great stone at his feet and the one and only Lancelot before him, Itto gave a cry that gave terror to the armies, causing even deer and rabbits to appear from the forest and make haste for the higher hills.

At the same time as a showdown was developing between Lancelot (who fully believed he would perish under the great fists of the monster, and in falling, would motivate the armies to use numbers to fell the Giant) and Itto, conflicts were arising amongst the Tribes.

A battle standard was clumsily knocked down.

Dirt was accidentally kicked upon supplies.

The Cornovii protested their flanked position, and eleven sub-tribes of the Ordovices each had two minor complaints (summing twenty-two squabbles).

Owain ap Urien, an impatient and undisciplined young man ever ready to spring up and fight (and especially disdainful of the Silure rank and file, even though he loved Arthur) was rebel-rousing.

Arthur, seeing the debacle developing before and around him (for this army, even when sharpened by the iron of steady war, had its internal skirmish and distress in delicate knitting of North and South), realized in an instant the reason that Itto had begun his bewitched siege against the Northern kingdom of Gwynedd.

"Think before you act."

Merlin was not there in the flesh, but his words lived. And as his words lived, thus did he.

"Maelgwn, please fall back – *fall back,* Maelgwn!" Arthur silenced the bards and the choirs, hushing music and song so the great knight could hear. "Maelgwn, fall back!"

Itto helped.

"I think the King of Kings calls you; go to him. I'll be here." Itto spoke with half mockery, half respect, for even devils and gods are quickly enamored with King Arthur Pendragon.

Maelgwn was irritated as he returned to the restless battle camp. He wanted to fight, not hear Arthur's revelation. His head crooked under the entrance of the pavilion, where an anxious friend awaited.

"You see this army? The cost of food, the complaints of the locals, who are your very people, the damage to property, the politics that will surely follow? By us even being here, he wins!" Arthur was articulate; Arthur was right. No army of such a magnitude had been assembled in over three years. It was a Golden Age disrupted. And this was the plan by Itto. *By whoever or whatever was controlling Itto.*

"One battle begets another. We must find another way," Arthur continued.

Some back-and-forth ensued, and as he and Maelgwn spoke, the Iron Bear remembered another of his old wizard's lessons. *"The past informs the present; NEVER forget your history."* At that moment, he knew his next steps.

Brutus and Gogmagog! Recalling how that ancient founder had spared thousands of men by challenging that Titan to single combat, the Pendragon knew his course. He would emulate his forefather and wrestle Itto Mawr, unarmed.

"No," said Maelgwn.

"It is the only way. No more war, Lancelot. We promised the people. We promised our children."

"Granted, but this is my land. Let me represent my people."

"He will only agree to terms with me. He wants my beard, not your locks." Lancelot never wore a beard. "He wants the High King." Arthur would not relent on his intents. The Round

Table Champion continued to protest until at last, Arthur was forced to do something rare and contrary to his nature. He *ordered* Lancelot to cease contesting him. He *ordered* the Son of Cadwallon Lawhir to fall in and support the words of his High King.

And the men of the Son of Cadwallon heard the order delivered with the tone of rebuke.

Maelgwn's bubble returned. Anger welled, but he said no more. His head brooded low, and he 'fell in' and walked three paces behind Arthur as the two alone went out to speak with Itto Mawr.

Prior to this, they informed Gwalchmai that he would be Wledig (as he was not qualified to be a Pendragon, being not of the paternal line of the Silures), should Arthur perish.

Itto's cheeks were flushed red, and the curl of his smile made his great grey beard lift and bounce; a jolly beard.

"Do you come to offer me your beard and end this conflict, Lord Arthur?"

"I desire no protracted war with you or whatever army you might raise." As though Itto needed an army. Arthur scratched at his short beard, sand-colored and well formed. "Neither will I give you my beard, which would represent surrender to you. That is an untenable selection. I offer this instead. Do you remember Brutus?"

Itto fell to both knees, had wine brought for the three, and listened to Arthur's history lesson and proposition.

Meanwhile the confederacy of Britons, growing impatient by the moment, asked for scouts and reports. And finally, with the sun soon to go into his chamber, word came.

"King Arthur fully disarmed of sword and scabbard, of dagger, of shield, of spear and cloak.

He has gone to the summit of a hill called Bwlch Y Groes," a messenger declared.

"To wrestle Itto Mawr," added another.

"To what end?!" the crowd charged.

"To the winner goes the binding and ultimate victory. If Arthur wins, the Giant shall return whence he came."

"And if the Titan prevails?" another asked.

Maelgwn interrupted the herald and finished the conversation. "Then Itto will have one more beard for his odd collection, and the Hawk of May will be our Battle Duke. There will be no fight today, no loss of life and no bloodshed. Because of Arthur, we have already won the day. Make ready to home."

Maelgwn's bubble stretched and stretched, as the seed of public slight and public offence found fertile soil in the complex man's soul. His only defense against the bubble was filling his mind with the debauchery and foul deeds he would commit to satisfy its demands. Then, he surmised, he would return to Camlan, or even visit the forests of Caledonia. He also planned then and there to found four churches and give gold to the bishops and to the bards.

Meanwhile, Arthur climbed the hill, talking to and getting acquainted with his opponent.

CHAPTER 7
The Cup is a Cup

Vivien looked over the mazer, of no comely or peculiar design; a simple wooden 'wide cup', the kind used by many cultures in Arabia and Palestine at the time of Christ. Its only distinguishing features were the many bite-marks and grooves where desperate partakers had surmised that, by biting bits of the cup, their chances of healing would increase.

The extraordinary Lady continued to abase herself for suppressing the Marian Mysteries. For so long had she fought the corruption and encroach of the Christian Church; she had forgotten the fundamental truth that Christ Himself would have nothing to do with it. And that the druids and the *real Christians* were *almost* on the same team.

Well, Merlin merged the teams, didn't he? she thought, looking at the Oak.

"You wanted this to come to me. How did you know Meirchion would compel Cadfan to break ground upon Enlli and put all these secrets at the shovel and plow of the Roman Church? You risked your mortal coil to learn the truth, to share your truth, and yet made a nonsensical trip north to get this, only to return south again to the ports.

And now I hold the Grail, far away from Cadfan and danger." She caressed the oaken prison where slept the wizard. "If I survive those who did this to you, my love..." She continued her conversation with one who could neither hear her nor give response. "You thought Lancelot would be here, unscathed and stained with Latin blood, ready to encompass me with an impenetrable shield of protection."

A singular, and swift, tear formed, escaping quickly over the curvature of her chin.

"You didn't drag my son along for you. You brought him here for me." She looked at Lancelot, sleeping soundly, his head wound freshly dressed. "How did you know all?!"

The one tear gathered a hundred friends.

"You are the Merlin of Britain. And there was none like you. Of course you did all this; you are *you.*"

The Lady of the Lake wept sorely.

***

To understand the Cup of Christ, it is imperative to understand dispensational truth. Israel was a nation gestated out of captivity and set apart with a specific purpose (namely, as God's agency for restitution and eviction of the current god of the world, the Devil), special covenants (amongst these being the Abrahamic, the Old and the New), and a promised inheritance (the earth), far different from the Gentile kingdoms.

God set apart this peculiar people to bring forth His word, His Son, His King. This required separation, contracts and perseverance. And, as an Israelite is a fallen man just as any other, God had to add the Law (over six hundred and twelve of them) to show them that they could not obtain right standing with Him on their own merits. The Law was not given to make them good, nor could it. Rather, it was made to stop their boastful mouths, showing them their need for a savior. For The Saviour. Though closest to the Creator of Heaven and earth, they were unbelieving and rebellious in their generations, always requiring signs and wonders. To this end, a longsuffering and patient God delivered the same. At sundry times and for specific purposes, to validate a Man, a Ministry or a Message, God either gave or allowed men to give signs. The benefit of these was not for those who believed, but as a witness to those weak of faith who believed not.

Nowhere did this aspect of the divine accord manifest more openly than in the manifold prophecies concerning the visitation of the long-awaited Messiah. When the Son of God arrived on the scene, His signature included casting out unclean spirits, causing the blind to see, and many other like miraculous manifestations, validating beyond disputation *who* He was, and *what* He was saying.

He came unto His own, and His own received Him not.

So great was to be the declaration of His Son's might and clarity of His arrival that the Father allowed one tenth of the disembodied spirits – the offspring of those Watchers who, in the Days of Noah, had lain with the daughters of men – to freely roam the earth, to gather in Jerusalem and, along with more recent ghosts from their kin slain by Joshua and Caleb, launch an attack on God's people. All for the express purpose of the Lord Jesus defeating them, casting thousands of them into the Deep, using only His word; a rehearsal for the epic conflict at the End of Days wherein all of them would fall to His sword.

And He healed the sick. In diverse ways and with diverse instruments, often to teach some great analogy or truth, not for the one being healed but, rather, for the unbelieving eyewitnesses.

Prior to going to His Cross to die for His people (for it was not known by men, angels or devils that the secret of the Cross contained the Son of Man becoming sin for all of mankind. This secret was well concealed for, had it been known, the enemy of God would have prevented, rather than caused, the Lord's death), the Lord supped with His twelve (after this pattern do the Cymry kings hold twelve elect men in close companionship with the king, and likewise do the greater kings keep twelve bards besides, for twelve is God's number for *governance)* in a patternistic feast which was a repeat of the meal the Lord had enjoyed with Melchizedek long millennia ago, and would be enjoyed again when the Lord joined His twelve Apostles in their City and their Kingdom in ages to come. The wine that the Lord blessed was symbolic of the blood of His New Covenant with Israel (which supplanted the Law of Moses, containing therein precious things it could not, having a better sacrifice, a better priesthood and a better hope). And thus the cup represented deep fellowship, healing and doctrine. To partake of one's cup is to partake of all that they are, all that they stand upon.

And Vivien, four hundred eighty and four years later, held that very cup.

After the Lord was crucified and received up into Heaven to sit at the right hand of the Father, His message and promises to Israel continued for a time through the efficacy of His twelve apostles, whom He gifted with powers, by the Holy Spirit, like unto Himself. Through handkerchiefs, through oils, through rods or other tangible talismans did they heal and cast out remnant unclean spirits. As sayeth the Scriptures, seas of ink could not contain all the good deeds that Jesus and His twelve did, and there were countless healings during the short season between the time of the crucifixion and the stoning of the Preacher, Steven. Here again, the signature gifts and healings were in acquiescence to an unbelieving and untoward generation; one that had murdered their own Saviour, even begging the heavens for a divine curse to be put upon their own heads, and their children's heads, thirsting for the guilt of His blood to be on their accounts. Though evil through and through, a merciful and longsuffering God allowed healings and miracles to continue, looking for but a remnant few to grant residency in the glorious kingdom of Heaven He had prepared for them.

But in parallel, God started to do something different.

He saved the chief of the rebellion.

A young Benjamite Pharisee, a Roman citizen born under the sign and sigil of the Bull, a *Hebrew of Hebrews* and a *Gentile of Gentiles* melded in one body, a picture of the Antichrist whose career was on projection to qualify for being he.

A blasphemer of the Holy Ghost and hunter of Messianic believers from the Church of Jerusalem. This man persecuted the early Church, scattering and wasting it.

Outside of the reach of salvation under Israel's gospel, God made of His greatest enemy an example for all times of His undiluted grace.

He saved Paul, ushering in a new dispensation. Grace.

As the believing Jews were sorely afraid of him and the unbelieving Jews hated and mocked their one-time kinsman, leader and ally, and as many Jews scattered at his own hand knew little about Jesus, the Lord allowed the signature gifts to continue, in Paul. Proving to the unbelieving Jews his Apostleship by many infallible proofs, he went forth, also using tokens and relics, and *cups*, to heal the sick.

As Paul's mysteries were slowly revealed while the sun set on Israel (for God no longer reckoned them as special amongst the nations, instead saving individuals on the merit of Christ's blood alone) for a time (for surely God will restore His favored nation, surely they will inherit their kingdom), God began to fill Heaven with the souls of those who trusted Paul's gospel. Whereas the earthly message required works and covenants and rules, Paul's Mystery required none of these things. An era and long hour of grace ensued and the signature gifts ceased, having no further purpose.

But the cessation was not permanent.

The sign-gifts waxed old (as did the Law), diminishing over time rather than vanishing in an instant. Some Jews were scattered as far as the Blessed Isles or other remote areas. For this cause, some of the supernatural characteristics of the earthly kingdom offering carried on as a trickling, drying stream.

And besides this, the Devil, who is cunning and crafty beyond comprehension, employs his favorite wile; namely, using *yesterday's truth as today's lies.* If he can get man caught up in doing and seeing (things necessary in the accompaniment of faith in times past, but wholly unnecessary this side of the finished work of the Cross), rather than trusting and resting, then he can do his greatest harm. More effective to hide the open manifestation of evil and rather encourage the soft and lethal deception of man-made religion. To this end, Satan himself was permitted to *charge* relics that had a past use for good, and repurpose them for evil; beguiling men to place their trust in things and spectacles that bring awe, forgetting the Lord who bought them.

Thus the Grail, with its deep representations of doctrine and fellowship and, in times past, healing and power, became a venerated and worshipped idol. Grail cults sprang forth all over Britannia and in Eire. Cauldrons came to represent fellowship, doctrine and power, only inverted and attached to powerful false goddesses instead of the Lord.

Blessed Mary foresaw this and did all to hide the relics until her Son would come again in the clouds, clothed with glory and victory, once again to enjoy the supper ritual with His twelve (and although she was sure any cup would do, Mary's heart was softened over *this cup*, for she was still a mother above all things and could not destroy it, though many times she tried).

Not only did the religious seek the Grail, but the very bones of Mary herself.

Knowing first the emptiness of idolatry and the unpredictable perversion and drunkenness of power, and then later learning the Pauline Mysteries as to *why* times had changed, a certain sect of the druids from Glamorgan made a pact with sweet Mary to forever hide these things.

And now Vivien held it in her hands as Lancelot lay healing from his wounds and, surely, the villains not far from the scene.

***

A woman of the strongest constitution, Vivien allocated herself no further time for weeping. She kissed once more the natural tomb that housed her most cherished friend and returned to the guest house (the very one where Lancelot had stumbled). Knowing he was too big for her to move, the Lady opted for combat instead of concealment. She hastened to the chamber within the northern-most peak of her castle: her very own bedchamber. A far more sophisticated and gaudy apartment than her simple little cottage at Llyn Fawr (tunnels, nay, an underground and underwater city, connected the Castle of the Lady of the Lake to her sacred lake in the Rhondda Valley, and other lakes besides, allowing her to travel much faster than waterborne vessel or steed between Cymru and the Continent). She opened a large silver chest, the perfect box to house its matching silvery contents.

Tiny faeries, who were as fireflies, zipped in orbiting spirals, helping her adorn herself in her very best armor, making a dramatic, albeit private, spectacle.

Vivien allotted herself one brief smile.

This set of protective wear was not just a breastplate with accompanying shin and forearm sleeves. This was *full armor* (rarely worn by the Cymry, even in full combat). It encompassed torso and pelvis in the mid-section, skin-tight and v-shaped. The whole of her collar and shoulder joints were encased within complex silver steel rivets. The ridges were finned high, peaking near the level of her chin. Similarly, fins surrounded the thigh, knee joints and the length of her calves as well. The helmet was a singular piece, formed to fit tightly over the nose; its sides formed two additional fins, guarding cheek to the base of the jaw, its only opening beneath the mouth down to the center of the throat.

Her under-armor was a soft but impenetrable white leather, with thousands of silver rings threading to compose a light mail. And she bore no cloak. To look upon the Lady was to look upon a silver-skinned goddess with not so much as a finger of pink flesh.

Merlin had known, at the dawn of the Saxon Wars, that the tribes and clans must not only possess the desperate bravery that accompanies the defense of one's soil, but also a skill that differentiated them from so many other cultures that had fallen under the insatiable Long Knife of the invading Germans. He witnessed Vivien's style when the priestesses would engage in sport or ceremony, and charged her to embark upon a great experiment. Seeing the superior balance and fluidity of the female warriors made famous by Buddug, or Boudica, of the Iceni Tribe (but spanning back millennia before), Merlin bade Vivien create a martial art that adapted her sect's *dance* with a radical commitment to counter-fighting (for the Saxons were ever overly aggressive and Merlin sought to take advantage of this, turning the imbalance of rage into a mortal liability).

Lastly, he requested awkwardly that the method must possess no enchantment or heathen arts. The common soldier, who farmed and practiced carpentry and often knew little of Jesus (save the pomp or corruption of the bishops who bore his name) and much more about fertility and harvest gods, would embrace such practices; but the rulers, wholly committed to the Christian faith, would reject it. Although priests and priestesses to the indigenous gods were found at all battles, using the power of music and hurling enchanted missives at the Saxon menace, the rank and file soldier could hardly incorporate those arts into the official martial art of the confederate armies.

The Lady understood the times and was mindful not to make the Cymry counter-fighting *dance* 'too pagan', and she and Merlin laughed oft at how even killing methods had been politicized.

The style of the armor she wore she had passed onto her foster-son, Lancelot, who in turn passed it onto the several Royal Clans and Tribes of the Cymry.

The Round Table Fellowship decided by consensus what to wear (aside from the standard shoulder shield that fasted cloak to armor) for each battle depending upon the terrain, whether the engagement was upon water or dry land, the weather, and lastly, for what manner of message they aimed to send to the enemy. On the occasions when all the confederated armies wore *this style of armor*, accompanied by their own sigils and banners, they were a brilliant, shining sea of silver stars, ready to shed blood with flawless grace. They sent the Saxons squirming back to the coasts, or to Germania, telling tales of immortals in magical armor; killing instruments who would not easily yield their lands, cattle or daughters.

And now the Lady who had taught the Britons how to fight, and to dress for a fight, encased in her full regalia, readied for a fight of her own.

And the Adder soon arrived for that fight.

It was evident that Merlin's body and scattered garments had been, as suspected, buried or taken. He searched around *Nimue's Fountain* and the branching streams it fed, still tinted crimson.

Nothing. The anti-druid then turned to the guesthouse.

The faeries had sealed every entrance so that he couldn't slay Lancelot in his slumber as a coward. Frustrated with fruitless pounding and kicking, he turned his attention on the castle, finding the great hall wide open.

Candlesticks and torches lit the hall, making it clear that either the Lady herself was in residence, or else one of her many guests was lodging there by happenstance. The Adder had a mazer to find and Giants to rouse, and whoever lit the hall knew something of the whereabouts of the Counselor of Britain's corpse and the contents of his robe. He hollered out disingenuous greetings, opting to be coy. He hollered once more, beseeching response from the master of the home. *Or the mistress.*

None make an entrance like the Lady of the Lake. Whether by climbing up the heart of a sacred lake through the roof-ceiling of her forebear's underwater cities, causing her to appear to literally *walk upon water,* or by instantaneously manifesting as a floating lily beneath the surface of a stream (using abilities to hold her breath for unnatural spans of time, on account of the traits passed down to her from her mother), always accompanied by flutes or harps or other chimes played by the water spirits who were her maidservants - always with drama and purpose she appeared.

This time the flames licked her silver skin, and the dusky sky made of her a frightful and beautiful shadow; a silver shadow on fire. The Lady of the Lake made a flaming torch.

She stood, or floated, upon a marble base atop the flat top of a spiral stairwell, a full story above her unwanted visitor.

"Is that you, Vivien?" The Wise Man saw the slenderness of the form; elsewise it could have surely been a Cymry warrior, clad for the field. At that moment her arm swiveled, and the Dynion Hysbys saw the likeness of a weapon he had recently seen spill Italian blood.

A battle dirk.

So the mother favors the same unique instrument as the son, he noted, clearly identifying Vivien, as none but Lancelot wielded such a shaft, and this person was far too small to be he.

"I am not your enemy. Merlin betrayed us all and would have stamped out our kind forever with his grace message. He aims to end religion. Merlin is your enemy; we answer to the same council, Lady!"

How she was so soon at his throat is unknowable. She neither descended the stairwell, nor did she fly. At the outrage of the traitor uttering the name of her beloved twice, she would not suffer the black-robed shaman to speak it again.

"We are Cymry. We answer to no council. We bow before no league of that which congresses in murky places, laboring shamefully in the dark to enslave men. We are a country of laws and not of men. As our sovereign, the High King himself, decrees" – she pressed the spike into the side of the neck, the pressure causing a wincing push of panicked air – "let men worship what gods they will, only that they don't kill their neighbors for it."

The Adder's walking stick had a head that was hard onyx with an inverted and blasphemous Awen engraved over its crown. With both of Vivien's hands gripping the battle spike, he made a desperate swing towards her knees.

The fabled silver armor made this a purposeless strike, but to anger the Lady. The broken stick clacked and clapped along the stone floor, resting upon a great yellow rug.

Vivien countered with a direct thrust to the fleshy part of the intruder's right shoulder, stabbing and turning the weapon with surgical violence.

His black robe became soaked with blood, quickly.

Then she clipped his left heel. Great screams bounced through the hall, the walls protesting by throwing them back at their source.

Lancelot had used this technique hundreds of times. By taking a right arm and a left leg, no weight distribution was available, no side could be favored. As a result, the opponent, processing his plight, just stood there, ripe for a quick kill.

The Lady snatched at the nape of his robe and pulled The Adder close. Leaving her helmet on, dropping her voice with authoritative indignation, she exclaimed, "Whatever your council did to my Merlin is of no god. You will live, should you escape the vast Wood of Broceliande, to tell your master that the Council will never have that which they seek." Playing with her bleeding prey, the Lady unveiled the Cup in all its simple splendor. "Now make haste to leave this place, lest you bleed out."

And haste he made, but not before turning just beyond the gate to mumble, "I overheard much during Merlin's final initiation." Followed by a mocking shout: "Why do you help men, when you are but the child of the woeful damned? YOU ARE DAMNED!"

Undaunted by his goad, she responded. "If you have only just now learned this, your thirty-

and-nine years of training must be no greater than oils and charms and marketplace tricks."

He cursed her, still in a limping and lumbering run, gushing blood.

"YOU ARE DAMNED!"

***

Vivien helped restore Maelgwn, caring for and spending time with him until Gwalchmai arrived to fetch away the great warrior to help him escort Gwenhwyfar ferch Ogyrfan Fawr to be queried of Meurig and Onbrawst.

Although having Maelgwn alone with Gwenhwyfar presented risk, greater was the risk that more of the Council of Nine's lapdogs would follow. *Would they leave? Or would they continue to besiege her estate until at last she was overwhelmed and the Cup of Christ lost*? In the end, she calculated that the secret order was a far greater threat than her foster-son's erratic appetites.

Thus, she begged the Hawk of May take the contents of Merlin's pouch, providing no other direction than to deliver it privily to his mother, Gwyar, who was Morgaine of the Faeries and the Lady of the Isle of Apples. Vivien gave Gwalchmai knowledge of secret and seemingly nonsensical paths to conceal his discovery without compromising speed.

Thus, Gwalchmai would bear the Grail to Morgaine.

And thus Lancelot would escort the future queen to Arthur, alone.

Vivien disappeared into exile. She was not to be seen again by the world of men, save for her foster-son, who would from time to time ensure she did well, for many years.

CHAPTER 8
The Infidelity Punisher

The raven-haired Queen Gwenhwyfar, whose tiny hands beheld the face whose large eyes beheld their mirror, whose repaired heart beheld its equal, whispered morosely and gravely to her true love.

"Mordred. You cannot remain here. This cannot endure."

His throat undulated and his mouth became dry. Bereft of sound, his *'cry-talking'*, with broken spaces betwixt each word, could muster little protest.

Through simple deduction, the lovers would be discovered. Their capital crime exposed.

Gwyar's absence.

The undue time nursing Bedwyr, who was mending rapidly.

The return of the king.

Gwalchmai's investigative looks.

The ongoing and unrepentant treasonous acts enjoyed by the covert couple risked ruining the only other thing they coveted in this life. Even their love and passion could not blind this aim. An aim they had shared in perfect unison well before they had met: the rule of Cymru.

Rule without Arthur.

Gwenhwyfar formerly had wanted power for its own sake. To do as she pleased, when she pleased, *with whom she pleased*, minus the cords of the Christian King.

Mordred, like his mother, had at first been drawn to the darker paths of Rhiannon and Hafgan. And he fancied the dragon god Hu. From his youth, he had been obsessed with categorizing the otherworldly beings and documenting their attributes in beautiful Latin script, which he had learned of his father King Llew and his grandfather, Meirchion. Mordred had cataloged four major categories, which he grouped as:

The people from the sky or the far-off north;

Their offspring with the daughters of men;

The spirits of these offspring, which he rendered as 'demons';

Elemental spirits.

Having skill of insight and foreknowledge just as otherworldly as the creatures he sketched on scrolls and in drawings and scripts, Mordred began to disregard the pomp and awe of his native gods. Before the age of sixteen, the lad had already concluded that the pantheon of Cymreig and Goidelic deities were nothing more than the worship of demons by the fearful and the opportunistic. This he did without reading one line of Scripture. His powerful mother worshipped, or was, a *real goddess,* and he could not discuss this with her for the dread of offending her.

Also like his mother, Mordred wed into a Northern family with Roman Catholic leanings and fidelities.

He was fond of, but did not love, the fair and pious Kwyllog ferch Caw. But through the union of the house of Cynfarch with the house of Caw, the offspring of Mordred would render the North finally stable, at last restored to the glory of those long-ago years, after Rome and before the Boar, where they had been equal in power, right and might to the Silures of the South. *And the house of Mordred even branched back to the line of Meurig through Gwyar, making a singularly unique case for a Pendragon based in the North.*

Thus, following the Catholic path, albeit nominally, was the only course. The North and their Royal Clans stabilized by religious Rome, versus the South and their Royal Clans stabilized by the primitive Church of the Britons and by the Merlin and his boy-king. *And Merlin had been missing three and more years.*

And so, as Mordred suffered the silliness of the Romish priests and dabbled with his demons, an emptiness grew within, of largely unknown origin.

This abyss was replenished when King Arthur and Queen Gwenhwyfar I sent their son, the prince Amr, for fosterage and training in the northern coasts. The youths were assigned the same patrols, and instant bonds were forged. A friend closer than a brother, Mordred found joy in his drab life in the person of Amr.

Then, by chance, the sharp dagger of a soot-blackened malefactor of no significance to anyone took Amr from Mordred in a senseless and meaningless act of murder.

This brought a finality of confirmation that justice was an illusion and that men were the playthings of demons and the pets of sky creatures. Mordred drank the lie, gulping the meaninglessness of existence. *Men were as cattle, and the less miserable of the cattle were the cattle allotted rule over other cattle.*

For this cause Mordred became a dark and

empty thing, positioning and posturing quietly, as an adder glides within the thrush. A man of no reputation, and overlooked by the glowing and wildly popular Gwalchmai and his other speckled and sparkling brothers – Aggravaine, Gareth and Gaheris (all who served Arthur and his Summer Kingdom with disgustingly consistent virtue and honor) – Mordred was a shadow man in the kingdoms of Cymru.

But for his lack of charisma, the politicians and priests would have long ago truly considered that the eldest son of Gwyar had the better claim to succeed Arthur, whose new wife had yet to give him sons.

And Simon Magus paid him no regard besides.

Embarrassed that he had even baptized himself in gold to appear as if from Heaven, to bedazzle and impress (or, if this failed, to bully and badger) the High King, a disgust for the object of his love's cuckold gestated.

If not now, then in the fullness of times will my sons qualify to replace you; the South will fall. And then I will consume my sons as a Cronos, and rule all of Britannia, and the Emerald Isles, and the Continent besides.

Even in the fantasies unfolding in his mind, there was never a thought that he could actually defeat Arthur.

Mordred removed her hands from his cheeks softly, then clasped them taut. "I will not leave your side."

"You must."

"Gwen."

"Mordred, my love." What her past had arrested, love had wrought. In her third decade, she at last possessed what blossoms in most women by seventeen: wisdom and prudence.

The sensual creature who had once sought only to consume and devour had now given way to a soft-spoken, powerful lady, desperately trapped in an unwinnable battle. She began to speak to Mordred of *endurance* and patience. Of how rulers, even as mighty as Arthur, fall to injury, lose their vitality or throne. Where Mordred would blaze the embers of civil war and leave but a smoldering heap upon which to rule, Gwyar would have him make the intentional choice to be born again; to be a charismatic, kind and heroic noble that so captivated the Tribes, the bishops and the landholders that Gwalchmai would be supplanted, and the eldest of Arthur's sister's sons would naturally be promoted to heir.

Then, should the king fall ill or suffer tragedy, there would be hope that the people would accept Mordred as a stand-in, though married, as a titular benefactor to Gwenhwyfar.

She and Mordred never quarreled, but found no consensus; when they parted they were respectfully and carefully considering the views and possibilities put forth by the other. Both knowing that they would have their field and farmhouse whenever fortune and time smiled on their infidelity. Both knowing that they would have to wear the mask of faithful spouse to Kwyllog and to Arthur.

But could so strong a love even feign a neighborly church kiss, let alone lie with another?

***

Fortune and time did not smile on scores of other young lovers who entered into adultery or infidelity. The thing that was in Gwyar (or part of Gwyar) had secured an almost permanent residence in the forefront of her mind and spirit. Using her anger and confusion to take her vengeful mind perpetually under the executioner's tent, where exotic killing instruments were spread before her upon a great table in her mind's eye, she gave herself to no other occupation than luring the guilty into the forest that she, the goddess, might visit justice on them more ferocious than a priest or God Himself could construct.

She had fashioned a garment after her custom, upon which, starting at her heart and spanning the length of her torso, was sewn a black spider with a red hourglass-dyed abdomen, in the concentric knot-work style of her kind. A singular grey piece that fit all but her feet and hands. Her black hair, which she had conformed to the conservative fashions of court, was yet again a thousand grey and black marble beads, such that bead and lock were indistinguishable.

Thus the Lady of the Lake and the Lady of Avalon were self-exiled in the same vast enchanted wood of Broceliande; the one for her role in committing a murder, the other for the purpose *of* committing murder. And, at that, many murders.

Morgaine of the Faeries made use of a method of scrying that involved a large basin finished with black glass filled with still, green, spring water. Through her unmatched skill working these arts, it was most effortless for her to discover or *see* adulterers, or uncover the untoward deeds of adulteresses. Once discovered, she sent familiar spirits sheathed in the skin of Fire Salamanders to influence the minds of the lovers, enticing them with irresistible drawings to an exciting, exhilarating and forbidden indulgence of the flesh in mystical and romantic Little Britain.

With her snug little circular huts for the

modest and her large privy estates for the rich, and her waterfalls and lakes, her vineyards and intoxicating apples, her flowers and sunsets and, above all, her enchanted woods, Brittany herself was a seductress; an alluring, irresistible bosom for lovers.

Morgaine's warty and crested newts (the female salamander lacked a crest, being identified by an orange stripe along her lower back or tail) slithered as unknown bedmates into where the lovers would lie, combining the newts' love juices with their treacherous emulsions. The resultant mixture would create a toxin that decreased the mind's defenses, making it moldable, lacking in discernment, subject to suggestion – especially where carnal pleasures and impulse were concerned.

The salamander would create in the lovers an unquenchable flame only to be extinguished by traveling, whether near or far, to the romps of Broceliande. The spirit within the crawling thing would whisper all through the night until, at last, at the mercy of their sin and poisoning, they would make for holiday in Little Britain, for the dark spider Morgaine.

Forgetting her station and her vows, Morgaine could see not but Gwenhwyfar ferch Ogyrfan betraying her brother, could feel not but her brother betrayed by her son. She did not often agree with Arthur's strict neutrality when it came to matters of gods and religion, nor his insistence on combatting the corruption of central overreach, hurting her deeply when he had refused to stop Rome from invading Ynys Enlli with their church and pilgrims.

But Arthur was loyal.

But Arthur respected women.

But Arthur did not go a-whoring.

But Arthur did not seek a damsel, or even a dally.

He had chosen his love and loved his choice.

Morgaine intimately respected the virtue of her brother King Arthur, the erotic hauntings of his past notwithstanding. It pained the sorceress that she herself was the one, guised in ritual veneer, within a grove, in a cave, who had robbed him of the same.

Guilt, respect, perversion and above all the failings of the mortal condition, love of Cymru bound the witch to the boy-king and she came under conviction solid as brick, inseparable as set mortar; if a terminal clash was inevitable between son and brother, Morgaine would choose brother. She favored Arthur above Mordred – though she loved them both.

And she would punish others as a proxy for her son. Using her rage in adjudication of Gwen and Mordred's high crimes upon wayward lovers, she made no grand speeches, no riddles or sleight of wordplay upon her victims ere she killed them. Simple and direct, she would cry in a whisper, "How would your spouse feel?"

And then she would add them to a stack of skeletons, a bony altar of judgment.

CHAPTER 9
All the Snakes have Driven Themselves out of Cymru

"Are you prepared to die, Lord Arthur?"

The weight of the Giant's hand upon Arthur's shoulder was as six horses tethered to the stony, domed vault of a church, all concentrated upon one joint, which crackled and shifted in protest. The Pendragon winced, and his mind gasped at the feat that lay ahead. *How do I find victory this time?* These were hard thoughts for an undefeated warrior. One direct blow from Itto Gawr would be deformity at best and at worst, and more likely, the gruesome death of the mighty ruler of the Britons.

Curiously, the Giant's query was not threatening, nor in the pitch and manner that pricks the inception of combat. It sounded rather like the deep discussions that best friends have over cider, as if the Giant was genuinely interested in Arthur's personal peace with mortality.

The Merlin had taught Arthur to always answer as a mirror, except when the opponent is angry (and then with firm confidence, salted with grace and understanding). When they are jolly, be jolly in return; when grave, recompense with gravity. When mourning, cry with those who mourn.

Following the lesson in this scenario, Arthur was contemplative. And honest.

"I am not prepared to die."

"Oh?" Itto's left hand combed at his great beard, desperate to learn more of this great man.

"Not for myself, but for those to whom I am accountable. I bear a great weight" - here the Pendragon sought an opening for humor, shifting uncomfortably and giving an audible groan - "a burden nearly as heavy as your great hand upon my tiny shoulder."

Though his face seemed to be up above the clouds and his head just below the ceiling of the firmament, Arthur was almost sure he saw a blush. And a smile.

The shy laugh confirmed the king's assumption.

"Of course, of course. I am sorry." Itto removed his hand, causing Arthur to expel great breaths of relief, at once feeling several stones lighter. "I have walked this earth since not long after Noah's Flood. I've collected beards, gotten and lost many sons, vanquished armies, won damsels and raised the horn of victory scores of times. Scores. I have seen the best of men, and men's evil worst. And I tell you, Lord Arthur, something is afoot that rivals the malevolence from before the Flood."

"And when did your walks from ancient of days bring you to Gwynedd? For during the sum of the Saxon Wars, and yet by these three and one-half years of summer, how did someone, anyone, not - well," Arthur maintained a humorous, albeit timid, tenor, *"see you?"* Arthur's neck ached from looking straight up, only to see the braided grey beard swinging down as a great rope from Heaven.

"Cymru is my homeland!" Whilst conversing, the two had come to the peak of Bwlch y Groes, upon which opened a small plain cleared of trees, with no obstacles save a few large, craggy rocks like natural borders, making a rim along the cliff of the mount.

The perfect setting for the two actors to recreate the drama of King Brutus and King Gogmagog.

Itto inhaled the view, still struck by awe after so many lifetimes enjoying the valleys spreading below. For the beauty of Cymru; of waterfalls and woods, of mysterious caves and caverns under the ground and yet in the waters, the winding vales and rocky gorges, the greens and blues found in no other land. Cymru brought wonderment and reverence, even to the otherworldly beings.

He continued. "I don't know where my father came from, other than that it was from somewhere called *the remote North*. As for my mother, I knew her not, only that she was a princess of striking beauty from Machynlleth, less than a morning's walk from here." Now Itto recompensed a laugh. "Or less than an hour, with the stride of these walkers." Bending them, he made a stool of a tree stump that had the circumference of the Sun, and sat. It was humid and the mighty thing sweated as pools that, when meeting with the dirt, immediately caused the dry summer ground to be as a muddy creek or farmer's trench. Wringing buckets of salty muck from his beard, he explained to Arthur things that not even Merlin had known.

"Know you how that our Isles have hundreds of stone circles and faerie rings, or in some cases Giant rings, and that the scholars and scribes rumor more here in Cymru and Eire than anywhere else the world over?"

"My friend taught me as much, aye."

"The Merlin? Of course. I shall come back to the subject of your friend. I came to learn that once, all land masses were one great breadth of earth; these were in the days of a man called Peleg, and his generation marks the time that the High God broke apart the nations. Thousands of diverse kinds of damnable things like me were either isolated, or subsequently fled here, because the Isles, when they were not Isles, were located near the northern strongholds of the Giants near the north, or center of the earth.

"As the land mass was broken up, the residue became the Blessed Isles in the Sea, upon which we now stand.

"That the stone circles are as the sands of the sea is because each of them represents a principle that threads all spirituality, and all religion: *"As Above, So Below"*. Every circle down here represents a formation of stars, or a tracing of their courses up there." One of Itto's six fingers pointed to the heavens. Arthur was transfigured back to his youth, when Illtud or Merlin would teach on these things. Hundreds of questions rushed into his mind, and he couldn't wait to hear more. "The Fae dance for the stars and build circles for the stars, cones of ethereal power where men ought never to tread. Giants erect gargantuan stone circles, bury their dead, and perform rituals to the very same stars."

"The legends say that Giants and the Fae are bitter rivals."

"Aye. But mark and remember the tale of Brutus and Gogmagog, Lord Arthur." Once more, the Giant pointed to the skies. "They may hate each other, but they have the same ancestry, the same stars, the same angels! And there is more." Now Itto stood, releasing another spout of sweat that muddied the surrounding dirt. "Many of these hills, in what the Romans called *the Celtic Wilds*, are where some of my kind sleep. The armies of Brutus, and other migrations of men, decimated our numbers and then, above five hundred years ago, Jesus came into and went out of the world of men."

Arthur minded not the stench and sweaty mud. He had to hear more, wishing that he and the great man towering above were enjoying cider together. The way Itto moved his hands in gestures, accompanying his oratory, impressed Arthur. Had he not wanted Arthur's beard and been moved to displace the Northern princes, the monster and the king were meet to be great friends. "And what did the Lord do?!" Arthur asked, now inquisitive as a small child.

"Within about a generation of His ascension, we began to simply go to the caves, enclaves or other dark places, some as deep as the Abyss itself, and fall into long, irresistible slumber. A sleep like death, yet not dead.

"Now, I don't understand all of this, and only share what I have gathered over too many lifetimes. It would seem that we were only ever allowed to draw breath in the first place to show the power of God's Son in defeating us. Beasts for the Hero to slay. Or, from another perspective: what the Fallen Ones meant for evil, God repurposed for good. And it would seem that we were meant to sleep, that we are *reserved* for a similar future purpose as well."

Here Arthur exercised his uncanny gift of deduction.

"So, if you are awake, then…"

"Correct; the end of the world is nigh. Or someone would us have, through their arcane arts, to make it as so."

"But there have been Giants and monsters, though rare, since the time of Jesus."

"I concur, Lord Arthur. We are only ever roused by some dark science or occultic arts, and these exceptions are so isolated as to be off the table as part of God's plan for the Ages. Anomalies. Moreover, some of the small descendants of our kind do walk amongst us. Most are inactive. Some engage in minor mischief, in service to the leaders of men who likewise render themselves sons of gods."

The discourse here caused Arthur to think towards his father-in-law, the Chief Ogyrfan.

Itto continued. "This 'unwilling awakening' is different, and a thousand times graver. This time, a black-robed druid brought me from the Deep. Through his spells, he put it into my mind so to see dozens more made to rise, and his enchantment drives me to kill all, even you, to devour and drink blood, making hell on earth before the Son of Man comes with His elect angels to send me unto my place.

"I think, Lord Arthur, that Merlin may have known something of the plans of these druids to bring about the end of the Age, and that calamity befell him for this cause."

The bewitchment that drove Itto to seek and kill and destroy welled, a miserable, gentile spirit with no soul, under witchcraft from the pit of Hell, driving and harassing and compelling him.

"Ask me if I am prepared to die," he beseeched the king.

"Are you, my friend Itto Gawr, prepared to die?"

Being rendered as *friend* by the one for whom

he had such regard greatly aided him in mustering the courage to finish his course. "Do you see those stones near the cliff?"

Arthur turned and then verified the outlay of the field of battle. "I do."

"When I rush upon you, I pray you have the speed of Lancelot. Roll to the side of my wounded ankle."

Arthur withdrew himself, gave ground to near the cliff, and spake these words, which live on in the songs of the bards. They memorialize the great thing done by Itto, who could have slain the king, but spared him, and thus the whole of Cymru.

The quote did something greater than exercising mercy; it gave the monster humanity.

"Itto Gawr is the bravest *man* King Arthur has *ever* known," said the Pendragon.

Hearing this, a contented and gaping smile developed under the perfect grey beard, coinciding with the very moment he made his rush upon the king. Missing the mark, he stumbled upon the stones, plunging from a height that rivaled the fall of his kinsman Gogmagog.

And thus the Giant resisted the dark power and died for the dream of Caermelyn and the hope of King Arthur, whom he had come to revere deeply.

***

The stanzas, poetries and ballad-songs of the bards spread rapidly throughout Cymru and abroad, celebrating how Arthur, far from idle in the Britons' era of tranquility, had saved the North and all of Britannia from the menace of Itto Gawr.

The Saxon slayer now the Mighty Giant Hunter.

Whereas many had prognosticated that Baedan would be the height of his star, Arthur was becoming as popular as Jesus.

But not all loved the Silure king.

That such a victory was enjoyed in the lands of Caw and Meirchion and Cynfarch *and Maelgwn* further unified some of the Ravens, whose affection for the High King, who had risked all to come champion them, intensified. However, others viewed it as an insult, a condescending example of the fact that once again the race of Silures had had to do what they could not. *A protective uncle who kills the wolves only when the village can see him pound upon his chest before all.*

And of course those who coveted the profits of war loathed his act of single combat mitigating loss of life, and expenses. And debt.

As for Maelgwn Gwynedd, he had wanted this rare moment, *the greatest warrior versus the greatest threat,* to champion his people. His credibility waxed and waned with the ebb and flow of his fractured personages and roving residences. For the first time ever, he empathized with the negative sentiments from the leaders of the Old North.

Stealing away to one of the tiny islands apart from the mainland, his bubble overcame him, resulting in his engaging in a wine-soaked orgy with flesh of his own kind (for his unbridled lust was not limited in scope to just women). Trying to slay himself afterwards with Merlin's ghostly dagger, he bled much, and slept long, but died not.

Taliesin learned of the untoward acts and chastised Maelgwn unrelentingly for his wanton thirsts and for the sake of his children, who were bastard sons and daughters of either the painted

Picts or deflowered Cymry girls.

Because the bubble burst and went to its temporary abode, and not for Taliesin's calls for repentance, Maelgwn was overcome with great guilt (though he showed little emotion when alone, and none in public). Instead, he established six chapels under the Bishopric of Llandaff, and gave himself to the memorization of hundreds of additional Scripture verses to temper his flesh.

Mordred scraped himself from Gwen (for the two were as one flesh) and returned to his father's lands, determined to feign being a *good man* to rival Gwalchmai. To earn a seat at the Round Table, should one of the twenty-and-four retire or pass on, to make an unspoken case for the throne.

Gwen II faced an impossible personal and political quandary. The tribes wanted male heirs from their famed liege and their famed liege wanted daily to lie with his wife, for she was his life's love and Arthur had discovered nothing of Gwen's infidelity. Since coming to Caerleon to be queen, she had forced herself upon a dozen men, continually violating the king's bedchamber and her own body with their members. Now a part of her died each time her own husband lay with her. *Now it was adultery against Mordred, the only man she would have talk to her, let alone touch her painted body.*

Her whole life was a ruse and a deception; formerly of want, now of necessity.

But for how long? There were no wars, no invaders, and only the occasional Giant, which Arthur and Gwalchmai would quickly vanquish.

Mordred and Gwenhwyfar II wove a yarn about Gwyar being urgently called away to provide nursing for a dying kinsman of her estranged spouse so that Arthur would have no cause to investigate her abrupt exit from Caerleon. Though, during her time at court, Gwyar and Arthur had grown closer, theirs was the kind of relationship where many moons could pass without letter or visit, then, when at last they met again, to resume as if there had been no interruption. Moreover, the distraction of finally getting to have the woman he had always wanted created a sort of fog that separated brother and sister.

And so, a year became three, and then two more, and Cymru approached the median of twenty years of peace and greatness. *Halfway through the Golden Age*. And a golden light it was, one of the too few chapters in the generations of Man where liberty, prosperity, and peace reigned. The stains of Saxon blood, of invasion, violation and constant terror, faded upon a satin of Cymreig greatness.

But, as the common person had joy in recreation, occupation and procreation, the rulers toiled with actual monsters roaming the countryside, with territorial tensions, with vain genealogies, with threats both external and of their own design. The heaven on earth was hell to maintain.

And Gwyar, now so many years a spider, had herself woven a hell of her own. She did not lure, trap and kill wayward unfaithful lovers for the sum of this time. At the first, oft; later, intermittently; at the last, seldom. Rather, she would brood and curse all that was called good for the despair that she could neither tell her brother of his harlot's treachery by her own son, nor stand with her immoral son against her righteous brother.

After some time, the days came where she simply hated infidelity, but hated solitude more.

Thus the same enchantress who had once coveted her days alone on Ynys Enlli tending plants and birds, streams and orchards, sulked about, lonely, ever longing for a tea, a cider, or a walk with her sons, her brother or Vivien.

Vivien!

Mother!

The Lady of Lake.

She goes as the wind, where she listeth, but could she have remained here all these years? Broceliande was vast as it was mysterious, its breadth that of a small country. The silvery mistress had been neither seen nor even whispered of during Gwyar's years at court. Had she returned to the affairs of men or, like Gwyar, had she convicted herself of some personal crime, likely in connection to whatever conspiracy and malevolence had killed the Merlin, handing down a strong sentence of shackles of loneliness far away from all? Alone with sins and mistakes, regret her ever-companion…

If Gwyar could practice scrying to discover strangers, surely her *Sight* could discover her foster-mother.

"Merlin's pouch!" she hollered aloud, to none save an attentive audience of owls and salamanders.

The contents of the haversack were well known to Gwyar; protecting it was part of her function as Lady of Avalon, and it was now safely concealed and under her control. The worn leather that held it would now be the conduit for finding the Lady of the Lake, for surely she had touched it while giving the Cup to Gwalchmai.

It was an early winter morning when she exercised the scrying basin. The waters, once still, began to swirl, changing from green to the darkest blue. Swirling, swirling and thrice more; then still as a looking-glass it became. Clipping five tiny shavings from the strap of the pouch, she gently laid them upon the looking-glass and spoke her imprecations, charging the god of forces to guide her eyes and make true their aim.

Gwyar's head jerked up from the basin, startled at her own folly.

"All this sorcery and magick, and lo, the Lady is simply home in her estate!" Gwyar laughed. At herself. "Perhaps reason and logic first before bothering the spirits, eh?" She could have sworn that the owls also mocked her with well-timed hooting.

Then her light moment became weighted, as her eyes were again drawn to the scrying bowl. Vivien's castle was still apparent, and the Lady sweeping and singing and of warm disposition as clear in vision as if she were in flesh. The scene widened, broadening further and then narrowing rapidly to fix upon a tree of oak which seemed somehow the elder of its neighbors; the ancient of the ancient oaks. *Next to?* – nay, *in* the oak was the form of a person revealed.

Gwyar peered hard. Perhaps a servant of Vivien's estate had also touched the pouch and had thus been brought into view? Perhaps it was an apparition or the incessant mischief of the Fae, who loved to bewilder and distract by making game and sport of the serious affairs of men.

Yet it was none of these things.

'Twas the form of a man – yet only in form, as he was enveloped by an orb of the whitest light.

"Merlin?" The words were an involuntary mutter, no more.

The still waters swirled, this time in reverse. Thrice and thrice again, and then still again; the scrying bowl would reveal no more.

Though the finding her was swift, the journey was slow. For the woods seemed infinite. Vast Broceliande.

When Gwyar finally approached the archway to the fore-entry, one hundred and seventy thousand petite faeries illuminated the path, lighting each of her steps and then disappearing with the next, as though fireflies with appetites for dramatic entry.

If only harps and Illtud's choirs accompanied this, she mused.

The otherworldly beings, as a swarm of bees, labored in concert to open the heavy double-doors and then burst asunder again to their places, finding perfect sockets from which to illuminate the great hall.

Standing at the base of the spiral stairway, in the self-same spot where had stood The Adder so many years ago, now stood legend's most infamous black witch, looking straight up at legend's most revered white witch; hair perfect, dress perfect, face glittering and shimmering, looking down on her foster-daughter with a smile so bright that the little faeries became jealous and dimmed, then chuckled and shone again, straining to compete.

After an embrace that stopped time and seemingly healed the world, *or at least their world,* the Lady of the Lake started.

Influenced by growing years in Brittany, she asked, "And how is Arthur's *Camelot,* daughter?" Correcting her own diction and accent, she restated, "*Caermelyn.* How is Arthur's golden fortress and glorious kingdom?"

"Camelot. I like how that feels upon the tongue," replied Morgaine. "Oh, I really like it! I feel that *Camelot* will be the word that long endures, outliving us in bardic ballads and minstrel's songs." Taking her foster-mother by both hands, she giggled. "Camelot shines, Mother, and freedom yet shines with her!" Seeing through the joy of reunion and discovering the melancholy that was in the Mistress, Morgaine sought out words of comfort to lend to the great Lady.

"You are the very foundation of Arthur's Camelot." Morgaine retained one hand, using the other to guide a stroll. "Excalibur, the Sword of Power." The little helpers, engrossed in the conversation, shone brighter still, making a similitude of the sword and emulating its legendary slashing whistle, lending drama to Morgaine's kind and edifying compliment. "Forged from the saber of angels that protected knowledge and access to eternal life when Man left his first estate, the authority and virility of the Land, whose holder is rightful king, whose granter was" – again Morgaine gave a sprawling grin, perfect white teeth emerging as the sunrise – "you, Vivien."

"And now I hear whispers that priests are the kingmakers and that the Tribes have no voice save that of the local bishops, themselves royalty with no interest but to hold power and land. And more, that the druids grow few and weak and that only the vulgar superstitions of the Dynion Hysbys hold sway."

"Well, your political fervor has not diminished," quipped Morgaine, still all beams.

More like pithy dialogue ensued for the space of about half an hour, and then the Lady of the Lake cut to the quick.

"I cannot return to Cymru, daughter."

Morgaine's rejoicing turned to tears, and the

sun set on her grin. "You cannot return, and I know not why you even left. It has been ten years."

The witches' walk had brought the two out along the stony outdoor spiral surrounding the turret of a high tower. No faeries provided light here, with only the starry onlookers above winking and giving sporadic and stingy illumination betwixt and between nighttime clouds.

"I am held hostage by an old, old man." Vivien's words were cryptic. For the residue of guilt. And for Morgaine's protection. Should she know all, she could be counted an accomplice after the deed, and her life be put in great peril (though Vivien did reckon that it would take Lancelot and a small army to vanquish the little woman, full of darkness and kindness, adorned in black from head to foot, before her).

"You are the Lady of Lake and answer to no man!" Morgaine tried the lever of feminine resilience and pride.

The trap sprang not.

Temperate and guarded, Vivien continued.

"I bargained with the only thing that had real power. The flesh betwixt a woman's legs."

Morgaine's eyebrow lifted. "Bargained for what?"

"To preserve our goddess. To ensure that she outlives Rome." Vivien looked down into the abyss of the treetops below.

The dark enchantress was becoming impatient, and now bewildered, with the scrambled discourse of her polar mistress. An interruption was offered: "Our goddess cannot die. She is eternal."

At this intentionally naïve untruth, the Lady of the Lake pressed upon Morgaine's heart, her fingertips greeting the thing that was in, or was part of, or was, Gwyar. "My little Queen of the Faeries, you know this is not so. Many of the old gods died in the waters from above the heavens, and many more have had their flames at last exhausted." The palm joined the fingertips and pressed harder. "And some use occultic tricks to continue themselves. Only one God is eternal."

"You sound like the priests, Lady, if so be that you are referencing the Hebrew God." Gwyar's bronze eyes were brazen.

"Nay, child, they do ever pervert every detail about the Father of Lights. And herein is my great sin." Vivien paused whilst Gwyar's fuming was assuaged, desperate to know why she had lost her foster-mother for so many years. "I allowed my hatred of those men. And o, that I hate them" – lightning crackled through the night, followed by the shriek of owls – "to blind my hatred of the One they misrepresent."

"An easy snare to fall upon; I do this oft," offered Gwyar.

"I do not know the Eternal God, but for the hatred of his false emissaries, I sought to hurt one whom I knew had joined him. One whom, I allowed myself to be convinced, would destroy, not with sword or army but with word and persuasion, all religions. Even our own."

In her grace, Gwyar chose not to utter the wizard's name, her tongue holding. Barely.

"And so." Great shame intoned Vivien's words. "I struck a bargain to protect our goddess in exchange for stopping that special one from making league with this God."

"Speak plainly, I beg you." The foundation of the tower shifted.

"Our goddess will live forever, as the Church

of Rome will suffer us to keep her. This was the bargain in exchange for releasing Nimue to rid of us of our newly-become common enemy."

Now the gravity and weight of the matter was known by Gwyar.

"But I repented at the course and sought to arrest the plot," she went on. "I am shackled for plotting with an old man who promised to keep my goddess alive."

"Alive by folding her into Mary."

"Yes."

At this, and at last, Vivien had shared at least the bits and pieces of her swerve from sanity so many years ago, and right before the Cymry's triumph at Mynydd Baedan, with another soul.

Now Maelgwn and Gwyar knew. Both of her foster-children. Connected by an old lie, an older love, and the future challenge of what would become of it all.

Morgaine buried her face in her hands. She had killed. She had lied; she was no better or no worse than Vivien. Error was no respecter of station or persons. The impact of Vivien's plot had a further reach: this alone was the matter. Grace wrestled against the creature within Gwyar. And grace won. She brought her head aright. Fixing the problem was paramount, nothing more. "What old man, mother?!" she demanded.

"Your grandfather."

Morgaine's countenance recovered, and hope returned in the twinkling of an eye. She gave a seemingly out-of-place, silly response. "My grandfather Tewdrig is long buried at his well in the village Mathern; was he not your friend?"

"You would make me say the Crone's name?" Vivien had not yet comprehended Gwyar's redirection. "Your husband's grandfather, Meirchion the Mad."

The dark little one roared in laughter. "We have exiled ourselves over folly, and you are in prison for–"

"I hardly see the humor, Gwyar–"

"Meirchion the Mad is dead, Vivien. Dead!" The sorceress then delivered the hug of hugs, followed by: "And Arthur, our just king, will reject all hearsay not delivered from the Crone's accusatory lips himself!"

"Dead lips?" Vivien dared to hope.

"Dead lips!" Morgaine affirmed.

Morgaine of the Faeries looked long at Vivien, the Lady of the Lake. Two flawed goddesses. Two brilliant women, who were more Christian in so many ways than the pseudo-Christians they loathed (for the ladies were continuously learning experientially what the Merlin had learned academically from the mysterious preacher).

"Let us make haste to win our country back," Morgaine declared.

Every gesture of Vivien's agreed. Fists pumped in the air (for she was a warrior and knight, as well as a regal and maternal figurehead for the Tribes).

As she gathered and packed her things, a query arose.

"My little daughter. You said '*we*' have exiled ourselves. Why have *you* been long in these forests of your own accord?"

Gwyar sputtered, and muttered, "I shall tell you along the way. Along the way *home*."

CHAPTER 10
If One More of My Pagan Friends Disappears

"I will not abide lies," Arthur's voice bellowed, and the bishops to a man cowered with chin tucked to chest and left shoulder elevated, as a child squirming from the switch.

"We have summonsed him to court, but he was delayed in his coming."

The blue of the king's eyes was eclipsed by the black, becoming all pupil in a glare of disbelief conjoined with disrespect. "Delayed?" he said. And his teeth did not separate.

"He cited lack of familiarity with the roads, having not visited the vales in many years." Bedwini was Arthur's chief counselor (except for Taliesin, who was often occupied with herding the lost sheep that were Maelgwn's ongoing mischief). His voice calmed any storm, and neither friend nor foe ever had ought to say against the gentle presbyter. "If I might inquire, friend," he continued, disregarding the rickety excuse of the indicted, truant visitor, "what caused you to suspect dishonesty out of the–"

"The Whelp." Arthur had to come to refer to him by this designation. And only this.

Arthur could not tell the clergy how he had been provoked to explore the *real* whereabouts of his sister, now gone for so many seasons' turnings.

His nocturnal demoness had begun to return, levitating and calling to him from above his bed. And this was how he reckoned that something was amiss with Gwyar.

The Pendragon had objectively studied the nature of his curse and, now in the fourth decade of his life, had drawn a few conclusions (though, he acknowledged, he did not comprehend the matter).

As done a hundred times over the years, his thoughts summarized his hypotheses:

Gwenhwyfar II was Arthur's one true love.

When sent away, as a mere boy, to be made king of Glamorgan and Gwent, the Tribes demanded the spring rites.

Arthur and Gwyar were the actors. He as virility, she as fertility. She was masked and painted as the vicar of both the land and the moon; Arthur, unknowingly, lay with his sister. And not just intercourse. A ritualistic act that involved every nerve-ending and created an in-between space of body and spirit.

Being so young, Gwyar became a type of replacement for Gwenhwyfar in Arthur's heart. For as a youth, his fantasies of Gwen matched the realities of the acts with Gwyar.

Gwyar was a witch, somehow, and just maybe the legendary Primal Witch from the Ancient of Days. When the Fallen Angels knew the daughters of men and got children by them, there was a first witch 'created'. She was the true Goddess above all Goddesses, by reason of her primacy and power. Too many rumors held the propensity of truth about Gwyar being one and the same with this Goddess's, or more precisely, demigoddess's, disembodied spirit, though Gwyar came forth innocent from Queen Onbrawst's blessed womb.

Through no fault of Gwyar's, a curse or connection tethered the siblings. Thus, for diverse reasons, Arthur felt, she would reach out to him through the apparition and recreate the forbidden deed, and remind him of their bonds, causing him to cry out to both loves of his youth in terrorized and erotic delusion.

Whether Gwyar knowingly did this or whether by the control of the vexing spirit, Arthur knew not. Gwyar was years away from court, and the king doubted he would engage her about it, were she there.

As Gwenhwyfar II had re-entered Arthur's life, the void had been filled and the visitations had ceased. Indeed, life was *heaven on earth* with his queen; yet Gwyar had begun to 'visit' Arthur again. Terrorizing and relentless, and only when Gwen did not, for this reason or that, share the king's bed.

The king's conclusion was that some trouble or peril or need had befallen his sister.

That the incompleteness was caused by a problem in his own bed and his own marriage never received a passing thought by the happy regent.

After three recurring 'visits', he decided to make the simplest of inquiries to the North.

Validation was swift and clear.

Gwyar had never been summonsed to her husband. There was no ill relative, no need for a healer or nurse. And of a certainty, she had not simply decided to stay in the North with her Catholic spouse. Moreover, none in the kingdoms of Gwynedd, Rheged or Ynys Mon had seen her, for the sum of the time she had been absent from Caerleon.

Now Arthur felt burden and guilt for letting himself wander so adrift between Gwenhwyfar's legs. And when not distracted there, so preoccupied facilitating quests, slaying Giants (though none were the equal of Itto for valor, or skill, or courage) and administering his Golden Age that he had failed to long ago inquire about his sister.

A problem he would cure, with swiftness and ferocity.

Returning to Bishop Bedwini, his response was short. Vague. "It has been about five years. At some point I would need my sister, or she would need me. It was a matter of time. How much longer?"

"He approaches, Lord."

Arthur did not convene the Round Table Fellowship for discourse about Gwyar. He suspected Church involvement, and would not be triangulated by fluid versions of their accounts. And so, as had been done so many years ago, all the renowned clergy – be they of Popish or British persuasion – were convened.

He made them stand in a semi-circle in the middle of the great amphitheater of Caerleon. Like ants under a looking-glass. Empty of the throngs and cheers of a chariot race, the ruckus and rants at the games of arms, or the articulate screaming of a clamorous political debate. Instead, only the howl of the wind and the rush of the Usk River provided accompaniment. These rendered the men, who thought themselves somewhat, small. And Arthur, pacing and circumambulating them, an echo following each word, immense.

Even before the guest was within range to hear them, Arthur had already lashed into them.

He was not tarrying for the Whelp.

"Ten years ago, in this very spot, we won our country but lost its most precious treasure; all in the self-same night! Right here." Excalibur was thrust forcefully into the stone tiles, sparks erupting as the sword met stone. And the stone gave way. "Right here! Right here was the last place I saw my friend, my counselor, MY MERLIN!"

The Whelp was now the opposite side of the bishops and priests and directly behind Arthur. The Pendragon's head swiveled and cocked with the motions of a dragon, befitting the man who bore its banner when fighting. "And I will not lose my sister over another vain theological conspiracy!"

Arthur was conflating the real conspiracy to remove Merlin (and his influence) from the king's ear with Morgaine of the Faeries' absence. A reasonable assumption, but the fuming liege had missed his mark; the Churchmen, though glad to be rid of one more heathen, were ignorant as to the cause of her supposed demise. However, so rare was it that the just and temperate king spoke in anger, let alone rage, that there was no winning by words. So each of them looked to the theatre floor, in silent innocence.

But the other invited guest was not innocent.

Cadfan, now fully installed as bishop of the Popish parish on Ynys Enlli, tried to match eyes with the visitor, tried to warn him that saying little was good, saying nothing would be better. Cadfan was unaware of a plot to displace Gwyar, but he was well aware of the connivings of the late Meirchion the Mad. And to him was the visitor intimately connected.

"Mordred."

"Lord Arthur Pendragon ap Meurig ap Tewdrig, King of all Cymru and Emperor of the world, I salute you, uncle." A bend at the waist with eyes up; by no means a full bow.

King Arthur's face was devoid of emotion,

and he spoke through the pretentious salutation, giving it no regard.

"You lied."

"It was five years ago."

"Unlike men, lies do not wax old with age; like wine, they only become more potent over time."

"I was just a boy," Mordred offered.

"How old?" queried the king.

"Twenty and four," Mordred responded.

"But fourteen years younger than I. And speaking of fourteen, at that age, a full decade ere you blame youth for dishonesty, I was — "

"King of Glamorgan and Gwent, the Pendragon of all the Tribes. Lord Arthur." Mordred continued with his pretense of formality and flattery. "Second to only the Nazarene, there is but one Arthur. I am not you. I *am no Arthur.*"

"Enough!" Freeing the legendary blade from the breached floor, the king gazed upon the hilt and its famous scripting. "I have but two questions, Raven." (Though Mordred was half Silure, Arthur here associated him with his paternal line, showing frustration that, yet again, problems pointed north). He sheathed Excalibur, notably in a scabbard fashioned by his sister, and stepped aggressively towards her son. Taller than the younger man, Arthur peered down into his eyes as if it was God Himself looking upon a trembling lost soul, quivering without excuse at the Judgment Day.

Mordred felt it.

Did the Saxons who fell by his sword feel it too?

Authority. Real power and authority.

The Bear of Glamorgan was not just king because some vain genealogy and the consent of the tribes had made him so. He was king *because he was a king.* A will like unto a piece of iron was upon Mordred, and he bent underneath it. That Mordred was doing as he pleased with every part of Gwenhwyfar's body now brought a terror through him, causing his pale skin to turn hues of white as the paints and dyes used upon houses.

Ghostly and slave to Arthur's will, he dropped to a knee, nearly confessing all, barely able to muster a lie.

Mordred's thoughts went unto earlier in the morning.

He had not been truant in his entrance to Caerleon.

He had not grown unfamiliar with the roads from Gwynedd to Gwent.

Far from foreign to him, he traversed them at least once a fortnight; in hours where none labored and all slept, and ever under cloak, and ever with a different steed.

He had arrived early and had audience with his life's love, the Queen of the Britons.

In a moment of sheer panic, Gwenhwyfar had deduced that Arthur's harshness over the one lie was a ruse to manifest *the real lie,* or five years of lies. That he had convened the Church, and no warriors or chieftains, rendered the matter all the more dire. Perhaps Arthur had discovered the affair and was to shame Mordred for adultery (and for treason) before God's representatives, making straight the pathway to kill him then and there. Though it was unhealed wounds of losing Merlin enraging the king, the two that lived ever under a shadow of guilt thought that this day might be their comeuppance.

They did not make love; there were no impassioned embraces or poetic meetings of the lips.

Mordred had tried, over the time of the affair,

to be a better man, to earn his renown – yet his face was not yet known by any knights of significance, save his own household. Arthur grew in strength and fame and majesty, and the plan to 'endure to the end and then assert as the rightful heir' seemed as a far-off and unreachable country. Arthur was only ten-and-four years older than Mordred and, should calamity or accident not befall the Cymreig Emperor, they would both be very old together, with Arthur enjoying Gwen's bed and Mordred relegated to a hidden plaything in a child's cupboard.

If Gwenhwyfar murdered the king, then the overwhelming consent of the Tribes would promote Gwalchmai, who had already been granted Pembroke as a sub-kingdom over which to rule and practice for a broader role as Wledig, or Battle Commander, over all the kingdoms of the Britons.

This would profit the forbidden lovers in no wise.

No; Mordred must gain favor with court and amongst men so that, when Arthur fell, they would accept Mordred being steward of his kingdom, and his wife, with minimal murmuring.

So, in misery, they had suffered the waiting.

And then the emissaries of the king demanded Mordred make haste unto Caerleon, to answer charges of lying to the Pendragon regarding the whereabouts of Gwenhwyfar's ever-thorn, Morgaine of the Fairies.

Did she know?

If so, why had she not simply exposed Gwen, to whom she was no ally, and been done with it?

The couple often wondered these things. As days gave way to months and months faded into years, Morgaine's failure to make manifest the affair could now be viewed as her deliberately withholding the matter from Arthur, rendering her an accomplice. Justice delayed, seeping into advocacy of the behavior.

Or had something else befallen her?

The not knowing, blended with the summons by Arthur himself, left Mordred and Gwen just looking upon one another, with high probability that this would be the last day they would see one another. They gave themselves to love's gaze and love's stare until his departure could no longer be put off.

Gwenhwyfar implored Mordred to deny any charges of infidelity and assert the right of appeal to the Round Table, that his peers might judge the case. He would go unarmed, as he was no match with sword, fist or spear for Cymru's second greatest warrior (for only Maelgwn had more might or skill at arms than did Arthur, son of Meurig), and a confrontation would be to no profitable end.

Deny the affair, feign a thoughtful motive for the lie about his mother. This was the course.

"I love you, Mordred."

"I love you, Gwen."

And out he went, in partial contrition and partial sophistry.

To a second knee he fell now, a few drops of urine escaping trouser. And with real fear.

"Your best friend Bedwyr was maimed, monsters were roaming the land, and I had no idea where my mother had gone. I wished not to add to your despair, and spared the worry by lying. I thought she would surely return soon, and when she did not, I feared greatly the snare of my own lie. To this day, I do not know what became of her. Please, lord, forgive me." The words were broken, and the contrition appeared sincere.

The subject appeared to be *the only subject*, and not a snare to delve into other matters...

Arthur grasped a handful of Mordred's curly locks. "Dark as your mother's. Rise to your feet." The Iron Bear's ferocity was only surpassed by the Iron Bear's grace. Something was deeply untrustworthy about the constitution of his sister's son, but Arthur believed him guiltless *on this matter*. Gently lifting Mordred by his hair and then delivering a brotherly wallop upon his shoulder, Arthur turned back to the gods of the villages, the deities of the cantrefs, the lords of the kingdoms, the gatekeepers of men's souls. On this day they were as grasshoppers before the son of Meurig.

He walked up and down amongst them again, pent up with ten years of not knowing what they had done to his wizard, his eyes stalking them as if to say: *He may have lied, but you made her disappear, didn't you?!*

Arthur roared a great lamentation. "Let men worship what gods they will, only that they don't kill their neighbors for it! Was this law, and the rights it contains, too grievous to bear?! Where is she?"

On many, many occasions these men had been great friends to Arthur and his family; on many more they had given authoritative pieces of advice that were more edicts than they were counsel to the king. He had signed land grants to and with many of the assembled. Dyfrig, Teilo, Cadoc, Illtud, Cadfan, Bedwini, Aiden; legends with stars as bright as Arthur's, heroes and legends in their own rights.

But on this day, Gwyar was officially missing, and answers must start with the same collective who surrounded the mystery of Merlin.

They had no answers for the sovereign. No explanation to provide. No narrative. Their mumblings and shrugs were as dry hay, their promises of innocence as stubble, and the king's anger as an all-consuming fire.

The interrogation carried on, Arthur surgically excising all facts from the time period, no stone of motive or intent not flipped on itself.

Another lamentation volleyed upward into the heavens. "*If one more of my pagan friends disappears!* Just one! I will raze every church and burn every chapel! And I say unto you that I don't think Jesus would blame me!"

The clergy understood Arthur's pain and would rebuke him not for his blasphemy. Their only objective, an objective that finally brought unity amongst the brethren, was to survive this, to limp out of the amphitheater alive, and hope to God that the witch would turn up, alive and well.

Suddenly the voice of another mighty Silure that possessed Arthur's similar innate authority, albeit in a tiny, brooding little body, filled the stadium with the shadow of its substance.

The bishops' wish was granted.

"I don't think Jesus would blame you either, brother, but unfortunately no churches will you set to the flame. For here I am." Morgaine looked upon hateful Aiden, crouched with his fellows, winked, and asked, "So, how is your arm?"

The Popish presbyter gave no pious Scripture, nor did he preach at the sorceress this time. He only gave a fearful sneer and an involuntary pestering of an old hurt.

Morgaine had no space to vex the rest of the assembly, either in jest or in earnest, as she was immediately enveloped in a great bear hug. An

Iron Bear's hug. As he held his sister, the first words were peculiar.

"Merlin. Did you see him?" he asked.

"Only in visions and whispers and mists, brother." Her expression was comforting but sorrowful.

"Then hope remains," asserted the king.

"Of course."

Now Arthur surveyed the assembly. Here at the same moment were brought together his treasured sister and her son. Accustomed to strange happenings on the Blessed Isles, even a confident king knows not when to pry and when to leave be. As his next words were forming, he saw another sprinting through the west arches, making haste to join them, her stride measured but urgent (as one runs upon a hurt child and loathes having to see, but needs to see all the more).

"Gwen?" Arthur's expression was puzzled.

Gwenhwyfar, not knowing how the examination was proceeding, had lost herself to despair and was racing to save Mordred; perhaps to kill Arthur and flee, perhaps to trade her life for his own, perhaps to snatch him away and throw them into the Usk. She had no strategy, no course; she was running to save her love, no more.

A quick glimpse.

He is safe. He smiles.

Must concoct a lie, rapidly.

"My lord, my husband – my love!"

Two men were addressed by the cunning queen, but only one understood the meaning. Mordred crimsoned with a blush. Arthur looked upon his wife as he had ever: with absolute adoration.

"Your sister, Gwyar. She returns!" Where

Hercules and the Hebrew Samson have no equals in history or legend for strength, the daughter of the Giant Ogyrfan Fawr had no rival for swift and effortless lies. She was naturally naughty, and the Faerie King had taken those natural inclinations and multiplied them a thousandfold. Even in her rebirth of true love, the old nature remained, and pivoting towards self-preserving deception was as natural to her as the lacing of a boot.

"Oh!" Arthur laughed. "My love, she is here, and still so tiny you did not see her behind my cloak." (Of course, Gwen had seen her during her gallop, only feigning receiving the news before her *hasty run*). Arthur laughed again, then finished his jest. "It is not as if she's grown taller in the past five years!"

Gwen gathered herself. "Queen Gwyar, wife of King Llew, you are most welcome home."

Gwyar measured Gwenhwyfar. And spoke not.

Arthur turned to the clergy and remembered the Merlin's lesson: *When wrong, apologize quickly and sincerely. The err can't be recovered, but you can always control how you respond.*

"Illtud, cousin, teacher and friend. I am sorry for suspecting something malicious of you. I have let a hurt from yesterday cloud the judgment of today. Please forgive me." And Arthur engaged each of the Elders, whether he liked them or not, with individual, real apologies, which left none of them with aught to say against so marvelous a king and so honorable a man.

As the Churchmen left the theatre, the tension did not abate; rather, it simply shifted. Now in the empty stadium remained four: Gwyar and Gwen, Arthur and Mordred.

Arthur recognized instantly that Mordred, as son, must have grieved in equal measure as had the brother. "I know you greatly covet time with your mam; pray you give me a few hours, and I shall send her unto you." He then turned to his wife, the actress misted over with the fullness of disingenuous hospitality. "Gwen, please escort my nephew back into the city - perhaps have your attendants see to it that he enjoys the ancient baths - and later, we will all sup, yes?"

"Straightaway, husband." The kiss of a proud adder that had just survived the farmer's plow and fanged his ankle followed.

No. This is why I left! He has delivered his one true love into the hands of HER LOVER FOR THE AFTERNOON! Gwyar's soul screamed, but her mouth moved not.

Gwenhwyfar and Mordred exited.

***

"The roaming mares and wild yellow flowers call for you; to our fortress we must!" Arthur gently turned Gwyar so that their vantage allowed them to see Lodge Hill, their special place, looking down, ever protecting them. At least from enemies without.

Gwyar gave no protest. Llyn Fawr (whence Vivien had gone when returning to Cymru with Gwyar), Ynys Enlli and Lodge Hill. These were, in no special ranking, her favorite places, and though she knew not which words she would choose for her brother, she knew that any discourse would be better conducted up the old trails in the mystical stronghold. At least they could gaze across the whole of the Vale of Glamorgan, the heart and capital of the Summer Kingdom.

Instantly, they were no longer alone in the arena.

While they yet gazed towards the hills, a gentle hand alighted upon each of their shoulders. Barely present, yet each could somehow see the *color* of the fingers.

Red.

The fingers tapped and rattled first upon Arthur; next, Gwyar, followed by a greeting that matched the order of the tapping, rudely: "Blessings and Cursings upon the line of Uther Pendragon."

The mortal king spun round to face the immortal. Arthur had never met him, but legends and reports abounded.

"This arena is my stone circle, lord of the Tylwyth Teg; by what infraction or infringement do you lay charge?"

"You have the resolve of your mother, Iron Bear." The echo of the voice vibrated and rippled, as if the thing were speaking under water. *Oddly, the deepness and tone that came out of the devil reminded Arthur of Maelgwn's voice.*

The provocation agitated the Saxon Slayer, the Giant Hunter, the Undefeated Warrior, who began to unsheath his blade. But Gwyar stayed his hand, preventing a futile enterprise.

"You know not our mother, and are being impish, which is below the station of a lord of such an ancient and noble race."

"Remarkable," the Tylwyth Teg's chief of mischief mused at the introductory missives. "The one I blessed put hand to sword and would battle me; the one I cursed did bless me with courtly edifications."

"Bless those that curse you," said Gwyar.

"And in so doing you shall leap coals upon

their heads." Arthur finished the Scriptural saying. "She always was the wiser of us."

A Bible-quoting witch, a god-king overreacting all morning and having a most out-of-character day, and the most powerful of the Fair Folk standing in Caerleon in broad daylight. The spectacle was not lost on the participants. They each met eyes and enjoyed a short laugh.

"The Tylwyth Teg don't just promenade through amphitheaters in the openness of the day in this most Christian of kingdoms. What mean you by being here" - Arthur's statesmanship returned - "my Fair Lord?"

"This was my land ere it was yours, Son of Adam. Are not all interactions amongst our kind about inheritance? Do we not ever guard what you do or do not do with our islands?"

"There was a time that I could acquiesce to the logic of your premise." Arthur took caution in his tone, but posited his view with great conviction. "A time where I would have agreed that we were regrettably, at one time - millennia ago - the very invaders that we now loathe. But that is not so."

The Fae puffed his chest, his green tunic stressing at the seams. But he fiddled with his beard, and listened on.

"My new Merlin—"

"Oh, Taliesin, son of Ceridwen, a Glamorgan lad; I know him well," the Fae King interrupted.

"Yes, Taliesin provided greater insight than did *my Merlin* about the origin of otherworldly beings. He explained that Man was placed here first and was to be the sole heir of salvation and God's agency to rule and reign upon the earth." Here Arthur was very careful to avoid insulting the Fae's ancestors, whom they worshiped with absolute religious devotion. "And that your kind share a common ancestor with my kind, demanding that Man, or more accurately the daughters of Man, were here first. Your kind is very ancient but, o king, you are the original visitors and not us."

"So Taliesin has grown bold. Your Merlin feared he would tell you of these and other mysteries. What else, I beseech you, Arthur Pendragon – what else has Taliesin taught you in your counselor's stead?"

"Oh, this and that." Arthur minimized the matter. "He is Maelgwn's bard, but we have had some fascinating conversations and I have entertained his theories. Now, I in turn beseech you: what more do you know of my Merlin? Do you know if he lives or if he fell, how, and who and why?"

"What gift would the Pendragon give the Fair Folk for such knowledge? Would you dance with us?"

"Yes."

"Arthur, stop," commanded Gwyar, upon deaf ears.

"Would you rid the land of all iron and ore, forever?"

"By command the mining guilds would begin on the morrow."

"Arthur, please."

"Would you abdicate your throne?"

The answer was immediate. And immediately 'No'.

"I am king for my people and for all the Tribes, Clans, Cantrefs and Kingdoms of Cymru and the Isles in the Sea. I would not gain this knowledge whilst the people suffered for it."

Gwyar gave a sigh, thankful that *Arthur was still Arthur.*

"Ah, Arthur ap Meurig, son of the pious Queen Onbrawst, you are my favorite of all the Sons of Adam who have ever lived. The better part of the answers you seek reside not with me, but with your new Merlin himself. Ask Taliesin what became of your dear wizard."

Arthur knew not how to respond to this and was not given space to; the Fae King continued.

"Yes, my favorite of all the Sons of Adam. Your Golden Age must run its course; the land prospers, the people prosper, peace reigns and our Isles free from the invading Boar. It is best for all that Arthur be king until the Summer Kingdom waxes old, and then the winter shall come. You are in great peril."

Soon it was evident that the otherworldly being had come, after pricking and poking and harassing as was his manner, to warn Arthur.

"There are visitors coming who are and are not what they seem."

Arthur had been reared on riddles, being raised at the feet of the Merlin. He knew that demanding plain speech was vain, and instead listened to what was said, inferred or withheld, with the focus of an archer left with but one arrow in the quiver. He assumed that the creature was referring to emissaries from Rome, who were visiting within the month, and rumors that the Bishop of Rome would finally come to see golden Caermelyn and stately Caerleon.

"At all costs, the thing that your sister here" – an unfriendly and unflattering pointing at Gwyar – "and her foster-mother so glibly and carelessly trek about with, paying insufficient regard to its import, must not be here when they are here. Should they possess it, your kingdom will end."

"Sister, what thing?"

Now Gwyar was doing the ignoring. Instead, she protested, "But where can we take it? The Isle of Apples is under endless siege by pilgrims and her magic wanes. And if the *other treasures were found,* then all hope would be lost."

Remarkably, the unpredictable Fae King gave a reasonable response. "Merlin thought best to hide it forever in Broceliande. Now those woods are breeched. Methinks your Ynys Enlli still remains the most difficult daughter island to access from the mainland. Get thee hence back to Avalon, and try to make it your stronghold once more. Recruit maidens, rebuild, divert and misdirect the Church and the inquisitive. Move the cup between there and Llyn Fawr oft, and make this thy and thy foster-mother's occupation. Guard the Grail."

"What thing?!" Arthur demanded.

Gwyar took Arthur by the hand and stated softly, "Remember our good secret in exchange for the bad? 'Tis one of her relics, that when charged and charmed is rumored to be capable of perversion, wrath and malice."

"Or healing," the old elf added.

"Oh - the cup of Christ. Can it be? You have it, sister?"

"Vivien and I have concealed it. It is near."

"The Lady of the Lake!" Though Arthur counted her amongst his beloved *missing pagans,* there were reports that she had simply retired to Lesser Britain and that Maelgwn visited her oft. That she was active again in the affairs of men thrilled Arthur, causing him to feel partially like his wizard had returned with her. The king eschewed the warning of danger, instead brimming with excitement.

"This sounds like a—"

"Quest." The Fae King smothered the whole

of his red face with his spiky fingers, partially amused. "Sons of Adam and their quests. Heed me, Arthur. Get Morgaine of the Faeries far from your Popish guests, or lose the kingdom you shall."

Lastly, the chief of the Tylwyth Teg looked upon Gwyar as a father looks upon a daughter – and in many respects, her father he was. He had *made* Morgaine, above forty years ago. Instead of retribution in kind at Onbrawst's offense with a simple changeling, ugly and insufferable, the Fae King had made something else entirely of the babe who *was Gwyar.*

Communicating only in thought that so that the king would hear him not: "I owed the Primal Witch a favor, but knew not that fate would add to black magic incest and perversion. The Morrigan hath begotten a twisted thing. He will bring winter upon our Summer Kingdom before the time." He was not greater in power than Morgaine, but was able to cause her head to turn back to road towards the city whence Mordred now made respite, surely, after finishing with the king's wife. "Had I foreseen the Whelp, I would've rendered you barren. For this, I mourn for you, my child."

Tears streamed down Gwyar's cheeks.

Two abominations, part human, part devil, acting as gods – but no gods stood with the innocent and loyal king. The moment was not lost on Gwyar, and she cried a great cry.

King Arthur understood that his sister was a peculiar, troubled and enchanted being and somehow deeply entwined with the Fae, hence her popular name amongst the Tribes, and because he knew this, he knew when to abstain from pressing for information that would not be given, and if given, not be understood. Instead, he let the arcane remain such. The Fae King vanished, and Arthur said simple words.

"This time, send messengers monthly and visit oft, and I will do the same. Guard this *relic* until you feel your course is complete, and then come back to me."

"Our thoughts are aligned, brother." She embraced him and warned, "Guard your heart carefully, and let our toil continue whilst others enjoy the sun."

"As always," he mused. They shared words of love, and Morgaine departed for the Isle of Apples, concerning herself not with seeing Mordred.

CHAPTER 11
Visitors from Rome

For many seasons preceding the arrival of 'the Whelp' to court (first to give an answer for beguiling the High King, and then, once reconciled of that matter, to make a name for himself), Arthur and Lancelot were greatly enjoying each other's company.

The offense over Arthur preferring himself versus Itto was long dormant, put far away into the corridors of Lancelot's complex and troubled mind. Skirmishes, raids, sundry quests and monsters gave the two warriors what they needed: combat.

The raids were mainly by pirates from Eire who were harassing coastal villages in the North. The clans that governed the Emerald Isles denounced the activity, and generations of intermarriage through the line of Silures ensured an iron-clad and lasting peace. To this end, Arthur recognized that the actions were wrought by criminals, individuals, and not by his neighbor nation in the western sea.

Nevertheless, the lasting peace had to be guarded with ferocious zeal, and extreme vigilance. For this cause, Arthur engaged Lancelot and Gwalchmai, rather than lesser-known guards or patrolling part-time soldiers, to send the loudest possible message abroad that examples would be made, punishment would be harsh, the behavior stamped out.

Lancelot, now in his fourth decade, was remarkably better than at the peak of his youth. More effortless, more swift, cleaner in his killing strokes; a perfect simulation of Vivien's dance, only enhanced by the strength of a demigod. He was a long man, lending him a great advantage in reach, rendering his battle spike as a spear on account of arm-span. Still cleanly shaven, still with mid-length curly raven's hair, Lancelot was *the Cymreig Warrior the Saxons feared in the night;* he and his Hosts from the North were the difference in the long and long-ago Saxon Wars.

He used the raiders for practice. Training with real steel. Arthur and Gwalchmai marveled at his techniques, and much fellowship, many laughs and little adventures became big memories for the troop.

Lancelot had forced himself to be more present for the Round Table Fellowship, but only when he could affirm that Gwenhwyfar II would not be at Caermelyn. On those occasions he would lie without hesitation, habitually breaking vows of honesty that were in the fiber of his identity, to protect the kingdom – *from himself.*

Gwalchmai, a young man burdened with Gwyar's observational genius and Arthur's wisdom, alone (save Taliesin) marked the patternistic behavior. And because he suspected Mordred of some malevolence with the queen, the added oddity of Lancelot's conduct doubly oppressed him. So many times, direct accusation welled but was held back, causing the sunny and shiny one sadness, gloom and pain.

Shortly after Gwyar's return (and too-soon departure, yet again), Arthur, Cai, Gwlachmai and Lancelot were about the coast, again *enjoying* quelling a small raid; twenty men of Eire and a few rogue Britons purloining cattle and harassing miners in a coastal village on Ynys Mon.

"Let's give the appearance of an army, rather than a collection of concerned citizens." Arthur beamed with excitement.

"The silver armor, red cape, tribal sigils?" Lancelot matched his king's beam.

"Precisely!"

"The special garb!" Cai was as a child about to rummage the chest for his favorite doll or plaything.

"The helmet cannot contain my hair, and it hurts," protested Gwalchmai, withholding his chuckle.

"Call the sunshine, Hawk of May" - for it had rained for four days without ceasing - "and then ride without helm," countered his happy lord.

Only criminals and villains covet actual *war.* And only baser men seek out violence. None of the Round Table Fellowship wanted war. The prolonged conflict with the invading Germans had torn at the collective soul of Cymru - multigenerational trauma that would long linger and never be forgotten.

However, all boys need to periodically fight. To engage in combat, to compete, to protect and show brawn and skill and will. Here and there, warriors must war, only to hope that they never *go to war.* And these men, who had been but boys during most of their famous twelve battles, knew this truth and, grown full of wisdom, often wondered how invincible they would be now, having the benefit of years and hard lessons. To this end, they relished the occasional raid.

Whilst they were reposing for a brief meal to discuss how to deal with the raiders and prepare for the battle, the sun broke the clouds, casting his rays of glory upon the heroes, gathered round a small fire, surrounded by ancient trees.

The Hawk of May shook his helmet off violently, making a show of it. The others gave such laughter that Cai complained that his ribs might leap from their cages. Gwalchmai glared at them, a mess of auburn hair with two eyes for a face.

"Well done, Gwalchmai!" Arthur looked upon the blue face of the firmament. He allowed the joviality to simmer and then made use of the time for more serious matters. A short discussion ensued about the task at hand. During the discourse, the Pendragon interjected.

"When we return to Caermelyn, there are two openings amongst our twenty-four by reason of retirement. It is time to consider the next generation of Round Table Knights. What of Peredur?"

All agreed to the nomination with great excitement over the upstart, who had seen no wars but possessed every quality of the special responsibility demanded by the coveted station.

"And your brother Mordred? What of him, Gwalchmai?"

"So long have I been with your House in the South, I don't know him with sufficient comfort to stand by an answer." Gwalchmai politicized the response.

"A great king you will make one day," Cai smiled at the burly but polished knight, "never giving a straight answer."

"Ha!" Arthur struck Cai upon the shoulder,

and then embraced him as they all enjoyed another portion of merriment. Then the Pendragon turned to his champion, tall as a cedar. "Your son Rhun has long been amongst our best, yet the bards say Rhufawn is the greater swordsman."

"Greater than even you!" In chorus, Gwalchmai and Cai both goaded the Lancelot.

"All good fathers desire that their sons exceed and surpass them, except in good looks," replied the Bloodhound Prince, himself fully capable of political recourse.

"Amen!" agreed Arthur. And the gaiety continued.

"In the same way that your brother Madoc lives upon the Sea, and your brothers serve the Church, my thorn begs me not to place Rhufawn for consideration for *our life*. He is vague and annoying about this, but I tend to heed him," said Maelgwn.

"Merlins tend to be vague and annoying. I understand." Arthur smiled and nodded.

Maelgwn knew nothing of Mordred, save that he was Gwyar's son and Gwalchmai's brother. A man with blood of North and South. In an effort to be helpful against never-ending ripples over territorial and tribal stressors, he put forth an idea. "Mordred seems to be worthy of this opportunity. Perhaps a probationary assignment? Perhaps we bring him on our next *quest or adventure*. Give him a go. Yes?"

Gwalchmai simply did not agree, nor would he ever. He discerned great evil residing within the Whelp. But the Hawk of May remained silent. A wordless and reserved protest.

"Sound thinking; this we shall do." Arthur liked the idea of the Fellowship being restored to its proper census. For twelve is the number of government. Twelve for Arthur, twelve for his champion, King Maelgwn Gwynedd. He then made an end of a horn of cider: one impressive gulp and – gone. "There is one other matter." His hand wiped some remnant of nectar from his short mustache, still colored as a sandy shore, still without grey.

"We have criminals to corral. Didn't know I was invited to a council." It was rare that Maelgwn jested, but on this day, he was just *one of four boys enjoying a moment in the sun.*

Seeing his Lancelot happy was Arthur's joy and, he knew, the ongoing salvation of Cymru. *And fleeting*. The thought was a moment of reality as the single angry cloud on a sunny day.

"Yes, yes, I shall be swift. The Church is hosting visitors." And now a moment of gravity. "From Rome."

There was an audible gasp, followed by an instant silence.

"It is an envoy of men in high places within the Church of Rome. A congregation for peace, and extension of hospitality in an effort to work out ever-growing differences, especially as it relates to the policy of baptism and church membership amongst the children living in Lloegyr." Here Arthur opted not to name the kingdom of Cedric, a thriving Germanic confederacy that was allowed to survive, on account of women and children and the values that the Cymry placed on innocent life.

However, the Native Church refused to teach them Scripture, to baptize them (in opposition to their own hard-fought and hard-won policies), or even to sup with them unless they suffered the dining party to go through a ceremonial washing. They viewed and treated the Saxons, Jutes, Angles and Gewessi as *gentile dogs.*

The Roman Church was more opportunistic. They were converting these *dogs*, or rather, *the Boar*, by the hundreds – and rapidly.

But none of that represented Arthur's primary concern.

"Maelgwn."

"My lord?"

"As you know, men of an Italian band are deeply woven into the schemes that both sponsored my sons' plots against me and the intrigue in Brittany ten years ago, which took our great one from us."

Maelgwn gave a frustrated nod. He knew more than he could share, on account of his foster-mother.

"We have never attacked another nation. This is not the way of the Cymry. But I shall never forget this wrong. And justice do I ever seek. Continue to investigate we must. All of us must be at Caerleon; all must be vigilant. Ask questions. Probe, prod. Be good hosts, but listen to what is said and not said. By Excalibur I swear…" Arthur motioned for a second cider, treating it as the first. "If we find some cell amongst the church, some actors in the conspiracy, or that the Church itself did these things, I swear by my right as king of these Isles that attack we shall."

Maelgwn had stopped listening. Though not his intention, the words washed over him as hot oil upon a pot, not sticking, of no import. Rather, he was consumed by the test before him. The test of Gwenhwyfar. *I must lodge at Caerleon during this visit!*

"What is the duration of the visit?" he queried the king.

"Seven nights," stated King Arthur.

King Maelgwn of Gwynedd, the Lancelot who

had forsaken all to serve the Iron Bear, had one week to tame thoughts and feelings that could well resurrect his bubble.

He fought flawlessly as the fully-clad Round Table Companions recreated past fame. The raiders were put to flight or to the sword. The men gasped and marveled at Maelgwn's skill. The joy of delivering justice and securing the realm brought youth and glee to the troop, transporting both Arthur and Maelgwn back to a time when they, and their two classmates, had conquered all enemies of land and sea in the kingdom of their youthful minds. A simple time of being children; boys and girls. Both sovereigns savored the moment and stole many glances at each other, redeeming the time and enjoying their small portion of the Summer Kingdom ere they returned to the trials and devils that surely awaited them back in their golden city.

***

Hormisdas, the Bishop of Rome, "died" in August, five hundred and twenty-three years after the Passion of the Lord.

The renowned ambassador of reconciliation had labored tirelessly for unity; unity at any cost. *There is no truth but oneness* and *endeavoring for the unity of the spirit in the bonds of peace* were the banner and sigil of his public administration.

He had healed schisms through diplomacy, stood with unwavering resolve before an emperor who had sought to discredit and destroy him, made of this foe a friend, and unified the Senate behind the Church, her councils, synods and edicts; this had strengthened waning Rome against the rising tide of the Ostrogoth and

Ishmaelian Empires that had eclipsed her.

All of these achievements and maneuvers had helped position Rome to rise again, only after a different manner. Never again could she use the soldier and the sword; now she would use the vestments and the Cross to meet her aims, guilt and reward to conquer the world.

To be used for his aims. To conquer the world under his boot.

The unity, the diplomacy, the beguiling of principled men to compromise, to sell soul in order to sit under one big tent, appears good, even godly.

'Tis not so.

Unity without truth is simply the best device for gathering all of the sheep into one corral – and then slaughtering them.

Hormisdas. The Bishop of Rome. The man from Frusino with a profound accent, such that he was hard to be understood, especially when he spoke Gaelic or needed to use Cymraeg.

Hormisdas, the Bishop of Rome. While toiling and working on dominating his ecclesiastical body, too many years were passing, the sands slipping far too fast through the hourglass; his hero pawns in Less Britain and the Isles in the Sea beginning, just so, to age.

Hormisdas. Simon Magus. The leader of the Council of Nine. A man in direct congress with the Dark Lord, the Lord of the Flies and the Father of Lies. The horned and hooved one whom the Cymreig called Arddu and who went by many names; the Prince of the Power of the Air, that Dragon, the Devil, Satan.

Arddu gave Magus ruthless stripes for his lack of progress, forcing the bishop to feign his death and develop a new scheme.

No longer would Arddu's vicar publicly rule from the direct seat of power. Too much bureaucracy and accountability rendered this illogical and inefficient. Nay. Henceforth, Simon Magus, and should the Lord tarry, his successors, would rule and reign from the shadows as *Black Popes* through the use of puppet Holy Fathers, whom they would personally promote and demote as served the ends of the Nine.

This was not accomplished without difficulty at first. Choosing the very elderly and pliable John I, the illuminated brotherhood were instantly at odds with his compromises and the intrigue in which he entangled himself amongst the politicians of Constantinople. This angered the Society, and the emperor of the Ostrogoths, who slung the old man into a dank and damp cell, leaving him to die from neglect and starvation in his own filth. Simon Magus would do better in his subsequent selection, placing Felix IV on the papal throne.

Having his new instrument in place, Magus would redouble his efforts to build up, and then destroy, the kingdoms of the Briton Arthur, elsewise Childebert. And so, ten years removed from *initiating Merlin,* he would go to the court of Arthur himself, to look in upon his top candidate to serve as vessel for the Son of Perdition, the conduit to bring about the End of Days.

He now took the part of a silent archbishop, mysteriously disfigured and confined to a mask for the cause of Christ: a part of the tapestry and dramatic scenery of Romish pageantry, barely noticeable and hardly noteworthy, save the mask.

Caution was paramount. No action must ignite conflict with the Tribes of the Cymry. Magus had spent most of his days since youth amongst the warring Boar that had toppled Rome. The viciousness of the Saxons, the wanton calamity of the Vandals, the cold cruelty of the Ostrogoths who 'ruled' at the present time over Simon's homeland (yet they all ultimately were ruled by him, who in turn was ruled by the capstone of a societal pyramid, Arddu the Horned God). None of these would be victorious over the Britons, who could not even be subdued in times past by Rome at the height of her Empire. The Britons could not, and would not, be beaten.

The irony of the People of Arthur was that they *could* conquer the world, but would not. No tribe of the Britons had ever usurped the sovereignty of another nation.

Rather, they could only be defeated through division, intrigue, subtle machinations and usurpations. And Simon's chief usurper in the Blessed Isles was the Adder, leader of the loosely-knit heathen wise men whose superstition yet controlled many of the common folk.

The Dynion Hysbys had served the Council well, rousing Giants oft and distracting the Round Table Knights by whispering of horrors, monsters and devilish threats to the realm; ever stamping as a boot upon the toes of the Summer Kingdom, ever irritating it with pricks and needles that, at any time, winter may fall.

Pertaining to Giants and phantoms, well; but pertaining to the Cup, heretofore, failure. Its guardian's keep could not be breached and, when it had been, the Cup had not been found. Rather, it had moved. Long years had passed, and the Adder was no closer to finding the Grail than finding a thimble in a wheat field.

Simon Magus was confident that he would put that commission right and recover the relic quickly.

And he wanted to know more of how the Merlin had come upon the tome, containing such a peculiar inscription, full of words that brought eternal life. And more than how, who *had given it to the old druid.*

***

Maelgwn wore a new road in the wild thicket on account of his pacing.

Hidden safely in a wood between Caerdydd and Caerleon, all of his selves were alone, to bring themselves under subjection and support Arthur by attending Court.

Frequently misunderstood, there was never a time when the champion of Cymru didn't *want* to be at Caerleon or Caermelyn; rather, how to perform the same and spare his mind was the matter, and his mind cared not about his wanting.

Arthur and his First Knight were truly enjoying a season likened unto their days at Illtud's before the Saxon Wars. Provided that Maelgwn could manipulate affairs to avoid Gwenhwyfar, which he could, and manipulate his bubble to leave him at peace, which he had for some time suppressed, the two enjoyed, and would continue to relish, many days of reaping their twenty years of sacrifice to win the war - reaping freedom and friendship.

But Arthur's request was wise. Was correct.

If Maelgwn, or any of Arthur's closest companions, could learn more about Rome's involvement in the seditious conspiracy to remove the king so long ago in favor of his sons, then justice might finally be wrought, the truth finally known.

The sentinel event that had been Mynydd Baedan was too grand. Too expensive. Too contrary to the nature of the Germanic Tribes. That a people who eschewed union and breathed factionism would unite under three kings and conduct the campaign that they had defied reason.

They had had help.

Nay: they had been used. An end to some unknown means.

Maelgwn believed that the Pendragon planned to give the religious overture of the meeting one to two hours for posturing over the primacy of who had the right to baptize and save men's souls and then, once annoyed by it all, to directly interrogate them about Baedan, about his sons, and about his Merlin.

Maelgwn must needs be in attendance. *Though it meant sitting in a hall near, possibly next to, her.*

He paced again.

And more pacing.

Then, suddenly, the winds shifted. A mist manifested and then a glimpse, faint and vague, of a shadowy personage peering at him through the thick fog, poised to attack.

The attacker's height and build was a mirror of Maelgwn.

The attacker's diagonal fighting stance was a mirror of Maelgwn.

The attacker's fluidity was a mirror of Maelgwn.

The mist was breaking apart and then merging again, swirling and twirling. And when it parted, the opponent could, for fleeting seconds, be seen.

The attacker's hair was a mirror of Maelgwn.

The attacker's flawless crystal eyes were a mirror of Maelgwn.

Then the weapon was brandished, picking out little dots of daylight, outlined by the mist. The battle spike, a mirror of Maelgwn's.

Seeing oneself is the greatest fear, and upon seeing it, truly seeing it, the Round Table champion, renowned for being void of fear, a hard man without tear ducts, felt the anvil of fear, the wellspring of tears. Its weight dried his mouth so that for a moment, he could neither swallow nor draw breath.

Containing the want to cry out at the specter, else his twin, only a broken whisper escaped his lips. "Maelgwn? Are you—"

"Talking to yourself, King Gwynedd?"

The mirror broke into ten thousand imperfect shards, exploding as ethereal dust. The mist gave way, revealing instead humpbacked little Taliesin, looking up at the hero with great curiosity and mirth.

"Or rather, talking to yourself *again?"* the bard snickered.

"Taliesin," rebuked Maelgwn, "you drive me to madness." A sigh followed the mystified and confused fighter, who had not ceased to think on Gwenhwyfar even as his foggy *other self* had come to slay him.

"You were expecting maybe the Bishop of Rome?" Taliesin gave a high, arching cackle. "I don't *think* he is joining the envoy but" - his arm motioned towards Maelgwn as though a shepherd's crook - "let's make haste to the city and find out."

"Never present when summonsed, always a bur when unwanted." Maelgwn meant these words, but fully knew that Taliesin was rather *present when the timing was just right* and, overcome with a coursing current of feelings that the small man had just somehow saved his life, allowed a half smile to escape towards his old thorn. His old friend.

"To Caerleon," he insisted. As they departed the thatch, the bard put his arm around the waist of Maelgwn, guiding the Bloodhound Prince as an aging father guides a grown son who has long outgrown the act but allows it anyhow, for respect and for love. (Though malformed Taliesin was younger than the Northern king.)

Seeing the ground worn, the jesting and jeering persisted. "Tilling the ground to farm?"

Maelgwn had long since calculated that the more the Taliesin goaded him, the more he already knew. Silent, he allowed the shepherd's hook around his waist, along with the goading, and the two made for Caerleon.

Compelled for a final look back to the forest, Maelgwn saw *himself* once more, peering at him from the side of a girthy tree. He quickly jumped behind it, vanishing in the twinkling of an eye.

***

The Church of Rome had sent twelve bishops, two archbishops (and Simon Magus in his guise accounting for one of them), and a small company of soldiers to visit the famous King Arthur at his estate in Caerleon.

The king's own brother, Prince Madoc the Sea Master, met with their vessel south of the horn of the Isles, guiding safe passage to the port of Newydd and then, transitioning from sea to river, up the winding Usk River into Caerleon.

Madoc prepared a parade upon the waters so that the ecclesiastical guests were greeted with a shower of high-arching fiery arrows tipped with powder, clashing in the air, giving bursts of light in unusual and spectacular shapes. Hundreds of streamers of gold and great banners adorned with the Red Dragon were posted at three paces apart on either side of the riverbank, making the river as a road paved and decorated with pageantry, splendor and merriment. Sculptures of art wobbled on stationary platforms that Taliesin and Madoc had engineered to float. Moreover, all the musical enchantment of the Blessed Isles was in its fullest, most prominent display. Illtud's choirs sang in unison with the rush and whistle of the river, creating a vibratory thunder of pious hymns, battlecries and love songs. Harps and horns complemented the singing, and Rome herself, even at the zenith of her external beauty and grandeur, gave no welcome that was equal to the Silures of Caerleon.

As Simon's boot met Cymry soil, the land cried out its protest. Gwyar, above the city center tending to ponies along the rim of Lodge Hill, heard Cymru's cry. Repulsed at a congress of pseudo-Christians, she gritted her teeth and made haste, descending by the path most swift into the city.

The saints were the first to greet their Italian counterparts. Helpers (for no Cymry citizen was a servant or a slave in his own land, even if a person of lower estate or employed as the hireling of a household) brought gifts of foods and delights and fabrics and tin and copper, but Arthur forbade gifts of gold. The Catholics received the gifts with humble gratitude and exchanged brotherly kisses with all, save Magus who, limited by his mask, simply bowed.

The prominent clergy of the Britons, including both those who favored and those who opposed Rome, served as hosts. Amongst these were Dyfrig, the Evangelist of Ergyng, who also crowned Arthur; Teilo and Samson, his pupils; Illtud the Wise; Bedwini, who was Arthur's personal bishop; Cadfan, who had rooted himself on Ynys Enlli and governed the Llyn Peninsula; Dewi of Henfynyw; and Caw of the Old North, who had brought his son Gildas. He was but eleven, but had been gifted from birth to quickly master all known languages and to work in scripts from any of the tribes and kindreds upon the earth. The boy would serve as a scribe, recording the visit.

A replenishing visit to the ancient baths, and the visitors retired for the night.

Gwyar was at Gwenhywfar and Arthur's apartment, rousing them with a violent knock. The king eschewed the grump of sleepiness and favored humor.

Rubbing his eyes: "Did you kill Cai then, sister?"

"Your steward lives."

"She is so short, brother; I often miss mice that sneak into your chamber as well." Cai hurled humor down the corridor, never far away from the one he'd pledged his life to protect.

Cai was a stoic, hard man. *The watchman of all watchmen.* His jest was so out of character that it caused the royal siblings' eyes to widen and foreheads to startle at the same time, and raucous laughter had no choice but to burst from them both at the same time.

They embraced.

A naked, immodest figure appeared in the shadow of the arched doorway. Cai, who was pleased with himself that he had been able to form a jest, had nearly joined where they were standing when he saw a flash of flesh and recoiled back into the hallway.

"I thought we agreed you would see to your orchards and bones and relics, far from here."

Gwyar's eyes met Gwenhwyfar's.

The room's hearth was not burning, for the weather was temperate, and blankets sufficed. But the moonlight revealed all of the Giant's little daughter nonetheless. Her tribal markings, decorating her body in spirals and tribal knotwork, seduced any two eyes to follow their circuits, to her navel and down to the flower, which was cleanly shorn and designed to be the ruin of men.

"My love." Arthur's visage begged his wife to consider a modicum of modesty.

She fetched a thin, silky gown and gave false eyes of wifely support.

"The Lady of Avalon goes where she will. And where she ought," Gwyar responded. "Besides, the Lady of Lake is at her turn as custodian of the Cup. Now…" She attempted to dismiss the queen and positioned her body towards her brother alone. "Will you hear me, or think you that I came banging upon your door hours before dawn for the pleasure of it?"

"By all means." Gwen was impossible to dismiss. Impossible to ignore. She placed her half-naked body in the midst of the siblings, an unspoken gesture insisting that she be part of whatever message was forthcoming.

In doing this, quite by chance, Gwen's hands brushed upon Arthur's and Gwyar's at the same time, forming a chain of contact.

'Twas but half a second in duration, and Gwen's carnality rendered her blind to the incident, but not so for Arthur and Gwyar.

Arthur, in the nether time between night and day where the senses are confused and gateways are opened, conjoined to his first love and his first *lover*, saw the form of his night terror rise.

Only it did not come forth from Gwyar. The succubus pushed up and out of his very own chest. Beautiful. The White Phantom with flowing black hair that was at once *there and not there, wisping between the worlds*. The ancient goddess of sovereignty and war swam in and out and around the three of them, then back into the king, and once more spiraled out of Arthur's body towards the vaults above.

"Morgana," he gasped, bereft of breath. The creature was an exact composite of Gwyar and Gwen, but that it had glowing white fangs of a wolf. "Morgana!" A second gasp.

As lightning, the goddess struck straight for Arthur again, finding her mark, disappearing within his head. He fell to a knee, *the first time any foe had brought the Pendragon to a knee,* and started again to call out to her.

Meanwhile, Gwyar labored hard and, at the last moment, pulled away, breaking the conduit. Moving quickly, she conjured a binding spell in the language of Heaven and pleaded with Arthur, "Say not her other name! Brother, my love, you must not!"

The half-second ticked away, and the ordeal abated. Gwyar looked upon her brother, worried and alarmed. He did not look well. King Arthur was never sick, never lame; the comfort and rock of Cymru, the Iron Bear. To see him ill, even for a moment, gave Gwyar great pause, frightening her more than the sorcery and witchcraft and malevolence that ever accompanied her goings.

"I have a terrible ache within my head and must return to my bed. Please hasten to tell me quickly the purpose your visit, that I might retire."

Gwyar was direct. Gwen scoffed, complete

with the rolling of eyes and the tapping of foot, but spake not.

"The leader of the Council of Nine, that shadow college that murdered our Merlin." She clutched both of the king's hands and pulled him closer. "He is here, in Caerleon. He is amongst the visitors from Rome."

CHAPTER 12
The Standoff

Ogyrfan Gawr loved his daughter. *In his own way.* He wanted her to obtain her ambition. A reckless, undisciplined love of libertinism, matched with coy statesmanship and political pandering.

To be queen: achieved.

But more. To do as she pleased and have the whole of Britannia grovel at her feet as she puffed and proudly lorded over them: not yet achieved.

A local chieftain, his fortress was impenetrable, set atop a gargantuan natural mound within a plain, easily defended on all sides by superbly drawn tracts of land that formed an expertly designed city. Caer Ogyrfan was the gateway to the Midlands, and the key crossway between North and South.

Having no particular god save Ambition, Ogyrfan gave consistent offerings to both the Church of the Britons and the Roman Church. Cattle and pigs and tracts of lands he gave to the druids and to the Dynion Hysbys. Aloof and neutral and brooding, he paid all but was friend to none.

And he was a Giant. He did possess the extra fingers and toes, and wore thick black leather gloves always so that, with time, few ever noticed the aberration. The extra row of teeth was present as well, but only on the lower jaw and limited to half a rung. This made him jowly but not overtly deformed.

Tiny compared to Itto Gawr, Ogyrfan was identical in height to Maelgwn Gwynedd, though wider at the shoulder. A massive man; a small Giant.

His stature was on account of the dilution of angelic blood in his lineage. Ogyrfan was composed of much more man than god and as such was incredibly difficult to bewitch and activate, as Simon's identified *next monster* to harass and trouble the Summer Kingdom.

"I am the High King's father-in-law!" he bellowed. "What you ask of me is treason and would cost my Gwen the throne. And more! I will not!"

"You will." Simon had calmly removed the mask. "Tomorrow you will attack the king before all. He will slay you and increase in stature, or you will slay him, leaving an open throne. Either way, any potential ire towards Rome is distracted. Either way, our great work continues."

"I know nothing of your great work, and care for none of your politics. My daughter and I – we have our own politics."

Simon Magus ceased wasting time reasoning with the thing that was mostly man but part monster. He summonsed the Adder, already skulking around in the shadows.

"Take his will and bend it. Make him loyal unto the death. Loyal unto me."

The anti-druid nodded, setting out to do his sorcery upon the queen's father. Magus smiled, returned his face back to its mask, and retired to the guesthouse provided for him at Caerleon.

***

After a hearty meal to break the fast, the Roman visitors were permitted, under the careful custody of Cai and a few select men of Maelgwn's Hosts (the most elite of all fighters on the Blessed Isles), to make the short carriage ride to Caermelyn and see the famed Round Table. Little Gildas was allowed to draw and document their wonder at Merlin's creation, but they would not meet in that famed hall, not argue religion in those gilded seats. Rather, they were back to Caerleon by midday.

Returning to Arthur's estate, they convened in an ornate grange with checkered floors of marble that featured a large stage that fanned outward, then sloped down towards an open hall, where dancing and games of sport and skill were conducted.

The Cymry were seated at one long table on the stage, facing their guests, whose table was twelve steps below them. Less than subtle, the arrangement sought to check the hubris of Rome.

Simon Magus, in his guise as a crippled archbishop covering up some unknown facial deformity, was concealed from head to toe in a crimson cloak; likewise was his mask blood-red. His vestments were ruddy as well, rendering him a scarlet rush, a candle of ecclesiastical peculiarity. The garb was an odd selection for one who coveted darkness and anonymity. On this day he needed to draw Arthur out, and measure him. However, he must not provoke the Bear, for if he did, the Romans would add to the bones of other invaders that now fertilized plant and tree and graveled the riverbeds. *Provoke, learn, and leave.*

The other archbishop was a very old man. Well into retirement, he had cited a deep longing to see Britannia before going into the sleep of death as the cause for his strong petition to head the envoy. As Bishop of Salona, Magus knew his politics and his military history and had discerned him harmless enough; the perfect prattler to get the bishops babbling, so that Magus could take advantage of the clamor and engage Arthur.

The archbishop had actually served for a time as western emperor for the whole of the Roman Empire several decades ago and, like Arthur's grandfather Tewdrig, had retired in favor of a religious life when spent were his political years.

Devils are smart; however, devils are not omniscient. What Magus was unaware of was that the elderly and feeble man harbored a visceral hatred of the Silures. Eighty and nine years of contempt dating back to the dusk of the Imperial Era, combined with the vanishing concern for discretion or manners that sometimes accompanies advanced age, had made him very unpredictable.

And dangerous.

Knowing none of this, Magus gingerly seated the elderly priest in the center chair at the long guest table and looked up to Arthur, Bedwini and the company of renowned Britons. He quietly spoke.

"Glycerius, ought not you ask the great Arthur of the Britons if you can bless this gathering with prayer ere we begin reason of matters plain and precious to the cause of Christ and His Holy Church?"

Honored and opportunistic, Archbishop Glycerius responded, "By your grace, you have fulfilled an old man's dying dreams."

"To it, then." Magus motioned his hand up towards the Cymreig assembly.

But the old priest's fulfillment would have to tarry as some of the guests were still assembling, the hall a loud bustle of deafening conversation and *settling in for what heated action might satisfy their itchy ears.*

Gwenhwyfar II entered, making procession to the host table. Accompanied by song from the bards, she was as a swan, gracefully dancing across the floor. Her gown was two sleeves, with the lower portion but a sophisticated woven wrap of green silk. Decorative red lacings threaded the sleeves, the small of her back and her bosom. Every jaw at once fell agape. Arthur beamed.

Four thin golden necklaces decorated her neck, several torques her wrists and sleek, perfect arms. The gold accented her speckled eyes; the most alluring eyes in all of Britannia.

Though her love for Mordred had reformed her outlook and softened her disposition, the fundamental core of her being - namely, disdain for men and thirst for power for its own sake - was starting to seep back through the cracks of external repair. The long years of pressure to give Arthur an heir and her chronic lies and façades to facilitate making love to her Mordred were *bringing back the monster.* She fought this, but the people took note… save her husband, as yet blinded by love as on the first day he had seen her.

On this day she was regal, and her authority gave great edification and confidence to the host bishops and elders, *for a strong woman supporting men always makes men stronger, and strong men as gods.*

Her eyes met with Maelgwn's.

Please don't sit here. The king of Gwynedd jiggled, desperately yearning to leap from both skin and seat.

"Please, dear wife." The king of Glamorgan and Gwent motioned for her to occupy the sole empty chair: between him and Lancelot.

Arthur, Gwenhwyfar, Lancelot; three of the four cords present.

And now, Morgaine of the Faeries.

"Cai, if you please, move a space that I might sit by my brother."

The four cords. The invincible schoolmates. At the same table, looking down upon former conquerors and potentially present conspirators; and a constant nuisance to the soul of the Isles besides. That the Cymry now condescended to the very institution that reckoned itself above the Nations and would have all men bend the knee to her ways was a relished moment. The Ostrogoths in the present generation had their way with the remnant shadow of imperial Rome, whom it behooved to behave in comely ways and sedately here in the House of Arthur, lest the Britons do the same.

Lancelot could think on none of these things. Nor could he appreciate the moment. His heart and loins burned for Gwen.

Gwen's heart and whole body ached for Mordred.

Lancelot noted her glow, and mistook its object.

The royal siblings rose above demons, pride, passion and hauntings of the past, focused as a bird of prey on matters pertaining to the preservation of the people. For this cause, Morgaine and Arthur were the greater members of the quartet.

Arthur made one more change to the seating

arrangement, asking that the lad, Gildas ap Caw, sit to his right, but for a special moment. The Iron Bear had observed that nerves and distress were overcoming the young genius and sought to encourage the boy. Though his father was a rival, *a rival approaching the measure of enemy,* Arthur had vowed never to visit the sins of the father upon the sons. Because of this principle, because Arthur treated every individual on his or her own merits, many Northerners loved the Silure king, and factions were held at bay.

The situation was overwhelming Gildas: a child charged with memorializing history's mightiest empire come to visit history's most legendary king.

"Look." A great warm smile erupted from the Pendragon. "Even the bards envy you, little Gildas."

"They do?"

"Yes. Your memory and gift for understanding tongues exceeds theirs." A fatherly pat upon the head and tug of the hair. "What you can do at ten takes them a lifetime of study."

"Eleven." Kind words gave the boy confidence. Confidence to correct a king!

Arthur had completed his task, engendering a calming joy within the boy. Recalling how Caw's youngest, and most famous, son had been born the year of Mynydd Baedan, Arthur replied, "Has it been eleven years?"

The boy hugged Arthur, pulling him close with all of his might, never forgetting the kindness of the king, then scurried off quickly to his own father and a comfortable position to prepare scroll and ink.

"Eleven years of peace and liberty." Morgaine's hand gently found the king's wrist. "Let's try and make it twelve. Yes?" Her disposition beseeched Arthur to stop suffering children and get back to dealing with the Roman Church. Arthur gave a short sigh, pursued by a shorter smile at his sister, straightened his shoulders, and allowed the congress to commence.

At last, as ready to burst as a ripe fruit, the retired emperor looked Arthur directly in the eye. "May I bless this assembly?"

"Of course." Hospitality and caution salted the response.

There was no salutation. No *thank you* offered.

"May the Lord God give the bishops of our brethren in Britannia and Eire the wisdom to bow the knee before our Holy Father, the Bishop of Rome, and cede her position and possession to the One True Church, commissioned to occupy until the Lord come!"

Magus wished for death inside his mask. For the old man had surely brought the sword upon them all.

"What is this *madness?*" It was Illtud who offered the retort. And Arthur gave him leave to continue.

Arthur was unarmed. Excalibur was displayed on the wall, well out of reach, along with one of the other swords of Britain. The sword of Caesar, raised by the king at his crowning in Londinium, accompanied the Sword of Power: a grand display and message as to the primacy and potency of Cymru. His dagger and other famed armaments were in his chamber or under the careful watch of Peredur. As the venom of religious factionism spewed so immediately, the king wondered whether he had erred in not having some means of protection, or attack, on his person. *Assassinations start after loud insults that result in a room of chaos.* Another lesson from his Merlin flooded his memories.

Archbishop Glycerius was at the ready to articulate his accusation.

"You require your princes and chieftains to pay a penance of land and cattle to your Church. In turn, you only allow princes and chieftains to enter into the clergy, thus protecting your own lands in perpetuity. It is a political mechanism. A circular fraud. A farce. A façade. A mockery of the Scriptures."

The old man was not wrong. The Church of the Britons, far older than Rome in spite of her claims, misinterpreted both Moses and John, asserting that those in ecclesiastical authority must be priests and kings. They did well to separate the two (unlike Rome), but did err in creating priest-class made wholly of immediate and strong bloodlines. This allowed frequent transfers of land, protecting Cymry soil for all times.

"And you would have all lands ceded to the Church. For you think the keys of temporal and heavenly rule are thine, yes?" Illtud fired back, yelling.

"The Bible says—"

"It has been given to me to understand that NONE OF YOU are Scriptural. It is part of your furniture, a decoration, a tool of selective misuse and no authority." Arthur winked at Taliesin, stooped in the back of the hall, forming a great and proud smile. *The Merlin would be proud too.*

"Enough theology today." The king rose. "To enjoy our rivers, bask in our baths and waterfalls, be revived by our forests, surely attempt to enjoy our women." The gathered crowd chuckled, including the bishops. "To tour our fellowship hall where all men are equal under God - only to recompense the gesture by launching into an immediate insult of our national faith. Such guile." Arthur shook his head, calming himself. "It will certainly make some story, laughing around the hearth with cider."

"I have a story for you, Celt." Glycerius used Caesar's pejorative. "I noticed that in all your hospitality and openness, you failed to take us to see the abandoned barracks of the Legionnaires, the housing of our brave soldiers in the days when we put the lash to you barbarians."

"Speak no more, Archbishop." Magus pointed his long spiny finger, motioning in vain to stop the rogue priest.

The spiny plated finger jostled a memory in Lancelot. He shifted forward but slightly.

But it was Arthur that spoke.

"Barbarian? O, Roman propaganda. My grandfather, the Pendragon King Tewdrig, told my father all about this. We taught your would-be Roman conquerors to understand Greek. Our druids taught you how to build canals, to conduct water and to live in cleanliness. As for the lash, we loaned you senators and chieftains. You were a tenuous and oft-unwelcomed guest here; never a conqueror. This is the land of Bran and Caradoc. Your mythology and hubris won't be sold for truth here, emperor."

Bedwyr, using his left hand, skated a leather-wrapped steel cup, brimming with cider, past three seated onlookers. It perfectly found rest in Arthur's palm.

"Grandfather? Yes. Let us speak on grandfathers." The delirious old priest's chest plumed, but the rest of him trembled. "I am here because of MY grandfather. For my grandfather. He was stationed HERE. He slept in your wretched barracks, pissed in your magical pools, and found your women – o, the Cymreig women that the whole of the world covets – he found them uncomely yapping dogs! You animals killed him. He fell at the tip of a Silure spear, his body never transported back to Mother Rome!"

"Perhaps you would join him?" Many Saxons had heard this particular tone, the final sounds that filled their ears ere they fell to Arthur's steel.

Unafraid, the elderly symbol of the proud but crumbled empire continued his untoward spectacle. "You will give tribute to Rome and fidelity to her Church, THE ONLY TRUE CHURCH, and to the Bishop our Father, or—"

Magus opened his armored hand. Using his unnaturally long fingers as four tethered whips, he smote the old man flush about the face. The lips split in twain, vertically. A fount instantly watered the table red and baptized the Catholic presbyters, sprinkling them with shock, spittle and much blood.

Through that massive curtain in the pagan tabernacle, I saw such a slap.

Lancelot rose so quickly it was as if he had been standing the entire time. He leaped over the long table with no more effort than a stag hops over a ditch, then majestically bounds into the deep of the forest. Also unarmed, he made for the wall, freeing the mounted Sword of Power from the hooks upon which it rested. Excalibur in hand, he rushed upon not the raging old man mourning a long-dead Roman, but rather the masked villain sitting next to him.

When the Masked Man perished, there would be no answers to rest Arthur's soul, no final closure to the wound. No healing for the loss of the Merlin. And this pained Lancelot, even as he brandished the blade overhead, preparing for the terminal stroke. However, he would here make an end of the Kingdom's most dire and secret threat. The shadow menace would fall. Whatever this man and his Council of Nine were, the means by which they coerced and controlled whole nations, or their ultimate aims for mankind, the details were not relevant. They were pure evil. And the head of that snake would be severed, today. Though Arthur would not have opportunity to interrogate his great secret enemy, he would be rid of him, and Lancelot was content with that outcome.

And in killing the Masked Man, the misdeeds of Vivien would never see the light of day, her sins dying with him.

Excalibur, so sharp and wielded with Lancelot's speed, rent the sky itself, flying swiftly to visit judgment upon Simon's neck.

Judgment deferred.

A club that was as a small oak tree intercepted and deflected its course. Though the club was cut through and through by the famed blade, which still found its mark, the blow was slowed, and the wound not fatal. Simon was knocked to the ground and opened, but the flesh wound was minor.

Lancelot's vision ascended slowly from where the masked priest lay to the height of the tabletop and at last, fully standing, to his eye level. Face to face and waiting for him to recompose himself was a wide and brawny form, a second club already in hand to replace the one severed and rolling away on the marble floor.

The stare was both empty and intense, filled only with malevolent intent. It belonged to the father of one whom Lancelot loved.

Ogyrfan the Giant had protected the red

Roman, and his eyes warned that he was set to execute the whole of the assembly.

Lancelot put the sword to the neck of Magus, still down, to stop the encroach of the large man, or conversely, to simply finish the task, even if the cost was absorbing a fatal blow from his newly-made foe.

Dumbfounded, Arthur's command stilled the whole of the hall.

"Lancelot, stop!" Bewilderment. "The crippled cardinal stayed the mouth of this rude collection of bones masquerading as an emperor. You launched out at the wrong masked man."

"Lancelot would not miss his aim, brother."

In a complex and closing vice, Lancelot responded to his friends, careful to conceal any indictment of his foster-mother. Haste was also demanded, given the burly opponent yet prepared to engage him.

"Lord, Gwyar." That deep and metallic voice long told in bardic song and poets' prose uttered its reply. "This man is chief of the shadow government. I saw him in the Lady of the Lake's forest so long ago. He is the one." The tip of Excalibur pressed to Simon's wound, twisting just so. Lucifer's disciple refused to reward Lancelot and cried out not.

"The one that—?"

"The one behind the mystery of Merlin, my lord."

That the Cymry were unarmed wasn't exactly true. Although the individual guests, heroes and knights did not bring their personal arms to the peaceful accord, no leader from the days of Vortigern to the present time would allow another Night of Long Knives to occur under their watch. To this end, several leaves, shortswords of the finest craftsmanship, lightweight killing instruments designed for a quick kill in a defensive situation, were concealed in ornate, thin, hollow boxes that served as under-bases for food salvers and chargers. In a move well-rehearsed and well-practiced for such an occasion, the food dish could be lifted and gently set aside, the box unhinged, Cymry steel revealed.

Arthur gave the command, his calm matching Lancelot's answer, both of them mastering emotion, both of them assessing the whole of the room, both of them transported from assembly hall to forest, field or riverbed. Unlike in other battle settings, children and defenseless citizens abounded.

Within three seconds Bedwyr, Gwalchmai, Urien, King Meurig, Mordred, Gaheris, Cai, Peredur, Geraint, Lancelot's sons Rhun and Rhufawn, along with the Bloodhound Prince, who brandished the king's own sword, were upright. Leaves swiveling, hilts rolling in ready and anxious palms, Vivien's battle stances engaged.

Sounds of the calamity reached the troop of Roman guards, who reposed outside the hall. They and their spears forced themselves inside.

"My beloved friend, and champion of all Britannia." Arthur was calm. "In your haste to protect us from such a villain, you did err." The way the king spoke was neither condemning nor offensive towards Lancelot and was followed by, "I would have done the same thing, having discovered the one who stole Britain's Treasure." (And by this, he spake of Merlin).

Lancelot had no argument for what came next.

"Rather not to slay him. Instead, brother, arrest! Detain! Let us finally discover the truth that has so long darkened our Summer Kingdom."

In an irony of fortune, Lancelot needed not make a reply. Like a mad, diseased bull or ram, Ogyrfan, having given a few more moments of breath to the one lording over his thoughts and deeds, turned towards *his target*. Stooping into an attack pose, shoulders low and squared, he barreled into the host table, splintering it as a twig, violently knocking many to the floor, causing scrapes and wounds but no major injury. Arthur had stood and jumped backward at the onset of the assault, but the Giant was before him, *and the club was already midflight.*

Lancelot's flight was much faster than the twirling club.

"Have any more?" Lancelot cocked his head at Ogyrfan, then looked at yet another weapon rendered as wood for the hearth by Excalibur. "That's two." The champion of the Round Table wiggled two fingers, goading the attacker to assault him rather than the king.

The events were unfolding with such surreal haste that none knew whether they should kill, or *could kill,* the queen's father. While Lancelot was cultivating distraction through taunting, granting them time to think, Gwalchmai usurped the process and, wrapping his hand with a strap of leather from his belt, grasped his curved sword by the blade and struck the Giant violently upon the back of his head with the sword's hilt. Then he recovered the hilt and raised the blade high, seeking a fatal blow. *Treachery is no respecter of persons.* This was the Hawk of May's reasoning.

But now.

But now a scene that no bard could dam the tears to tell, could channel away the overmuch sorrow to utter.

Now the tip of the Sword of Power pressed

into the side of Gwalchmai's neck, its bulging veins swelling at the fear, pulsating from a rapid and roaring heart. Through the droplets of sweat, Gwalchmai peered down the plane of the blade to see an oak of a man as a statue; no movement, no emotion, ready to kill.

Thinking only of his one true love, regarding neither law nor politic, Lancelot would slay Gwalchmai, or one thousand Gwalchmais, rather than suffer Gwenhwyfar to see her father slain.

Gwalchmai's sword remained at the throat of Ogyrfan.

Lancelot's sword remained at the throat of Gwalchmai.

"Gwyar, please, no." Arthur's words were for naught.

The only person in the realm, nay, any realm, that could challenge Lancelot by reason of her sorceries and her skill (and he knew as much and respected the threat) could not reach Lancelot's throat, as he was twice her height. Rather, Gwyar put a small dagger, rivaling Excalibur for sharpness and forged on the same Isle, to his kidney. She cared *for country and for her son,* and his remaining alive was best for both causes.

Gwalchmai's sword upon Ogyrfan.

Lancelot's sword upon Gwalchmai.

Gwyar's dagger upon Lancelot.

And the Roman soldiers closing in, under no obligation to delay their encroach or give space for the Briton's internal strife to reconcile itself.

Meanwhile, Magus and Glycerius used the standoff to stand and recover. Both bleeding, only one giving thought for his own life. The retired emperor, too old for combat, nonetheless attacked the mighty King Arthur.

Whilst the other Round Table Knights and

Companions used hidden compartments to conceal reserve weaponry amongst lamb and beef and cakes, Cai simply kept his famed club inside his cloak - always. He tossed it to the twice-attacked-in-one-day Pendragon who, in one motion, both caught the wooden instrument and brought it hard across the Roman's jaw.

A club is light at the handle, weighted at the head. A menacing weapon. Arthur rotated explosively from his core, generating maximum torque: a colossal blow.

A dislodged eye bounced, ultimately finding rest upon a broken plate on what remained of the host table. Teeth clacked and spread over the floor. No facial structure remained; just a white face smashed, a lump of folded dough with nostrils. The bitter man was liberated of the shackles of his mortal coil, released from his hatred of the Silures by a Silure.

And so, whilst his most beloved friends were frozen in the snare, the High King of the Britons slew a Roman emperor.

Next came a command, yelled in unison by the king and his champion.

"Cai, remove the queen. Hasten her to safety!"

"At once," Cai answered them both. "Shall I send signal to Lodge Hill and rouse our soldiers?" The steward could relay a message from Caerleon up to the fortress within three minutes and the guards, using fire and mirrors, could have a hundred men at arms at the hall seven minutes after that.

Arthur looked on his men and their quandary. And upon the Romans. "No, Cai. If we manage to not kill ourselves off, we will quickly add more Romans to our soil."

Gwenhwyfar was as befuddled and bewildered over her father's behavior as any of the attendees. She had no answers, and she worried for him, but gave no protest. She glanced at him, helpless before the Hawk of May, and then kept her gaze at Mordred constant until she was out of the hall and he out of her sight.

As their leader was *busy,* the warriors furthest from the standoff, and thus nearest to the Romans, tarried not for command or instruction. Rather, *action.*

Taliesin did all to discourage Rhufawn, for he had a special affinity for Maelgwn Gwynedd's son, but the young man could not be withheld from the fight. Indeed, becoming a marvel and spectacle to all, he *was the fight.*

Rhufawn had a similar build to his father, but was of just above average height. Where Maelgwn's hair was curly and black, his was as the sandy shores, like Arthur. The young warrior seemed to be the product of God, taking the best ingredients of the two great men and blending them into a flawless, perfect knight, gifting to the world Rhufawn ap Maelgwn, whom the bards record as Galahad*, which is a Hebrew derivative of the word Gilead, and by interpretation means 'healing balm'.*

Rhufawn, the bastard son of a Glamorgan damsel, favored the simple midnight-blue tunic worn so oft by Maelgwn, the color, when coupled with crimson, of the Silures. But he loved his father and the Tribes of the North as well. For this cause, his cape was black, ensigned with a beautiful white raven. *A walking symbol of peace, unity and individuality amongst the Cymry.*

On days where he sought a shinier, statelier expression (though he was ever humble in disposition, impossible to anger, impossible to speak against), he enjoyed the gold-styled armor popular amongst the children of both Arthur and Maelgwn. When decked in gold, the lasses swooned (though endowed like his father, the boy knew no woman, vowing only to give his virginity to one wife) and the poets sang, all the while Taliesin laboring to protect him from the world.

Rhufawn had not known war. Had never known the terror of the Saxon's Long Knife, his mind not bent with the horrors of the ever-threat of ambush and torture and annihilation.

A healthy mind, but wanton for quest.

A natural warrior, he held back in training exercises, cautious and careful never to injure his opponents, his kinsmen. But natural talent is often overcome through hard work. Heeding this lesson from Taliesin, Rhufawn was a picture of *both.* Never taking the skill passed to him from Lancelot for granted, he practiced with radical commitment.

Naturally better than others, more humble, harder working.

And now a real combat situation was before him and his kinsmen and friends.

The first Roman soldier swung his spear sloppily at the young man, putting undue faith in the advantage of reach. Rhufawn not only ducked the lazy swipe but, during its flight, circled from front to back, round his opponent, slashed him in the only space between armor and spine and recoiled, watching the attacker fall paralyzed, with an agonizing death soon to follow.

He followed this, *dancing Vivien's dance* through the Romans. Always at a diagonal position, always countering, never initiating, always killing instantly. His movements were at once a tempest and a swan. As he ran one Roman through, his blade was withdrawn and already taking limb and ear from the next in one motion.

Neither clip, nor bruise, nor scrape found him. The only time he was touched was when Urien caught the lad by his tunic and chastised him, screaming, "Save us one!"

Rhufawn's singular massacre of an old invader in a new era lasted a short time.

Lovemaking and fights alike seem to last forever, but are over in minutes.

Maelgwn, though never moving from his vantage point upon Gwalchmai, whom he believed would surely strike down the queen's father minus the steel upon his throat, was able to see it all. And for him it *did* seem to last forever. The Northern king had been in battles with Rhun, a fine soldier and great young man who had already earned his own bards' songs. Thus, he was accustomed to the threat of losing that son.

But not so Rhufawn.

Maelgwn's emotions undulated as a strong spiderweb. *Fear for his safety. Dread that he now knew the stealing of another man's breath; pride over what he witnessed.*

Could it be?

Nimrod.

Hercules.

Achilles.

This was the company of fighters that Maelgwn Gwynedd kept. Invincible. Unstoppable. Grace and power personified.

But also, madness and instability.

Rhufawn had proven in his years as a boy and young man to possess none of the latter; he here showed the fullness of the former. Could it be?

Speed.

Use of balance and imbalance.

Counter-fighting skills to an extreme degree, where the opponent's next two moves could be *seen* before he began the first two.

Precise maiming skills when desired.

Killing strokes from hundreds of angles and approaches.

Fluidity.

Defense.

Could it be?

For as long as tales of valor and skill would be told and soldiers ranked, the matter would never be settled. But Maelgwn first saw his glorious son vanquish a troop as an effortless and beautiful angel delivering death with grace.

Could it be?

Yes, Galahad was greater than Lancelot. The greatest warrior to ever live.

A father's tear formed, and Maelgwn cared not to contain it.

Meanwhile, the High King was directing a battle on two fronts. He took one of the priests by the neck of his robe and demanded, "Which amongst you is a boatman? He is of the laity, the troop, or one of you?" Arthur's authority and power was delivered in Latin with the same precision and want of immediate response as when delivered in Cymraeg. "I will only ask once," he finished.

The priest, soaking his robe with urine, trembling, pointed to one of the soldiers, barely enunciating, "Sail, sail the boat."

Arthur unhanded the clergyman and threw his voice, as a javelin is hoisted through the skies at Grecian games, down the long hall. "Urien!"

The ferocious fighter paused in a kill and found the source hollering his name.

"Him." Arthur pointed and gestured frantically. "Spare him!"

But two minutes later, the Roman troop was dead. With the exception of the sailor, all had perished. All tilled at the plow by famed Round Table Knights of old, *and new.*

The civilian guests found a crack in the chaos, a collective feeling of safety, and vacated the hall. This was more dangerous than the inferior insurgency by the Italians.

Simon Magus took full advantage of the fleeing frenzy, snatching the child Gildas, who was too big to be carried and too small to push men and women aside, from his father's custody.

An evil laugh projected, louder and sharper than the king's own voice had been moments ago.

"Let's add one more knife to this tension, one more wooden piece to this game of *gwyddbwyll.* After all" – through the mask his eyes peered over the checkered floor, now a calamity of teeth and organs, broken furniture and broken bones – "we are already upon the game board, yes?" A second laugh.

"This is no game," struck back the Pendragon, taking a strong stride towards the masked priest.

"O, my king." Awe, mixed with mockery, stirred with teaching, followed. "All life is a game of *gwyddbwyll.*" A short black dagger was now upon the child's neck, his pens and parchments fumbled away, his hands pushing at the priest's red robes. "Don't move, lad; not another movement." The dagger pressed. "And don't you move either."

Arthur stopped as though a statue, ceasing to tempt the villain.

The scene quieting and settling, with the fighting assuaged, begat the accusations and strained discourse amongst the chain of prisoners and prison-keepers.

"How dare you draw your sword upon my son!" Morgaine of the Faeries the first to break the silence in their deadly game.

"How dare your son attempt to kill my—"

"Your what!" Gwalchmai swelled with righteous indignation, sensing that Lancelot was primed to out himself, to snare his leg in the trap of his own adultery, and by his own words no less.

As the battle of threats and accusations proceeded, and as message had not been sent to Lodge Hill to signal for additional warriors, *other visitors were arriving.*

Lancelot captured his confession ere it fully left his lips, swallowing it back and recovering with, "My king's father-in-law. What is it you accuse me of? Use plain speech." Here, Lancelot evoked an evil and ancient technique, used by the guilty since the dawn of man. When caught in a grave and unspeakable sin, boldly dare the accuser to verbalize it, making it sound shocking and absurd, diminishing the credibility simply through its saying, though it is true.

Morgaine found her son's eyes with her own and forbade him to speak, knowing it would undo the Summer Kingdom.

Lancelot's rationalization went on. "Before we execute this man, we must understand the aberration of his action. A quiet fellow who gives alms to all and loves his daughter and her king."

"Such love manifested as an attempt to murder the king, whom you say he loves." Gwalchmai tried to corral his words, obeying his mother as he could, but alas, he could not fully. "You protect him for love of the queen, not our lord."

But Arthur had found reason in Lancelot's

words, and dismissed the weight of Gwalchmai's half-concealed warning. "You are right, Maelgwn. I have seen this before. A just man atop a great hill in the north also sought to kill me. The toil in my father-in-law's eyes matches those of Itto Gawr, a just and goodly creature."

Arthur's glare turned again towards Magus. "Somehow, Ogyrfan is bewitched and no traitor, yes?"

The Leader of the Council of Nine ignored the query.

"Gwalchmai, stand down. Mordred, would you and," Arthur found the awing Rhufawn amongst the onlookers, "this" – the enamored king wanted for words – "extraordinary young man please bind Ogyrfan and see him back to his lands? There confine him in exile until we discover how to cure the kingdom of this witchcraft. Station many soldiers there; make the arrangements and see to it swiftly. As for you," now Arthur spoke directly to the Giant who had but minutes ago made attempt on his life, "you shan't be charged with treason at this time. However, see that you tether yourself to Caer Ogyrfan, and leave not."

Then the king attended to the others. "Lancelot would not have hurt your son, Gwyar. Please." His hands made a motion to withdraw the weapon. At this point, with Gwalchmai released and Lancelot's sword no longer occupied, he could have turned and engaged the sorceress. But he counted the cost, selecting to let Arthur mediate and resolve the conflict, for he had grown up at the feet of powerful women and, to him, they were somehow different creatures entirely than maidens and farm girls, or the Picts who aided him in emptying his lusts from time to time. To him there were *goddesses and girls,* and Morgaine of the Faeries was a *goddess of goddesses.*

Arthur pleaded, repeating his motions once more. "Gwyar, he forgot himself for a moment in the chaos of confusion. He is our brother, our champion, our friend."

The sorceress drew so close that none but Lancelot could hear her. Though impossible on account of their proportions, she was in his ear.

"I have been in love too, Maelgwn." Here she spoke of the only time she had really loved a man, and that years ago foiled through Vivien's prerogative. "And I didn't let it consume and control and change me." *No, lying with your brother in ritual intercourse did that, followed by your soul shattering at the seeing of your son inside your brother's wife.* Her conscience judged her hypocrisy harshly, but she repelled those thoughts. "Get thy head out of thy loins and serve Cymru to your fullest potential." Having concluded the impassioned and maternal lecture, she at last recoiled.

Now all were free of pointed things upon their throats and vital organs.

All save little Gildas, hostage, and the sole means by which Magus might walk out of the hall alive.

"O, King Arthur, son of Meurig and Onbrawst, you cannot be defeated and your kingdom can never fail, even when conflict arises from within. Your career hath not disappointed me. I am most certain that nothing frightens you."

Her son safe and her attention fixed, Morgaine heard the words and shrieked; candles that were unlit blazed, curtains that were closed and knotted flew open, and windows clinched and cracked. His phrases, his arrogance and false flattery. She had met this Italian before.

"Dynion Hysbys!" she cried. "Dynion Hysbys!"

"Druids in the Church of Rome? His identity you mistake." Illtud was aghast at the notion.

"And what a match I did make, little Raven." Magus looked upon Arthur and Gwyar with violating and debased expression.

King Arthur spoke to the chieftain Caw. That they had had land disputes, territorial controversies and bruised history for the whole of the Iron Bear's life was irrelevant. "Sir, your son will be safe, worry not."

Then he looked down to the frightened boy. "Gildas, be calm. Breathe. This will make some story to be added to the histories that you will memorialize for our people. Our official historian."

Gildas managed to smile through the terror and feel safe. *And this was the majesty of Arthur, the lamp in darkest times.*

"Brilliant, Briton. Brilliant." Magus stalled, confident that rescuers of his own would arrive. "What will you give me that I might refrain from opening the lad like a fish here and now?"

"You would give your life to harm a child? If Maelgwn and Gwyar are correct, you are some great one. Would that be your end? Rhufawn hasn't left with the Giant yet; I am sure he could get to you before your blade gets to my young friend."

Rhufawn's father and Urien shared a grin. That the king would threaten the priest with Rhufawn instead of Lancelot was noteworthy, and increased Lancelot's pride o'er his boy.

"O, Arthur, if you knew my God you would know that harming a virgin male child" – he looked for words to further offend the Britons – "is not only a frequent requirement, but a great joy."

"What do you want?" The king tired of

contests of words with the unwanted visitor.

"Two things." Now Magus's recourse was likewise blunt.

With one arm he strangled Gildas, using his forearm, whilst holding the dagger in the same hand. With the other he reached into the folds of his garb. "This book – from whence did it come?"

"I am Taliesin and men call me Merlin; I am Merlin, but men call me Taliesin." The hump-backed bard, with a staff to aid his gait, made straight for the Devil's own man, unafraid. "It was passed down through my family, given to my ancestor centuries ago by the one whose message you fear the most."

"So." All fell silent. "You are the one that converted the Merlin and delayed my plans. Yet, unlike the Merlin, these pseudo-Christians here" – the bishops and elders buckled that such an overtly vile thing would judge them false – "you are allowed to live, freely accessing the king, serving as the new Merlin. Why?"

"In the Body there are many members and diverse offices, as it pleases the Lord." The boy Gildas was nearly within arm's reach of Taliesin now. "My role is to look after one who will carry the truth long after the cosmic dust has rolled up our Island as a scroll and fire from Heaven discarded her. I teach individuals and influence where I can but Merlin, o, the Merlin – his voice and influence would have changed the world and filled the Body of Christ by actually saving souls and edifying saints through the gospel of the grace of God!"

A clamor and howling of heresy filled the hall.

And Magus's other guests gaining distance, soon to arrive.

"Gwyar?" Taliesin looked for aid and the

sorceress obliged, causing the flames to change from shades of yellow to greens and reds and blues, rattling candlestick and curtain rod, fastening the mouths of the bishops through fear.

"And because of Merlin's mystery, which revealed how God forgave all men living in this dispensation above five hundred years ago, not imputing their trespasses against them, that salvation is a function of simply trusting that good news and being forever secured, at peace with a God that already did it all. Because neither these bishops and their works or religion, nor you and your Devil worship, can stop God's plan to reconcile heavenly places with the simple and the foolish, the beggar and the commoner, men and women of no report, because of this simple message of grace." Taliesin was a very soft-spoken man who usually used quips and humor to teach, or harassed his students with witty short allegories. Here he raised his voice, booming with righteous fury. "Because of this, *you killed the Merlin.*"

Hearing this pronouncement, Rhufawn and Mordred stopped short of the wide, arching doorways that were in the anteroom of the hall, one of two entrances to the place. Ogyrfan was bound, head dangling low in shame, confusion and externally-operated rage. Then his ear perked up, as that of a hound that hears a hare whilst hunting in the wood.

Lancelot had returned the shimmering rapier forged on Ynys Enlli to its rightful wielder.

Arthur was gazing upon its scripted hilt. The masked fiend denied nothing and the fact that Arthur was in the same room with the man, hiding behind his guise, who had killed his beloved wizard, challenged his soul to sacrifice the boy and strike Simon down. Teeth gritted, fists clenched, breathing somewhere between weeping and screaming, he managed a final question.

"And the second demand?"

"O Arthur. Your temperance and will, your mastery over passions, over self. How I will enjoy redirecting it."

"Your second demand!"

"The cup that accompanied this." Simon Magus slung the ancient text at the feet of Taliesin, improving his ability to shield himself using the dagger and the boy. "The Grail. I came to witness how you govern, to get but a glimpse of the legendary sovereign, and I came for the Grail. And the visit, the foolish emperor notwithstanding – of course most emperors are dullards and dumb – has been wildly successful, to this point."

"You won't see another sunset, yet you reckon the day a success?"

"I will outlive you, son of Meurig." Magus gave a confident response. "Now, the cup; where is it?"

The doors of the anteroom exploded open, knocking Mordred and Rhufawn back several paces and rendering Ogyrfan unconscious. Rays of light and fog filled the hall. A spectre entered. Gracefully strolling upon the fog, she at once ascended as a dove, with pillowed sleeves and long yellow hair. She was adorned all in white, clad with silver armor. Spiraling towards the ceiling, she soared in and out amongst the long timber rafters.

But 'twas no spectre, for 'twas the Lady of the Lake.

Rhufawn's might in battle exceeding Lancelot had been the first marvel. The Lady of the Lake appearing, bearing in her very hands the Cup of Christ, was the second.

Simon Magus let Gildas loose. Into Arthur's arms he sprinted and in turn, Arthur gently guided him to Caw, who actually embraced his foe. Every witness stood silent and agape. Many swords, satchels or staffs simply dropped to the hard floor below.

The maser was borne as if by an angel, and when she tipped it down towards the watchers below, revealing the mouth of the cup, all saw through their own eyes the next world.

Rhufawn, though raised at the feet of Taliesin and grounded in his mysteries, yearned for it most. And such did it touch him that his heart thumped not for any maiden, his mind drawn away to no other thought save partaking of or *achieving the Grail.*

Taliesin noted that it vexed him.

The Roman Catholic visitors saw it.

The Primal Church of the Britons saw it.

The Round Table Fellowship present saw it.

Morgaine of the Faeries had seen it before, but never as this.

Sundry warriors, stately ladies, minor chieftains, cooks, keepers of the estate and bards looked and saw it.

Little Gildas, the historian and scribe, saw it too.

And then the Lady, as a glowing white phantom, spoke to none else but Simon Magus, the Devil's vicar upon the earth.

"They worship the creature in the stead of the Creator, and you want men to swear by this. A wicked and adulterous nation seeketh after a sign. But a sign you shall have not, and you will never have the Grail! It was given to the druids to guard, and the druids will guard it." The sound of her voice was as many rushing waters, her sermon turning unto the clergy. "And neither shall you!" She cursed the priests and vanished, the whole of the hall falling into pitch black, the silence of darkness.

Morgaine wondered if she ever she would see the Lady again. She had resurrected the purpose of their Order; she had retained her gall for the corruption of the Church, but discovered that Christ and His mother were not to blame for their deeds and had, indeed, endowed her with a sacred trust. She had become fully empowered, transfigured, and glorious. 'Twas no longer needed for the two to move the cup to and fro about the land. It was in Vivien's hands now, to keep or to destroy, to keep from the reach of the wickedness of men forever.

Simon's other expected visitors finally arrived.

Whereas the Lady of Lake had entered through the anteroom, destroying the doorway, these unwanted guests blasted through the front doors.

Two Giants. Thrice the size of Ogyrfan, with green, ghastly skin, horny brows and fanged teeth. No sooner had Urien and Cai restored some light to the hall than were the monsters upon them. Swift as four-footed beasts of the field, they barreled through the crowd. One snatched up Simon with the same effort that a child expends in snatching up a doll when it is time to clean her chamber. The other led the escape, providing a shield of flesh, absorbing sword and spear as they sprinted from the hall, adding further destruction to a place now filled with disarray and desolation. All snarls and no words, they were at once in full sprint across the fields, into the muck of the riverbeds, and gone.

Maelgwn Gwynedd thought only of

Gwenhwyfar, departing at once to see her. The bubble within, no respecter of time or place or propriety, was building in him yet again.

CHAPTER 13
The Abduction of Queen Gwenhwyfar by Maelgwn
The Rescue of Queen Gwenhwyfar by Lancelot

Though lacking the Holy Grail's fame, the king had a special chalice as well. Heavy, ornate, wood inlaid with pewter; the Awen symbol sprawled the circumference of its base. Most importantly of all, the Merlin had gifted it to Arthur after the boy-king had earned his first victory in the Saxon Wars. They had enjoyed a scrumpy together so many long years ago, and with a rare but earned drunkenness, many victory cries. The poor pewter cup was dented by virtue of victorious hammerings into tables and shelves.

No longer a boy, the son of Meurig hammered it down upon a small end-table now. Scrumpy hissed, and not a few drops of the cider streamed about the surface.

Illtud, cousin to Arthur and, due to Dyfrig's advancing years, the most influential amongst the clergy, was the king's drinking companion. And his friend besides.

There was no cause for statesmanship amongst friends, not ensuing the day they had both witnessed and endured. "By Heaven and Hell, Illtud, what just happened?"

"I think I aged three lifetimes in one day!" They both laughed; the chuckle of trauma.

The king became serious, yet no less friendly. "Illtud, you maintain that education and knowledge must diffuse throughout Cymru, from beggar to prince. Moreover, that every person above twelve ought to be able to speak in Latin for commerce, to entertain strangers, and to have some Greek and Hebrew to reason the Scriptures."

"Absolutely, lord. An educated populace has a higher propensity to eschew tyranny, being enlightened by the precepts of liberty."

Arthur swallowed hard another gulp, then replenished the scrumpy. "Then why not consider what my Merlin taught? Why preach liberty and then silence those who would take you up on the very offer you make – namely, to reason from the Scriptures? The words of the elders are at variance with your deeds."

"I know today's events have reopened your greatest wound," said Illtud. "But we did not conspire to murder your counselor. He was my friend too."

Arthur was unsatisfied by the response and responded not, opting to drink and wait for more information.

"The theology that the druid discovered, and that Taliesin the bard champions, is not a new revelation." Illtud was respectful but continued with conviction. "Variants of it have been studied and affirmed as heresy since the times of Caradoc and his daughter Eurgaine. We find that such a mode of study slices the Scriptures like bread, selects favorable passages and ignores a balanced and holistic view of the full counsel of God. Where Taliesin would cry 'grace through faith!', we would counter with 'show me your faith by your works'."

Another swallow. "Does not their way simply maintain that consideration should be given of to whom a letter, poem or prose is speaking in the Holy Book and that audience and context matter?"

Illtud countered, "We also maintain that tradition has equal weight as Scripture, and that, when interpreted without at least some guidance by one called to teach and oversee the flock, gross error and divergent sects will emerge, fracturing the Body." Illtud proceeded to give Arthur what he coveted: direct truth. "We were going to do all to force Merlin to retire and not put his message upon your ear, lest he turn the world upside down, but by the Saviour Himself, none amongst our sect sought to injure our friend."

"You feared he might be right and you might be rendered less necessary. Or unnecessary. Would he not say that your traditions have made the word of God of no effect?"

"He might." Illtud offered candor. This pleased the king more than smokescreens and distraction.

"I don't know if Taliesin and Merlin hold the truth, or if you do, or if it lies somewhere betwixt and between. My station in this life is not to be a master of letters, but rather to secure religious liberty for every man. Even for the Romanists that we sent back to their See with tail between leg and official demands that they investigate deep corruption from within. Do you understand?"

"I do, and I agree. We let fear best us, but again, I promise—"

"I believe you, cousin. This red-robed villain is connected to the Dynion Hysbys and connected to Rome. Whether by infiltration or coercion or alliance. I find no such alliance to the druids or to our primitive Church at this point. What befell our Merlin was of fiendish design by this masked devil. We must settle the tension between the court and pulpit, and focus on his capture and deposition. Madoc will secure every port. He must not leave the Blessed Isles. We have spent the whole of our lives evicting invaders; this time every effort must be made to keep him away from his *secret society* and confined to our soil." Then Arthur eased the gravity, seasoning it with some levity. "Grace versus faith plus works we can debate another day, over much more cider - agreed?"

"Of course!"

Illtud and the king embraced. And no sooner had they embraced than there was a familiar and coordinated knock upon the king's door.

Arthur's countenance dropped as he hollered, "Cai, come. What is it?" He looked at Illtud, exclaiming, "Giants, masked red devils, Roman emperors, a demigod boy warrior and Vivien transfigured with the most precious of our Isle's relics. What else could happen today?" Equal parts smile and dismay.

"Perfectly summarized, Iron Bear. Perfectly summarized." The preacher's disposition matched his friend's.

"The Queen Gwenhwyfar," Cai panted, struggling to moisten his mouth sufficiently to form words. "Abducted. The queen abducted!"

***

"Unhand me!" Gwen II screeched. "You would destroy Cymru for your lust, end an era of peace for an hour of pleasure?"

Maelgwn's bubble had swelled as never before. More so than when he had murdered his uncle to have his wife, or later, arranged for his nephew's murder to bed down Rhufawn's young mother.

Discernment gone.

Temperance abandoned.

The queen was not bound, save by Maelgwn's hands, one of which eclipsed both of hers. He sat behind her, and she was pinned between the trunk of his torso, as a great muscular stone, and the saddle horn of Maelgwn's stallion.

He pressed hard against the small of her back, fully aroused. He freed his massive member from the folds of his trousers and forced her hand to reach round and stroke it.

Prior to her transformative affair with Mordred, she would have happily succumbed to his, or those of any fit and handsome lad, aggressive advances just for the intrigue and fleshly pleasure of it. But she had changed. Had *been changed* for years. Maelgwn simply knew this not. He was accosting a woman loyal to her true love. The loyal adulteress.

When she did not comply with fondling and pleasuring Maelgwn with her hand, he groaned as a dumb animal chained and just out of reach of food, and relinquished her hand. However, he left himself out of his trousers, grinding upon her bottom as they rode.

"Where will we die?" she asked, crying out to reason with the Round Table champion. "For when discovered, we shall both be put to the grave. And you know this. Arthur doth love me above all, and not even your battle dirk will prevent his sword."

Ignoring the ominous sentence of death, he answered the question. "Pictish land. The settlement of Megiel, near to the capital, Peairt. They crown kings there and view me as one of their own; they will protect our entry."

Gwenhwyfar scoffed at the tall warrior. "You would make me your Caledonian whore queen? Arthur will lay waste to the Picts, and to you—"

"Mention not his name again." The pressure from the pelvis of her abductor made the severity of the demand very serious. He could crush her, and in his current state, quite without intending to do so. She needed a different tack.

And she had help.

"When it comes time to do that which you would do—"

"Stop your mouth, wizard!" The famed low voice became a scream. A scream to none but the owls, who responded through the dark of night.

Hearing one once so dear speaking unto unknown voices, obviously originating from his own head, increased the queen's fright. She ceased talking and thought on Mordred and the few happy thoughts of a life shredded by abuse and sticky secret sins. *I have reaped what I have sowed, perhaps,* she thought. *He will be the avenging angel of the dozens of boys and men I have used. Why, in the end, would I not be likewise used?*

Megiel was in center of Alba, a four-day journey by horse or carriage; three if they continued at Maelgwn's relentless pace.

"When it comes time to do that which you would do, for the sake of your country, and for Arthur, do it

not." The phantom voice palpable, substantive. Real. Yet not real.

Arousal and distress caused the warrior to thirst, and thirst caused the warrior to divert his thinking from Gwenhywfar's painted body, and, being diverted, he tried to fight his bubble.

"We will camp here tonight," he stated bluntly.

They had made it as far as the midlands and were in a deep thicket, the forest itself serving as the queen's bonds. Knowing this, Maelgwn gave no thought to leaving her near their fire, that he might find a stream. Bringing them water soon afterward, indeed she had moved not.

The insane man fashioned some random rules.

"Will you give yourself to me? I'll not force myself upon you."

"With all my heart, I will not," came the reply.

Maelgwn held her through the cold night, respecting her decision, forcing himself to abstain from forcing her.

The following night brought the same exchange.

"Will you give yourself to me? I'll not force myself upon you."

"With all my heart, I will not." This time Gwen pressed the one who had pressed her. "After all these years and all the maidens you've enjoyed, your reputation as a lover spreading from the Isles to the Continent, why do you yet dote over me?" That he was respecting her rejections gave her some bravery. "Is it the simple jealousy of men, or the forbidden fruit – that you covet what you cannot have?"

Lying next to the fire, he erected himself on one elbow, the position causing the veins of his neck, thick as a python, to pop and pulsate. *There was a time that those veins alone would have driven me to disrobe and throw myself at him,* she thought. And then he uttered the secret unspoken for more than twenty and five years.

"Cannot have AGAIN, you mean, my love."

And there it was. Before the lord of the Tylwyth Teg had known and changed her, making her a weapon to trouble and disrupt the world of men, there had been Maelgwn. The troubled young man from Gwynedd, tucked away in the Southeast at Illtud's school over some great scandal. Too important to prosecute and bring to account for his actions; rather, exiled until it could be sorted. *Had she forgotten? No. Tucked away in the tiny remnant of a mostly dark heart was one room, tinier still, a room indeed that belonged yet to Maelgwn.*

"Had the Iron Bear bothered to ask me, instead of his repetitive diatribe of *seeing you first,* I would've made it known that seeing you first was not knowing you first, AND I KNEW YOU FIRST." Now tears streamed. "But curse of curses, I loved him too much to tell him."

"And this secret has undone you, my sweet." She kissed him in a friendly and maternal way, not romantically.

"I was undone before meeting you or our High King. It was but another stone to the press, another burden to bear." He pushed her away gently, then pulled her close again. "Gwenhwyfar, my" - he had no proper name for it - "impulse has not passed. You must sleep in the cold, or I will ravish you. May I ravish you?"

Softly, she declined.

"What has changed since that night ere I brought you to Caerleon? What has changed since you looked upon me three days ago?"

Now Gwen's tears arrived too.

"O, Maelgwn. You intercepted a look intended

for another, and assumed it unto yourself. I am sorry. You were my first love, and I thought, devoid of hope, my last. But" – she trembled – "and I pray you not slay me, I have changed. For I am in love."

***

King Arthur was overwrought. A man of command, anticipation and confident control, he had become a walking corpse of helplessness. The most logical conclusion was that Giants had made off with the queen. There was no demand for ransom, no evidence of struggle, no witnesses of anything. The queen had simply vanished into the night.

The priests and elders prayed and fasted, seeking God for a vision. Not for their support of the barren queen, but rather for the wellbeing of their sovereign. Strife and wrangling and positioning for power notwithstanding, Arthur's policies had created an enduring kingdom that afforded all factions, sects and religions the *freedom* to strive and wrangle. And though they sometimes hated him in the moment, when calm were the storms of religious passion, they loved and appreciated him.

Gwyar attempted use of the Sight, to no avail.

"And Maelgwn has vanished as well." Gwalchmai's statement of fact, dripping with obvious connection, flirting with direct accusation. Again, his mother both begged and commanded him to arrest his course with unspoken pleas and desperate gestures.

"You are right," responded the red-eyed and weary king. Yet again, the blindness of love fogged his discernment. The one who could detect a ruse or perceive a dishonest eye, from merchant to priest to ambassador to fellow sovereign, neither heard nor saw any of the warnings of late increasingly launched by his nephew. "And that is the hope of our nation. He is the hope of our nation. My Lancelot must have seen the abductors that night and given chase. He knows every forest, every crag, every fortress, every settlement, the circuit of every ancient road and modern highway. If not ambushed and slain by whomever or whatever took our queen, then he is out there, and Lancelot will save her."

***

"Who is he who has won your heart?" asked Maelgwn.

***

Mordred was brought news of the queen's abduction while reposing in his white pavilion, erected at the base of Caer Ogyrfan.

A natural first act of investigation was to validate that the queen's father, bewitched and only days removed from his attempts to assassinate the king, had not somehow managed to escape from his appointed custodians and hold his daughter captive in his formidable fortress.

The appropriate point of departure for the investigation; but of no avail. Rhufawn and Mordred were both resting, vigilant but relaxed, having rapidly rendered the fortress a home-prison for Ogyrfan Gawr, who sulked in his own chamber. Mordred's eyes clamped tight, forcing away tears that would betray him, *and betray her*. He must present himself as a concerned soldier, citizen and nephew, no more. The scales of his sorrowed response must be no greater, nor lesser, than what was meet for the situation. *Especially if Rhufawn son of Maelgwn was as observant and intelligent as he was radiant and fair.*

Worst of all, the king had charged him and Rhufawn to remain at Caer Ogyrfan until a just solution could be delivered upon the queen's father, or until the enchantment wore off. *Mordred thus knew that he was bound to midlands for a while, helpless to launch out and find his one true love.*

***

"It is King Arthur Pendragon, mine own husband. And none else." Gwen did not hesitate. She lied quickly. And she lied convincingly. "Ere you brought me to him, I would have let my heart go back to our time together at school. He was a fine boy and a great friend back then but he was not..." Gwenhwyfar's words were contrived but conciliatory. "He was not you."

"And after? I was the very one to deliver you to he who would replace me in your heart?" Maelgwn's mind was all splinters, and he grasped with all that he could for one of the more benign shards. "He saw you first, and finally, in the end—"

"In the end I saw him. When you and I met it was as diving into a pool, naked." Her naughty allegory gave the tall, hurt warrior a happy moment and a short laugh. "An instant shock! Followed by pleasure and joy. By contrast, loving Arthur was rather like getting up before the break of dawn, preparing a great meal, laboring to carry it up the trails and finally, with sweat upon brow and growl within belly, reaching journey's end, and feasting. It was a slow, grinding journey to know the man. Less splendor, less splash – but yes, Maelgwn, I came to love Arthur. And you know." She took him by the hand. "You love him too."

Indeed, Maelgwn did love Arthur. A love that withheld provocation by the sons of Cunedda to engage in apocalyptic civil war and wrest the paramount of the monarchy from the Silures. A love that kept Arthur on the throne in the stead of Maelgwn. A love that kept the armies of the Cymry undefeated and shining to the world, their internal squabbles notwithstanding. He loved Arthur because Arthur was all that he was not; loyal, temperate, consistent, stable. All men who have lived through an era of war are broken; all have suffered loss. Arthur had lost all of his sons and his mind was yet healthy, his character full of humor and grace. Maelgwn's sons were all well and thriving, slashing villains, achieving quests, wrestling and playing with their father. And yet their father was a mess of contradiction, sorrow, brooding and instability. Jealousy burned Maelgwn, cooled by love and respect.

Maelgwn received Gwen's words with tact and surprising grace; he offered deep apology for the abduction and for forcing himself upon her.

Then irony entered. *And irony is a cruel master, a cold trickster.*

As Maelgwn apologized and behaved himself in a comely fashion, Gwenhwyfar was at instant taken back to their youth. The piece of her heart given him as a lass still glowed, a tiny ember. But tiny embers have set whole forests ablaze.

She looked on Maelgwn, his face truly as of the gods, his body as warm marble. Reminiscence and distance bring betrayal to the doorstep. And lust knocks hard upon the doorknob.

Mordred surely withholds not himself from Kwyllog in their marriage bed, and I sleep with Arthur. What is the difference?

It has been so long. Arthur has befallen no misfortune; we are no closer to Mordred upon the throne than we were after our first tryst in the field. What is the difference?

I have already lain with Maelgwn. He was my first lover. This cannot be undone, so to have him now – what is the difference?

If we cannot conjure a ruse for my abduction, he or we are as the walking dead. WHAT IS THE DIFFERENCE?

"Maelgwn. The Bloodhound Prince." She made her eyes impossibly large, her mouth as honey before a starving bear. "We are near Alba. Show me this land of the Picts and, provided it is but one time and brings no ongoing scandal, we may revisit the passion of our youth, and you may have me. But once!"

The bubble burst! This time not in relieving itself with debauchery or some erotic crime, but rather with the satisfied glory of lovemaking yet to come. Maelgwn gently mounted the lady upon his steed, making haste and pace as the wind unto the realms of the Cymry's neighbors to the north.

"Now the High King of the confederacy of the Picts is King Drest, son of Girom. Similar to our Arthur, he is a Christian man presiding over a pagan majority. He is pious, speaks seven languages, is apt with spear and bow, and, though a friend, would not play shelter to our scandal." Maelgwn felt Gwen resting upon him, this time comfortably behind him. He controlled the gallop and absorbed her weight, which was to him as a small child resting upon a parent. "Thus we must lean upon another tribe to guide our passage into Mìgeil, as discreetly as possible."

Accusations of barbarism by Roman historians volleyed against the Picts are false. Their villages and small cities were well planned to include sanitary water and waste contrivances, means of using the sun to warm homes, residential circular huts commingled with places of commerce and market, and churches and temples to old gods and the One True God. This ethnos, second only to the Cymry in rights of primacy to the Isles, was advanced and bore no resemblance to Latin tales to the contrary.

Yes, they honored their water deities, from whence they believed all life emanated, drawing on their power in warfare through smearing the woad paint their bodies over. But war paint doth not barbarism equal; neither ferocity.

Any tribe appears ferocious and barbaric when defending their farms, their churches, their homes and their daughters from the invader.

And so the little village of Mìgeil hummed of this sophisticated and ancient beauty.

"Sojourners, travelers and traders remark that Cymru is the most beautiful of all countries in the creation. But the greens up here have no equal, nor the waters so clear. Almost more—"

"Careful, my lady; our vales and mounts stand alone—"

"Almost *equal* to the beauty of Cymru." They laughed, Gwenhwyfar being overtaken with enamor of the place.

"Mark this, my queen," said Maelgwn. "Remember the roads, the trails, the short barge we took. Note well every part of the journey. This little fortress..." He had her look up at the single tower, a horseshoe in shape, an ornate spiral staircase twisting up its side, no gate, the only entrance near the top, beautiful and quaint apartments and chambers within. "And the chapel there to the west. These are considered my lands by the decree of the Picts who, embarrassingly" – a blush from the mighty champion of the Britons – "venerate me as a god." He shook his head, clearly disagreeing with their assessment. "If ever you are in danger, if ever you and Arthur or any of our Fellowship is in dire need to hide, to heal, or to disappear, this is the abode. These tribes will die for me and my own."

They scaled the stairwell and worked together to kindle a fire, which crackled as it matured. They rose and washed the soot from their garments, and he showed her the east from the chamber terrace, resuming the earlier discourse. "However, as with our clan and tribal rivalries, there are factions in Alba. Go not there. Ever. For they claim closer lineage to King Drest and do not favor the locals here doting over me. Avoid them. Their sigil is the skull of a seal, for they are a seafaring and hunting tribe, and no easy match in battle."

At once, Gwenhwyfar's traits seeped through her reformed exterior. Savvy and fleshly libertinism. "Maelgwn, lest you can find the head of a Giant to bag and throw across our horseback, some of these Picts must perish. Or we must. Is having me" – here she bared the top crescent of both breasts, teasing her old and would-be-again lover anew – "worth all this?"

"You must not die, for in your death dies Arthur, and in his death dies the Summer Kingdom." Maelgwn's sophistry was truthful and dark by implication.

Would that he did die, that Mordred and I could

reign and love in the open of the day, or rather in the bright night of a Winter Kingdom of our own, thought Gwen.

"What ruse would you have us conjure?" he enquired.

"There was an abduction. We need an abductor. We are in Pictland; clearly the Picts, whose king favors the Popish way of the Church, used the distraction of the visit to steal me away in the night, intending to demand that the mighty Arthur bow down to the Bishop of Rome, lest he fall by the sword."

Any rational person would pause greatly at the woman's ability to lie so fluidly, so without effort, *spoken as if she believed her own lies.* But the breasts of Gwen II made Maelgwn far from rational.

"But only a small faction; them!" Again Maelgwn pointed to the east of the tower. "The good and valorous chief of the Picts would denounce the acts of his own in the same way Arthur denounces cattle raiders from the house of Caw! Drest would surely stand down and give us passage for my elite Hosts to crush the faction that stole you, helping my mates here, giving us breath for another day."

"Preserving the Summer Kingdom another day." Her hand was already between his legs. "Taken by Picts, rescued by the famed Lancelot, returned safely home to Caerleon." She loved him with her hand outside of his undergarment. "But not home just yet."

"Just one time," he said.

"Just one more time." She used his extreme preoccupation with their past to seduce him all the more. Moving him to a luxurious bed that was *all blankets and pillows,* she was in control.

He disrobed, and they began to kiss hard. Her

eyes noted, and could not avoid, the wound where the 'V' of his muscles conjoined low on his pelvis. Not just the scar of a sloppy and poor puncture wound, but a wound atop a wound atop a wound. He paused the passionate embrace, noticed her noticing, allowing the obvious question to be posed.

"No one has breached your defenses. You are undefeated, invincible, and if the bards don't exaggerate, usually unscathed. What is this?" A gentle circumference made about the wound with her skilled fingers.

"The bards ALWAYS exaggerate." He deflected with humor.

She pressed.

"It's an old complaint, and it heals not."

"By some witchcraft?"

"Well, Gwyar and I were reared by the same foster-mother…" More nervous humor.

Knowing she would garner no further information, the task of having Maelgwn resumed. She had put herself back at Saint Illtud's. She could smell the Cymreig breeze off the shores, the sands of Ogmore beach between her toes, the fullness of young Maelgwn inside her.

But he was NOT inside her.

When it comes time to do that which you would do, for the sake of Arthur, and for Cymru, do it not.

Maelgwn was utterly naked, at the very door of fulfilling above thirty years of frustration and crazed madness.

And yet.

Instead of anger, Maelgwn cried into the night, cried from the bed within the solitary tower of Mìgeil.

"Merlin! Merlin, I need you! I cannot do this without you. Wizard! Friend! Help me!" Maelgwn had at last exhausted self-effort, coming to the end of himself.

***

Within the hollow of an enchanted oak, or perhaps in the hollow of the abyss itself, olden eyes did shift behind their lids. A bright light outlined a door there and not there within the tree.

***

I am never here when you call me and always present when unwanted, but I am never late.

Suddenly, mounted atop the daughter of the Giant, legs spread, ready to have her though the kingdom be damned, Maelgwn saw all the enemies of Arthur as if they were in the room; Caw and his impetuous sons, Meirchion the Mad, though long dead, his upstart son Mark of Cornwall, Llew ap Cynfarch, Cedric and his Gewessii. And one figure besides, shadowy and formless. A fleeting name, *Mordred,* puffed as dust, then was gone. The fall of Cymru and the sovereignty of the Blessed Isles was before him.

At the sentinel moment, Maelgwn was Lancelot. The champion of the Round Table, the first knight.

"Gwenhwyfar."

"I know, Lancelot."

Gwenhwyfar's thoughts returned to Mordred, her love. The two almost-lovers sent for a messenger to deliver tidings of the queen's rescue to Caerleon, congressed on the details that would implicate the Picts, and went unto separate beds within the tower.

In the early hours of the following morning,

great pains rushed upon Lancelot, who, needing privily to combat the pain, fled into the forest, bleeding from the old wound.

CHAPTER 14
The Prophecies of Merlin

The Golden Age of King Arthur was never to last beyond twenty years.

If King Arthur was a second King David, his reign was thirty-three and seven years.

If he was a rehearsal for the heavenly kingdom on earth of Jesus Christ, also thirty-three and seven years. For the Lord came and announced His kingdom and endowed His Twelve with special powers; their ministry lasted thirty-three years prior to the *great interruption,* with seven years remaining unto the coming of the King and the ushering in of His government.

Arthur had been crowned four hundred and ninety-seven years after the birth of Christ. His famed victories during the Saxon Wars spanned twenty years, culminating in the decisive and history-altering victory at Mynydd Baedan. Thus, after that, if he be the Child of Prophecy, but twenty more were determined on him, terminating the Cymreig Golden Age in the year *Five Hundred and Thirty-Seven.*

But Merlin needed no Scriptural analysis of God's prophetic plans, neither soothsaying, neither indigenous nor tribal messianic prophecies to affirm and know this beyond disputation.

For he knew the circuits and patterns of the heavenly bodies, and they declared with a shout the lifespan of the boy-king and his gilded and glorious kingdom, commencing with the visitation of *the Red Dragon* the very year that Arthur was born.

What the stars, wandering stars and other astral bodies were, Merlin did not fully comprehend, and the nature of their composition he knew not, save that they were closely associated with gods or angels. In time, he came to understand that the heavenly hosts were made for Man; for seasons, and harvest, and travel measurements, and for signs. They declared the glory of the one unknowable creator by holding their heavenly courts within the firmament in constant pattern, day and night proclaiming the plan, purpose and grandeur of God.

But some rebelled.

These were the wandering stars, doomed to run contrary to the course of the other hosts until the Judgment Day.

Moreover, others, from time to time, broke free from their appointed routes and tried to bring devastation upon the Sons of Adam, whom they hated. Those heavenly hosts loyal to their Creator would wrestle with these and either restore them to their appointed circuit or bring them crashing to the earth, where their disembodied spirit, having been freed of its star, lay crushed in so many pieces as an egg dropped from its basket.

Men of vain sciences devoid of God, especially amongst the Greeks, called these *comets*; but Merlin and the druids, even prior to the foundation stone of Christ being laid upon the Blessed Isles in the Sea by the Princess Eurgaine, knew them to be fiery ethereal dragons. And none were more dangerous than the one that broke free of its chain, declaring the birth of the Pendragon, when Arthur was born.

Hailed with great anticipation, his coming had two meanings.

Dread and celebration.

Dread for the devastation and great loss of life the Cymry would have to endure, and celebration that the Cymry would defeat and endure his fire.

Thus the Red Dragon became the banner of the Pendragons, sharing space with the Bear as co-sigils for the royal clans of the South. Never was the dragon a heathen symbol, or a nod to the devil, as the priests would falsely accuse, but rather it was a symbol of the resilience of the Britons, ever at threat from invaders seeking to annihilate them and steal their coveted islands.

But Merlin knew the Red Dragon would come again. He was mentored in gazing upon the stars, and his knowledge of both math and astronomy had no equal. He could not know if the gods or angels would be victorious yet again when, on his next orbit over the isles, the Dragon would endeavor to hurl himself upon the earth. There was no equation of arithmetic or mapping of star patterns to know this, nor could it be divined, rather only speculated.

Only one spike of the dragon's tail had found soil the year of the birth of the king. It had caused men's eyes to melt within their faces, a plague to form within their bowels, and, where contact was direct, evaporation that left no corpse and little ash.

Merlin *believed* the Red Dragon would strike in the Isles, in whole or in part, fifty-three years hence that awesome and dreadful first pronouncement, because he was given many prophecies.

Prophecies based upon wise speculation and understanding of the times.

Prophecies of ecstatic utterances in trances and meditations.

Prophecies using divination.

Prophecies after ingesting mushrooms, herbs or other yield of the earth that enabled a link into the world of the spirit.

In those visions, he saw that the Boar would take the sovereignty from Cymru through intrigue and cowardice (never through victory at arms). Or he saw calamity and devastation that allowed foreign migrants to simply *come ashore and colonize, unaccosted.*

His prophetic visions detailed imagery of the Boar dancing with the Raven and the Harp, and the Silures falling from their place of primacy - but surviving.

He saw a dark age like no other since the foundation of the world, where the light of liberty was all but extinguished; a thousand years of terror, ignorance and dread. All the old gods appeared as dead; an age of men and money and empty atheism or emptier rote religion reigned.

Further down the corridor of time, he saw mechanical monsters that he could describe not, neither could his mind comprehend their construction; evil inventions that could heap death upon the earth by land, sea and air.

But in the midst of the dark was found a struggling little light. The flicker of but one candle.

And the candle had a name. And the name of the candle was Hope. And a sandy-haired young man with a blue hood and a shield upon his shoulder was the keeper of Hope. The candlestick he held in his left hand and lo, Excalibur in his right.

The Age of Arthur was not to survive the days

of the king. When gone was Arthur, so too would be gone his ministry to bring hope to all men. Not hope for heaven on earth, for this belonged to God Himself, but hope that men could love their neighbors in spite of their differences, until God Himself returned. Not hope that knowledge would transform the world, as the wisdom of men is foolishness compared to the wisdom of God, but rather hope that the common man would have access to the same knowledge as the rulers and that, for some measure of the time, justice would prevail. Hope for the arts. Hope for sciences. Hope to challenge rulers lawfully; hope that the common man could live a quiet and peaceful life of liberty.

The Age of Arthur would survive as a little candle to alight a brutal and fallen world. A thousand thousand years hence, men would look back upon these heroes, their challenges, trials, failures and triumph. This was the burden of the prophecies of Merlin, and the burden of King Arthur and his Round Table Companions. They were the stewards of the flame of liberty. But that stewardship would come at great cost for all involved in its calling.

These were the prophecies and visions of the Merlin of Britain.

And with the visions, a mandate was implicit.

First, the Cymry must unite under the Pendragon for a generation, holding in ambience the infighting that had ever left them susceptible to first the Roman, and later the Long Knife.

Second, they must be undefeated. Their deeds in battle must be unblemished so that future generations amongst all tribes and nations reckoned these Britons as the standard by which all armies, and all men of valor, would be measured.

To remain undefeated against the wave upon wave of Saxon menace required Maelgwn Gwynedd. There could be no Summer Kingdom without him, for he and his Hosts were greater in battle than even those famed warriors of Sparta, more elite than the renowned assassins of Persia.

Thus, third was keeping the unstable Maelgwn *stable enough* throughout the duration of the Saxon Wars, and then mitigating any damage he might do to legacy and reputation thereafter.

Fourth, to protect Arthur's gentle heart, which only ever wanted to find a love to match what he saw displayed by his parents – one of the grandest couples that ever loved.

For all the complexities of nation-building, policy-making and statecraft and through all the machinations of a country shifting from paganism to the Christian God, these four imperatives were paramount above all.

The prophecies of Merlin haunted him, being not favorable in any category.

"Fate is not written." Taliesin would challenge the troubled wizard over long talks and deep horns of cider. "Only God has foreknowledge; He alone knows the ending from the beginning."

As Merlin began to know the way of Grace from Taliesin's teaching, as he obtained what he believed to be his personal salvation, the old wizard began to doubt the veracity of the prophecies.

Becoming fully persuaded that *real and valid* prophecies from God were centered on Israel, and only by extension and exception the Gentile kingdoms, and that they concerned Israel's reclamation of her land and her rise to reign under David and the Lord in ages to come, Merlin began to question his own visions.

He came to understand that God had but seven years remaining in His prophetic dealings with man and that over five hundred years had passed without the resumption of that week of years. As if the sundial had been paused, God was no longer dealing with man on the basis of prophecy. Rather, He was dealing with individual men on the merits of Christ's work on the Cross, regardless of Israel's position and covenants; dispensing grace to any who would, simply by faith, lay hold of eternal life. In this regard, grace had nothing to do with prophecy and prophecy nothing to do with grace.

So what of Merlin's prophecies?

The Prophets of the Old Testament Scriptures were never wrong. Never. If one detail did not come to pass, then they were marked as False Prophets and stoned to death. Far from being harsh, this was a divinely instituted protective measure between God and His People, so that they would know true Prophets from swindlers and pretenders. Many of Merlin's prophecies were slightly wrong on this or that particular (and many came to pass in precise fulfillment), and he certainly did not meet God's standards for a Prophet.

Merlin had only come to see Paul's Mystery as presented to him by Taliesin for a short time before Nimue and Simon Magus had sent him to his oaky grave. In their few discussions about the meaning of Merlin's visions (from which he had suffered from his youth) and activities as a Seer, the two drew some conclusions.

First, the Devil was the god of this world. As such, he was manipulating events and seeking to control outcomes. And thus, he could give *prophecies* to an extent, because his plan and purpose was controlling the very outcomes he was showing to those whom he was revealing, or tricking, with visions.

Second, the visions had to include much truth mixed with some lies. If the Serpent saw a great kingdom unfolding amongst the Cymry, it would behoove him to reveal as much truth as possible to beguile and entrap the Seers, leaders and visionaries. None will swallow a whole lie, but a drop of poison in otherwise clean water will render one just as dead. Thus, the greater parts of Merlin's visions were true, albeit positioned for malevolent purposes.

Additionally, some of the angelic host, ever at war with the Fallen Ones, might wink their eye at the ignorance of heathen folk who knew nothing of the Devil but worship amiss. Taliesin did not rule out that Merlin must have received some angelic or divine assistance along the way in knowing the course of his people.

Outside of these postulations, Merlin was unsure how the Council of Nine fit, if at all, into the Prince of Darkness's schemes. Though Taliesin had a greater grasp than some of how the Old Mystery School religions led to dark, murky paths, both had some hope that the Council *might* be benevolent - a secret college of men grasping the greater mysteries of godliness. As Merlin discovered firsthand, this was not so. Thus, one of his final thoughts as his lungs filled with water, his throat already closed and clamped with swelling and trauma, was that the prophecies had been Satan *showing him* what might come to pass and then endeavoring to seduce him into partaking of it.

Speculation.

All that could be known and measured was

that, whether by God or by Devil, by intuition or hallucination or a combination of the same, *there was still the Red Dragon. The comet was still coming. And with him, the end of the Summer Kingdom.*

And of the magnitude of the colossal calamity coming, the only one who could warn the people remained in his oaky grave.

CHAPTER 15
No Help from the Fair Folk

Simon Magus must find the Grail. He had seen its splendor, felt its power, knew it would indeed be the very vessel from which the nations would become drunk on the outpoured wine of pseudo-peace, only then to swoon in their drunkenness into deep sleep, offering no resistance to the coming worldwide butchery of his Antichrist.

He must find it immediately.

He must immanentize the eschaton.

And if it could be immanentized, then delayed.

Always the urge to bring about the end of the world *now,* and if not now, *back to plotting and waiting.*

With or without the coveted relic, he must escape the Isles and return to Rome where he could resume his great work with the Council of Nine.

The former emperor had wrought calamity and chaos of Simon's first firsthand view of the Pendragon. It had not gone as expected. However, calm and ever seeing the next three, nay, the next five maneuvers in advance of his opponents, he was able to make great use of the debacle.

The next immediate action was ensuring that his kinsmen, the priests of Rome, charged, under threat of all-out war, by Arthur himself with initiating a comprehensive investigation to discover and root out the secret societies corroding and corrupting from within their fair institution, *would never leave the Island he so desired to leave.* They would never reach Rome. He would. They would die here, adding more ghosts to haunt the scary British woods. He would not. They would never give report of their visit, never bear witness to the things they saw, never give testimony against the Masked Priest.

Simon met with no difficulty in achieving this. The king of the Britons, in his pathetic mercy and uncomely regard for all men, especially his enemies (who thus could never say aught against him or defame his name), had allocated twelve guards divided upon two ships, along with the boatman he had spared to escort the clergy to safe waters.

Using flat-bottomed barges designed for speed, the Cymry flanked the Roman boat, protectively escorting her from the Usk in Caerleon to the ports near Caerdydd.

Killing Arthur's brother, the Prince Madoc, was an option but was not expedient for the attention it would beget. Rather, they waited for the master at sea to break from the party, getting supplies and victuals for the less experienced sailors. An outgoing, neighborly and loving man, he sought ever toward the good of his neighbor and the care for their safe and comfortable journey.

His affable and brotherly love rendered him chatty, and a door for ambush was made ajar as he buzzed about the market, discussing winds and squalls, linens and rope, oars and oils, embracing and laughing with merchants and friends, imbibing not a few ciders.

The two Giants, now joined by two besides, crept up on the Cymry guard. Though after long fighting slain, they fought well; died well the warrior's death. But the priests mustered no physical protest and perished as whimpering dogs and no men.

The monsters made off with the bodies, burning some, eating portions of others. The ships were left tethered and calm as Madoc returned to blood splattered and pooled upon the soil, making a black mud. Brain matter and innards were strung along the reeds and tall grass, bones and jewelry garnishing the sandy pebbles of the port that the bards would come to call Penarth.

His identity contained, Simon Magus labored next on how he might return home. In the meantime, he lodged with the Adder and a select few of the Dynion Hysbys, those complicated traitors who had transgressed well past the point of return in betraying their own kind to the Prince of Darkness.

***

"We will search every hut, estate, fortress and castle. No closet unsearched, no bed not turned over. From the horn of the mainland to the daughter islands above Pictland, we will bring the masked villain to justice." Bishop Aiden was proud in his proclamation, believing his words would please his lord.

"What think you of the bishop's words, Mordred?"

Happy for a reprieve from guarding the chained and depressed father of his lover, exhausted from the detail, he wanted none of Arthur's politics, and less than none of his moral lessons. Alas, knowing what was wanted by way of response, his lip service formed the right words.

"I don't think we *can* do any of those things."

Arthur looked pleased, then onto Rhufawn. "And what think you?"

Here the lingering obsession was revealed. "His capture would surely lead to more knowledge about the whereabouts of the Grail. Whatever needs to be done."

Arthur was gentle but direct. "That it might, Rhufawn. But the son of my sister has spoken true. We surely will do none of those things."

"But—"

The just king's irritated hand motion stayed the bishop's tongue.

"Every citizen under his own roof is greater than the king. More powerful than the sovereign. Remember that the law rules from Caermelyn. We will not become a kingdom of raids and incursions, a government of reaction and over-reach and encroach. Our women will not be within the bath, ever anxious that their time of relaxation will be disrupted; neither will the farmer be at the plow ever with one eye on his goods being turned over, his storehouse seized."

"These things would not happen," rebutted Aiden.

"These things *always happen,* when liberty is ransomed under the banner of security. Though the Devil himself be hiding in my neighbor's home, it is not for me to encroach. This right of privacy is inalienable and is no respecter of sect, creed or god. Our State shall not do these things." Arthur loved liberty as he loved Gwenhwyfar, a love that gives all until spent - and then gives more. "We will find another way."

The Pendragon motioned. Prince Madoc entered.

"Brother. We make no changes to the law with respect to hearth and home. But the ports are a different matter. Use Merlin's fortress rings; launch signals throughout the land. Freeze the ports."

Madoc quickly realized that this would be the great work of his life. Even in Arthur's Summer Kingdom, many tribes were not fond of each other. Corrupt trade deals were made in secret rooms and other nations, offering spices and silks for tin and coal, pitting brother versus brother for gold, position and privilege. Madoc had never sought a seat at the Round Table, neither a throne nor principality. But in every way he was a king. The king of commerce. Where the import and export of goods, people and services was concerned, he was Protector and Duke of the Isles. In this regard, he was second of import only to Arthur himself.

He never questioned his older brother. Ever the response was "how?", never "why?".

"Freeze the ports." Verbalizing it frightened the prince. "For how long?"

"Until you have developed a systematic approach for ensuring that nothing leaves, nor enters, these islands without the approval of you and your designates."

"Our friends and kinsmen in Brittany will give full cooperation, as will the remnants of Lloegyr. The Scots, Picts and clans of Eire—" Here Madoc paused.

"Make your speech direct and with my authority, brother, saying unto them that King Arthur will raise the Round Table Fellowship once more, a silvery chorus of death and a song of graves and woe upon them." Arthur again confirmed his instruction. "Freeze the ports. The murderer of Merlin will not leave these Isles. We will find him" - an unkind glance upon Aiden and his opinion - "lawfully. Elsewise, he will die of old age here."

***

"I will not die of old age here!" One devil shouted his voice hoarse unto another devil, who answered desperation with laughter.

Conjuring the Fair Folk is rumored as impossible, yet the dark shamanism of the Adder had been able, somehow, to achieve this. Bound in a cyclone of mystical winds swirling at a great speed and rising as a funnel to the height of a small tree, the Fae was in a prison of demonic powers. Bordered in a ring of stones, he had not only been conjured but also caught. Not far from that field where Mordred and Gwen would often betray spouse, country and history, the king of the Tylwyth Teg, summonsed and held unwillingly, was before Simon Magus.

There was nothing Magus or his anti-druids could do to harm the otherworldly being. It was as the corralling of a bull with hopes that it would calm down for long enough to brand and then release it.

"Why will you not help me?! My order—"

"I owed your order, your god and the old witch a debt. Favor paid," he barked back, still cackling and dismayed that they had somehow managed to capture him in the first place.

"He is your god too, elf."

***

But this was not so. At least not directly. Later Christian tradition, in an effort to gather its perceived enemies into one barrel, confining them for an easy kill, created the false understanding that all spiritual beings save the Elect Angels of God are in league with Satan.

This is simply not so.

If Christendom, being full of supposed good men, is divided, then how is the kingdom of Satan, whose composition is of men and creaturekind evil and corrupt, ever to be in a state of unison and concord? If bishops of Galicia loathe bishops of Milan, then why is it assumed that oracles of Crete love the Korrigan spirits of Brittany?

This false assumption has led to ignorance, voids of compassion, tyranny and superstition.

Now the truth of the matter is this.

Many witches greatly dreaded the Devil, fearing that, if they so much as grazed the smallest twig of Mountain Ash, he would come for them (as they believed he did in the Blessed Isles every seven years) and drag them to Hell for eternal judgment.

In this regard, they viewed the Devil as God's agency, His hypocrisy of using evil to fight evil. Whether having merit or being amiss, these witches were not in league with the Devil, hating him greatly in favor of their own goddesses.

Some did not acknowledge the Christian concept of a supreme God presiding over the other gods. True polytheists, their gods came from other gods whose origins of ancient times were *intelligences* that had gathered themselves together to form gods, who formed the worlds. These were the harmless pagans who gathered mushrooms and herbs, made love without restriction or reservation, were ever kind to all, embraced their perceived duality of nature (and of nature's gods), and wanted nothing of the Christians' God, Jesus or Devil.

Still other beings were sold wholly to the Devil's scheme, feeling that the creature would somehow supplant the Creator, winning a successful rebellion in the end.

Lastly, some hoped against hope for redemption. If they helped children, fed widows, swept homes, and gave coins, would the God of Heaven and earth spare them? Would he at least let them simply cease to exist in favor of an eternity in Tartarus, or worse, the Lake of Fire?

And so, as with every son of Adam, matters of faith, of belief, of death, issues of personal eschatology and soteriology were highly individual. Yes, Satan was the god of the Tylwyth Teg because Satan's two hundred hosts originally sinned, violated creation and begat children by the daughters of men. This they did for wanton lust, but also to prevent prophecies of the Saviour, who was foretold to come of the seed of the woman. From the beginning, he manipulated the lusts and shortcomings of others to achieve his long-term ends: becoming as the Most High God. Yes, the deceived and the unbelieving were equally lost, and yes, their destiny the Devil shared… whether they hated the fallen cherub or not.

***

"There be gods many and lords many." The Fae continue to mock his desperate captor.

"Know you not what Arddu will do for this insolence? What infliction he will unleash upon those who betray him?"

"Yes, and how much greater the One that created *him?*"

"Oh, you fear God? Is that it?"

"For the devils believe and tremble, as says the Christian Scripture," he responded.

"The unseen and unknowable One never knew you and would cast you into the Deep, were He here to look upon you. You are a walking reminder of perversion, abomination and disappointment. Better to serve one who finds beauty in your ugliness, value in your otherworldly powers."

"Say the word again, Magus." Tired of the ruse, and inflamed at something the Devil's disciple had said, the Fae gave but a wave of his hand and a mouthful of ancient incantations. The cone of ethereal bonds burst asunder; the ring of stones resumed being just another formation of pretty and benign Cymreig rocks. The towering chief that ruled *the in between* summonsed a hundred of his mates, who surrounded the Dynion Hysbys, planting by their wiles visions of terror and fright, causing all to drop to the knees - save brave Simon Magus.

"Where is your Horned God now? 'Tis you who are in the snare." A long red finger tic-tocked left to right, chastising and lecturing without words.

Showing the same calm resolve demonstrated when but recently at the mercy of Excalibur's strident edge, Simon condescended by retort and sigh: "Which word would you like me to repeat?"

"Perversion." Here, emotion bested the king of the Fair Folk. It would seem that the residue of humanity within the Nephilim and their progeny were all the worst bits; the offal of the human condition. And the top of the refuse heap of these was *assumption.* Gifted with a broad range of powers of divination, sorcery and special knowledge but never *all-knowing,* the elf's *assumption* resulted in him gifting Magus the pathway to victory.

Perversion.

Incest between siblings.

In every culture, religion and sect, it was viewed as abomination. Cursed abomination to be avoided without exception. When royal families did it - disease and madness. Rome fell because of it, and even the ancient bloodlines that maintained their purity in an ongoing effort to rule the world were careful to diversify their inbreeding, never procreating inside the branch of first cousin. When the line would degenerate and mother would bed son, or son would have intercourse with sister, it was never to a good end.

Even the heathen and the faeries held to this. The notions of right and wrong that are memorialized for the Christian in Scripture are revealed to heathens by conscience.

"Perversion. I brought the primal witch out from her mournful wanderings in the Underworld, her anguish in the valley of the graves of her sons. Then I stole the girl-child of Onbrawst and Meurig and made her one with the mother of goddesses. A Pendragon and a Fae in one shell. So bound are the twain that they are one flesh, yet separate; one soul, yet a host and a parasite." The chief paused in contemplation. "I don't even think they know who or what they are. But I do know that when is final the Matter of Britain, Morgaine of the Faeries will survive all."

"Yes! Morgaine of the Faeries. Your finest work, blessed be Arddu. Is this the perversion that vexes thee?"

"No! That I owed her this deed, and that she

would bed her brother, forging a soul tie and a gateway to resurrect your son of perdition in him–"

Magus interrupted, further agitating the towering menace before him. "Ah, you who have violated daughters by the batch, damsels by the bundle, are bothered that the siblings would lie together? For so many years this has troubled you?" Instead of the natural fear of being squashed at the whim of a greater foe that would possess and paralyze a normal man, he was genuinely interested in the strange set of codes and ordinances that governed the perplexing ways of the olden Fae.

Here the goading and inquiries finished their course, and the assumption accidentally delivered.

"Not the deed or the ritual, but its issue that will destroy this land! I shall not help you or your Horned God expedite our demise. For all of the mystery of the Tylwyth Teg, let it be made simple for you and your conniving secret society. I simply like King Arthur more than I like you." Sometimes the faeries act in this way, and their mysteries are no deep thing but rather a pithy moment or a jovial whim. "Blessings and Cursings from the line of Pendragon. We choose the Blessing."

Brilliant and sinister Simon had stopped listening to the sermonizing of what he perceived as diatribe by the hypocritical elf.

"What issue?" he asked. "Did our schema produce not just a soul tie but a soul? *A child begotten of the boy-king and his witch sister?*"

Instantly realizing what he had done, what dark knowledge had been gifted, the red-eyed chief gave out a cry that startled stags, disrupted hares, and displaced wolves. The forest responded to his cry, crying in return.

He became vapor, and vanished. His hosts and mates burst into mushrooms and daffodils, squealing in anger and protest at the woeful exchange.

The anti-druids rose.

"Arthur will fall and Mordred will reign," they said, gleeful.

"Nay." Magus dismissed them, not so much as acknowledging those who had not been initiated into his level of sacred mysteries. Instead, he spoke to only the Adder. "Mordred will rise, in time. He will bruise Arthur's head, and Arthur will resurrect in glory. We have our villain. Nothing changes. Order these men's tongues be put to the sickle, find the Grail, and get me off this Island."

Even traitors have pride. Even rogues possess patriotism. "Prince Madoc controls the coasts and ports. The Isles are now a scroll, the ports as a lump of warm wax, and Madoc is the king's signet. None will leave unauthorized; none will arrive unawares. And surely not without some otherworldly succor, which seems to have" – the Dynion Hysbys shaman looked at the now empty faerie ring – "vanished angrily. Would you tear out the tongues of these who would harbor you? The faithful who would hide you from the High King? The Cymry abhor rudeness. It is a violation of our most ancient codes of hospitality. Sir, you are stuck."

Hubris had landed Simon Magus in a temporary vice. Seeing no other immediate option, he feigned sorrow for the directive (the taste of apology as bile in his throat) and processed his options. His mind pondered exile amongst those who had obviously grown weary of years conjuring monsters and disturbing the Summer

Kingdom, all the while seeing the Catholic Church grow and the native pagan religions continue to diminish.

The threads were becoming few and thin by which he tethered the alliance between the old gods and their priests (who would be discarded when their purpose fulfilled) and the Church of Rome and their priests (who would be used to absorb and destroy all religions, forming One Church to subjugate the earth).

Honorable men see schemes quickly. Corrupt men come around. Exposure ruins the plotting of secret societies. For this cause, Simon Magus opted to say little, and to leave the custody and protection of the Dynion Hysbys.

The Masked Man made off into the forest. A scream in the thickest of Italian accents: "I must get off this island!"

CHAPTER 16
More of Taliesin's Quiet Years

Simon Magus did not get off the Island.

As a vagabond and a fugitive, he slithered, as face-down, in muck and wood and thicket, in hut and hovel, winding ever north up beyond the borders of Arthur's long and brawny arm.

King Arthur was not sovereign over the Picts or the Scots; neither did he desire to be, for the Cymry never sought to rule men of other nations.

However, the Bear of Glamorgan did assert his authority over the ports, the rivers and the causeways, even unto the northernmost tips and daughter islands of Alba, even unto the horny tip of Land's End in the vassal kingdoms south of Cymru. The murderer of Merlin could hide within, but lest he grew wings and tempted Arthur's control of the air, he would find no liberty without.

A man in direct league with the Devil, Magus retained confidence in the most dire circumstances. Where all seemed lost, he simply moved onto the next opportunity. The adaptable Luciferian found refuge in the company of a wealthy landowner who, having kin in the

North and the South who were ever embroiled in controversy and malicious strife over cattle and sheep and grazing lands, had given up all and became a hermit. This man had distanced himself from the tidings and gossip of the day, becoming a kind of solitary recluse. A complicated fellow, having fear of the Lord and an affinity for the Roman tradition, but also a curiosity for herbs and benign folk magic, the wanderer had abandoned wife and children, cousin and steward, the whole of his hired household and all friends.

Loathing of those who loved wealth and things more than people brought him from Glamorgan to the far north and Pictish Wilds.

Chance brought him into Caledonia.

Misfortune brought him to Simon Magus.

Having no need of garbs of concealment, Simon's mask and vestments had been put away, substituted for a simple blue robe and walking stick. The hermit was instantly enamored by the seductive knowledge of his new friend, happy to barter lodging in the Caledonian forest for lessons in herbs, in astronomy, in the mechanisms of wind and the sciences of magnetics and water. And as he valued his own privacy and seclusion, he never asked about Simon's reasons for abdication from dwelling amongst the civilized. Two hermits in the vast Pictish wood; a master and an apprentice.

In time, Simon came to corrupt the hermit's Christian name, calling him Merlin Wyllt: *the Merlin of the Wild*. This he did to mock the king who had imprisoned him. Simon had killed one Merlin in the wood and given birth to another. *And he hoped this one would engage the Fae that had shunned him, using him, if it were possible, to escape the Isles and make his return to Rome.*

Thus was the third Merlin *born.*

***

Lancelot had succeeded in not doing that which he would do when the opportunity was naked and spread open before him. *But would it be enough?* He continued to touch her improperly (and she gave no protest, often guiding hand or lips) during the journey home. Her heart was glad that she had not given herself to him and was fixed upon being home, with her husband's nephew, but her body could not resist the touch of one such as Lancelot. Neither could any woman's.

In the end, they contained and restrained. After the sticky fondlings and hundreds of wet, aggressive kisses and clinches that were too close, lasting too long, the infamous legends, pulsating, moist and frustrated, saw in their immediate vision the welcoming flags of the red dragon, the streamers decorating the streets of Caerleon.

They had done it. They had made it back to court without doing *it*.

A message had been sent in advance that Lancelot had rescued Gwenhwyfar ferch Ogyrfan Gawr from the Picts. The bards were already singing the tale, concocting details of the brave rescue as befitted the song or prose. Gildas had taken pen to parchment to memorialize this history that had never happened.

The welcome celebration would be grand.

During the journey home, the only thing Lancelot and Gwen did more than touch each other was rehearse the facts. Lying was natural for Gwen, but a part of Lancelot died each time he dealt in dishonesty. Not only did Merlin haunt him regarding his proclivities towards adultery, but Taliesin's voice plagued him about honesty and ethics. *Consider how this act (of debauchery or roguery) will impact your children* was deeply planted, always orbiting round in his head, thanks to the Chief Bard of Britain.

But lie he would. Expertly.

King Arthur's relief had not yet caught up with and reconciled his worry, his rage. He looked beleaguered, starved of sleep. After embracing both wife and friend he, naturally, wanted facts. Ever thoughtful of his queen, ever considering her feelings and well-being above his own, he encouraged her to leave the chapel where they were talking: "Rest, my love, you need not live through it again during Maelgwn's telling." The chapel was very near to her private apartment, and the field where she often betrayed the king with her younger consort.

"I would." Three bats of big eyes. "But I cannot leave your side, my husband; the distress is too great. I will suffer my beloved rescuer's telling of it, if only to drape upon thy arm." Beguiling Gwenhwyfar II, lying to protect two lives, and perhaps extend the life of a nation, was in perfect character; deceiving and abusing the fond feelings of a cuckolded husband, the love-blindness of the famous king.

The lie was plausible. A tribe of Picts, converted to the Roman sect, had used the distraction of the visit to abduct the queen. Their ransom? A desperate attempt to demand borderlands be declared for the Bishop of Rome and placed under Maelgwn's protection. Knowing none of the fantastic activities in the hall that day, the only abductors were but there to support and strengthen the position of their Roman allies, desperate to control the Isles.

The Bloodhound Prince offered his son, the mighty prince Rhun, to deploy Maelgwn's Hosts and a small company of soldiers to smash the offending tribe, making a decisive and swift example of them.

Arthur approved the action.

The lie was whispered, and as lies are whispered, embellished and nurtured upon lips of men everywhere. Even the tribe of Picts accused came to believe that they had committed the deed. By reason of repetition, the farce became fact. Maelgwn's Hosts easily smashed the painted warriors of Alba. Souls went to the grave on account of Lancelot and Gwenhwyfar's lies. He was celebrated as the queen's protector.

Arthur, making use of his supreme vision and wisdom, privately went to meet with King Drest of the Picts, and supped with him in Perth.

He ordered that his Round Table Companions gather as many of the Dynion Hysbys as could be found. They were directed to assemble before the Silure sovereign at water's edge, along the shore of the beach at Ogmore. With the ocean to their backs they faced twelve famed knights, helmed and armed with long spears, pressing upon them as a cook uses a long stick to plunge potatoes into the cawl, wreaking great fear of a watery death.

The Round Table Knights were a frightful sight, and the waters menacing, but Bedwyr and Urien and Cadog were a welcome end compared to the real presence of fear upon the scene, for Morgaine of the Faeries herself stood in the midst of the Round Table Knights. As she opened her tiny fists, the waves would wax; when clinched they would wane. When she lifted her dark eyes to the firmament, the skies crackled and popped; when to the ground, the sand shifted. All that witnessed this swore by their deity that the weather itself obeyed her mood.

And her mood was vengeance, driven by embarrassment.

Now what had been deduced by her brother's first wife, the *First Gwenhwyfar,* was known before all; that she had had carnal relations with her own brother during the king-making rites. That the Church would weaponize this when advantage manifested was a certainty. That she would access the seething powers of her ancient *other self* and render the shaman, or even the whole of the beach, desolate was a probability.

But something peculiar happened on the beach. In the stead of shame and political posturing, whether because Arthur himself was implicated or because the men saw the one equal in power to Lancelot rendered helpless - her countenance brought to such low depths that pity prevailed - is unknown. Where opportunity shone as the sun slowly lights a room, the curtain closed, bringing back shadows of rest, kindness and grace. Each of the knights and the bishops alike were tender-voiced and protective of the Lady of Avalon, putting her secret back in a dark and safe room as they were able to.

"Can you identify him?" asked Owain ap Urien softly.

"Take your time; they are going nowhere, my lady." Young Peredur offered comforting words.

Morgaine the Witch buckled at the kindness, tears of frustration and thankfulness in equal measure contorting her face. Composing herself, she looked over each in the line as a hound sniffs out thieves for its master.

The men continued to help.

"Which of you are the archbishop, or high priest, or—" Urien struggled for the proper description.

His brutish and indomitable lad helped. "Who is head heathen? Identify yourself and step forward from your fellows!" he barked.

"Unlike you Christians, we have no hierarchy, no ladder of lords or tower of bureaucrats to lord over men," snapped back a black robe (although marked within their bodies in diverse knotwork, sigil and symbol, all of the Dynion Hysbys were dressed alike, with no distinguishing features of dress or vestment).

"Just the tyranny of superstition and the wiles of the Devil to frighten and control the pig farmer and the corn grower." Owain moved forward a pace, his spear now a pace closer to the head of one of the heathens. "The gods you conjure, even the most faithful pagan disdains! How long will you bind the people in fear and superstition?"

"Sounds like the Christian Church." Morgaine had to slip in one protesting jab at the obvious irony of odd bedfellows when corruption reigns. Owain's rare grin indicated that he did not agree. "He is not amongst them." She was thorough, looking for the memorably ugly teeth that had lisped at her so long ago, calling her 'little crow'. "Not amongst them, I am certain," she confirmed.

Bedwyr took the lead, shifting from an eyewitness identification scenario to a full military-style interrogation. Upon his demanding to know where they were hiding the Masked Priest, the Dynion Hysbys held fast, offering nothing upon pain of death. Innocence was easy to proclaim, given that the shadowy figure had parted from their company.

"How did a foreign leader of some secret order come to lead you" - good-natured Bedwyr lent no humor or jest to his speech - "you who have no leader? How then did he gain position and privilege amongst you to make the very selection of the priestess who would be the proxy for *your* goddess in the spring rites that accompanied the crowning of a Pendragon? A once-in-ten-thousand-lifetimes honor, and you would have us believe that this intruder just tossed a hood about his shoulders and made himself head of your order?" With a motion of his hand, the other warriors now also advanced their spears by one pace.

"It was above thirty years ago!" the Adder answered. "We have few conferences, fewer councils and no central order. These men serve the Tribes and the old gods of stream and pool, of wind and rain. We know not how this occurred, and some of us were not yet weaned from our mother's breasts!"

"Merlin's killer chose Arthur's sister to participate in your rituals—"

"Not our rituals; the people, *your* people, demand that the king identify with the land and that the land yield its bounty in accord with the virility of the king. For this cause, the goddess chooses whom she chooses." The Adder boldly interrupted Cadog.

As the interrogation lumbered on, Morgaine actually found relief that it was now known what had happened between her and her brother at the rites. Her reaction to seeing Magus had prevented any concealment of the source of her distress. *Perhaps the burden will help him as well,* she thought.

"Some offenses do not rust over with time,"

she declared. "Some sins have consequences that last for a lifetime."

The Dynion Hysbys understood the double meaning of her words, but spake not of Mordred, for they yet feared Magus, and above Magus, the Horned God Arddu. Rather, they pursued the angle of perceived hypocrisy.

"This condemnation does not sound like the grace your Merlin preached. We have the greatest king in the history of the world; why cleave to this grievance? Clearly the goddess selected well, and certainly your unique union with our king has gifted him with verve unfettered!"

Morgaine ignored the whole of the vain speech. "I am not Merlin."

Many of the saints were next to her and Bedwyr upon the sandy shore. Those with fealty to the Apostolic Church of the Britons alone were permitted, with no Catholics amongst them.

"I am sorry you have not found the author of such a vile offense, my child."

Morgaine respected the kind of words of old Dyfrig. He feared her but was genuine and kind. Though she felt him misguided and mistaken, she was flattered at the words he offered in concern for the healing of her soul. She even accepted an embrace from the bishop.

As the masked villain was neither present, nor identified, Bishop Dyfrig made certain that Morgaine had completed her questions. Finding that she had, grateful that she had not used her sorcery to kill the lot of them, he revealed that King Arthur himself had commissioned him to pronounce a decree upon the wise men of the Tribes.

And this was the decree given by Dyfrig.

"By the authority of the twelve and twelve

and the champion who serve Arthur, who serves Caermelyn, that shimmering city which serves the royal clans, tribes, kingdoms, cantrefs and hundreds of Cymru, to those who identify with the Dynion Hysbys, the *jealous and the hateful of the Merlin from the time in the days of Vortigern when he shamed you for the folly of your sorceries*, have been found to be in league with and conspirators both before and after the fact with the murderer of the Chief Counselor of the High King. And by his authority, and with the complete accord of both the regular druids, whom you so often impersonate, and the Primitive Church, founded here by Joseph and by Princess Eurgaine in the days of Peter and Paul themselves, we declare an end to the rituals, practices and ordinances by the Dynion Hysbys unto the time of the discovery and arrest of the murderer or unto the ninth generation of your sons' sons."

"Let men worship what gods they will—" the Adder began his protest, trying to misuse one of Arthur's oft-quoted sayings.

"But you *did* kill your neighbor for it." Cai smothered the attempt to twist the king's words. "The degree violates no liberty or principle of freedom. We have cause; we have witness of this masked devil by both Maelgwn and Gwyar. Bring him to us, or you are no more. And that is the end of the matter."

Bedwyr nodded at Cai, supporting the piercing words given by the Pendragon's steward.

"The druids are dying out or converting to the new God. The people will never accept this." The Adder was resolute.

"We trust that every Cymreig citizen knows right from wrong and will understand our decision. And we will hear those who disagree, giving them freedom to voice the grievance when next, and whenever, we again at the Round Table convene," said Bedwyr.

"They will understand, provided the harvest does not fail and the Iron Bear gives the land an heir to raise Excalibur afresh when limp becomes the current Pendragon. How goes that?"

Peredur smote the Adder square upon the cheek. The twelve put the anti-druids to flight, considering it gracious that they did not put them all to the spear; but they yet needed them to hand over the masked man, to trip and lie, to be boastful or full of wine and accidentally reveal. Perhaps this extreme measure would finally bring justice, delivering judgment upon the one who had stolen the wizard from the sandy-haired boy-king.

***

With Simon Magus imprisoned in the Caledonian forest, world politics changed. And the world itself slowed again, into those times Taliesin the bard called 'less weighty years', for surely one day is not equal to the next, and some seasons are indeed quiet.

Although subordinate fraternities, guilds and covert orders continued to pursue the great work of simultaneously bringing about and yet delaying the End of Days, the head of the snake was lost. And with him, finality of direction and decision. Satan's organization was run by one apostle at the top, driving paramount decisions downward through a group of nine, then of twelve, then of seventy, then of three hundred, then onto lower ranks in trade, commerce, currency, the pseudo-sciences and religion. If the Dark Lord was to raise up another Magus, he had not yet done so, nor did he intervene supernaturally to liberate his Chief Disciple from the Isles in the Sea.

Ironically, the diverse creaturekind and woeful Children of the Damned could manifest more otherworldly powers in this time than could their ancient relatives who ruled the skies. As this was the Dispensation of the Grace of God, where faith reigned, the gift of signs had ceased, and miracles of God gone too. 'Twas a doctrinal age where what men believed trumped what men saw. The powers of the Faeries, the Giants, the nymphs and elemental spirits were the leftover crumbs of a moldering slice of bread that would soon, through the process of time, become as dust and be gone, forever. Because such beings were outside of the creation, they were outside of the dispensational guidelines that governed the creation. Thus the powers of devils (which were the disembodied spirits of a Nephilim, or other like abominations against the creation) persisted, whilst the power of Fallen Angels were strictly limited to deception, excepting when they broke free of their heavenly patterns and could do direct harm unto the earth and the Sons of Adam.

And so, with Magus stuck in his little circular hut in Caledonia with his neighbor, the Wild Man of the Woods, the Church of Rome was less corrupt; the governments of Constantinople and Rome did increase in mutual respect, wars were few, and an air of production, prosperity and freedom was felt by citizens of most nations worldwide. Arthur's golden age was credited, and well deserved, but the *absence of organized and directed evil* did as much to enable men to leave quiet, peaceable lives as did *directed good and justice.*

Amongst the famed living legends at court, *the routine* resumed as well.

Lancelot could scarcely be at Caerleon or Caermelyn and gave most of his time to missing his foster-mother, founding chapels, giving alms, and memorizing long sections of Scripture. When not about these, he secluded himself up in Gwynedd, hunting on his lands in Camlan, training with his sons, and enjoying many diverse women. His ache for Gwenhwyfar II was never assuaged and the cracks it left upon his soul were as broken glass, resulting in tiny shards broken away forever from the whole. *Shards of insanity*. During this time a daughter was born unto him, and she was called Eurgaine.

For Mordred, his *name and fame* did cultivate and grow at last during these quiet years. His deeds became noteworthy, his tongue edifying, his disposition perceived as warm by every man. Earning the adoration of his neighbors begat the softest of whispers, suggesting that perhaps the older nephew of Arthur was a perfectly fit heir to the childless king. Though not exposed to the front lines of the Saxon Wars nor battletested like the favored heir, Gwalchmai, some thought that it might behoove a peacetime ruler to *not* be hardened and haunted by war.

In his inward parts, the man had not changed. Mordred still believed that people were the playthings and cattle of superior spirits. He still wanted to be the preferred amongst the herd, he still lusted after power, and he was still reformed, or corralled, by his love for Gwenhwyfar II. Although they loved yet, circumstance required Mordred to relocate his wife, the godly and pious Kwyllog, from her lands in the North to Caerleon. His sons remained North, being at fosterage with their kinsmen of the House of Caw. And although Mordred missed his young children, their absence left only his wife to dodge and deceive when desiring to lie with the queen. *One being easier to sneak around than three.*

For Gwen, the sliver of her heart that she had given to Lancelot as a child when she also gave him her flower was an ember that could appear as choked out, smothered, or giving dying puffs. Dying but not dead, ever to be re-ignited by the subtlest breeze. The rest of her belonged to Mordred, and nothing did she reserve for her husband.

Vivien vanished after her appearance with the Cup of Christ and was not seen during the quiet years, which were five. Many questioned their own memories, though they had witnessed it firsthand, thinking the specter but a vision, a temporary fit or delusion shared by a distressed crowd. Many who heard of it secondhand came to even think it a legend or a myth. The sacred lakes and streams were still as hard glass, and not even a glimpse of the Grail was reported. Men began to forget about the relic, but Rhufawn ap Maelgwn affixed on nothing else, day and night, which grieved Taliesin.

As Vivien was transfigured, transformed, retired, or dead, Gwyar returned to Ynys Enlli, where she gave the whole of her forbidden powers to hiding the Treasures of Britain and keeping the little island's secrets and sacred groves away from Cadfan's parishioners. Though a small island, her mysticism kept the hidden parts hidden, at great toil and taxation to her health. Drawing down the Dragon's Breath, or mist, causing pilgrims to go left from the path one day and veer right from the same road the next, was not an occupation that she could sustain forever. The Fair Folk helped her at certain times, foiled her efforts at others; ever impish and under some unknowable rules of engagement were they.

Keeping her vow, however, she visited court oft, spending many fond afternoons atop Lodge Hill with Arthur. Her pattern was to visit with her brother, look in upon her son, investigate where she could to ensure that no plot was in place by the lovers to kill her brother, and then make haste and leave.

Although Arthur had Bedwyr, his closest friend, and Cai, his steward, and although both Onbrawst and Meurig, as with all Silures, were ageless, vibrant and always a supportive shadow to the sun that was their son, with Merlin gone, the two that Arthur *needed* most in his life were the two too often absent from court.

Maelgwn, because of his forbidden love for Gwenhwyfar.

Gwyar, because of her forbidden witness of Gwenhwyfar with her lover.

Druids and priestesses continued to convert to the Christian faith, and those benign orders diminished. The Dynion Hysbys sometimes conducted the rites at great peril, disobeying Dyfrig's edict. Arthur had authorized the ordinance and found it just but refused to dispatch soldiers to enforce the ban, never wanting to bring the sword of the State into the pulpit or altar of religion. However, these men *had harbored or allowed an evil murderer a place as pillar in their sect.* Thus, with each violation, Arthur would engage the local chieftains to make arrests, demand testimony, and gather information in whatever manner their local jurisdiction deemed fit. Because of this, many Dynion Hysbys were put to the sword or to the noose.

Gwenhwyfar continued to be barren, but the crops and harvests were strong, so the people suffered the dispute between the court and their wise men. Were the crops to fail and Arthur to have no son, the Tribes would unite and force an abdication in favor of either Gwalchmai or Mordred. Because King Meurig had abdicated immediately upon the injury to his loins, and because Arthur had risen in his father's *fall*, endorsed even by Excalibur, the supreme symbol of virility, Meurig lived in peaceful retirement, with no fear of further superstitious or religious requirement from the masses.

Not so if Arthur, fully healthy, produced no heir AND the land gave no yield.

In this circumstance, an aging king would be offered in sacrifice, dying with his dying lands, a new king rising in his stead. The Christian faith, in five centuries of practice on the Isles, had not distinguished the rite of the Sacral King.

This was not a present danger, but the lack of a babe suckling Gwenhwyfar II gave rise to periodic gossip and grumbles. *Increasingly so.*

At times during the five more quiet years, the bishops, elders and Round Table Companions would also conference to gauge the threat or propensity for civil war. Wisdom dictated that they be vigilant, given the disunity and rivalry that tugged at the middle kingdoms and the West Country, the way two fighting sisters pull upon the legs and arms of their favorite doll. In this case *the pullers and tuggers* were the men from the Old North and the powerful Silures from the South.

Cymru was a loose confederacy of sovereign kingdoms. It recognized a High King and the Round Table as a "unique and special counsel", primarily on matters that impacted the borderlands between Cymru and Lloegyr to the east, Alba to the north, and the Emerald Isle to the far west, or on material threats to the people as a whole; elsewise the local kingdoms ruled themselves. And although independent kingdoms can be coopted into civil war, brilliant political marriages and a generation of peace made the notion extremely unlikely. *Almost impossible.*

For example, King Urien's mother was from Glamorgan, whilst his father hailed from the renowned line of mighty kings and queens of Gwynedd. Even if his loyalties swayed towards one parent or the other, his son Owain was fully *blended* with beloved kin, cousins and uncles from both ends of the Isle. Though a Northman by paternal descent, would he really put the spear to a Silure who might be a first cousin, or slay an elder who might be a former neighbor of his Silure grandmother?

The similitude of this wonderfully impossible strait was engineered strategically over and over again throughout the land. Gwalchmai: mother from the South, father from the North. Rhun ap Maelgwn the same, and scores more. Purebloods like Arthur, Maelgwn, Bedwyr and Taliesin were becoming a minority amongst the prominent and the powerful, which was a good thing. Prominent, powerful women had sacrificed their very hearts for the good of *the next generation*. For their selfless devotion, it was said of them: *"They lie with princes, but their marriage is to Cymru."*

A religious war had to ride atop the backs of a territorial war and thus was also unrealistic, for the same reasons. Catholics and Apostolic Britons continued to gnash and hack upon each other about baptism, the authority of the Bishop of Rome, tonsuring, how bells were to be transported, and the policy and method of converting and integrating the Germanic tribes amongst them into the Church. The sentiments and conduct were rarely friendly and ever tense – BUT the key decision-makers resided in all kingdoms and would be forced to fight their own kind, their own families.

Tensions? Yes.

Skirmishes? Plenty.

Disputes and murders? Seldom, but yes.

War? Impossible.

Except.

If Arthur perished without a direct heir and Maelgwn did not favor the selection, he could take the throne at will. His Hosts were too powerful, his reach of dread mixed with love and awe too long. This one man could turn the tide for good or for ill, resurrect regional differences and perhaps successfully pit brother versus brother.

It was rumored that Maelgwn itched to reclaim rule of his lands in Gwynedd, but there was never evidence of any ambitions beyond that, which was his right. And yet the possibility, especially during his long absences, was considered from time to time. *If the Pendragon produces not a son, the future of the Summer Kingdom rests upon the relationship between Maelgwn and Gwalchmai.*

And that relationship was strained.

Gwalchmai, whether by natural wisdom and perception or by a measure of the Sight passed onto him from his mother, perceived accurately the conflict in Maelgwn's soul over Gwenhwyfar. And *all* perceived, most accurately, *what she was*. Gwalchmai threaded the two perceptions together, weaving in his mind a vision of the future. *A future where an adulterer and adulteress might kill his king in the night and take his crown the following morning.*

As Gwyar was paralyzed to expose Gwenhwyfar for fear it would break Arthur, and having broken him, break the country, so too was her gilded and happy son ever melancholy, ever given to moods of dread over exposing Maelgwn, for the same reason. Those who loved Arthur would rather perish from within, slow and with wanton pain, than hurt their beloved king. Just and kind, undefeated in battle, fair and balanced in religion, principled in politics, the War King and the Giant Slayer. The hope of Britannia. Never, never must he know of the betrayal of she whose head rested upon a pillow but inches from his own.

And so five years passed. A half-decade more of marvelous quests, legendary adventures, pith and contentment amongst the Britons, whose hearts shone as the golden rooftops of Caermelyn and Caerleon.

Five years passed from the appearancc of the Grail and the visitors from Rome.

Five remained unto the coming of the Red Dragon of Merlin's prophecy.

Then Kwyllog, wife of the traitor Mordred, took ill and died young. And Autumn fell on the Summer Kingdom.

CHAPTER 17
The False Gwenhwyfar

Seed 4 – "You put me in a vice where, behold, though I win yet will I lose."

Ogyrfan Gawr, the only Giant to have survived being *activated* by the bewitching beguilement of the Adder, did sorrowful penance for his behavior in the great hall during the Roman's visit. Though he could not control his actions, his contrition was real. An opportunist seeking security and wealth does not attack rulers, for they are his best customers. Instead, an opportunist deals in commerce, and goods, *and children.*

And this crafty brute possessed additional capital for commerce in the form of another strikingly fair daughter. A mirror image of her older sister. So uncanny was their resemblance that, though separated by two decades, one could not be distinguished from the other. Ogyrfan's second daughter was called Gwenhwyfach.

Mordred came to know the one who was as a twin to his true love whilst serving as the principal guard at a type of garrison Arthur had stationed at Caer Ogyrfan. Over long months of idle time (for Ogyrfan was of no real danger to the king, especially with Simon Magus landlocked and inactive), Mordred came to sup many times with the lass, to hunt in her father's fertile lands atop steed, and to visit the markets for trinkets or supplies for Ogyrfan's fortress and estates.

Mordred was captivated, marveling and smitten.

The eyes, the same.

The build and curves, the same.

The seductive sophistry, identical.

The sensuality and touch that could fell nations? Yet unknown.

But Mordred burned to know. With Kwyllog deceased, and with increasing access to Arthur's own ear, Mordred convinced Arthur to remove the chains upon Ogyrfan; and in return for his advocacy, Ogyrfan gave Gwenhwyfach to Mordred, making her his betrothed.

Gwenhwyfar raged.

"Your saintly wife dead not one moon and you must needs already get this wet" – she grabbed at his trousers, but not romantically – "when you can have me right here in this field, as oft as you can arrange it!" Gwen actually spat on Mordred, and then on the ground, as does a vulgar man full of too much strong drink.

"My lady." Mordred locked up Gwen's wrist, causing her to release his privates, clutched painfully in her hand. "It is political. With my spouse dead, I could not just hover and swirl as some vulture above, waiting for your spouse to do the same. How would that look before all?"

Liars loathe the lies of other liars.

"This is about the lines upon my cheeks and sag upon my breasts."

"You are as a lass of eighteen! Stop now."

"This is as a knight putting down his old

war horse. If white, doth he not always replace it with white, and if spotted, is it not the same? You are treating me as an old war horse, or as one of Arthur's goddamned war dogs! The pup becomes a dog – get a new pup!" she seethed. "Beware the fang of this war dog, Mordred!" She whipped the back of her hand, filled with costly and jagged rings, across the Whelp's jaw, opening three gashes. Gwen had killed often. She had not the supernatural powers (save the rose betwixt her legs) of her sister-in-law, but was just as lethal. "There are games tomorrow, and the Lancelot is confirmed at court. If you lie with my sister, I will see to it that you face him at swordplay. And I will see to it that his sword is not blunted like the rest of the field. You are mine! How many long years have we endured grass and mud upon our naked arses in the stead of down and silk? You are mine!"

Mordred applied pressure to his wounds, but they yet bled in globby, chunky, circular drops.

"I am yet yours." His answer was vague. His eyes were empty.

***

The games were vital for fighting men, both old and young. The land had been so long at peace, and some of the Round Table Fellowship were beginning to be on the wrong side of their prime. Arthur was yet in his fourth decade, but fifty was hunting him as a pack of nearby wolves, and Lancelot had recently reached the half-century mark. These were special men, during a special time, and they aged differently. But they aged nevertheless. A twinge in the knee, a pang in the shoulder, a complaint in the lower back when rising from bed. The games were critical to make the men feel young and exercised and to combat the subtle enemy of time, which was constantly trying to remind them all that even Arthur and his twenty-four would one day lose at least one battle, that time would ultimately be the sole undefeated warrior.

But not on this day.

On this day, the warriors were brilliant. *Still brilliant.*

At archery, all possessed the eyes of the eagle, with contests amongst many masters won by the smallest measurements.

At grappling all were advanced martial artists. Locks and holds, leverage and speed; each match was as if the Cymry had invented the sport instead of the Greeks. Many jested that Zeus himself must have first visited the Isles in the Sea on account of the quality of the wrestling. The lists were careful not to match Arthur, the second-best wrestler, with the Champion of Britain. Instead, Cai met Lancelot in the final match; an epic display of force and elegance in a contrasting and well-fought dance.

The splendor of the games was second only to the noble character of the mighty men. Cool heads surpassed hot valor. None gave way to emotion; victors were humble (knowing they could just as easily fall at the next go), and the vanquished were resolute but not given to anger. The games were sport, but also training, and the participants knew this. The younger men were grappling and sparring with soldiers who had fought in the Saxon Wars. *In actual war.* When Urien or Cadoc put the staff to one's hinderside, one felt as struck by a demigod and learned much. Priceless access to greatness witnessed by fortunate few, greatness that might never be again.

The young warriors, such as Peredur and Gwrgi, deeply appreciated the lessons, the bruises notwithstanding.

Rhufawn communicated deep regret (for all would see him pitted against his father in a wondrous clash of Titans for the ages) at his absence from the games. A rumor had surfaced of a Grail sighting in a chapel in Glastenn, and he was off as hound to the scent, hunting hard.

Rhun was present, working up the lads, leading in some sibling mockery and roll of the eyes as brothers do, many having an innocent laugh over the adventures of Galahad.

But Taliesin looked at his thumb, burnt, disfigured and scarred. Taliesin laughed not.

The final event was swordplay. Head-to-head matches were fought with blunted blades and small shields that were only about the twice the circumference of the hand. These shields were designed to protect against broken knuckles or hand injuries; they were not large shields for fending off arrow or long weapon.

The combatant was not regulated regarding armor and could celebrate tribe or kingdom with ornate helm and plating, or choose simple leather cuffs and scales, or fight with bare chest as desired. Lateral slashes were executed with the flat of the blade instead of the edge so that gashes and cuts were incidental and rare, less dangerous bruises and contusions common.

Three points, defined by a clean blow to the navel, chest or head, ended the match, or an injured or overpowered contestant could yield prior to the third blow.

Bedwyr, having retired on account of the loss

of his right hand, and Illtud, who loved combat but had left such things to serve God, were judges, and their determination of a score was to be respected as final by tradition of the games.

The day's matches were contested on a large rectangular pitch near the amphitheater. Wooden benches were stacked and staggered to the east of the pitch and canopied with colored fabrics, silks and tassels, looking very much as a long half-stadium, similar in style to the chariot sprints conducted in Greece and Rome.

The most honored of guests were seated on a covered platform situated lowest to the pitch, where the clash and clank of sword and shield could actually be heard, aerial projectiles of teeth actually seen, the sweaty splash of musclebound youths actually felt.

Gwenhwyfar II, Queen Onbrawst and King Meurig were amongst the nobles watching from here. Gwenhwyfach the newcomer was seated amongst them as well. The glare of the older sister was upon the younger, without ceasing. When trumpets were blown so loudly that words were drowned, Gwen would curse the lass, though unheard. She had not reconciled the situation, had not calmed her storm from the prior day, and had all but forgotten *the long game* played by her and her love for well over a decade. She had been scorn and scorn's hell personified throughout the games, and earlier that day at home as well.

That Mordred would soon know her sister ceased not to cripple the Adulteress Queen's hypocritical heart.

Have I not changed?

Have I not been mostly good?

She screamed at God, bartering with a deity

unknown to her, and she beat her fists against the air.

Worse, she carried her anger in the open of the day and volleyed it at her faithful husband. Contrary to the sum of her life, this time the *Mistress of Compartmentalization* could not separate out her segments, the slices of her trafficking in lies and diverse lives. No mask of modesty or doting wife adorned her; she was raw, nasty and rude.

And Arthur noted it.

It was impossible for him not to note it, being the object of her tirade.

She screamed about the chamber being unkempt.

She insulted the breaking of the fast, and those who had labored to prepare it.

She shrieked about misplaced bracelets.

When dessert was served, she screeched that the custard was off.

She stamped around, protesting having to sit in the summer sun at the games, which she professed were the vanity of men who refused to cease acting as boys.

And she laced Arthur with vitriol regarding his dogs.

"I will not sit and smell this shit of your mastiffs for three hours under the beating sun. Move the dogs, or move me."

King Arthur abhorred rudeness. He did not abide it in his own men when engaging each other, nor when negotiating with a foe.

"Think before reacting. When a person is taken in extreme anger, there is a matter behind the matter, and the matter at which they yell and holler is a projection, and not the matter."

Arthur had been sixteen when the Merlin

had taught him this lesson, and the king recalled clearly his response: "That's a lot of matters!" Even Merlin had laughed at his own bardic prose. But the use of unique word combinations, humor or harshness, always with love, had anchored these lessons into the core of Arthur's being, allowing him to draw from them at just the right moment – making him the greatest of kings.

Oblivious to the chronic and ongoing wrongs done unto him by Mordred, the arrival of Gwenhwyfach should have been noted as a variable, but was not. To the contrary, Arthur had become quite fond of him. Mordred wore black often, celebrating his Ravens from the North, and his presence gave Arthur a feeling of 'familiarity', most probably associated with the closeness he felt for Mordred's mother.

Pressing and pressing in his mind, he landed on another option: *Lancelot.* Away so frequently from court, and especially from Caerleon where Gwenhwyfar made her permanent home (for Arthur's residences were plenary, requiring him to lodge in diverse locations throughout the year in administration of his kingdom), the presence of the champion was the only known disruption or irregularity to the day. Arthur tried to dismiss this notion. A fog was starting to lift… slowly. Were Gwalchmai's whispers starting to creep in? Was the wisdom-filled, silent disdain of his mother at last finding fertile soil?

Women know things. They are smarter than we. Especially about other women.

The rude seductress before him suddenly caused Arthur, for the first time since they had mutually ended their marriage, to miss the company of Queen Gwenhwyfar the White, his red-headed lady, who was stately, a patriot, a

Christian and maternal. A powerful, wonderful woman.

Whilst Gwen II was flirtatious, giggly, or overtly doting on the king, he could see none of the malignant sores spread over the whole of her constitution – the fester of opportunistic stink and sludge that was her character. Because she had fallen so deeply in love with Mordred, a good shell had formed about a bad egg. Acting was easy. Flawless. She could (and did) look on Arthur as if he was Mordred and engage in theatre under the name of marriage. But with the shell now cracked, the yolk did seep: a black yolk.

And this one outburst over dogs and meals and the daily happenings of every couple was able to start, albeit slowly at first, to awaken the king in the one sphere of his life where he was woefully asleep. *For the abused start to see that they are being cheated upon; if you are to cheat, be nice, ever.*

But prudence requires evidence. Thus, Arthur tucked away the concern about Lancelot for another time and took an alternative course.

"My love," he opened, countering anger with love. "Are you yet unwell because of your cycle and what happened?"

The fool hath given me easy escape! The evil queen glistened.

Arthur was referring to a potential miscarriage (of a truth, to an unknown father) that was but recent, and hard on Gwen's health. Her recovery was slow; her appetite suffered. That she would be faint and of ill disposition was not an unreasonable assumption.

Discerning that the calm king was upset at her outbursts, and underestimating his ability to see her as she was, she seized upon his suggested diagnosis. (He let her do the same to deescalate the situation, allowing him to monitor her next move. *And Maelgwn's.)*

"I deeply apologize, handsome." The actress was resurrected. "Yes, I am of foul mood, but 'tis a matter of health and not anger towards you. I love you so."

The transformation was immediate. Instantly, in her effort to restore *the fog*, she was upon her knees, loving Arthur with her mouth, making endless doting comments about his coming victories in the games, finishing him quickly so that they could enjoy banter with cider and jest ere he was off to compete.

Her efforts exceeded impressive. But Arthur was not fully fooled as they parted for the afternoon's contests.

His eye would be keen on Maelgwn.

Her foulness would resume the moment she saw Gwenhwyfach.

***

Maelgwn, having been away from court, had dearly missed his friends (for it was never his desire to be separated by them, but only for his madness) and his youthful verve, though he was aged fifty, was on full display during the contests of sword. He let several young aspiring warriors, thirty years or more his junior, have at him first.

The champion's objective was to teach the younger, but also not to embarrass or humiliate them, but also to win. Only the Lancelot could carry out such contradictory objectives with his grace and skill. Each opponent learned much, was allowed to fight long enough (for he could have ended each contest with a stroke or two and instead carried the lads for a few minutes apiece) to gain priceless experience, and left the day with memories that would invigorate them forever, improving their potential military careers.

And Maelgwn, the Lancelot of Britannia, shone with the sun.

Then the weather turned.

In Caerleon, the winds can hit the "river low and the hilltops high", changing the most pleasant summery day into a miserably cold wine-press of bone-chilling air. The hot day rapidly became cold.

Warm weather helps warm manners, and warm muscles are injured less.

Cold weather brings grit and grumpiness, and muscles strain and are injured more.

The whole temperament of the day seemed to change with the redirection of the weather. Combatants didn't offer a hand when their fellows fell; curse-words and complaints of fouls increased, and good sportsmanship disappeared as the sun vanished behind the clouds. Saint Illtud and Bedwyr could feel the change and engaged Arthur privily, inquiring as to whether or not they should proceed, or perhaps postpone the swordplay to the following day.

During the interlude, Gwenhwyfar II called Lancelot to the platform where she was seated, in the plain view of all. The exchange looked inappropriate. Not because she was doing something untoward, but rather because she had come to her decision regarding her threat to place Mordred in the path of Maelgwn's sword.

He had done poorly in the lists, losing far more matches than he had won. Because of this, and because of the myriad of times he had looked discreetly upon her throughout the day, saying

"I promise not to touch her" with his eyes, she decided to forgo it. But she wanted Mordred to feel the threat of Lancelot's might - so she beckoned him over, only to discuss neighborly and non-essential matters.

But between Lancelot and Gwenhwyfar, nothing is neighborly and non-essential. He was still full of post-battle glow and glisten, the only warrior unfazed by the cruel winds and, forgetting himself, was *too familiar with Gwenhwyfar*, leaning in close, approaching a kiss.

"Would you betray our lord before all?!" A red-haired Round Table Knight called Gwalchmai made the accusation.

Lancelot withdrew from the lady and ignored the son of Morgaine, instead looking to Arthur.

The only variable is you. The king was still fixed on the morning's assault by his queen, who had become all smiles at the presence of the Briton's tallest knight. Knowing that Lancelot desired him to reprimand his heir, he would not.

Morgaine was not present. Had she been there, surely she would have stopped Gwalchmai's tongue, by maternal authority, or else by sorcery. The cold weather and long hours of competition, sweat and manly pride, mixed with years of suspicion, caused the tea-kettle of Gwalchmai's temperance to bubble and at last boil over.

"Do you accuse the queen?" Lancelot posed the question, whilst Arthur was stoic, and whilst a crowd gathered and constricted.

"You are our bravest and our best, yet your absence far outweighs your presence. Where a man's time is, there too is his affection."

"Then he must be wildly in love with the sheep that graze upon his hilly farm." Bedwyr volleyed humor to quell the development - to no avail.

The wind become angrier; the sunny day become vile. The throngs agitated, forming an immense half-circle of humanity around the two heroes, now pinned by the platform stage on one side, and three to four hundred souls pressing them from the other.

"Do you accuse the queen?!" Lancelot demanded a second time.

"Let the queen account to her husband. I accuse *you*."

Gwalchmai was taller than Arthur. Lancelot turned, pulling his shoulders back hard, posturing to full height, his chest plumed as a peacock, towering over the Hawk of May as a grown man in a scolding position above a small child.

Neither man had a blunted sword, as they were between matches and had their usual arms, making the incident thrice as dangerous.

The King of Gwnyedd's forearms and hands were all silver, armed in the fashion of his foster-mother. His biceps and shoulders were bare, as the day had started full of merriment and celebratory competition, and naked were his arms to bring swoons and cheers from the damsels in the stands. His breastplate was wrought of very thin metal fastened with thirty rivets upon thick leather, knotwork outlining the piece. His shins were protected, and his thighs were as his arms.

And the famous battle dirk rested in two custom leather loops along the left side of his belt. History's most accomplished killing instrument in the hands of the offended Bloodhound.

Gwalchmai was all leather scales shined with beautiful green lacquer. The lacquer was an enamel that sealed the leather and added some additional deflection and displacement on blows. Arthur's father, Meurig, made use of a dark blue enamel and had popularized the style of enamel atop leather. This kind of armor was as an extra layer of skin; fitted tight without joint or rivet, fashioned for speed and comfort, woven to be at once as a fishnet over the whole of the body but designed to 'breathe' as well.

The two curved swords, sleeping at the moment in matching green lacquered sheaths, were nearly as famous as Lancelot's battle dirk, nearly as deadly.

Neither man had a helmet.

Lancelot grumbled under his breath and looked to Arthur to intervene.

But Arthur doubted.

The queen's outlandish rudeness.

Lancelot's erratic, maddening behavior.

The *kidnapping.*

And now today's little exchange, which provoked the Hawk of May.

Arthur doubted. And Arthur remained silent.

Gwalchmai did not.

Like so many living in this transitional, and not a little confusing, era, Gwalchmai loved Jesus very much, to the extent that he understood Him. He also had no moral conflict with fluidly floating in and out of his pagan worldview. Gwalchmai was an example of tens of thousands of Britons who were 'betwixt and between'. And this was the testament to Arthur's brilliance as king. *He managed the transition, slowly.* Abrupt changes would result in rebellion, unrest, chaos and endless opportunities for the powerful to orchestrate religious wars for no god other than their bellies. It meant suffering some superstitions and customs, from both the Church and the heathen; it meant endless nuance complex decisions and directional shifts, and sometimes, it meant nearly impossible scenarios.

The Hawk of May, who was perhaps part magical creature on account of his mother, the witch-goddess Morgaine of the Faeries, or was perhaps simply a *transitional man in a transitional age*, called upon a custom as old as the Isles.

"Trial by combat!" he screamed, drawing both swords with a graceful anger. He stepped towards Lancelot, fearing not the oak tree with arms looming over him. And where he stepped, the clouds parted and rays of sun warmed him, but Lancelot remained beset by the pressing, windy and now rain-filled storm.

Lancelot now audibly appealed to the Pendragon. "If I am accused of conduct inappropriate with our queen, of the which I am surely innocent, then logic, reason and evidence should try me, not a seldom-evoked mystical custom."

Trial by combat. The belief amongst the druids held that, when one who is a warrior is accused of a great wrong and engages in such a trial, the spirit of the land would ensure that the one who was true would win versus the one who was false. That fate and right would win out over brawn and skill. The ritual did not apply to farmer or poet, and the words of the Lord were borrowed when articulating the druids' position: *"He who lives by the sword shall die by the sword."* The intent was to mitigate false accusations, creating a healthy fear that the gods, the forces of nature, or even the Fae would help the wrongly impugned.

Arthur, the Christian Sovereign, surveyed the multitude, who was demanding that he respect the customs. He gracefully ducked behind Meurig and retched, but none saw save his mother, Queen Onbrawst, who used the breadth of her gown to screen her son, giving him the two seconds he needed to rally. Anguished in his spirit; in his mind, curious. *Is there truth behind trial by combat?* And moreso, *What might I learn as these men engage; what truth will fall out of their mouths?* The risk was indeed great.

King Arthur appeared in the midst of the complainant and defendant.

"I will allow it. Only that it be conducted with blunted blade, and that when either has gained an advantage near victory, he will grant mercy to the other upon my command."

The crowd loved the king's judgment. He had retained and respected custom, but modified it so that the two great men would also keep their heads. All seem pleased but Lancelot, who was crimsoned.

At this very moment, another seed plunged deep into soil, another root of offense and deepest hurt.

Yet again a seed tossed on dangerous soil. A sowing stamped with foot and watered, surely to take root. A molten anger wrought by his lifelong friend's refusal to declare him innocent. Another instance of Arthur not lending his unconditional support to his First Knight. *Your painted wife panted wet and ready before me; if you are to kill my reputation here over mere words, why did I suffer and deny myself?* Instead, regardless of outcome, Lancelot would leave the pitch the loser; a man with the public accusation of impropriety of the highest order now ever upon his head. The Tribes might love custom, might declare him divinely innocent by right of victory, but the Tribes venerated but one thing above their ancient customs… gossip.

The hot animosity that sizzled towards Arthur he would redirect towards Gwalchmai. *The son of Gwyar I will not bless to be king when gone is Arthur.*

Mordred will be High King if on that day I feel not like taking the diadem; elsewise Rhun or Rhufawn. Lancelot himself was most surprised that his mind ran to politics when fury welled. He accepted the blunted sword – "I'll take two, please" – and made his way to the place designated for the trial.

Gwenhywfach took her new husband by the elbow, removing him from the main stage, endeavoring to go and stand amongst the people, closing to the fighting, curiosity needing a better vantage. Arthur saw her from the corner of his eye. Though suspicious of his spouse, and hoping against hope that the lifelong friendship between her and Maelgwn had remained as amicable siblings and not lovers, opted for edification and love in the place of the unfounded daggers that are hurtful words.

"Your younger sister looks like you," he remarked plainly.

"Some say we are twins, twenty years removed." Gwen's response was dry.

"Similar, to be certain. But you are far more beautiful than she, my wife. I pity her."

"Oh?"

"Aye; she will ever be in the shadow of a sister more fair. Poor thing."

The one whom Gwenhwyfar loved had put her to the stables as an old mare.

The one whom she never loved revered her, preferred her and respected her.

The result was not that good sense and reason would pour in upon her, or that misplaced affection for Mordred might at least decrease. Rather, apathy towards Arthur's affections increased.

The trial by combat commenced.

Lancelot circled and waited.

Circled and waited.

He would use counter-fighting to an extreme, waging a defensive and slower strategy against his bulky red-haired opponent.

Gwalchmai had fought and bled with Lancelot during the final years of the Saxon Wars, and during countless real-combat raids. He knew the philosophical approach, and would not be goaded.

Thus, they danced.

And danced.

To stimulate action, Lancelot finally faked a looping, swooshing slice towards Gwalchmai's lead leg. Gwalchmai made a perfect blocking pose with his sword at the hip, but used two hands upon his hilt, and the strike never came. This exposed his head to Lancelot, who came forward hard, spinning and putting back of his fist hard upon Gwalchmai's mouth, splitting his lip in twain.

No stranger to his own blood, for Gwalchmai was a warrior of grit and grind, not flawless and scarless like Lancelot, he recoiled calmly and started yet again.

Years of frustration towards Lancelot helped the Hawk of May fight well above the fullness of his abilities. Like his mother, he was a patriot above all and felt that the Champion of Britain was a monumental underachiever. A man enslaved by passion and the shortcomings of the god Narcissus, ever putting personal tribulations over the public good. The shining city on the hill had many enemies but only one real threat: that it would crumble in upon itself on account of some scandal or crime of passion. *One real threat: Lancelot.*

***

A tremor jolted Gwyar in the center of her back, betwixt the blades of her shoulder; a supernatural flood of knowledge, a feeling of dread accompanied by the manifestation of real pain. She had once grown too accustomed to like feelings when her brother would position Gwalchmai on the front lines, or some especially precarious assignment during the Saxon Wars. But never so intensely. Never so present. A twang and a twinge would pinch when her brother would select Gwalchmai, and always Gwalchmai, to join him in the hunt for a Giant or other monstrosity of cave, wood or deep. Arthur did it for trust, for mentorship, and for love (for he greatly wanted the people to hear of Gwalchmai's deeds and achievements, that they might accept him as king).

And for the same love, she hated it. Wishing her lad ever to be safe and bringing joy to any village, warmth to any city, song and merriment to every singing tribe. These were his natural dispositions. A shaggy, auburn-curled, jolly leader of men. He possessed the best bits of grandfather Meurig and uncle Arthur, and a pinch of mother Morgaine of the Faeries. He was meant to rule one day, not to fall to the Long Knife or be eaten by some otherworldly abomination.

This danger transcended the others. *'Twas mortal.*

"I must see!"

She darted away from the small cell that had become her simple abode towards the enchanted castle she had long ago abandoned. And not by choice. She had traded marble and precious stones for thatch and mud of necessity, for Bishop Cadfan and his pilgrims were, with each passing day, closer to finding one of the little island's sacred treasures. *The treasure* that would change everything. Thus it behooved Gwyar to become as an old hag guarding a cauldron, living by her possession day and night, as a crone chasing away inquisitive children with a stick.

"My son, my son. I must see!"

Mists and enchantments were her primary instruments to keep the Catholics away. She did not frighten them. Rather, she kept them perpetually lost, perpetually unable to chart and map the small island, the surface of which was but a moderate mound with a steep, sloping opening to wood and then beach. The mystical island, called by some *Avalon,* floated as an imperfect little dumpling just beyond the outreached finger of the Llyn Peninsula. Her task was to render it as a perpetual maze, as the cornstalk labyrinths hewn for children's games during the harvest rites and festivals.

This, though, was no game. This was for the survival of her spirituality, and for the real Christians of every sect and stripe.

Distracted completely from her task as mist-weaver and path-changer, she made for a black marble scrying bowl, which was centerpiece to the upper room in the loftiest tower within the bastion. All focus went unto summonsing or becoming her *other self* and taking command of the Sight to seek out and, if possible, aid her son.

"A hawk and your keen eyes for my Hawk and his pure soul. Help me see him." Gwyar had fetched the bird that shared her boy's namesake. Her dagger, sharper than any sword amongst the Britons save Arthur's legendary armaments, was through the hawk's neck with no effort; its blood was upon the still green waters of the scrying basin. With a physician's skill, she dissected its eyes, discarding all but the lenses, which she held in her tiny left hand. With her right hand she etched the seven-pointed star of the Fae into the rowan-wood pulpit that held her instruments, located next to the watery looking-glass.

The primal witch who dwelt in unison with her essence bore a special pain for losing children, as God Almighty, in the days of Noah, had bound her in chains and fixed her eyes open, sentencing her to watch each of her children perish as He opened the windows of the vault above, drowning them without mercy. All the while the witch had screamed her repentance to the Father, who had ceased striving with her kind. Her screams had been met with the coldest of responses. Silence. A silent heaven, far crueler than an angry hell. The Most High had charged her father, who was a Watcher, to teach men about governance and patriotism, even yet in the times before man's boundaries and habitations were apportioned. Moreover, the Watcher gave men wisdom of herb and plant, seed and silk, and the proper moderate use of the like. Her father had taken a mortal wife, who had brought her into the world. He in turn had lain with his daughter, the primal witch (though she knew not he was her father, as she had been raised an orphan, her mother dying in childbirth), begetting sons that were more god than man. Sons of double abomination.

Taking the mantle from her father-lover, the arts she had taught the Sons of Adam were soon corrupted, developing into a forbidden body of esoteric wisdom that sinful man could not manage and, because of it, should not learn. Intended, from her perspective, for good, but always to wreak disaster and evil outcomes. In her pride she disobeyed; in her passion, she meddled.

God was right and she was wrong. The potter

understood the vessel better than did the clay. *But why no mercy upon my children?*

And so, this confusion of reverence for God and Country melded with an unyielding, dominating drive to be overly protective of her young passed from her substance into Gwyar, who was relentless in her need to see Gwalchmai and his brothers safe. But not so for the oldest; the same need was not so present towards Mordred.

The meddling was passed on to Gwyar as well.

Her lenses became fused with the lenses of the hawk, empowering to her to see at great, supernaturally long, distances. The 'hawk-eyed' sorceress gazed upon the waters, setting about to scry.

Her efforts did not return void.

There in the black marble the green mirror showed her past true love, *her only true love,* steadily and increasingly dominating his bout with her son. Lancelot was punishing Gwalchmai. Where he could end the contest with minimal injury to his opponent, Lancelot would pause and go no further, allowing Gwalchmai to recuperate some strength, alongside false hope, only to punish him again. Morgaine could not see her brother, who was judging the bout; nor could she tell that the swords were blunted for training and sport. The perceived mortal danger outweighed any holistic evaluation of her vision.

Crying out to any and all gods, imploring all forces, she begged, "If Maelgwn ap Cadawalhir hath any past wound, open it; hath any weakness, manifest it! No matter how small, grant my son hope! Give my Hawk of May one ray of sun, one sliver of light, I pray!"

Meanwhile, whilst she was fully distracted, Bishop Cadfan himself found it.

***

Gwalchmai was losing. Losing badly. Battered, cut, ashen. By the precepts of trial by combat, he would soon have to declare Maelgwn's innocence and his allegation false. This circumstance usually resulted in the death of the accuser, but Arthur had modified the custom. He might live. Life henceforth would ever be accompanied with the shame and aggravation of knowing that an affair would crumble the Summer Kingdom. The misery of knowing that he had fallen short, the ancient custom having failed the Green Knight. Perhaps it *was* fact alone that reigned, and not who could swing a piece of steel better. A great disappointment splashed over the romantic and discouraged warrior.

As he retreated five paces and began to offer the rote words of *innocence,* it was instead Maelgwn who let out a great cry. His naked left thigh, high up near his loins, was awash in fresh blood, falling in uniform and heavy splashes as a waterfall upon his shin and calf armor, then bouncing down to the soil below.

Neither participant was to stab or poke, rather only to strike with the flat edge of the blade. Incidental cuts abounded, but this was an actual *wound.* The two had been closely engaged on a few passes in the match, but none had seen the source of this injury.

Arthur rose to speak, but Lancelot stayed his words.

"It is an old wound, my lord, the scar of which opens betimes. The Hawk did nothing afoul."

The blood brought a reminder, and the reminder was of Merlin. Lancelot was not innocent. That he had not consummated his lust in Perth did not abdicate him of hundreds of kisses and *martial eye service;* transcending the physical indiscretions, he loved the king's wife. He had caused men to die for her, neglected his mates for her, abused women for her. The blood judged him guilty. Deserving of the penalty of death, each day a borrowed and unfair day. In the very next moment, the shattered Lancelot might change his mind, might be haughty, might disagree with his own assessment, slay both Gwalchmai and Arthur, and plop the diadem upon his own crown. But in this moment, he was dripping blood and looking at a hopeless man below him. A good man. A man to whom the bards had given a place as one of Arthur's twelve. And rightly so.

Morgaine's meddling and Merlin's ghost dagger saved Gwalchmai's life.

"Iron Bear." Maelgwn humbled himself before the Pendragon. "May we please end this madness? Or would you have me bleed out right here on the field?"

But, as the Scriptures record, *jealousy is the rage of men.*

"This recurring hurt." The king's tone added the words *that none of us have ever heard of.* "How long will it take to mend?"

Surprised by the response, Maelgwn answered, "But a day or two."

"Three days will suffice." The winds remained relentless, causing Arthur's red cape to flow and flip wildly, making him look as an angry, menacing god. "This contest is finished. The Lancelot of Britannia is the victor, and by right of trial by combat, innocent of Gwalchmai's rail." The crowd warmed themselves with raucous cheers, horn and stringed instrument adding deafening praises of the mighty knight.

Because the Hawk of May had made accusation of impropriety before all, and because the test of arms had favored Maelgwn, life would henceforth forever be very different for Gwalchmai. And by extension, for the kingdom. The common man and the soldier, and a few of the clergy, who lived under the old codes, traditions and manners, were forced, by their own logic, to conclude Gwalchmai as a false accuser: a sower of discord amongst the Cymry. Because of this, his star diminished somewhat, and his chance of being the popular choice to succeed King Arthur was damaged greatly. From this day, many men amongst the Tribes began to pledge their swords to Mordred, the oldest of Arthur's nephews.

"This contest is finished." The king repeated himself. But Arthur was not finished. Frustrated, he settled the grumbly throng; at last they quieted. "This contest is over. But the games are not. Maelgwn is in first position, and" – the king studied the lists and results of the day, confirming how he might beguile the accused for more information – "I am in second position."

"The weather has turned vile. Let there be no more games today!" Bedwini beseeched the king.

"I said 'three days'." Arthur reprimanded his counselor, who looked to the earth and spoke not again. "Maelgwn, heal thyself, and in three days you and I will meet here and conclude the games. That is my judgment." He turned to Gwalchmai, who required assistance from two men, firmly supporting one arm apiece, to stand. "Nephew, you fought well."

The crowd was shocked that Arthur had declared thus, but with the winds mixed with rain mixed with coming dusk (and none wore cloak or coat, for the day had begun hot, with skies blue and clear), they made haste to cottage, estate or hall. The coming championship was the sole subject of conversation and buzz for every woman and man.

But Maelgwn would have none of it. He made for the woods of Gwent immediately after dressing his wound.

Knowing he would do the same, Arthur disguised himself, and followed.

CHAPTER 18
Did You Lie with My Wife? Breaking What Could Not Be Broken

Seed 5 – "Forty years undefeated. You take all, and would now ruin that too?"

Morgaine crushed the hawk's lenses in her hand, discarding them upon the ground. Her unholy looking-glass confirming her son lived, and without a moment to contemplate why Maelgwn would do battle with her son, or whether this would make him her enemy, or whether it was less grave – *boys must fight from time to time, after all* – she was on to the next peril. As a cat giving his chase to its own tail, back to the treasure she hastened.

The foul weather from the south had traveled northward, resulting in heavy rainfall upon Ynys Enlli. The overcast was full, with not one luminary visible in the night sky. A grey and black shell covered the whole of the isle, and the waters dashed against the shores, shrieking in symphony with the high winds.

Morgaine had been away from the hut where

she served as guardian for approximately three hours. The weather had only turned in the past two. This left a one-hour window, if misfortune befell her, for a vessel to have left Ynys Enlli for the mainland. The odds were in her favor… but *ill luck comes in bunches.*

If pilgrims had found the site, but not prepared letter or messenger, nor launched to sea, then the problem could be *contained.* Gwyar would simply kill those who had found what they ought not to have sought, slay those who had seen what was meant to be concealed. *No survivors, no breach.*

At full gallop, her steed lost its footing, for the deluge mixed the dirt roads rapidly into a cake-batter-like mud and threw the sorceress. "Not so tasty as the batter we put to spoon and belly ere we put pan to oven!" she mused, her face full of the road and a little blood.

She rose quickly. Her hood was of the kind where the stretched, pointed end fell well below her lower back, designed for fashion and not function. With both hands she positioned it on her head, a wet, heavy leather cone that flopped to one side. She looked all the part of a frightful druid priestess about to do devilish deeds for the Creator God. The irony was not lost on her. She looked up to the pitch black and imagined Him, presently laughing from His throne, just above the clouds, at her. She smiled.

"At least Moses had Michael to wrestle for and hide his body. Yet the precious lady gets only devils and the bungling children of the damned for her cause. Truly, God must be a man!"

Levity gave way to horror as she finally arrived at the site: torches and many men surrounding the innocuous grave.

A sect of the druids from Glamorgan, who had

seen the light of the gospel but held to many of their native traditions, had made a pact with the Blessed Lady, and with Princess Eurgaine. The relics of the Christians would be hidden amongst the druids, lest the Christians find and make idols of them, falling into corruption like God's chosen people, Israel, before them. Pagans hid Christian things so that Christians would not become as Pagans. This was the pact.

And the relics, or *treasures*, were these:

The cup, or *Holy Grail.*

The alabaster box.

The true Cross.

The second coffin of the Law (for the first had ascended into the heavens afore time).

The spear that had opened the Saviour's side.

The nails that had pierced Him.

The shroud used to wrap His precious body.

And an eighth.

The coffin of Mary, the Mother of Jesus.

Some of the relics had magical or unpredictable properties; some of them were wholly untouched, with powers unknown.

The concern over the body of Mary was not one of mysticism, but rather of history and the nature of men. Men swear by graves. They become a source of revenue to those who control them and a source of false doctrine to those who require that the presbytery come and bow down before them. Men kiss the feet of other men - more so those of other *dead* men. Mary feared that she would be venerated as a goddess, though her bones lay in a box; that an entire religion would be erected around her, appealing to all, spreading the world over, redirecting the praise and worship due the Lord alone unto the mortal woman whose womb had carried Him.

Such was the fear that the druids refused, under any condition, to disclose her location to the Church of the Britons and, over time, denied outright that she had even passed away upon Avalon. Thus, even as the bishops and elders defamed, abused and slandered the druids wherever they could, their enemies did no such thing; rather, they were protectors and guardians against the foes of all men, which are iniquity and idolatry and institutional power drunkenness.

With Vivien transfigured, and Taliesin preoccupied with politics and court and his struggles in keeping the next generation's guardian from falling into the forbidden trap of being seduced by the very thing he or she was to protect, the task fell to Morgaine, the Lady of Avalon. *Independent,* with no special affinity for any group, sect or claimant of god or goddess. A radical patriot who disagreed with much but cherished Arthur's love of liberty and religious freedom.

Perhaps it was right that it should fall to me.

But I have failed.

And, in the time of the reign of King Arthur, the Roman Catholic Church discovered the coffin of Mary, the Mother of Jesus Christ.

Shovels had already unearthed the stone coffin. A marker lay over the sarcophagus; rather than stuck upright in the ground at the head of the corpse, it was buried well beneath the earth and lay flat atop the box, per the custom of the early saints in Cymru. The inscription read, in the Coelbren script of the bards, "Son, behold thy Mother". These were the words the Lord Jesus said unto Mary, distancing Himself from the Lady whilst He became our sin on the Cross. This was an act of love and no malice, for the Son of Man knew well that man would seek to worship her.

Cadfan the Meek had grown up to be Cadfan the Bold. Meirchion the Mad had poisoned his head with arrogance and self-importance and ill purpose, and no part of the kind, quiet-minded Christianity of Brittany remained in him. Taking full advantage of his lineage and entitlement to lands in Llyn, and by extension Ynys Enlli, he was every bit the thorn to Morgaine, Vivien and Taliesin that Meirchion and Caw had been, in their time, to Arthur and Merlin.

He was happy to let the downpour ruin his best vestments, provided he looked the part of the proud priest: the legend who had found the coffin of the Mother of God.

His time drawing breath to enjoy the fame might not survive the rainstorm, for Morgaine of the Faeries approached.

His men had torches, producing a rectangle of lights around the gravesite. She produced an illumination of her own; a purple, thick and substantive light enveloped her. She and it moved quickly, right for him. As she drew close, he could somehow see her eyes, all black to match her raven's hair, strands of which were matted against her forehead and down her cheeks, emerging as vines from the hood of her garb. Unsure of what manner of words would stop her from going right on through him with no more effort than a fox wastes on the hen pen, he opted for truth with slight.

"Lady Gwyar. None will know Mary rests here, and pilgrims will henceforth visit a façade I shall erect upon the mainland, leaving this place be. I assure thee!" He trembled, hoping the fox would hear the hen. "The pact between Meirchion and Vivien I will honor!"

The latter stopped the sorceress. The dagger was momentarily sheathed. She was not prepared to hear him, however, until her assessment was complete. Eight men and a boy - the young historian Gildas ap Caw (who lifted up Arthur in his heart with special adoration, on account of Arthur having saved the boy's life from the macabre talons of the crazed archbishop). *Jesus and Mary outweigh the loss of the lad Gildas, unfortunately,* she reasoned.

Fanning her pillowed sleeves as a great black cobra, her one question was delivered, her voice causing such terrific trembling that none could run; all were as frozen.

"Has an emissary left for Llyn with news of your *discovered treasure?*"

"No, my lady." Cadfan was frightened but coy. "Three boats have departed. Not for Cymru, but for Rome."

"Prince Madoc or his faithful stewards of the sea will stop them."

"On what grounds? What charges? What authority? Monks make pilgrimages and clerics attend sundry councils. Does not liberty still reign in our peaceful and glorious kingdom of light and summer? The masked villain who posed falsely as one of us will not be found amongst them, and to Rome they will freely go with news of the Blessed Mother, unless the sea makes an end of them." Three he had sent, knowing the likelihood that but one might reach its destination. "Would you kill the whole of Rome with your *unique* gifts to cover this truth, Gwyar?" A protective arm was now flung about the soaking and freezing young historian's shoulders. "Would you kill this boy?"

Gwyar had murdered before. Her composition

and traumatic experiences caused her to loathe infidelity in any form and, if she could not contain herself by agony of will, she would give herself to judge these men and the boy here and now. However, Bishop Cadfan was correct. If the discovery had left the little island, it would reach the big island (whether he was lying about Rome made no matter), and if one spoke of it, soon so would a thousand. Her situation would not be improved by sending eight souls to the Underworld. Hearing his intentions seemed to be her best, if not only, recourse.

"What will you do with the body, priest?" she asked, bluntly.

"*The body.* I am so thankful you asked in just that manner." As he started to speak, Cadfan's eyes met Gwyar's. Seeing Death itself staring back at him, he at once discerned that wordplay and boasting was best smothered – immediately. Looking towards his boots, steadily sinking into the relentless rainy mud, he continued, with a tone and tenor of extreme caution. "Your concern about the Blessed Mother's body, with the greatest of respect, has been misplaced. There is an accord between the Lady of the Lake and my late master, Meirchion the Mad. That pact demands that we honor your goddess, though the world comes to Christ."

Gwyar knew there was deception and guile forthcoming, not knowing only what form it would take. She held her tongue.

Cadfan continued. "Where Illtud and Dyfrig would convert you all, we would rather assimilate you. You are not lost sinners doomed for a cruel, fiery hell. Rather, you are all simply departed Catholic brothers and sisters who have lost your way. Hell is a sentence served in portions and degrees, not a place of finality. We believe we can shorten your time working your way out of Hell by joining to us this side of the veil." There was little conviction behind Cadfan's discourse on Hell, and Gwyar wondered if he believed his own words. Were she pressed, Gwyar would reckon Cadfan a traditionalist, an opportunist, and an atheist.

"Instead of denouncing and forcing rejection of your goddess" – he took two contested steps in the thickening, soupy dirt away from the sorceress to deliver his next words – "we will simply appropriate her, and all goddesses in their myriad of forms, to Mary. In her will your goddess live on."

"In pretending to be kind, you would inflict cruelty and compromise upon men of all faiths! No two goddesses are compatible in characteristic, origin or purpose. None will accept that *all the gods are one God, or Goddess!*" she protested, using simple logic.

But his logic was superior, or at least more realistic. "If there is no such thing as an actual goddess, and the thousands of local deities the world over are but tribal expressions of the same *one Mother*, they will swallow the whole of our doctrine. All men want to serve a woman, to slay a dragon, to have a fair maiden, to be in the bosom of the safe harbor of a mother. We will supply all these to the faithful, in the person of Mary. She is the end of your religion."

Gwyar knew he was right, but protested just the same. "You have seen *my power!* Am I a myth or a local cultural expression?"

"Surely not. But men forget all in a generation's time. Our king is removing the land of all the Giants; the *real witches* attack villages and children and fall at his sword or axe, or else those of this or that great Round Table Knight. When the supernatural prints and smudges on this land diminish, our propaganda will ensure that they all become restated as legend. You, my lady, are real today but two centuries from now will be a child's bedtime story."

The evil genius of Cadfan's presentation exceeded his levels of intelligence. He was parroting information passed down from the Masked Priest, surely.

"Even King Arthur will be a myth."

"That is treason!" Gwyar hissed.

"It is what will be. We will take the coffin of Mary to the mainland and erect a chapel there. Pilgrims will come to the chapel of Saint Mary and bow down to her *empty tomb.* Great statues and images we will erect to celebrate her. And slowly and methodically we will teach that the coffin is empty because the Mother, the *goddess,* to the Tribes, hath ascended to heaven, leaving us a memorial to honor her but no body, for she lives, like the Saviour, at the right hand of the Heavenly Father."

"You will create an enterprise built on lies."

He ignored her and went on, "Your pact with the Glamorgan line of druids and the ancient promises made to Mary and Eurgaine may, of course, continue. Protect these bones; do as you will. None will believe that they are hers."

"The truth, like water, seeks its level. The truth will prevail. My brother, the greatest of all kings, will hear of this, for he loves Mary, for different reasons. He knows of the secret, and he knows of this place. Even if you overcome a little witch like me, how will you defeat Arthur ap Meurig?!"

"Did he not do the same thing at Mynydd Baedan? Did he not bear an image of Mary vague enough to be repurposed and embraced by heathens?"

"What he did was borne of respect and no guile!" she hissed.

"Nevertheless, the king faces problems and perils of his own. I doubt not that he will be much entangled in the rumors and wrangling of rival religions over bones and relics."

Cadfan's confidence was an indication that the mantle had passed from Meirchion. She surmised that he was a low-level initiate in league with the Masked Priest, who must be active from his hiding places within the Isles. Cadfan was as a breadcrumb, and for this reason, Gwyar let him live. The Church's strategy of assimilation was *a slow game* that might win the day, but not *this day*. In his boasts and revelations he had manifested his plans. He possessed a box with old scratches upon it, no more. Gwyar's only course was to stay the course.

As the tempest tendered no grace, pounding Avalon without mercy well into the early hours of the next day, the little raven managed, by herself, to labor for the whole of the night in muck and soak, in sleet and mud. She managed to reinter the earthly mother of Jesus beneath the flooring of the circular thatch hut that had recently become Gwyar's temporary home. Busy hands begat a racing brain. Her thoughts went randomly here then there as she hastened to finish the task.

First to Mary. The burden of a mother and the impossible plight that is womanhood. *To be the mother of an innocent man, to see Him slain before your very eyes. To flee beyond the fingertips of Rome, to hide from the Jews, to never have rest.* Then to Gwalchmai. *My son, my Green Knight, the brightness of our Isle. What embarrassment and shame hath Lancelot brought to you, innocent and just now spotted and smudged by a crazy man!* The involuntary reflections increased the speed of hand and accelerated anger; unrelenting visions of Maelgwn smiting her boy joined the rains soaking and troubling her soul. Lastly, to Gwenhwyfar. The kernel and core of all that distressed Cymru. *A woman is no woman who has not known the birthing of a child. She is a well without water, a dry spring. She knows not the burden of anything save ambition.*

At last she finished, the thoughts somewhat assuaged. She looked upon the new concealed place. It was arranged with love and respect and, above all, discretion.

***

Both royal siblings had braved the night's summer storm.

"He makes camp at Llyn Fawr. At his foster-mother's posts, just beyond the waters."

Arthur quickly unclothed himself, throwing his soaked robes (for this time he had been guised as a bard, complete with harp and scroll) and accessories into the creel, next to a massive freestanding closet in the anteroom that joined to his and Gwenhwyfar's bedchamber. She half listened, giving the greater heed to the mud tracked in upon the floor, and the chaotic and wet greetings of Arthur's dogs, whom she rushed out of the room with intolerant and vulgar words.

She began to speak, but the king gave her no place, nor space. Replacing the disguise he had donned to follow the Lancelot with a simple flesh-colored robe and placing a circlet upon his head, though she was his only audience and the sun was not yet in his chamber, he authoritatively drew to within inches of her, and questioned the queen.

"In three days I will meet our childhood friend in a *game of sport*. Have you anything to tell me, whether in regard to the privy exchange that set my nephew at such variance, or any untoward deed or thought of past or present?"

"You have been at it all night hunting the Bloodhound. And remain yet eloquent. Yet virile, and strong. I am as innocent as the trial declared, husband," she responded.

What his heart wanted to believe, his head forbade. She was Arthur's first love, his only love. But the glow she had around *him,* the *look*… Never gave she these to Arthur. He knew that nothing revealed love so much as a lovers' quarrel. Her anger, her investment of emotion, betrayed her words to be false, though Arthur mistook what was on account of Mordred, laying Maelgwn to blame. Far from conclusive, the scales were falling, yet slow as an inchworm, from his eyes.

"Think you that I am as strong as he?" He tested the queen.

The actress, still obsessed with the probable present congress of her love with the False Gwenhwyfar, could not suffer even the briefest of exchanges of this sort.

"Oh, the two of you!" The beauty snarled, the left side of her lip raised, teeth shown as a trapped predator, giving warning before the strike. "He is stronger. Or you. You are more handsome. Or perhaps he. By my soul, I care not, for I am WEARY of you both. Ever from our youth, 'twas always the same. Will we go to our graves abiding such nonsense? Not I!" Though the aggressor, the lady retreated three steps. "Get these cursed dogs out of our room, Arthur!"

"This hatred of the pets. Is it new, or like other matters, newly revealed?" Calm words, though his heart raced as the sprinters from yesterday's games.

"I would not enumerate the things I detest, for the new day is not long enough."

Merlin had taught Arthur that extreme anger revealed one of two truths that were unfortunately negating, revealing nothing; the twin angers of innocence and guilt.

Thus, more information was needed. Information that would not be had under the current cloud of ill sentiment. In her indignation, his spouse, who was as a mouse before him, was yet intimidating; but Arthur was not subdued. He encroached further, his very breath now felt upon her forehead.

"It has been a miserable day, which has wrought hasty words. Forget not thyself, and see that you disrespect never the king, especially in his own estate."

To look upon King Arthur Pendragon when he drew upon his innate and natural authority was to look at Death itself. She suddenly felt as scores of Saxons of old had felt before Excalibur had run them through, which was a pleasant alternative to the menacing imposition of the Great Sovereign.

The actress. The politician. Seeing that she had overstepped and noting well that Arthur had transitioned office from husband to king, she forced herself to stop thinking about Mordred and Gwenhwyfach for a moment and to focus on surviving the moment. "Yes; the storm, and the moons of womanhood. Forgive me. Of course I love you alone. Please let us rest, my love." Her countenance shifted from hunter to seductress. The snarl waxed into a smile. "And yes, husband, I have always hated those damn dogs!"

They giggled, and he bade Cai put them with the horses.

The sun rose and the fair weather returned, the clear sky causing the majestic Severn to shine as a crystal river.

Surrendering to a few hours of sleep, lids too heavy to uphold, Gwen's final waking thoughts: *Mordred is having intercourse with my sister!*

***

Mordred was having intercourse with Gwen's sister.

Not all lovemaking is the same. Not all privy parts are a delicious counterpart. The wonderful friend Mordred had made at Caer Ogyrfan, the courtship so enticing, so alluring and confirming; the *newer Gwenhwyfar. The little sister, the 'bach' or tiny Gwen,* now beneath Mordred. His wife, his legitimate lover.

And yet.

In the very act of knowing her, with feigned looks of pleasure, the heavens themselves began to crash, the world ending in apocalyptic fashion.

She is boring.

She is not good at this.

What have I done?!

The dark magic betwixt Gwenhwyfar's thighs wrought by nature, else by the Tylwyth Teg, had ruined Mordred (and many other unfortunate souls besides) for all women, the realization thereof drowning him – not in a slow coming to terms, but as the highest tides climaxing upon hard rocks.

She is boring.

I do not like this!

What have I done?

Mordred, yet still in the act of loving, peered into the eyes of his wife, who sincerely returned his gaze with ecstatic adoration. His glance had become academic, curious, and mindful of history.

Knowing the fullness of what might come, he marveled at her. *I am looking at the one who will be the ruin of Britain.* Then he finished, and slept.

***

Arthur instructed Bedwyr and Cai to send word to many that the championship contest was at hand, only that the venue had changed. Both knights, uneasy, faithfully executed their charges.

Maelgwn rested under a tree, gazing upon the lake, hoping desperately to see Vivien, or the wizard, or any otherworldly being that might bewitch him to forget her and resurrect his love for him. That Arthur had allowed one swing of a blunted sword by Gwalchmai rivaled his thoughtlessness of many times afore. Denying the king of Gwynedd the chance *to defend Gwynedd,* and other hurts, boiled and boiled. And the boil produced a bubble.

Perhaps two great kings are two too many. For this cause, perhaps there can only be one. Maelgwn wrested with vivid and detailed thoughts of violence against Arthur.

And then the very object of his malicious contemplations presented itself above him, the form a familiar regal shadow. *And three hundred onlookers besides.*

"Making your leave before the final match?"

Maelgwn did not rise, but remained flat on his back beneath the tree, as a felled, dead oak fixed hard against one that was yet upright. His present foe was not Arthur; rather, the bubble.

"Yes, the match is asinine. Ought not cooling our hot heads and the more noble angels of our grace prevail?"

"You speak of the Trial by Combat," came the retort. "That was between you and the Hawk of May. Of a truth, this is in no wise related to that. Come; let us show our skills, that our peacetime warriors become not as a rusted axe and our next generation learns of your foster-mother's martial art. Let us dance her dance." Arthur's empty hand indicated the sacred lake. Lakes, mountains and waterfalls; the romance and grandeur of Cymru consolidated in one sanctified place. "A three-point match, sir."

"Nay." Maelgwn tilted his head, rather annoyed that so many boots would tread upon a spot that should only accommodate rare and discreet visitors in three or four. Instead, a hundred times as many were rendering the scene as half amphitheater bordered by a body of water. An arena composed of men and women.

The gathering spectators included Rhufawn, returned from a fruitless questing after the Grail, and Gwyar, who had come from Ynys Enlli to the mainland by barge, then by hired carriage to Caerleon. She had not yet found Gwalchmai as she politely elbowed her way towards the front. She would find him. And she would confront Maelgwn. For she was rested, and in want of answers.

Gwalchmai and Urien, along with Peredur

and Owain, were present as well, Bishop Bedwini and Illtud and not a few noble women mixing with the crowd.

"How did you find me here?" Maelgwn continued his horizontal repose.

"You saw me on the steep; were you not of such height, our eyes would've met, though mine were shaded by a hood."

"I saw none but an old, grey-bearded Glamorgan bard braving the rain—"

Arthur produced the grey, silky deception, lifelike and remarkably realistic, and dangled it over the King of Gwynedd. Laughing and provoking, he said, "Master of disguises. With this beard in hand, and the crowd before us, we look as if we are performing theatre; I as Itto Gawr and you *as me.*" Arthur offered not levity of laughter with his jest. The intent thereof was directed to mean: *You wish you were me and I the Giant whom I slayed, championing the people you could not.*

Maelgwn rose upon an elbow, partially taking the bait. Then he recovered himself. "You and your disguises. Perhaps you, more than any of the Round Table Fellowship, understand why the chief of the secret society that vexes this land hides behind his mask as he does." Insult for insult. "Perhaps you ARE he."

Arthur gritted and ground his perfect teeth. "Rise, Lancelot. A match we will have."

Maelgwn's eyes panned round the mob. Cadog was present; Illtud appeared nervous. Queen Gwenhwyfar, in simple green gown with long brown boots suited for horseback, climbing or trudging through mud, stood amongst the damsels. *Gwenhwyfach and Mordred were not present.*

"I shall not." Standing fast, but giving the

response in his familiar killing voice.

"Very well. Bedwyr." Arthur looked about for his friend.

"Yes, lord, I am here."

"Bring forth Rhufawn the Radiant, son of Maelgwn Gwynedd. As he was absent from the games and neither suffered losses nor earned wins, he will be a fair substitute. He will be his father's proxy. Go to, now; get me the lad and four blunted weapons." Then Arthur manifested *his* killing voice, glaring at his old friend. "Perhaps the son of Lancelot will learn much in fighting the High King today, and I will certainly learn much about you in felling him."

Each hero had violated unwritten boundaries, even when angered. Maelgwn intimating that Arthur was the very villain who had launched the plot resulting in his own sons' deaths, essentially *creating a reason to kill his own seed.* Arthur hinting at doing the same to Maelgwn's lad. Severe insults with thin veils and known meanings, as fiery arrows shot.

"No!" Maelgwn was on his feet so quickly that it startled Arthur, who withdrew to gather himself. The knight made quickly for the lakehouse where he had lodged. He emerged with such haste that the faeries must have dressed him, for he was fully armored save his helm. *The silver armor. The special occasion armor.* And he held no blunted sport weapon, but rather that legendary battle spike, and was at full gallop upon the king, screaming, "No! Let us stand together!"

Arthur was calm. The War King revised his request of Bedwyr, bidding him fetch Rhon, the king's enchanted spear, along with a curved shield that stood in height to an average man's torso.

Excalibur remained sheathed and in Bedwyr's custody, several yards away from the combatants.

The façade of sport had dissolved, replaced by a titanic clash. Not between Arthur and Lancelot, for their *right-minded selves* were now also as spectators. The battle between Arthur's jealousy and Maelgwn's jealousy had begun.

Maelgwn slid inside the reach of Arthur's long weapon, bringing the hook that appended the guard of his battle spike down hard on the Iron Bear's shoulder; a spraying array of blood arched high, splattering upon the spongy ground near the lake. The next maneuver would be to clip Arthur's right knee or ankle. With left shoulder and right leg debilitated, he would have no side to favor, nowhere to redistribute pain. This would result in a moment of inactivity, ensued by a violent and clean deathblow.

I have seen the steps of this dance danced scores and scores times more upon the Saxon and the Pict. Arthur had the advantage of knowing, borne of the intimacy of repetition, where Maelgwn would go. *Right knee or ankle!* In an instant, Arthur positioned his shield upon his right leg and spun away from the taller opponent's crouched striking attempt, thrusting his spear towards the Bloodhound's thigh in the same motion.

The crowd, in concert as if they were veteran members of Illtud's choir, voiced their awe, their shock. And not over the bloody wound that was the king's left shoulder.

Rhon's tip had breached the Perfect Knight's armor. Lancelot was cut!

Maelgwn Gwynedd was fifty. Maelgwn Gwynedd had been a man of sword and spear since age fourteen. Excepting the mystery of Merlin's dagger and its peculiar stab wound, and a tiny scar upon his scalp secondary to his fall in Broceliande, Maelgwn was wholly unscathed. Thirty-six years. Not a broken bone, nor a disjointed knee, nor a smashed nose. No slashes; no other scars. He was as perfect, creamy marble carving. Flawless and untouched.

By contrast, Arthur had seen two fewer winters than the Bloodhound, but his body was far more battleworn. His knees complained periodically, as did his left shoulder. He had suffered a few broken bones, and a few near-kill slashes had left permanent signatures upon both his chest and back. Still, both men possessed the speed, verve and appearance of young men in their twenties.

Now Maelgwn joined his friend and opponent in bleeding.

"Do we rush upon them, tackle them, and end this?" Bedwyr asked his fellows, desperately.

"Yes," said Meurig. The old king knew that rage had displaced reason and that his son was in peril; as was Cymru, a confederacy of kingdoms, tribes, clans and cantrefs, seeing the blood of its fatherless king crimsoning the green grass. Meurig noted, and Gwen neglected to mention, that Arthur had brought a Silure death mask in his satchel. The burial helmet was all silver, save the eye sockets and outlines of the moustache and mouth, which were pure gold. The helmet was inlaid with a jeweled diadem, and ornate Latin scriptures were etched to appear as in orbit around the crown. A golden mail shirt and shiny trousers trimmed in gold were folded neatly beneath the helmet. Meurig's son was prepared to die this very day; moreover, he was controlling the action, intentionally provoking a fight under the pretext of a sport.

In the moments of hesitation as his closest allies and friends pondered intervention, a remarkable, shocking development manifested.

Arthur was winning.

The skill of the Iron Bear in hand-to-hand combat and grappling had no equal save that of the massive man he now enjoyed a slight advantage over. Both men disarmed of long weapon in the scrum, Arthur was mounted upon Lancelot, both legs hooked, flattening the longer man. Chest to chest upon the ground, Arthur would recoil upward, creating separation, and then bring his elbow down hard upon Lancelot's head and cheek, opening gash upon gash with each strike.

Clutched so close, words followed. The three hundred witnesses could hear that the combatants spoke, but discern their words they could not, for they were closely engaged.

"Second! I am sick of being second!" Arthur lamented. "Second in handsomeness, second to be looked upon by our fair damsels." (Now, Arthur was a noble man who did not lust after other women, nor seek their coquettish affections. But *all men* desire to be revered as handsome, and the incessant rankings in gossip, at feasts, in buzzes and hearsays, had worn upon the king's soul. *Better to be a reproach than to be the second most handsome man in the kingdom).* "Second with sword. Second in valor. Second in glory. I am" – another elbow found Lancelot's nose – "sick of being second!"

Lancelot finally caught a free-flinging wrist, locked it, and flipped Arthur. So much taller was the Bloodhound than the Iron Bear that the scene now looked as an older boy atop his infant brother, bullying him.

Arthur's defense was excellent. His jealousy, rage, and the confidence filling him as the tide pools rapidly upon the shore enhanced his skill, when usually such attributes imbalance a man. He blocked every shot. And now Lancelot, who was bleeding *all over Arthur*, recompensed jealousies.

"*I* am sick of being second! Second!" Another attempted crushing blow was shucked by the valiant king. "Second in decision-making, second in strategy, second in regard by the ladies." (For all women would choose to lie once with Lancelot but would, each and every one, take Arthur to husband. Pleasure for a few minutes, or romance and respect and reverence for a lifetime? Women, being smarter than men, would always choose the latter. Lancelot knew the same. Arthur, a handsome and fantastic lover in his own right, envied the taller, more godlike man, and could not see that he was the preferred choice.) Another strike went amiss. Lancelot abandoned course and stood, literally lifting Arthur with him, flinging him hard against the tree.

Lancelot's attendant ran quickly, efficiently rearming the silver knight with both his battle spike and leaf-shaped sword.

Bedwyr did the same for Arthur, but was rebuked.

"Not that sword. Fetch thou me the Sword of Power. Fetch thou me Excalibur."

But Bedwyr disobeyed, as Meurig shouted, "Will you not stop this?!"

Bedwyr followed with, "My lord. You are Arthur of the authority of the Three Swords, the possessor of the Two Swords of Britain. Wield not the sword with vanity, I beseech you."

King Arthur's eyes were now as the Red Dragon that had hailed his birth. "Bedwyr. It is not for you to determine how to bear the sword, but rather to deliver the sword. DELIVER THE SWORD."

"My lord." The trustworthy knight yielded that famed steel unto the Pendragon.

Some weeping began to replace sport-lust and curiosity.

The reality of combat, as with lovemaking, is that most sessions are very short in reality and long in legend. Actual fights typically last but a few strokes. Not so for these men.

Ten strikes given. Ten blocked or dodged. Vivien's diagonal dance executed to perfection. Spiral steps and remarkable speed; a symphony of steel.

Where the shore of lake met the high grass near where they battled was a marshy area that appeared as a stream adjoined to the lake. Tall reeds grew in the 'betwixt and between' of lake and shore and the water, in spots, rose as high as the armpits of an average man. Lancelot was pushing Arthur backwards towards the stream, where his height would give him decisive advantage, as he could stand in the waters whereas Arthur could not.

As they hacked and whacked, two figures emerged on either side of the marshy area.

Morgaine of the Faeries.

Gwenhywfar II.

Arthur stood to the north, firm upon the land.

Lancelot to the south, now in the water.

Gwen was to west, her eyes aflame as fire.

Morgaine to the east; she seemed elevated above her stature, her hair wisping about as the wind.

The four cords.

Breaking.

Gwen could here demotivate and disarm Arthur with cruel words, giving Lancelot the victory and, perhaps, Mordred a pathway to the throne.

Morgaine could use her dark magick to shift the tide for Arthur, ending the misery of the troubled beast that was Lancelot forever. *But her magick could not make Gwen return love to Arthur, or even treat him well.*

The four cords.

Breaking.

Lancelot's eyes met Gwen's. Arthur saw this, and advanced, enraged. This had been Lancelot's aim, as it drew the men deeper into the marshy waters. But Lancelot, though better on every other day, was again bested by the Pendragon's next move as Excalibur knocked Lancelot's sword cleanly from his hand, leaving him with his battle spike and no secondary weapon versus Excalibur. Arthur brought down unyielding overhand strikes, remembering the cause of the day. *Information. Truth!*

"Did you lie with my wife?" Overhand strike.

"Did you lie with my wife?" Again. Overhand strike.

"Did you lie with my wife?" Overhand strike. Again.

The volley caused Lancelot to give way and fall. His knees reached the bottom of the stream, giving Arthur the high ground. The famed battle spike was held as a broom handle by both hands above Lancelot's head, in a purely defensive pose.

"Did you lie with my wife?"

"Yes."

All sound stopped. As did Arthur. As did Lancelot.

"Adultery against the High King! This is

treason!" Saint Illtud hollered as an authoritative judge and executioner.

"Nay," said Lancelot, still upon one knee, the other plunged into the bloody pink foam of the marshy stream. "Yes, I have known the queen, but queen she was not, for we were but sixteen!"

At the confirmation that Lancelot had been intimate with his life's true love, all spittle evaporated from Arthur's mouth. He could not breathe, nor control the pounding, irregular drumming of his heart.

"All of your 'I saw her first' prodding and goading and demands made it impossible to find any forum to tell you. She was MY childhood love. You are so humble in matters myriad but so arrogant on this matter. Had you but asked—"

"You withheld this from me for over thirty years!" Arthur was not addressing Lancelot alone. His statement was generalized, though his anger was acute. "Sister? Did you know? Gwenhwyfar, you withheld this as well? Were you all in league to shame your king?"

"Not to shame you, lord. To protect you," Gwyar offered, weeping.

"Rather to die under the weight of truth than to live under the false security of a lie!" Arthur, then, full of jealous rage, looked to Excalibur and spoke words ancient and powerful; words whose origins he knew not, for they formed of themselves. The Sword of Power became emerald green and the blade vibrated as if to sing a deafening song of vengeance. One more overhand strike followed, the force of which had not been matched since the foundation of the world, neither has it since.

"I SAW HER FIRST!"

Excalibur cleaved Lancelot's battle spike in

twain as the famed blade made shattered glass of Lancelot's breastplate, reaching his chest, piercing flesh and bone, very near unto the heart. He reflexively slung the two shards of his battle spike into the lake and stood to counterstrike but closed his arms just as quickly, grasping his opened chest, crumpling in pain, toppling into the waters.

Excalibur also was two pieces in the stead of one.

Arthur's heart was as broken as the legendary blade. It had been made from angelic protectors of Eden, its ores now witness to two *falls.*

Llyn Fawr, the most sacred of lakes upon the Blessed Isles in the Sea, rumbled and rushed.

Lancelot, the invincible knight, lay defeated – lay dying. Undefeated no more. Arthur had broken the Bloodhound Prince; the greater had succumbed to the lesser.

Suddenly a mist emerged from the center of the lake, spiraling clockwise, filling the entire basin. Visibility became limited to shadows and forms, the summer day fighting the spontaneous shadows.

"Sister, cease," came the command.

"'Tis not I," said Gwyar.

A hooded druid appeared beneath the oak tree whence the fateful match had commenced. His robes seemed grey and he was tall, as tall as Lancelot.

For the shame of his act, Arthur had dropped the hilt and shards of the sword that had been his ever companion since gifted to him by the Lady of Llyn Fawr above three decades ago. Something caused him to turn to the druid; an eerie silence was over all. None were protesting the mist, none were chaotic over the fog. The events witnessed rendered them all yet silent, nothing remaining that could surprise them.

Then the voice came.

"You have broken what could not be broken. Hope is broken. When he could have taken the South by force, he did not; when he could have taken the queen at his whim, he did forbear, suffering himself not. You would allow Caermelyn to crumble over a youthful tumble. Little Bear, let not the sun set on your anger; yield not to wrath."

The mist and the lake and my emotions do deceive me. Arthur suffered himself not to say the name of the man, apparition, or devil that spoke unto him. *I am beside myself. This is my conscience speaking. I am beside myself. But the apparition speaks truth.*

A faint, faint whisper escaped his lips. "Merlin?"

As he turned back from the vision towards where Lancelot had slumped in collapse, laboring hard to prevent him from drowning in the stream, the fog abated, but only above Arthur and Lancelot. In the stream, another lost friend appeared.

Both Lancelot and Arthur saw her.

Contrasting Morgaine's dress, black as night, was the white gown scaled in sparkly samite, flowing in elegance, one with the water, just beneath the stream. She illuminated the marsh as a second sun. The brightness and grandeur caused Arthur to cover his eyes with blood-soaked hands. As he peeled his fingers away, he witnessed two arms fixed straight, emerging from the water, holding a sword.

"Take me up!" The voice of the shadowy druid quoted the words etched into the obverse side of Excalibur's hilt, the reverse side reading *Cast me away!* "The Lady of the Lake! Take me up!

It is not thy time!" The voice begged Arthur to understand.

Slowly, and frightened, King Arthur approached the floating water spirit. The height of the stream where she held tight the sword reached well above his chest, causing him partially to swim, partially to walk.

"Take it!" the voice implored.

Delicately, the erstwhile boy-king handled what had been, for the sum of his adult life, a metal extension of himself. As he reverently put his right hand upon the hilt, the Lady's hands gently retreated from the blade and recoiled into the waters.

"How can it be?" asked the king, bewildered. For Excalibur it was! Whole, original, as if never harmed, as if newly forged. The Lady of the Lake gracefully sank into the marsh, and was then at once seen in white spots and splashes dashing away from Arthur, then beneath the surface of the lake of Llyn Fawr. Then into its center, then gone.

The fog was completely burned off by the heat of the sun, the crowd seeing their hero holding the symbol of his virility and power. They cheered and cheered the victorious king. But Arthur silenced them.

"Sister, heal him." His directive gave room neither for response or debate.

Though Arthur sorrowed greatly over the ordeal, his jealousy had not been assuaged. Every other thought was of the taller, more handsome man pleasing his exquisite wife. He wished not for Maelgwn to die, but he wished not to look upon the half portion of his misery.

Barely conscious, Maelgwn was alert enough to hear his sentence.

"Withholding the truth is the same as a lie. You

are forthwith demitted from the Round Table Fellowship, unwelcome in its courts, ineligible for its adjudications. You are the champion no more. Unless it be, from time to time, to have fellowship with thy sons, see to it that you do not oft visit these lands. This is my sentence, and it will be enforced, with arms as necessary." Soft banishment, with a garnish of the value of family, was the sentence of the hurting and good king.

Taking Gwyar by the hand, he gave one more utterance. "This will not be a kingdom of secrets and lampshades and bushels. When the news is good, my people will celebrate it; when ill, my people will hear of it - and endure it. No more will we try to save people from themselves, heaping decades of lies in the process. NO MORE SECRETS."

Morgaine of the Faeries ought to have here shared that Mordred was the bastard son of the spring rites but, risking her relationship with her brother whom she so deeply loved - or worse, her head - she discerned that she must yet continue to shelter the king's head from truth for the sake of his heart. *For the sake of Cymru.*

Acknowledging him with her eyes, she spake not, but instructed four men to place Lancelot in her carriage, that she might take him to Avalon and heal him.

CHAPTER 19
Arthur versus Cynwyl Gawr the Last

The barge bore Lancelot to Ynys Enlli, under the care and custody of Morgaine of the Faeries.

I could kill you now for the hurts you put upon my son, report that you perished by Excalibur. But then my brother would bear the guilt of it. The sorceress recalled her dagger from his throat. Replacing the malice of steel with the soothing of herbs, she ensured that that his sleep was deep and his complaints mild. Possessing complete mastery of every herb of the field, treating him was much easier than looking upon him.

She had loved him when a lass, later revered him as warrior, was thankful to him for fifteen years of plenty and peace, but otherwise shared the collective emotion of the whole of Cymru: frustration.

Unpredictable.

Dangerous.

Volatile.

Inconsistent.

Disquieting.

These were the attributes that marked and defined the greatest knight in the history of the world from the Creation to Galahad. *Perhaps he will right your wrongs.*

His woes began on the Isle of Apples – reflection changed Morgaine's attitude by some measure – *perhaps he can find reconciliation and restoration here as well.*

The Merlin Taliesin had arrived in advance of the king's sister, greeting her warmly as her barge skidded and bobbed, docking upon Avalon's tricky port.

***

He nearly slayed an invincible man, a demigod amongst grasshoppers. What might the Iron Bear do unto me? Gwenhywfar the Actress conducted herself with extreme checks of her behavior. Heaping scores of apologies for not disclosing the intimacy she had shared with Maelgwn *before* her marriage to Arthur, she tried all to earn his favor and garner forgiveness.

Her years suggesting that her womb might be dry, she was now a beautiful liability, a tarnished trophy, a queen quite replaceable. Mordred had taken a young wife and had led Arthur to live under a veil of deception for fifteen years. Her situation was precarious, her disposition deflated and depressed; her instincts to survive were all that kept the lady from falling into a deep woe or removing herself from the realm of the living.

Two things saved Gwenhwyfar from divorce, or worse.

First, Arthur, though embroiled by jealousy (for he too was but a man), was no hypocrite. He possessed empathy for all, even his rivals, even his enemies, and especially his wife. Arthur's youth had deeply affected him as well; fosterage away from his parents, with whom he was very close, the spring rites to validate himself amongst the Tribes, the carnal yet mystical act required of him, fighting and killing too young, fame, accountability, pressure.

I had relations with one of the four cords too, and surely I spoke not of it either. Why would I expect Gwen to do what I would not? Or, for that matter, my champion. Whether a good memory or ill, their incident shaped them. And was private. Provided that they continued not this love, nor knew one another after I wedded the queen, they are innocent. And I am wrong.

Arthur had been taught to immediately admit his transgressions, possess them, and move forward. That he could admit his wrongs in the presence of a woman differentiated him from all men who have ever lived.

Secondly, Merlin.

The quest and long-dormant hope to find the one who had taught him this lesson had been resurrected, distracting him greatly from involuntary thoughts and images of Gwen and Maelgwn doing things that poisoned his mind. No one, save perhaps Maelgwn (who was at present being nursed by Gwyar), had heard the voice, nor seen the grey druid. But Arthur was convinced. *It was his voice. Merlin was there. The fog confused the ears and distorted the eyes of the crowd. Was it a vision? Or does he live?!* An excited man with a work to do has little time to dwell upon private hurts or be governed by natural insecurities.

In light of these, the king dealt graciously with his disloyal, loathsome wife.

"We have long reigned, you and I," he opened.

She felt her kneecap knock involuntarily upon its counterpart.

"Our reign," he continued, "has had no Saxon invasions. No fear. No sending boys to marry and fight at fourteen, neither robbing the damsels of their precious youths. Art, science, enterprise, freedom. We have done well." Arthur smiled. "A question I have for you, fair Gwenhwyfar."

"Ask; I shall not answer amiss." She looked to the floor, unable to face the uncertain direction of the discourse.

"Have we Round Table Companions, we bishops and wizards, we powerful and stately women, such as you…" The good king took up a drinking horn, polished with such shine that it reflected his face. He looked upon himself for the twinkling of an eye, then gulped down his scrumpy. "Have we written enough in The Great Conversation? Woven enough in The Great Thread? Have we done all to inspire future generations to look back and to know that, for whatever short season this Summer Kingdom did endure, liberty and good can prevail? Have we lit the bright light of liberty?"

Gwen discerned that encouragement might save her neck. "One hundred or one thousand years from now, the governments of men will measure themselves by what Arthur ap Meurig achieved. You are the candle in a world ever on the brink of total darkness, the pole star that demands the clouds below him to scatter, though he be the only flicker visible on a stormy night. We have had peace on earth in our time."

"I am Arthur, the Iron Bear of Glamorgan. The War King, the Giant Slayer." A blush crimsoned his cheeks.

"You are!" she agreed.

"But you will never look upon me as you look upon him."

Not so much him as upon Mordred… but aye, never upon you.

"Not so, husband; I lo—"

"Let us not speak of love. You are innocent, and I am the fool. My mother once said that a person 'loves who they love'. What love you possess for me is eclipsed by your love for him."

Conciliatory.

"Will you put me away?"

"All things change, Gwenhwyfar. The Summer Kingdom is not buildings of gold, neither song nor merriment. It is more than loving your neighbor above yourself, more than the leaders living under the very laws they subject the people to. In the end it is not even such noble things."

"What is it?"

"It is the ambassadorship of truth whilst we tarry in a fallen world. We will not make heaven on earth, neither will we replant Eden. Rather, we shall point men towards the hope of Heaven, and the promise of Eden. That is for God Himself to deliver, and He will keep His promise. Burn our estates and castles, export our gold, scorch our crops, level our chapels. All things change, all things fail. But *HOPE* never fails. We are hope."

He is going to put me away. Or worse. And abdicate!

"I will not put you away."

Tears of relief welled, this time the actress pretending not.

Arthur was direct, and crestfallen. "My heart breaks at our plight. But we must endure. The Silures must not crumble on account of such a thing. The Midlands and the North are not strong enough to unite our land, and enemies are always at the door."

"A political marriage?"

"A half political marriage. I love you yet with my whole heart." Arthur sighed and laughed. "I owe Lancelot an apology. To the Isle of Apples I must go."

"Which disguise will you choose that you be not accosted on the roads, or hassled by Cai?"

They both laughed and the sorrowful moment, no less sorrowful, was eased. Arthur still operated under a heap of Gwenhwyfar's lies and deceit, but the little truth that he did know relieved her, and her disposition relieved him.

Arthur selected an old costume. One that rendered him a derelict: a beggar or thief. "I wore this years ago when traveling on a horrible assignment; a task as commissioned from Hell itself. As I made my way north I reposed, in these very garments, within a shout of your bedroom. Thoughts of you warmed me through a night of bitter cold."

"May the guise keep you hidden and the selfsame thoughts keep you warm. I will be here upon your return." Gwenhwyfar embraced her husband, all the while leaping in her inward parts at the prospect of a few days with her lover. Whether in their field, the chapel or her little apartment mattered not. To see him, to peel him away from his younger lover, *or to kill him.*

Softly nestling one of her tiny hands in his, he jested: "And yes, I will take the dogs with me."

Arthur, relishing his brief moment away from the burden of the throne, selected a horse that was not his (adding to the façade), a rugged, aged but happy companion and carrier of men. He lumbered along with the war dogs, mastiffs nearly as tall as the horse, grunting and rejoicing in the change of routine.

"Don't *they* compromise the ruse, lord?"

Bedwyr gave a roaring laugh, stopping King Arthur on the stone bridge that connected Caerleon to the old roads and the valleys.

"Only within the view of these golden roofs. When wood and night become my allies, the pups will be of no consequence." Roaring laughter was matched and returned.

Bedwyr alone, as Arthur's greatest of friends, could truly distract the sovereign with pith and wit, or intellectual barbs and humor. Even as they jousted back and forth for a few minutes, Bedwyr opted not to embrace the king for the intentional musk and pungency clouding off his cloak and trousers. "You spared no detail! Even your face is blackened!"

In spite of the happy farewell, Bedwyr detected a melancholy, and was greatly alarmed. Nevertheless, he bid his friend Godspeed and departed unto his own estate, demanding that the king instantly report his return from the Isle of Apples.

The happy farewell also delayed the departure, endangering the plots of Mordred, who was making haste, rehearsed with pretended reason to look in on the queen. He also met Arthur *the beggar thief* on the way.

In the twinkling of an eye, the adulterer feigned heroism.

Quickly at the quiver, bow drawn, and from a high-ground position, the son of Morgaine of the Faeries was poised to lob arrows at the king.

"Thief!" He screeched. "You would purloin the king's own hounds? As you are in the act, I could put two in you presently, sending you to sleep in the pits of the destitute and fatherless!"

Arthur removed his cap, then used the back of his thick glove to smear off the better part of his moustache, dark as pitch and made of coarse animal hair bound with a gummy glue. Standing in direct line of a taut bow, the point of the arrow shrinking to but a dot, rebuke was offered, and no fear.

"That is NOT what our law states, Whelp." That commanding sound, which many reckoned to be how God the Father had sounded when speaking to Moses, was unmistakable, regardless of the tattered, blackened rags that covered the speaker. "By the mouth of two or three witnesses let all things be established. As a resident, or long-term *guest,* in this cantref, we detain and investigate; we do not slay first and inspect after."

"My king. Forgive me. I saw this thief with your very own dogs and I—" Mordred paused. The king had not hushed his words, neither refused to listen; rather, Mordred's own memory paralyzed him, suspending his speech.

The dirty beggar.

The garments.

The gloves.

The mannerisms too stately and measured for a derelict vagabond.

I have seen this man before!

"You wanted to impress your uncle with some brave deed of spoiling a thief in the very act. Overzealous, young man. If you are to rule when lame, retired or dead am I, you must temper passion, demoting it in favor of objective adjudication of the law. Control your feelings. Do you understand?"

The way you did when you put the Sword of Power into the chest of Cymru's Champion? Hypocrite.

"Yes, uncle. I forgot myself and will improve."

"Excellent!" Arthur seemed pleased. Full of grace, he mused, "Now I must go and fix my face."

Mordred gave a sheepish smile. "The bards say you can trick any audience, concealing yourself amongst monk, farmer, or shipman. Or even take on the appearance of a bull or an eagle!"

"This time, the bards exaggerate not!" Arthur chortled, for he reveled in this.

"I doubt it not. Tell me, have you taken up this particular visage before – perhaps in the North?"

The eyes locked.

Sharing Morgaine in common, the eyes were the same.

Mirrored eyes speaking without words, saying in concert. *You were there the last time I wore these rags, the day Amr was slain.*

The silence was awkward. And building.

Arthur made no provision for further spectacle, tragedy or intrigue.

"I must visit King Maelgwn. The voyage will be long and I wish to make my way, privately. I bid you communicate the time of my tardy departure to Cai and to Bedwyr. And please appoint thyself unto Gwenhywfar. She enjoys your company and a visit by you and your new bride would be well received in my stead."

Half true. So wise and yet so ignorant of the doings in your own chamber.

Though the shallow and reactive voice within mocked the High King, a deeper, more contemplative voice anchored his spirit, bringing him down into an abyss of desperate fear. Mordred was a man of no moral constitution, an accomplished adulterer, pretender and sophist. For years he had betrayed the Iron Bear without repentance. Although the campaign to concoct a political career had been successful, so much so that he was known at court as Mordred of the Golden Tongue, the list of men he had defrauded and swindled was as long as Itto Gawr's famed beard. A criminal, a lecher and more, and yet – *Even I could not kill my own children. If this man would do that to those of his own house, what might he do to me?*

The inside voice stopped mocking. And a tremble set in. Mordred hated this man more than any man ever hated; but the hate was now matched with terror.

"Mordred."

The Whelp was lost in thought and too many dark realizations.

"Mordred?"

"With great haste, Lord Arthur."

Arthur terminated the conversation, beginning his solitary journey to the Llyn Peninsula and, if the summer winds behaved, to Ynys Enlli.

Mordred the Traitor was so troubled that he lost all desire to lie with Gwenhwyfar. Instead he turned back and returned to his own place.

***

"I am sure they hated being tossed to and fro. Look at the poor pups."

"Taliesin!" Arthur hailed his new Merlin (although his predecessor had been reckoned as dead for above fifteen years) but embraced him not; both he and his war dogs were green from the tempestuous crossing from Porth Madwy to Ynys Enlli.

"A cider?" offered the Chief Bard.

Arthur pinched his chin, tempted, but his nausea offered a counter-response. "A cup of tea, perhaps."

After recovering himself, and marveling at how many pilgrims successfully made for the island's shore and how many perished during their personal quests, he made straightaway for Lancelot, who was convalescing in Morgaine's castle of glass.

Seeing several maidens attending the wounded knight, too long for the frame of any bed in the whole of the house, convalescing awkwardly as they doted on him, Arthur's eyes found his sister and offered a jest. "Recruiting?"

Morgaine joined her brother in a laugh at the scene. Six damsels and a fifty-year-old man whose fair looks were not only that of one twenty-and-five, but were improving as he aged. "Nurses will be needed even when your bishops and the Church have conquered these lands."

"With care such as this, I am sure your numbers will replenish threefold."

"And though 'tis my chest you ran through, I ever complain that my thigh and earlobes give complaint!"

"Lancelot!" That the complex and unstable man opened with intelligent humor that synced and cinched with the other adults greatly convinced Arthur that he was in his right mind. Sparing no moment, the king dismissed the priestesses and knelt upon a knee, placing his palm upon his friend's forehead, brushing back the curly black hair.

"You can no longer call me by that designate. I am no longer *the greater serving the lesser.* As if I ever was. You defeated me."

"Aye, with unfair advantage of a magical sword. You are the greatest of Round Table Knights; my First Knight, my Champion, my Lancelot."

"Forgive—"

Arthur interrupted. "No. Forgive me, my

friend. What happened in your youth belonged to you."

"We" – Lancelot's eyes made connection with Morgaine – "protect you from certain painful truths because our Land will fall unless you are happy and whole." Lancelot now sat aright upon the small metal framed bed. "But one lie begets another, and soon the webs of deceptions outweigh the original offense."

"Sometimes they do, sometimes they don't," offered the king.

"You did see her first. I should not have yielded to youthful lusts." Tears voiced their anguish, parading down Lancelot's chiseled and perfect jawline.

"And I put my position square in your handsome face, didn't I? Forgive me, if you can." And herein lay the greatness of King Arthur, the most noble king save the Saviour Himself: that, though brokenhearted and freshly awakened to the cold reality that Gwenhwyfar would never be to him what his mother was to his father, he sought out not his own needs but rather to mend his friend, and his friendship.

Apology and tearshed met, embraced and danced.

Then the weightiest of questions loomed, Arthur brave enough to make the query.

"What do we do now?"

Lancelot was well prepared with his answer. Honestly and sensitively, he proceeded.

"I love her, Lord Arthur." All present could feel the room shift with tension. "But I love you too. And I love Cymru." He peered at Morgaine, prayerful that the sentiment would earn him some favor.

It did.

"You have defeated me. It gave me great perspective, great liberty and great release. It is hard to describe, but…" Lancelot now struggled for words. "I love her, and I love you. It is misery and tension and damnable pain to be at court. You have defeated me."

Where is he taking this discourse? thought the Iron Bear.

"Instead of contriving pretexts to be away and shouting my agony at trees and in caves I am going to take my defeat, and retire."

Arthur gasped. As did Morgaine. As did Taliesin.

"It gives me a legitimate cause and removes the drama, gossip and intrigue of it. The life of a monk I shall lead, and into the Holy Writ my oversized head shall go." Lancelot looked lighter, happier and different upon the honest uttering of such things.

"We need you," they all said, nearly in chorus.

"I cannot be at court. My sons you have, and they are as fleet of foot and deadly as I."

"And young," Taliesin barbed.

"We won those wars because of you. I'll not lose you," protested Arthur.

"If the Long Knife returns, or your strait is dire, I will come. Elsewise, I must retire, my friend. Visit me oft at Camlan, or at Illtud's. What have you said in no less than eight of your speeches before the armies?"

"When have you listened to any speech?"

"Shut thy mouth, bard!" Lancelot now took Arthur by the hand. "All things—"

"Change," said Arthur. "All things change."

Not to be convinced otherwise, he asked of another matter.

"Did my battle frenzy cause me to hallucinate?"

Knowing the subject, having no need of exposition: "No, lord. I saw him too. Merlin. Or an imposter, or a ghost. No, I am sure it was he; Merlin lives! And in his breath of life is my foster-mother vindicated."

Too burdened with past hurts, the Pendragon looked only forward, a fount of undiluted grace. "Yes! Whatever troubles befell that famed pair, 'twas the hands of the Masked One that slew our wizard, and no Briton. But he is not slain; he lives!"

"My friend." Lancelot clasped Arthur 'forearm in forearm'. "I believe he does."

Here King Arthur and Lancelot said sorrowful goodbyes and intimate words that no bard knows, and if he knows, shan't utter: only that Arthur bound Lancelot to return to shimmering Caermelyn, should calamity or dire urgency require it.

Having made amends, the two men parted, both in love with one woman – who, at that very moment, paced in circumambulatory rage, smashing vessel and looking-glass, renting cloth and curtain, cursing the creation that Mordred, the one *she loved*, had spurned her.

Morgaine struggled to find a sentence of discourse with her brother, so full of excitement and hope of finding his wizard was he.

As he herded the massive mastiffs into his little barge, wishing it were Madoc and not some other boatman to safely conduct him back to the Llyn Peninsula, she was at last forced to holler. "Brother, there is another matter! Hear me!"

"If problems were meat, my plate would be overly full. State the next dish."

"Our good secret in the stead of the bad."

Arthur leapt from the boat, the dogs and his sister yelping at the splashes.

"Because of the Masked Man's encroach upon our hall, most know the bad secret," he stated.

"Aye, and now the Catholics have uncovered the good. Literally."

Arthur's face became ashen. He hailed the boatman, beseeching him to wait a space of three hours so he could discuss the grave matter with his sister.

***

When Arthur returned home, his new reality began. He did not lie often with Queen Gwenhwyfar II. Periodically he was overcome by wanting her, for he loved her so, and she protested not, though took no pleasure in it. And there was the matter of no heir begotten of the king's seed and Gwen's womb.

Cymreig kings are selected by election often, and it is not given that the son can govern simply because his father did well. However, the line of Tewdrig and Meurig and Arthur was strong, just and long-enduring. The ease of two hundred different scenarios, all wrought with strife and friction, would be all but alleviated were there a son to take the diadem when Arthur returned to the ground, or else entered into a happy retirement.

For this cause, they periodically knew one another. However, his painted queen was two score and ten, and the Tribes grumbled, aided by the needling of the scorned Dynion Hysbys.

The queen was careful not to be cold towards the king, nor overly warm. For he was tuned to her acting. The lukewarm middle made life reasonably pleasant. To stitch the heart that tore here a little, there a little, day after day, Arthur obsessed himself with finding the Merlin. A year had passed since the unpleasant match with the Bloodhound Prince, and with that year no hint of the old druid.

Arthur convened the Round Table Companions and demanded report of each of the twenty-four. No bards were to give song, neither was drink to be served. "Report, and next actions, and accountability," the king demanded, didactically.

The men were exhausted.

"We defeated the Saxon Horde, which sacked Rome, but we cannot locate two old men."

Many heads dropped, embarrassed and disappointed.

"The Masked Devil, not found. The Merlin of Britain, not found."

"Maybe the Merlin found the Masked Devil and resolved, well, half our problem," Bedwyr offered. The expression on his face could have warmed ice and caused a monk under vows of silence to bellow in giddy laughter.

It worked. Arthur laughed. "One of my theories is that Merlin lives, and is about that very enterprise. If there is anyone who knows where the adepts of secret orders hide and lurk, it is he." Arthur's countenance lightened, even casual surmising about his wizard lifting his spirits. "Forgive my curtness, brethren. For warriors, quests don't fill the void of war. Peace is difficult. The summer is hot. Let us rest for a season. Enjoy your wives, your farms, your children."

As he was dismissing the fellowship, the guards of the hall suddenly escorted a vexed visitor, an older boy, injured, who could barely walk. The tattered messenger limped and lumbered but hastened, finally reaching the king's ear. They spoke softly, but the implication was clear and few words were needed. Gwalchmai slowly flapped his arms, crossing them at the chest, then as far back as they would go. Then he rolled his neck side to side. His curved swords were drawn with the grace of a swan and the speed of a stag. "Excalibur or Rhon, lord?"

"Rhon and Carnwenhau. The Sword of Power remains sheathed." Arthur had not used Excalibur, though magically mended and 'as new', since his battle with Lancelot at Llyn Fawr. He bore a burden of guilt at using one of the treasures of the Cymry with malice and jealousy, and believed himself yet unworthy to wield her again so soon.

"What foe hath Hell vomited up upon our peaceful kingdom?" Cai followed Gwalchmai, warming his muscles, swinging his club at the air.

The boy spoke. "A Giant. And a witch."

"Where?"

"In Caermarthen. The destruction of home and chapel is as 'tis the world ending. Many innocent lives lost. Including babes!"

Caermarthen. The very birthplace of Merlin himself. The irony lost on none, many volunteered.

Arthur embraced the shaken lad, clearly a resident suffering personal affliction from the assault. Steadying his men: "Giant hunting is not well conducted by large numbers, but rather by a small and trained troop." The king's blue eyes gleamed. "Home to your wives, friends. Cai, Gwalchmai and I shall go."

"And I," the knight insisted. Bedwyr with one hand was superior to most with two.

***

Caermarthen was rent in pieces; a shamble, a dung pit. In the center of the village, every shop had suffered damage such that none could conduct commerce, sell silks, eggs or other goods. Even the large, glorious oak tree that honored the city's favorite son had been snapped, charred and nearly ruined. *But the base of Merlin's oak remained, and the tree would be replenished.*

It was not difficult to approximate the dwelling that the assailants had taken. Their trail, one of slime and sludge, bones and bile, painted a trail that ran to a cluster of caves not far from Caermarthen. The caves dotted the shoreline of the West Country of Cymru and had been a site of splendor, a retreat for lovers, an ancient place of worship, a spot of beauty; no more.

Henceforth the bards would call the largest of the cluster Ogof Pentywyn: the *Bone Cave.*

The cave was of the sort that had no solid floor, for the waters of the sea sought their level, creating a shallow *lake within a cave*. The rock formations jutting up from the watery bottom were as large as men and imperfectly shaped, looking as an army turned to stone mid-battle, frozen in time. The Tribes took great care to ensure that the cave was illuminated and safe. In this regard, several iron torch sheaths were fastened to the walls, ropes were available to help those who slipped in the murky waters, and markings were etched into the walls, providing directions to those who might lose their way in the winding hollow.

When Arthur and his fellows reached the mouth of the cavern, dusk was upon them, but many torches rendered the place an illuminated splendor.

"They have fighting men in their company," Bedwyr remarked.

"Nay, look." Arthur pointed out that the tall humanoid shadows were indeed but rocks.

The warriors proceeded through the water, holding satchel and sword high, Arthur's famous spear picking up shards of light as he marched.

In the waters floated massive folios of Scripture, much longer and wider than even the most ornate works created by the monks. These were either a special piece of art purloined from the town chapel and desecrated, or they had been brought with the Giant and dropped or cast away in haste. The sheer size of what remained of some great tome suggested to Arthur the latter. Additionally, several more torn pages were stuck against the inner walling of the cavern. The scene reminded Arthur of what a strong-willed child does in their youth when scolded, damaging their own books and bedroom things in protest.

A tantrum occurred here. He was sure of it.

The cave narrowed, becoming, for a time, more like a tunnel broad only the shoulder-width of an average man. Arthur led the men, and as the tunnel opened he was first to see the witch.

Likewise, she saw him.

The torch light manifested the whole of her. Hideous, green. Rotted teeth and rainbow-shaped nose. A dark blue corpse beneath a hooded grey cape that was more holes than whole. She was the subject of every small child's nightmares.

And she was twice as wide as Arthur and taller than Maelgwn.

Crying in a variant of the Pictish tongue, the hag levitated above the waters and darted at Arthur. As she was too broad to breech the tunnel, the seasoned fighter simply retreated five paces, pushing his men back with him.

Crouched low, Arthur slowly turned round and spoke to Gwalchmai, who was by chance nearest him in the line of knights momentarily trapped as rats in a narrow maze. Cai filed directly behind the Hawk of May.

"Are you aware of the verse in Scripture?" he began.

"Suffer not a witch to live," quick-witted Gwalchmai whispered back.

"That verse was not written about heathens who have different beliefs to those who follow Christ."

"No?"

"No; it was written about monsters like *that,* flying around the countryside, killing the livestock and passing the children through fire. All witches are not witches. This witch is a witch and no man."

Gwalchmai comprehended. "Or woman, I think."

The men broke out in laughter at the hideousness of the devil that sought to make of them dinner (or worse) just several yards away.

"We are undefeated. We will not have our end here in some watery underground grave under the fangs of a supernatural, oversized crone! Avenge the city!" Bedwyr emboldened the troop.

"She attacks in a straight line, easy to counter. I will slay the witch. It is critical that you look not upon me. Rather, emerge from this passage and fan out, finding ground, at the ready for her companion. We know nothing of the Giant save the destruction he wrought."

Arthur drew his enchanted dagger, Carnwenhau, and emerged a second time from the mouth of the passage. Predictably, the witch was yet shrieking her Pictish imprecatory chants. Even the bravest mortal would knock at the knees seeing her. Hideous, strong as a bear and fast as a hound.

But she faced the Silure War King and no mortal. King Arthur, the Bear of Glamorgan. Every thought was about preservation of his people and their season of liberty. He would live because he must live *for them.* This made him uniquely accountable and fearless.

Her speed was impressive. But he was much faster. Instead of fleeing from her attack, he used the forward and diagonal dance now, by reason of three decades of training and practice, more natural to him than drinking water or lacing his boots.

Sliding just to the right of her line of attack, Arthur countered aerial assault, stepping well inside her looping slashes with taloned hands, and caught her under her left breast, the blade plunging through her heart, clinking and redirecting as it finally notched into her backbone. Rapidly withdrawing Carnwenhau brought a fount of black, bile-like blood. Somehow, instead of falling to prostrate to the ground, she slowly descended and stood, a waterfall of blood.

"I will save the interrogation for thy partner, thou killer of babes!" Arthur made a lateral slash from his left to right, such that the follow-through of his blade hand finished wide of, and well behind, his own back.

The one monster was now in two parts, for he had cleaved the witch in twain.

The Iron Bear had not long to admire his work as Gwalchmai crashed hard upon him, knocking both warriors into the muck. Cai tumbled and crumpled a few paces away, suffering a blow to his head. The injury was not serious. Arthur's steward shook it off and stood aright, cursing at the air, preparing for another go.

Scooping sludge from his brow, the king stood

and clutched Gwalchmai's hand. "Up we go. Looks like you found the Giant?" He laughed.

"That we did!" came Bedwyr's yell. "Help!"

The monster looked as a man, similar to Ogyrfan Fawr. He had a massive pot-belly and disproportionately long, slender arms that, when drooping, reached well past his feet. The appendages were all bone and muscle attached to curled, lifeless hands. They swiveled constantly at the shoulder, which were out of joint, deformed permanently from birth; designed to crush and destroy. He had no need of club or axe, for his were weapons of flesh.

The arms smashed down cyclically, looking as a waterwheel, but with the rapidity of a wasp's wings. And because of the deformity, the Giant was ever in great pain, causing him to make horrible noises.

There was limited space to fight in the cavern, and it was difficult for the knights to find range and avoid the unorthodox opponent. Thus, they were absorbing damage. Even blocking the thrashes was battering the famed mighty men. They fought well but were losing by reason of attrition, of exhaustion. Arthur could find no opening to join the fight and was constrained, having the tunnel behind and a wall of three of his fighting men before him. By fortune, he had brought his spear, giving him advantage in the circumstance. Finally, with a frustrated holler, he commanded, "Gwalchmai, move one pace to the left!"

Rhongomyniad whistled in flight; even with the absence of air in the enclosure, the Pendragon's aim was true.

"You could've done that half an hour ago," Cai protested.

"The three of you needed the work."

The Round Table Knights appreciated the moment. Four men who had executed complex battle strategies against the Saxon hordes. Flanks and ditches, volleys and lines. Yet here they were, soaked in the stench of a seaside inlet cave, fighting monsters that reasonable people would doubt existed. *Yet better the occasional monster than a generation of invasion, terror and war.* Bedwyr jested about their sorry state, but as the men celebrated, they sensed movement.

The Giant rose, the enchanted spear lodged in his chest, disabling his right arm completely. With his left he extracted the spear, guiding it along the path of *most pain,* so that the tip came back out whence it had entered. His scream released clouds of dust, dislodged from their resting places along walls and crevices in the cavern, uninterrupted for thousands of years.

The beast wailed, then flung soggy torn pages of Scripture at the men with his working arm. Finding an artery deeper yet in the hollow, he retreated.

"Yield." Arthur directed his three to abort the chase. "I will finish this."

Cai was unable to lift his weapon. Bedwyr and Gwalchmai, bruised, beaten and cold, offered no protest. Relieved, they responded, "We will have your favorite cider waiting. This one is thine, lord."

Arthur gave chase. Alone.

The inquiry and investigation began during the pursuit. He paced quickly but there was no cause to run, for the thing's blood upon the cavern wall and pooled in black blobby botches on the watery flooring of the cave guided the way. With torch in left hand and magical dagger in right,

Arthur's only complaint was the water, causing him some chill and surely ruining his boots.

"Sir," he called, recalling how respect was the most powerful agent when dealing with these sorry fellows, *all* of whom were under the dark enchantment; miserable creatures acting not of their own accord. "Sir, why are you destroying the Book of the Law? Talk to me about why you might ruin such a large, ornate and lovely work of art."

Arthur mentioned nothing of the murder and wanton destruction levied by the Giant upon Caermarthen. Neither was there judgment in his voice, only curiosity and discovery.

Additionally, Arthur added personalization. Itto and the myriad other slain otherworldly creatures had responded best when their humanity was acknowledged. The Iron Bear deployed the same tactic here.

"Sir. What are you called?"

The tactic worked.

From a hundred paces and down within the leftmost of three arteries in the hollow came the response. A voice so soft that it in no wise matched the form of its owner.

"Cynwyl," he said. "I am called Cynwyl. Are you that king? Or do I wait for another?" The sounds and echoes caused by the voice were static. The thing had stopped moving. "He said you would come."

"Aye. I am a king. Glamorgan and Gwent are my people."

"Unnecessary humility," grumped the Giant. "You are King Arthur, the High King of the Britons and Emperor of the Isles in the Sea."

"I am."

During the salutation, Arthur had closed

ground and now stood before Cynwyl, within range of his monstrous strokes, yet unafraid.

"Reason with me, Cynwyl Gawr. What shall we make of all this?"

Defeated and repentant, the Giant found a stone standing out of the water and sat, the full weight of his gargantuan head falling upon his curled, deformed hand, arm bent at elbow, supporting the chin.

These beings respected the office of the real kings of the Sons of Adam. Kings that were kings indeed and not pretenders chosen by the cunning and policies of corrupt Man. Above all sovereigns they loved Arthur, though they were bewitched to harass and bring havoc to his lands. Though he slayed them, they adored him still. An awe came over them in his presence, and he had authority over them. *The Giant Hunter.*

Never much above a whisper, Cynwyl began to plainly state what had befallen him. And what had befallen Caermarthen.

The Giant inhabited this very cave, or when the Tribes were performing their ancient rates, that cave or another. Ever in the hollow hills of Cymru. Slumbering for decades at a time, he would wake to hunt stag or hare, read his Bible, then return to the groggy hibernation of the monsters reserved to be awakened at the End of Days.

To eat. To read. To sleep. And never in his unnaturally long days had he harmed mankind.

Then a Wildman of the Wood, a Northern Cymry shaman, presented himself in his cave. Cynwyl recalled that, as he had been roused, that the Wildman had protested that he was beguiled, that a conflict had ensued, that the yelling was much, and the scene confusing.

"A masked priest misused the magic of the shaman."

"For he has no power in and of himself."

"You know of this evil man?" Cynwyl asked.

"He is the thorn in my flesh – for decades ere I knew he existed. He the gold that financed the Saxon Wars and the divisive hate that feeds the Religious Wars. A shadow, a secret, a whisper. He is trapped on these Isles and clearly has found someone to serve as his agency to strike calamity within the bars of his own cage."

The Giant was engrossed in learning more of the wickedness of men. Then the tale demanded that he confess his own dark deeds. The spell had caused him to dash and slash at his Book, and then sprint into the city as a feral beast of the field, killing and destroying at random.

"The city was yours to sack. What caused you to stop?"

"A Christian druid." He fumbled at his words, the seeming oxymoron lost on neither monster nor king.

"Like Taliesin, my bard?" queried the king.

"Bring the torch closer." The deformed vine of an arm lifted high, beckoning forth the Iron Bear. "Closer."

Having no fear, but dagger ready to thrust as it must, Arthur obliged.

The light of the torch revealed the face, a large pear shape with but four or five strands of silver hair. When he had had all of his teeth there would have been two rungs; but now only pits and three yellow kernels remained. One eye wandered, as if it were a rivet with no attachment to its socket. The other eye could see but was encumbered by a heavy, drooping lid that covered all but the smallest crescent.

"No, Emperor Arthur son of Meurig. Not like your bard Taliesin of Glamorgan. Rather like his predecessor, born here."

"Merlin!" All spittle left the king's mouth, and a great lump manifested in his throat.

"He gave chase and I fled back to this cave. He saw my Book in tatters and asked about it, as you did." Cynwyl Gawr snatched up a page and arrested the conversation, straining to read, studying and contemplating.

Though the king could not bear it, feeling years of loss and hopelessness about to break, giving way to a new dawn with his old wizard, he knew that the Giant could not be rushed. At last he let the page fall as a feather upon the water. He watched it sink.

Cynwyl went on to explain that he studied Scripture for six hours each day that slumber did not possess him. And that he did so in hopes he would find the truth of what he was and, peradventure, eternal life. Concluding that he was damned, an abomination, and well outside the scope of God's creation, he hoped only to never harm a soul that the Lord would show mercy, sentencing him to some other torment besides the Lake of Fire. A woeful, sorrowful existence.

But Merlin had given him hope. He had explained that life was in the blood and the blood was passed down from the father. Through much mating, the probability of a chain of male Nephilim begetting sons only, and never a daughter to lie with a man (whose soul was redeemable), was low. Being neither a first, nor a second, but perhaps up to the eleventh generation, Cynwyl was young for his ancient race.

"Merlin shared with me grace. He said that I was a godly man, but that being godly wasn't enough. Rather that I must trust Christ alone. Whether I be salvageable or a woeful child of the damned, only God knows. And if a man, or the better part a man, then forgiven. Moreover, Merlin said that he was…" Another long pause.

"Please." Arthur could no longer contain himself. "Please tell me what else my Merlin said."

"He said that he was like me. Whether god or man, saint or monster. He shared that he and I were the same."

"And the witch? Whence came she?"

"Pict." He answered straightway. "The shaman and the masked priest brought her with them from Caledonia."

"And where did Merlin go?" Now Arthur was the one moving closer. And closer. "Is my Merlin yet in these caves?"

"No. But he said you would come. And he said he would rid Cymru of Simon Magus, the—"

"The Masked Priest!" Arthur pumped his fist excitedly. His Round Table Companions had spoken true; Merlin had joined them in the hunt.

"Then as suddenly as he appeared at the great oak in the center of the town, he vanished. I know not if he was here in the flesh, or a ghost or apparition."

"You are a godly man, Cynwyl Gawr. I too am most persuaded and amazed at this message of grace that Taliesin gave to the Merlin. I hope there is salvation for you, sir." Arthur's dagger opened the man's throat so wide that the base of the tongue was exposed. Arthur snatched at the tongue and tore the whole of Cynwyl's throat out. His wandering eye blossomed as a flower, then turned hoary; a violent but instant death. "Find your salvation or damnation in Heaven, else in the Underworld. You killed my kinsman, and must needs be removed from this land."

***

"How are you, men?" Arthur emerged from the cave, a minor cough developing on account of the damp and the cold.

"Is it possible that you inquire this of us when covered are you in tarry, sludge and slime? You look awful, lord!" Bedwyr gave a mighty laugh. "You sliced a witch in twain and slew a man that whipped, literally, the three of us" - even after decades of witnessing the valor and wonder of the sandy haired boy-king, the men were awestricken by their friend - "and you ask how *we* are?"

The troop found their triumphant king an oaky scrumpy while the remainder of them drank strong ale. Then they began to mourn that such death and loss could occur in the Summer Kingdom; the journey back to Caerleon was quiet, having much contemplation and little banter.

CHAPTER 20
The Madness of Maelgwn

When Arthur departed from Maelgwn, a *soft reconciliation* had been wrought between two men who loved the same woman. Some light of truth now allowed the proud warriors to at least *make the best of things*. Both men were of sufficient intelligence to know that more secrets and lies lurked. However, both men were of sufficient wisdom to not overly seek details of the same. Arthur believed to the depth of his sinew, the fiber and core, that his champion had not betrayed him *during* the fifteen years of marriage, and that left a thread of hope that they could live peaceably – finding some enjoyment themselves in the age of peace they had given to multitudes of others. Arthur further hoped that the single thread might, in time, lengthen, loop, double back and twist again and again, by the healing salve that is Time, to once again become the cord of strength and reliance that, though frayed, could never be severed. *That was the faith of Arthur.*

Moments before boarding his barge, Gwyar had made Arthur to know of the most recent insult of the Roman Church: this time desecrating the sarcophagus of Mary herself. Setting to revising and rewriting her history, laboring slowly to venerate her as a goddess and appropriate her atop all other goddesses the world over, using cultural and spiritual assimilation and annihilation in the stead of overt genocide.

Because of his radical commitment to liberty for all sects, and his refusal to allow the State to compel any man to follow one or the other, the Silure king was respected by most clergy, hated by a few, but popular with none. But now agnostic policy was impossible, for the transgression of the Roman Church was too great. Their deed had caused direct outrage, followed by official condemnation from the king. Arthur had openly fallen out with the Church. He had spent the greater part of a year handling that schism, upon his renewed quest to find his counselor, be he ghost or vision or flesh, and upon the new reality of his *situation at home.* Because of these three preoccupations, Arthur assumed that Maelgwn did well, that Gwyar and her new priestesses had brought him back to full health, and that he was at the plow in Gwynedd, or at contemplative study amongst the monks and students at Saint Illtud's.

But Maelgwn did not mend as expected.

Following the friendly words, Maelgwn fell unconscious for several hours, and when awake 'twas a *sleeping feverish awakening,* followed by more sleep. It was difficult for Gwyar to discern if the overly tall warrior spilling like four great weeds over her longest bed was succumbing to the enchantment within Excalibur's blade, which had surely breeched the sternum and perhaps nicked the heart, or to illness, or to despair, pride and shame; or to the sum of all of these things.

Taliesin and Gwyar studied and pondered upon what course of care might recover the renowned knight. Finally the Chief Bard declared,

"When the present is confused and disjointed, let it look to the past, not for judgment, but rather for answers." As something in times past had befallen Maelgwn, by happenstance on the very isle where he lay in the dire, Taliesin and Gwyar sought to understand *that event* that it might guide resolution to *this event.*

But in order to transcend gossip, rumor and tale, to gain the fullness of *that event* required direct witness from one who had been there. Maelgwn's foster-mother.

Prior to her appearance in the streamy marsh that fed Llyn Fawr, none had seen the Lady of the Lake for years.

Taliesin, a Christian, could not endorse the means of making contact, but as Gwyar sat about to summon that witch of olden that was inside of her, *and was her,* he remarked, "We are not under the Law, but under Grace. We can do nothing against the truth but for the truth."

She enjoyed these words. Then she helped his conscience by closing the door upon the slight sage, that she might do her deeds beyond his view.

Though it exhausted her tiny body, ironically rendering her nearly as ill as the one she was seeking to save, the most powerful of all Britons met with success. Using the Sight, violating and perverting nature and its laws, she made contact with the Lady of the Lake.

She awoke, seemingly a day or more removed from the encounter, in a bed that had been prepared next to Maelgwn. As her groggy eyes were unhinged and the painful sunlight greeted her eyes, Taliesin's wit greeted her ears.

"This chamber is now more as the convalescence tent of wounded field warriors than the mystical abode of the Queen of Avalon!"

"This is why you banish him from court, isn't it?"

Maelgwn mustered a smile. "Aye. I fear not even this deathbed will free me from the dwarfish thorn. Could it be? Did you see our foster-mother?"

"Through the still waters that were as a looking-glass, yes. We spoke, then I fainted and remember not since."

Taliesin had beckoned one of the nine maidens to bring her a special tea, and gave her space to gather her wits. As she rallied, she waited for Maelgwn to drift back into sickly sleep, then she made known the Lady's words to the bard.

She shared how Vivien had retired to one of Cymru's myriad daughter islands that speckled the coast, and that a small but ancient castle – all but ruined by shifting shorelines and the merciless erosion caused by sand – was her abode. There, she and others guarded the Grail, desperate to keep it from Simon Magus at all costs. Because the Grail Guardians disagreed with Taliesin's theology, they viewed Rhufawn the Fair, whose obsessive love for the relic had become well known o'er the whole of the Isles and the Continent, as a desirous candidate to possess and guard it.

Vivien had gone on to say that she was aging and could not protect the Cup forever. Vivien had a mortal father, Budic I, who had been beguiled and seduced by a Korrigan. As her father was mortal, Vivien would one day sleep the sleep of death. And because her father was mortal, she had hope of resurrection. She yet learned little of the Christian God and cleaved to her goddess (who also had an origin), but hoped that her protection of the Cup that the Nazarene would sip when He returned to dine with His Twelve in the Jew's kingdom would be enough to earn her salvation.

Her concern was the Pendragon and *his twelve,* and the untoward designs on the Summer Kingdoms by dangerous foes without – and within. She made Gwyar to understand what had befallen the young Maelgwn, before the bards called him Lancelot. But first she bade Gwyar remember, above all things, to warn Arthur that Howell the Great, her kinsman and his ally, would soon need the Iron Bear to bring an army to Little Britain. For a confederacy was rising, knit of men with different tongues; a monster with many small horns under the leadership of two great horns: Childebert the Merovingian and the upstart Mark, the son of the late Meirchion the Mad. The confederacy was succored by Roman gold and strengthened with Teutonic muscle.

Gwyar recalled gasping at the news and had vowed to make her brother to know.

As for Maelgwn…

When just a boy, overtaken by the lusts of youth, he had forced himself upon his uncle's wife, and known her. The deed was discovered and, in the conflict that ensued, the uncle was slain. Some suggested murder; others maintained that the offender had committed manslaughter, defending himself.

Only an intimate circle of the influential and the powerful knew of the matter. They caused the deed to disappear, along with the innocent woman involved, violating the moral code of every Briton – that kings, queens and princes and bishops live under the very laws they required of the people. Corruption for one was corruption for all. The decision haunted otherwise principled and moral men and women. Vivien and Dyfrig and even the High King Meurig, a man devoted to justice, made exception for the boy.

This was by reason of his abilities with fist, bow, spear and sword. Not since Achilles could one dominate the field as could Maelgwn. By the age of fifteen it was evident to all that he was a legend, a god in his own time. And by reason of the loyal group of boys, *his Hosts,* as they came to be called, who surrounded him and were very near his skill. By reason of the Saxon menace. By reason of compromise and the failings of all men, the circle allied to wash away the crime.

Maelgwn was sent to train on the Continent with Vivien herself, and the two perfected her martial art. When not there, he would be tempered and controlled by the rod of the Christian Religion at Saint Illtud's. When residing in neither place, Ynys Enlli.

There he met the Merlin, who was not involved in the plot, and there he was, from time to time, left to wander and explore in the sanctuary of the enchanted isle.

Peradventure one day, suffering from an intense, abnormal thirst after training, he was drawn to, and possessing no regard for sacred restrictions, profaned the Sacred Grove. There he lay with a Cymry damsel under the green canopy of its tops, loving her in its cool blue shade. As they embraced afterward, she stood with a jolt, and at once transformed before the young knight. Drums beat and horns bugled. Stringed instruments strummed. And the well-known mist filled the whole of the orchard.

The damsel now revealed herself as a radiant Fae, adorned in white apparel. Not a thumb's space upon her bosom, ribcage or arms were not filled with the ornate markings and the concentric knotwork of the Tylwyth Teg. A white owl rested upon her shoulder.

She beheld a wooden saucer filled with strong drink from a forbidden tree, sprung forth from the apple that Brutus had sought. Select druids and priestesses used some of the fruit, carefully crafting multivarietal ciders for healing and enjoyment by the Cymry. Only ever in small measures; always mixed, never whole.

Men were forbidden to enter the grove unless they be under the guidance and authority of the druids, and it was evidently by bewitchment that the boy Maelgwn had been led there in the first place. The whole of the orchard smelled of the musk of seduction, sang of lust, tasted of allure, looked as an altar of warmest pleasure.

The fermented product of the seven-seeded apple changed Maelgwn. *It radically intensified all that he already was. Plus more.*

He left the orchard with the remnants of an old war, which survived in the flesh of the fruit, now part of his blood.

The Dragon.

The Giant.

The Korrigan water spirit.

And Man.

The attributes, memories, perpetually-conflicted disposition, incompatibility, anger towards the creation itself, misery, power, strange beauty and all the good and bad of the Otherworld entered him.

Yet he remained but a man. A man poisoned by the residue of a lost and dark time.

Pleased with her work, the Fae brushed away the dark and curly locks, and kissed the tall prince upon his forehead. And vanished.

The faerie had gifted Maelgwn a curious silver cruciform featuring symbolism that represented each of the four elements that had joined to become the seven seeds. It just *was* about his neck, a simple leather strap and a pendant. None had seen the likes of the cruciform and, when spotted at sup or sport, it engendered endless assumptions by experts who caused Maelgwn to laugh, knowing nothing.

But Vivien, his mother, knew the meaning of the cross and its symbols.

"A cursed apple from a forbidden tree given him by a shining angel caused him to be this way?" Taliesin challenged.

"Sounds incredible."

"Agreed!"

"Of course, I just spoke to a woman older than my mother whose appearance is younger than mine by means of a pool of water, and sometimes I possess the strength of five armies and can crack marble with my mind. Let's not start doubting the nature of these peculiar times now, bard."

They laughed hard at the observation.

"Does this mean he is not responsible for the ill and evil he has done?"

"We are all responsible for the ill and evil we do," Gwyar responded.

She continued Vivien's account.

"The Lady of Lake went on to say that the cruciform is ever with Maelgwn, and not even Arthur knows the meaning of it. The apple was indeed his curse, but now he is inseparable from it, and in this regard, it may save and sustain him."

"Poison given to the poisoned." Taliesin nodded, understanding. "'Tis true in nature."

"'Tis true in love."

They laughed again. The kind of chuckle that precedes peril.

"That apple has faded into legend. What if it was simply conjured by the faeries for the purpose of the ruse?" Taliesin, a man flowing with *the Awen*, or divine inspiration, given him when he achieved knowing the mysteries of God, knew not of the veracity of the legend, for this secret was hidden from even the adepts.

"You know what words Jesus gave Paul when he ascended to the third heaven but know not where reside the seven-seeded apple trees upon the island of bards?" The sorceress playfully goaded her Christian ally.

"We all have our specialties, my lady. Is it real? Does it yet exist?"

"It is. It does." She spoke plainly. "And all who drink of it drink unto themselves death." She and the Chief Bard stood, looking down upon the sickly warrior.

Taliesin took her hand in his palms. "My dear Morgaine. Worry not. When the last stone of golden Caermelyn hath toppled and the mighty men of this epoch sleep in the ground, I believe that YOU and HE shall outlive us all. I believe this will be YOUR story to tell."

"Then I must make haste to save him," she responded.

Bishop Cadfan and his pilgrims had not breeched Gwyar's grove. It was surrounded by a great vault of green semi-transparent glass, which protected the trees and other scarce plants from the harsh, salty winds of Ynys Enlli. The original Brutus Trees, as the druids came to call them, were gone. But, through the expertise and art of grafting, they had been reborn and three of them flourished amongst Gwyar's trees, which boasted nine other Cymreig varieties besides. The seven-seeded apples were shaken, not picked, and allowed to turn in the enchanted soils prior to being pressed and fermented in woodchips within great icy steel cauldrons, which were sealed for the life-cycle of the fermentation. Once the cider, or when left in the cauldron longer, a spirit, was ready, a few drops were added to other ciders during the final stages of their cycle. It was never blended early in the process and never processed and served on its own.

But Gwyar collected a small quantity that was set aside for blending. She protected it in a drinking bladder that was very small, capped and ready to serve unto Maelgwn. The total sum was a spoonful or two, as elixir given to a sickly babe.

The cider, an accelerant, made straightway for Maelgwn's bloodstream. His blood remembered the sup and the special interaction it had shared. And the dark-painted faerie who had made use of it for the poisoning. All these quickened the Bloodhound Prince, and he woke with a feverish shout of "Gwenhywfar!"

***

Maelgwn lived, resurrected from the netherland between the living and the dead. He lived, but his love of Gwenhwyfar II now burned afresh, his mind seeing her markings all day, his thoughts ever upon her visage, never quite to grasp that the markings upon her were the same as those upon the elvish creature transformed from damsel so long ago.

The Champion of the Britons, the peculiar 'sometimes King of Gwynedd', divested himself once more of his Hosts, who wept sorely, and his bards, who sang at him from coast to coast, and retired into extreme monasticism, spending the greater part of his days in a small chapel in Abergwaun, located in the west country of Deheubarth, which the bards would later call Pembroke. They had all witnessed him waive his rule over petty politics, land strife or when quest and desire outweighed the administration of tax and cattle. But all perceived the difference in this abeyance. Lancelot's heart had been pierced long before Excalibur pricked it.

Ironically, Gwalchmai governed the very lands of Maelgwn's abode in the role of a type of consultative governor. He did not infringe upon the local chiefs and tribal leaders, but was given an office to support them as training and practice should he one day ascend to the throne of Pendragon. After the Trial of Arms, Gwalchmai's reputation was severely damaged and the office had devalued to that of an empty title; a figurehead with no power or authority. In Cymru, the people loaned power to the rulers and, ultimately, the rulers were subject to the law. This was the heart of the light of liberty cast upon a dark world by an ancient people who refused to live under the boot of the very few reigning over the very many. When a leader fell out of favor amongst the Tribes, there was an unspoken shunning and shift of mood in the wind that typically preceded a visit by the druids or bishops, who gathered the will and directives of the people. Gwalchmai had not been deposed or asked to leave Deheubarth, but that they had lost confidence in him was a thick and ever-present reality.

Still, he did what he could to serve farmers, to assist with building villages, to train guards, to try and practice being a good leader as Arthur would have him do.

From time to time Gwalchmai would bring food to Maelgwn, who betimes did not regard his own nutrition. The two did not like one another. Possibly they never had. But they were brothers under the codes and precepts of the Round Table, had killed Saxons together, doing things unmentionable to preserve the nation. They both knew what prolonged war did to men and they both extended a kind of cold grace, speaking of nothing save sport and weather.

Thus two of Arthur's best suffered great loss at *the games.* While Caerleon and Caermelyn were trumpets and gold and commerce and great loudness of children at play and choirs at song, the West Country was sleepy, and rainy, and grit and brood and hard labor. And also lovely and quiet. In this regard, it suited both the Hawk of May, now less bright, and the old Lancelot of Cymru and Brittany, now in service to none save his own obsessions.

Taliesin demanded that Maelgwn make himself presentable and receive his son, Rhufawn. The troubled knight loved his son deeply, so much so that each visit would cause a temporary rest from the torments of thinking on Gwenhwyfar, or upon *Arthur and Gwenhwyfar.* When the lad would return, so would the thoughts and, with them, the torments. Such was his low state that Taliesin began to wonder whether he and Gwyar had been more cruel than kind in saving him, for the poison had surely magnified his pain.

Then Rhufawn stopped visiting.

A quest for the Cup of Christ, with two other brave young and worthy knights, came the tidings. *Rhufawn has discovered the Grail Castle; trials to follow.*

Months became a year and a year became three. And reports grew scarce.

Disdaining Taliesin's chides, Maelgwn refused to see him. Isolated in self-imposed exile but never truly alone.

For there were many Maelgwns in Maelgwn.

In the forest he would oft encounter his other selves and make combat with them, but they would always disappear the instant his blow was about to find flesh. Moreover, his other selves would audibly whisper or hiss, accusing and condemning him. This time in his own voice, that time in the voice of hag, or else that of a he-goat or some devil.

Just beyond a plot of graves that garnished the pitch outside his chapel was a great yew tree. Its sap was constant and the consistency and color of blood. Working the edges and curves of his cruciform pendant, the fallen knight gave the whole of his weight to the tree, embracing its sticky crimson issue. His black curls matted with sweat, pasted against the chiseled cheek, the broken god-man Lancelot fell upon both knees and lamented; the base of the tree and his splinters were the only audience to hear him.

I cannot kill myself, for I cannot be defeated in battle, save by the Silure.

She is my sun and my moon. The rotation of the heavens as my heart towards her. Always twirling, ever in their circuits, never to rest upon her bosom.

She regards my best friend and I regard her. She is my first love, though she were made to be his last.

Let me go down into the Deep. Disjoint my shoulders and make my knees to shake out of their places for the weight of this loss causeth me not to stand.

Violence and tremors, malice and envy and all

good gone in the rage of my jealousy. And towards him it waxes.

Yet towards him it waxes not. Men will do what men will do. For we are beasts all. It kindles rather towards her. Gwenhwyfar, how I loathe thee.

Your eyes do disrobe yourself and your lips invite us to the snare. Your hair is woven of deceit and at the small of thy back are bars to the hot gates of Hades whence none return.

Where is the Christ? Does He not promise to set the captives free? Where is Rhiannon; does she not protect those who serve the sovereignty of the Cymry?

Merlin, I have done what you bade and cannot die, though I die daily. Is the kingdom worth the eternal punishment of one man? Would that the Saxons reign, that she make her bed with mine!

Can I not squash Arthur as the crawling thing, cannot my Hosts devour the Silures? Their blue war paint frightens not the Ravens of the North.

Victory! But what victory to be won when she hath chosen him?

Him! Arthur the Emperor. Arthur the Temperate. Arthur the Wise. Arthur the Son of Prophecy and Messiah of his people. A man who knows not want, for he is given all by right in the stead of merit. A man who knows not to covet, for all is already his. Arthur the Just! They would make him as the Saviour Himself. But neither hath saved me!

I am more comely than thee, King Arthur. Of more brawn and girth, I give more pleasure for the gazing, and the swooning. Every damsel save YOURS freely giveth her life for me. And to me. You are a stalky, average fellow. You are not my equal!

But you are my greater, and I am the lesser. Beauty fades as the grass and muscle weakens year by year, but your character and command, your honesty and grace, endures forever.

You are my king; let you have what woman you will and if your choice, though the beautiful Cymry women are as the sands of the sea, be the only one I want, then it is well. I shall love you both from this pit, and all my days I shall battle the bubble that makes me a monster and the untenable love that makes me mad.

Where goes my son? Why is he not near that I might love him? He is my rock and my salvation. The flame of Arthur shall never perish, as it passes on to the son of Maelgwn. Protect my son, o Christ, and let one strand of hair be distressed under the wing of thy shadow, o Rhiannon. Let him have no regard for women, that love ruins him not, and pray ye gods and the God of Gods, that the best of me and the best of the Silure Lord combine in him, defiled not by triangles of affection and unrequited love. For we have been great; but save ye him and this and he will be threefold better.

The coasts, as they do in the West Country, brought an instant and unrelenting rain. The giant yew offered some shelter to the prostrate knight, but the storm was too great. The rush of waters cleansed him of the sap, but rendered him looking as a black salamander struggling in a soup made of blood.

CHAPTER 21
Magus Finds His Mark

In the final years of the Summer Kingdom, King Arthur was - *King Arthur.*

A cold peace at home that fell disgracefully short of his aspirations of being like his parents (who were yet as vibrant, giddy and yet stately as ever).

Open disputes and unsolvable complexities of politics with the Roman Church.

In accord with Vivien's warning by the mouth of Gwyar issued, a new threat burgeoned on the Continent, issued from the loins of a defeated and long-dead foe.

Magus not found.

Merlin, though hope was high and rumors many, remained unconfirmed as truly amongst the living.

The Dynion Hysbys brooding.

The druids worrying.

The bishops *bishopping.*

But there was no war. No Saxon menace. No invaders ruining innocence and frightening the soul of the nation. No Civil War. The Kingdoms, Royal Clans, Tribes, Cantrefs and hundreds still functioned as local principalities with Arthur as their High King and the twenty-and-four as their High Council. Cymru had long endured, approaching half a generation of prosperity and unparalleled tranquility for the common citizen.

Since the day he had cleaved the witch in twain and slain the Bible-toting menace in the dank bowels of the inlet cove of Caermarthen, a slight cough had entered Arthur's lungs, and remained. A minor and irregular complaint, it projected no indication of weakness or impotence, as the harvests were yet strong year over year.

Yet there was no direct heir. But one of Arthur's younger brothers, Frioc, dabbled in politics or in military matters, and the remainder of his kin were either devoted to the monk's robe, or else some other enterprise. His sisters had been married, quite contrary to the norms and customs of the Cymry, to Northern princes for strategic purposes decades ago, and their stock produced fine nephews such as Gwalchmai and Gareth, who could bear the mantle but *were no Arthurs.*

Rhufawn, as the bastard son of a daughter of Gwent, could be promoted to Pendragon, or at minimum declared Wledig or 'Battle Commander' by the Tribes.

Then there was Mordred.

The Whelp.

Only fourteen years younger than the king, he had crystalized his reputation as a man of flattering tongue and sneaky blade. He would compliment a farmer with feigned words with the crowing of the cock and plunder the same man through corruption or legal manipulation by the setting of the sun the selfsame day. He knew Arthur had slain Amr, and Mordred knew that Arthur knew.

The son of Gwyar had left court the very day of the uncomfortable exchange at the bridge upon the Usk River, returning to his father's lands. His fear of the Iron Bear dominated and controlled him, driving him to approximate Lancelot's lowly condition. Mordred rarely lay with Gwenhwyfach, and when he did, it was only when he could imagine her as Gwenhwyfar. On nights when he couldn't, they didn't. His affair had run nearly the sum of the Summer Kingdom, but the light of that unholy candle had been pinched, smoldering to a flicker. Gwenhwyfar periodically sent him letters. Then either sender or recipient would slay the messenger, that there be no trail of discovery. Dreading being found out and brimming with suspicion, correspondence was seldom and brief. Thus Mordred sought to make the most of an unhappy life with his pretend-Gwenhywfar whilst the authentic queen did the same with her preoccupied, inwardly distressed and outwardly perfect husband. Having neither Mordred nor Lancelot to bed rendered her miserable and cold; her only thaw the *hope* that one day Arthur would stumble from some great tower or slip into a holy well - else that Mordred might garner the gumption to overtly seize the throne.

Alas, to Arthur the challenges *behind the throne* were a light wage in exchange for the smiles of the children and the hearty embraces of farmers that the Iron Bear enjoyed every morning during his walks up to Lodge Hill.

Gwyar visited him less often and their walks grew few as she focused on raising up her nine maidens that the Roman Church might not, through their plot to elevate Mary as the new goddess, remove her faith entirely from the earth, causing it to be relegated to the corridors of the supposed superstitions of ancient man. Knowing Arthur bore too many burdens, she blamed him not but wished greatly that he would do more to aid the very vanishing sect that had gifted him his Sword of Power, validating him as king before all.

***

In Brittany – where Cymreig migrants had in times past settled peacefully and established a small kingdom during the Saxon Wars to protect their ports and provide for defense against pirates and invaders – the long protective reach of the Pendragon banner was vexed and torn, as diverse Germanic, Frankish and Gallic tribes, along with bitter rivals and menacing new enemies of their own kind, were encroaching upon Breton soils.

So close was the kinship between Cymru and Little Britain that corresponding 'sister cities' on the Continent bore the names of their predecessors on the Isles whence they had come. King Hoel Mawr ruled from both Kerne-Brittany and Leon-Brittany, whilst his ally King Arthur ap Meurig held court in Cernw in Gwent and also Caerleon in Cymru.

The mightiest of Hoel's foes was Childebert the Merovingian and he, tragically, was succored by one of Glamorgan's own.

Long ago when Mad Mark Meirchion had conspired to murder the Merlin of Britain, King Arthur, lacking sufficient evidence to execute him, had dispossessed the old Catholic king. The bishops studiously memorialized the transfer of his ancestral lands in south Cymru in the margins of an oversized Bible; many princes and influential landowners witnessed the document. Though the North, with its Romanist leanings, did not follow course, Arthur made Meirchion abdicate his principalities and transfer those lands to his grandson, Urien Rheged. Meirchion was thus made a vagabond who owned nothing and died mired in shame and destitution.

Although Meirchion had been born in the south of Cymru, his religious, political and military allies resided in the Old North, as did his wife and many children. One of them, Cynfarch, begat a son, Llew, and Llew of the Old North was married to Arthur's sister, the princess Gwyar.

For this cause, and for the ripple that would rise as a tide from the North and peradventure smash and crash down upon the Midland Tribes and the Silures, Arthur chose mercy instead of the blade for Mad Mark.

The sinister old man spent the last of his days far down in the horn of the Isles amongst the Cornovii tribes. Knowing he would soon pass, he bade them raise his youngest son, Prince Mark, as their own. This they did until they witnessed the hate and corruption cursed upon the son by the father. Mark too was a *banished man* without a country.

Then Simon Magus, the imprisoned leader of the Council of Nine, found him.

From the hut that was his abode in the darkness of the Caledonian wood, the Masked One used Merlin Wyllt as his pawn – his means of divination. The recluse possessed the Sight and, with above three years of discipleship, was able to serve as the probing and scouring eyes of a hawk for Simon. Roaming the land through these forbidden means, Simon discovered a jaded lad that had done something, quite on a small scale, that thoroughly impressed the architect of the long-prophesied New Order for the Ages: confederacy.

Confederacy, save not of those of his own blood, but of those from many nations. Mark had located the discarded, the angry, the bitter and the violent from amongst the Tribes of Eire – the Picts, the Jutes, the Angles, the Saxons and some Ravens who hated *the tyrant Arthur besides.* A band of criminals, accorded of men whose native kingdoms were often at war and, where Briton and Saxon were concerned, had not been in league since the time of Vortigern the Traitor.

But this rabble was no army. Three hundred men who would be stamped underfoot without notice by the elite armies of either the Britons or the Bretons.

However, Magus saw potential. In the stead of three hundred outcasts, he saw a confederacy of six nations, and Mark as their king.

He also, at last, envisioned the means of his escape from the Isles.

Mark subdivided his three hundred into troops of twenty and, through negotiation, corruption and patience, placed his men privily into employ at posts both upon the harbors and the ports. Trade was very active, as was religious pilgrimage, making boats and barges the perfect place to hide vagrants and baser men. Prince Madoc's maritime guard meticulously searched every vessel that left or entered, but these were of no reputation. Provided Magus could convince one troop to sacrifice all to ambush and kill Madoc's men at one of the more remote, less friendly Pictish shores (for they were hot with displeasure that the Britons had intruded upon their ports for the sake of one criminal), Magus could slip away and make land on the Continent. There, his Merovingian alternative to the Pendragon would receive and restore him.

Because Mark was a devout practitioner of Christianity after the Roman Catholic tradition, Magus was careful not to overtly use means of sorcery or devilish practices to facilitate introductions. This could prove difficult, given that Mark was either in Eire or on the Continent (circumambulating the mother island as a frightened but resolute dog circles a wolf threatening the herd), whilst Magus was in Alba. As the Merovingians shared no such opposition to occultic practices, Magus instead, through the channel of Merlin Wyllt, engaged the friendly ear of a general, who then in turn gave word to Mark of a *friend in the shadows who could help him overthrow Arthur and Hoel, and restore Mark's lands.*

Through the course of many like messages, a trust was forged with the young renegade and Magus, *the Shadow Man,* began to make Mark his pawn. Building upon his model of finding traitorous men who could be forged and molded into an *angry confederacy loyal to none save each other,* Magus taught Mark many tactics and tricks of Statecraft, and his numbers increased tenfold. A man born of any nation save the Vandals or the Visigoths (for they were the only army that could defeat the Britons, and Magus sought to not disrupt them with politics. They were to be his *final move* in creating a great war that would result in either Arthur or Childebert ascending to the dark throne of Antichrist on behalf of Simon's master, Arddu) could join their ranks.

Unpleasant to look upon just as his father had been, Mark had the ears of a donkey and a great cleft in his chin. The men followed him not for his fairness or skill with blade or spear. Rather, the allure that bound them was restoration for their sundry wrongs, real or imagined, or - for the more fully corrupted - vengeance and violence for its own sake.

Some Gewissi conscripts gave some of Mark's confederacy ongoing lodging in the far northwest of the Emerald Island, and they made a sort of settlement on the borderlands of Brittany. Magus taught Mark to have his men harass and withdraw, to garner attention and then vanish. To be a thorn and a whisper. At the same time, he bade Childebert initiate war with Hoel Mawr and his sons.

Just as a victory would be at hand for the Breton, extra brawn of no particular battle standard would manifest and sway the battle in favor of the Merovingians. Mark's confederacy of six nations was the difference, tilting all in favor of the King Childebert.

An easily-dismissed rumor became first a curiosity (that Briton would fight elbow to elbow with Saxon), then it burgeoned into an urgent threat to the sovereignty, and potentially the existence of, Cymru's greatest ally. Thus Arthur requested that Amwn Ddu, *the Black Knight*, who was brother to King Hoel, join him that they might personally inquire of the matter. Amwn was husband to Arthur's sister, Anna, and he possessed knowledge of every inch of Brittany save the unknowable corridors and twists of the Broceliande forest. He was also lethal with sword and beloved by Hoel; the perfect escort for the Pendragon.

In the guise of bards adorned in simple garb, the Round Table Companions watched a small skirmish from afar. The soldiers knew not what famous men were just above them on the ridge. The Bretons used Vivien's martial arts and, to Arthur, looked as forty Lancelots fighting in one accord in the valley below. Leaning upon the arching branch of a tree older than time, the master of disguise removed his hood and lost himself in the scene below. *All warriors miss the fight.* A rush of reminiscence, jealousy and longing for his troubled friend overcame the king. Such did his countenance shift that Amwn worried after him.

"Do you need to sit and rest, lord? May I fetch you water?"

"Cider," smiled the king, recovering back to the present. "I do well. Look how your people, my cousins, fight as one."

Then the battle before them, small in scope and number, unveiled the microcosm of the problem. Amwn and Arthur saw the fatal difficulty in fighting Mark's Six Nations Confederacy; hesitation.

The Breton made no pause when felling a Jute or putting a Saxon to flight. Not so with a Briton or a native of the Emerald Isles. Treachery and defection has ever been part of war. But not a composite army made wholly of men with no regard for their own nation. Not an army of traitors. In the marvel of it the Bretons would halt mid-stroke and beg their adversary to turn from their treachery, reminding them that their newfound allies aimed for the annihilation of all Brythonic and Goidelic peoples. In mid-sentence the Breton knight would catch an arrow to the bosom, or an axe to the gullet.

"We are not designed to kill our own kind on the field of military combat," observed Arthur. "When it is a cattle war or a land skirmish, we gnaw and devour our own, but the line is drawn when an official war with mounted horse, flanks and fire, banner and songs ensues. Our patriotism, so great a strength as 'tis…"

"…Is strength become weakness." The Black Knight finished the king's sentence.

"We must make haste back to Caermelyn and present the case for raising an army to lend aid to Hoel. The Continent hums with tension and feels as if it is on the brink of all-out war. Should Little Britain fall to this or any other abomination—"

"They would be at our doorstep next."

***

"A wizard sought here amongst the owls and mushrooms and heather." Merlin Wyllt smirked at Magus, who had returned from some privy preparations for his escape attempt.

"Oh?" Magus expressed little concern. "A crookbacked slight wizard with a walking stick and too many scrolls?" The Italian meant to mock Taliesin.

"Contrary. A tall Briton. Taller than any Briton I've beheld. He beseeched me cease training with you, informed me that the depths of your ill intentions reached the gates of Hell herself, and that you were a false prophet and an Antichrist. He was persuasive and had command of his words; an impressive, unusual man!"

"What else can you tell me about this sojourner that impressed you so?"

"He said that his name was already loaned to another and he called me by my Christian name, Laolkien. That would make his name—"

"Merlin." Magus dropped his satchel and stood agape. "But that's impossible."

"Nothing is impossible for the woeful damned. At least, not during their time amongst mortals."

"No. I was there. Impossible. My Lord Arddu would have told me." Magus began to rumble. His expression became *all* concern.

"I fled politics and strife. I know not what this Merlin was, and I possess no desire to validate or disqualify any his invectives cast. My hermitage is intentional. I am far removed from Cymru and I like it so." The hermit turned and puffed up in effort to be authoritative, an effort to repossess his home. "I think it is time for you to make your escape. I think it is time for you to leave."

But the hermit spake to the air, for Magus was already gone, already mounted and riding, making his way to the designated spot for his escape – an old road above the Firth of Forth and north-east to a Pictish port.

The new *Mystery of Merlin* notwithstanding, the Council of Nine's newest iteration for immanetizing the eschaton crystalized within its leader's corrupt mind as he made for the port:

Use Mark son of Meirchion to draw Arthur to the Continent here, to the Eire there. Let the threat make the armies of the Round Table reborn. Stretch them thin and tax them with frequent travel.

Once overstretched and distressed abroad, manifest the scandal of the Whelp Mordred at home. Let the Church and the heathens alike determine how to manage Arthur's firstborn son being a bastard born of incest.

Fractured and factionalized, let Merlin's long-prophesied comet come! May his tail set the Isle ablaze, furthering our Great Work!

And then, when the familiar trauma of perpetual war hath returned to the Cymry and the hope of liberty slipping as despair rises, and when the people feel as if God Himself has predestined their fall; when their low disposition seems to have descended to ocean's floor; when they can take no more – then. Then we release the Vandal Horde. The Black Boar. Like the Iron Bear, undefeated. Two Titans. One will be fit and ready and full of verve, the other hearing its bards singing its own death songs. The Black Boar will hunt the Dragon and the Raven alike.

Arthur will be destroyed or, against hope, will rise from grievous wounds over the enemy I have yet again created for him. Judas Iscariot will rise from his place and, should we find that damned cup, place it in Arthur through the same means that Mordred was begotten.

Arthur will be Antichrist.

Else, Childebert the Merovingian will form an accord with the Vandal Horde and the Nations and simply walk onto the rubble of Caermelyn, rebuilding the Kingdom of Heaven over the grave of King Arthur.

***

"Whence come the greater portion of their recruits?" Arthur and Amwn ceased not to talk about the matter as their flat boat was about an hour from reaching the mainland of Cymru. The confluence was at the posterior of the Severn, and they would simply sail all the way to Caerleon, not having to step foot upon land and travel by carriage or horse until the last short leg of the journey from Caerleon to Caermelyn.

"It seemed that the greater part of their numbers were Saxon," Amwn observed.

"I agree," Arthur concurred. "Has time at last caught up with us? Are the Saxons now producing men of fighting age? That army could not *all* be the disenfranchised and the banished. A Saxon has no regard for kin or countrymen, provided the wage is meet…"

"Conscripts," they both surmised, speaking at the same time.

"The Cymry do not invade nor encroach upon the sovereignty of another people. We protect our soil, and our just cause for doing this is that our soil is *ours,* and by extension, their soil is *theirs.*"

"Aye," the Black Knight confirmed.

"But…" Arthur paused. "In this case, although we will not invade, we will spy. I need a man who knows Brittany well and can study these men. Their dress, their dialect, their manners. Then, and I believe not that I am saying this—"

"Lord?"

"That same man must then sneak into Germania and validate whether or not these men are being exported to Gaul for the cause of bolstering this odd collective." Arthur used fingers in the air to summarize, speaking with his hands. "Find a man. Study the Germans in Gaul and Brittany. Study the Germans in Germania and the surrounding countries. Report the findings to the Round Table Fellowship. Can you find me such a man?"

"He is aged, but yes, there is such a man whose adventures qualify him for this task. Greidawl, father of your ally Gwythyr, whose vast lands span Leon, has been to Germania more than any Briton. He is your man, my lord."

"An excellent recommendation, brother-in-law. After we congress with our mates, please spend a fortnight with Anna and your children for then we, along with Bedwyr, must return again to the Continent and visit Leon, where I will personally give charges to Greidawl. I do apologize that I am removing you from hearth and home to go to and fro upon boats and vessels."

"In light of what we saw in the lands of Hoel, I think the reality of our future *is* going 'to and fro'," Amwn Ddu responded.

CHAPTER 22
Crop Failure

The year five hundred and thirty-and-five after the Incarnation of the Lord Jesus Christ was the last of what Arthur's Chief Bard referred to as the precious and priceless *quiet years* in the Summer Kingdom.

But for Arthur it was neither quiet nor restful. It was a year of travel for the sandy-haired one-time *boy-king,* now beyond the midpoint of life. *The War King, the Giant Slayer,* now *the Traveling King.*

First, Magus did escape. He purchased the blood of nineteen of Mark's men, mostly Picts, who hacked and whacked, delivering him at long last upon a departing boat. This occurred at the very time Arthur was returning with Amwn from Little Britain. At the same time, Prince Madoc was away at sea on an expedition. Timing, poor fortune, and the use of force finally allowed the serpent to slip by the rake, through the grass, and out of the garden.

Six of Mark's men died, but for the port guards, both of Pictish and Cymreig blood, every living soul perished in the ambush. As there were no witnesses left drawing breath, Arthur himself went to investigate and deduced, based upon the scene, the evidence and the circumstance, that Magus had made use of Mark's confederacy to make his escape from the Isles in the Sea.

The incident demanded that the Pendragon once again sup with King Drest son of Girom, once again speaking eye to eye about the grave risks associated with yet another incident that had seen Pictish souls sent to the sleep of death on account of Cymreig politics. The Pictish lord adored Arthur, but grew weary of drawing criticism and objection from his vassal tribes. When pressed, Arthur reminded the Picts through his authoritative statements to their High King that the loss of life in three score raids and one hundred skirmishes could not outweigh the blood that was upon the head of the Picts for conducting the Saxons into Gwynedd, the Old North and Powys in times past when the Saxon Wars were beginning. Moreover, the Boar would surely have turned upon their hosts and devoured the whole of Alba if not for the victory earned by the Tribes of the Britons.

The Picts owed their freedom to turn to the Christian God or retain their native gods and goddesses to the Cymry king. And ultimately, they suffered some insult and encroach on account of this.

The greater sum of the year was spent making the case for the sons of Briton to die for the sons of Brittany. *We are the same sons,* argued well the High King. For nearly two decades, mothers had grown accustomed to seeing their sons grow, court, farm, play and marry. The age of manhood had slackened to eighteen; and why shouldn't it? A fourteen-year-old is a babe and no man, unless imminent and endless war and a death rate that exceeds the birth rate demands it. Only then must the boys become men, the girls mothers too soon.

Slow to win over, Arthur and his closest retinue traveled oft, at last gathering an army of Powys, of Deubarth, of the Midlands, of Silures and Ravens once more. Vivien and Lancelot's silver armor shone again as the undefeated Britons made ready to bring hell from above upon the Franks or other German tribes, or the renegades of Mark, as needed.

Arthur tired some from the travel, the political speeches, and the knots and tangles of promising a people that they were yet at peace whilst clearly preparing for war.

Rhun ap Maelgwn and Owain ap Urien were Arthur's strongmen from the Old North. Needing extra help, he sent for Maelgwn himself. The request went, and then remained, without response.

"Go and chastise him until he polishes his famed spike and wields it once more," Arthur commanded Taliesin.

"And remove myself from guarding the hearts and motives of Rhufawn? Even Vivien's magic is no match for his tenacity," Taliesin objected.

Arthur proposed a compromise. He suggested that Rhufawn be allowed to handle the Cup, thus satisfying his obsession, and then that it be buried with the *other relics* upon Ynys Enlli, where Gwyar herself would guard it. "Perhaps a periodic pilgrimage will tame the boy's noble lust?" offered Arthur. "If he is to be king after my passing, balance he must find."

"I don't think temperance accompanies handling the Cup of Christ. It will either consume him, that he never unhand it, or he will guard it all his days. However, none can impede him on account of his blade. His good graces alone would be all to constrain him.

Thrice he has requested the company of three. Your approach may work…" Taliesin was full of doubt. And fear. "I will reason with him. Then I will go to Deheubarth and pull Maelgwn out from whatever cave he has made his dwelling place, from under whichever wood he has made his home."

"He is a special young man; have faith, Taliesin."

Gwalchmai and Mordred remained the other clear candidates for succession.

Mordred.

That Arthur had not sought him out whatsoever for inquiry (or an outright secret slaying) further proved that the king of the Britons had indeed murdered his own son, and that he knew that Mordred knew as much. Though a spineless fear of the Pendragon was ever in his bowels, Mordred became emboldened and, with Arthur ever traveling to Eire, to Alba and to Brittany as the war drums began to prattle, he began again to slither into court, causing Gwenhwyfar's bedchamber to be very active during the *last quiet year.* Moreover, Mordred kindled embers of ire amongst the Dynion Hysbys, and tested the waters of speaking against Uncle Arthur. Though they loathed Mordred's outward Catholicism, they received him and, over time, his true beliefs, his religion of *the meaningless of it all* and *keeping your head long enough to get what you want* became clearly known – and embraced.

After all, Arthur the hypocrite, while sermonizing about religious liberty, had shut down their rites. Why? Over the flimsy connection to an unproven murder of a wizard who now appeared likely not dead! *And moreso,*

Arthur the hypocrite, sermonizing yet more about the right to worship whatsoever gods one pleases, now openly opposes and fans public accusations against the beauty and grandeur of Rome. Why? Over a box and a shrine!

Mordred began to garner the unspoken endorsement of the Dynion Hysbys. And, for so many tribes, whether in the remote North, Powys or Land's End, the Dynion Hysbys held captive the voice and directional will of the people.

***

It was winter of the year five hundred and thirty-and-five when Morgaine of the Faeries was near her birth home, tending to the harsh season's preparations at Llyn Fawr. Evening gave way to night and no star twinkled. 'Twas black as pitch.

"At some point I must question the stability of my own mind, that red eyes staring down at me – nay, through me – are as natural as being happened upon by a bunny or a house pet."

The king of the Tylwyth Teg clicked forefinger against thumb, and his hand became a torch, that the eyes could reveal the outline of a familiar and mostly unwanted elf erect as a great marble pillar before the tiny sorceress.

"Daughter," he began.

"You are not my father!" she snapped and, where a man's knees would knock out of joint for terror, started towards the otherworldly being.

"Your position is rather ambiguous, is it not? How know you that you are not a changeling and of my very loins?"

"Because you cursed the line of the Silures, not that of your own seed!"

Gasps and cackles of impress were let loose.

"So wise. Still, look at you. Ambiguous, I say! But the matter of *your seed* be the purpose of my call tonight."

"Gwalchmai? Is he in danger? I had no Sight over it! What is wrong—"

"Not the Hawk of May. Rather, the son of Arthur and Morgaine."

The cruel verbalizing of it brought a rush of tears, not likely concealed by the night.

"Put your dagger away," continued the rude spirit. "I come to beg you, Morgaine of the Fae."

"What would you possibly beg of me?" She was as mouse before a moose, and the moose kept a fearful distance.

Struggling on how to form the words, he fumbled and bumbled, seeking tact that was contrary to his nature. "You must do what is contrary to nature for every mother. I know you love him without condition. I know you to be warm, to be kind—"

"Beg of me to do what!" The mouse now seemed thrice the height and double the girth of the moose.

"Kill Mordred."

"You had a direct hand in bringing him into the world of men, and now you would have me take him out of it?" Instead of the primal witch rising within and perhaps slaying the prince of elves, she was incapacitated by the very notion of the deed, grieving and shrieking at the thought of it as though it were already done. Knowing some riddle-ish explanation would ensue, she gave way to bawling and screaming *why* at the king of the Tylwyth Teg again and again. *Why? Why! Why must I do this thing?*

"We faeries live under peculiar laws and peculiar ways, daughter. It must be done lest not just your *Camelot,* but the whole of the world of men, fall."

"Is that not what you want? Why to you is that a bad thing?" she fired back.

"Man is a foolish, proud, and arrogant master of the earth, respecting not those who ruled before, but he is far better than who will rule in the next Age. An aeon of tyranny and evil unbridled, a hammer to the head of all creaturekind." He stooped and took the tiny hands of the trembling mother. "And the abomination that *we* wrought unlocks the key to those *Dark Designs."*

Morgaine gave the Fae the whole of her weight, which he barely noticed. "Then *you* do it."

"I cannot; neither can the Fair Folk."

"Why not?"

"We woeful and sorry damned live under peculiar laws and peculiar ways."

"No mother can put her son to the sword. I cannot bear the burden of even thinking it." Morgaine's thoughts wandered towards Queen Gwenhwyfar I. A rush of regret punished her for the cruelest of words.

The Fae King discerned those thoughts. "You must do what your brother, King Arthur the Just, had the courage to do."

"There is only one King Arthur. I will do it NOT!" She pumped her fists as small mallets upon his chest.

And at once, he had vanished. The wind swooshing over Llyn Fawr was her only company. Gwyar, who was known as Morgaine of the Faeries, wept sore knowing the time was upon her that her secret sins would soon be manifest before all. That the rightful heir, though the wrongful man, was soon to be on the move lest the Tylwyth Teg tortured her for his own amusement.

Darkness arrived early and the fullness of winter came, colder than usual, but no more than reasonable.

Arthur gave Cai a few complaints about his knee on this day, else his shoulder on the other, his steward having none of it and showing him his own myriad of scars and dents, the two knights goading one another in an effort to remain young.

And the petulant cough that lived in Arthur's lungs roared more frequently, but no more than reasonable.

The twelfth month passed, and the year *Five Hundred and Thirty-Six arrived.*

***

Armies seldom attack in winter, but rogues and villains are no respecters of the weather.

Mark, son of Meirchion the Mad, dispatched above five hundred of his confederacy of the rejected and the spiteful to harass and sack Catholic churches all about the north of Gwynedd. Visiting violence on his own allies (and ensuring that neither priest nor bishop was ever present or ever harmed) would force Arthur's hand, drawing him out to either give troops and resources to protect his religious enemies or, better yet, to do nothing and lose credibility amongst the Tribes.

Conducting an atrocity against one's own people as a pretext for war or some great sacrifice of liberty is as old as the lying tongue of prince and man himself. Simon Magus had taught Mark the art, and the uncomely rogue perfected it.

But Arthur, an undefeated leader and genius of tactic and method, sniffed out the ruse.

Two thousand silver-skinned equestrians made an intentionally dramatic, slow tread through the tundra of mud and sleet that was the January soil in Gwynedd. The battle horns screamed, and the use of drum and trumpet mixed with song aided the beauty and terror of the Briton's army, against whom none could stand.

The sum of them, still mounted upon armored steeds, formed a ring of men and metal around one of the chapels, freshly ransacked, smoldering and ruined.

"You're too late!" Two clergymen emerged from the ornate wooden double doors that would not, from the shambled looks of the building, welcome the faithful on this Sunday, or the next. By happenstance, one of the men was Bishop Cadfan. Success and promotion had made the once-timid boy a haughty and arrogant man. He had survived Morgaine; now he would take on her brother. "You surround the shell of a building, robbed of artifacts, relics and gold. Dereliction of duty and no regard for the Holy Church!"

Meurig, still lively as a stag, joined his son but was unarmed and in simple coat and tunic, looking the part of a druid or bard, though in reality he was but a father enjoying the field with his lad in the eventide of their years. "A tongue so full of spite ought not to wag; who but a priest would speak thus to the Pendragon of Britain?"

"The head of the dragons. The title fits the man. And look, I have the pleasure of having TWO Pendragons on the scene three hours late with the damage done and the enemy halfway to Eire, or to Mars, by now!"

At the direct and malignant conduct towards his father, Arthur himself was off his horse and eye to eye with Cadfan, whom he smote hard across the cheek, feeling the cowardly cleric crumble and cry out before him.

"Stand," Arthur commanded.

And Cadfan, his crimson arrogance trickling down from his cheek, pooling upon his collar, *stood.*

"You are not entitled for men to leave wife and child, plow and pig, to come and bleed and die for your relics."

"So you will not help us?"

"Stay thy mouth!" Arthur hollered. "You shall not tax the people, nor demand of their treasury to make yourselves fat as you dupe them with your traditions."

"There have been five attacks this month, likened unto this one," Meurig interjected; equal to his cub, this Bear was also a menace and a marvel with command of tones and words. "And we have investigated and heard report of each."

The second priest opted for the cordial approach. "Thanks be to the Lord for your assistance and protection. What evidences have you found? What cause of such outrage against the Lord's Flock?"

"Evidences." Meurig smiled. "Evidences and trends." He folded his arms, already proud of words not yet spoken. "Each time, the relics and gold are stolen with such care and lack of disruption that the marauders either are dainty as water sprites, or have complete and intimate understanding of the layout of the chapel – down to the placement of every bench and pew."

Bishop Cadfan realized he was in the presence of smarter men, and stepped back four paces, placing himself in the shadow of the double doors.

"And more," old King Meurig continued.

"May I have a go?" Arthur clutched at his father's elbow. Every mounted warrior laughed with the unison of Illtud's choir. A horn added musical accompaniment to the light moment.

"Fine," the senior sovereign grumped, and grinned.

"In each case, no bishop or clergymen are found on the scene, and only the laity are assaulted. When, EVER, is a church empty of its clergy amongst your sect? Oft-times you live at the church!"

Cadfan gulped hard.

"No supposedly stolen gold, nothing of real damage save the structures themselves and a few tapestries, priests magically missing." Then the Pendragon gave his judgment. "You attack yourselves to raise a flag and rally the people falsely into war! You wanted my army?" Arthur twirled his famed spear thrice in the air and then pointed it towards Owain and Urien, a sample of mighty ones invincible and sharpened from recent and intense training. "Here we are."

"I swear it is not so, my king. 'Tis the confederacy of the son of Meirchion—"

"Meirchion, your mentor. You are the disciple of your pretend enemy!" Arthur cut off the priest hard, giving no place to his games. "Say what you will to the people. I just trust that they can discern truth." Arthur motioned for a young man of eighteen to be brought forth.

The young man brimmed with excitement and thankfulness every time fortune allowed him to be in the presence of the just and great king. With quill and vellum at the ready, the historian Gildas looked as a starving soldier before some great feast.

"Document these things, my historian." The Iron Bear hugged the boy hard.

Cadfan hissed within, as Arthur had made

a close ally of a son of his most bitter rival in the North (as he had done with the sons of Maelgwn and all the line of Cunedda). Gildas ap Caw, though of the Roman sect himself, hated corruption and the abuses of power, and was happy to document the historical facts and conclusions objectively.

"The raids will cease. You will not damage roads or fences or farms, or frighten damsels and the youth in your theatre." Arthur was using the pitch and tone he used to use ere he slayed a Saxon invader. Cadfan's heart began to fail for fear, and even some of the younger knights were phantom-white with dread and awe, having had no exposure to *real military authority* in their happy lives of fat and feast and no want.

"The army is here," Arthur again asserted, making a simple hand signal that caused the circle to close as a slow vice round the church. "And you speak of relics. The coffin of the Blessed Lady. You will return it to Ynys Enlli in a fortnight, or I will raze every church of your denomination from tip to top in these Isles. You will make an idol of her no more!"

"I beg you to believe my innocence, for the raiders desecrated the shrine of the Heavenly Mother but yesterday, leaving only splinters of the box. Of course there is no body, no bones, for like the Lord, she ascended!"

Arthur now, as his sister had learned afore, realized the full magnitude of the plot to deify Mary. The false attacks were not just to bring criticism upon Arthur's increasingly harsh polices against Rome and her encroachments. More than this, they served as cover to forever control the coffin of Mary and force Arthur to either reveal that he and the Mistress of Avalon were hiding her bones from the people, or to allow the lie of her nature and essence to go forward. This was a losing prospect in either event, as men would simply worship the bones as had Israel worshiped the Brazen Serpent, the rod of Aaron, the bones of Moses should Michael make known their resting place, and so many other material things associated with the spiritual and the good. *Oh, the idolatry of man! The death toll and expense of bones and rings and cups!*

"I will make it known by policy that your doctrine is a lie."

"That is not the place of the State, lord." Cadfan found courage.

"Men can believe as they will, but Caermelyn will not remain neutral on this matter. Of your baptisms and tonsures and vestments and robes, we care not for the empty squabbles of vain men."

"You sound like the demented wizard who spewed his blasphemous words against the traditions of the Church. Meirchion was right to—"

Arthur thrust *Rhon,* his spear, down hard through the foot of Cadfan as a master fisherman, patient and still, at once strikes violently to pierce a great fish, pinning him to the ground. The spear plunged as if to the heart of the earth itself. The screams and cries of the *Man of God* and his pleas for relief moved not the Iron Bear.

"But of your lies about Mary, we will not remain neutral for as long as I have breath yet in me. I have firsthand knowledge of your lies and it is no violation of liberty for a leader, who is but a man, to share the truth of a thing with his neighbor, though he sits at a public council." Arthur gave Rhon a twist, making dust of the small bones in Cadfan's foot. "Do you maintain that these *raiders* stole the coffin, or will I have it in a fortnight?"

Knowing the punishment of Magus exceeded the justice of Arthur, Cadfan the Crippled held taut the line of his lie. "The rebel Mark's men have it, lord, not the Church of God."

Arthur's visage added to the pain of his pierced foot caused Cadfan to swoon and fall, unconscious.

"No more raids!" the Iron Bear screamed at the inert body.

The army helped rebuild and repair damages to farm or land near the chapel, tended the wounded, and returned to Caermelyn, Arthur thinking of his Merlin without ceasing on the journey home.

***

"Taliesin." Arthur gazed into the hearth that gave warmth to a large hall of books and scrolls, organized from floorboard to vault. The king was at once happy and saddened to be home. "My *first Merlin* and I spent a lifetime of hours in this library, seemingly three lifetimes ago. His manifestation during the bout with Lancelot. His appearances. His supposed hunt for the Masked Priest. I heard his voice. Maelgwn heard his voice. We saw him. Or did we? Are these—"

"The illusions begotten by hope?" Taliesin offered a conclusion, knowing his lord worried that he was slipping into bereaved madness.

"Yes." Direct, full of melancholy.

"As your *current Merlin,* I say to you that too many witnesses have seen your childhood mentor and beloved friend. The Scriptures declare, in the practical wisdom, *'by the mouth of two or three witnesses, let all things be established.'*"

Arthur's countenance lifted somewhat. "Speaking of Scriptures, what does your unique theology hold regarding Merlin? Did he return from the grave? What is he? Give me your understanding, bard."

"The dead cannot contact the living. Thus, he is not an apparition. This leaves a few possibilities."

Arthur was aglow with interest, begging the Merlin Taliesin to pause his teaching that he might fetch a cider, remove his boots, repose and listen. Doing this (and it pleased Taliesin to see his sovereign allow himself to ease upon a long Roman-styled couch in the library) and clutching a simple sword, as all warriors do when they rest, he bade Taliesin continue.

The little Christian druid pointed at the weapon. "It is time to wield Excalibur again, Arthur. What is the king without his sword?"

"What is a king who strikes his ally in jealousy wrought by speculation and not fact?" Erect upon an elbow, the king became irritated, yet not angered. "Back to Merlin!"

"Well. Either Merlin survived what befell him in Broceliande, which is unlikely. Or Merlin is not a man, which seems probable, and if not a man, is not subject to the laws of man. Or, lastly, the Fae are involved. And there is no Bible for what the Fair Folk do!"

They laughed.

"If Merlin is not mortal, can he be saved?"

"The question that plagues us all, Lord Arthur. In this dispensation of the Grace of God, how will He handle the remnants of times past? I know not – only that I can only trust His grace and mercy."

"It is hard to answer the question, which plagues beggar and lord nightly, about what becomes of any of us when we pass into the sleep of death. The greater burden for me" - Arthur's throat tightened and his voice cracked - "is this. Why, if he be alive or half alive or a quarter part alive, why is he not here? Why not return, in whatever his state, to Glamorgan?"

"Drink your cider down quickly. And then have another," Taliesin insisted, and Arthur did the same. The bard, with uneven gait, bungled about in a closet, revealing a perfectly folded, stained and war-tattered battle standard. Unfolding the flag with reverence, he pointed to the Red Dragon, the symbol of victory, the sigil of peace. "Forget not Merlin's prophecies ere he came to see the Mysteries of God given us by Paul. Whether given by devil, by intuition, or by special knowledge, Merlin saw that the days of the Summer Kingdom were numbered." Taliesin made a great pause, that the statement would settle within the king, whose ears and heart were opened to hearing it by mild drunkenness.

"The comet," the rosy-cheeked Bear stated.

"Aye. You were born under its sign, and you are meant to emerge victorious from what dread might come should it return."

"You can't offer me the strong scrumpy sup and then layer upon me comments vague and broad. Plain words, *New Merlin*, speak plainly!"

The men laughed, for Arthur, a model of self-control and moderation had, in the self-same day, angrily run through a priest's foot with an enchanted spear and become drunk on potent apple spirits.

"Very well." Taliesin smiled. "I speculate. I theorize. But I do not know. Perhaps Merlin knows that he cannot stop the end of the Summer Kingdom, so he is trying to stop the end of the world. He cannot control a fiery serpent from above hurling itself upon mountain, valley and wood. But he can find and stop your adversary. He can kill the man who has funded wars and turned Silures into traitors and used whole nations as pawns to further his iniquity. If Merlin can find him, then he serves us being better out there than in here."

Somber words aided rapid sobriety. "But the Evil One escaped our grasp. Will Merlin hunt him the world over that he returns not? For I miss him sore."

"Are you not afraid of the comet?" asked Taliesin.

"We are undefeated against men and steed and steel. Giants and witches and monsters that befit children's fables have we slain in our lifetime. But against a calamity like that, I have no answer and no fear. If the sky is to fall, then let us do good and keep the light of our glorious kingdom shining bright until that day. And let our conduct be as if that day will never come, and as though it will come tomorrow."

"And you bade me speak in plain words."

The friends enjoyed another laugh.

"What about Gwenhwyfar?" Arthur posed a curious open question to the bard he had borrowed from Maelgwn.

"Lord?"

"Does Merlin *the phantom* stay away because he likes her not and cannot be around our *situation?*"

"Like you, Merlin had one great love and one great lust in his life. And like you, he struggled greatly to untangle the heart's fog that mists the senses and impedes discernment over which is which. Were he here, he would see much of himself in you. It would bother him and he would pester you with goads and riddles and unwanted advice."

"Like unto you and Maelgwn."

"Precisely!" Taliesin grinned. He traced the dragon a few times and then put away the flag. "But no, Lord Arthur, he would not stay away or forsake you on account of *her*."

"Thank you, Chief of Bards. Any other wisdom, druidic or Christian, to pass on ere I repose for the night? The hour is advanced, and I am certain that Cai wants me to sleep that he might do the same soon."

"The Catholics," Taliesin offered.

"Need I another cider ere I hear this?" said Arthur, half musingly.

"Maybe." Taliesin touched his sovereign upon the shoulder. Though younger than Arthur, Taliesin had had a paternal manner about him from his youth; he was a man full of divine inspiration, *the Awen*. "Remember the lesson that Merlin gave you about leaders and people?"

Arthur perked up, remembering it well. How Merlin had said that sometimes good people had bad leaders and other times bad people had good leaders, and that the truly special times in history were when good people were supported by good leaders. Unspoken communication ensued, then Taliesin followed with few words.

"The Catholic people are the most beautiful souls. They love the Lord, they care for the poor with devotion and sincerity; in morality there are none better, in kindness, none softer. We Britons are not evangelical. Though intensely spiritual, we are inward; they are outward. If Christ is to go to the nations, it will be because of Rome, not Britannia. Fight their corruption, but be mindful not to lose the people in the process."

King Arthur, a humble king receptive to the wisdom of others and never above reproach, absorbed the words. Many candles were spent, meeting their waxy, nubby ends, as he remained silent in the library for hours, pondering the complex problem that Magus, the Northern kings given to Church-sanctioned corruption, and the bishops presented; a canker gnawing upon his Summer Kingdom. *Be mindful not to lose the people.*

Prior to twilight he looked up, peering at the top of a great shelf, filled from floorboard to ceiling with tomes and scrolls. Filled with memories of sitting at the feet of Merlin.

"Merlin! Where are you?" he cried, his stately voice giving way to a mourning that would not abate. "I need you!"

Suddenly one scroll, provoked by chance or by magic, was dislodged from its slot and fluttered down to the floor. A folio of Scripture, penned with ink of the highest quality, scribed in ornate Latin, lighted gentle as a feather upon Arthur's feet (for he had not moved from the cushion of his chair) at the place where the Scripture read: *'And there appeared another wonder in heaven: and behold a great Red Dragon.'*

***

The bitter winter of the first two moons of the year ended, and spring was nigh.

***

The People.

The Common Man.

The cattleman.

The sower and the reaper.

The carpenter.

The miner.

These cared not about a missing wizard. They cared that they could eat. They cared not about Maelgwn Gwynedd, his bubble or his madness, and certainly not his propensity for other men's wives - especially of his kinsmen and close friends. They cared that they had eggs and milk and hay. These men, and the women that loved them, had no regard for a meddling Devil-worshipper puppeteering politicians from the shadow. They cared about the harvest, good wood and the ability to heat their homes.

But they did care about Arthur the Silure Lord and Emperor of the Isles in the Sea.

He was more than a crimson cape and blue-helmeted highborn to them. He was their hope, he was their kinsman, he was the reason the crops never failed and the hens gave eggs and the calves were fat. Remove all the dross from the golden city of Caerleon and the shimmering fortress of Caermelyn, and what remained that was of value to the common man was the crop and King Arthur. King Arthur and the crop.

Spring came.

The crop failed.

An orange haze arrived with the winds and lingered, ever filling the air, night or day. Smokey, with grit and content, yet air. A cough and an issue of blood among the weak and the young soon followed the haze. The yield of fruit and grain was the lowest in memory, even amongst the elders who had witnessed many springs, had reaped many harvests.

Mark's collection of rebels continued to harass Hoel in Britanny. Also, they hacked and carved and raided until at last they had won a lasting presence in Kernwy, a cooperative vassal kingdom and partner-state to the Silures. This gave Mark a southern position below Arthur. Though still too small to be a grave threat or resurrect the *War Years,* the thorn was growing, causing the Round Table many expeditions to the Continent (or south to the horn of the Isles). The frequent and ongoing absences resulted in a void whereby the opportunistic bishops and Dynion Hysbys could stir the people, speculating and upsetting the masses with theory and speculation over the cause of the crop failure.

The Roman Catholics blamed, of course, Arthur's sins in refusing to provide financial and military support in obedience to the needs of the Church. And not a few whispers of his taking a second wife and being smitten with impotence by an angry God found many ears in pubs and fields and times of gossip. His sins, compounded with the Cymry bishops' continued refusal to eat with, baptize or read Scripture to the Saxon tribes under Cedric in Lloegyr, had brought the judgment of God, so said the priests.

Saints Illtud and Bedwini instead hurled accusation at Rome for desecrating the resting place of the Sacred Lady. This was a misplaced strategy that allowed Rome to simply state that Mary had been translated into heaven, unless the Britons could produce her body. As the Church *could not* and Gwyar *would not,* the mythos and cult of Mary blossomed even as the crops slept.

Ironically, the majority of citizens, those not princes and priests, scoffed at the superstitious jangling of both sects, yet with religious devotion cleaved unto the old gods. They turned to the Dynion Hysbys to understand the haze, the illness, and the arrested growth of fruit, vegetable and tree.

"The cough that is in our lord's chest has manifested as a cough and diseased lung upon our land. He is sick, having no heir. Heal Arthur and heal the land."

"But he is not here! He fights the Son of Cornwall and the Franks o'er in Brittany!" The collective and recurring cry of the people.

"Then let us look to one to rule in his stead until he returns. Let us turn to the most eligible and proper heir, Mordred son of Cynfarch ap Meirchion and Gwyar ferch Meurig Pendragon. Let him unify the land as a proxy whilst our High King restores Brittany and once again frees his mighty sword from the stone, erecting it in splendor towards the Sun that it might find fertile soil and yield again." These were the words, or similar, spoken oft by the Adder. He was full of double meaning and plotting, for the people knew Mordred to be the rightful heir on account of being the son of Arthur, not the son of a Northern Chieftain. These impish anti-druids, playing games upon men as if they were the Tylwyth Teg, would insert Mordred as an "Aliteryn" or sub-king, and when the crops yet failed and plague yet scarred and sickened, they would reveal with feigned awe and dismay that they had unknowingly put forth a bastard born of incest on the throne, manifesting the *real curse* upon the land. This would force Arthur to abdicate, or worse. Mordred would be rejected as well, and Mark or a son of Caw, or even Maelgwn the Mad Exiled Hound, would ascend the throne.

At last they would have revenge on the wizard who had spurned them; at last the Council of Nine or the corrupt within the Church would rule the land, leaving the Dynion Hysbys installed to mystify, regulate and control the masses on behalf of whatever wickedness reigned from high places.

And so it was, with spring vegetables scarce and trees giving no spring bud, with children coughing blood and elderly men swooning with dehydration never to rise, that Simon Magus through his puppet Mark set about to destroy Cymru from the Continent, and the Dynion Hysbys to replace Arthur from within.

But the heathen tribal leaders miscalculated the degree to which the people loved Arthur. For those who are devoid of love can never appreciate the love extended by others.

"We will not yet entertain the proposal of Mordred as a proxy. Find another way." This was the collective command of the Tribes from Ynys Mons to Deheubarth, and all tribes and clans in between besides.

CHAPTER 23
The Red Dragon, the Sword, and the Cup

Seed 6 – "Not my son! You have now let the rituals of the Tribes ruin two more lives."

The will of the people was made known to the local chieftains and princes, who in turn passed their judgment to Taliesin, who presented the news privately to Meurig, Onbrawst, Ittud, Bedwini, Dewi and Cadfan.

"First." The hunchbacked sage looked more weighty and distressed than ever, speaking as though he were carrying nine oxen. "I have convinced them to give us more time. One failed harvest and a mysterious gaseous wind shall not remove the diadem from our Pendragon!"

"How much time?" Meurig, more than any present or living, understood the verity of the ancient customs that connected High King to the output of the land.

"The fall harvest." Taliesin was ashen, grave. "A baby or a crop yield by fall."

"There are but seven months until autumn! It is one mandate and no choice!"

"I agree, my lady," responded Taliesin. "The people would have you validate that Gwenhywfar is not these past few months with child. They are being slow and diligent and hoping against hope that an heir doth grow in her belly even now."

Onbrawst was dignified in her indignance. "I have not the closeness of relationship with *our queen* to examine her fingernails, let alone her womb."

"My love, have a nursemaid accompany you; I pray you do it." Meurig was sensitive to his true love. "It is for our son. They will slay him."

At the saying of this, tears welled and ran freely from all, save Cadfan, who was as stone.

"And if there be no heir and no crop by the tenth month of the year? What then would the Cymry do with their Pendragon and" – Meurig the Cheerful's voice broke, giving lumpy and disjointed words – "my son? What then would the people do with my son, my King Arthur?"

"Will it be the nephew Mordred, or perhaps will affections return to the Hawk of May?" asked Bishop Bedwini.

"It will not be a son of Gwyar." Taliesin spoke plainly. "It will be Arthur." He panned the room, nodding and confirming, and bewildering them. "They want to keep their King Arthur as much as we do."

"Then what befalls in autumn?" Onbrawst was understandably confused.

"A prince full of virtue and virility will draw the sword and stand as substitute, dying for the king, and the king will rise in his stead, reborn anew for another cycle of seasons."

"Are we not a nation of logic and reason?" Cadfan interjected, unable to bite his tongue. "If

Arthur were to be lame and unable to lead in battle or facilitate matters of strategy and course then by all means, do a little ritual and retire him. But this ritual is nonsensical. Let us just take a firm hand and insert Mordred if and when Arthur should fall."

The bishops of the Britons did not disagree with part of Cadfan's assessment. However, the light of Christ had not penetrated the working and farming classes. Though a Christian nation in its foundational rights of man and natural law, the new faith remained yet a novelty for the rich in the minds of the agrarians who spent day and night tilling, watering, planting or hunting. Disregard for the most serious of their rites and customs would result in a refusal from them to send sons to become soldiers and knights, a refusal to sell or trade in the markets. The Cymry did not favor laws to solve problems, neither brute force or tyranny; rather, the power of abstinence, peaceful opposition and withdrawing from free markets. The power was with the people, and the slow conversion to Christ and the swap of Church superstition for pagan was not yet.

After hearing and promptly silencing the dissenting voice, Taliesin revealed the candidate selected to *give his life that Arthur might live.*

"The slain and risen king will be Rhufawn the Fair, son of Maelgwn, the Galahad of the Isles in the Sea."

It seemed that for three minutes, even the birds of heaven and the rush of the manifold streams that treated Cymru with their song were silent. There was no sound. There was nothing to debate.

The next harvest or a babe must come.

"If the time comes, I will be the one to inform

to Lancelot." Taliesin had spent the sum of Galahad's life rearing him to replace Arthur, but not after this manner. And his whole life rebuking and spurning Lancelot, because though the new Merlin hated the sins, he loved the man.

***

No babe grew within the belly of Gwenhwyfar the Adulteress.

***

Beltane came. The cloudy orange haze had not abated; rather, matters worsened, as an ash of unknown origin swirled about for hours every day.

"It is the coals burning in the lanterns of the dragon's nostrils, is it not?" Arthur knew the answer to his own question. He and Madoc and Amwn Ddu walked along the river ports in Gwent, overseeing a plentitude of ships provisioning for departure. Taliesin with his uneven, nigh-hobbled gait lagged behind.

"I believe it is, lord; the comet is slowly making its way to the earth, and his breath hides the Sun and rains poison and ash."

"So be it, bard. I am not leaving."

But the Black Knight was emphatic. "You must. We know not how much worse this will wax; the Royal Family must live, and return to reign again. Moreover, we need your leadership; Hoel—"

"I'm sorry, brother, Hoel must fight this one alone. I will not leave whilst my people choke and suffer boils and blisters and starve from this sickness." Arthur paused his promenade and waited for his counselor to join his pace. "Taliesin, what would Merlin do?"

"Merlin saw these things, and it would appear they are coming to pass. He would make you leave as Amwn bids you. You are their hope, even in exile. There is no glory in dying with them in this way."

Arthur abruptly changed the subject. He turned to his brother, the Sea Master, Prince Madoc. "Get thee hence from the Isles. We are neither conquerors nor invaders, but if there be land overrun by wild beast or Giant or creeping thing that can sustain us, find it and return unto me with tidings and findings and charts." Arthur embraced his brother hard and shared with him how much he loved him and how proud of him he was for safely guarding the entryway to Cymru for so many decades. Knowing the expedition might not include a return voyage, many fond recollections were shared, and farewells were forbidden. "Take the vessels with bolts and rivets of wood and see that supplies of iron are minimized."

Madoc obeyed, readying ships designed for long voyages. These boats could not be shaken apart by the magnetism of the vast sea or the circuits of the moon. Many thousands of men fled Cymru by way of the Usk River, which fed the sea.

"Amwn, has Greidawl returned from his mission in the Nordic lands?"

"He awaits you in Lyon, lord." The Black Knight attempted to lure the king by any means onto a barge.

"What news then? You give the report." The effort was blocked.

Amwn Ddu acquiesced and reported. "Climate

change and local tyrants are causing many Geats and Danes to join King Mark upon the Continent. They are viewed as criminals and banished men and their local tribes neither regard nor miss them. Greidawl was discovered by a young king called Beowulf. They met in single combat and Greidawl was injured. Beowulf followed Greidawl back to the cave that was made his hiding place and the Geatish King saw the mother of Greidawl, who even in her advanced age is fair, being rumored a child of the Fae."

"A fair Fae like unto her cousin Vivien she is." Arthur paused, reflected and smiled. "So these tribes of the Geats and Danes raise no army to invade Cymru?"

"Nay, lord. Mark gathers only vagabonds and desperate criminals."

"Send Greidawl back but once more to the Germanic lands, and ensure the same."

Suddenly Bedwyr appeared, upon steed. Cai was complicit in the loving but disobedient plot, and already aboard the king's ship. Arthur's hinder side was unprotected and his sword sheathed. Bedwyr leapt from his mount and tackled Arthur hard to the ground. The Black Knight controlled the wrists of the mighty king, who was eating dirt and spewing curses not befitting his office. Three more men joined, and they were needed. The struggle cost some dignity, some a few teeth, but at last King Arthur was upon a vessel meant to leave for Brittany.

Before apologies could be spoken, the Red Dragon arrived.

The sun darkened, and the moon gave not her light. The stars appeared to have fled, and only a red spike from the tail of the dragon could be seen; a red bolt of lightning contrasted against a black night (though it were yet daytime). The spike itself was taller than Cymru's tallest mountain, and it cut through the earth as a table saw finishes its final draw. Instead of sawdust and flakes of birch, the spike drew lava and rock from well beneath the surface of the earth.

The screams and confusion were deafening.

The hilltop fortress of Caermelyn *melted.* The white marble that was not thrown to the plain below was molten and became part of the mountain top; white splotches were where the gilded city had once stood.

Caerleon was on fire, yet stood.

There were no screams at first. Those who died simply vanished, consumed by the dragon. Scores were caught in the path of the spike and now part of the ash that covered the mountain. Trees were victims as well, reduced to stumps, to nubs, or to nothing.

Then the spike withdrew and the dragon flew straight up, up, towards the heavens. His ascent revealed the sun and let the living witness the devastation. Moreover, pitch and oils had begun to boil the river and pockets of flames rested upon the waters, creating lanterns, illuminating the deaths.

Now came the screams.

The rattles.

The moans of dismay.

From the river could be seen the little monastery where dwelt Queen Gwenhywfar I, and next to that, another small hall connected to the church that was used as a school. Knowing it as a safe and sturdy place, many children fled to the school.

By chance, Arthur glanced upon the monastery and caught a glimpse of the children, at risk of perishing as fires surrounded the hall, its roof giving way. The vessel had shifted from the port's bank; its tethers burned away, it began to drift. Arthur dove into the boiling water, the great cries of his kinsman and mates shouting in protest above him.

At once he appeared upon the shore, blackened, hair singed, cape ablaze, boots gashed or gone. Discarding his burning garments without breaking stride, the High King was soon upon Gwenhwyfar's cell.

Their eyes met.

But six words were spoken. "I do well! To the children!"

He did not speak, but Arthur embraced his former spouse, who felt as a skeleton in his strong arms. She vanished quickly, making haste towards her abode of old, navigating small side streets, running a labyrinth of flame and screechy chaos.

Meanwhile, he was at once inside the ancient stone structure joined to the church.

One by one he carried them to a tavern located across the bridge. It had not been stricken by the comet and was afforded some protection by the river, surrounded by a small pitch with no dry foliage to burn, nor trees to help the fires skip rooftops and devour the building.

The Red Dragon beguiled the Cymry, feigning that it was making ready to fly on to the destruction of some other country. Instead it reached its zenith, turned and plunged again towards the earth, in effortless free fall as a bird of prey.

Arthur held the last of the children in his arms; his outline was visible below a small arch in an anteroom where he might leap from the church, which was no longer the grey and brown of stone and oak but rather the whites and oranges, the blues, of angry coal. The mass of the celestial serpent rendered the summer's day pitch black once more, the tip of its tail making Gwent a wasteland. Witnesses saw a tall hooded figure absorb Arthur and the small child at the very moment that they were in turn absorbed by flame and ash. Arthur was absorbed by shadow.

***

As suddenly as judgment had come upon Britain, he was gone. Next came Eire, which looked as a burning lantern bobbing and rolling in the sea. Then the Dragon volleyed three-hundred-score balls of fire into the oceans, breaching the crust of the earth and the gates of the Deep. Volcanoes erupted and ash covered much of the earth. Though it was summer, a winter of ash and darkness beset the land - all lands, but especially the Isles in the Sea.

The new version of *dawn* came, and with it, some daylight. Reality was suddenly a dusk that gave way to darkness by noon time.

One thousand times one thousand Cymry were cremated by the Red Dragon.

But the luminary serpent rogue visited a death count much higher upon the Tribes of Lloegyr. What twenty years of repair and replenish had begotten (for these tribes had been located nearest the Saxon Shores during the war years and were yet recovering from decades of rape, plunder and butchery) was annihilated in the space of thirteen minutes. Two thirds of the population, dead.

The Northern invaders, were they organized

and intending to do the same, could have walked onto the whole of the eastern half of Britannia and simply settled it as their own. Conquest by Comet. However, thanks to the might of Maelgwn, the strategy of Merlin, and the leadership of Arthur, the Germans had no present intention. They were still not ready. Twenty years was not long enough to make enough fighting-aged boys and train them for another go at the undefeated Britons.

By fortune or chance, Cedric and his small kingdom of Wessex, which had been peaceful and kept the covenants placed upon it by the Silures, was not visited by the Red Dragon, who killed with the precision of a surgeon's blade but three hundred yards from the Saxon borders.

The songs of the bards recorded how the Summer Kingdom, born in December of the year five hundred and sixteen, received its first of three great death blows in June of five hundred and thirty-six.

Merlin had predicted and dreaded that the days of the Golden Age were numbered. In accord with his visions, he had hidden well the treasures, all of which survived and were safely concealed upon Ynys Enlli, save for the Grail, which was held on an island castle that was unharmed by the serpent's assault. As for evacuating or displacing the people, this was not possible. There was no preventing what came to pass, nor adding to the years of such a gilded age; rather only the redeeming cherish of the years that they had had.

And cherish them Arthur and his noble companions did, their sins and failings notwithstanding.

His land lay dying, but the High King lived.

How he had escaped the school, and who had

shielded and then carried him to safety, was a mystery.

Arthur was conducted to a teeny daughter isle called Flat Holm, where seventy guards kept rotated watch over him day and night without ceasing.

The cantrefs were full of disease and filth without exception. Taliesin and Illtud calculated that it would take two years or more to clean and remove the ash. A country filled with satins and silks and white marble where the architecture had been a bright and clean striking contrast against the greens and romantic overcast of Cymru was now simply and impossibly *dirty.*

The water supplies were poisoned, both by the Dragon's venom and by human waste. Illtud was a master of both sanitation and the mechanisms of sea and fresh water, and set about diverting bad water and cycle in good through a complex system of dykes and purification centers. But the process would be slow and arduous.

All of the Round Table Knights had survived. All princesses, princes, and chieftains too. Like Arthur, the renowned were forbidden from stepping foot upon the mainland, even if they had to be kept away by the edge of sword, or the tip of arrow.

The concern was twofold. First that the Dragon might return to finish his ugly work. Secondly, that disease or plague would eat the living and the dead.

The leadership was thus removed whilst the Dynion Hysbys, locally, and the Church, nationally, determined what must be done.

***

Simon Magus and his secret college watched the Isles in the Sea burn from an exceedingly high place in Tours.

"Is this the Tribulation, and the End of Days?" asked one of the Nine.

"If Israel had received Christ, then John the Baptist would have been—" He paused, demanding that his subordinates continue to demonstrate their understanding of the principle of 'delay' found throughout the Scriptures.

"Elijah," answered another.

"Indeed." Magus beamed. "Much remains to be seen - if the wandering luminary be Wormwood, or if we look for another."

"What must occur next?"

"Taliesin's *rapture*, I suppose." A mocking laughter by each of the Nine was as crackle and pop added to the flames. "The Cup of Christ: it must fall into the hands of the daughter of Pendragon, for the ancient evil that indwells her can bring again Judas Iscariot from his place, and put him within Arthur." Simon looked hard at the smolder and ruin of the Coveted Isles. "Much to manipulate and prepare, if that peculiar place is to rise from despair and bring forth a King of Kings." His excited breaths panged off the inner metal shell of the mask. "The Holy Grail must be found."

***

Three months later, The Holy Grail was found.

Though this be another bard's song, Peredur was there, and his mate Gwrgi too. But 'twas Rhufawn the Fair who achieved it. *And Vivien wailed sore and vexed herself nigh unto death that she could not prevent this.*

But Rhufawn did well with the burden of it at the first. He possessed it; it did not possess him. Taliesin's dread had just begun to be tempered when word came from the druids and the Dynion Hysbys.

It is a fearful thing when all sects and denominations agree. Unison typically means bad tidings and that confusion, or error, or superstition is running unchecked. Disunity and opposition provoke thought; dissent guards against the mob, contrarianism shields liberty.

There would be no dissent here.

"This is what it means to be free, to be ruled by the Law, to be subordinate to the people. We are but stewards and no overlords." King Meurig held Taliesin as a father holds a small child who has lost a parent, *or faces the loss of a son.* Tears and sweat rushed from every pore, the ground ran damp with his sorrow, and the great senior king minded not the mess. "Your Awen allows no possibility that it might work."

"None." The Christian bard had been forged hard by the Pauline Mysteries passed down from his family, and his worldview and belief demanded that the Grail was a dead idol at best, a thing allowed to be used as a toy for Satan at worst. But as an instrument for bringing miracles, this was a thing of times past and for Israel alone; no. This was contrary to the dispensational truth found in God's word. "It is an hour of grace, which demands it be an hour of faith and belief, not signs and sight."

"And the fiery beast that laid waste to field and stream, menaced village and castle, killed with indifferent discretion. Was he not a sign?" Meurig questioned the weeping sage with all sincerity.

"No." Taliesin's answer was immediate and

authoritative. "The heavenly beings run in circuits, declaring the veracity of the Creator from before men could read or write. In the principalities and dominions above something went awry, and the hosts of heaven rebelled." More weeping. "Merlin used mathematics to calculate the return of the wandering monster, not prophecy or sign or mysticism. Its cause is well known in that realm but to us, it was a random cataclysm. Chance."

"And God did not intervene."

"He could not."

"You flirt with blasphemy, or atheism." Meurig's voice flared.

"Grace looks like atheism, for it sees not an angel behind every sneeze, a sign under every rock. God intervenes not upon this crude matter." Suddenly, the bard clasped the brawn of Meurig's shoulder. "He has a plan for the living part of us, the *spirit*. He did not do this to us."

"And He didn't stop it either." Meurig doubted. "We have no choice, Taliesin. When I was incapacitated, they demanded that I retire. I had Arthur and he…" These words choked up the old king, leaving two men weeping. "And he has Rhufawn." Meurig gave Taliesin instruction that he find Lancelot and inform him that his son would serve as proxy in sacrificing Arthur to the land, in hopes that Arthur would rise again. The people would not wait for the Fall harvest.

Lancelot, along with Gwalchmai, were the only two Round Table Knights unaccounted for during the forced temporary exiles. Even many of the Royal Clans' animals and livestock were relocated to Brittany or to remote finger-islands unscathed by the catastrophe. Even Arthur's war dogs had been found, but the Hawk of May was rumored lost and none dared try and forcefully evacuate Lancelot.

***

However, the Hawk of May was not lost; he was spying on Lancelot, whom he crept upon as he slept beneath the bleeding Yew Tree, very near to the forest where he made his home.

The curls were still present, but the raven-black hair had given way to the look of polished silver coin. The eyes were yet the best of blues and the chin was still chiseled, now covered with a perfect short beard (though never cut, never trimmed, never groomed). Even as a hermit, Lancelot was magnificent.

"I hate you." Gwalchmai kicked at his wartime companion, who was in and out of sleep, or perhaps in a trance. The kick was playful, in part. "But I love you. Without you, we would speak the Saxon tongue, if we had breath to speak at all."

Lancelot rose, a towering menace, a bloodhound that durst not be provoked. "I hate you." The voice was a steel fork raking across a panel of brass. "But I love you. Without you, we would be a nation of slaves and no men. Better miserable and free than a fed slave." A moment of mutual glaring ensued. Lancelot's gaze, as steel, broke first as he caught a glimpse of Gwalchmai's wild red hair and freckled glow. Lancelot broke first, and embraced his Round Table fellow.

Crisis drives some apart; some it brings together.

"I would have killed you years ago, but—"

"Then my mother would have killed you!" Gwalchmai smiled. "You fear her."

"Precisely." The solitary warrior, oft alone save

his *others*, welcomed the jostling that only men-at-arms understand. "I do fear her. Moreover" – his tone turned thoughtful – "she and I are childhood friends. Real friends. Four cords we were, inseparable. She sacrificed much, and you are here because she set aside her own needs for those of her kinsman. Never could I harm the issue of the patriot and war goddess Gwyar, for I greatly revere her. And I greatly respect you."

Here then were Gwalchmai and Lancelot reconciled, and none present to witness it. For but one positive word, one report of good gossip, would have placed Gwalchmai on the throne, with Arthur's full blessing and with Lancelot's backing. Thus would the kingdom have been salvaged; thus would the Summer Kingdom have continued.

"What has become of our Blessed Isle?" Gwalchmai moaned.

"Would that I could find my foster-mother; she would know whether or not this is the end of the Age." Lancelot looked round – the forest was filthy with ash, the air barely breathable. "Give me leave to make some preparations and return unto me again at eventide, and we will set out to find the Lady of Lake."

"A quest for two old knights?" Gwalchmai beamed, and a single shard of sun fought desperately, breaking through the chalky sky.

Lancelot nodded.

Three minutes after Gwalchmai departed, Taliesin arrived.

***

"A full day for guests here at the edge of the world," the tall Briton snarked.

"It is good to see you too," the short Briton rebutted.

Seeing Taliesin's disposition, his bloodshot eyes and inability to look upward, Lancelot knew the tidings were poor.

"Gwenhwyfar - is she—?"

"The queen is safe. She was conducted to Leon in Brittany and her health is well, save that she grieves her father, whom the Dragon took."

"Was the body recovered?" Lancelot asked, hurting for his true love.

"Nay; amongst those disintegrated upon impact, a necklace charm alone remaining to indicate that it was he."

"I am very sorry to hear this." Lancelot clutched at the special cruciform about his own neck. "And Arthur?"

"He is ill, but yet has life, and has been put into exile until the air is again clean."

"The air will never again be clean," offered the king of the North.

"Our darkest days are not even yet, Maelgwn. We must endure."

Puzzled at the usually hopeful Taliesin's lack of optimism, Lancelot's questions of his random guest shifted to his children. The bard gave account of each of them, and then ran out of space for delay.

"And Rhufawn?"

"Your son, known home and abroad as the Perfect Knight, the chosen vessel, and the Galahad—" Taliesin's voice broke, and his words and thoughts became disorganized. "Arthur is sick. The Land is sick. Tribes fear starvation. Arthur is sick."

Maelgwn Gwynedd, on account of his unique and diversified upbringing, had had exposure to all the sundry religions and competing worldviews amongst the especially spiritual people of the Isles. When his madness pestered him not, he studied, and read, and studied more. More than a mountain of muscle and an insatiable male member, the complex person living as a hermit in a prison of his own sins and lusts fully understood the garbled nonsense of his former bard.

"He has achieved the Grail?"

"He has," Taliesin answered.

"And my mother?"

"We know not how it was achieved. Only that she shared our concerns for the young man and desired not these things. And is herself missing, feared taken by the Dragon."

A single sentence. A double loss. Maelgwn breathed it in, stopped breathing, and then exhaled violently. "The Lady of the Lake cannot be slain by some fire serpent; she lives."

"I hope you are right, and I believe the same." Taliesin drew some strength from Maelgwn's resolve, and verbalized what the Bloodhound Prince already knew. "Galahad has achieved the Grail, and he will heal the land, and be king." Maelgwn fully comprehended the layers of these words. "Arthur will never suffer this to be so." Taliesin did not argue the point, for he assumed that Maelgwn knew that Arthur was kept from the fullness of the ritual and would simply stop the ceremony when discovering its aim.

"When is the king-making rite?" Maelgwn asked.

"One full moon before the autumn harvest."

"That is a fortnight hence!" Dread overcame Maelgwn. Typically he could rapidly assemble his elite Hosts, but due to the calamity, he knew not where they were. And if a military action did usurp the will of the Tribes, what then? He would save his son and lose his people? An army acting arbitrarily and contrary to the will of the people is an army of despots. Would he save his son only to deliver the lad into a life of being an outcast in his own land? Maelgwn concluded that only Arthur could stop what was coming.

***

Arthur knew not what was coming.

When a proxy was selected for the Slain and Risen King rite, the dying king was not given to know anything beyond *the dying portion.* In this way, the casting-off of his old self was full and sincere. Often, the ruler would simply be told by his druids that he was being made to retire in favor of a younger successor, thus thinking that the ceremony was an abdication rather than a sacrifice.

The Dynion Hysbys and the sects of druids from Powys, from Deheubarth, and from Ynys Mon and the Old North were all of one accord about the carrying out of the rite in this manner. The minority sect of the Silures, to whom Taliesin's lineage belonged, agreed to remain silent, but abstained from participation or endorsement of the same.

But the Merlin Taliesin was tasked with delivering the message, along with Saint Illtud.

"You will abdicate your office as Pendragon."

"For Galahad?"

"Yes, lord."

"My heart hurts for Gwalchmai, but rejoices for Galahad. It is a fine selection. May the malice that plagues us pass, and a young man lead us yet into a brighter and better iteration of our Summer Kingdom." The sockets of the ailing king's sunken eyes were blackened, his face flushed and his countenance grim. Damage had filled his lungs when he had saved the children; his left knee was badly damaged, but mainly his vexation was melancholy for the suffering of his people.

Rhufawn, who was called Galahad, was a Christian Prince and had been reared on the Pauline traditions passed on to him from his mother's line, and from Taliesin. Thus, twisting of words and deception was required to convince him to enact the ritual.

Taliesin would not participate; neither Talhaearn the Elder (a retired, older bard who had mentored both Merlin and Taliesin), but they would not condemn the ceremony either. In their silent abstinence, the officiating fell to the Adder, the most influential of the local wise men who controlled and feigned representation of the Tribes.

A seasoned liar, he used many partial truths to gain Galahad's comfort.

First, there would be a sword pulled from a stone. The sword, 'down' and in the earth, represented a king's impotence and need for renewal. The meaning of this was softened and altered, presented to Galahad as simply meaning that 'hope would be renewed' should he be able to free the sword, hold it high and present it to the ailing king.

Secondly, the actor must be in water. Water was the source of all life to the Britons and held spiritual significance of great import. Thus, a floating platform supporting a great stone would be constructed for the two participants and the Adder.

Lastly, the Cup would represent agricultural

rebirth. The circle of the cup would represent the womb and its wine the placental blood of a new era. Moreover, the passing of the cup would represent fellowship, a type of oath or acceptance on behalf of the giver and receiver.

In Christian dressing, the cup was simply a vessel of healing, looking to the One who had first passed it ere He went and sacrificed Himself for His people.

Galahad could not be allowed to know that he was being made king, and Arthur could not be allowed to know that the ritual was more than an abdication. The shining prince thought he was presenting the cup and sword to an ailing king to bring hope for a return of the harvest and health (and many believed that the Grail might heal Arthur and the land as well), and the Iron Bear was made to understand that he was retiring in favor of a younger, qualified and ready man whose mother was a Silure and whose father was the greatest of all the Sons of Cunedda, that powerful line from the North.

Two actors operating on half-truths.

The darkest of pagan rituals, with a dash of Christian nomenclature and a pinch of benign symbolism, can pass for harmless without much difficulty.

The place of ritual was in Gwent, where the river passed by the very cave where Arthur had been *made king the first time.* This time, as then, many representatives and witnesses from the whole of Britain were present; the consummation of that ritual had been performed in a shadow and this one in the daylight. That first had finished with a crowning as king by the pious Bishop Dyfrig; this one would conclude with whatever the local shaman had for him. Cymru had been the first to claim Christ and the last to let go of the old gods. *A peculiar and wondrous people are we,* Arthur reckoned. For thirty and nine years he had reigned, twenty as War King, a decade and nine years as Giant Slayer. *And the sum of it as Child Executioner and Failure at Love.* The people had enjoyed the rest of peace, and the happy lethargy of plenty, but never truly the king.

Now his heart and mind were locked as behind an iron vault, scarred and numb, even to his own self, but it appeared that he welcomed the coming rest.

His only company for months had been his war dogs, the great mastiffs that were in height above some small horses, and the guardians of Flat Holm. He favored the company of the dogs, but the soldiers smelled better. *Now I understand why Gwen puts them out with the horses when I am away.* He wondered if she would be in attendance for the retirement ceremony. And his thoughts went to Mordred. Whereas criminals harbor dozens of minor secrets and sleep well, Arthur was a just and righteous man with very few secrets and slept poorly; for with secrecy it is magnitude and impact, and not quantity, that eats a man.

Will he use what he knows about Amr to promote himself, or shame me? Arthur distrusted the Whelp, and wondered if he was scheming or, like so many others, simply trying to find sustenance and clean shelter… and survive.

***

One moon before the harvest, at dawn, masses from every hundred, cantref, kingdom and Royal Clan gathered about the riverbanks of Gwent. Cedric had asked permission for his Gewissi to attend, and of Picts and men of the Emerald Island there were not a few. The clergy did all to Christianize the overtly heathen event, giving sermons and promising mercy from a just and concerned God. Here the first offerings to Mary the Mother of God were encouraged, and her favor from the heavens evoked.

Arthur was directed to wear black. He wore no armor; rather, long-sleeved, simple garb and boots. Sandy hair and a simple gold circlet were the only contrasting colors in his attire.

And he was made to wear an ancient black mask that represented death. Ghastly and beautiful, it was a bearded visage of horror itself.

Simple, black, death.

A custom suit of armor had been fashioned for Galahad. The style of Vivien's metal skin was retained, then enameled with white, over and over again. Every piece, every shell, every rivet was rendered white as a dove. Gold dust was added to the enamel and a large red plume fixed to the helm, which bore the fins and traits of a Pendragon. Similar in style to a Corinthian helmet, it was only cut and soldered at the nose, revealing the whole of Galahad's face from the cheeks down. There was no mask, as Galahad possessed the face of an angel, a living mask of the ceremony.

Galahad wielded a replica of his father's battle spike, save that it too was white-enameled. The stitching of both the Ravens of the North and the Bear Claw of the south decorated his cape, also in a white thread one shade removed from the host. The three rays of the Awen, stitched in gold, collared the front chest piece of the armor.

Ornate, white, life.

Arthur was unarmed.

The participants were forbidden to speak.

All of Arthur's famed companions were present; Bedwyr, Cai, Gwalchmai, Amwn Ddu, Caradog, Gaheris, Owain, Urien, Rhun, and scores more. Each of these had been carefully given a slight variation on the course of the day's events and none knew exactly how they ought to feel, nor what would be. The common man knew they were there to witness the Sacral Rite; but the leaders had been away, and were in confusion. The orchestration of lies begat an orchestration of silence... and inaction.

Maelgwn was there too, and greatly feared. He worried for his son, but knew Arthur would find a way to do right in the situation, *in any situation,* as he always had.

But Arthur did not know what right needed to be done, and Maelgwn understood this not.

Morgaine of the Faeries looked on as well, standing next to her son, Mordred, all the while being harassed by the Tylwyth Teg who, unseen to all others assembled, pulled at her skirt, poking and tugging her, begging in concert for her to *kill the Whelp, kill him now.* For all her powers, she could not stop the mouths of the tormenting spirits, so she rebelled against them by hugging her son tighter and tighter. A man of no affection, he accepted the hug as a person accepts tea – giving surface gratitude and then leaving the cup half full.

Gwenhywfar remained yet in Little Britain, convalescing on the estate of Gwythyr ap Greidawl, an ally to the Silures likened unto King Hoel.

The morning, as had been for nearly four moons, was an orange and yellow translucent fog, a lingering poison of congested despair. The

Adder would have to hasten the ritual lest he lose the support of the crowd, who would soon retreat to their homes or other shelter.

A low drum beat.

Rhythmic.

Borrowing from Illtud and Merlin's mastery of sound and its manipulation of the emotions, alertness and very directional thoughts and passions of men, the Adder's choice of musical accompaniment was the zenith of intentional drama.

The three stepped upon the platform.

Maelgwn emerged from the shade, positioning himself as close to the river as he could. Arthur saw him not.

Morgaine did the same.

"Speak the words," bade the shaman unto Galahad.

"Take," opened Rhufawn, full of the nerves of a youth giving his first public address; "this cup is the new testament in my blood, which is shed for you."

Arthur found no malice in the verse, thinking that Galahad spake of the Lord.

Galahad revealed the mazer, which he had encased in an iron egg-shaped protective case. The case was brilliant, covered in a mural of Bible scenes. The case ornate, the contents simple.

The crowd was awed, being witnesses to living history – seeing the Cup of Christ and one of the Treasures of Cymru in open display.

"If thou be the One, raise the sword." The Adder gave his line, scripted, expressions to match the drumming.

"What blade is limp and bound in the heart of the earth?" Galahad responded.

"King Arthur acts in the authority of the Three

Swords, but he possesses but two. Today, for the first time in the history of our Isles, and the world, one king will possess them all."

The sword of Troy! How did the Dynion Hysbys find it? And what other treasures upon my Ynys Enlli have been breached? Morgaine tightened her fists; the still waters became unsettled.

"I be the One to restore the land." Galahad believed he said these words in the stead of Christ: an honorarium, a prayer. He knew not that he was declaring his kingship.

Arthur took no offense, for another legend was being born in his view, another boy drawing a sword. Arthur coveted not his glory at the expense of others and enjoyed the success of all – even in his supplanting.

Galahad drew the Sword of Troy. The blade had been brought to the Isles by Brutus, given him by Aeneas, who fled as the Island of the Cymry's ancestors fell in flames on account of adultery and the greed and lust of princes and demigods.

The sword was a marvel. Like Excalibur, its hilt bore ancient script, and like Excalibur, it seemed to hum or sing when wielded. As the sword was freed from the stone, the platform floated away from the shore (whether by witchcraft or whether the Adder arranged it by tethers and pullies below the platform that were set in motion by the moving of the sword is debated by the bards, and known by none).

Galahad placed the sword laterally and flat upon Arthur's outstretched arms, in a pose of *receiving.*

"You and the land are one, my lord," said Galahad. "Drink and be healed."

Arthur's hands were full, so Galahad lifted up his mask and helped his lord drink, just as the

Jesus Christ had been helped to sip upon vinegar whilst on the Cross.

"Take up the sword again and drink, Galahad."

The lad did as instructed. And the power and kingship shifted to the new boy-king.

"The people would have Arthur continue as Pendragon for all seasons and all times," declared the Adder.

"Stop him!" Maelgwn was at once in the water, but the platform had gained overmuch distance and was too deep for the Bloodhound, who had to shift from running to swimming, and lacked time to reach his son.

"Rhufawn ap Maelgwn, you are forthwith king and Wledig."

"What?" The young man was confused, as the people cheered and horns and stringed instruments joined the drumming.

Then the drumming stopped.

"The king is dead!" cried out the Wise Man with evangelical heat. He then drew a sickle-shaped short knife across Galahad's throat. An instant and mortal gash; the white enamel, the stone, and the base of the platform were awash in hot red blood. "Without the shedding of blood there is no remission of sin" – the heathen mocked Scripture and Scripture's God – "long live the king! The perfect lamb has shed his blood for you, Arthur, and you are born again."

"Long live the king!" the mob shouted. The music resumed.

"Arthur!" Maelgwn reached the platform, his black-clad sovereign holding the dead hero Galahad in his arms.

"I knew not, I knew not!"

Suddenly the sun broke through, and the regular light of morning descended upon the river and the forest and the mouth of the cave.

"The boy achieved the Grail; Heaven accepted him and has healed our land!" The Adder basked in victory, and in real and timely actual sunlight.

Maelgwn wrested Rhufawn from Arthur and his eyes moved not from the king. His eyes were filled with rage. With hurt, with disbelief.

"I knew not," Arthur wept. "I knew not!"

Maelgwn could not slay Arthur or the devilish anti-druid, for the people rejoiced at the name of Rhufawn, which was all that remained and endured of Lancelot's son – for Galahad the Grail Guardian was no more.

CHAPTER 24
Despise Not the Wife of Thy Youth
The Seventh Seed

"Fornicating with his sister was meant only to traumatize the boy, creating a pathway into his soul, by which we could insert a spirit and possess him. That the deed brought forth a bastard maniac to be our pawn is just a delicious dividend!" No cackle can equal that cackle which is cackled in Italian. "I am so glad you have forgiven me my little *tongue* comment, and that we can again resume our Great Work, my Cymreig friend."

"And I'm glad you've graced our welcoming Isles yet again with your presence." The Adder knew well that Simon Magus hated Britannia, mostly for being made to sleep on hay and stubble, or else in mud, during his long seasons of confinement. They shared a common goal and a common enemy, but the anti-druid had no renewed affinity for the Professional Meddler in the Affairs of Men.

"Do you have one more activation spell in the workings?"

"If there be Giants left, I know not of one." The Adder was puzzled.

"No, no. We need to unleash a different monster." Magus schemed his schemed.

"Mordred?"

"Yes!"

"Not possible." The puppet protested against the puppet master.

"Why not?" Magus patronized with false patience.

"He fears Arthur. An unnatural, controlling fear that he thinks is concealed but is stained as a bright dye upon his visage at all times."

"Would the Weasel fear the Bear if he had a…" Magus, full of hubris, full of glee, playfully taunted. After much pause he revealed, "…A Bloodhound?"

"Maelgwn Gwynedd? He would put me to the sword or worse for my role in giving his son to the gods."

"The balances of power are tilted by Maelgwn Gwynedd. If the people reject Arthur and find that *he* advocated a proxy die in his stead under false pretenses when an actual heir was available... If they find he extended his reign through lies and manipulation, then will Galahad's death be in vain and his glory turned to pity or worse in the bards' songs. Then you will have your Bloodhound Prince. And with him his hosts, and with them, victory."

The Adder, seeing he was in the presence of a greater deceiver than he, acquiesced to the plan. Magus instructed him to convince Mordred to proclaim himself heir and, harvest or no, the rightful ruler in the stead of the fallen Bear of Glamorgan. Moreover, Mordred would be open and loud about being caused to live as the son of

Llew ap Cynfarch under false pretenses, as a ruse to plant yet another Royal from the South in the Northern lands of Cynfarch.

Though appalled at Mordred's origins, the plotters were sure that the majority would be more disgusted with the procreators than the procreated.

It was time that Mordred transitioned from a Whelp to a usurper and traitor.

With the promise of men and succor from both the cantrefs and kingdoms of the North, and of Mark's confederacy of rebels, and of Maelgwn himself, Mordred would have hope of vanquishing the undefeated Silures.

Hope of finally having the crown.

Hope of finally having Gwenhwyfar in the open.

***

The harvest did come.

A glorious, bountiful harvest.

Because of the mixing of words and imagery at the Sacral Rites, the Tribes knew not whether to celebrate Rhiannon, Arianrhod, Blodeuwedd, Jesus or Mary. Thus, they celebrated each of them and, in doing that, celebrated Arddu the Deceiver unawares.

The birth pangs of the Dragon entering the atmosphere had caused the temperatures to lower in spring, ruining the harvest; his fullness and battery of the Isles caused the temperatures to rise, bringing a temporary and false sense of plenty. In reality, the weather was erratic and the four winds, along with the circuits of the sun and moon, disjointed. But there were leeks and potatoes for cawl, and rhubarb for pies, and tiny glimpses of what had been had reappeared in less than two months' time.

Winter drew nigh, and Arthur determined to visit Hoel and to fetch his wife home from Brittany. Moreover, there were reports that Mark would harass Brittany once more before the fighting would give way to the cold. Thus, Arthur set to the channels with seven hundred upon his vessel.

And in his absence Mordred dropped the pebble of a rumor into a pond. It rippled, so he skipped a larger stone. It rippled yet more – a larger. And yet again the ripple swelled. Soon the rumor became a boulder and the subject of Arthur's bastard son a giant wave at high tide, becoming the sole subject of all discourse and gossip in every market, every Sunday assembly, every tavern and every place where men and women gather when itching are their ears.

***

"Please kill him, lady, I beg thee!"

"Why do you not cease to trouble me? I will not!" Gwyar bore the weight of sufficient burden in rehearsing her words, traveling north to confront her husband and confess that, though she had brought him many sons, his *firstborn* was in fact Arthur's. A repentant elf lacking gumption to act was the final stone stacked upon the scale. "Perhaps the only killing that need occur today is that I kill you."

The king of the Tylwyth Teg sighed. "How do you end the damned? Or destroy the accursed thing, lady?"

"Indeed," she seethed. "Which is why you and I will outlive them all, eh?" In her next breath, the elf was gone.

The Northern chieftain Llew ruled a region of the Old North in conjunction with his brother, Urien. Their grandfather, Meirchion the Mad, had called the area Rheged after his territory in Glamorgan in the days when the Silures had reappropriated Southern men for Northern princesses that the line of Cunedda might survive. As an elderly man, Meirchion begat Mark, making the enemy of Arthur Llew's uncle (though a significantly younger man).

Urien ranked amongst Arthur's closest allies and fondest friends. Llew became poisoned with fraternal rivalry and regional envy from his youth, and was devout about the Roman way. Under pressure that felt as if at the tip of a sword, he married into the household of Meurig and begat Northern sons with Southern blood. A brilliant political strategy. But such maneuvers, which work well on ink and parchment, impact real people who, like Llew and Gwyar, have empty or even malicious relationships.

As soon as the children were put to fosterage, Gwyar left Llew to return to her craft (and to look after Arthur), and the couple only made appearances as were meet for public and political needs.

Still, Llew was as all men. And all men hate the notion of being lied to about matters of loins and lovers.

Gwyar entered the hall of her hilltop estate and walked, shoulders pulled back and chin up, to face Llew face-to-face, though the tip of her head only reached his navel.

Jealousy and shame beget false bravery, and false bravery impulse, and impulse begets death.

With no exchange of words, no argument, accusation, consideration or investigation, the grandson of Meirchion the Mad became mad himself and slapped Gwyar hard across the face, sending the slight Fae violently backward and to the ground.

Gwyar went down; Morgaine came up. Looming as a tower above the impulsive chieftain. The primal witch rose such that she had to stoop her back to avoid breaching the vaults of the hall. Llew had known, as he let his hand fly, that death was sure. His wife was the daughter of Meurig and Onbrawst, or Meurig and the Devil, or Onbrawst and Satan. There had ever been something wrong with her, always something otherworldly.

In the twinkling of an eye, Morgaine had recoiled and reshaped - was tiny again.

Loyalty.

Fidelity.

Honesty.

How would you feel if you were a man and the boy you raised as your own was sired by another?

Morgaine came down and Gwyar came up. She suffered the strike, a bloodied lip the fair wage for forty years of false pretense.

"I am sorry, Llew." She turned and made her leave of Rheged, departing for Ynys Enlli where she might hide the Grail. Her brother had hastily handed it to her while he and Maelgwn squirmed and slipped, scrambling in a pool of Galahad's blood, laboring in vain to stop the fount from his neck and revive the lifeless boy.

As a result, the very person who must not bear the Cup possessed the same, Simon's plan positioning and posturing by both chance and intention.

***

Word of Mordred's machinations had not reached

Brittany by the time Arthur and his troops arrived in Leon. The weather was bitterly cold, and all bore layer upon layer of skins and caps in an effort not to freeze. Every hearth was ablaze and additional copper basins were placed throughout Gwythyr's castle, mobile fire pits that were fair to look upon, and functional besides.

Arthur saw his wife, bundled in white furs, as an adorable bunny, the flames flickering in her magical eyes, and he fell in love with her afresh.

She was indifferent to his coming, and rather enjoyed the rolling estates and Breton wines. *But she longed to see Mordred or Lancelot as an acceptable second. For this reason alone she was glad to see her escort home. And happier still when she learned that he was only come to greet her and would stay behind to lend support to Mark.*

"I heard your knee was injured and that you were restricted in breathing. Are you certain you should do this? Would that you were home instead." She kissed the king as she lied and flattered, knowing how alluring she looked, and how he looked upon her. *For often it is more attractive to conceal rather than to reveal.*

"Hard as iron and ferocious as a bear, love." Arthur used jovial wordplay with his own name.

"I see this," she remarked. "You appear as born again." These words were used to inflict a stab of pain upon Arthur, *for this is the operation of those who abuse; first with flattery, then with insult.* For she knew well that Arthur was born again; under the coming of the Red Dragon, from the bloody sacrifice of the innocent came the *new Bear* in the worldview of the Tribes. Such a thought was awkward and repugnant to Arthur, the death of Galahad haunting a man who was now twice afflicted in his soul by rites and rituals.

Before he could hold his untoward spouse accountable for her subtle strokes, Gwythyr presented himself, throwing an enfolding embrace about the Pendragon.

Hoel was present as well, and these two were the foundation and backbone of Brittany. Cousins to the Cymry, but with their own cultural style and sophistication, it was *as being home but not, the same but different* for Arthur and his kinsmen. And they greatly loved the Bretons.

The discussions soon shifted to battle strategy and how that they must prepare for one more strike from Mark prior to the fullness of December causing all men to stay in the warmth of their homes. If it was not the return of the *war days*, then it was surely nigh, for the conversations, preparations and emotions took Arthur back to those legendary times where Saxon fell to Briton sword again and again. The threat itself invigorated the aging sovereign, who was fifty-and-three, talks of strategy causing him to miss his Merlin exceedingly.

A young woman rested her shoulders along the railing of a spiral stairway, carved of ivory, etched with knotwork and sigils, a story above those gathered in the great hall. She enjoyed the cold and allowed her yellow locks to serve as her only cap; they fell gracefully over her shoulders. A princess, aged twenty-and-three years and never wed, she governed the home and estates of her father, Gwythyr. His land holdings in Brittany were massive and she his only heiress. The people loved her and put a twist upon the name of their region; feminizing it in honor of their future queen, they called her Gwenhwyfar, the queen of Lyonesse.

Hers was a natural beauty, equal in allure yet

opposite in nature to the High King's wife. Her beauty emanated from her soul and her character first, her bosom and form secondly.

Gwenhwyfar ferch Gwythyr had never met Arthur, always missing the chance, being at the market or some assembly, misfortune delaying the occasion. Like every person alive, she knew of the living legend by his legends, but longed to meet the man, whom she somehow loved ere they met. She found his eyes amongst the hundreds of skins and cloaks bustling below. She looked into them, and loved him so.

But though he looked directly at her, he noticed her not, his troubled affection and affliction fixed still on Gwenhwyfar the daughter of the Giant, who was making her departure and would soon be back in Caerleon, betraying her husband with one of his own house.

Mordred grew emboldened, making passionate speeches how that his *father* had authored the ruse to keep himself on the throne in spite of the calamity that ravaged the land, how he proclaimed a false freedom erstwhile putting restrictions on the Dynion Hysbys that violated their rites, and their rights, and the same allegation made he on behalf of the Catholic Church. Moreover, he promised that he would place his sons, born of Kwyllog ferch Caw, on the throne for generations to come, finally restoring the North to a position of equality and prominence.

His seductions found willing bedfellows amongst many of the sons of Caw, and among the lines of Cynfarch, not a few. But many of those houses rejected the Whelp, seeing his treachery from the beginning.

In all, approximately two of ten from those of age and ability to fight joined unto Mordred.

Sufficient to be branded an insurrection; hardly enough to ignite a revolt, or a civil war. *Maelgwn and his Hosts would be needed to draw men unto Mordred, and his treachery would be quickly crushed.*

Mordred had drawn no sword, had scorched no farm, harmed not the hair of one child of Glamorgan. Thus far it had been a volley of words and accusations and no arrows.

Gwenhywfar II was overfilled with joy, singing and laughing aloud, celebrating that her paramour had finally found the stones to do what he ought to have done nearly two decades ago. *Finally! I have years of love yet to give King Mordred, though it be during the dusk of my years.* Of paramount import was that she keep great distance from the Traitor, that none suspect him at the last. They forsook engagements in their forest, avoided the farmhouse, the tiny apartment and the chapel (all places marked with the fluids of their betrayal time and again through the years).

But as her joy begat burning lust, Gwen could no longer contain herself, and took quill and ink to parchment, expressing whimsical, youthful love and naughty and explicit demands of her longing.

As Gwenhwyfar's sister, Gwenhwyfach, was wed to Mordred, she was able to use the cover of suing Mordred for peace in the stead of her husband, and for the love of her sister, to send the letter. Mordred would bring troops and would meet in public feigning discussions of good faith with the Round Table Fellows then, under the blanket of winter night, would steal away unto the bed of Gwenhwyfar.

The Deceptress informed Bedwyr and Bishop Bedwini of her course, and they found the maneuver stately and profitable, hoping that the softer words of women would quell the hotter, more impulsive aims of men.

Finding relief that she didn't have to dispose of another messenger, she sealed and released the letter.

Seven days later, one hundred of Mordred's newly formed army, mostly Ravens, met below Lodge Hill on an open plain that lay between the amphitheater and the hilltop fort. If desired, the Silures could have descended from the fort and slayed the rebels in the space of minutes. That Mordred had agreed to meet in a place of obvious and easy slaughter was an act of peaceful posturing, or overt arrogance. *Or, alternatively, that his wife had forced him to meet there.*

Bedwyr brought only fifty, Gwalchmai, Cai and Peredur amongst them.

Both armies were mounted upon steed and met 'line to line' on the pitch.

The Adder served as a dark Anti-Merlin to Mordred, and stood in the midst of the men, salivating to assist with Mordred's allegations and assertions as opportunity yielded him. But it was Gwenhywfar's meeting, so he let her speak first.

But she could utter but three words of welcome before her sister was upon her.

"Please read this aloud, sister." *Gwenhwyfach had discovered the letter.*

"Before you do that, might I speak?" A metal-skinned god interrupted.

"Lancelot!" Bedwyr rejoiced.

Mordred's own men were instantly deflated. As King Arthur had calculated that he might be long at war, and as rumor of Mordred's insurrection had reached his ears, he had evoked an old promise betwixt the strained and troubled friends.

"I too have received written charges: that I

might be Protector of this kingdom whilst our lord is on the Continent. Apparently the Iron Bear finds this weasel a real threat to we Undefeated. I see it not," Lancelot goaded. "But a promise is a promise and here I be, my Hosts with me." Suddenly seventy more *Lancelots* filed in behind their commander, a troop that would cause the fabled Spartans to quake, the Romans to run. The Hosts of Maelgwn were the reason the Britons had remained so long impenetrable. And they gave appearance of rest, sharpness and hunger – for battle.

As for himself, Mordred was but a doll or lifeless piece of furniture on this day. His wife had intercepted the love letter and threatened to hand deliver it to Arthur if he did not comply with the place and course of the meeting. The affair was soon to be found out; moreover, the Lancelot had joined with Arthur, despite the Adder's promises to the contrary. *We underestimated the mad knight's sense of duty and commitment to his own words.* Now Mordred was living as a dead man, moment to moment, gulping for one more, one more breath at a time.

Lancelot's arrival pleased Gwenhwyfach all the more, and she hoped to see his Hosts make a quick meal of Mordred's wretches.

"Welcome, King Maelgwn Gwynedd. I am certain our Lord Arthur is pleased to have you back in Caerleon. As I am sure my sister the queen is to be under your protective wings, my angel." Gwenhwyfach flattered *the difference-maker*. "Now, sister, please take and read."

Gwenhywfar was indignant, feared nothing and, much like Simon Magus, always held out for a way out. "It is not for the High Queen to receive orders, but rather to give them."

"Read it!" her sister barked.

Gwenhywfar II repeated her stance. And then yet again the third time.

Frustrated that the Adulteress would not confess her crimes before all, Gwenhwyfach struck Gwenhywfar hard upon the jaw.

To smite a queen or king in public is an act of highest treason by the ancient laws and customs of the Cymry. The act represented more than the deed itself, and was a stroke against the king, who *was the people*. This type of rebellion wrought chaos and disorder and tyranny, and could not be abided or given place or grace.

The Adder ran to Gwenhywfach's aid, hoping to find words to defend her and regain control of the situation, *which was about Mordred shaming Arthur for his incest and lust of power and manifold sins, not the squabbles of women!* But his coming forward was mistaken as aggressive, as an assault against Bedwyr's line to follow Gwenhwyfach's blow. Perceiving the same, Cai unfastened the leather strap that fixed his double-headed battle-axe to the back plate of his armor. In but two movements the axe was in hand and the Adder was cleaved in twain, spilling his guts upon the plain.

Here then, *the slap and the slaying of the Adder* were the second death blows to the Summer Kingdom.

Bravely, but in vain, Mordred's men rushed Bedwyr's line, perceiving that they must fight desperately or perish, being put under the shadow of a military fortress in enemy lands by the foolishness of women. The battle was no battle; rather a ten-minute training exercise for the Silures and their allies, the Hosts of Maelgwn. As Briton was fighting Briton, quarter was extended where possible and deaths were few. Mercy was given, and mendable broken bones took the place of death strokes. In the fracas of fighting Mordred put dagger to his own wife's back, seized the queen, and fled the battle, riding hard, harder still until he reached Arthur's very own home.

And Lancelot seized the letter, crumpled upon the frozen ground, listless as the dead lass next to it.

***

"It is over. Our life ends at the conclusion of this pretended abduction." Gwenhwyfar was realistic, and hopeless.

Mordred had declared Arthur false and taken his wife *prisoner,* and the people scoffed and mocked the move. Troops were assembled and besieged the chamber where he held her. Making contrived threats to put her to death, he sued Arthur to come and meet him; battle man to man, father to son.

The scandal of Arthur having a secret son by his sister had fermented and the nation wanted to hear of it from their king. Thus, they desired that he come home and face Mordred and the people.

Illtud and Bedwini distanced themselves from the situation, using the occasion to speak against heathen rites, and the druids claimed ignorance and misfortune in the stead of perversion at the selection of Gwyar to lie with her brother during his king-making. Many called for the deposing of both men due to the scandal and shame of it all, creating an open throne for this interest or that interest. At once the notion of Arthur as the *forever king* was losing its appeal, and the oldest of rivalries between North and South intensified. Smarter men than Mordred, such as Llew and Caw, could use the king's bastard as an instrument of great gain, and then discard the Whelp. And these sent emissaries and some soldiers to Caerleon, hoping to negotiate and ask for peace on his behalf, blaming his deceased wife for starting the skirmish.

Mark's latest surge quelled and, Leon-Brittany secured, Arthur braved dreadful winter seas, hastening home to his seat of power, which was occupied by another.

Rumors of the letter were confused and disjointed and fell unto Arthur's ears as written from his wife *to Lancelot*. This, and not nephew Mordred acting out as an insolent youth recently drunken at the knowledge of inheritance, dominated Arthur's every thought. Such was his rage that the frosty air and icy water was unnoticed; he could have swum across the channel, propelled by forty years of jealousy and misplaced adoration.

He stood quite alone, insisting upon solitude as the vessel cut through the waters, approaching the confluence of sea and freshwater – the inlet mouth artery that would ultimately take him to Caerleon. It was early morning, prior to the rising of the sun, and he stared upon the waves, his thoughts about Lancelot inside his wife in one instant, his approach to defeating Lancelot again in the next. Lancelot's marbled chest upon her painted frame in one thought, Arthur's spear opening the marble in the next.

He was quite alone with the racing thoughts. Then a familiar voice came, originating somehow from the rush and ebb below: *Foolish is the man who judges a matter before he heareth it,* and a moment later, *By the mouth of two or three witnesses let all things be established.*

"The cold tricks my brain. My lost wizard counsels me from the sea," he said, to no one and to any who might be eavesdropping. Still, the proverbs tempered the Iron Bear just enough that he pinched a thread of reason, a hair of patience, that would last until he was come into his own country.

'Twas Lancelot himself that met him on the bridge o'er the Usk.

Arthur's salutation was with his fists.

"You lay with my wife *AND NOT AS PUPPIES IN LOVE AT SCHOOL*; you who are Protector and First Knight, you are as my Judas Iscariot!"

"When one or more are involved in delivering a message, you can be sure that its meaning and intent will be changed thrice." Maelgwn remained calm. In this instant, Maelgwn had kept his head more so than the typically temperate and logical king. Maelgwn *knew* that it was Mordred and not he whom the queen favored, that his one true love would have neither of the *four cords*, that his heart was desperately foolish and vain. Yet he looked to Arthur's feelings, as the overmuch sadness over Galahad and the truth about Gwen and Mordred had softened the warrior, giving him introspection as substitute for power and lashing out in raw emotion.

But Arthur was in a different state. And was landing meaningful blows.

Risking injury, Lancelot did tackle and subdue the Iron Bear.

"I love the queen with all of me," he said plainly. "You know this."

"You mock me! Stand and fight, else unhand me, else strangle and slay me!" Arthur gave screaming, desperate orders.

"I touched her not. I honored thy bed, my lord!"

"I dined with the king of the Picts. I KNOW you killed men as a ruse and that you lodged with her in his lands."

Arthur was five times smarter than any man and could indeed see through any conspiracy. But he had no way of calculating that the abduction of Gwenhwyfar, that her subsequent seduction, had been arrested and that honor had been upheld. The appearance of evil was too great. Maelgwn opted for cold and abrupt honesty. He controlled the left arm and head of Arthur in a side lock, using the force of both as a type of triangle, and squeezed with heavy pressure and much leverage, forcing Arthur to listen.

"I did abduct the queen, I did take her to my stronghold in Pictland, I did falsely accuse a rival tribe and lay her kidnapping at their charge, I did lead my sons to victory and in the slaying of many painted men on account of my lies. For this, do unto me as you would according to our customs. But when the moment came that I might know her, the Merlin came, and stopped me. And I love you, and stopped myself."

Arthur was losing air, but managed to continue cursing.

Maelgwn released him and rapidly went for the crumpled letter, scribed in Arthur's wife's own hand. "Read this." Maelgwn absorbed another punch, clean to the nose. "Read this, Bear, please."

More cursing and punches.

Read it! A familiar voice descended and swirled as a cone or whirlwind about both great men. Arthur relented. And read.

After a long pause, Arthur looked towards his

estate, still filthy from the calamitous debris.

"She has enchanted and bewitched you the whole of your life, hasn't she?"

"Longer than even I understand, my king."

"It is Mordred whom she loves, in the comfort of my own home, in the heart of my own lands." Arthur's face was as stone. Maelgwn had been in twelve major battles with Arthur, and more than sixty minor conflicts, and this look – this look he had never witnessed. This was Arthur's authoritative death look tenfold.

Maelgwn prayed the look was directed at Mordred and not Gwenhwyfar.

"She is a troubled creature from our youth, Bear," Maelgwn offered.

"We all have night terrors, we all wrestle with devils. She owns her actions, as do you, as do I." Arthur straightened his attire and made for his estate. "Come, Lancelot, I know a secret way into my bedchamber. I've used it for years."

"You and your disguises." A friendly, brotherly smile.

"Don't worry about a few dozen Picts, my First Knight; come with me."

Arthur *loved* his disguises, secret passages, minor escapes from the stresses of governance and simulation of other characters who suffered not from unrequited love. As a result, he knew of three different means of accessing not only the mansion that contained his and Gwen II's bedchamber, but also a covert entrance into the bedchamber itself.

Chieftains and priests and bishops had gathered, wanting to negotiate the return of Gwenhwyfar and the voluntary surrender of Mordred. The matter was exceedingly complex. He was the king's son (if the rumors were true, and Gwyar had validated them with the brevity of her repentance towards her estranged husband) – his first son. As a result, he had rights under ancient codes and customs. He was also a traitor, a usurper, a claimant to the throne. The magnitude of the situation brought an uneasy curiosity and fascination to the assembled renowned, those given charge to manage such things.

Knowing all this, and that none were to soon barge in upon them, Mordred put the vigor of a lifetime of lovemaking into one encounter. Their time together was at once animalistic and romantic, gentle and hedonistic, an explosion of lust and a conduit of sweet, truest love. Mordred had bound his mistress queen to a bed post, thrusting and pounding upon her from behind, exploring all that her painted body offered, when Arthur and Maelgwn burst through a secret door connected to the anterior of a large wardrobe closet.

Arthur saw her pleasure. Her satisfaction. Her involvement. Her vulnerability. Her ecstasy.

Maelgwn, on this day, was the wiser, forcing himself to look away.

Mordred pulled himself out of the queen, gathered trouser, then dagger, which he turned upon Gwenhwyfar's throat.

"Ready for more blood, Father?" Pupils black, eyes black, soul black. "Step back, or you will be the widowed king."

In spite of the open betrayal and blatant encroach of living decades of lies, Arthur loved Gwenhwyfar, as did Lancelot.

Maelgwn touched Arthur upon the forearm. "Let them run. In the end, where will they go? The law rules in Caermelyn."

"Caermelyn is fallen." Arthur transcended

hurt; his visage said *butchery and revenge.*

Maelgwn did all to help. "You are Caermelyn, lord. And you yet breathe. We have survived Saxons, and Giants, and monsters indescribable. We WILL survive this scandal. You are King Arthur. She never loved either of us. Let it go. Let the law judge them."

"I must have audience with my wife," said Arthur.

"My lord?" Maelgwn responded, confused.

Arthur ignored Maelgwn momentarily. Turning to the couple before him: "You would no more harm her than would he." He pointed to his First Knight. "So go on." A judgment dwelt in Arthur's eyes that were as from God Himself. "Go on; run. What befalls you both will be far from here."

Mordred needed no further encouragement or warning, and scurried from the chamber as a rat scurries from a well-lit barn.

Arthur returned to his friend. "It was never you; it was he. The golden-armored boy who has ever coveted my crown and, now we know, my wife besides. I charge thee, best of all knights, I charge thee remain as Protector for a time yet. To Gwenhwyfar the First I must."

"As you wish, my king," Maelgwn answered, knowing he would disobey the mandate, and closely following the Iron Bear. Maelgwn was numb, but his bubble and his *others* harassed him not. On this day he was more stable than Arthur, who saw much and bore too much more.

Gwenhwyfar I's cell had survived the comet; the adjoining school-house had not. A light snowfall covered the ruin, which was but a foundation stone and four or five charred bits of wood. An aroma of despair lingered and visiting the place was not desirous, let alone abiding there. But there she abided. The crimson-haired ghost. Her lodging included a narrow, short bed with drawers built into the frame, a small table that could accommodate two children at study or tea, and a basin. In the cell a simple iron cross engraved with knotwork hung upon the east wall. These and a few gowns were the sum of the queen's possessions.

"I knew you would come," she said, her lips tightened as one concealing a great secret that everyone already knows.

"Well, you stole my sword."

"That I did." She smiled. Gwenhywfar I was full of wisdom and foresight. In the chaos of calamity, hearing though gossip that he had ceased to wield it, she had hazarded her life to retrieve, and protect, the Sword of Power.

"How did you know?" asked an inquisitive former spouse.

"Women know things."

They shared this moment and a few moments more. The subject of Llacheu and Amr was never mentioned but her grief, now twenty years on, was fresh as the morning's snowfall and just as unyielding. Finding the right moment, she took her husband by the hand. "You aren't here for Excalibur, are you, Bear? Rather a man of routine, you are here for hugs and holding, for consent's embrace."

"Yes; I come for your strength ere I…" He could not say it.

Where men falter, women have an anchor of resolve. She made the words for him. "You must kill another son."

He broke into sobbing, more for the memory of past trauma than future duty.

The wife that Arthur had put away held him tight. She then reached below the blankets of the bed upon which they sat and revealed a long object, wrapped in white silk, tied about both ends. Loosening one end revealed the hilt.

"Kill that bastard with this, forgive yourself, and wield *your sword,* my king."

Arthur beheld Excalibur as if he were again fourteen, seeing her glow for the first time.

"In the next world, when this office is done with me and we are but man and woman, mother and father, and friends—"

"Then I will see you out and claim you as all. You are a man just and righteous. Get thee now once more and one last time; do what only you can do."

Arthur embraced the wife of his youth once more and set out to pursue Mordred and Gwenhywfar II.

He knew exactly where they were bound and, after a few hours trailing Arthur on the path, so did Maelgwn.

Dread found Maelgwn early in the journey, for he could calculate all the outcomes, and none were good. *Mìgeil. They make for Mìgeil. She thinks it is her refuge and salvation, but knows not that Arthur discovered our lies! The Pictish king will either refuse their passage or kill them on the spot.* Maelgwn felt in his sinews that Gwen was fleeing from arrest in Caerleon to execution in Alba. *And I will stop it.*

Accompanying Arthur were Cai, Bedwyr and the Hawk of May, his *famed Giant Hunters.* And the dogs that she so loathed were leading the way.

***

"They venerate Maelgwn as a god, and they will protect me." Gwenhwyfar half believed her own words. "And I will protect you."

The forbidden couple knew their plight was dire, and chances of success grim. By fleeing they solidified their guilt; by fleeing they cut themselves off from Mordred's remaining loyal men; by fleeing they put themselves at the mercy of the painted warriors from Alba. After four days of hard riding and no food they arrived at the very tower where Lancelot had passed his test, where he had not done what he would have done, where loyalty to Arthur had overcome lust. *Would Arthur's loyalty to the law overcome rage?* Gwen's only aim was to extend her days, through hiding, then trial, then negotiation, then escape. Escape by way of a window or secret passage, or escape by way of a noose or blade, it mattered not. *Extend my days. Live as I please. And when I can extend them no more, escape.* She hungered; weak and dehydrated, she swooned and slumped forward on her horse.

Mordred sensed that the sentinels at the remote village gates were too complicit in giving them passage. Slender, muscular, half-naked men smeared in white paint, wearing the skins of Fisher Cats, the frightful guards were too calm, too accommodating, too easy. Assured that the safe haven was no such thing, and placing no trust in Maelgwn's year-old promises of sanctuary and safe conduct for his past lover, the bastard son of King Arthur did what was in his nature to do. Kissing his mistress, yet unconscious, upon her brow, he whispered, "Do your wiles to again manipulate your husband, and survive this if you may, my love."

Doing what cowards do, Mordred slithered

away into the Caledonian Wood, preparing to battle winter as preference to Arthur's sword or Cai's club. He lit a fire for Gwen and placed her gently upon three bear skins. He made a fire and looked at her, in deep sickly sleep in the very spot where Lancelot had almost had her. He looked back once more, and vanished.

Three hours later Gwenhywfar roused to a sound she'd suffered for years. Barking. Howling. A deep but whimpering bark. A bark that sounded like the moaning words 'I love you, I love you'. Hundreds of times - nay, by the thousands - she had been forced to hear the cursed 'I love you' bark. Wits not yet gathered, she sat straight up, confused, thinking she was home.

"Arthur, else Cai, come and put these cursed dogs to the stable! Filthy wretches all, would that they were put to the butcher!"

The dogs were there, but she was not home. This she realized after her half-asleep yell had already been ejected from her lips.

"The dogs. No. He is here." Tears began to stream. She yelled for Mordred and ran to the arched windows, then onto the tower ledge. "Mordred!" she screamed and screamed and screamed. Into the December night, her cries were void. Below she saw them. The dogs. The cursed, damned dogs.

The hot breath of a man well rested, full of strength, fuller of cider and with the authority of God suddenly whispered upon her neck, clutching both of her wrists in the same action. "Have you the Sight, mistress? Did you always know they would feast upon thy painted flesh, that they would pluck and pop and play with your copper-speckled eyes? YOU are the dog—"

"Please, no—"

"And the dog returns always to its own vomit!" Arthur used the leverage of Gwenhwyfar's wrists, turning them in on themselves; they crackled and snapped. Then he flung her from the tower as a maid tosses a bag of rubbish.

She landed far below, slamming down upon her stomach, her spine severed, resulting in paralysis, adrenaline mitigating the pain. This made her aware of when the first dog took a section of calf muscle, and when a second shook loose her foot.

Arthur's war dogs feasted on the cheating queen, the king himself looking down from above, as God looking down on Satan being cast to the bottomless pit. His obsession, his lust, his love, the object of many of the troubles that befell both the man and the kingdom, was bones and chunks below.

He saw her first.

He saw her last.

King Arthur didn't see Gwalchmai dying; rather he only heard the gurgle, and the thud.

Maelgwn had tried to stop Arthur. His battle dirk swirling and ready, he meant to clip the king behind the shoulder blade, causing a minor wound but incapacitating him with sufficient time to rescue the queen. It was a maneuver both men had executed ten score times when training or when desiring prisoners instead of corpses. There was no intent of injury.

But the Hawk of May could not discern Maelgwn's aims in the flicker of snow and sleet and minimal light within the small turret. He saw Maelgwn making the stabbing motion towards the Pendragon and, lacking time to draw either of his famed twin blades, threw himself between Maelgwn and Arthur.

The spike went through Gwalchmai's back. Though layered with manifold skins and coats, the killing instrument breached his heart. The blood was minimal, else hidden by his attire, and death quick. One death rattle and a free-fall to the broken, rocky floor below.

Arthur had judged Gwenhywfar by intent, and Lancelot had killed Gwalchmai by accident.

Here was delivered the third deathblow that wrought the fall of the Summer Kingdom.

Arthur drew Excalibur, and Lancelot assumed the diagonal fighting stance of the Britons. Both titans grit their teeth; the Bear versus the Bloodhound Prince.

Cai and Bedwyr, lagging but moments behind, rushed upon both men, beseeching the Picts to help them as well. At last nine men subdued the two, preventing further bloodshed. Lancelot freed his neck from the great vines that were Cai's arms and, though unable to strike out at the king, achieved a clasp of his cloak. Pulling Arthur close, so close that the tickle of spray and spittle of words was upon the king's cheeks, so near that Arthur was able to smell the salt of Lancelot's tears, Lancelot said, stoic and devoid of emotion:

"Now you will have your Civil War."

CHAPTER 25
The Winter of Magic's Return

Arthur revitalized himself at the baths in Caerleon, the springs cleansing him of blood and grime, but doing naught to wash away tears or pain. After, he retired to the library, where he hoped to redeem a moment to himself to think about what lay ahead.

He fell into a familiar chair at a long reading table, the top of which was worn as a smooth stone by his very own elbows from years of childhood study. *How my Merlin made me read, then read more. But woe, there is no writ for this calamity!* He gazed upon at the scrolls, the single papyri, the bound books stacked to heights where only owls and bats could read them. *But I have read them,* he reflected.

He was not long at reflecting when the wind blew and the doors were flung open. Many parchments protested the dramatic force by rolling from the table, while three large tomes crashed upon one another, making chaos of Arthur's favorite shelf.

The king, wearing his midnight blue trousers and tunic, didn't look towards the door, assuming Cai was simply overzealous in rushing in to look upon him, as was his caring but clumsy custom. Instead, the Iron Bear remained fixed on his books, preparing to chide, utter a desperate holler, a demand for a moment of solitude.

"War King. If there is to be a war, there must be a—"

"War strategy," Arthur responded by rote.

"War strategy." The coned traveling cap of a wizard, grey and worn, was flung upon the table, spinning and landing upon Arthur's hand. A humorous jest Arthur had witnessed two hundred score times, each time followed by profound words or esoteric lessons. Dust flew. The wind rushed. Night-time critters howled.

Arthur's ears had been fooled before, and his eyes, by visions he could not trust. Reluctantly, he touched the cap. 'Twas real. His posture straightened, though he felt faint; his mouth dried and his heart stopped. He touched the hat again, twisting and folding it; then he allowed himself to look.

"Merlin!"

THE ARTHURIAD VOLUME THREE

THE MISERY OF
MORGAINE

God versus the gods
North versus South
Champion versus King
Father versus Son

The Battle of Camlan

ZANE NEWITT

'Prince Llew, forced to fight alongside a man whom he raised as his own but revealed to be sired by another.

The Northern Chieftain Caw's favorite child adores the South and is historian and scribe for the very Throne he would usurp.

Urien strains to slay his own brothers and kinsmen, else turn on the king.

Maelgwn to take arms against the man who slaughtered his love, and in so doing ally with the man whom his love loved.

Gwyar to avenge Gwalchmai's death, but in doing so cause another son to fall; else to watch her brother perish.

Roman Catholics to fight their rivals, but join with heathens.

The Church of the Britons to see the burgeoning yoke of Rome break, but the tax is joining with Druids and Witches.

King Arthur of the Cymru to protect the Tribes from splintering into two weak principalities, ceasing to be one nation. And then, once weakened by division, ceasing to be altogether; for the Long Knife is rested.

One more traitor to execute, one more villain to fell.

To kill a third son, or to see tyranny consume the Land.

With such impossible conflict, does it not become needless? With so many weeds and entangled loyalties and deceptions, ought not they neutralize and cancel one another, revealing another way to find reconciliation, or restitution?

But alas, evil men have struck the spark, and mortal men must burn in their desires to make war over one another. Thus Civil War for the Cymru is embroiled.'

Dr. Zane Newitt
Fall, 2019

'The Strife of Camlann in which Arthur and Medraut fell and there was plague in Britain and in Ireland…' Annales Cambrae

PROLOGUE I
Authority Obeys the Dying King

Markings glowed, a flashing ember of mystical letters upon the hilt. From Eden to Avalon, through time itself, it sang haunting warnings to its wielder. *Cast Me Away. Cast Me Away!*

"Fling it not! Yield to it not! Stay it within thy hand!" Morgaine of the Faeries: a visage of loss, a mask of pain, eyes as a well whose bottom was filled with grey stones and speckled gold, only bereft of water. Face once as olive, now as phantom; the pain of both the North and the South, the woe of the ruin of Britain, centered and balanced as a great winepress upon one little grape. One slight Faerie. "Bedwyr!" she beseeched. "Fling it not!"

She labored in contested strides through the waters until the depth overcame her. Then she swam. At other times she appeared to run upon the face of it. Her cries continued; pleading, begging cries.

Suddenly her cries were arrested.

Morgaine had come unto the midst of the pool.

She beheld first the fingertips, red and full

of youth, sparkling. The fingers were forming a loosely-held fist, as though it were holding an invisible sword. *Or waiting to soon catch one most real and visible… and near.* Next she saw the wrist; lastly, the forearm of the silver-skinned Breton. That unmistakable armor adorned in white samite.

It was the rising, silent call of the Lady of the Lake, outstretched and ready to accept Excalibur. Ready to accept the passing of King Arthur.

"Mother, no!"

The awesome and awful power of the rare appearance of the water spirit now passed, silence broke. Morgaine pressed past the gilded arm protruding from the sacred waves, resuming her way towards the knight standing despondent and bleeding, wobbling in the watery reeds, near the shore.

***

Bedwyr.

The loyal.

A friend closer than a brother.

The joy in a time of mourning.

A fabled and unfailing knight.

One deserving of twelve bards' songs.

A survivor, one of scant and few, of bloody Camlan.

Bedwyr the True.

Yet twice he had disobeyed his lord. But now, the third time… to be true.

Even so, he paused. His eyes closed tight; bile and clotty black blood from his liver had climbed his throat and escaped. The nature of his wounds murdered dignity, and he vomited out the blood with violence, giving no regard for cleaning himself after.

His eyelids flittered in osculation.

How can it be? How so that Llyn Fawr is undefiled amongst the desolation of our cursed isle? Have I passed into the hereafter?

Bedwyr long gazed at the lake as he reflected upon these things.

By chance, a faulty latch had caused his armor to fail at Camlan. Early in the first day a Saxon battle-axe had found his guts and gashed them. For the sum of the clash, which had lasted three days, his insides desperately sought to escape to the light of air and bring him the mercy of death. But Bedwyr had work to do ere he yielded to his spirit's now constant effort of exodus and release.

Bedwyr pressured the gaping wound with his right arm, the nub of his missing hand a seal upon the canyon where his seared bowels swam.

Yet he tarried, though he knew he would soon unseam, and perish. Tarrying, relishing the waters that served as an aromatic footstool beneath the highest peak in the most mountainous region of the tribal kingdoms of the Britons. Tarrying perhaps to capture but once a glimpse of the damsel to whom he had been sent, and bask in the mystical peace of her sacred abode. A moment of peace, covered neither in soot nor char, an air of happy fowl and innumerable flowers generous to give their musk. A moment of remembrance of the Summer Kingdom. *Maybe I have already crossed over, and will be granted rest in Llyn Fawr always,* he thought.

He stood upon the very spot where a Pendragon, King Meurig ap Tewdrig, had retired and returned his sword to the Lady. And it was here where the Sword of Power she had loaned to the Merlin, who passed it to a sandy-haired boy, that he might be king. The greatest of kings.

And now that very king, forty years hence, lay in a small chapel at Aberdaron, near the shores of passage to Isle of Apples at Porth Meudwy, surely soon to die. Too lame to journey to Glamorgan, and even were that not so, too damaged to walk into the waters and return the symbol of his virility and vitality to its source. Thus Bedwyr was charged by proxy to the task.

Twice he had ridden from the North. His saddle was now as red leather, the whole of his horse as dipped in crimson dye. Twice the sword had been brandished high, only to be withdrawn again. For he could not, though the sky had broken and the kingdom fallen. No, he would not. He would not fling *hope* into the lake, casting away the time of his Iron Bear forever.

But Bedwyr the True had found his resolve once more.

I will not forget the authority of my slain lord. He is my king and my friend; how can I dishonor him at last?

"A day will come more dire than this day," the king had said.

"More dire than the End of the World?" Bedwyr had mused, cradling his king. Bedwyr had ever used humor, during each of the Twelve Battles, even upon the lines at Mynydd Baedan. "By definition, that cannot be."

There was a medicinal comfort from the smiles Bedwyr wrought. And it had worked then as well.

"The world's end is not nigh; be not deceived, old friend. Now, heed me, for my breath thins and my light goes."

"My lord?" Bedwyr had harkened.

"A day will come more dire than this day. At the hour of Cymru's greatest need, a king shall come, and the sword will rise. Take. Return to her. Be not thrice untrue. Go!"

Bedwyr had seen that look, that authority divine, that real and just power; he recalled it now, and his resolve doubled.

The knight clasped Excalibur by the tip and reared to cast it away.

"No! Must not! Cannot!" The witch was upon him, and stayed his hand.

"Gwyar," asked Bedwyr, "how came we to this dreadful end?"

PROLOGUE II
Merlin Confronts Maelgwn

The Pictish strait called Mìgeil is shaped as a flexing forearm divided by three wanton and puffy veins, three crooking creeks. Although the unbearable freeze was most intense near the waters, Mordred would cling to the banks; for the veins would lead to villages, and the villages to harbor, and harbor to escape.

Mordred.

Whelp.

Coward.

Which of the three creeks would he choose? The one most expedient of terrain, for he was a soft man and would choose the easy path.

Thus Maelgwn made for the northernmost, leaving the drama of the crumpled corpse of Gwalchmai, cradled in the arms of the raging Pendragon, and the dismembered queen, whose fresh blood cried from the icy blackened earth: one hundred - now five hundred feet behind.

Maelgwn immediately sensed that he was being followed; the pursuer himself pursued. He stopped abruptly. Then he dipped his shoulders to the left but in the same motion jolted hard to the right, ducking behind an overgrown ash tree for cover.

Hoarfrost and not a few shifting grimy rocks betrayed his would-be attacker, whose weighted approach was near. Soon Maelgwn, fastened as a shadow to the trunk of the tree, could see, and feel, the breath of his follower billow; a misty cloud in starless pitch. Closer he drew. Again closer. Soon they shared obverse sides of the same tree.

A weapon was drawn. Maelgwn either felt or saw this. A weapon was swinging – *Making for my head!* The skill of the strike was advanced; a professional killer. Maelgwn avoided the blow by the most narrow of margins. In withdrawing and dodging, he retreated from the tree and backed up hard, crashing into a third participant.

But I sensed only one attacker!

The two attackers were not two. They were seven. The silence by which all save one of them had earned positions on Maelgwn bewildered and disoriented him, and the foe he had crashed into shoved him hard to the ground. When he rose, he was surrounded by a perfect circle of knights. A circle of perfect knights.

He was in the center and they as seven sunrays. Each of them diverse in their armor.

A red knight.

A green knight.

A yellow knight.

A knight of light blue.

A violet-clad knight.

A white knight.

Lastly, a knight from brow to toe-tip in a metal skin of black.

Each knight's long sword in color corresponded to the knight to his left, so that the Black Knight's blade was white and the White Knight's blade was violet, and this was the pattern throughout the company.

Maelgwn found his balance, and his battle dirk, just as the seven began to orbit, swords held in an overhead but parallel position. In perfect concert, the swords were all erected into an overhand striking pose; the spiral closed and they were upon Maelgwn, soon to overcome and slay him.

"Enough! Return into him, else flee to another place!" The command of the Merlin of Britain pierced the night and rattled the forest.

Seven helms turned as one to acknowledge the bark, then disregarded it. The brief pause gave Maelgwn a moment to look closer upon the multi-colored troop. A glimpse into their forms, a glimpse into their eyes.

It cannot be. They are all… they are all ME!

Resuming their pose, each of the seven colored knights fixed again upon Maelgwn and made ready to deliver.

"Have you had quite enough? Assemble thyself. Quit you like a man, Lancelot!"

Ancient words followed the castigation, delivering a spell that caused the warriors to disintegrate, becoming a sparkly dust; a dust of red, and yellow, and light blue, and green, a shiny sand of violet and white, speckled with flakes of black.

A mild rush of wind finished the task, and Lancelot lay alone.

Alone with Merlin.

Eye to eye on the barge to Broceliande, eye to eye in the makeshift tabernacle of the Council of Nine, eye to eye in the guesthouse ere a stumble redirected history's course.

These heroes had shared much peril together and normally found a fondness in looking level at equal eyes seven feet from the earth, a fondness born of rarity and equal stature. Both were weary of stooping to greet men, else giving salutations upon balding crowns.

But this time, Maelgwn was consumed of haste and hate, and desired no reunion, least of all with the *other* tall Briton. And from Merlin's eyes emanated an authority, a hot white urgency that made the whole of his face shine as an avenging, angry angel.

Maelgwn made a strong fist about the bottom of his battle dirk with his left hand, a loose fist about the top with his right.

"Excalibur cleaved the spike of Lancelot. And yet I behold it whole."

"My mother restored the steel of both Titans, only mine privily." Maelgwn postured, somehow becoming as tall as the frozen trees that compassed them. "That when we stood together again our arms would be equal."

Merlin suffered not one more word, and brought the tall tree low, disarming the Bloodhound Prince with the fluidity and grace of a Cymreig maiden spiraling in frolic at festival or feast. In one move the dirk had changed hands; in the next it whistled, lost in the dark of the thicket; the third move put the head of the walking stick of the old druid upon the neck of Maelgwn, now shifting to his throat that he could not speak. Or breathe.

"The Lady of the Lake mended the weapons of Lancelot and Arthur that they have peace, forever retire AND NEVER REPEAT such a sorrowful day. Grace and love in the stead of the seeds of strife. For they are a vine that choke upon your soul. She mended metal as symbol of your reconciliation – she did not forge instruments to renew your division, thou fool!"

Merlin released the staff, and then continued. "I bade you do one thing above all else. Tell me, if your lust gives way to reason and your envy gives place to recollection, what was the thing?" demanded the wizard.

"You charged me watch over my son above all else." Maelgwn answered true.

"When you were conducting pretend searches for me, watched you over him?"

"My mother would have been executed as a murderer, as YOUR murderer, had one found you out."

Merlin disregarded the retort.

"When you swam in self-pity and bathed thyself in the blood of boys, watched you over him?"

"That was MY Giant to fight!"

"Always an excuse - always towards yourself, never towards the good of our kinsmen." The rebuke intensified.

"The Cup of Christ took my son, our future High King, and none of my failings could have prevented that, neither the new Merlin." Maelgwn shoved the old man, or ghost, or devil, or invention of Maelgwn's shattered mind.

This appearance of Merlin, however, was no shadow. The druid stood, and brandished steel of his own.

Maelgwn was not impressed. "That dagger has breached my loins two score. Again, I fight myself and no man."

Where Merlin the apparition would pierce the warrior in bloody reminder that passion would beget death, Merlin 'the actual' presented the weapon's edge, and opted for a different tactic.

"Lancelot. See thou the tip?"

"Aye."

"Galahad perished due to the treachery and manipulation of the Dynion Hysbys. Gwalchmai is slain due to the folly of mighty men, the failing of princes. The Healing Balm and the Hawk of May - dead! There is no clear heir. Arthur's brothers and uncles are pledged to the Presbytery, and your Ravens are pretenders! The land is desolate. Children starve, cattle are walking ribcages." The blade's edge was presented to the very tip of Maelgwn's perfect nose. "The Long Knife has new children reared to take up axe and shield. And the Council of Nine plots their ceaseless apocalyptic designs on these Isles. The survival of Cymru rests upon the edge of this knife."

Merlin's magick presently caused a large snowflake, ornate, spectacular and fragile, to light upon the blade. "When it comes time to do that which you would do, for Cymru's sake, I beg you, do it n—"

Maelgwn pinched, causing the snowflake that was Cymru to evaporate in a prick of blood. "I did not do that which I would, and now she makes her grave at the snout and paw of dogs! Her blood begs for vengeance, and I swear it, she will be avenged."

"Will freezing men fight for lust? And the starving lend their battle axe for adultery?" Merlin made a final appeal to the *Unreasonable One* with reason.

"The Hosts of Maelgwn Gwynedd will fight for the Sons of Cunedda and to right the calamity wrought by the Silures. No other reason need they."

Seeing that Maelgwn's delusional justification was set in mortar, and his intention as brick, Merlin gave a great sigh, its puff of frustration filling the icy dark.

"You would be in league with the Traitor that bedded your true love against the man who executed your true love?" The Merlin allowed for no reply. "But you murdered the brother of the Traitor you would support. Putting you in an impossible strait, for Morgaine will not succor you, and may remove you from the plane of the living."

"Neither will she suffer her brother the king to kill *their* son." Warm spit left the snarling prince's lips, freezing as a trail of anger and hurt upon his marble chin. "My own counsel will I keep with regard to whom I lend my Hosts. And those to whom I lend them - they will be the victors. The Sorceress has no power in warfare, as demonstrated during the Saxon Wars. Let her kill me in my chamber; the outcome will not be altered."

"That *Sorceress* is amongst your very best of friends, from the time of your youth. Have you forgotten, in the Madness of Maelgwn, that she has ever loved you?"

"Nay, I've not forgotten." Maelgwn recovered his dirk from the thicket and fled. Turning, he added, "I've not forgotten. I'm counting on it."

CHAPTER 1
Keep a Few Drops of That Poison in You, for You Will Need It
There Will Be Civil War

The desolation growing within Arthur was filled, nay, distracted, by the reunion of all reunions. The long-dead resurrected, the longing and cureless woe undone.

The library seemed to revert to brighter days; the very countenance and composition of the room was glowing, reminding the embattled Britons of the glistening times when the Boy with the Sword and his Merlin were invincible.

Arthur rose, snatching up the wizard's coned cap. A slap of dust. And another. Somewhere high above the lofts and shelves a barn owl shrieked, protesting that it should share in the night's discourse. Arthur approached the figure filling the doorway with folds and folds of robe, wave of white wavy hair, yet more dust, and splendor.

"A strategy." Arthur smiled, absent of judgment. "What counsel givest thou to me, wizard?"

Arthur's tact in treating two decades of

dearth and disappointment as vapor, twenty years of bearing a heartache, of not knowing, as a parenthesis that never happened, disarmed the Merlin, who was set to give what answer he could.

"We will speak of strategy, of method and aim – soon, my lord." A lump and a rasp. Merlin himself could not calculate how much he had missed the king and the power of his presence.

But by saying nothing, the student had become his master. Arthur's pause was endless, his gaze all awe and no gall. The power of silence compelled Merlin to give answer where no query was made.

"I was dead," Merlin stated plainly, then followed it with crypt and riddle. "But death means many things to we Britons, and many more to we Woeful and Sorry Damned."

The Pendragon remained silent, his beam constant, eyes fixed upon his mentor, his counselor, his friend.

"It was for me to serve you in bringing about the Summer Kingdom, and not for me to serve you in governing it. I forfeited seeing you bring rays of Heaven to earth, and for missing it, I am truly sorry. You did beyond all we who love mankind and cherish peace could ever have hoped for, Little Bear. You did it."

"You speak of summer. You talk of heaven." The smile fell. "But the whole of Glamorgan is beneath winter. The sum of Gwent buried in Hell. The great red dragon I could neither prevent nor contain." The tall druid stooped, his eyes finding the marbled floor. "You were *dead,* and by my very soul, 'twas by men and motives foul. Who wounded you unto death? This Mystery of yours, did you discover the meaning of it?"

"Let the secrets and peculiarities of wizards remain veiled; his ways are not our ways, his days not likened unto ours." The owner of these words spake with authority not unlike that of the Merlin himself.

"Dyfrig, old friend!" Merlin turned to see not only the bishop but Arthur's father as well, carrying themselves as two overbearing parents interrogating a young man with endless questions three minutes removed from being left by a damsel.

Loving but annoying, and now there be three of them. Arthur collected his poise, and reverence. "Three old Wise Men and a young prince," he mused. The context and scene were not lost on him.

"At four years and five decades, you are not so young, my sovereign." Dyfrig bowed, chuckled, and bowed again.

"Any jest that renders him aged renders me ancient!" Meurig contributed with a huff. "Let Arthur of Caerleon a lad be, and let him ever a lad remain!"

By imposing upon the discourse, Bishop Dyfrig had achieved what he sought - distraction and delay. He did not so soon want Merlin in the king's ear, with his heretical views on ending ecclesiastical orders and rendering meaningless the sacerdotal rites of baptism and tonsure. Though the land lay in ruin and the rotting smell of bloodlust and rancor was as a pungent cloud sprinkling the Tribes with constant fear, the politics of religion were still paramount for the old bishop. And, though Dyfrig and Merlin were friends indeed, the bishop was glad for the Christian bard's long absence.

Thankfully, as the dread of recent events

and the end of the kingdom were at hand, the distraction worked well, and the four men were onto other subjects.

Subjects far less comfortable for King Arthur.

"In pursuing the traitor Mordred ap Llew, your wife, his captive, was accidentally slain, and no bard will sing of it otherwise." Meurig was resolute, the just and jolly retired lord advocating lies for his firstborn.

"No." Arthur looked upon the three wise men. Three grey beards that loved the Cymry and shared in the greatness of her Golden Age. Arthur knew that his fall from grace would represent their defamation as well; for all heroes of the age would be recorded *as Arthur*. "A dishonored king executed judgment upon a traitor caught in the very deed of plot, the very act of overthrow, under the very candlelight of two witnesses. In this case, there needs be no counsel; I acted in accord with our most ancient laws."

"All things are lawful, but not all things are expedient," said the Merlin.

"Yes," Arthur acquiesced. "I brought no honor to our nation, no glory to Cymry; rather, only suffering and loss for a love oh so unrequited."

"Sometimes love is as a poison rather than a clear spring, my son. I am so thankful for your mam, and so very sorry for your long years governing with a troubled heart. Whatever comes next, whatever you need, I am here for you, to the ends of the world."

"You are very fortunate to have never supped from this chalice," Arthur responded – an acknowledgment of admiration, and not a little envy.

"The poison will pass." King Meurig continued to offer consolation.

"Let it not pass." Merlin surprised the assembly. "The battle dirk of Maelgwn Gwynedd that punctured Gwalchmai was meant not for the Hawk of May. It was meant for YOU! The Whelp surely makes for Eire, or worse, to appeal to the Long Knife, and the son of Meirchion is a cancer upon the Continent. Your enemies in the North will feast upon calamity; for the loyalty of a man is limited only by his opportunity."

Arthur groaned at hearing all these things. "Despair reigns; add no more words to what is plainly seen with the eye. For all men see everywhere that the sky itself shatters upon us."

"Despair reigns not." Merlin increased his stature and, with a puff of dust, approached the Pendragon, as he had but presently done upon the Bloodhound Prince. Only, this time, the Merlin stooped. "*You* reign, Lord Arthur." The druid took the cheeks of the king into his hands, paternally and with great authority. "You can still save us. But in order to do so, you must abandon mercy, you must suspend regard."

"We cannot become that which we oppose, Merlin," the bishop offered.

Merlin ignored his colleague of old, continuing his plea. "From the days when our accord with Rome shattered to now, we have labored to prevent what will now surely come to pass." The wizard panned the room, still holding the head of the king as one talks to his mates in the kitchen whilst holding a hot kettle. "There will be Civil War." His words were both a boom and a razor. "Our enemies are not just carnal; the Devil himself would rule this land to fulfill his wicked purpose. If we are to mitigate great slaughter, even the passing of our diadem from this Island, we must commit deeds never imagined. Only terror can arrest a war in its youth; only deeds that bring nightmares can create hope to end war before it, in earnest, begins. There are dark deeds necessary to end the night and allow for the birth of a new day."

Merlin the Orator has returned to us indeed! thought all collectively.

Meanwhile Arthur's right hand clasped the wizard's left, whose fingers still coiled about his face. Merlin used to fasten upon the Iron Bear's cheeks in this manner oft when giving ill tidings, else a hard lesson. *Merlin the Teacher. Merlin the Sage.* Arthur knew he had grieved these twenty years, but he had mis-measured the depths, until present was his friend. Arthur allowed himself to escape the despair, to free himself of the hurt, surrendering all heady weight into his druid's hands. Merlin granted him the moment, suffering the weight of twenty years of ruling and the misery that accompanies great men. Whilst the people rejoiced and reveled in freedom, Arthur the Saxon Killer, the Giant Slayer, the Executioner of Treacherous Children, the Cuckolded Husband, and the Just Man, had had hard years.

"The Northern kings will be in league with Rome, and with Rome"s Church. This will be a match of gwyddbwyll, and the clay game pieces will be heirs. We have peered down the corridors of time; we have proactively anticipated this very day. By placing southern princes in the North and begetting children with allegiances to both, we have positioned this generation to retain and respect their Tribe but to venerate the People over local differences. We have created a generation of children with so many conflated and complex alliances that they are forced to be truly Cymry, less so Silure or Ordovice." The men listened.

Merlin released Arthur's face, and continued.

"But, nevertheless, the Houses of Caw and Cynfarch Oer have young candidates in the persons of Mordred's sons by Kwyllog ferch Caw."

"What claim has Cynfarch to the sons of Mordred? For Mordred is—" Dyfrig found not words to finish his question delicately.

"For Mordred is *my* son," answered Arthur, "and your grandson." Meurig did not like hearing these words, neither Arthur in posing them.

"Llew ap Cynfarch has claim to the line of Mordred by marriage to your sister, Gwyar. The House will decry the intrigue and claim beguilement, or even ignore the fact that the children are of the Pendragon line. Else, they may claim to put forth a son of Mordred in the guise of unifying the Tribes with one born of both great Houses."

"There are a few candidates for the High King that could trouble us," Meurig agreed. "But this has ever been the case, the unfortunate circumstances of Mordred's beginnings notwithstanding. This is politics, and no cause for terror."

"Mordred's sole existence is fixed upon killing the man who killed the only thing he ever loved—" Merlin started.

"Two things—" Arthur began to interrupt.

"Son, stop, I beseech you."

The Iron Bear raised his hand, staying his father. "As I said afore, no more secrets, as they are the canker that eats at the soul of the Cymry. This empty creature Mordred adored his *brother,* Amr. And did see me visit justice upon the lad. This happened during Merlin's sleep of death, and though the bard knew much, and divined more, this he saw not."

"Double the reason to hear me." The revelation only strengthened Merlin's perception of the first maneuver in the coming war. "Likewise, Maelgwn's sole existence is fixed upon killing the man who killed the only thing he ever loved."

Assuming the conclusion, Dyfrig and Meurig protested in unison. "Maelgwn will NEVER take up arms aside the Whelp!"

Merlin pressed on. "Mark's sole existence is killing the man who deposed his father of all possession and title, causing Mark to be born in Cernu, a vagabond and an outcast with no land. Which of these," the druid posed, "is most dangerous to Arthur?"

Meurig thought on this for a great while. "Mark," he finally answered.

The Merlin smiled. "Why?"

"Mordred's is a motive of jealousy and passion and unbalance. His danger comes only from those who would make use of him. He is a puppet."

"Brilliant," Merlin approved, "and the other?"

"I was Pendragon for many years too, bard." Meurig poked at the rib of the tall druid, reminding him that retirement had not robbed him of his skill in statecraft. The poke was soon followed by a smile and embrace between the two heroes of old.

"True, true, King Meurig." Merlin gave a crinkle-nosed grin. "And the other?"

"Maelgwn is dangerous, to be certain. If his Hosts really do engage us, the task will be formidable. But his is a motive of jealousy and hurt, and he trusts not his own judgment. He is as unpredictable as he is dangerous."

"Agreed!" contributed Arthur.

"And he may not survive the fortnight, having killed a son of Gwyar. Who can fathom what wrath he hath begotten in her?" Dyfrig added.

"Mordred and Maelgwn are both lethal threats, but Mark the greater on account of the truth of *recency*." Merlin the Teacher may as well have been at pulpit or in lecture hall, ushering his truths and views with fluid form. The living dead man truly most quickened when teaching.

"Though the former enemies," it pained Merlin to nominate Maelgwn so, "may have borne malice for years, the recency of the act that pushed them to war is fresh. They are imbalanced and illogical. By contrast, Mark has been under the mentorship of the Council of Nine," Arthur shuddered as Merlin revealed this, "plotting and cultivating his hate for decades - raising an actual army for years."

Merlin went on to draw the men's attention back to the sons of Mordred, tying a perfect knot before delivering his decree. "Arthur's greatest threat was wrought of our mercy. He was created because we were kind. If we are to truly spoil this insurgence, and utterly stamp out the rebel Mordred—" Merlin paused.

The moon cast her blue light through the highest windows, bending it into a funnel that lit upon the Merlin. He continued in silence until at last Arthur commanded him to speak. "Mordred's heirs and mercy upon Mark's father - what, Merlin? What is the connection?"

"When you slew the painted queen, did your pain and hurt rush out of you? Is the hole now filled? And the heart mended?"

"What has that to do with—"

"Answer you me, little Bear. Did it make things better? Or for the worse?"

"I thought that by taking her breath I might have a surety that she'd not share her bed with others, or know that at any moment that she looks upon another in the way I desperately longed for her to look upon me. I thought it would be over."

"But the poison remains?"

"Yes, Merlin, the poison remains, that it would overcome and drown my soul." The anguish of the king emanated forth, seemingly an actual substance that greyed the blue light resting majestically upon the resurrected druid.

"I want you to heal, but that will be far off, my lord." Now Merlin delivered the decree. "Save some drops of that poison, suspend conscience. Order the death of the immediate house of Mordred. His deceased first wife's children; male or female, young or grown. Put to the sword animals, and whatever of his estates the comet spared, raze. There will be no second coming of Mark the Mad in the person of Mordred's seed. Order this, and then get thee an army to the Continent."

"We must do this?" Meurig whimpered.

Now Merlin clasped the cheeks of the Senior King, as he had but presently with the younger. "There will be Civil War. I am of a single mind to lessen the souls it sends to the Underworld." Merlin turned to Arthur, uttering thrice more, "There will be Civil War."

The nobleman and the aged bishop understood the bard's reasoning, but whether they could perform their charges, they knew not.

CHAPTER 2
I Will Kill Maelgwn
There Will Be No Civil War

Gwyar ferch Meurig and Llew ap Cynfarch Oer presided over the interment of their son, the famed Round Table Knight Gwalchmai. The body was borne from Pictish land whence Lancelot had killed him, through dreadful winter and broken roads.

The Tribes in the South West of Deheubarth had made Gwalchmai their prince, and he had adored his little village, Castell Gwalchmai. It was meet that he should be buried here. Though his coastal village was now an ashy grave covered thickly with ice, having nine of ten trees uprooted, else reduced to ringed stumps, and though dark billows were perpetual as Illtud's choirs, the corpse caused an array of light and beauty to shine about the whole of the region. This caused the bards to sing, *'Even in death doth the Hawk of May bring the Sun to woeful Deheubarth. Year after year, the Green Knight shall renew us.'*

Where the river Peryddon met the western sea, beneath the shadow of a little stone house of prayer Gwalchmai had favored and lodged in oft (especially in the times he had buckled under the shame after his defeat to Lancelot), was Gwalchmai laid to rest. *Yet not the whole of him.*

Llew insisted upon a proper Catholic burial. To this did Gwyar consent. The funeral rites were somber but celebratory, honoring and full of love, and even the Sorceress appreciated the grandeur of the Roman customs. His burial chamber was ornate, a deposit well beneath the earth filled with yellow plaster and bricked with gold-speckled black marble. Two of his steeds joined him in the ground, along with his shield, and his twin curved swords, of such smithmanship that they were suited only to his form. Additionally, there were placed with him five treasures of Cymru.

The Hawk of May himself was clothed in silver skin, shined and without blemish. His wild crimson locks were tamed, a simple torque about his neck. He looked perfect. As the young soldier, unblemished, transfigured to the early years of the Saxon Wars.

When was finished the Catholic ceremony, little Gwyar rose and approached the body, which had not yet been wrapped and lowered. Llew stood betwixt the Witch and the Hawk of May, appealing with both palms.

"We have an accord." Gwyar's four words reminded her disaffected spouse that she had agreed to a Christian funeral and that bartering with the Fae was without repentance. He gave ground.

One of Gwyar's Nine Maidens presented the Lady of Avalon with the helm of Gwalchmai, which she placed o'er the head of her dead son. Her tiny fingers clutched hard upon the plume – and then her dagger flashed.

"Sirs, please lower him. Bring the Sun to the

hereafter until the end of days when you will rise again, and reign with Arthur and his kinsman and companions. *You are the Summer Kingdom, my son.*" A fount of tears spilled from the Lady as the body was lowered. She erected herself and turned to the assembled guests.

Gwalchmai's brothers, all present save Mordred, surrounding the shoreline mound, saw it first and gasped with great hurt.

The helmet containing the head of the massive curly-haired warrior was wider than Gwyar's chest, and she struggled to hoist it. At one point she nearly dropped it, then recovered, and, at last, with dagger in left hand and head in right, proclaimed: "For as long as Cymry do rule the Blessed Isles in the Sea, the head of Gwalchmai ap Llew ap Cynfarch ap Meirchion ap Gwrwst ap Ceneu ap King Coel shall be paramount amongst all the relics in your place of worship, be it heathen or Christian or whatsoever label future men may apply to their false religions. Never shall it suffer corruption, and year by year shall it renew, that it be a reproach to all men, a reminder to men throughout all ages that Lancelot did wound the innocent and that passion did kill justice. Look upon it and marvel, look upon it and fear, for soon Lancelot's head will give my son's company, only on a spike!"

Gwyar was taken by full consummation of the Primal Witch. She levitated from the ground, her eyes set aflame, a wrathful glare upon Llew. "There will be no Civil War. I will find Maelgwn Gwynedd the Manslayer and Adulterer, and I will kill him."

***

The weather increased in violence. Gwyar and the Nine Maidens could not return to Ynys Enlli, but Caerleon was less than one day's ride from Castell Gwalchmai. Thus, she sought lodging there. And to be near her brother. Though the burial arrangements had been made in haste and it was not uncommon for friends and kinsmen to make pilgrimage to the resting places of the lost in their own timing, it concerned Gwyar that the king had not been there. Perhaps it was out of respect for Gwalchmai, knowing embers kindled between the Pendragon and King Llew over the revelation of Mordred's paternity. Or perhaps Arthur was in too much disrepair over the loss of his Gwenhwyfar to make public pretenses. Whatever his motive, Gwyar worried after her brother, and hastened to Caerleon knowing not in what state of mind he might be.

Arthur, however, was not at home in his burnt city; neither Bedwyr, neither Cai, neither Cadoc.

Gwyar perceived a sense of withheld communication and half-truths from those who received her but dismissed it. *Even with Cymry reduced to rubble, boys are off politicking.* She did look in on her mother, Queen Onbrawst, who – like all Britons, blasted by the Comet, the knowledge of Arthur's bastard traitor, the execution of the queen, the death of the Hawk of May and the brooding and moaning of the Land itself – paced without purpose in cold halls, or remained in bed all day succumbing to deep depression.

"It is the last day of December." Onbrawst sipped at her tea, sitting up in bed. Gwyar sat upon a couch pulled up hard to the post, her hand upon her mother's forearm. She anticipated the humor that was forthcoming, for she knew her mother well. "By Caesar's reckoning, tomorrow is the new year."

"We are a full fourth into the year by our reckoning," Gwyar responded, and paused with a smile.

"Let the Romans be right for once, that the year five hundred and thirty-seven be better than thirty-six."

"Aye, we will give them this, only that the days will be better." Gwyar appreciated the Senior Queen's hope, lip-service as it was, for both knew that only darker days coiled as a snake at the door, ready to strike and kill them all.

"My little faerie. Woe is me that I offended the Sovereign of the other realm, and that the Fair Folk have punished you so. I was a horrible mother to you, child," Onbrawst lamented.

"You loved me enough to see me reared by own kind, Lady." Gwyar was gentle, full of grace to the mother whose only mistake in an honorable life had been rejecting the advances of a Devil. "I'm hard to love," Gwyar chuckled.

The changeling witch and the pious Christian sat for a long time at tea, speaking of all things save politics and religion. Onbrawst drifted back into sleep whilst there was yet daylight (though day and night were hard to distinguish, as Caerleon had been impacted most by the Red Dragon, and was day by day in its shadow, else covered by a yellow gas), and, against her judgment, Gwyar felt drawn to go outdoors and walk. Drawn to the spot where Cymry fell. Drawn to Mordred's Thicket, the Field of Malevolence.

Llaniltern was untouched by the apocalypse that made of Caerleon desolation. Gwenhwyfar

II's dwelling was intact, clean and beautiful. The pitch yet green. No snow, neither ice, neither soot. As if cut upon by a butcher with cruel, cruel humor, the place of ongoing and perpetual adultery and betrayal was spared.

Gwyar, knowing not whether to curse God or Arddu, shook her fist at the firmament, shouting imprecations at both, and wept.

This is my fault.

I traded long-term peace for temporal happiness for my brother. For Arthur. I let him have his whore that his night terrors lessen and his great quest for love like our parents' be fulfilled, though it were false fulfillment.

To cover for a lie, or to not speak against a lie discovered, is to be part of that lie. I am a liar, I am an adulteress, I am Mordred and Gwenhwyfar. I spared the king and killed the country. And I killed my own son! My Gwalchmai…

A generation has not known war, not known rape, not known raising revenues for armies that ought to be raised for art. A generation has enjoyed the liberty to argue about God and gods, the freedom to wrestle about baptism and tonsure. An entire generation was spared the Saxon Axe because of my concealment. I protected Arthur, and he did above and beyond all that could be expected of fallen Man! And, at that, with Giants preying upon the hills and crooks!

Was it worth it?! My head says yes but, dear Gwalchmai, my heart is an open sepulcher – my bosom says no!

Mordred.

My son.

A twig to the womb at sixteen would have the Kingdom saved!

A swig of herbs and an hour of rough issue would

have my brother's honor preserved!

But for a mother's love, I could not kill you then.

"Neither can I yet kill you," she said aloud.

"But you will slay the Lancelot, eh?" The Elf was behind her, then at once twirling in the center of The Field of Melwas. "A lovely spot to cast a circle and dance, wouldn't you agree? So pristine, so undefiled." He mocked the Sorceress, consistent with his nature, though he wrestled with it as he could.

"No, I cannot." She loathed the Faerie King's presence but had no will for the banter, no joy in the joust.

"Blind passion and the illogic of a mother's love. From even before the Flood, you possessed a love of your children, though they be abominations and monsters. Break your cycle, or Cymry will pass into shadow and Germans will rule this dirt."

"I will not kill him, neither will I suffer my brother to do so." Gwyar had once accepted that Arthur would defeat and execute Mordred, but time had changed even that. She supported Arthur, but she would sue him for mercy. *Banish the man, imprison his family, but murder the last of his line, and lose another son, the priestess could not.*

She set about to scold the Elf for his imposition but alas, he was gone, a circle of stones left in the field.

This is my fault, she reiterated, but nevertheless sought out Maelgwn that she might kill him, and after this Arthur, that he may not kill Mordred or his heirs.

***

January AD 537

The Julian New Year began as the old year had ended, with a lethal freeze. Though the sense of the Kingdom was that *it was at war already,* none would fight in this blister. *Wherever Arthur and his Companions are going, I do hope they are warm.* Gwyar had no Sight for the matter, and mused within herself that she was too cold to practice divination. Rather than magick, the Faerie used deductive reasoning. *Maelgwn will pursue Mordred, the lover of his love. Perhaps to make alliance, perhaps to eat his soul. In either case, where Mordred is, there will Maelgwn openly be. None will pursue him until the curse of this winter thaws – if it ever thaws.*

What she reasoned was so. *For women know things.* Making for the ports and traversing the sea over to the Continent (and to his ally, Mark) was not possible. But rousing fellowship and followers amongst the Gewessi was obtainable. By following the river south to Aberhonddu into the kingdom of Brychan Brycheniog (the old but virile chieftain who was son to Arthur's aunt, Marchel) the Traitor could find like-minded men, as a cell of the rebels of Eire had settled in these parts, sharing lineage with Brychan.

Marchel, aged, had affection for Mordred and would give him haven, food and rest. And with rest, rejuvenation, and with rejuvenation, recruitment. Queen Marchel had learned the darkest of occult arts amongst the Dynion Hysbys, and amongst the secret druids that rejected the good news of Padraig (thus *a few snakes* remained in Ireland) in her husband's lands in Eire. A conjurer and a meddler, all done under the absent nose of her late husband, the very pious, very Catholic and very poisoned-to-death Prince Anlach. Ceridwen the mother of Taliesin had taught Marchel about herbs, and she took advantage of and corrupted what was received.

History and legend would later call Marchel *Queen Morgause, aunt of Arthur and friend to Morgaine of the Faeries.* But Morgaine and Morgause were no kindred spirits. All that Morgaine did was for the sovereignty of Cymru and the survival of liberty. All Morgause did was for Morgause. In this regard, though beyond years and lacking strength to pose a serious threat to Arthur, she was a perfect help for the fleeing, scared and desperate Whelp.

The sub-kingdom of Brychan was not far from Glamorgan and Gwent. Every one of Brychan's twenty-six children and grandchildren were loyal to the Pendragon, but he was not; neither were the rank and file of his men, as they were given wholly to the Popish denomination of the Christian faith. Because of King Brychan's disaffection towards Arthur, especially towards Bishop Bedwini and old Dyfrig, he could be swayed to help Mordred, whether openly or privily.

Thus, once again, both the radically religious and the radically devilish stood against the High King, whose friends were druids and the old Church, who didn't much like one another.

Mordred was hiding in a barn, cowering behind the stalls as a dog that had taken the meat from the master's table instead of waiting patiently for the scraps. Slithery, sneaky, and warm with a full belly.

By chance, Maelgwn Gwynedd, who was alone, and Morgaine of the Faeries, with her company of Nine Maidens, reached the double hinges of the barn door at the same time.

The night was far spent and Marchel was not found, but looked down upon the scene from a tower room where she sat by a giant iron cauldron, scrying both night and day.

A heavy log that lay across two iron hooks separated Maelgwn from the door that led to Mordred. No sooner had he lifted one side of the log from its hook did it slam back down with a violent crash. The mighty man could not cause it again to budge. He turned. Bewildered, he looked round, then down.

Nine torches suddenly helped him discover the invisible door-locker. Surrounded by priestesses, he sensed that his comeuppance for Gwalchmai was at hand.

Mordred fixed ear to barn doors, but did not present himself.

"I saved you, I healed you, I brought you back from the realm of the dead, only for you to replace yourself there with my son!"

"Would that you had suffered me to perish, Gwyar. But your brother has slain my—"

"Your what?" Morgaine growled. "Your wife? No. Your sister? Nay. Maybe your mam? Again, no. What was she to you that you would put your spike in my son's back?"

"She was one my true love, and Arthur must die." Sorrow now absent, the burst-bubble version of Maelgwn's self manifested; the greatest warrior of all time versus the Primal Witch engaged.

The bards do not agree upon whom attacked first, but Maelgwn lay quickly in a pool of his own blood. Lightning proceeded from the fingertips of Morgaine, inflicting sting after mystical sting upon the invincible Son of Cunedda. From his crumpled position, his dirk swung low, severing her dark blue coating at the midriff, but reaching no flesh.

He found his feet and sought an overhand strike, blocked by her little dirk with fluidity and minimal effort. He stepped inside her strike and brought the hook of his spike down her shoulder blade. He hoped for a scream; she lent him only laughter, recoiling and examining her wound.

"I am no stranger to blood, mine or that of adulterers. Why must men cheat? Why must men betray?" The bolts came with ferocity now, bringing Maelgwn to his knees, his black curly hair now grey, now white. Jaw broken, his eyes rolled to back of the skull; the full weight of the oak of a man fell. And yet would not die.

Twenty more times, as a demoniac scorpion, she stung him.

"Why won't you die? Die!" She screamed this until her voice became hoarse and exhaustion overtook her. Then her screech became a whisper and a whimper. "Why won't you die?"

"For the same reason you cannot use your powers in an open field of battle. Was it not the same in the Saxon Wars?"

"What means this?" the most powerful of the Britons sobbed.

The king of the Tylwyth Teg traced his crimson fingernails along her tiny brow, collecting and then sloshing the sweat off. Then he brushed back her raven's hair. "It means Cymru *is* officially at war. The Creator will only let our kind punish men unto death, yet we can kill them not. A rehearsal for our role in the End of Days. His glory we are not to subrogate." The Elf embraced the slight Faerie. "We faeries live under peculiar laws and peculiar ways, daughter. An actual *man* must kill this fallen hero, and moreso the coward that watches beyond that door."

"What was the act of war in the Christian God's mind? The two armies lining up and arguing at each other ere the Adder was slain? Surely a cattle raid is more akin to a war than that! Why cannot we save lives with our gifts, or curses, or whatever they be?" Morgaine was shaking.

He continued to hold her. "His ways are not our ways, my child. I am sure you can still kill" – he laughed – "simply not in the context of battle." He lifted her chin. "Besides, you love him; some part of you wants him to live; let us not blame God for that." He pointed to a large stone. "If I am wrong, smash the Lancelot about the head with that stone."

Morgaine knew there was truth in the Elf's words, lack of timing or decorum notwithstanding. She offered no response.

She did not open the door, did not force her Mordred to conjure the courage to face her. Instead she spoke through the door. "My son. I do love you. I will beg of my brother to give you mercy. See that you do nothing to add to these troubles, that your days drawing breath in this life might be multiplied."

Marchel was lurking, and Morgaine knew this.

"Gather him up and give him your herbs if it pleases you, Crone."

The Nine Maidens marveled.

They and Morgaine vacated the place, seeking King Arthur.

CHAPTER 3
Making a Three-Front Attack a One-Front Attack

Mordred ap Llew possessed a *hundred* (a division of land within a cantref) in the Northern kingdoms ruled by his father. His first wife (who was taken ill and had been deceased for several years) was a kind, godly woman and had founded a chapel that the bards would, after her, call Llangwyllog. And her chapel, along with a humble dedicatory shrine, were revered by the people, and located within his hundred.

Though he was ever absent from his estate - for before the manifestation of his great sin he was ever at Caerleon or Caermelyn, exercising his forked tongue and flattery to make a reputable name for himself, whilst simultaneously and perpetually defrauding the king's bed - Mordred's sons and daughters maintained a pious, warm and lovely home. Each of these were in their teenage years, the firstborn being Melou, and had been reared by Mordred's cousins, bards and steward.

They were all home when the mounted soldiers arrived. Home, doing what the rest of Cymru was about - staying warm. The comet had not damaged this cantref, but the air was foul and the cold extreme.

Thus, while Gwyar sought her brother in the south, desperate to have audience and make appeal for leniency upon Mordred and his immediate House, Arthur was north, directing his men to deliver a steely message devoid of mercy.

Arthur had two hundred and two score soldiers, the Merlin, Taliesin, Bishop Bedwini, and Meurig in his company. Bedwyr, Cadoc, Amwn Ddu and Cai were present as well.

"Our most ancient customs will demand an answer from the Northern Tribes, should we see this strategy fulfilled," Bedwyr reminded Arthur. And Bedwyr had no pun nor humor to add. Even he whose role was to lighten the mood bore a burden too heavy.

But Merlin would suffer not this downtrodden disposition amongst the men. He was the real architect of the twelve major battles (and sixty smaller besides), his resolve unlike any other man's, save perhaps that of Maelgwn Gwynedd. Merlin would see Mordred uprooted, and he would not risk hesitation or withdrawal.

He spake on behalf of the Iron Bear. "The Red Dragon that smote our Island is as a gnat upon the beard compared to the death that organizes itself from all sides against justice, and hope, and liberty, and the Round Table itself." He then pointed at the Pendragon with his staff, dramatically. "And against our Hope himself!"

Merlin took Arthur aside; he puffed his pipe, then chewed upon its stem as if he were angry with it. "The poison, Bear: some yet courses through thy veins, yes?"

"Much." But Arthur did not look upon his beloved wizard. "I see no Northern Tribes, neither their princes. Bedwyr," he hollered, "where is Caw? Or his tempestuous robber sons? Why is not the House of Cynfarch here to stand in the gap for Mordred? Where are these Mighty Ones of the Old North who ever boast that they can rule better than we, but would put us under the yoke of a State Religion? I am standing here in the open, and we number but a few. Come! Let us stand together!" he called at shadows. In challenging the list of all of his domestic foes under heaven, he failed to enumerate Maelgwn or his Hosts, the most dangerous of all Ravens - and the lack of mention was noteworthy.

Arthur himself was compelled to wait in the chapel, and not to look upon the execution of his grandchildren. He stared long at the shrine of the daughter-in-law that never had been, imagining for a moment sitting at tea with her, or showing her the golden city of Caerleon. *I am sorry, daughter; sorry I begat, and you married, a monster. Sorry for the monstrosity that must needs be.* He gave the formal order, then put himself behind the chapel doors, and stood with arms folded in prayerful contemplation before the altar.

Merlin joined him.

"There will never be another 'Mark uprising', and the terror of your ferocity and resolve will slow this war and, peradventure, end it."

Arthur's eyes were bloodshot and his countenance bleak. Thoughts of the Traitor's spouse brought a rush of thoughts about his own. Involuntarily, his mind fixed upon Gwenhwyfar II. He could see, taste and smell her being passionately used by Mordred. In the twinkling of an eye he was again looking down, his massive war dogs feasting upon her. Lastly, he relived Maelgwn's declaration of coming war. He withdrew from daytime visions and fixed upon his wizard, in exile during *heaven on earth* but now returned, full of passion and verve, when hell reigned over Camelot. Merlin always knew what to do, and now he *was here*.

"We have never visited such terror, even upon the most barbaric Germans." Arthur voiced one final reservation, one last protest. "But should it give Mordred pause ere he raise an army – should it cause his knees to wobble and turn him away from seducing the Gewessi of Eire against us – let it be. Only… never speak of it again."

Merlin bobbed his head a few times, listening, understanding.

"Bring me the lad Iddawg ap Mynyo for to be our herald, please," Arthur requested.

***

The Noble Round Table Knights brought slaughter upon the children of Mordred. Dreadful, unparalleled slaughter. No beast survived with beating heart, nor manservant, nor maiden. Such was the desolation that the wailing reached the western sea, the weeping unto the southern tip of Britannia.

The bards referred to the tragedy as 'The Tremendous Slaughter of Cymru' and sang long songs of the ordeal; some used it as a warning against treachery and commended the Round Table Companions, while others condemned the same, calling the brewing conflict 'The Foolish War'.

***

Iddawg ap Mynyo, selected to lead an envoy for

the court, differed little from any of the Silure lads that had come into their twenties during the Summer Kingdom.

The Round Table Fellowship had drastically reduced the size and scope of the military, ensuring that no central power would be tempted with corruption to leech the people of resources, gold, cattle and freedom. Ever at long study of the histories of fallen empires, and apt to heed their failings, the Cymry recognized that most governments turn on their own people in times of peace and devour them. And armies are the brawny arm of governments, puppets of the rich and powerful that control them.

Tyranny must be checked, but defense of the Islands was still paramount. Professional soldiers were employed at the borders and ports, and the web of fortresses that guarded the kingdoms of Glamorgan and Gwent continued on, manned at all times.

Training and readiness remained, but training for a battle can never simulate the reality of *real war.* Thus young men were left to strike upon wooden shields with dulled swords, their verve and passion fueled by aged living legends teaching them and telling tales of old. *And by their loins, for boys must fight.* Four thousand lectures about the horror of confronting the Saxon invasion could not convince a growing boy to pray for peace, nor focus more upon the plow than the buckler. Young male minds see only the glamour of the triumphant return of shining skin, a procession of flowing banners; young male imaginations are filled at all times with the fight, hearing betwixt the ears trumpets blasting sounds of victory, cymbals and drumbeats of glory.

Only those who have never warred covet war.

Behind metal faces are broken minds, and beneath metal skin shattered souls. Fractured knuckles that calcify and will not heal, disjointed shoulders that slip in and out of socket nightly, never allowing full rest, nocturnal sweats, bowel irregularities and nervous fits are the real spoils of war. But of this, the peacetime youths cannot be convinced.

And Iddawg was a peacetime youth.

He wanted to see Arthur wield Excalibur in person, burned to witness Urien and Owen as rapiers thrashing their foes. Sought just once to view the sons of Gwyar and Llew, or Cadog or the Black Knight, or any of the famed warriors engaged but once in *Vivien's Dance;* to view the perfection, fluidity and skill of the Briton warrior.

Iddawg was amongst those who cared not for what had happened between Arthur and his witch-sister during some heathen rite four decades ago. Those given to reason knew that the birth of Mordred was either by happenstance, misfortune, or political intrigue. What Iddawg cared about was the harvest, the freedom to keep the fruits of his family's land, and giving the allegiance of his sword, if ever required, to a local chieftain that defended justice and regarded the poor. Though the harvest had failed Arthur, Iddawg (as with most common men in the south) clung to the promise that Arthur was the best hope to restore the land over which he had so long reigned. And reigned so well. That Mordred would raise an army, kidnap the queen, betray the Sovereign and join with criminals and worse, Rome, caused the lad to *want war,* if only to see Mordred bend knee and give his head for his crimes.

But the articulate speaker, who had learned diplomacy and decorum at the feet of both Taliesin and Illtud, wore none of these predispositions upon his visage, giving neither Arthur nor the Merlin pause in deploying him to communicate with the Whelp. Heralds were not to be harmed, and their words considered proxy for the king himself.

Arthur bade Iddawg find Mordred and communicate with somber grace and calm temperament that traitors would no more have heirs to corrupt the Cymry, that the woeful example of Mordred must deter the debased and the haughty.

Moreover, the king instructed his herald to be direct, with unmatched clarity of communication. *If Mordred will forthwith withdraw claims to a throne upon which he will never sit, and should he halt to stir the North, should he end the provocation of the urges of starving and desperate men. If he no more lures them to enraged ambition and folly in chasing after the false promise of the spoils of supplanting the Pendragon. If he wholly abandons his course instantly, then will Arthur let Mordred live out his days under the house arrest of his mother, Morgaine of the Faeries.*

Then would the Civil War end ere in earnest it began.

"Finding Mordred will be impossible; he is as a thimble in a wheat field. If only we had one with the Sight, for to seek the enemy out." Arthur smiled at the lad, looking up at his wizard.

"I cannot." Merlin could feel Arthur's disappointment.

"My Christian druid." The Iron Bear now fully understood that, whatever Merlin was, surely he was changed. "We will find another way. Have you objection to others practicing such things?"

"A man is at liberty to do as he wills—"

Arthur was honored that the great orator

would borrow and cite his proverb. The men said in concert, "Only that he doesn't kill his neighbor for it."

Iddawg was charged to search the land to make the declaration of the king. Others would investigate and seek to find the Whelp, by whatever means, and fortnightly meet the messenger with reports of progress, potential and leads.

Meanwhile, Arthur would sail to the Continent.

Unlike Mordred the Coward, he did not fear the winter sea. Whereas Arthur would follow the next step of Merlin's strategy to the letter, the Traitor remained in stealth, hiding with Marchel until which time he could present himself to the Gewessi that occupied the hills of the Brecon Beacons. It was most unlikely that Brychan Brycheniog would war against the High King, but if it came to it, he would surely discreetly feed the rebels of Eire, and provide arms and aid to the bastard son of Arthur. But if indicted regarding Mordred's whereabouts, Brychan in full and intentional ignorance would remain.

***

Caermelyn. The golden fortress whose halls had housed Merlin's invention, the Round Table, was rubble. So too the table formless shards, chunky blocks and snapped bolts. The calamity from the heavens had rent the spectacular castle, even defying nature and melting white marble, which in parts were now mixed with soils in the foundations and ramparts.

"We don't go to a fellowship hall; we *are* the fellowship. Our capital is laid low, yet we endure." The resolute king, adorned in his dark blue and crimson, gathered his knights, their regal wives in gowns fair and hair jeweled. And the bishops and notable of the Church of the Britons besides.

Resilience personified assembled. In spite of the assembly's resolve of spirit and defiance of the cold, regardless of their grit and defiance of the dire strait and collective focus on seeing the dark days through to a morning light that must surely, and soon, come, there was great and audible lamentation at the absence of Rhufawn, Maelgwn and Gwalchmai. Two empty chairs and one missing Champion. The twenty-and-six now twenty-and-three.

Moreover, the resurrected wizard was not in attendance.

"You scourged both the Roman Church and the Dynion Hysbys over a murder that, well, may or may not have even occurred. I am a distraction, a source of suspicious wonder," he had confided half an hour before the assembly to the Iron Bear.

"Rome threatens the liberty of all men who would exercise the freedom of conscience in worship. And the Dynion Hysbys were bewitched by our enemy. Our *actual enemy*. The leader of your Order." Arthur did not covet this uncomfortable conversation. "When we survive this and the land is healed, I will mend the Dynion Hysbys; I will loosen my grip and encourage those who revere the old ways to restore their rites and worship as they will."

"Former Order." Merlin flipped his hood upon his head. "And until we chop the head of the hydra, and his peers or superiors' heads also, our sovereignty of these Isles will not endure."

"Peers? Superiors? Whose ill whims command the Masked Priest but the Devil alone? Surely he tops the stairwell."

"Everyone answers to someone with greater authority than themselves, even he," Merlin replied. "Everyone but the Emperor, Lord Arthur ap Meurig." He grinned. "Now, unto your assembly go, and explain why you must take the battle to Mark, why you must leave."

So Merlin kept some distance from court, and Arthur convened the Round Table Fellowship.

The strategy had two preliminary objectives.

First, strike terror into the Silures' would-be opponents by exterminating the line of Mordred. The blood-bathed warning would slow, if not fully arrest, any faction, especially those in the North, from action. Arthur was renowned for carrying out the strategies of Merlin and Illtud to the smallest detail, possessing unmatched gifts of execution, having fearlessly executed risky maneuvers in his twelve victories against the Saxons. This time infamy might replace fame, and he might rather be called a tyrant or a terrorist in place of a hero.

But if the strategy worked, and if the land recovered, heating cold lands and cooling hot heads, then the bards would well record that his harsh act saved thousands of lives – and spared a nation from the mental, moral and spiritual consequences of war.

Saxon Slayer, Giant Killer, Executioner of Rebel Sons. These were his monikers, and he wore them willingly that the people enjoy their twenty years of summer. With the hope of yet a few more to come.

Secondly, Arthur would take three ships of one thousand soldiers to Brittany. These were soldiers, some of old fame but for the better part new, that were volunteer reserves. Farmers, pig and cattlemen, artisans. Leaving their homes, whether huts or fortresses, was a hardship on their loved ones and livelihoods, and the sacrifice great.

Cai and Bedwyr personally lent their celebrity to asking the Tribes to raise troops, and this act, the *asking for lives,* made it finally feel like the Times of War had returned. Having spent the sum of their youth in perpetual conflict, the two famed knights liked not the feeling.

The three thousand would serve a subordinate role, lending muscle and support to King Hoel and Amwn Ddu, who were flanked by Mark's confederacy. Due to the season, there was not currently active fighting, just encampments and positions and empty negotiations laced with real threats.

Merlin would have the Silures pick a fight with Mark, and drastically reduce his numbers. And then back unto Caerleon. If the first strategy faltered and Mordred did activate an army, then he could be taken on more directly, Arthur having crippled a supportive front. If the first strategy was successful and none of the kinsmen of the Cymru took arms, then the play upon the Continent would serve to position Hoel to at last defeat Mark, and subsequently the Merovingians, and end what was now becoming a slow-bleeding and protracted war.

No army in the history of mankind has ever, neither can they, win a war contested on two fronts. The risk was material that Arthur would have to conduct, or rather endure, a three-front war; from the Continent, from the North, and from Irish raiders embroiled by Gewessi.

Frighten the North into staying home and pummel the encamped enemies in Brittany, presently warming themselves, layered and snug under many skins, in their pavilions.

Kill Mordred's children, punch Mark directly in his mouth.

Make a three-front war… one front.

What Maelgwn Gwynedd would do next was unknown. The biggest threat, the least discussed. Although the slaughter of Mordred's house would deter Caw and Llew from giving supplies and men to Maelgwn, it was unspoken and self-evident that he was viewed separately from his Northern kinsmen. There was no calculating whether he would be holed in some cave for a hundred years, or present with his Hosts to crush the Silures the very next morning. Merlin encouraged all to plan around what was known, not to fret about what was unknown. If Maelgwn did represent a type of fourth front, the whole of Cymry would fall anyhow.

This was Merlin's strategy.

The Round Table Companions, the loyal chieftains, the noble ladies, and those of wealth and repute, along with the bishops and druids, received Arthur's words and understood with great clarity his course.

Shivering but proud, and cleaving to the hope that three thousand souls, even if lost, would yield peace for above one million, they bade Arthur Godspeed. At this, the prologue of the Civil War officially began. All prayed that the early operations would abridge the tome, and that the days would be shortened.

Urien and Owain, Cadog, and Cai were notable amongst those who would join the Pendragon himself in Less Britain.

Meurig, feeling virile and spry despite his age, would serve in Arthur's stead (and he jested, making all to know that he might not yield back the throne to his boy, causing levity and the medicine of laughter for all).

Bedwyr would stay behind, being principally accountable for seeing that Iddawg was successful in locating Mordred and delivering Arthur's decree, and secondarily receiving Gwyar, as it was reported that she sought the king.

Rhun ap Maelgwn not only supported Arthur but was given charge of a ship, one third of the men.

This, and so many like scenarios, continued to bewilder many who could not conceive of Maelgwn clashing with his own son, whom he loved exceedingly. The whole Matter of Britain simmered with madness and boiled with calamity, but simmered nevertheless.

Seeing the final ship leave the port and find stride in the icy, deadly waters, then fade out of range of vision, Taliesin the bard murmured, "Who can sort out this foolish war?"

CHAPTER 4
Sorting it All Out
Interlude

Before King Arthur departed he tended to his cough with honey, tea and herbs. Merlin noticed the complaint and harassed him without ceasing, beseeching him to spend time round the fire pits and avoid the decks and the winds at all costs. At fifty and four, Arthur still looked a young man, especially to a paternal old wizard.

Also the king spent a precious few moments with Gildas, the chief scribe of the court, and the youngest son of Arthur's enemy, Caw.

Gildas was twenty and had been in every way Arthur's foster-son for half the lad's life. The historian was deeply troubled and implored the king not to slay his older brothers should they meet upon the field. The Pendragon desired the injury of no Cymry, even the base rogues of the House of Caw.

"Do you feel that the judgment brought to the sons of Mordred will cause my brothers to unhand spear and stay home?" Gildas asked.

"Merlin believes it will engender both shock and awe amongst them. And that they will indeed stay home. But even if they do, Mark and his confederacy of the disenfranchised grows like a cancer. There will always be angry men from every tribe, and every kindred under the heavens. This is the nature of man, my son." Arthur enjoyed mentoring Gildas. "Though the unhappy and the discontent, and those who worship themselves above their neighbors, will always be with us. What is different about the threat to our kinsmen in Brittany is that disenfranchisement has become organized. Periodically villains come about, bring very bad men together, and covet our liberty and our very lives."

"Can Mark defeat the Round Table Companions?"

"No." Arthur answered a plain question plainly. "A professional army of long-haired Salians hailing from the Rhine River in Germania have united with Mark." *And not by happenstance,* thought Arthur, his mind going to the Masked Man who embroiled the nations. "Thus, even were we not beset by Civil War, we would have to fight on the Continent to defend our friends, and ourselves."

"Were we not divided, we would crush those Franks with no more effort than an eager winebibber crushes a grape!" Gildas recognized that disunity alone might change the future of his world, being of a younger generation, and that a far different Cymru might lie ahead.

"Yes!" Arthur smiled. "You are wise - perhaps the next Merlin?"

"None are as smart as he," Gildas countered.

Arthur roared with laughter, still less popular than the celebrity druid. "I have important charges for you ere I go."

"Lord?" Gildas nodded.

"Get thee to the monastic cells in Neath. They are safe, and reports indicate unharmed by the Red Dragon. There, draft a register of my lineage to Noah. Of the sons of Cunedda to Noah. Of the sons of Llyr to Noah. Of the landholdings, weddings, guests of weddings, grants to any ecclesiastical body, and of the noble women to Noah as well. Add not opinion or bent, nor narrative."

No explanation was required. Before all the Bear of Glamorgan exuded only calm confidence; kingly, stately, comforting. But this confidential charge was the act of a realistic sovereign who recognized that the line of his people might be wiped from the Earth, the request of one who hoped that a scroll or parchment would be the stuff of future study. That Arthur might clearly live by the ink and scroll of Gildas, who loved nothing more than to write of the famed king and his fabled companions.

A register of Neath to record the times of Arthur.

***

"Foolish strife, to no good end. Foolish war," Taliesin reiterated four, now five more times. Chastising the air. Frustrated, disgusted as the last ship left the reach of his perspective.

The Chief Bard pondered how any could sort out who would stand against Arthur, and why, and who would yet keep their fidelity to the Pendragon, and why. In his mind did he start to list the principal actors in the coming folly.

Llew ap Cynfarch Oer will stand against Arthur.

As for Urien, Llew's brother, for Arthur. And Owain ap Urien for.

Mark the brother of Cynfarch and uncle, though with fewer years, of Urien and Llew will stand against Arthur.

Gareth ap Llew for Arthur.

Ogyrfan (not that Giant, but rather the youngest son of Gwyar and Llew, whom history would record as Aggravaine) for Arthur.

Mordred the Traitor, son of Llew by marriage and Arthur by blood, against.

Geraint ap Erbin for King Arthur, but Caw ap Geraint against.

Gildas ap Caw for King Arthur, but Hueil the Cattle Thief, most violent of Caw's sons, against the High King.

And the remnant of daughters and sons of Caw, devout saints all, divided in their allegiances to Arthur versus their father.

The Chieftain Brychan against his kinsman Arthur, but Cadoc ap Brychan for.

The myriad of children by Brychan's three wives for Arthur.

In Powys the youthful prince Cynan Garwyn against Arthur, by reason of jealousy of the men of Gwent.

In Dyfed, Gwerthefyr against Arthur, as he burns with envy that Gwalchmai ruled in his cantrefs.

In Rhos, Cynlas Goch, who serves as captain of cavalry and is tip of the spear for countless wedges made of human skin with silver flesh shielding the Iron Bear himself, will favor his cousin Maelgwn against Lord Arthur.

Bedwyr for Arthur.

Peredur for Arthur.

Cai for Arthur.

King Hoel Mawr of the Bretons for Arthur.

Amwn Ddu, the Black Knight, for Arthur.

And Rhun ap Maelgwn for Arthur.

The High King of the Picts, Drest, though offended at Maelgwn for his fallaciousness and murder, knowing his tribes do worship the Bloodhound Prince, will align against his friend, King Arthur of the Silures.

And Cedric of West Saxons against the Briton who gave him mercy.

And I, the Merlin-Taliesin, along with my Merlin, do fight for Arthur always and always.

And Maelgwn and Gwyar, what will you do?

CHAPTER 5
Stones Do Not Fall From Heaven
No Help From Rome

February
AD 537

The devout, faithful Catholics in Rome began to wax furious against their leaders, who continued to demonstrate extreme and overt dereliction of duty, open corruption, and utter disconnection from their parishioners.

The two great Islands in the sea had been wasted, first set ablaze and now becoming as a glacier of ice, by an astronomical catastrophe. Rome and Greece were mostly unharmed, suffering unusual cold and some change of composition in the winds. The damage to these storied nations was, for the better part, inconsequential. Their "cometary disasters" were the Visigoth and Ostrogoth hordes, now matured into fully functioning 'states'. They had split the old Empire in twain, and plunged the indigenous Italians into an ongoing Gothic War.

The Long Knife that had invaded the Britons with neither mercy nor rest, until at last repelled by Arthur at Baedan, had even more vicious kinsmen in these, who were known as the Wild Boar. The undefeated Cymry had not yet faced these conquerors and masters of North Africa, vast tracts of land above the Rhine, and much of Italy besides. *Neither did they want to, hearing of what brutality they had visited upon their conquered hosts.*

Downtrodden and exhausted, and shackled by religious bindings, the people of Rome had acquiesced to foreign rulers upon the throne and puppets in the Holy See. For their brothers and sisters in Christ starving to death over in the Isles, they demanded that the wealth and generosity of the Church be engaged; yet She engaged not.

From the shadows, Hormisdas, or Simon Magus, who *was* the Adept of the Council of Nine, installed his own son, Silverius, as Bishop and Holy Father of the Church of Rome. Hormisdas controlled King Theodahad of the Ostrogoths and bade him consecrate Silverius Pope, against the will of the Church and the people. Magus did this to create unrest, chaos and resentment.

He controlled the Visigoths and Ostrogoths, and the Merovingians, and the Cymreig traitor Mark ap Meirchion. He caused schisms only to resolve them, wrought confusion only to replace it with false clarity, created debt and desperation only to bring about the stability of slavery. He embroiled the western world, making up for the time lost when Madoc, the brother of the Silure King, had penned him in Caledonia for so many years. *And a Golden Age had blossomed with the Illuminati High Priest bound.*

Now the mighty ones of the Earth were his pawns - save King Arthur, whom he had hoped aforetime to control through contrived wars, then through his druid, and now through his sins. The world itself would at once turn on the coveted isles and their legendary king, and he would rise from the calamity as Nimrod of Old, the mighty hunter and world leader before the Lord.

Else the Merovingian would put Arthur the Tyrant's head on a spike, and that mantle take.

But the rising protests of the faithful, which amused Magus, were overwhelming Silverius, and had to be dealt with as the immediate imperative.

The Britons had given Rome tin, copper, silks and grains throughout their tempestuous relationship. They had also loaned the diminishing empire heroes, leaders and souls. There never was a *Roman Britain,* nor were the Britons ever conquered by any nation. Rather, like oil with water, the two endeavored - through treaty and politics and not a few blood-soaked fields - to share the same bowl, but never mix. Finally, Eudaf Hen had chased the Romans away for good less than two centuries ago. But relations remained. Sometimes for ill, ofttimes good, and primarily ecclesiastical.

The primitive church of the Britons and the Popish Church ever conducted Synods, Councils and Conferences, always seeking to scratch itching ears, perpetually yearning to hear some new thing. Debate, chest-pounding, pride and the desperate need for white-haired men to be something above their fellows and to bask in the cheers and claps of their own preaching fueled the connections between the proud nations.

As Christian men under the headship of the

same Saviour, regardless of seasons of hate or hours of affection, they always fed one another. When Rome suffered draught, the Britons gave food and clean water. When a diseased calf spread its malaise, killing the herds of three cantrefs, the Roman Church brought relief and meat unto the Cymry. Whatever squabbles of state, or border, or Scripture caused the leaders and the elite to burn towards one and another, the churches of both the Romans and the Cymry lent charity unto the poor, be they of another race, or even amongst the heathen.

But Silverius the Stingy was breaking this custom. Breaking it dramatically.

Although neither aging Dyfrig nor Bishops Bedwini and Illtud sought aid from the Roman Church, many of those with Catholic leanings did. Amongst them was Dewi, whose renown as an orator and influential saint was on the rise. Though he suffered willingly, choosing that path of punishing the flesh for the benefit of the spirit, the same imposition he wished not for the flock, nor for any person in the cantrefs in the southwest. He and others throughout the whole of the island (save the Silures) sent letters to Rome, beseeching her to send food, undamaged and dry woods for burning, pelts, blankets and fats. The letters moaned and sang of the suffering wrought by the Celestial Judgment. The Comet was described as a volley of so many stones, showered from heaven.

The answer Silverius gave was made on theological grounds.

"Heresy," he directed his emissaries to write. "Rocks do not float in the heavens, and the only stones of fire are upon the Mount of God Himself. And if the Cymry Tribes fancy themselves worthy of God Himself wasting the stones of His garden upon them, they are guilty of pride and arrogance, and if not, then lying outright."

"They are not proposing an atheistic explanation, nor stating that the stars are rocks, only that the luminary encasement becomes as rock when it enters the horizon of the first heaven," came the collective protest by the emissaries, wanting not children and the elderly to perish over the mysteries of the construct of the cosmos and the prattling over words.

"Rocks floating in the heavens is an absurd insult to the created order of our God. Let them suffer that they may not blaspheme. This is my decree; answer me again not in thy insolence."

And so the public Pope gave the words that the dark Pope in the shadows uttered, and the freezing Catholics in Deheubarth, in Powys, in the spectacular knolls of Brecon, in the midlands, in Gwynedd and in the Old North would receive no provisions from the wealthy coffers of Rome. Empty barges would screech and halt upon the ports, transporting scant people and even fewer supplies throughout the sum of February.

However, the compulsion for tithes from the parishioners was not relieved.

"Father, will our refusal to help the *Walles* not cause them to turn against our bishoprics there, and bring about unwanted reconciliation with the Silure bishops?"

"Let them grow a little more desperate yet." Magus assumed his educational voice, coupled with his Italian laugh. "When spring is yet cold, else comes not at all, we will forgive the ignorance of their claims and offer a bargain of charity." The sinister laugh was chilling, even to his own seed, who recoiled. "At the first, the Saxons preferred greatly to emigrate to Britannia as guests, conscripts, and subordinate barbarians to their advanced Brythonic and Gaelic superiors. Our gold caused them to imitate and, over time, *become* a monster for the lust of it. 'Twill be the same for the tribes that adore the Faith after the Roman customs – only we will buy their allegiance with blankets and cheese, with lard and biscuits, rather than with gold. They will pledge their fighting-aged men to us against the Round Table Companions, or the carrion will feast on frozen *Walles* flesh."

After he gave these icy words, Magus made for Brittany to look in upon the Merovingians and Mark's confederacy, wanting to evaluate their progress in harassing and, if possible, displacing the Cymreig sister-cities.

The twenty years of waiting and goading had passed. Many young Saxons had grown to fighting age; the Cymry were wearied and tattered from Giants, from unnatural beasts, from scandal, and the deep, growing hurts of unrequited love poisoning the breaking heart of their celebrated king. And, above all, from the flaming pestilence wrought from above.

Childebert ruled Orleans and Paris. He wielded a magical spear with Biblical connotations, had a Blessed Lady to guide and balance him and remained a lovely alternative should the line of Meurig ap Tewdrig fail. He lusted to rule the surreal and magical twin of Caerleon upon the Continent, the famed Lyonesse. Gwythyr the Just and Hoel the Good alone were as a great wall of truth and warmth against the serpent and the door – the tribe of Merovee.

When Rome grew disgusted with the Church, and the Church's chief bishop, the Wild Boar would take pretended offense that their appointed Pontiff was so despised, and crush Rome. Then they would lend allegiance to Mark and Childebert on the Continent to do the same. A Holy War would erupt, with the pretender Christ's children the victors.

But the pesky Bretons, who shared the undefeated pride of their Silure cousins, were a key cog. And thus Simon would see for himself how best to eradicate their position.

He knew not that the Iron Bear too was visiting his Breton kinsmen.

***

Arthur and his select three thousand were clad in grey leather with light mail and black helmets. Nothing about their attire brought undue attention, calling them out as the famed warriors from the Summer Kingdom in the Blessed Isles.

They were subordinate by design. There to help and to hack, discreetly.

Gwythyr and Hoel's men wore dark blue checkered silks atop their metal skin, the former with a red horsehair plume and serpent-finned helm. The headwear of the leader. Arthur was glorious because he was not jealous of, but rather filled with joy over, the success and achievement of others. He grinned from ear to ear seeing Hoel ap Budic II direct the men.

Mark's army were encamped in the border forests of Bro-Wened, but two hundred yards from Kerne, which formed a natural buffer between the invaders and Leon.

King Hoel's personal bugler blasted the trump of warning to the enemy, proving the Breton sovereign's honor. It was a surprise attack in winter, but no cowardly ambush. Hoel bellowed out warnings that the Confederates should dress, should bathe, should eat, should organize their women and their infirm – and then leave expeditiously. Else be scourged by men simply protecting their homes, their loves, and their lives.

A space of three hours was given.

The Confederates of Mark feigned surrender and organized a retreat, claiming that they would return again at Beltane to renew swords, and to stand together yet again with the Bretons.

But just as the protectors would relax and return to hearth and home (or in Arthur's case, to the extravagance of Gwythyr's lodging in the sides of the north in Leon), a line of four hundred rushed upon the Bretons.

Calm, regal, and stoic, Hoel was not fooled. "Side volleys, and see that our ranks move not to flank."

This skirmish, or minor battle, was in an open field at the edge of a forest and the area demanded a traditional 'line versus line' battle. The army that earned a flanked position, or better yet double flanks, would win the day. There was no high-ground position to be gained.

Instead of hastening to earn a flank, Hoel divided Mark's lines into three by lobbing arrows near the middle right and middle left. Because Hoel knew he had Arthur and Urien and Rhun's men at the ready, he favored an unconventional tactic and created three separate 'circles of men' fighting. Rather than an elongated battle earning a flank, at much loss of life for both sides, Hoel desired three quick 'surround and surrender' scraps.

Cymreig bowmen are the best that history has ever produced. Precise, artistic, lethal. The average bowman could draw and loose three ere his enemy could string one.

"Slay not our disgruntled kinsmen amongst them; imprison the Franks, kill the Danes and the Geats, grant no mercy to any tribe of the Long Knife," Hoel instructed.

Arrows showered down, fastening some by foot to frozen tundra, clipping others in the neck. Some found shelter beneath wooden shields and were filled with mortal fear at the whistle, thud and stick of some many hundred missiles as angry hornets upon them. Many lost the contents of their bowels; some broke the line and sprinted into the forest, taken down as a stag during the hunt by Cymreig arrowhead.

Hoel signaled unto Urien, Rhun ap Maelgwn and to the Pendragon, each of whom rushed upon the three divisions and rapidly encircled them.

Simon Magus's carriage presently arrived. A servant helped him to a footstool, and then to the ground.

"Where be Mark?" he asked of no one in particular. A young soldier who spoke Latin with moderate skill and low intelligence answered.

"We are ambushed; he is not here this day." The lad searched for proper words. "But the long-haired ones are here, they have charge of the men out there." The boy pointed towards the Tribes of Merovee, receiving a harsh lesson in Silure and Raven steel. *For the Cymry cannot be defeated when unified, cannot be overcome when fighting as one.*

Simon Magus approached. Closer. Closer still. Yes, his assumption was soon validated. *Could these be Arthur's men? Arthur's men these are! And their form is as if twenty years were but a fortnight. Even those with greying beards are swifter than the youthful Long Knives.* Simon was as a man looking through an enchanted mirror back through the corridors of time. A witness to the fighting spirit that had birthed and protected the Summer Kingdom. *Though they starve and freeze and their halls are filled with sin and scandal, the spirit strives and thrives. They are not yet broken.*

Simon witnessed Urien mercifully let five run into the wood, disarming two more, now sending yet four more retreating to the pavilions. The objective was to defeat Mark, not to send more Cymry souls to the Underworld – to see the Cymry traitors, discouraged and without hope of victory, abort their cause and return to farm or cattle, and forsake the sword. The honor and grace of the Cymry granted to their own, but in equal measure withheld from men of other tongue and tribe, engendered an idea within Simon, one that he would hide in the storehouse of his mind for later withdrawal.

Could the Silure himself be amongst them? Could he be providing live training to his younger men under the guise of supporting the Bretons? Magus looked through the clamor and clank, looking for King Arthur himself.

But King Childebert had found him first.

The fighting was diminishing, as the final few minutes of the fire within a cooking stove: a few final wisps, then silence. Three circles of Britons and Bretons fully surrounded three circles of confederate rogues. The fighting had ceased, the incursion assuaged.

The Merovingian had given no heed to the trumps of warning and preparation offered by King Hoel and rushed to the fight late, in only kingly winter robes in flattering red leather boots and feathered frontlet. Thinking oneself a god provides confidence, and confidence seems to beget luck. He thrust himself without worry into the division where Arthur discreetly made combat. It would seem that royalty knew its own.

"Your bards say you favor disguise. And that you can take the form of a bear, or an eagle." The pompous Merovingian spoke in a deep, intentional Latin. "I believe the former; the latter is part of your mythos. Am I correct, Arthur son of Meurig son of Tewdrig?"

Friend and foe gasped. That celebrity might be amongst them seemed to slow time and heat up the field. Arthur, found out, kept his helmet low, eyes fixed upon the dirt.

A loud, bellowing and celebratory laugh diffused the mystery. "Of course he is King Arthur. And he is my kinsman and best of friends!"

"Hoel." The Iron Bear quickly stood erect, with shoulders brought back and chest squared. "This is your day - not mine, not ours." He looked to his Round Table Companions. He locked eyes with the Breton. They laughed together, relishing the moment. Another victory.

"It is *our* day, and your discretion let you do your surgical work so well. Perhaps I should come and lead your armies in Caerleon in Cymru?"

"Please do!" Arthur cared for results, not glory.

But the Merovingian understood none of these principles.

"Why would a god hide? Perhaps for the shame of your house?"

And here King Arthur the Pendragon stood eye to eye with King Childebert the Merovingian.

Magus was petrified but could not reveal himself, lest Arthur slay him instantly upon discovery. All of his wagers were upon one chariot, all eggs cooking in the same pot, with none in reserve. Both of his Anti-Christs upon the same field! A name-seeking youth with a dagger, an ambitious, zealous archer, a duel, a fall, a misstep. Should one perish, both would perish. *And my life's work perish. By Lord Lucifer, these men were not meant to meet on this insignificant field!*

Magus prayed that Arthur's character would outweigh Childebert's guile, that grace would outweigh provocation, that kindness would subdue arrogance. *Let everything I loathe win the day for a space of five minutes, that my Merovingian might leave the field alive, and free.*

Arthur did not bear Excalibur in this battle, lest the Sword of Power be identified and distract the men. But, symbolically, Excalibur stood face to face with the Spear of Destiny. The Briton and the Frank. The one who adored Mary against the one who claimed descent of the same.

Hoel, Rhun, Urien and the others had overwhelmingly won the day. The message was ringing and clear. Kerne and Leon were not to be won. And Arthur did choose honor, and mercy.

"Put some clothes on; this is a field of a battle, not a festival dance for those that favor young boys." Arthur then drew up his authoritative *kill voice*, causing his proud opponent to tremble. "Live today, to give Mark MY notification. Leave these lands; disband the Confederacy, or when spring hath come and blood and skin has warmed… the armies of Hoel, the Ravens of the North, and mine own Silures will return, and crush him." Arthur paced three steps closer, looking up at the taller Frankish Lord.

Dark Lord, no, let not Arthur run him through! Simon prayed.

"And I personally will crush you," Arthur concluded. "Should you or he find in your blackened souls a love for life and the sparing of men, come and face me, or any of my Fellowship, in single combat to determine the outcome of this pathetic invasion. I will lodge with Gwythyr ap Greidawl. You or your herald will have safe conduct. Take this message, and take your leave, *king.*"

Magus sighed a great sigh, and became as the shadows of the Wood.

***

Arthur rested for three blissful weeks in the dreamlike manors of Lyonesse, and then a messenger arrived.

His messenger.

"Iddawg. Lad. Welcome! You have discovered the hiding place of the Whelp. What tidings?"

The boy did not give direct response to the inquiry of his lord but rather skipped salutation, handshake, embrace or nod.

"Arthur, you must return to Caerleon at once! At once!"

CHAPTER 6
The Last Lie Ere Arrows Fly

March
AD 537

The three weeks before Iddawg presented himself in a frenzy at the manor gates of Gwythyr were a calm and desperately-needed respite for King Arthur, with one exception.

The nocturnal apparition had returned.

That Gwenhwyfar II had never loved him, never been true, was ever an opportunist, and had defiled their bed with his own son tormented Arthur. That he must slay his own son, *another son,* that tyranny might not shackle the remnant of the Britons bent the Iron Bear's iron will to the point of breaking.

But King Arthur cannot be broken. And the ongoing company of true friends was good medicine.

Walking the shoreline alone was good medicine too. Cai looked on from a defensible position and a small troop of awe-stricken children with wooden swords interlaced his legs. This was as *alone* as the king could be.

Lyonesse was second only in beauty to Caerleon. Indeed, the twin city was as a twin, only the seaside views were of deepest blue instead of the greens and browns of the Usk River. *Maybe this Caerleon is fairer than mine,* Arthur marveled; then his mind saw the golden roofs, the banners, the markets, the amphitheater, the wild horses ever at play, guarding the city below with their whinnies and mirth from Lodge Hill. He could almost smell the springs and feel the baths. *Almost as fair as mine.* He smiled, forgetting for a moment as he breathed in the blissful ocean air that his Caerleon was now as a wasteland from the Biblical apocalypse. The seahawks seemed to sing to him in the Breton tongue, and retirement in a simple hut was a heavenly proposition to the embattled Sovereign.

A fortnight and a week to rest, and then again to the lines.

Arthur and Amwn Ddu were greatly concerned that Danes and Geats had joined with Mark's vagabonds, contrary to Greidawl's reports, but remained confident that the Britons and the Bretons would crush the insurgents at the next go, stamping out the threat upon the Continent entirely. Arthur would go unto the land of Beowulf and beseech him for an audience, imploring those tribes not to join their Germanic cousins in donating their blood to Britain's shores. These Germans could be reasoned with and were not like unto sons of Hengest and Horsa, having only yellow hair and blue eyes in common.

But Mark continued to attract traitors and debased men of every sigil, with every pelt, under heaven. His nomadic nations spoke above five languages and had taken lands in Eire, in Corneu, and on the Continent. A radical Catholic in charge of radical Arians (else heathens who worshiped the gods of Valhalla), the lot of them were a mixture of oil and water, new threads with old, spotted cattle with single fur, a monstrous rolling rock gathering moss.

Thus far, none of the house of Hoel, nor Gwythyr, had betrayed their Silure allies and joined to Mark. Only treachery or intrigue of that sort or some other could defeat the Round Table, whose three thousand, combined with thirty-and-five thousand of Hoel's own, would force Mark out of the field and down deep into the Broceliande Forest and thoroughly defeat them.

Like unto the days preceding Mynydd Baedan, a policy had to be designed and planned on how to administer the victory.

Mark would be beheaded by Hoel.

Most Saxons would be killed and buried in collective graves, their princes' and mighty ones' heads sent as a strong message that Cymru would not soon suffer another wave of Saxon invaders after twenty years of external peace.

Geats and Danes, prisoners to be used in preventative negotiations.

The Gewessi confederates whose swords belonged to Cedric, arrested and made to travel back to the Isles to be dealt with in West Saxons.

The Cymry traitors, seven years' penance above the wall in Caledonia (for the Britons were yet tired of bloodshed, most of all of their own.)

Unlike at Mynydd Baedan, there were no nauseating all-night debates about who would baptize, how a conquered foe would become part of this census or that flock, and who would get to claim which soul. Arthur was allied with the Primitive Church of the Britons, and with the remnant of druids that held to the old customs, but had no part with the Dynion Hysbys sects. Twenty years of politics and scandal and the *murder* of the Merlin had at least made those lines clear for the king.

Instead, the three weeks were of pleasant discourse, focused strategy discussions, much continued grieving and a deep inhalation of cider, shellfish and harp before the next move in the infant Civil War.

If Mark could be truly rooted out on the Continent, his cells on the Isles would be as gnats. And if the unspeakable judgment visited upon the House of Mordred caused the Ordovices to keep sword in sheath and Arthur's other rivals and enemies to bite the tongue and stay home, then would Cymru be saved - and given space to heal.

***

None of the three thousand brought to aid Hoel and Gwythyr were slain in the winter attack. None received even a scratch. Their *carve with arrows and circle smaller divisions* strategy was executed with precision. No battle rust shown by legendary and aging warriors, no fear or impulse by the new generation of knights.

Not one drop of blood spilled, save for that of King Arthur, who gashed the top of his left hand wrestling with his beloved war dogs but two nights removed from the victorious romp.

A hundred men sat at meat in Gwythyr's palatial hall, and a hundred men jested with the king as a droning chorus over this. "We fight the perfect battle, with nary a turned ankle, our unblemished record as marble, only to suffer one casualty - and that our own king by a pup!"

The whole of the hall laughed and laughed, as did their Pendragon, who also coughed betwixt ciders and reveled in insults at his own expense.

These men loved Arthur, and he they. Failed harvests and Grail rituals gone awry and which fellow put his member into which lass did not remove from that love by neither jot nor tittle.

Enter Gwenhwyfar.

Gwenhwyfar ferch Gwythyr, heiress to Lyonesse and, to the reckoning of many, the whole of Brittany.

Gwenhwyfar I was tall.

Gwenhwyfar II was as slight as the Faeries.

The daughter of Gwythyr was of average height for a woman, a median of the former two.

Arthur was sitting on a simple stool at a long bench, taking the drubbing and goading of his men, gulping the scrumpy, and coughing, when her hand was suddenly upon his. She was standing and had stooped down, fresh wrappings and a chalice of an herb concoction being negotiated and balanced with her free hand.

"Boys will jest and revel while infection sets in, else whilst our High King bleeds out." One lock of dark brown hair disobeyed her hairnet, which was made of thinnest silk and silver thread, and ran freely down her crimson cheek, fully hiding one of her eyes, which were regal and happy.

Arthur, ever attentive to others, respectfully pushed the cascading lock from the lady's face, and their eyes met – directly.

Gwenhwyfar of Lyonesse had seen him but a few times, and a few times known she was smitten. Now eye-to-eye enamor begat love, and love begat true love. A transcendent love that surpasses physical or romantic attraction is heavier than the fondness of mind, or the welcomed comforts of shared interest. Nay, this was a spiritual, deep, once-in-four-thousand-lifetimes, never-to-be-repeated-or-replicated, one and true love. She looked upon Arthur more intensely than Queen Onbrawst on the old king.

Periodically the bards wrote of this kind of love, and most dismissed it as mythology. Even the Cymry, who dwelt amongst faeries, wizards, wandering beasts, monsters and flying things, rejected and mocked to scorn the notion of such a love as possessed Gwenhwyfar for Arthur.

For all of this, the sandy-haired king noticed her but as the daughter of his ally, the poison of his recent betrayal too fresh, his heart closed; in the way he needed to see her, woe to Arthur, he was blind. But friendly nonetheless: he was gracious for the attention to his wound, and to his cough, which had agitated his throat and made it sore.

He took his rest early, thankful for sleep. But his sleep was disruptive, and, as the equinox of night and morning came, so too did the female apparition so much part of his years as a younger man.

Gwyar and he had shared their *theories about it,* then let it pass into the corridors of fog as a lost memory.

Is she reaching out to me? In vengeance? My manhunt for Mordred and my rage for Gwen resulted in the death of the Hawk of May, and then the act of war upon her grandchildren, guilty only of proceeding from the loins of the Whelp. Does she now hate me? Or need me?

The visitation was not lustful, nor sensual. It did not consummate in ritual and taboo acts as before. Rather, the night-witch embraced Arthur with four perversely long vine-like arms, drawing him close as a spider does with a woven and rolled fly. Aware but unable to move, in the clutches of the paralytic grasp of his uninvited bedmate, he called out "Morgana, Morgana - Gwen—!" and awoke, sure that the incident had been real and unable to find again rest for the sum of the night.

And this was the pattern every few nights for the course of his respite from the victory on the forest borders of Kerne until the arrival of Iddawg the Emissary; pleasant days, strategic planning and splendid camaraderie with the men in the evening, early to bed, and Gwyar - else some devil - sharing his sheets and pillows at night.

Gwenhwyfar ferch Gwythyr created every reason to steal a moment with King Arthur during those days.

None of Mark's men, nor Childebert's, nor any of the Saxon Tribes answered the Silures' challenge and offered their sword in a single match of champions. Thus the drums of war continued their low rattle…

***

As a hunting hound that will jump over a cliff or run upon a frozen pond for his master did Iddawg pursue Mordred to deliver the king's decree.

His primary method was to have a standard bearer wave the red dragon of Arthur overtly and openly in the streets, along with a bright yellow flag that indicated *neutrality*. Neither hot nor cold, yellow was the lukewarm color of messengers. Iddawg was ambitious and full of verve and chased down every lead and whisper, most of them false.

At last the chieftain Brychan, fully aware of the fact that Marchel lodged the lad (and fearful of hiding this truth from Arthur, whom he feared but did not favor) discreetly made Iddawg aware of the barn where dwelt Mordred.

Marchel, ancient and mischievous, was a person who meddled and enjoyed strife for its own sake. She carried unspoken bitterness for being married off to the Gaels for the sake of *war prevention,* received little accolade for her role in securing peace for the Summer Kingdom on countless occasions (for the raiders of Eire were both at once friends with, and desirous to rob the cattle, gold and land of, the Cymry), and she had been systematically oppressed by her late husband's religious overreach. Thus, in the boredom and jade of life's twilight, she feared neither noose nor axe, and quite reveled in the opportunity to rebuild The Monster Mordred, though it would be direct treachery against her brother Meurig and her nephew, King Arthur.

Thus the bards would call her Morgause of vile villainy against Two Pendragons.

Her dark arts and the knowledge she stole from Ceridwen (the mother of the second Merlin, the bard Taliesin) gave Mordred an artificial bravery and recovery of purpose, though she could not exorcise his petrifying fear of the man he had cuckolded. Marchel employed a smith, doubling his compensation to labor for long nights, restoring Mordred to his Mab the Dive Child, helm and taut armor, though this iteration was dull silver enameled with blacks and greys in the place of its gold-plated predecessor.

He received Iddawg, not knowing the ill tidings that had befallen his children, manservants, livestock, and property.

The emissary, full of verve and patriotism, had rehearsed Arthur's sentence hundreds of times.

He ate the words and slept with them upon his brow. When he bathed, he bathed in them, and when he dressed they were his trouser, and his shirt.

But being face to face (or rather face to masked face) with the *Judas Iscariot of Britain* caused anger to supplant duty, and the fantasizing of battle to replace reason.

Mordred exuded arrogance. He *was hubris.* Iddawg beheld the man, and hated him.

The messenger of the king did not want Mordred to live a life of exile; being fed, reading, exercising, seeing the light of another day. Such was the temptation that Iddawg perverted the king's sayings, baiting the snake to emerge from the hole.

"Travel without arrest or harassment under my banner of peace to Llangwyllog. The High King's own guard will conduct you. Inspect the status of your home. We will meet there in three days' time, and I will provide further instruction."

Of course, none of this was authorized by Arthur, Merlin, the bishops, the Royal Tribes, or any person of authority. Iddawg should have communicated the somber news about the execution and then offered a life of house arrest, and an end of the rebellion. Instead, he goaded and poked upon the Traitor.

"And if I stay here, choosing rather the protection of the beacons and the cauldron of my great-aunt to nourish me, what then? Will father Arthur come and crush me?"

The response came. A direct lie; the err of answering evil with evil.

"Arthur will crush you in any wise. The army readies now, sharpening skill, using live action against the son of Meirchion to ready three thousand elite soldiers, all cavalry, in Little Britain. And a thousand thousands to be raised. The message is found at your estate in Llangwyllog. And it is a portent of greater judgment to come. There will be no pardon. Sue not for peace. Go you, Sir Mordred son of Cynfarch Oer, inspect. And give me answer that I might give your response to our lord."

Mordred juddered but mustered a question.

"Sure you are, lad, that these are the king's words?" For messengers are usually of a neutral tone, careful to interject not emotion, nor vigor, nor tone in their delivery. But Iddawg emoted these all.

Nevertheless, dishonesty reaches a point where reversal is impossible, and the foolish Iddawg had exceeded the juncture where reason could be regained – and lives saved. "The message of King Arthur ap Meurig ap Tewdrig to you, Mordred son of Cynfarch," again intimating that no matter the Whelp's lineage, he was no heir, "has been delivered by my authorized hand. And now, farewell."

At this time, Iddawg relished his lies, believing fully that Mordred would raise some men – after all, his *golden tongue* had seduced some – and be dispatched quickly by Arthur or his Round Table Fellows. Mordred the Traitor would perish, and the boy's small provocation prove inconsequential; nay, helpful.

But Maelgwn, who *was* the Lancelot of the court of King Arthur and his famed twenty-and-four, convalesced also in the same household (save that he was brave and did not hide, rather resting in the same abode as Brychan, accepting herbs and salves of Marchel). The perceived hubris of Arthur by the mouth of Iddawg reached Maelgwn, and every sown seed of rage and anger and hurt was nourished threefold.

And then tenfold when Maelgwn, who followed Mordred and his conductors to Llanwgwyllog openly but from afar, witnessed the place of slaughter.

Mordred was prostrate upon the muddy, freezing dirt for hours.

Maelgwn observed.

This is so much overkill, thought the war veteran. *Were it not for the herald's words, I would think this is a terror to deter, and no military action. Arthur's madness over what we saw in his bedchamber lingers long; he will murder Mordred, all the whole of the Northern princes, lest I stand against him.*

But Mordred had been the lover of Lancelot's love too, in the same person of Gwenhwyfar ferch Ogyrfan Gawr. Having no present desire to speak with the bastard son of the king, Maelgwn instead sent one of his bards.

"Rise," the bard beseeched Mordred.

"Yes, rise, and give response." Iddawg was on the scene, the allotted time period having fulfilled its days.

Mordred was prepared to surrender in the face of so much devastation. His wanton lust and abyss of empathy had resulted in the loss of all.

Of Gwen…

Of his sons and daughters…

Of cousins who resided at his estates…

Of property and livestock…

Of freedom of mobility.

Though his lungs were filled with air, he was dead, his time borrowed, the debt soon to be recompensed.

The empty brain-pan of a father's son will cause such a pause in ambition, the blood of his daughters painting warnings and curses upon the side of the barn.

Maelgwn's bard spoke instead. "Mordred will repay and revenge. Let Arthur his war paint apply; Maelgwn will champion the North, and the armies of Mordred."

Iddawg was numb. He had overstepped. Knowing not that the Lancelot and the Traitor would so soon converge paths, or even ally at all, he had hoped for a skirmish, a brawl, a two-hour burst resulting in Excalibur buried in the chest of the Pretender, with his curly metal locks.

What now but to give the message, and hope that one legend from his youth would best the other?

That the Bloodhound Prince and his Hosts (the chief of all warriors amongst the Cymry; ferocity and skill exceeding even that of the Silures) would fight for him gave Mordred courage. And courage fed revenge.

"Suffer me two days more, lad," he said.

"To reconsider the hasty words by the representative of Gwynedd?"

"Two days, I beg of thee." Mordred gave fake courtesy, his tone sneaky, reptilian. "Get you back to Caerleon, else to Caermelyn, and I will come unto you with the response that I desire you, on your honor, to return to your king, my father King Arthur." Mordred's eyes saw Lancelot atop his steed, two or more feet taller than his company, the shadow of dusk outlining a god amongst boys. "Travel south, and take thy rest, and we will congress soon."

Maelgwn did not want an end of Cymry, just an end of Arthur. Neither an end of the Summer Kingdom, just a change of he who held the diadem - *For he killed my true love and wronged me too grievously.* His ideal scenario involved drawing the Pendragon into singular combat, felling him, and ending this madness. Though he had never coveted the throne, and hated politics, the greatest warrior in the world would occupy the seat until some young lad would rise; be him a son of Cunedda or of the house of Tewdrig, no matter (although Mordred would not reign). Maelgwn was wrestling his demons to find honor and reason, and all evidence presented to him, on account of the false words of Iddawg the Herald, suggested that Arthur had switched roles, becoming as Maelgwn had been for so many years.

Mordred had darker designs.

Due to the countless years at court, either to bed Gwen or to posture and politic, he had become an expert on the terrain, access points, lesser-known streams and hidden roads in Caerleon. He knew Gelliwig better than the locals. Deception and *the adulterer's sneak* beget expertise.

Thus, the effort was minimal for Mordred to conduct fifty privily into Caerleon.

Firstly, he traveled openly, a *defeated foe traveling to the court of Arthur to surrender to the Herald of the absent king.* Or so he pretended. Openly he presented in Caerleon with ten.

Secondly, he hid the other forty, blinded even from the eyes of the watchful hillforts. For treacherous and devious Mordred knew how to hide; and to hide men.

***

As night fell, having but twenty-four hours until Iddawg was to convene with him for to hear his response, and see it borne to Arthur, Mordred and his fifty were upon the doorstep of the humble cell of Gwenhwyfar I, the retired queen, the lovely Lady and Honorable Mother of the Blessed Isles in the Sea. A stone circular structure with a hearth that served as a pole and a thatched roof that looked like unto a floppy wizard's cap. The humble dwelling of a stately woman who, in the years when she ought to have thrived and flourished, toiled in solitary brokenness and despair.

A humble dwelling, too easy to breach for creeping criminals.

Mordred's men butchered her chickens. Drowned her cats. Speared her great fish. Abused her dogs.

She was as a monk, yet a dame, and alone most of the time. But three guards were at the watch, diligently minding her home in nearby quarters of their own. They launched a fiery missile into the Cymreig March night just as arrows filled their bosoms, pierced their throats, impaled the soft tissues of cheek and thigh and, as they turned to fall and die, their hindersides as well.

Their alert brought ten quickly, who were overcome by Mordred's numbers.

The slaughter matched, by intention, that which had been visited upon the Whelp's children.

Vicious, violent, murderous, wrathful.

Entrails and bone.

Unnecessary slices, unneeded thrusts upon those surely already at the door of death.

Mordred himself found the former High Queen, who was yet queenly.

She knew what he was about and flinched not, drawing the authority of her former husband; in grit and valor an *Iron Bear too was she.*

He abused and used her, and she filled him

with gaping gashes that would never close in return. Each of her fingers snapped and dislocated in protest. Her nails were torn away, left in the chest and shoulders of her assailant. Resilience never abandoned the *real queen*. He put the blade to her throat and finished her as he finished inside her.

"Now I have had BOTH Gwenhwyfars." He drooled, crimson spittle dripping upon her pale cheek. He tugged on her locks as a maniac tears at a grasshopper. "Gwenhwyfar the Black," another yank, and a proud admiration of the trophy now in his hand, "and Gwenhwyfar the Red."

"Flesh becomes dust with the passing, but the Spirit transcends all. And the Spirit of Britannia is Arthur's. Arthur *is spirit.* We are all Arthur. And you but flesh. My husband's only misfortune is having spoiled, awful sons! And glad am I that he killed them all." Her eyes pierced the villain, speaking of him as though he was already dead.

She then, or perhaps from its inception, separated her mind and soul from his assault upon her body. No matter the depth of his evil design, her dignity remained intact, for he could not rob her of it. He was not her equal, and her disposition in the final moments of life defeated him all the more.

Gwenhwyfar I here passed into glory, murdered by the cowardice of Mordred.

The Whelp etched his crude response in her torso for Iddawg to find.

The self-same day, Queen Onbrawst, who had long battled illness, gave up the ghost, and died.

Thus the Cymry lost two Elect Ladies. And weeping and gnashing of teeth was great throughout the land.

CHAPTER 7
Reinventing the Anglo-Saxon

Iddawg congressed with Arthur privately, giving false report that exile had been offered and rejected by Mordred, with avarice and hubris. After hearing the lie, Arthur was anxious to receive a counter-proposal, or new terms, from his rebellious bastard son.

"You have done well, lad." Arthur handed the young emissary a wooden cup, brimming with the sparkling cider of the Bretons: made from varieties of ancient apples blessed by the water faeries, and by Giants, and rivaled in quality only by the sacred orchards on Bardsey Island, which is Avalon.

Iddawg accepted the offer, and drank hastily, wanting courage, from any source, to help him through the thorns and thistles of the lies he had sown.

"Hand me the letter, please." King Arthur was ever polite, treating the man who cleaned the pigpen with equal respect to the high-ranking knight, and he who minded stables as an Archbishop.

"Parchment and papers have I none." Iddawg trembled.

"A verbal response then? Proceed."

"The response *was* written, my lord."

Seeing Iddawg shake, but not knowing that the tremors were of what his deceit had wrought and not just the weight of the matter, the king attempted to calm and steady the boy.

"You are distressed and confused; sit." Arthur assisted him in sitting at a small round table in the king's chamber. "And I think I know why." Arthur scratched at his chin, proud of his deduction.

"You do?" Iddawg's eyes were as wide as two great moons. *A poor liar assumes; a good liar waits.* Though his lies were the layered sort of youth and verve, he was the kind that waited, rather than revealing more than what was known by uttering one sentence beyond that which was directly required.

"I think so." The king's face looked beyond the boy, into the memory of his own youth. "When I was your age, the Merlin bade me deliver a decree, penned by the Lady of Llyn Fawr herself, to Bishop Dyfrig. The Church and the druids were, of course, debating this point or that point." Arthur laughed, recalling when the harvests had been full and men fat and merry, hungering only to gnaw upon one another regarding gods and mysteries of the afterlife. "It was of such import that my wizard pleaded with me to deliver it to the old bishop personally. Cai and I rode late into the night, until exhaustion overcame us. We stoked a small fire and warmed ourselves on spiced mead. Finding ourselves overslept, fogged and grogged the next morning, we hastily packed our horses and continued our errand."

Arthur crimsoned, even now, upon the recollection.

"I presented myself to Dyfrig and his disciples

at Llanilltud, proud and stately. And under a barrage of pulse and stab, a ferocious headache secondary to the mead, reached into my cloak - nothing! Then the side pouch - bereft. The ante-pocket where I hide important trinkets, scrolls, and medicines - void." Arthur's cheeks were as crimson as his famed cloak, and so hearty was his laugh that both hands clutched a corresponding knee as he bent at the waist, shaking his head. "Vivien looked as though she was going to turn me into a toad or repossess Excalibur when Merlin made me ride all the way back and tell her in person what I had done!" *Many rumors surrounded the Lady of the Lake. Many disturbing reports, conclusions and assumptions. But Merlin had returned; why not Merlin's peer and partner? Why not the goddess who had once commanded the Tribes? Arthur greatly missed the squabbling of his Christian and pagan friends.*

"You lost the document, didn't you?" A conciliatory smile remained. "These things hap—"

"No; the reply was not misplaced." The space for delay was no more and Iddawg battled a fainting spell, which was tugging upon his neck, his shoulders, and his consciousness as a great iron anchor. Candor and brevity remained. He shared how Mordred had invaded Caerleon with a small company of men and exacted dramatic revenge.

As he listened, King Arthur was transported back through time. Before his days as peacetime leader, or the legendary protector against Giants and foul beasts. Before the dawn of the Summer Kingdom. Prior to all of these things, from the time he was fourteen, Arthur ap Meurig had been *the War King*. A man with a resolve as marble, a constitution as granite. He had seen things that no person ought to be made to see, and he had seen them a hundred times over.

Teeth spiked into bark.

Brain matter splattered on the ferns.

Fingers and toes garnishing the ground as mushrooms upon leafy green dishes.

The jelly of the eye.

Hearts exploding, painting men in fresh, bright red blood.

And more.

The War King did not flinch when the dread and woe visited upon his kinsmen, and upon the wife of his youth, was described. *The strategy has failed. Mordred answered terror with terror. His bravery we have miscalculated. Merlin and I must adjust.*

Arthur had just one query of the boy whose lies had embroiled the kingdom in Civil War. "What was the record carved in the flesh of our Queen Gwenhwyfar?" This he asked in that authoritative tone known across the Isles, o'er the breadth of the Earth.

"War," Iddawg replied.

***

"Your three thousand superior warriors tip the balance here; we can end this phase of the war, my lord!" Hoel was visibly upset, scurrying about, trying to stop crates and barrels from being loaded upon the fleet. Ships were returning home.

"Mordred struck at the very heart of Gwent." Arthur was filled with compassion, yet not sufficient unto the changing of his mind. "O, Hoel, would that we could stay, but our capital and the center of our hill fortresses are at risk." The Pendragon could not help but glance at Rhun, who busied himself loading and organizing faster than his men, distracted, bewildered and sad. "Especially if the Maelgwn has joined unto him."

Hoel pleaded, as did Gwythyr, his daughter Gwenhwyfar on his arm.

"I love you, Hoel. You are my greatest ally. And my kinsman. I beg of you, hold the line against Mark and Childebert. Distract them, delay them, earn but a draw to buy time." Arthur now looked upon Gwythyr, doing all to impart the confidence and influence of real leaders. "And I will return to Brittany, and you will defeat Mark. This I promise."

"You cannot be convinced elsewise?"

"I cannot."

Like Arthur, King Hoel ap Budic II was a legendary, remarkable man and chief. Selfless, wise and full of grace, knowing that a protracted conflict similar to the Saxon Wars lay upon his doorstep, he ceased from negotiating and did the opposite of what most men would have done - and exactly what Arthur would expect of him. Having less, he offered more; having little, he gave.

"We will defend Brittany. Moreover, if Mordred gathers numbers more expeditiously than you can resurrect the armies of our old Summer Kingdom, we will send all that I can supply in men, in horse, and in steel, to support you."

"May we sack him quickly and your men remain." Arthur's face full of thanksgiving. He then turned to Gwythyr and embraced him. And lastly, to the stately young woman who carried herself amongst men, emanating her presence as an equal (for their equal she was), but having mastered the grace and technique of not usurping the delicate pride of men, none of whom know how to respond, let alone relate to or with, a strong woman. But in her was no manipulation or seduction. She was regal. She was stately. She was strong. She simply possessed the temperance to wield her strength humbly and in good timing, like a mirror or counterpart to King Arthur.

But she felt neither power nor strength at this moment – only sorrow and longing. *I love him, and he sees it not, and but barely does he see me. But now does look upon me!* Sorrow and longing, combined with the helplessness of rushing skin and tumbling insides that accompanies falling deeply in love, vexed the damsel.

"The Lady of Lyonesse. Will you take care of these men for me while I ride forth with Excalibur once more, crushing villains and saving Britannia?"

He boasts in a jestful tone to garner my approval. Perhaps he dotes upon me yet knows not yet that he dotes! Yes, that is it! Gwenhwyfar ferch Gwythyr possessed the wisdom of Gwenhwyfar the First and, like unto her, *women know things.*

"Tend to thy cough, and to the wound upon thy hand, and come safely to thy home in Lyonesse as swiftly as the arrows loosed by our Cymreig longbow, my lord."

Arthur had suffered both of his wives murdered, and gruesomely so, in a span of three moons. His heart was a thousand shards. The light within guttered and wilted like the last wick curling ere the candle has no more wax to give and becomes nothing.

Yet Gwenhwyfar the Last's words bound one or two of the slivers, added wax, stoking the candle with just a bit more light. Arthur *saw* Gwenhwyfar, his anguish heretofore having blinded him of her beauty: a beauty that surpassed Gwenhwyfar the Adulteress, for its source was deep within the soul, and one with her composition. *She is rare and wonderful! There is hope for Cymru's future with heroes, and heroines, of whom the bards have not yet sung! Her husband will be most fortunate,* was all that Arthur's brokenness allowed himself. "Nay, dear friend. As swiftly as a Silure arrow, for our missiles are faster than any of the other Tribes."

The vaporous moment of levity vanished, and Arthur made one final request of Hoel.

"Iddawg will travel with our company. Will you please conduct envoys to Caerleon, informing the Merlin of our course?"

"What is the aim of thy vessels, if not for the Severn, or the Usk, lord?"

"We will sail around the horn of the Isles, then up north."

"For an assault? Your numbers are so few!" Hoel was bewildered.

"We will establish a beachhead with our three thousand, and then make ongoing targeted strikes, slowing his build of an army whilst purchasing time for us to do the same. Tell Merlin we make for Llongborth. Bid him make haste to send for warriors from the North."

Arthur would use a *pincer strategy,* attacking a beach from *below* and then bringing five thousand men from *above* in Rheged. Urien's men. He would use Ravens to fight Ravens, continuing to hope that soldiers from both sides would see the folly of such an enterprise, and discard blade and axe.

"I will see it accomplished," said Hoel, comprehending the king's design.

***

Though the comet had devastated Cymru, the loss of life and land to the east, in Lloegyr, was much worse - fivefold. Whole tribes had been removed from the face of the earth. The remnant, neighbors with the Cymry by blood and the Angles and Saxons by geography, did something unprecedented.

Within ninety days of their *apocalypse,* the Lloegrians conferred with Cedric - the vassal king given permission to live, and to rule, with generations of constraints and accords that kept the once invaders, now immigrants, in check and controlled - to make a proposal.

Cedric's lands, known later as West Saxons or *Wessex*, had suffered much less, causing the Saxon poets to cry that *God himself wanted the Celts destroyed.* This they boasted privately, that none of the mighty Britons might hear them. Still, the trauma of the catastrophe, and the strength that yet remained amongst the Silures and their allies in both the Midlands and the southwest, resulted in Saxon people having no appetite for war. Certainly none for finishing off a helpful people that would provoke the unifying of the Cymry in response.

Instead, both Lloegyr and Saxon took a different course. A monumental shift.

Cohabitation.

Saxon men were given unto daughters of the western and southwestern Britons. For survival. That any blood might remain of the original stock and that children be born native to the Isles to work the land; lest a Boar mightier than Cedric and his predecessors march upon the shores and easily wipe out the woeful and downtrodden inhabitants.

Grandmothers who had, in their youth, been

raped and used twig or herbs to rid their wombs of German seed now willingly permitted the fair daughters of Buddug to lie with men who were not their own. The catastrophe had created an air of gentleness and respect, and life surpassed bloodline. Cedric's Saxons and Gewissee matured in this crisis, laying aside their barbarism and treating the Briton girls as goddesses worthy of worship, respect and adoration. And from this moment the Iceni, the Catuvellauni, the Cantiaci and the Trinovantes, whose capital was Londoninium, began to integrate with the Angles, the Saxons, and the Jutes, becoming a new people – the former fading from history.

As for chief Cedric: if forced to choose between the upstart Mordred and the long-reigning High King, Cedric would cast his lot and sword with Mordred. Arthur had demonstrated a *cold grace* to the lone surviving liege of the confederacy that was comprised of *all of Germania* that had failed to overcome the Cymry, the sole surviving chieftain of Baedan. Rather than slaughter his tribes (who were diverse and numbered greater than twenty), Arthur let them exist. And for this, Cedric was thankful.

He did not hate Arthur for his deeds, nor did he care about the marital affairs, usurpers, conspiracies or schisms over the proper way to bow down before the Roman god, Jesus. If he hated the famed king it was for this: that he *was King Arthur, and perceived a better man than Cedric.* On account of this, Cedric had, for two decades, coveted a rematch. Though Mordred repulsed the Germanic noble and Maelgwn was an unstable man of fluid composition and no character, they were the catalyst to an end. An end that might give Cedric's blade one more go at Excalibur.

***

Arthur and Cai in their ship, and Urien and Owain in another, and Rhun ap Maelgwn Gwynedd and his one thousand Ravens, sailed for Cymry - the long and slow route round Kerneu, to attack what army Mordred could raise on the beaches in the north.

Learning of this, and knowing that the Sea Master Madoc ap Meurig had ventured to seek out new lands - and that the ports were no longer a vault of iron due to the loss of lives and resources - Simon Magus wagered that he could send a troop of spies, small in number, to bring message and instruction to Cedric (whom he *owned* by reason of gold and silver) in advance of Arthur's arrival.

Finding a scribe who could write in Latin amongst the brutish barbarians from the Rhine (and finding one surprised Simon, given the ignorance and illiteracy of the Saxons, who by practice refused to learn the tongues of other men, or conversely lacked the aptitude to do so), he instructed:

The Walles destroy themselves.

The Shining City on a Hill that gives light unto the world teeters upon the cliff, ready to plunge into the abyss. Sin, deception and immorality burn the nostrils as brimstone, avarice and corruption as sulfur.

Rome could not conquer them, having to govern by treaty and endless prostration and the kissing of Silure arse to trade and to engage in enterprise. Your kinsmen, the sons of Hengest and Horsa, the offspring of Odin himself, were made as a city of grave mounds before the longbow of the Celt.

They were the height of civilization until vanity was found in them. And now their enchanted island, worth more than any mortal could be made to grasp, is yours for the taking. The damage cannot be reversed if we but conduct the next campaigns with wisdom.

And herein is wisdom:

Let the Saxon change.

Let the Saxon start to become the example of grace, and literature, and art, and religion and civility, and let the Celt be as the barbarian.

Learn therefore the Christian Religion as packaged by Rome; and use it as your cloak of righteousness, discarding it when the objective be fulfilled.

Form orders and guilds. And make your most promising men as their bards.

Heave your black leathers and your wooden lacquered shields into the sea and make unto yourselves metal skin that shines with pride and craftsmanship.

Learn mercy.

When the Walles falls before your Long Knife, give him quarter. Bid him go in peace.

The moral authority is ready to shift unto a new people.

Mordred took their honor, Maelgwn their constancy, and Arthur showed rage in the place of justice. He is no god, and the people will fall to you not on account of your strength of battle, but rather because they see in you what once was.

One thousand years hence the Britons will be remembered as they are now rather than what they were, and the Saxon as you will become rather than as you are now.

Do these things, become these things, though only in pretense. Do them! And at last the Boar's tusk will have run through the Red Dragon.

- S

CHAPTER 8
Undefeated No More
The Battle of Llongborth

In the middle of March, five hundred and thirty-seven years after the Lord, Arthur's fleets achieved the shores of a beach in North Cymru in the region called Ceredig ap Cunedda, between Tresaith and Aberborth, upon the sands of Penbryn, next to the mansion recorded by the bards as *Llanborth.*

The landscape featured hilltop waterfalls that poured directly into the sea, long strips of beach, small hills and several pools of stagnant waters.

Maelgwn's Hosts, the best warriors in the world, numbered twenty-four times twenty-four, minus Rhufawn and Rhun. They calmly watched the three thousand arrive, studying, absorbing. Ready to move up the coast and engage upon the Bloodhound Prince's charges.

Maelgwn pulled his curly white hair, which had been made so in an instant by Morgaine the Sorceress, tight at the brow and then braided it with leather, and with gold. His jaw was yet misshapen on account of the selfsame encounter. For this cause, he abandoned his custom of ever presenting his youthful, chiseled face waxed and clean and now favored a wild, bushy beard, which was also white. With Rhufawn deceased, the mantle of *most handsome alive* had reverted back to Maelgwn, who was fifty years and six. He chose snow-white silks and capes to pair with his foster-mother's skin-tight, lightweight silver armor. His men chose what sigils of the Ordovices they would and he flew a black and gold dragon banner, making wavy protest that legitimacy as High King was no longer valid.

Twenty-four bards plus one hundred and nine trumpeters and drummers were configured at the base of the waterfall, making the music of war that motivates or terrorizes the hearer, depending upon perspective and battle line.

Continuing steadfast in the view that Arthur had entered into a state of madness without redemption, both against the late queen and the offspring of Mordred, and hoping to prevail by isolating and killing him whilst preserving life, Maelgwn gave specific instruction to the men.

"Injuring strikes only. Where possible, kill not. Where mercy is available, avail it! No arrows to be loosed, neither spear flung." Maelgwn grimaced, tears and wrinkles ruining perfect blue war paint. "And harm not my son!"

Mordred's upstarts numbered about five hundred. Most of his company were Picts who were still bitter over Maelgwn's use of their lands and the innocent blood spilled for his selfish lust. But fear swallows harder than gall. They feared Maelgwn as a god, imputing him into their pantheon of gods (though many had converted to the Christian faith), and thus aligned with Mordred.

Hueil ap Caw ap Geraint lent two hundred. Llew ap Cynfarch Oer gave one hundred and fifty more, as he prepared his constitution to stand against Urien, his brother, and his nephew Owain. These Northern ravens formed a straight line upon the beachhead, and would be first to meet Arthur's armies straightaway, with no deception or trickery.

Hueil the Cattle Thief and Llew the captain of the Old North first, then the Picts; last of all, Cedric and the Long Knife as a third wave.

And Maelgwn would engage surgically when and as desired.

***

King Arthur's instructions nearly mirrored those of Maelgwn.

Avoid mortal strikes.

Seek opportunities to extend mercy.

Look upon thy cousin, and father, and brother who bears shield and axe against you, and beg him reverse his aim, and make peace.

This Civil War is not one battle. It is three hundred thousand individual moral contests. Try first to win your personal assignment by imploring your opponent to simply drop his sword.

All of this wisdom and more gave he, but as rules of engagement for the Cymreig combatants alone.

The Saxon and the Pict slay, reminding them of our past glory, and their present position, for they will fill burial mounds here at Penbryn by the score, and by the hundred score!

Arthur and Urien expected no reinforcements above their present crew. For the Silures and her allies simply had not the time, nor armaments or supplies (for the Comet had destroyed many armaments, and many blacksmiths besides) to prepare a proper military force.

However, Arthur's choice to attack the beach in the Ceredigion region was not rash. It was swift, but not impulsive. Similar to Mark's scuffles and minor strikes on the border lands, Arthur's purpose was to establish a base. A place far from the ring of fortress hillforts, which served as protective eagles o'er the whole of southeast Britain, where the Silures could block supplies, replenish traversing troops, and tactically initiate minor conflicts meant to diminish the will of Mordred and *the others* gathered against him.

Though I wish Excalibur was in mine hands, that it might bathe in Saxon blood today! he complained.

"What is the boy-king without his famed steel? We would not want the bards to have to write into the tale details which did not of a truth occur! Yes?"

Suddenly a very tall druid cast a shadow from behind the Iron Bear. Although his wizard had randomly manifested over the years in visions, in dreams, in whispers and as a phantom upon the lakeshore, his voice never ceased to both startle and delight Arthur. Cai was in front of the king, looking up, beyond and behind him, grinning an unquenchable grin.

"Merlin! How?" Arthur exclaimed.

Turning, he saw. A fourth vessel, much smaller than the other three, had used the former as cover, and slid ashore as a swan glides from mere to soil. It was one of the platform-topped longboats designed for waging battles upon rivers, large pools or lakes. The commander of this longboat was none other than Geraint ap Erbin: an old ally who, in his youth, had been called *Geraint of the South* because he had been transplanted to the North, that royal houses might survive in the generation following the Night of Long Knives.

So long associated with the Old North was Geraint that he was now known as *Geraint of the North* (and so it was with many chiefs and elders at this time), or, more frequently, *Geraint father of Caw.*

So it was that Geraint came to join Arthur; both men at arms against their own sons.

Geraint was a master at sea and possessed many fleets. He had apparently sailed south, gathered Merlin, Bedwyr, Taliesin and other necessary men, and then returned back north to Penbryn in the same amount of time that Arthur and his captains made but one journey. His speed and skill amazed Arthur, who greeted him with accolades.

"Let us gain the beach and peradventure the cantref, and no more."

Geraint nodded; the two statesmen were of one accord.

But what does Merlin think of this maneuver? Arthur wondered.

He did not wonder long.

"I agree with your decision to suspend support of Hoel and poke the Whelp here in the North," the resurrected wizard encouraged the High King. He then cast a glare upon Iddawg the Emissary. "That Mordred did not place tail betwixt legs and disappear amongst the Picts, else Eire, befuddles me. You are sure you gave him the words *we gave you to give him,* lad?" The glare, ancient and searching, persisted.

"The very words." The lump consumed the circumference of the boy's throat; he swallowed four or five times, struggling to breathe, and withdrew amongst the men, looking *busy.*

Merlin doubted.

But the battle was at hand.

The wizard and the Pendragon surveyed the scene together, dispatching Urien and Owain to congress with Hueil and Caw concerning terms ere the battle commenced. They both noted that the Saxons carried themselves differently than afore; dignity in posture, discipline in alignment, an air of professional soldiering about them. And improved skill upon horseback, it appeared.

Meanwhile, Maelgwn's drums beat.

Thump. Boom. Pause.

Thump. Boom. Pause.

Coronet in single squealing note.

Repeat.

The peculiarity of the matter would have befuddled even the most creative bards. The Saxons in professional garb, calm with neither drool nor growl, helmets plumed, silks clean. Rough and callused Caw and his troop of traitors and lechers the same.

And there was Mordred, in his god mask, flying a golden dragon atop two red chevrons – borrowing from, yet perverting, the ancient sigils and symbolism of the Silures.

Against this *majestic force,* in this inverted and perverse moment, were *the invaders.* Freshly come from supporting Hoel the Great in discreet black and grey attire, the three thousand Britons looked more raiders and pirates than celebrities and demigods from the Summer Kingdom.

None of this strangeness was lost upon the mentor and the student, the counselor and the sovereign – the two great friends.

"Which would you prefer, Bear?" The nose crinkled and the pipe puffed. "Fish that looks good," puff, "or fish that tastes good?"

Arthur chuckled. "We used to taste *and* look good," he countered.

"But does any fish *smell good?*" Bedwyr contributed, ever adding brevity at just the right time.

The three heroes enjoyed the moment, the overly cold March winds howling in protest and sometimes in concert with Maelgwn's drums and horns.

"Lo, Urien returns." The tenor returned to gravity and the mood snapped back into focus. "What terms given by Hueil and Llew?" asked the Merlin.

"We have instigated a military threat to the Ordovices and all men of the Midlands and Northern Cymru. And are to return at once, else perish."

"I am amongst the *all men of the North,* and I stand with King Arthur Pendragon!" old Geraint the Sea Commander screamed, his war blood elevating above a simmer, en route to a boil.

"Archers?" asked Merlin.

"Withheld," came the answer.

"Prisoners?"

"Yes, save for those who were present at the—" Urien did not need to finish describing the deed accomplished against the House of Mordred.

"Pious for one who betrayed the throne for untold years and would usurp the Round Table Fellowship." Arthur gave scathing rebuke, his *authority voice* building, thunderous.

"Bishops and priests?" asked Merlin.

"Unharmed, safe conduct."

"The dead?" Merlin again.

"To be buried where they fall, unless our attendants can bear them away under threat of sword and spear. And the lads we have are fighting today, not cleaning pot, dressing wound, or fetching water." Urien looked upon the Saxons, assembled several hundred yards off, clearly separated as an additional *wave* against Arthur. "We will ensure *they* are in separate mounds, apart, from our Britons who may fall here."

"And may that number be few," Arthur concluded.

"Be there any warriors, excluding the Hosts of Maelgwn, that we should mark for exceptional skill or fleet of horse?" Merlin made his final inquiry. Perfect planning prevented poor performance, and the Merlin used to gather extreme amounts of intelligence; patterns and predictions, variables and dependencies, on individual infantry, cavalry, archers, hurlers, spearmen, commanders and notables amongst the enemy. The battle was over before it began on account of Merlin using information to drive decision-making and indicators for the course of strategy.

This, coupled with the valor, leadership attributes and mystique of Arthur and his famed Companions, resulted in an undefeated, invincible force.

But Merlin had been long in abeyance and could not apply the methods on this day.

"Mordred has found a champion that forms a vault o'er the coward at all times. He is called Eda Elyn Mawr. Mark him - note him. My son Owain grappled with him in sport and always seeking advantage by trickery is Eda Elyn Mawr."

"And he is a radical proponent of the Roman way, giving his sword to the Bishop of Rome over any *temporal* chief," contributed Owain ap Urien.

"Other?" Merlin pressed.

"Derfel ap Hoel ap Budic II, and his kin Alan Fyrgan, have deserted our beloved friends on the Continent, lending their sword to Lancelot,"

Urien said, pale at having to answer.

"So, the insanity of this war has crept into the houses of Brittany as well?" Arthur was crestfallen. "Amwn Ddu and Hoel must be grieved unto the sinews. Derfel is an honorable boy, his fame flowering. His likeness is as one of our Round Table Fellows from the Saxon Wars."

"The women swoon at his appearance and his spear has no equal save the battle-dirk of Lancelot, who also makes war against us." *Boom. Rattle. Thump.* The Hosts of Maelgwn taunted with haunting horns. Urien was disheartened.

"Be of good cheer, brother. May the day conclude with his capture, that we might reason with the lad." Arthur sought to comfort the man who surveyed the lines.

All agreed, for Derfel was a noble and powerful young warrior.

A final threat. "Leave these shores. And see to it that you leave now. Tyrant! Oppressor!" Caw bellowed. "Hop a-boat, and take my father with you!"

"This is my land too!" Geraint's retort matched the anger, exceeded the volume.

The clash began.

Arthur was as brilliant at the Battle of Llanborth as ever in his youth. Speed; grace; perfect counterstrikes. A complaining knee and a loose shoulder joint had no impact. He felt in top condition; he led by example, defeating twelve men in as many minutes, slaying none.

But something was *amiss* with the rest of the men. Mistakes were made; hesitations begat poor defense. The older warriors were *old,* and the younger men's inexperience threatened to undo the band.

Nevertheless, such was the might of the black-clad Silures and their allies that, by a narrow margin, they outlasted the Ravens, winning the first wave. Caw and Hueil retreated. Mordred never engaged, preferring to hide behind his *champion.* Fifty Britons broke bonds with Mordred and reunited with the Round Table confederacy. Derfel was brilliant but withdrew when the cause was lost.

The death count was less than five.

"They are in league with the Saxons and with the Picts. But, God be thanked, they are not commingling and combining the forces. They yet remain in well-defined, and separate, compartments. The Saxons come next," Bedwyr observed, breathed deeply, resetting his lungs. "And now they do come."

The second engagement was of a far different disposition.

The Saxons possessed the advantages of high ground and mounts (for though Arthur's armies had traveled oft with their steeds, very few had been taken with them to Brittany, on account of the bitter cold and the nature of the engagement). This was unfamiliar territory for the Britons, and a reverse of the normal scenario where a small number of mounted knights could best a large number of foot-soldiers.

Fortunately, Geraint had brought a *few horses* with him, giving them to the choicest knights, hoping to sway the balance of advantage. Cadog, Cai, Bedwyr, and Gareth cheered when they received stallions; they quickly saddled and rapidly clashed with the approaching Saxon, *horse rider to horse rider*.

The Saxons had improved.

But not enough.

Soon they were dismounted; next, harvested

like wheat. Arms and brain matter decorated the beachhead. Entrails fed the birds.

"Do not envy thy brother's steed, lord." Geraint beamed, jesting with the Pendragon.

"Can it be?" Arthur's smile was as the noonday sun, as the infant being surprised with his first puppy.

"The old wizard made me bring him, saying: 'Bards sing of swords and armor, men are immortalized in ink and lore, but every soldier knows 'tis the horse that wins the war'."

"My Chief Strategist turned Poet." Arthur embraced *his horse*, Hengroen. Time ceased for three seconds, as did the drums, as did the Germanic screams, as did the precise instructions and commands in the language of heaven, which filled the air. *The High King, Excalibur in his right hand, bridle of his horse in the left, was twenty-three again, cunning and quick, the savior of his people.*

If Merlin was a poet, then on this day Arthur was an artist; a painter with blade in the place of brush. *And o, how did Excalibur paint the shores red in German blood!*

The Britons were handling the Germans with ease. Then the Picts entered the fray, favoring slingshots and three-balled clubs, sprinting headlong into the lines.

The Ravens fought with great skill and order. The Saxons had improved, their motions and strikes similar to the Cymry. But the Picts were sloppy, dirty. Their chaos was their strength, their lack of apparent strategy *was their strategy*.

Harassed by the painted fellows from the side, the Saxons fully retreated – to the chagrin of Cedric, who was unable to get close enough to Arthur to even see him, let alone make a crying challenge for the opportunity at glory – and the

Bloodhound Prince slashed in from the other.

Arthur's men struggled to execute their charges where combat with their kinsmen was concerned. The kingdoms had degenerated into a Civil War in word and decree, but not in the heart. Maelgwn's men were a degree better. Their movements swifter, their power strikes more effective. Exercising mercy in obedience to his instructions, they but clipped their opponents. When Arthur or Urien's men fell, they were swift to help them aright, only requiring that they disarm.

The Picts slew a few of Arthur's men but in the confusion of battle, when a Pict raised club or axe against Rhun's troops, Maelgwn himself put battle-dirk to Pict, shouting reminders that his son was not to be harmed.

Where Cedric failed, the Lancelot succeeded. He did breach the Silure defenses and was upon King Arthur himself - the one target to whom no quarter would be extended.

"You fight shoulder to shoulder with Saxons. Traitor! Forever traitor!"

The words pierced Lancelot, running him through with greater force and precision, and pain, than the sharpest tip of the spear. Then the voice of Merlin, who was rushing to the place where Arthur and Cai stood - readying weapons to fight an unwinnable fight - but was well outside of earshot, whispered that familiar verse, as if it were added to Scripture itself: *"When it comes time to do that which you would do, do it not."*

One of the Lancelots in Lancelot considered the words, and his weapon began to lower. He did not speak. He could not believe himself on the side of Saxons, from whom he had saved Cymru. *Would you deliver Caerleon into the hands of the sons of Hengest and Horsa? Would you replace Vortigern, becoming the chief of treachery?*

Cai's club disrupted the introspection.

Maelgwn came back into focus, blocking the overhand strike one half-second ere it crushed his shoulder. Off the block, or rather at the same time, the Bloodhound countered, the shaft of his spike meeting Cai flush upon the cage that housed his heart and lungs. A follow-up kick below the knee to the left shin brought Cai down; a clean straight punch left him unconscious.

Cai heard the charges of Meurig as he drifted away, feeling failure and shame as the light gave way to darkness.

Lancelot and Arthur did not speak further.

Merlin arrived, dragging Cai away that he might attend to him, cursing Maelgwn with ancient pejorative, causing the sky to darken and the thunder to crackle upon the Sea.

Sword and fist cannot defeat the forces of magick and the way of the Otherworldly. Morgaine whipped me; if Merlin is to do as much, or kill me, let me first have my vengeance.

Therefore, Maelgwn made his rush quickly; the other combatants gave way, forming a circle about the two princes.

King and First Knight, to the death.

Meanwhile, the Hosts of Maelgwn were successful. These Britons were undefeated in their generation. In twelve major battles had they decisively bested Saxons, Jutes, Angles, Picts and the pirate raiders of Eire. Moreover, their sigils and chevrons had waved in glorious and proud victory on the field above sixty times after minor skirmishes or raids. But when undefeated faces undefeated, one will of necessity experience a new taste: the bitter bile of defeat.

'Twas Urien and Owain who tasted it. And bitter it was.

The combatants were evenly matched, but the Hosts prevailed through ferocity and greater speed. Many of Urien's younger, less experienced warriors were overcome by awe and legend as much as spear and shield, the moment being too big for them. They would live to fight again, as Maelgwn's men obeyed the mandate – injuring without killing, disarming without dismembering.

Urien and Owain could feel their numbers waning, their lines compromised. And o, the cursed drums of the Hosts of Maelgwn! *Boom. Rattle. Rattle. Boom.* When the percussion roared so near and so loudly that the dynamic father and son's commands were deafened, so much so that hand signal had to replace holler and bark, they could both feel *and hear* that defeat was upon them. Urien would fight to the death and have nothing of surrender, but the Hosts begged him to cease, imploring him to look yonder to the shore where Rhun was corralled and forcibly loaded upon his ship, along with the greater part of his retinue of one thousand, as if they were barrels of coal or blocks of cheese and no men.

If Maelgwn did here kill King Arthur, the destiny of Cymru would shift to his hands.

But Arthur, the second-best warrior amongst the Britons, ever fought above himself versus Lancelot.

Arthur blocked everything. Everything. Lancelot exhausted himself, the only scratch on Arthur being that which Gwenhwyfar ferch Gwythyr had already mended. Five more attempts – blocked. Now six more – eluded.

At last Lancelot threw down his long weapon and gave his low, guttural command. "Bow!" For he had in mind to kill the man who had killed his love at short range, with arrows in the stead of steel.

Arthur, finding himself surrounded and his army under the control of the enemy, was in new territory. New territory did not displace old bravery, for the courage of Arthur transcended time and circumstance.

He looked up at his taller foe, dropped Excalibur, and locked eyes. The Bear and the Bloodhound.

But Merlin was there as well, the thunder reminding Maelgwn that other allies had the king. "You will die in the twinkling of an eye, should you loose that arrow."

Maelgwn pretended to ignore the wizard, knowing his warning to be full of merit and no shallow plea. *Then in one twinkling of an eye will I be with Gwen.*

But a screeching, mournful, terrorized cry interrupted all.

All eyes scanned the source and found Caw, begging and commanding the fighting to cease. "The heathen killed a prince of the Britons! My father is slain. What have we wrought?"

"War is no respecter of persons," said Cedric, attempting to remain stately. "I do not condone what happened, but we *are in league* against the Round Table Fellowship and the enemies of the Bishop of Rome. Acquaint yourselves with killing your own, for this is but the beginning of it." With these words, Cedric motioned and his men left the field at once, without cursing, in graceful marching form, the dead being left where they lay.

Two youthful nobles of the Angles had taken advantage of the duel – a distraction that gave them cover to apprehend old Geraint. He had fled and tried to fight, making it as far as the manor estate called Llanborth (not far from Penbryn, where most of the fighting had occurred), which was the spot where they slew him.

The Angles, the Saxons, Jutes and Gewessi would immediately spread word near and far that a prince of the Britons had been killed. This would ignite a fire of hope that the Blessed Isles, should she recover from the dragon's flames, were at long last subject to defeat - and conquest.

Caw ap Geraint had killed, by proxy and allegiance, Geraint ap Erbin.

As the shock of looking upon the first noble to fall in the Civil War began to dissipate, more than fifty men from both sides placed themselves between King Arthur and King Maelgwn Gwynedd.

There would be no more fighting this day.

King Arthur and Urien ap Cynfarch Oer retreated, whilst Rhun returned to his homelands in Gwynedd to consider the matter.

The invincible Britons were undefeated no more.

CHAPTER 9
Unlikely Traitors
Derfel Gadarn and Alain Fyrgan

Though seven seeds - sprinkled, buried, and cultivated by many real and perceived hurts across forty years - provided the harvest of the Civil War, and though three woeful blows diminished the Summer Kingdom, leaving in its place a perpetual winter, the choice of side and allegiance for lesser nobles, heirs apparent, youthful heroes not yet famous, novice clergy and a myriad of other wondrous damsels and knights meriting of their own bardic songs was complicated - or else sometimes simple, but always tinted grey.

Arthur as hero. Mordred as villain. Lancelot to tilt the scale and achieve victory depending upon which of his fractured personas was in charge that morning.

Would that it was this simple.

The truth was that heroes were amongst the ranks of Mordred's men too.

Of note was Derfel ap Hoel Mawr. The ladies doted upon the lad, but seventeen, as if he were

Lancelot, and men envied his spear as if he were Galahad. His mind was as Taliesin's, humor as Meurig's, disposition as the Hawk of May's. The bards were already making these and other flattering comparisons, though Derfel had never met any of these men.

And yet he found himself amongst the ranks of Caw, of Llew ap Cynfarch… and Mordred.

Derfel's aunt was Gwen Teirbron, and her son was Cadfan, the Bishop of Llyn and thorn of Morgaine of the Faeries – the same who had established a chapel on Ynys Enlli.

Cadfan was his kinsman.

Cadfan and Derfel had been schooled in Glamorgan under Illtud.

Cadfan hated Illtud.

Derfel hated Illtud.

Illtud, as with all Elders cleaving unto the primitive Church of the Britons, was loyal to Arthur.

Thus Derfel, having no personal angst against the Pendragon, lent his spear to Mordred, breaking his father's heart.

Derfel also was secretly a druid, wanting to be closer, and closer still, to Cadfan as the Catholic priest possessed the sarcophagus of Mary, and, before the comet suspended his efforts, had relentlessly sought the other Treasures of Britain.

How many hundreds of men or more cast their lot for intimate, personal and like reasons on both sides!

Alain Fyrgan was another such. An unknown offense by Illtud swayed Derfel. The impossibility of promotion moved Alain, brother of Hoel (and Arthur's very own kinsman through the line of Alain's mother, Anowed). Alain was the unwanted, unintentional last son of Budic

II. Though a just and kind man and fair ruler, Budic had been so advanced in age when Alain was born that the boy had suffered neglect, lack of promotion, and frequent fosterage. That Alain could attain a place amongst the fabled and magical Breton nobles, or a famous name amongst the tribes, was beyond his grasp; that he might be made a Round Table Companion retired to the realm of the impossible. He would lead a troop and advance no further.

Thus the simple, fleeting thought that Alain could displace his older brothers and sisters, and succeed Hoel should he perish, caused Alain to take his men and leave Brittany, marching under the banner of Mordred.

Alain was elsewise an honest, upright and neighborly man; a kind fellow to his neighbors and of devout faith. Jealousy and lack of promotion was his motive and no other.

Thus Merlin would often observe that *the Sons of Adam's loyalty is limited by their opportunity.*

***

April
AD 537

An ornate stone coffin was borne to the Mansion Llanborth, where Prince Geraint was interred and celebrated. A chapel was erected to establish a place of pilgrimage for the saints to visit and give respect unto the first Cymreig noble slain by the Long Knife in over twenty years.

Arthur returned home to Caerleon, his resolve tested by defeat. What he found awaiting him suspended character lessons and sent the great man into a spiral of unmitigated sorrow and loss.

Wanting him to fix his talents upon the invasion at Penbryn, none had informed the Iron Bear of the passing of his mother, the beloved Queen Onbrawst.

Arthur had still been at sea when the process of time demanded that they bury her. But the celebration of life, and mourning of loss, continued. Meurig and Illtud had established a choir singing her favorite hymns at all hours, serving cakes and hot wine to the trail of visitors, who did not cease to come visit the beloved Lady.

Equitable respect was given for Queen Gwenhwyfar I. Though she had been out of the public life for two decades, the whole of Glamorgan and Gwent adored her, suffering the king to be happy with his *second Gwen* but never displacing their loyalty to the original Fair Damsel.

King Arthur was regal before all, graceful and strong. Privately, he wept much. Dread and concern filled him towards the senior sovereign in his home - his father, King Meurig. He was six decades and six, and only fourteen years older than Arthur. Moreover, the line of Silure kings had a propensity for living to an advanced age, sometimes into the hundredth year. Nevertheless, the son feared the passing of his remaining parent might not be many seasons hence.

His care and worry for the older Pendragon preoccupied Arthur's every thought for the space of three days, causing him to lose much sleep and retreat daily to the fortress of Lodge Hill, which all knew was *Arthur's sanctuary.* The fourth morning, bundled to brace the cold air, which was a bitter, whipping and constant reminder of a spring that would not come, Merlin and Bedwyr joined him.

"When two are truly in love - and I speak not

of the diluted and common use of the designation, but rather *really in love* – it is said that when one passes, the other, having no purpose and void of his or her very bone and flesh, soon passes as well, though outwardly healthy."

"Yes." Merlin blew his pipe, a long, polished bone pipe that billowed perfect rings of smoke, adding to the intentional drama of any druid, shaman or aged counselor (old Dyfrig the bishop smoked from an identical device, showing that grey-bearded contemplative men puffing away were no respecters of the gods). "It is said so."

"I will be here when you are too old to walk, boy!" Meurig had crept upon the company, covered in six pelts and a thick brown fur hood; yet his smile snuck through. Meurig saw how Bedwyr, Arthur's best friend, and Merlin, Arthur's wizard, worried for Arthur as he worried for his father. And they worried for Meurig too. Greatly moved by their love, the afflicted chose to be the one giving, instead of receiving, comfort. "Mother is gone, son. But I have reason to live." Meurig withdrew his hood. "Your brothers are a disastrous lot, ever praying and preaching and giving alms. They can't possibly function without me!" Each of the three heroes allowed themselves a teary smile, seeing how Meurig kept his humor in so dark a time. "And your sisters – where to start!" he continued.

Full laughter ensued.

"Arthur, son..." Now King Meurig was gentle, but grave.

The son could not give response to the father, his throat choked for sorrow, love and endearment. Meurig patted the head of his boy, then knuckled the scalp as mates do. Well past the median of life, but yet with only blonde, red, and brown and not one grey rebel amongst the waves of hair.

"I have YOU to be around for. I retired my sword and trusted our kingdom, and the very hope of the survival of Cymru, to you. You were far too young: a mere lad tasked to be as a god, a savior. The burden alone, however, we never allowed you to bear. Neither now shall we let you bear it." Meurig positioned himself slowly in his layers so that he could address the group. "Mourn for Onbrawst ferch Gwrgan Mawr, and for noble Queen Gwenhwyfar. Cry hard. Weep long. Remember them in bards' songs and tavern tales, and numb thyselves with much strong drink. But worry not for old Meurig. I promise that my love's spirit will carry me, and that she will sleep in the Lord until we are again together. At that moment 'twill be as if no time has passed at all."

***

The cold leverage of starvation, meanwhile, was driving many of the Catholics amongst the Tribes and clans to make their pledges to Llew and Caw.

Blankets and food in exchange for muscle, sinew and sword. Help from Rome as barter to displace the Church of the Britons and the king who had once claimed neutrality but now openly supported them.

Though Caw mourned the loss of his father, pride has a failing memory, and hate comes ever to displace and supplant reason – *so much so that he illogically blamed Arthur for Geraint's decease and not the Saxons of his own band that had done the deed.*

Orders were whispered that those faithful saints of Rome from Powys, from Deheubarth, from just north of Arthur in the lands of Brychan, extending to the extreme southern horn of the Isles, and even from Glamorgan and Gwent, should at once relocate to Ynys Mons or to any havens ready to host them in the cantrefs of Gwynedd. However, the harvest was so weak and the weather yet so bitter that travel was undesirable on most days, and on some days, perilous. As a result, there was no mass migration of fighting-age Catholic Christians to the North.

Instead, in the same village one home was pledged to the Round Table, ever at song about the glorious victories of the Golden Age, crying new hymns about its imminent return, whilst the next home gave its loyalty to the Bishop of Rome and a new future for Britannia and the world. This was the condition throughout the hundreds, cantrefs, sub-kingdoms, and kingdoms of the Cymry.

Resigned to the fact that armies must be raised, armed, and trained, the Round Table Fellowship experienced the same challenges. When asked how long it would take to properly engage Mordred, Cedric, Caw, Llew, Mark *and Maelgwn*, Merlin gave a blunt answer comprising of but two words: "Three months."

The Pendragon disliked the answer but sought optimism amidst the dreary state. "Good," he said. "I believe it will be warmer then. June. We finish this in June."

And whilst the kingdoms of the Britons continued to divide and dilute their strength, the Jutes, Angles, Gewessi and Saxons trained as one united force in Wessex, and in Lloegyr.

CHAPTER 10
No Song for Mordred

The enemy did not join his 'father', Llew (in Mordred's sorry circumstance, the bastard had neither step-father, nor foster-father, nor father-in-law in the person of Llew ap Cynfarch), in Gwnyedd.

Rather, he celebrated his first victory over the man who had violently murdered his love, his very own soul, sitting about Great-Aunt Marchel's cauldron, brooding noiselessly. Barefoot and wearing only trousers, she had covered him in the nine sacred herbs of the druids, which are:

Henbane,
Mistletoe,
Vervain,
Clover,
Wolfbane,
Primrose,
Mint,
Mugwort,
And, last, Anemone.

A lather of ivy salve spread the old crone about the warrior's torso, greasing his chest, back, arms and neck. Next, she placed idols to the four winds and to all directions save the North, which was left null to represent the place of the

Christian God, who was as repugnant darkness to the witch. Red candles were spread across the cold, blackened stone floor, forming the shape of a seven-sided star about the Cauldron, and about the Whelp.

She sought to conjure ellyllon, which are elves.

She sought to conjure the Coblynau (who were but a foot high to a man, but full of mischief and malignant designs).

She sought to call the Gwyllon, which are female demons of the night.

And many of the other Tylwyth Teg she invoked besides.

Whilst Mordred remained as a statue, sulking in his sulk, void of expression or response, the intermittent undulation of his chest the sole marker that he was yet living, one of the Fair Folk did give answer to Marchell's ritualistic beckoning.

"What would thou?"

She could hear him; Mordred could not.

"Bravery for the Son of Pendragon. Bravery like unto the gods!"

"Batwings and potions, salves and herbs. Will these not be enough for the Bastard to carry the day against the Iron Bear?" The tone was unkind. The very King of the Fae emerged from the shadows, now in open starlight, a great red tower directly opposite Mordred within the heptagram.

He looked upon the Traitor at length. Had the boundary of Mordred's mischief been harassment, theft, political intrigue and the occasional assassination - a thorn and a prick upon the Sons of Adam who ever boasted their dominance upon the sacred places of the Otherworldly, primal occupants of the Blessed

Isles – then would have the Tylwyth Chief done well. *Instead love found this imp, and love doth undo all, and maketh the imp the very Devil.* A celestial tear navigated the cheek of a creature supposed to be void of humanity.

"I made his mother, and caused her to be selected to make him. And I cursed his mother's mother." Then he roared, as a ravenous lion, "ONBRAWST! I AM SORRY!", knowing that his screams could not rouse the departed Lady. *Neither did the scream of repentance rouse Mordred, for the herbs had placed him fully in a trance, trapping him as a hare caught in the snare, lodged between two worlds.*

"Morgause." He addressed her in her *name of romance,* as already uttered in nighttime fables to scare naughty children over on the Continent. "You believe that by defeating Arthur and controlling this weasel you will purchase the continuation of your kind. But you believe amiss. The One who controls the ones who control the ones who control him reveres no god, neither anything that calls itself God. As a prostitute is used and discarded into the byways, else slain in the alley when shameful loins sober, so too will he be used. And the Wicked Thing that would replace these Britons, these pesky, horrible Celts, will be the destruction and merciless judgment of us all."

The old witch harkened, speaking not.

"I am manifest to arrest your works. The Fae will not aid you beyond what you've already lured into this chamber. But neither shall I send them away." He began to depart; then, turning, inquired, "Who was it that asked you to summon the Dormarch? For this notion came not forth of your own design."

"The Bloodhound Prince, Lancelot himself, requested these."

"Lancelot?"

"Aye."

Phantom snarls. Faint howls and growls from afar increased. No longer ghostly, real and present claws scraped, stepping out of the shadow; the drip and plop of drool soiled the floor. Soon a company of mystical and dreadful canines were present.

"He bade me fetch them from the Underworld, saying, 'Let Arthur know what it is to be hunted by dogs, dismembered by hounds.'"

Giving no reply, the King of the Tylwyth Teg left Morgause and Mordred to their devices.

***

I am meant never to rule.

Son of a witch, seed of incest, fated to be used by the religious and the ambitious.

There is no Song for Mordred. History will make me a profane thing, the sigil of dishonor.

Vortigern, whose treachery first filled Lloegyr's shores, inviting the Long Knife to our very hearths – even he will be forgotten and I remembered. Mordred the Traitor. Judas and Mordred; woe is me, I share infamy with the Son of Perdition himself!

Treachery, loyalty – I care for none of these designations and assumptions. We are pawns and cattle in the hands of inconsistent, impassioned angels who fancy themselves gods. How does a treacherous worm differ from a loyal one? Or who looks upon the ants below with individual condemnation?

By extension, my father too is a worm!

But woe and dread, how I tremble at THAT worm.

With a false face he hunted my brother Amr as a

stag, and privily he slew him! He swept his enemies away as does the broom sweep the hall, and then he reigned.

So long a reign! Emperor Arthur. Invincible. Promenading and strutting about the whole of the Isles in the Sea, hunting Giants and ridding the world of every creeping thing.

But not the monster in his own house.

When you were on the hunt I kissed her, and when adjudicating liberty and prosperity with your knights and bishops, she lived in the crescent of my arms.

You have ten thousand songs, but never once sang Gwenhwyfar to you. I am Mordred, and I have no song save how that Gwenhwyfar of the raven's hair did love me best.

You took my brother, and I took your wife, and would manufacture a good name that I might take your crown – but as month begat year and year begat decade, you would not die!

There is no song for Mordred, but the bards ought to sing a song of patience for the Traitor of Britain. Patient in the field, patient in the barn, patient in the chapel, patient in her ladies' lodgings, patient under the stars and in the brook and stream. Patient, loving her where I could, when I could, until the process of time and the cruelty of circumstance would that I take a second wife.

Gwenhyfach, the little Gwen. Contrasted by name from the beginning to shine less brightly than Gwenhwyfar, the great Gwen! The fair Lady! The favored child of Ogyrfan the Giant! Forgive me, my love, that I used your sister in my dark imagination, loving her by the name of Gwenhwyfar in my heart, yet my flesh wanting none of her! That I made my bed with another is my sole unpardonable sin, and I seek not acquittal, my heart!

There is no Song for Mordred. And Arthur would

do unto me as he did unto Amr, and his steward with indomitable club did against the skull of the Shimmering One! O, Llacheu and Amr, and Gwydre, my half-brothers, did not your father slay you all that he might long rule contrary to the parameters of nature? Or was Caw in league with the evil forces, as rumors report, saying that some Masked Villain of Italy manipulated all? We are worms; who is it that maneuvers us in our holes in the soil bed? Is not Arthur the master manipulator? Has he not beguiled Gildas ap Caw, recompensing one son for another?

Arthur will kill me thrice, the triple death of our ancestors. Poison will I drink, a thick noose wrapped and knotted that my throat shall close, the water to drown my lungs. And Excalibur the fabled blade will delight in my flesh, slow and skilled to bring sting but not death afore all this. Unless my mother save me!

Mother! I am your first son. The heir. The paramount. Yet you hid me in the safe lines, having me battle wanton sheep in the stead of invading Germans. Did you know I would find my own brother in the place where you hid me? Where your disgrace and shame was hidden? Then it was you that sent me to Caerleon. Your displacement and shamefacedness to look upon me gave me both my loves! Amr and Gwenhwyfar ferch Ogyrfan – they alone are angels and no worms!

But your I love yous, Morgaine of the Faeries, fall upon ears most deaf when Gwalchmai is placed at the right hand of the king, whilst I am as uncomely garments shoved into the dustiest compartment of the wardrobe chest.

The Hawk of May. He judged and accused correctly – only the participants he identified were half wrong! Oh, irony that his last years were under the shackle of a bad report, only to be killed by that very man who grieved him so. And both were innocent! Round Table undone by my vices! I defeat you, father, regardless of the outcome of this war amongst the Tribes.

But you will murder me and parade my head upon a spike, my four parts to herald the corners of Britain. Unless my mother uses her sorcery to hide me!

Mother! Cymru is your first priority, then Arthur and I by equal measure. Choose; tilt the scale! Will you not save me, for he slaughtered your grandchildren and boasted against our entire house? And unlike the one whose bones you guarded, he shows no mercy, extends no door outward. Morgaine and Arthur adore their Mary, but would the Son of Mary butcher children, or set war dogs upon women? Mother! The stack of your kills reaches unto the treetops – will you not add one more to your count, and in so doing save your son?

There is no Song for Mordred, only a lamentation for the fall of nations. And what will rise from our fall?

Mother! Your Lancelot has lent me his spear. Lancelot is the one you would have as my father. He now protects me against the coming day. Will you not join us, and let our Trinity rule and reign for a thousand years? Forsake your foolish oaths, your commitment to skeletons and Jewish prophets of old. They are perished. We live, while yet we live. Mother! Will you not use your powers that we might prevail? Moth –

"No, the Lady of Avalon will not help you. Because… she cannot."

A loud discourse between Morgause and the King of the Tylwyth Teg accompanied by the heavy gait of five devil dogs (whose breathing alone was as cracked, screeching trumpets) had not roused Mordred from his trance. But none of these are the mighty Maelgwn Gwynedd, *the Lancelot* of the Continent, the foster-son of the Lady of the Lake; the Champion of Britain.

Does he walk between the worlds as the Fae? How much did he hear? pondered Mordred.

Much.

"By ancient statutes that harken back to that Age when the old was overcome by the waters from above the heaven, the spirits cannot engage in open combat, cannot sway the outcome of war. Your mother appears to likewise fall under this restriction."

Mordred began to make the inquiry that all made, but Maelgwn dammed up his words ere they flowed: "I do not know *why;* perhaps only the Merlins know, or perhaps none know at all." Maelgwn had not presented himself for to surmise about theology and the mechanics of the End Times.

Each time Maelgwn looked upon the man he had witnessed in active, passionate congress with the one *he had loved first* an evaluation was made: *would Mordred be granted another day to fill his lungs with air? Would the tenuous allegiance continue?*

"Rise," he commanded.

And the Whelp arose.

"Fetch your garments."

The Whelp dressed himself.

"Is your objective to be king or to avenge Gwenhwyfar?" The evaluation began.

Mordred's answer was careful, thoughtful and honest. "Just presently, during this very ritual, I was made to understand that the only way to prolong my days is to slay the king and beg Rome and the influential amongst the Tribes to recognize me as ruler." Mordred paused, then delivered the wrinkle in his modified strategy. "But not for the whole of Cymru, as this can never be." Maelgwn seemed interested, honing in on the realism and resignation in the Traitor's words. "Ruler – not of Cymru. Just Gwent. Because of my parentage, and as my uncles are clergy and my aunts wedded to the Houses of Brittany, I can leverage the military support of Brychan, and – with Arthur dead – make claims in the South. But a Pendragon, nay. They will never accept me."

"You will kill to be king, to avoid being killed by a king?" The aggrandizement of the man reminded Maelgwn of himself, especially during those fits where his bubble was intolerable and the most bizarre and abstract behaviors were justified. Maelgwn felt at once great disdain and sympathy for Mordred. *After all, were our hearts not bewitched and held by the same Siren?*

"I will inform Llew and Caw of as much. The sons of Cunnedda shall rise again; I shall rule in the south and *they* shall raise a dragon in the North."

Maelgwn disagreed. "A Pendragon must needs be a Silure! From the earliest divisions of our tribes under Brutus it has been so. They may nominate an Wledig, but a dragon out of the North? Unthinkable. I flew the dragon sigil at Llongborth to protest Arthur, not to promote one of our own to the paramount position."

"All you say is true. But, Lord of Gwynedd, our world is upside down and traditions are suspended as the elderly freeze and the children grapple for an acorn. We are plunged into chaos. A fire serpent has wasted our land; the harvests have twice failed without the Royal Clans demanding Excalibur be returned back to Llyn Fawr. The old bishops have befriended their most ancient rivals in the druids, whilst the Roman Church is political bedfellow with the Dynion Hysbys.

"The vision came to me clearly." Mordred paused, contemplative. "This is the very hour where a man of the North *can ascend* to be head of the dragons."

"What man?" Maelgwn demanded.

The Dormarch gathered round the seven-foot embattled cedar; two sat erect as griffins, eyes flashing red then black, a blue mist swirling about them. The remaining three lay about his feet and cried as pups yearning a pat. The hounds of hell, claiming the Bloodhound as their master.

"You, Maelgwn Gwynedd." The cauldron gave a hiss, bubbles popping. "You will be Pendragon after Arthur."

CHAPTER 11
Gwenhwyfar Taunts Arthur From the Grave

Gwynllyw ap Glywys was a minor chieftain who once had governed a Hundred in the kingdom later known as *Glamorgan*. His domain extended from the port town of Castell Newydd to Afon Twyi.

A ferocious warrior and one of the scores of heroes worthy of songs and books from the Age of Arthur - *the Age of Heroes and Villains* - Gwynllyw adored the family of the Pendragon. Living so close to the courts and manors (and thus soldiers) of the High King, Gwynllyw possessed the deepest gratitude that Meurig, and then later Arthur, never interfered in the daily administration of his humble realm. The respect for local rule and the constant guards against over-reach of the Round Table, which functioned as a kind of central or *federal* principality, besotted Gwynllyw and many local chieftains to the more famous princes and knights that held seats in that lofty and renowned brotherhood.

At the terminal battle of Mynydd Baedan, Gwynllyw and his men had been amongst the disciplined Silures that waited as statues atop the hill, animating in the twinkling of an eye after such extended stationary time at the command of the Iron Bear. He had been a significant contributor in delivering ordered, methodical slaughter upon the Saxons as they made their vain ascent to defeat, their fateful climb to certain and violent death.

After Baedan, and like many other *survivors* of the Saxon Wars, the volume of fatalities and terror changed Gwynllyw. Having no more taste for combat, having had his soul bruised by reason of three hundred grotesque images of entrails and teeth flashing and clicking through his mind every night, never giving place to restful slumber, the warrior chieftain forsook his sword and instead took up candle, bell, incense and Bible.

When not serving in the church at Llandaff, Gwynllyw and a few other soldier-saints personally labored to build a chapel in Castell Newydd. The project was a labor that wrought healing by distracting his mind from the horrors of war. As for his lodging, Gwynllyw founded a hermitage at the place the bards would later call *Bryn Stow*. He much preferred the solitude of life in a humble cell, furnished only with cot and kettle atop a hill fort, to the courts and markets of Caerleon and Caermelyn.

Until he fell in love.

Then Gwynllyw could not be removed from the city, where dwelt Gwladys - who by misfortune was the daughter of the Chief Brychan, who cast his lot with Mordred the Traitor.

Gwladys owned a shop where she and three damsels under her employ made fine gowns. She was noted near and far for her silks (with which she adorned herself always, whether under angry winds or smiling sun). Such was her skill, and so coveted her wares, that she traded with merchants upon the Continent and with Rome, and even periodically hosted buyers from the Near East who came praying for a glimpse of Arthur and of his famed knights, and to procure the silks of Gwladys.

She was a brilliant, enterprising Cymreig woman full of verve. Pious but not haughty, faithful to the Lord but not given to empty religion, sensual but chaste, Gwladys was very much ingredients of Gwenhwyfar I and Onbrawst, with garnish of Gwenhwyfar II. *And her body was thirty years younger than the dead queen.*

It being yet early in April, the next major offensive in the Civil War was not to be contested for three moons. Knowing that the chiefs, captains and rulers were busy preparing their men, Brychan boldly entered into Caerleon, communicating with angry force to the two lovers that their union would never be.

The Twenty-Six (subtracting Rhun, who painfully considered whether he could war against his father; Rhufawn, deceased; Gwalchmai, deceased; Amwn Ddu, engaged presently on the Continent; Hoel, likewise; and Maelgwn, at variance with the High King, reduced the count to twenty) were indeed busy, refreshing the skills of veteran warriors and training young men of promise. Although having not a minute to spare, King Arthur himself interrupted his work of warfare to support Gwynllyw, whom the king viewed as a founder of Castell Newydd, and a dear friend.

Reports to the king communicated that Brychan and a few of his men had barricaded Gwladys in her store, along with her lover, and that the shouting and threats were intense. Gwynllyw, now every part hermit, carried no sword and was at a disadvantage, being surrounded. Even in the aftermath of the Red Dragon, some buying and selling had resumed (along with desperate bartering) and young children were at play in the streets of Caerleon, warming themselves, hoping to cause their bellies to forget deep and painful hunger.

The situation was dangerous to innocent citizens – and escalating.

Seeing a dual opportunity to at once enjoy an adventure that would allow him to seek the refuge of disguise and to see justice delivered against the imposition of an unwanted guest, Arthur planned to transform himself into a beggar and approach the shop.

As he carefully organized a pile of tattered rags in the king's chamber, Cai, half-musing and half-concerned, inquired, "In the east Cedric has tasted success, and rallies an old foe."

"Yes; the Saxon rises, even now," said Arthur, struggling with a hopelessly holed stocking.

"In Little Britain, Mark and Childebert would crush our friends and our kinsmen, and install a new order in Cornuaille, in Leon, and throughout the Lady's forests in Broceliande."

"Quite true, steward." Now Arthur's charcoal, which he masterfully applied to his eyes, was giving him fits. "Hasten to hand me that mirror."

Cai did so, with a grimace and eyeservice. "Llew and Caw would end the line of Pendragon, and make us two vassal kingdoms under the diadem of the Bishop of Rome and her Emperor."

"Frightening to consider." Arthur responded

passively, his care fully devoted to evaluating which cap to don.

"At home the Roman Church toys with us with her wealth, making bondservants of the faithful."

"Wherever religion is organized it degenerates into corruption, for it too is made up of men." Arthur was now practicing dragging his right leg while hitching his left shoulder higher than its counterpart.

Cai exhaled, watching a man full of honor and dignity feigning the role of a lame drunkard - and worse, loving the role! "Your son raises an army to unseat you."

"Where are the grey horsehairs I use for the beard?" It was now as if Arthur was fully ignoring his longtime protector.

"Lastly, Maelgwn Gwy—" Cai did not finish the name, seeing the Iron Bear's countenance change.

"That was a fine summary, brother." The lame beggar with the unsightly limp was gone, and the sovereign had returned. "You forgot to toss in a few thousand Picts and whomever else assembles as jealous vagabonds longing at last to see us wiped from the face of the earth. We are encompassed by enemies who are guided by the invisible hand of an ancient Order of powerful Devil worshippers. At the same time, we are ablaze by our own sins and failings. The winter falls on our Summer Kingdom."

"Yes!" Cai thought his friend was rousing him with a fiery speech, articulating the dire straits.

Not so.

"And we can neither delay nor hasten what comes, for a sort of *second Mynydd Baedan is approaching, and it will set the course of life on this Island for the next generation as Baedan did for ours.*

It is coming. The course is set, and we will not change who we are because of that circumstance!" Arthur was teaching, but some frustration had crept in, magnifying his point. "We fight for truth and justice, and truth and justice say we help our friends! We let *the situation* change us when we massacred the remnant of Mordred's line. Let us learn to never again react so. Rather, let us change the situation, and not suffer the situation to change us. Do you understand?"

The inflection suggested that a question had been asked, but when the king commanded his words in *that tone*, no response was expected, *or tolerated.* In his wisdom, Cai gave a simple, "Yes, my lord." After much pause, the steward then offered light words to reduce the king's ire. "Go with the long black beard; the grey is obviously like unto a costume worn by the bards during the solstice dancing festivals. It wouldn't fool a dullard, let alone clever Brychan. And your gait is wrong – walk like this."

Arthur roared with laughter and joined in the mocking, theatrical limp. "After so many years, Cai has become as Bedwyr and would cure all with merry and lightness of heart!"

The jesting spent, the serious Cai soon returned.

"Now, brother, what is the strategy?"

"Gwynllyw is a hermit, oft wearing rags as these." Arthur was beaming at the opportunity to misdirect and befuddle his foes. "I will walk into the shop under the pretext of being a poor saint, imploring the captors to make peaceful resolution with the forbidden pair. Then, once inside the door, I will turn and reveal."

"You're going to stroll into the heart of a conflict where our friends are pinned in by an enraged father and his *armed men* and then *reveal?"* Cai wasn't sure he wanted to hear the response, but let loose the question anyhow. "Reveal what?"

King Arthur rehearsed the matter before his steward. A leather tube designed to carry a map or scroll was hanging by a strap flopping sloppily around his left shoulder, appearing innocuous. With a swift twist, the top of the canister popped into the air; a pouring motion followed to empty the tube. In the place of scrolls and parchment, Carnwenhau poked its hilt out, as a snake emerging from the hollow of a tree to snatch its prey, and then disappeared into a shadowy sheath once again. *Along with casting a cone of darkness around its wielder, from which to work the blade with great advantage.*

"Armed soldiers, angry father, hermit's rags," Cai repeated himself for impact, "and a magical dagger…. What could go wrong?"

Arthur grinned, slapped Cai about the shoulder, communicating great confidence, and made directly for the markets of Caerleon.

***

Gwladys's silk shop was in an open market, outdoors. The back of the shop was a section of the city gate itself, the front two posts roofed by a thatched canvas. Three archers stood erect and drawn at the sides of the shop, greatly disrupting neighboring merchants (who had all struggled during the distress of the poor harvest and irregular, bitterly cold weather; the loss of even two buyers due to the conflict could represent not eating for the month), whilst Brychan and two men armed with longswords guarded the front entrance.

Gwynllyw and Gwladys were as penned

hogs. Curses and yells filled the air, and the hermit posited the sum of his body in front of his damsel, fearing greatly that hot heads might a missile sling.

As rehearsed, and without hesitation, *Arthur the hermit* limped up to the soldiers. "Cymry threatening Cymry at tip of arrow and edge of sword whilst the Saxons daily strengthen and recover their numbers. May Jesus save us – can we even spare one soul?" *That was almost too kingly,* Arthur thought, fighting back laughter that might betray him to quick-tempered Brychan.

"Mind your business, monk," said a soldier.

Brychan did not speak to the hermit, his glare and invectives fixed upon his daughter's unauthorized suitor.

Arthur did not need to win a philosophical debate, nor negotiate a release; he only needed to pontificate and plead for a few moments whilst positioning himself between the soldiers and the shop. *They perceive no threat, and surely will not strike me down.* He calculated quickly. The men found him as a gnat, not an opponent. They hollered at him a few more times, a mixture of mocking and frustration.

"We must attend to this matter! Preach elsewhere!" they cried.

Finally, Brychan allowed the hermit to divert his stare. As he formed the order "Remove him," Arthur had already gained three paces on the soldiers and was firmly under the fabric roofing of the shop. He turned to Gwynllyw, and, tearing at a portion of his fabricated beard, smiled at his old friend and ally.

"I will make the day as night in here; as I do, leave comely Gwladys and flee, sir."

"I cannot leave her, lord. She – "

"Her father treasures her as do you. She will be safe with him, and away from this situation. Then you will call a troop of your men out of retirement. We will give chase and recover her."

"But, lord…" A smitten man is void of reason, and protests.

"Trust me."

Gwynllyw remembered well the authority contained in that tone and nodded.

"Remove him. Cast him upon the road, else into the Usk River!" Brychan's agitation was at its zenith.

"Blessed is the peacemaker," said the hermit. "Let me pray with my friends, and then I shall withdraw."

Brychan had inherited a fear of God from his father, and suffered the fool to make his prayers lest Brychan suffer condemnation of the Church. He approved the request, his eyes rolling, and the sighs intensifying. "Make haste."

The hermit unfastened his leather tube; none questioned the act, each supposing some religious instruments were to accompany the prayers.

Carnwenhau, the enchanted dagger of King Arthur (and amongst his favorite armaments), was at once in hand, the disguise torn away, and a tattered but somehow stately Pendragon stood before all.

"You." Brychan ground his teeth together and flared his cheeks to such an extreme that his eyes disappeared in the folds of his face.

"Women possess their free agency in this land, Chieftain. She is of age; you have no just hold over her hand, or her heart." Upon saying these words, Arthur worked the dagger, causing it to cast darkness in a large cone around the king, Gwynllyw and Gwladys.

"Hypocrite! Foul! False! The foundation itself, decadent and tunneled with rot, of your *Summer Kingdom* is built upon arranged marriages and the use of women as political pawns!"

"Each lady who sacrificed, that peace might endure, had what you would now deny your daughter." Arthur pushed Gwladys from the cone with a gentle force, knowing that a soldier would catch her away. "Choice!"

Seeing his daughter safely removed from Arthur's *mystical cave,* King Brychan signaled the archers, who fired twenty and nine arrows into the shop. Next, the soldiers rushed into the shadow, returning only to report what Brychan already knew.

Arthur and Gwynllyw had vanished, untouched, unharmed, and surely far removed from the markets of Caerleon.

***

"I respect that you have forsaken this life, but if you pry the damsel from Brychan and make her your own..." The king handed Gwynllyw a silver breastplate, and Cai fastened the red cape of the Silures about his neck, lacing it over the armor. He still bore the ageless frown of protest that the Pendragon had once again put himself in danger.

"Why wearest thou the frown, brother?" Arthur asked. "Were I to have perished back in that storefront, would not Maelgwn and the Northern princes have laid down arms, called for a conference atop Caer Caradoc, and negotiated peace? It would be rather favorable were I to have gone to the place where the Merlin slept."

Cai did not contemplate the king's philosophical posit, not for one second, making immediate response. "Were Arthur ap Meurig slain, the Northern princes would strip the mines to barren, and use Cymreig gold to conscript Cedric and a host of other Boars, and cut through the South as the vineyard keeper thrashes the vine. We who lived would bow knee to the Bishop of Rome and, in a generation's time, German would be our native tongue."

Arthur looked soberly at Cai, then onto Gwynllyw, who was reluctantly reacquainting himself with the instruments of war. "I suppose I should be more careful then."

The three men shared the bellowing laughter of fellows, then entertained plans about abducting fair Gwladys.

***

Gwynllyw's popularity in his hundred had not waned. Moreover, hungry men would rather fight than bear the guilts and pains of entropy. It was not difficult to raise a company of three hundred, and to make for Talgarth, where stood the principal court of Brychan Brycheniog.

Unaware were the Silures that Maelgwn Gwynedd had but recently been nearby and left fifteen of his Hosts behind, aiming to add brawn to Brychan's position, which was north of Gwent, and a key passage into the Midlands.

Arthur, Cai, and Bedwyr were supportive but direct with Gwynllyw. This was his operation, led by him and his own clan. The Round Table Companions would provide secondary support and watch the action from the hill called Boch Rhiw Cam. Should trouble befall Gwynllyw, they, being positioned to see all, could descend quickly to provide aid from a high-ground location.

The three heroes rode fast ahead of the three hundred, and set up camp, bringing the gwyddbwyll board and much spiced mead (which they would heat upon the kettle) to pass the time. Cai and Bedwyr pitched a small pavilion to shield the trio from the cold, which gave no mercy, and against the freezing rains, which were as so many thousands of tiny razors upon the skin. Warmed by fire and mead, the men slept well.

The following morning Cai and Bedwyr resumed their gwyddbwyll, a contest intense - and emotional, when coupled with the aching head subsequent to mulled mead. Arthur favored the solitude of hiking and communicated that he would ascend to a vantage wherewith to look down on Talgarth and report the matter upon his return.

The idle time proved to be more enemy than Saxon knife to the heartbroken king. One share of his heart mourned for Queen Onbrawst, and the other agonized over the absence of Queen Gwenhwyfar ferch Ogyrfan the Giant. One chamber grieved the warm grief of fondness, a limitless stream of loving memories and fair times. The other chamber grieved the cold grief of unrequited love; of the self-doubt and questioning of one's worth when one loves something, and indeed must be near, that which reviles and dismisses him.

Hot grief.

Cold grief.

Such dichotomy threatened to burst the Iron Bear's spirit asunder. The pressure around and in his chest was great, the emotional and spiritual impacting the physical.

Hot grief.

Cold grief.

The fingertips of his right hand twitched. His

left arm presented a dull pain. His tongue dried as a forgotten sponge and then yelled at him, *Swallow me!*

Whilst Bedwyr tossed dice and Cai mused, *Now try it with your right hand…* And whilst Gwynllyw and his equestrian knights progressed to the beacons slowly, preserving wind for a tussle… And whilst love and hope swirled… Arthur swooned.

Gathering himself to one knee and giving his full weight to an old oak tree, the broken king readied himself to perish, literally, of a broken heart.

In that moment the temperate, honorable, loyal man peradventure captured a glimpse of Gwladys, staring up as if she were arguing with the clouds, pleading with them to give way to the sun. Brychan's palace was constructed primarily of wood, trimmed with gold; ornate, the beautiful round manors in the style of the ancients. An external stairway, painted in white and carved throughout with doves and owls and stags, coiled round, winding and winding until it terminated at the sixth story and transitioned into a balcony where this debate between damsel and nature was conducted.

Temperate.

Honorable.

Loyal.

Lustful!

Carnality, and nothing noble, rushed upon the king to stay his heart.

"Gwenhwyfar?" He peered down. He knew she was not Gwenhwyfar, for he had been first witness to her decease, having fed her but four months ago to the war dogs.

Feeling better, though deceiving himself and

healing nothing, the stately sovereign adorned a new mask – a typical man.

She is not Gwenhwyfar, and I love her not, but shall not a king lie with whom he pleases? Her comeliness is as a goddess, her disposition as an angel. Why not have her for myself?

"Why not have her for myself?" The second time was audible.

Best friends sense things. Cai and Bedwyr had shared the spur of concern quite at the same instant and were searching for their fellow.

Hearing those words, and the fleshly thoughts that begat them, caused both men to think their lord bewitched, ill or drunken. Not knowing how to respond, and distracted by shock, Bedwyr was unrestrained. "Because she loves another man, and you another woman – that is WHY!"

Cai followed that with, "You mourn and are not your right self."

"The woman I love sleeps beneath the dirt."

"That is her condition. Whether she draws breath or is dead as that log changes not your condition. Look not on another woman until the woman you love you no longer look upon. Who gave this proverb?" Bedwyr continued to be strict with his best friend.

Arthur fixed his stare upon Gwladys, but gave response. "Merlin did."

"If you must fill your bed with damsels, do so; yet not her," Cai pleaded. "We can ill afford scandal amongst our own tribes. Neither can we suffer ourselves to lose Gwynllyw to Mordred."

Is this what it feels like to be Lancelot? Arthur was rallying, reasoning with himself. *To give in to passion and do as you will? Is his crazed bubble lurking within me? Ought I not to learn the ways of my opponent?* The upright son of Onbrawst and respecter of women combatted the notion, and rejected it – in part.

"Brothers, you are right. My conduct is wrong. I feel faint and not well; forgive me."

"Nothing to forgive." Bedwyr supported the king at his elbows. "May this tussle conclude speedily that we might see you to your bed, resting and restoring yourself for the real clash that lies ahead."

Partial rejection.

"I do desire to be in my bedchamber, Bedwyr," the king stole one last, sustained gape at Gwladys, "and I will heal my heart with my loins and enjoy some women." Arthur smiled, but his companions were unsure, continuing to be startled by his uncharacteristic antics. "Not that woman, but *some* women," he reiterated, terminating the conversation.

Soon the capable soldiers of Gwynllyw's Hundred arrived at the base of Boch Rhiw Cam, ready to breach the wooden spires that surrounded Talgarth. Their smitten leader's disposition was regret and resolve.

Regret that he had to engage in arms of any kind after twenty years of peace.

Resolve that a tyrannical father, petty and power-mad, would no longer divide the lovers.

The three Round Table Companions could still see Gwladys. Her arms waved frantically, her motions easily confused from afar.

Excitement?

Instruction?

Fear?

Waving and pointing. Pointing and waving.

A deep, elongated and vibratory beat drummed. And then a rattle.

More waving. Desperate waving.

The drumming intensified; familiar horns gave instruction spoken in music.

"Ravens!" Bedwyr cried.

"And not just so – rather, the Hosts of Maelgwn! The lady's arms are begging retreat!" Cai started screaming for Gwynllyw to withdraw, searching for his steed in a hurried, upset fog of mind.

"They cannot hear us from up here." Arthur's was face ashen, filled with colorless shame. "I climbed too high. Gwenhwyfar haunted me from the grave, and I pulled us from the range where we might do good for our kinsmen."

Cai had found his steed and his fellows' besides, and they made haste.

It was so; Gwladys was doing all to wave off her betrothed abductor.

The Hosts of Maelgwn were but fifteen. *Fifteen professional killers who had seen real and ongoing combat for the sum of their youth. These were hard men; these were amongst those who had won the Saxon Wars for Cymru*. Each was aged above fifty, but fought with the vigor of a young warrior.

Though none were tall as cedars, as their master, each member of his Hosts were *as him*. The style, the movements, the invincibility. It was uncanny and rumored unnatural that there were so many emulations of the Bloodhound Prince. *And he had hundreds more in addition to these.*

But these were sufficient for the battle at hand.

As Maelgwn had moved on from the location, he was not present to give strong instruction and reminder of cautious and careful blows – of mercy and quarter. Without their lord to bid them behave, these Northmen slew the Silures with strokes and slashes empowered by the anger and rage reserved for the Long Knife, not for their own Cymry.

Fifteen killed two hundred. One hundred remained when Cai, Bedwyr and the sandy-haired, blue-eyed, fabled king at last arrived.

Gwynllyw bore a hurt upon his left arm, and his bloody cough revealed broken ribs. He did not judge the Round Table Fellows for the tardiness, thinking them to have been in the rear lines, else in the chaos of the fight, all along.

Arthur gave some confession, concealing more than he revealed. "The spirit in those hills detained us; forgive me, brother. In the space of one hour, with your life you shall be."

"Nothing to forgive, Emperor. Gratitude and thanksgiving that you rescued us from that villain, and have provided us hope that we may marry. I owe you all, o just and pure king, along with the renowned Cai and the indomitable Bedwyr!"

"Can you ride, old warrior?"

"I can, lord," he responded. "Only not well." The greying warrior-monk was anguished, bleeding and broken.

"Cadog is one of your own," Arthur offered an encouraging smile, *"and he is one of my own."* He motioned to the Round Table Knight. "Conduct him some yards hence, and encompass him with nine swords, that he might witness the remains of the day. We will deliver this damsel!" Excalibur was unsheathed, the ring and song of the Sword of Power overcoming the battle drums of Maelgwn.

Three corralled fifteen, allowing the remaining one-third of Gwynllyw's soldiers to breach the spires and extract the princess with great ease. King Brychan retreated with his guard, opting to renew swords another day.

"Hearken!" Arthur hollered. "They will counter, neither slashing nor swinging first. And their diagonal they will not break. See to it that you do the same. Be their mirror! Be their mirror!"

Bedwyr continued to master fighting in an inverse, left-handed stance. Illtud, who was a master of leverage and the relational impacts of weights and measures and force, had designed a sword that the Round Table Knight could wield with one hand, never needing to add the supportive weight and strength of the other. The distribution of weight achieved gave the approximate force and reach of a longsword, only with the dexterity of a dagger.

Assuming that deformity would equate to an easy kill, hubris consumed one of the Hosts, who abandoned his teaching and rushed upon Bedwyr.

The Raven's head rolled, spinning thrice and lighting at the feet of his fellows.

Arthur's three opponents were more calculated, precise, and difficult to overcome. The heat of battle had distracted the Iron Bear's broken heart; he felt recovered, healthy and strong. Whether false or temporary, the recovery served him well, for his opponents *were as mirrors. And the opponent in the mirror can neither be dodged, nor struck, tackled, nor run through.*

Excalibur clipped the heel of one, causing him to withdraw *(and Arthur was glad that a soul was spared, desperately hoping that this elite soldier would one day make his charges under the wavy red dragon banner once more)*, but the other two fought on.

Brute force wins some battles, and skill wins more. Strategy with skill translates into almost certain victory. However, when the scales are even – brute force equal, skill equivalent, strategy identical – 'tis one attribute that determines the victor.

Wind of lung.

For lovers and fighters, he who lasts longest wins. Many skilled lovers are laughed out the bedchamber one minute after they enter. Likewise, many who grapple possess knowledge of forty arm-locks and fifty holds to subdue a man, yet are winded in one minute and find themselves panting – and pinned.

King Arthur was fifty and four, and fatigue should have made his steel heavy and his movements slow. Rather, his verve only burgeoned as the conflict was prolonged. The Merlin had imparted to him secret methods on how to keep his heart (that muscle of flesh and not the spirit of the man) rate to differ little whether resting or running. He had learned this secret forty years ago, and it had enabled him to win countless protracted matches in games of skill, versus giants and hags, and when locked in real combat upon the field of battle.

The Hosts of Maelgwn did run long, but Arthur longer. Where Excalibur, and its wielder, was concerned, one tired error, no matter how minute, could mean death. And for the mighty men of Gwynedd, two more needless souls were added to the heap: a growing stack of bodies charged to the account of Arthur's offenses and Maelgwn's loins.

Having finished them, Excalibur paired with Cai's club to fell the remnant.

Victory.

But the wages were great.

"There remains no ambiguity. The Chieftain Brychan is as the gatekeeper between the North and South; and he is wholly devoted to Mordred, to Rome." Arthur sorrowed as he panned over the Ravens, lying dead or gurgling the last gasps and rattles of death all about the spires and gates of

Talgarth. A heavenly fortress and manor carved in wood, a dwelling of repose, hunting, merriment; a place to cease from vocation and appreciate the romantic beacons. *Blood stains cannot be removed from woodwork, nor the soil cleansed when watered with native blood; the Blessed Isles herself cries out that the Titans Arthur and Lancelot soon end their madness.*

"This will not soon end," Arthur stated plainly. "Neither can we suffer the enemy to establish himself so close to Caerleon. The hilltop ring guards should have easily noticed the swell of military activity here," he complained.

"Too many experienced watchmen perished by the fiery mouth of the cosmic dragon," Bedwyr responded.

"I know," Arthur conceded, and sighed. "We must train new watchmen rapidly. Moreover, we cannot suffer this war to be fought here. Our numbers are depleted, our people morose. It must not be so. We will give pursuit, the terminal battle of this war to be contested in the North."

***

Arthur, Bedwyr and Cai returned with doubled obsession to the matter of raising, training and preparing their army.

Gwynllyw and Gwladys married immediately, conceiving a son. So thankful were they that Cadoc had shielded and sheltered them (for he had conducted them safely to Gwynllyw's modest cell, and then remained, toiling with his own tools, hands and sweat to transform the dwelling into an abode befitting a dazzling and enterprising woman like Gwladys) that they called the newborn Cadwg, meaning *'battle glory'*, a variant of the original Round Table Knight's own name. Cadoc was greatly honored, finding joy in that babes in every cantref were called Arthur, but few were christened with his namesake.

CHAPTER 12
Finalizing the Lists
Urien Denied Again

May
AD 537

Some bards, using numerology and a smidge of theatre to teach and preserve the histories of the Cymry, cite but three souls escaping the Battle of Camlan (that fateful and dread pitch where Arthur and Mordred engaged at last) with their souls; others sing of seven; yet others twenty-four and two (matching in count the original Round Table Fellowship), that the death of one Administration hailed the beginning of the new.

Not discarding pedagogy for the cause of precision, 'tis true that the survivors, both among the faithful Britons and among the deceivers who found pleasure in opportunity and sophistry, giving their swords to the pleasure of Mordred the Traitor, were scant. However, many champions and heroes of the Age were not part of the census, counting as neither dead nor living, for they abstained from the battle itself.

The men and women of the fading generation, *Arthur's generation,* who had defended the sovereignty of Cymru, had paid a wage that wrought a life of despair, night-terrors, fits, incontinence, shakes and insanity. Their fractured condition had been caused primarily by engaging in gory and vile combat when in the flower and formation of youth - fourteen being the age by custom and necessity.

For this Civil War, Arthur refused to repeat the requirement and, to the credit of those confederated against him, so did his foes. Only warriors above twenty and five battled at Camlan.

Peredur and Gwrgi, the youthful Grail questers, were withheld, lacking years. Likewise Trystan.

Whereas some were too young, the Senior Monarch, Meurig, was persuaded to abstain from Camlan, with much protest, on account of having *too many* years. He had returned his sword to Llyn Fawr after suffering the injury that had brought fear (whether of superstition or substance) to the Royal Clans that the harvest, on account of his pierced loins, might fail. The wonderful commander had carried himself with a limp for the past forty years, but in all other measures of a man he had fully recovered. None would protest his assumption of a temporary office as King of Glamorgan should Arthur fall at Camlan. For this cause he would remain in Caerleon. *However, by those ancient decrees, he could never again serve as the Pendragon or High King of the Blessed Isles.*

Gildas the Scribe was ordered to remain at Neath, charged to continue penning his histories and registers. Gildas adored Arthur as a father, but he likewise adored his father by blood, with whom Arthur would soon war. Therefore Gildas was thankful to remain neutral, burying his head in scrolls and parchments far from the crooked river, rocky hills and waterfalls that fed the field of Maes-Camlan.

Mark remained on the Continent and would not be counted amongst the participants at Camlan. Not so his foes Hoel and Gwythyr, but Amwn Ddu, who is the *Black Knight* in the epic poetry of the Cymry, was strategically held from the field.

Arthur's older brothers were monks and no warriors, and monks they remained (though Frioc was privily developing ambition as he witnessed the chaos and calamity of the rulers, thinking, as many do, *I could govern for the better than these)* and many other Saints – and Sinners clothed in the vestments of Saints – did not perish at Camlan, *as they lacked the courage to be at Maes-Camlan in the first place.*

The noble Rhun ap Maelgwn Gwynedd agonized for two moons, eating little and sleeping less. Llongborth had given him a first-person witness to what would come to pass: fathers slaying sons, brothers slaying brothers, Cymry in league with Picts, Saxons improving in both technique and presentation. His witness was sufficient. He did not consult his father, neither druid nor bishop, and in the end, grieved with trepidation and uncertainty, he sent a message to King Arthur, informing him that he would lend two-thirds of his men – who, by individual election and full persuasion of mind, chose to continue with the Silures – but that he and the remaining one-third (including the sons of Rhun) would remain in the North, ensuring that a strong vein in the lines and branches of the Royal House of Cunedda would continue, though Maelgwn might fall.

Arthur accepted the Raven's offer and sent

blessings to his ally Rhun; bidding him Godspeed, beseeching him to rest from his distress, not begrudging his choice.

***

Arthur summoned Urien and his son Owain, inviting them to join the Pendragon for cider and custard pastries in the library - a favorite refuge for thought, reflection, strategy and solace for the king. Rebuilding the Round Table was not a priority when the army lacked armor and the people lacked supplies for basic daily living. Also, the king favored the spot because his wizard had returned to him here.

And Merlin did now join him, as did Meurig and Bishop Dyfrig.

Urien, coy, wise, grizzled, instantly knew the ambition of the summons when he saw the inner circle of Arthur's inner circle puffing upon their pipes, thickly filling the library with the smoke of meddling in the lives of other men.

"No." Urien objected ere his hand lifted from the iron ring fastened on the door.

"There now, my friend." The Iron Bear made efforts of consolation. "Drink here with us; elsewise let us ride to Lodge Hill."

"No." Not yelling, but directionally louder.

"Please, brothers, sit." Arthur cocked his head to the right, blue eyes welling with empathy, but honed with resolve.

"No!" This one a yell. A few old tomes creaked in response.

Owain, usually of hot temperament and reactive disposition, seeing that Urien was surrounded by Elders who would not be swayed, sought to cool his father. "Please, Da— "

"No! No! No!" It was followed by a steam of inarticulate cursing in tongues and diction older than the Merlin himself.

Presently the same rose.

"You are younger than Arthur; your lands are in the North. Should your brother Llew and the Traitor prevail, your father will surely negotiate a peaceful ongoing alliance with you." Rings of smoke sailed across the book-filled room, as a sailing vessel glides towards the setting sun. "Whether the Council of Nine scheme and conspire to beguile these shores, or whether the Saxons seek to expand by sword, or by fornication as they do now in Lloegyr, a remnant of what once was must remain, lest the future shadow hide the past in a blanket of dark lies and revision."

"The son of Meurig ap Tewdrig, the Emperor and Lord, Arthur, savior of the Britons, will take the head of Cynfarch Oer – whom you designate as *my father* – and Llew will follow him down into Hell!"

"May it be as you say." Arthur's voice broken. "Nevertheless, you and Owain, along with one third of your own…" the king was a friend first, and struggled to finish the edict, "…will not join us when June arrives and the Knights of Old drive north to face the menace of the Ages."

Urien was of stocky build but at the same time of great height, being a full head taller than Arthur. He had auburn and yellow hair, which was wild and curly upon his brow, but neatly tied into a dozen leather and jewel-decorated braids that fell about his shoulders. His beard was profound, and likewise braided. He was the type of knight that seemed to live in his armor, to sleep in his armor, and to take hold of every moment as if it were a dragon to slay, well pleased to one day die in his armor.

A hard man. A man of war. A man of order, of faith and of loyalty.

Owain had only witnessed his father weep once. And now the tears returned, for the same cause.

"I missed Mynydd Baedan, deployed on some vain quest to find this misplaced druid." Urien was frustration incarnate. "And now he prances back into our camp with the frolic and twirl of the water-sprites and I am made to miss the Siege of Mordred."

Merlin was not offended, knowing that Urien had given the whole of his life, another warrior hatched at fourteen, to the cause of unity, freedom and defense of Cymru. Urien did not relent, continuing to lash out at the wizard, even as his moustache became comically matted by tears and the issue of nose that accompanies crying.

"And where were you, Merlin? Give my quest, which was not voluntary, meaning - for surely your quest, which was at your whim, must have been to save Arthur himself!" Urien chose an extreme, not expecting the candor of response.

"It was to save Arthur himself. And I have not yet saved him, nor delivered him out of harm. For this cause have I returned."

Merlin's enigmatic words quieted the room.

Arthur wept. Urien wept. The three Elders made efforts at stoicism.

"When my chapter in the Songs hath ended, Urien will still be slaying Saxons, I promise." Arthur's words.

After a great pause and a nervous adjusting of his cape, a fidget with beard and brow, and the alleviation of his tears, Urien fixed his moustache, allowed his shoulders to slump, and calmed himself.

"What will you do if Owain and our Ravens arrive in a wave of thirty thousand? Will you turn your arrows from Mordred and loose them upon us? Will you refuse our aid? Or surrender?" The questions were a half-portion of jest.

"If it keeps you alive, and hope for the Summer Kingdom alive, then I will send Merlin to Brittany presently, and command you to go find him." The Bear of Glamorgan smiled. "But he is old, so sit with me and enjoy cider, giving him the lead by a week or two."

The heroes of Mynydd Baedan managed to turn tears into laughter, and mourning into fellowship. Two more of the original twenty-four and two would part the Fellowship, by design and by tactic.

Urien left his youngest son, Pasgen, to receive fosterage in his ancestral lands of Gwyr, which is in the cantref of Eginawc, in the realm of Deheubarth. Owain and his father and a large retinue parted company with their Round Table Companions, returning to the Old North; Llew and Caw dared not bring ambush or injury during their journey.

CHAPTER 13
The Summer Kingdom was False, and You Knew

The Lords of the Old North had promoted Mordred's idea many times afore. That Maelgwn should be High King was not a new notion. That which was new was that Maelgwn gave the concept place for consideration.

Maelgwn had witnessed, being side by side with the Pendragon during the unfolding, unraveling events, Arthur's *look* when they had caught Mordred and Gwen II in adultery - performing *the very act of adultery.* Arthur had not ceased being Arthur when he had fed the queen to his mastiffs; rather, in Maelgwn's opinion, his lifelong friend, and Sovereign, had been lost instantly, signified by *that look.*

Was that the look I wore all those years ago when bewitched in Avalon's sacred orchard? Does madness enter in an instant and immediately signify its birth with the expression of that look?

From age sixteen to the very moment of *the look,* Maelgwn had acquiesced to the following:

Arthur was more honorable - *until now.*

Arthur was more stable - *no longer.*

Arthur was less blemished by scandal, a ruler

beyond reproach – *reproach and defame aplenty now loom over the head of the Silure.*

Arthur was a man of reason, never under the spell of passion or impulse – *save when he hurled her from the tower to the hounds below.*

Arthur could better unite and galvanize the Tribes – *Rome versus our ancient relic of a church, the druids gnashing and gnawing upon the Dynion Hysbys, every tribe and household at variance under the reign of the son of Meurig.*

Arthur had better command of the customs and law – *I have twenty and four bards to help me with this, even if Taliesin has forsaken me.*

Arthur was the Prophesied One. It was his destiny. *Prophecies fail, portents oft interpreted by what the Seer wants instead of what the Seer sees.*

Maybe it is to time to think on Lancelot and Head of the Dragons.

The estranged Champion of the Round Table thought hard on these things, looking at Arthur in a new light, forgetting his own darkness.

Two of his other seven other-selves manifested to remind him.

Did King Arthur slay his uncle for three minutes betwixt the legs of his wife?

Did the Son Pendragon exhaust the flesh of youthful boys, brimming with life and virility, and then slay them that their protests or political leverage in the scandal might be buried in the Deep, silenced by the dirt?

Did the rightful High King betray a tribe of Picts, PICTS THAT ADORED AND WORSHIPPED US, that he might lie with the queen?

The Merlin gave you one charge, one command, one duty. Proclaim it in somber recollection. Proclaim it!

The splinter of Lancelot taunted Maelgwn in

this regard for the space of fifteen minutes.

Proclaim it!

"He charged me protect Galahad my son above all else. For in Galahad were all the wrongs of both Arthur and Lancelot made right. The North and the South united, and Camelot secure for a hundred generations."

And did you meet your charges?

"No."

No! Instead you distracted yourself with women, and jealousy, and self-aggrandizing madness! The Madness of Maelgwn shattered this kingdom, not the failings of the just and great king, or the manipulations of the Church, or the conspiracy of the satanic elite. You, High King of Cymru? You were to guard Galahad! Instead he chased after relics and lost his life to empty superstition! Taliesin said well, 'You are the ruin of Cymru'!

"Maelgwn–"

Interrupted by one of his bards, the Bloodhound Prince reassembled, decided that he did not deserve to rule, undecided whether he *wanted* to reign.

"I asked for solace." A dreadful, low voice.

"Forgive me, but urgency demands I disquiet you."

Maelgwn grimaced and nodded, for truly there remains no privacy during a time of war. He motioned for the bard to report.

"Warriors from Glamorgan overcame Talgarth, causing Brychan to flee. Many of your elect have fallen. The stronghold in the South - lost."

"We were discreet in that stationing. Surely word of our trespass so near Arthur will have come to the king's ears." Maelgwn assumed Arthur and his Fellows were ever occupied with training his inexperienced army, aghast that an offensive, small battle had been fought so soon after Llongborth.

"Cai was there," the bard stated. "Bedwyr too."

"Cai would not leave his lord's side. He is a protector and no commander," Maelgwn responded, shrugging his marble shoulders, his hands opening flat and elevating to the heavens, then clenching as an eagle snatches its kill upon the brook. "Arthur was with them!"

"Aye," answered the bard. "The bards say that he fought as a youth upon the field, that Excalibur twirled and whistled; that he was as a god with lightning bending and bowing to the will of his hands."

The jealous version of Lancelot manifested, capturing control of the host. "And what will the bards say when I slay the Lightning Bearer?"

Filled with fear, the bard responded, "That the Grandson of Cunedda has at last restored the diadem that has belonged here from the days of Brutus, long usurped by the dark tribes in the South."

The flattery allowed the replaceable bard to keep his head, and Maelgwn hastened the training of those opposed to Arthur, hoping desperately that the cold would abate, or at least give pause; that those declared against the Pendragon, dispersed over the whole of the Island, might have opportunity to leave their homes and voyage north where the efficiency of preparation, and of census, might be a thousandfold more efficient.

That Arthur had anticipated the placement of a garrison in Talgarth, and exterminated it, gave Maelgwn great cause for alarm. No further operations would be launched in the midlands, and certainly not in the south. Rather, he would prepare a defensive strategy, knowing in his bowels that the king was readying to face those confederated against him far away from Caermelyn and Caerleon; the Civil War would be conducted in the Northern realms of Cymru.

***

Mid-May
AD 537

Queen Onbrawst and King Meurig had taught their oldest son, both by the behavior they modeled and by direct instruction, that physical romance - kissing, holding hands, and intimacy - must be connected with love, lest an empty carnality develop in a man or a woman.

Though bewitched from his youth by the dark-haired Gwenhwyfar II, Arthur for the greater part lived these values, having had very few lovers in his fifty and four years.

Seeing the damsel whom he had perceived as the sole and exclusive love of his life willingly and hotly ravaged as an animal (enthralled by, and returning to the ravaging to, her true love) tormented the king. His knee ailed. He fought a slight cough that would not surrender his lungs, and his handsome face showed more than a few new wrinkles (though his appearance was that of a man in his early thirties, his sadness begat a false perception of aging, and the ugliness thereof).

Convinced full that he would now never enjoy what his parents possessed, a season in Arthur's life began where he chose to be as the world and dabble in fornication. After returning from the incident with Gwladys, he slept with three women in three days.

The polite, gentle, and *loving* (though absent of *love*) man remained, for he was kind, careful and engaging with each, building them with warm words and doting compliments.

After each occurrence, at the very moment the lass would robe and depart his chamber, an emptiness seven times worse after the act than before would overtake the king, causing him to make haste in dressing, hiding himself in his formal armor. He would then rush to the shrine of his first wife, Gwenhwyfar ferch Cywryd, *Gwenhwyfar the Red.*

Her place of rest was the chapel called after Saint Julian, a martyr slain in Gwent in Roman times. The malaise of freezing and unpredictable winds had not allowed a full reconstruction, but her stone sarcophagus was complete. It had been hewn with devotion, adoration, and regality, and expressed an artistic humility that was a perfect and lasting representation of the person whose body made permanent abode therein.

But Gwenhwyfar's spirit was not there. A stateswoman of faith in Christ and unwavering patriotism, a splendid Sovereign, and a better mother. She had been wholly devoted to her children. Then the Saxon Wars had broken her spirit, the act of surviving her own sons murdering her whilst she lived; a human shell hung upon a ghost haunting a nunnery.

Mordred had taken nothing that was not already gone and, in her final days, her last acts of wisdom, grace and reconciliation had imparted strength and a familiar comfort to Arthur, preparing him to once again do what he must, and what none else could. *To murder another son.*

And so Arthur would warm his flesh with

a damsel by night, and seek consolation and support from his deceased wife by day, kneeling before her grave, lost in deep contemplation. He donned the one-piece helm, fashioned in the Corinthian style (for the Britons come from that kind of stock, being Trojans) where the eyes and nose were fully encased, and the cheekbones as well, leaving but the lower lip and throat exposed. Arthur's helmet was silver, enameled with a blue as midnight, which matched the tunic and leather beneath his heavy armor. His cape was the crimson that all Royal Clans the world over seem to favor. He presented himself to the queen polished and shined. The image of the Blessed Mother, debossed upon a small oblong shield, was fastened to the left shoulder, the Iron Bear sigil about his neck served as meeting point for the ties of his cape; the Sword of Power was thrust deep, more than halfway up its shaft, into the clay floor at the base of her shrine.

"One more time, O wife of my youth, great friend, proper and true queen, one more time I will do what I must, though it render me without issue."

Arthur felt a great shadow behind him, cast by a dark faerie. Having no need to rise and validate with his eyes what his bosom already felt, a whisper vibrated up through the sides of his helmet: "Sister."

Gwyar, in this moment fused fully with *the Morrigan,* was raging with anger older than the Lakes, indignation deeper than the Bottomless Pit, a righteous fury that rattled and shook, an incensed, caged demon jerking and tugging violently at the bars that gate Hell.

Disregarding the greeting, the Sorceress Morgaine cut to the quick: "Nay, you will not."

A broken, disjointed exchange of phrases and

unilateral comments ensued – the kind that lacked order or sequence. The way that siblings long to resolve disputes but run round the issues instead of addressing them directly: in this manner did they speak. He remained kneeling, behind the midnight blue *mask*, and she stood behind him; whether in this moment she was three and a half feet or thirty stories tall (or at once, both), Arthur could not discern.

"My sons are Gareth, Gaheris, Ogyrfan, Gwalchmai and Mordred. Four of the five in preference choose you, their uncle, King Arthur of Caerleon, over their father Llew. Gwalchmai is fallen to Lancelot. Would you see the rest follow him to an early grave?"

"Women know things," Arthur said.

"I sought you out, hoping against hope that you would show Mordred mercy. In the place of mercy, you slaughtered an entire house of my cousins by marriage, of friends of our youth there employed. You slaughtered my grandchildren!" Thunder crackled.

"You knew." Arthur had no fear of the Sorceress Morgaine.

"Why did you not order me to Lodge Hill, that we might congress before actions so rash, so murderous, so *unArthur?*"

"Twenty years of peace through the Isles, but not in my own home! Twenty years a fool!" Arthur's voice was animated, rising and falling, but he was as a statue. "The sacred rite was to prove I was fit to rule, yet my seed begets only treachery and perversion."

"Gwalchmai gave his life – for you. He is gone. Galahad is gone, Llacheu and Amr too. Would you have every fighting-aged man under forty a corpse? Would you have the old Four Cords rule well beyond our season, governing over a pile of younger bones?"

"But three cords remain, for your rival Gwenhwyfar's blood feeds the soils of Cymru." This time, he responded to the fragmented statement.

"My rival!" This missile found its mark.

Arthur could feel a shift in the wind, his armor conducting heat to his flesh; soon he was a fount of perspiration trapped in a metal box. Yet anger continued to override fear. Fixed in a contemplative bow upon one knee, supporting his weight upon the hilt of Excalibur, he remained.

"You loved Lancelot, and she loved" - Arthur measured his words - "another." More measuring. "She sat upon a throne, having my ear and my attention, whilst you mastered herbs and fought with priests over enchanted relics. Lo, I declare, she was your rival."

"She was a whore and the ruin of Britain!"

"And you knew!"

"I love you!" Stone fell from stone, the power of her words making the chapel ruin *more ruined.* Then she shrank; the sweaty king, feeling her defeat and her suffering, rose and turned.

Little Gwyar ferch Onbrawst and Meurig the healer, protector, mother and patriot, stood before the king. He fully armed, she in two pieces of brown leather (a top and trousers) fastened by a heavy knotted rope - the attire one wears, be they man or woman, when a hard ride of great distance is required.

Sister.

Advisor.

Companion.

Sacred lover.

Friend.

The angry Bear slowly removed his helmet, and the two Silures looked long at each other, recollecting and reenacting much history and countless deeds in the looking-glass of the other's eyes.

"I love you too, Gwyar, more than any person who liveth."

"Any save your half-alive, half-apparition wizard." She smirked.

"Yes; second-most, then." Arthur patted his brow. "What exactly *is he?*"

"I only know that he and I meddle and manipulate and do our best to support you, Arthur. You are the hope of Cymru. And of mankind. We succeed, and we err. I did know."

Though the dispositions had cooled, the confirmation was as white-hot coals upon Arthur's head. He stayed his tongue, and did not respond in anger; the burning truth cracked as an egg, running in every direction down his face, then onto his chest and at last running off onto the floor below.

"I concealed the matter, and it almost destroyed me, bringing more shame than our *incident* in the cave. Putting the Harlot to the knife discreetly would have destroyed you, so happy and in love, the Summer Kingdom thriving. My own son, OUR own son, I could not slay, leaving me only to tell you, or for mercy's sake let us have our season in the sun."

"Mercy and secrets. Let's examine what mercy and secrets have over these many years wrought," Arthur began. "The wages of mercy upon Cedric is the imminent end of the Lloegyr from the face of the earth, and the rise of Saxons born not in the Nordic Wilds but a day's ride to the east of this very spot!" Arthur watched a few rays of sun, resilient and unwavering, brave their way through broken glass and charred wood, lighting beautifully upon the stone box that housed the queen. "For mercy's sake, Mark menaces the Continent. Dispossessed of land and cattle but not slain, that *mercy* has grown an army, here a little, there a little, that could shift power to the Franks and, worse, drive our cousins into the Sea. And his hooks in Cornwall could trouble our borders besides, should we survive the Civil War and be so fortunate as to draw breath and have heartbeat to entertain troubles." A few more rays touched upon Gwyar's raven hair and illuminated specks of gold in her large eyes. "Secrets taught Lancelot that he was above the Laws and Customs of the Tribes, and gave license to his madness. Mercy and secrets would I have none - only immediate justice and transparency. This is what I have sworn, and this is what I beseeched and begged of my companions, including you, sister."

Gwyar reached up, straining to reach her brother's shoulder-shield. At last she was able to trace a few lines around the image's outline. "Some secrets are good, brother. Did we protect the Mother of the Lord so long in vain?"

"Well, no—" Arthur began to frame a response.

"And mercy is its own reward, as saith both the Christian God and the benevolent goddesses of old. Foreswear neither mercy, nor the selective wisdom as to when it is meet to conceal a thing, Lord Arthur, for these are the hard prerogatives of princes; and you are the best of princes."

"Did my half-dead wizard script these things for you, sister?" Arthur smiled, his hand tracing the outline atop Gwyar's tiny fingers. "She was wholly dedicated to mercy, and we love the Blessed Lady."

"We very much love her, in spite of the priests' blasphemy and abuse and spite-filled treatment. And her walk and every moment was wholly given to mercy, grace, and truth. I find these things not in the Church that claims her, nor in the Creator God whose *Jewish King Arthur* she bore, but—"

"The second Merlin, Taliesin, has shared with me much about the distant and silent God and the purpose of His Son. Should we again have an hour of peace upon these lands, I would share his *secrets* with you."

"Mercy and secrets." She smiled, seeing the conversation come full circle.

"Aye, and cider." Regrettably, Arthur discontinued as brother and assumed his office for the next part of their discourse. "Gwyar," he began, "even were there no scandal associated with Mordred's birth, Gwalchmai's accusations, or Lancelot's guilt - and even if my offenses and missteps with the Champion of the Britons had never been - this war *would have come.* There is a force behind the Saxon Tribes, a force greater than and indeed controlling Rome, a force that our local diverse sects and colleges bow to as some enlightened guild when, of a truth, they are of darkest evil. Because Rome is as a toy on a string to this *force,* even now giving blankets and coal and victuals to the faithful in our own villages, using the leverage of feigned help in a crisis to control the masses, this war was inevitable.

"And the South must win. The Roman Church would rid the Isles of your gods and goddesses by assimilation—"

"And your bishops would banish us by statute!" she protested.

"Let us not take up again Vivien and Dyfrig's

debate at this time. For the survival of us all, the Round Table Fellowship must both wage this war, and prevail."

"I will not let you kill him." Gwyar was resolute. "He is our son."

"If he falls into the controlling hands of the Council and their masked master, what then?"

"We Ladies" (here she referred to herself as the Lady of Avalon and Vivien, the Lady of the Lake) "are good at hiding things."

"He is neither horn nor scabbard, treasure box nor chalice, but a man of flesh and bones. We must prevail, no matter the personal cost."

"I will not suffer you to slay our son!"

"Will you strike me down, as reports say of Maelgwn?"

Morgaine of the Faeries was unable to strike down Arthur Pendragon.

On the merits and mysteries of God's plan for the Ages, the otherworldly thing could not harm *the real king* (for Arthur was not a ruler promoted by the will of Man, but rather was set to fulfill some part of the Great Conversation, and the Consummation of All Things). Therefore, he could strike her down and not rather the reverse, though she be far exceeding in power. Knowing some measure of these things, her answer concealed much.

"I tried to prevent this Civil War, but did not slay him; neither will I bring my brother, whom I love, to be undone." A pleasant response, chased by eyes set aflame for the warning that followed: "Now this is the final time I give plea, prayer and warning. I will not suffer you to kill Mordred; and from the pitch of war, refrain to place Gareth, Gaheris and Ogryfan!"

"Round Table Knights all! They will join

the company, lead men and add more songs of praise and heroism to their names, bringing the confederacy of traitors to bow and beg – and, by the might of the Sword of Power, be scattered to the four corners of the world never again to make war upon these exhausted Isles!"

"Brother, I will call the Dragon. His breath will I direct to envelop and shelter my sons, creating a protection of confusion, that neither lance nor arrow shall find them. ALL of my sons. And the mist shall encompass and hide you as well." Morgaine was determined to this, intervening against the peculiar rules and laws that bound her kind to doctrines of non-interference. She would find a way, though the heavens fall.

"Have not the People presently had their fill of dragons?" Arthur demanded. "You will at once protect both Mordred, who fights with Rome, and the remnant of your sons, who stand with me?"

"I will not suffer my sons to perish."

"Your aims approach treachery, sister." Arthur freed Excalibur from the floor. It gave a metallic hiss, sparking as he freed it from the clay and stone. Sibling squabbling resumed. "In your *mercy and secrecy,* you knew these dark days would come. Whether it was a good thing to delay them, or a grievous sin in delaying this hour, we cannot say. I hate that you allowed me to live a lie! But I know you sought only to protect me, and give our tribes an age of peace and prosperity. My anger kindles, but the Merlin's lessons ever remind me, and us, to press on towards the mark ahead, not looking back at decisions for good or ill that brought us here." King Arthur then ordered Morgaine of the Faeries away. "In a fortnight we assemble and ride north to finish this. If you yet respect your Sovereign, exile thyself to Avalon and there remain until the dead have been buried and the lost mourned. Then return to Caermelyn and reconcile with me. Then let us yet embrace in ongoing and grievous mourning, and after this mourn more. When the sorrow is spent, we will draw breath yet and, seeing that the sun yet rises over the valleys and the birds sing and swoop over the lakes and brooks, we will heal this land."

"Into exile I go, obeying the Emperor of the Britons." Morgaine was not shaken by Arthur's attempts to see her physically removed from the scene. "Thunder and lightning, rains and MIST I can cast from anywhere, most especially from the Sacred Isle."

Siblings change subjects when subjects become painful. Rather than continue a circular, unwinnable dispute, Arthur succumbed to jest, that one last fair memory be created for the two heroes.

"Sister, what have you done with Cai? I can no more lift my face from the wash basin except a hand-towel be at the ready by the intrusive brute." Arthur laughed. "You didn't slay the king's Steward, did you?"

Gwyar allowed a smile to escape. "Herbs. The potion I gave him has given your childhood protector the best sleep he's had in forty years!" The smile gave way to a mutual laugh, then a strong embrace of merriment.

Arthur would do what he must. Morgaine of the Faeries the same. The faerie withdrew from the king, who immediately made for his helmet *mask*, returning to quiet contemplation at the side of Queen Gwenhwyfar.

CHAPTER 14
My Heart Turns to Camelot as the Floor Around Me Burns

Mid-May
AD 537

Gwenhwyfar applied a soft knock to the door; though it was barely a rustle, her parents knew the sound.

Gwythyr rolled to his side that he might face Alienor, who feigned sleep. Tickling her ribs and tugging an ear, he began to rouse her, then made her fully awake with a wet, childish kiss. "Your turn, my Swan."

"Gwythyr!" she protested. "'Tis your turn, and she is her father's child."

"You only disown her when it is the middle of the night. 'Tis YOUR turn, and by the by, she is the very image of her mother."

Slight knock. Rustle. More ironic mousey sounds came forth from the Lioness of Lyonesse at their bedchamber door.

"I am daughter to both! Hearken and let me in, I pray."

"She can command thousands with the wink of an eye, can cause wells to dry at the snapping of a finger, yet she whines and whimpers outside our door," Gwythur goaded the girl.

"I cannot sleep!" she exclaimed, still a mouse.

"She'll not relent," Alienor mused.

"She'll be out there until cock crows." Gwythyr made jesting protest.

"Da!" The Mouse-Lion heard the ongoing mocking.

Gwythyr protested about the hour, as parents do, and dressed, at last presenting himself at the door.

Before he could fully greet the princess she burst in and jumped upon the bed, then took her father's original spot, lying next to her mother.

"I supposed I could sit upon the footstool." Gwythyr sighed, and then laughed.

"Respite escapes me. My mind is disquieted. My head races in circles, running as children round the Maypole, not ceasing or easing. Is it true? Will I really lodge in Gwent two nights hence?"

"Aye, daughter, but brace yourself, for the golden city is in ruins and the people despair much," said Gwythyr.

"Turrets and towers, founts and theatres, minstrels and markets. These things do not render a city great. Rather, it is the liberty they stand with, such unrelenting resolve that ignites the flame of freedom within the bosom of every man and draws us to adore them. And that fire was kindled in our own lifetime in the south-east of Cymru, in that place we call Camelot. It is no trivial thing to be alive during a dispensation of heroes and legends. In my eyes, I know I will see it as it was. I will weep with honor for what it gave me, gave us, and rejoice with a forward-looking, longing hope that its best days may return."

"Even while the sun yet hides in his chamber she is stately." Gwythyr was the proudest of fathers.

***

Both parents deeply appreciated the maturity and optimism displayed by the heiress of Brittany, especially in light of the dire turn of events causing the Royal Clans to make haste from the Continent and *repatriate* to Cymru.

Hoel the Good and Gwythyr were losing ground in the protracted battles against Childebert the Merovingian and Mark ap Merichion. Lacking the reinforcement of the three hundred the Round Table Companions had provided was material; both morale and momentum was being lost as they abruptly returned to the Isles.

Moreover, the absence of Derfel upon the field was devastating. The *new Lancelot was in the company of the old,* instead of fighting invaders under the banner of his father. Where battles are concerned, one person can sway the tide, one hero make the difference. *True leadership and success are infectious, as often said the Merlin.*

These two factors were principal in the decision for Hoel, the greater portion of his sons and daughters, and Gwythyr and his whole house, along with other chieftains, bishops and thirty troops, which is nine thousand men, to abandon the sister-cities of Brittany and return to their ancestral homelands in Britain.

Gwythyr faced the truth that Mark would soon defile his very own bed, the women and soldiers soon to soil the baths and pools. There was little concern that the Merovingians or Mark's commanders would burn the villages, or in any way damage the castles, chapels, founts or dykes. Their aim was to conquer and occupy, not raze. Provided that they controlled their Germanic conscripts, the kingdom would be intact when Hoel and Gwythyr returned to restore their land and, one day, place the diadem on the deserving crown of Gwenhwyfar, the Lady of Lyonesse.

As for the residue of the Bretons, Amwn the Black Knight (Arthur's renowned brother-in-law by his sister, Anna) would lead an exile into the magical forests of Broceliande. Though the otherworldly beings who occupied the wood were given to mischief, they had an affinity for the Bretons, as the Bretons were Cymreig. The vastness of Broceliande could conceal thousands; provided their circles and groves were not disturbed, the Fae would be content to host. Sufficient soldiers were left behind to protect against the sweeps and manhunts Mark would surely conduct, but Hoel wagered he would be too busy erecting his new kingdom to be overly bothered with scattered and defeated refugees hiding in huts and tree-houses.

Amwn would serve as Protector of Brittany, keeping as many of the citizens alive as possible until Hoel (and peradventure, Arthur, Cai and Bedwyr themselves) should come again, and liberate them.

***

"Your restlessness comes not by reason of our defeat nor our hastened departure, does it, daughter?" Alienor asked.

"My heart commits treason," Gwenhwyfar responded. "Mother, where I should cry out over our world, which collapses into chaos, I can think ever and only about—"

"Your heart is no traitor. The barn could be on fire whilst you fed the horses and you wouldn't even smell the hay burning, nor feel your boots cooking, when under the consumption of this condition."

"I am the Lady of Lyonesse; no passion consumes me." Gwen made a vain effort at resistance of the open and plain truth.

"Were that 'twas only passion, for passions ebb and withdraw as the moon-tides." A mother's wisdom. "Just verbalize it. Let it out loudly; it may give you rest." A mother's instruction.

"Say it." Now Gwythyr goaded his daughter, making tea for the trio with clanks and clamors of protest and the disquieting of his rest. "Say it" - he served the princess the first cup - "and then" - he handed his beloved wife the second - "get thee back to thine own bed!"

"Well, then." Gwenhwyfar slurped the tea as a child, assuming the immaturity of her accusers. The family roared in laughter. They knew they faced a short but treacherous sail in the morning, a dangerous journey to a land where few had sufficient food for their own families. The worry about feeding nine thousand more would cause unease, and potential strife. Yet the family embraced, and mused, and were merry in the moment, knowing their lives would change forever not many hours hence.

"Well, then." A final gulp emptied the cup. Gwenhwyfar rose from the bed, straightened her gown, and ordered her hair, acting as if she was readying to make a prepared speech to an assembly of elders or bishops.

She paused. Gwythyr of Leon had repossessed

his spot in the bed and he and his wife sat against the headboard, leaning forward in anticipation, squeezing their pillows.

"I love him!" Gwenhwyfar declared. "I love him to distraction. The sea boils and the sky falls, and I think only on him. I love him such that it frightens me that I may lose myself."

"Who is the boy?"

Alienor smote her husband with one pillow, then two. "Don't embarrass our girl further, causing her tongue to identify what the whole of our little kingdom knows."

"Arthur," said Gwenhwyfar. When she proclaimed the Bear's name, she felt as if the sun arose anew in her heart, and dark times gave way to the light. "Arthur." And the sun rose again. "I love King Arthur of Camelot, and I shall love only he, forever."

"And we love you." Gwythyr stood and embraced his daughter. "Only corral your love, and let patience guard your precious vessel. For he must first win a war versus an opponent that outmatches him. Should he overcome, and be the victor, only then can he be of equal disposition to love you. And love you he must, else avoid him – though we love him – you must." He spoke not of Mordred, nor Lancelot. A father's wisdom.

***

"See them flee unto the Sea, the beginning of the extermination of the Walles on the Continent." Simon Magus was amused by his rhyme – a sinister self-aggrandizing cackle, amplified by thin black steel. "Son of Merovee, govern well here," admonished The Mask. "And mark thou Mark." More wordplay, more cackling. "After all, he is as crazed in the brain and mad as his father ever was."

Childebert beamed, seeing cowardly Frankish warriors clip at the heels and upon the backs of the last of the Bretons, frantically shoving off on their long platform boats. Some were maimed by chained whips, while others absorbed arrows flung chaotically and maniacally straight up in a blind arc; the invaders made sport, casting lots on how many would fall into huddled groups of women and children. Mercifully, the winds carried most missiles into the sea. But injuries and losses were many, such that foamy blood remained long after the final boat exceeded the sight of the devilish onlookers.

"And now, the Council of Nine likewise departs. Be not tyrannical, but rather kind, that you might earn the people's affection ere you close the fist of dominion over them. That celebratory slaying below," Magus spoke of the brutish behavior by the victorious Franks, "is uncomely. I adore the kills, but be smarter about such things." Every instruction Magus gave the king had the underpins of weighted threats, *for I favor Arthur as our puppet. Be a good second choice, for second choices are come by easily.*

***

Word by messenger was first given to Iddawg of the *exodus* of the Bretons. The lad had settled into the unspoken office of Emissary to the High King. His bloodlust spent, his lies consuming him, his face was either ashen or green at all times. The cataclysm of the comet had created diverse illnesses and maladies, allowing Iddawg a cover for his guilt.

Arthur and Cai were visiting with the Pendragon's uncle, Caradog Freichfras, calling another from the Saxon Wars out of the repose of retirement to once more take up the lance and defend Cymru. Caradog would lead a more permanent sacking of Talgarth, ensuring that Brychan could not recover and rear-flank the Silure-led armies. This was a final and necessary step before the armies rode north, and the interpretation was easy to understand; old Caradog would take the Beacons, and the larger army would move north, meeting the Ravens and their confederacy of Saxons, Picts, and the vagabonds of Mark somewhere above Powys but below Gwynedd.

Iddawg the Pale-Faced Liar, knowing the Iron Bear was absent, trembled as he approached the Merlin, who had vanquished seven ciders whilst sitting at tea with Illtud, for the peculiar Christian druid did ever glare into the boy's soul, and fill him with fright.

"Cornuaille, Vantes, and Leon have fallen, but perhaps their temporary defeat will gain a long-term victory by reason of numbers or arms." Illtud chose optimism, greatly vexed over his kinsmen, presently sailing to a war-torn land filled with sorrow and confusion.

Merlin engaged in the conversation, but his eyes never left the messenger. "I do not disagree," he said, contemplatively.

"You are the greatest war tactician since Caradoc ap Bran, old friend." Illtud sought to edify Merlin, who bore criticism spoken and unspoken due to the perception that his counsel to punish the House of Mordred and shock the North into a cessation of war-making designs had not only failed, but thrice-fold worsened the matter.

The wizard remained as an eagle upon Iddawg.

"Thank you, Illtud. However, my devices and schemes are better than Caradoc's, for I escaped my prison." The men laughed as historical enthusiasts do when none else in the room comprehend the reference.

"Your heretical faith yet concerns me. But I am your friend, your kinsman. Your strategy will be successful this time; faint not, Merlin." As intelligence is weighted, only Taliesin and Merlin were at the level of peer with Saint Illtud. And the respect of a peer was oft given by the schoolmaster.

Merlin saw the bottom of another scrumpy. Then a ninth. Flicking the sediments of the heavenly sup where they had splattered here and there on his beard, the bard rose. Standing, he towered, and towering, he emanated an authority such as a god toys with men as clay chess pieces upon the earth.

"The thing about my last strategy failing," he opened, causing Iddawg to stumble backwards and catch himself upon the stool where the Merlin had but presently sat, "is that it didn't."

My impish lies born of want that Arthur whip the Whelp are found out! The Merlin is no man, but like unto the legends about the seven, nay, ten-foot-tall elves that torture men for ten eternities in their hollow hills and their caverns beneath the lakes. I am undone!

"You look as if Death himself hath come for you, boy." Merlin knelt slowly and Iddawg recoiled, knowing judgment was nigh. Merlin clutched the boy by the nape of his neck, authoritatively, but having no outward malice, and pulled him close. To his own drinking horn.

"Sip on this - slowly, not rapidly like the master cider imbiber before you."

"How many legendary names and titles must be given the Merlin?" Illtud jested jealously.

"Well, we have a few for you, bishop." Merlin smiled. "The lad is ill. I pray you give us leave, my friend. Leave me to sit awhile with Iddawg and see to his recovery."

"Of course, I think tea and prayer in the stead of your hard drink will best bring the color back into him - but go to it. I will seek out Cai and Bedwyr, that we prepare to receive Hoel, and we will renew discourse of your schemes and strategy tomorrow." Illtud retired from the company, speculating that Bedwyr might be training in the valleys of Cwmbran, quite near to the Caerleon and the place of their discourse.

As Illtud was out of earshot, Merlin assumed a far different tone. "Why wait until tomorrow? Iddawg the Emissary, let us speak now of my strategy. The one they say failed. But we know the Merlin's strategies never fail, don't we, boy?"

CHAPTER 15
Whos Afraid of Morgaine Le Fay?
Cadfans Change of Heart

As men struggled to forage and hunt, and the ladies had scant success in merchandising or bartering in the village markets, Bishop Cadfan continued his schemes as agent for the Satanic Cult he served. Having previously made use of Mark's soldiers to vandalize and pillage his own parishioner's churches, he then turned to the very people he tortured, taking advantage of their calamity by offering blankets, munitions and food. In return he required that they acquiesce to one simple favor.

The continued deification of Mary, and diminishing of the local goddesses.

Traversing the North, he engaged village elders. If a bishop would allow Cadfan to change the name of their chapel, calling it after Mary to replace Michael, or Paul, or some great Cymreig saint or warrior, the town would eat; else, Cadfan would coldly and expeditiously pack his wagons and leave. Desperate for warmth and food, many churches became *Saint Mary's* in the five short months after the Red Dragon and before the final hours of the Civil War.

The enterprise of rebranding parishes, coupled with his ongoing taunts and hunts to wrest the remaining relics from the Lady of Avalon, rendered the bishop of Enlli exhausted. The travel was arduous and the weather ever in tumult. His foot would never heal, a constant reminder of the wages of treachery against the Iron Bear of Britain.

As the first days of June dawned, Cadfan found himself presently returned from a visit and *conversion* of another Saint Mary's, reposing in Ynys Mon at *the chapel* where resided the coffin where once had slept the Mother of the Lord. Even villains can be overwhelmed; even criminals can come to places of hard reflection when conscience confronts their crimes.

Cadfan made his home in a hermit's cell located to the east of the chapel. He hastened to his bed, his body at full rest whilst his mind would give him none.

Morgaine of the Faeries. For how many long years have you hidden the relics from me? Thy womb is closed, thy childbearing years long past. You could have put Llew away, found love, married anew for happiness instead of political obligation, enjoyed your old sons, and made new babies besides. Instead the prime of your days you have loaned to a God you know not, for a quest you never obliged, for the mother of a Jewish man your kind curse! Why? Why rather not let my Master align with you to charge the talismans and, using them, to rule the world?

Because Pagan and Christian alike know unprecedented evil, and any person who regards his neighbor would die ere he or she let powerful things fall into the hands of maniacs and devils. That is why!

Cadfan shot up in the bed, fevered, the debate

between his mind and his spirit spending him. His mouth as cotton, he swallowed and gulped at a bedside pitcher of water, hoping to rehydrate his deserty throat. Then sleep, or sleepless sleep, came again.

Morgaine of the Faeries. Rival. Enchantress. More character resides in one stray strand of your raven's hair than in the sum of my entire constitution. Why do I hate you for what Illtud has done? Why hate I any man? Am I not a Breton? Am I not Cymreig? Has my preference for the doctrines of Rome truly driven me to serve those who would enslave, nay, destroy my kin? What would it be to win? To rule over a field of bones and command councils of headstones? Morgaine is right to hide the Treasures of Britain from me – more so from the Council of Nine. Conviction fell upon his bosom, a weighted lightning bolt from heaven. Again he woke, ill, violently nauseous. Guilt brings forth pungent vomit.

Oak branches quickened and gave scratchy knock upon the chalky wall, rebuking him with a hair-raising scrape and chilling screech. The owls that own the night joined in; a chorus of clamor and judgment. A few hours ere the sun rose he slipped back into slumber. And the convictions continued.

King Arthur. The reason we have liberty to debate and disagree. He only sanctioned Rome when Rome maneuvered to deny him the freedom and power she coveted for herself. He moved against the Dynion Hysbys on the careful, thoughtful authority of several witnesses who implicated them in a plot to murder his friend and overthrow his government. That is not tyranny – rather, justice!

King Hoel Dda. Uncle. Never an unkind word. You provided gold and provision when I and eleven besides departed the Continent to receive schooling at Llaniltud Fawr. What happened there under the ill tides of Illtud was not your doing, neither were you aware of it. Did not Maelgwn Gwynedd have like passions? He wars against you, Uncle, and joins with a perverse, split man. And now you and thousands from our clans are displaced. You bring your bowmen and your swords, and your mystical fighting arts against the North – because the North is against the good.

Groans, tossing and turning.

And Derfel, the new Lancelot. Only minus the madness. You have joined me against reason. Loyalty over evaluation. O, the misplaced vigor of youth! I have led you into the snare. In what manner of world will you fulfill your years? If under Arthur, as a free man. If under Magus, a pawn or spear made of flesh meant to be discarded after the using.

Magus! At this, Bishop Cadfan was fully awake. His pierced foot continued to complain, and a fever coursed through him. He made tea. But it did not stay down.

Magus, you have seduced me. You are not the Church of Rome. The Church of Rome is beauty and charity and tradition. You are no successor to Peter, nor Clement, nor the Church Fathers. You are the anti-Pope, and the forerunner to the Anti-Christ. Why have I allowed you to seduce me? I fight for the wrong side no more –

When a man would return to God, that is when the Devil knocks on the door.

Rap. Scratch. Tap.

These were not the tree branches that tortured Cadfan throughout his sickly night. Heavier sounds, the product of hands. *Metallic, gloved hands.*

Rap. Scratch. Tap.

Injured, exhausted, nauseous, and combatting a sweaty fever, Cadfan opened the door to his cell, drawing one deep, contested and troubled breath, then exhaling. He looked up at the dark powers that had come to visit him at the holy chapel of the Blessed Lady in Ynys Mon.

***

Anger is like hot coals, which are enflamed by a light breeze or soft blowing, yet are extinguished by heavy winds.

So it is with leaders, parents, or men and women in authority. The day-to-day, tactical things enrage them. Incompetence, insubordination, minor errors. These are the light breezes that unleash the wrath of the mighty; even those of level heads and soft dispositions. Mothers spare not the rod when the daughter's room is disheveled, or the crockeries still stained. Yet those same mothers hold their daughters in the embrace of grace and consolation when an unwanted pregnancy occurs, offering herbs and solutions in the place of screaming and punishment.

Merlin was a hot coal. A white-hot coal.

The Summer Kingdom had been at the tip of the blade when Iddawg was charged with giving Mordred the Traitor Arthur's offer of *a way out*. When Iddawg betrayed the king's message, instead provoking Mordred to a desperate and violent answer, the blade penetrated, and the Summer Kingdom began in earnest to bleed, nigh unto death.

The lad's foolish act, his desire – having never seen the death in war – to see renowned heroes ride once more, vanquishing Giants and monsters and villains, would have been likewise committed by any of a dozen boys in a like position. This was a generation that listened to bardic poetry, and viewed bardic theatre, hearing and seeing the glory of battle, embellished and polished by professional minstrels and storytellers; never hearing the cries of mothers burying their sons, nor seeing bone and lung exposed in the field, nor breathing in the stench of black blood - a smell that lives in the nostrils decades after the fighting has ceased.

Merlin's anger was numbing. *How many souls will perish, how many lives be ruined over youthful lusts? How many will die, directly on account of this young man's lies?*

Merlin's anger was just, and capital. The boy had directly misrepresented the king's decree, made a shamble of the strategy - *My strategy!* - and proceeded to tell six score lies to cover the first. He was deserving of death. An immediate, painful death, that he might know in his final moments what so many thousands would soon know on account of him.

Grace.

Mercy.

These are stronger than anger, and love heavier than wrath. This is why a loving mother or father barks and hollers at little infractions but is soft and results-oriented where major sins occur, seeking solutions and not punishment for its own sake.

Mercy is the withholding of what the guilty deserve.

Grace is the giving of unmerited favor, the active gifting of what is not deserved.

God showed mercy in withholding His righteous judgment against a rebellious, evil world.

God showed grace in gifting salvation to every man, providing that they simply trust Him.

Taliesin had preached these things to the Merlin afore. And, when the wizard's anger burned hot, these truths were the heavy winds that cooled him.

Do we rank sins? No. Whether the mark is missed by the space of a thumb or by ten yards, the arrow still missed, and missed equally. None of us are good. None of us differs from the other. We all need mercy; we all should extend grace.

Arthur favored Iddawg. Merlin noted a paternal glance, the glow of a mentor from the Sovereign towards his messenger.

How many fighting-aged men will survive this Civil War? How many able men to serve their wives and children, and provide their muscle and skill to working the land? What profit is it to give one more Cymry warrior to the Isle? She is full of blood, and cries against it.

Merlin did not depose Iddawg. Iddawg knew that Merlin knew, and Merlin knew that Iddawg knew it.

"Far from the borders of Cymru, deep in the vast Wood of Caledonia, in the land of the Picts, resides a hermit called Laolkien. Go to him and there remain in exile." Merlin began his decree, Iddawg's head bowed submissively: the dog slumping beneath the banquet table, having been caught purloining meats from the children. "Arthur has beseeched those of us closest to him that transparency and truth, even disastrous, calamitous truth, reign, and that secrecy and scheming be put out of this land." The druid's tone intensified as he struggled not to smite the lad. "Therefore I will inform him of your gross lies." Grace and Mercy struggled back. "But I will delay for five days, giving you space; peradventure you may survive the roads, the raiders, the soldiers anxious to gain an early kill, and the Picts besides. Arthur may visit upon you triple portion of what befell his first wife, our rightful Queen Gwenhwyfar I." Grace and Mercy prevailed. "But I will beg of him to forgive you. In exile you will remain, pledging to only return if Arthur himself calls you back into service."

"And if he never calls?"

"Then your sentence will be a prison without walls. You will spend your days, and die, in that forest."

Iddawg wanted to bawl. To cry thanksgivings that he could keep his head, to blither a thousand remorseful words. He wanted to confess with his mouth, that it might lather his soul. But the Merlin permitted no such opportunity. The emissary of the king swore oath to accept the condition of the exile and departed the Round Table Fellowship to do penance with the Wild Man of the Woods, be it for a month… or a lifetime.

***

"Perfect timing, I perceive." The slithery Italian voice, once a seductive flavor, now tasted as gall in Cadfan's ears.

"The Continent has been converted. Childebert and Mark rule, the descendants of the Silures have fallen." The bishop robbed Magus of a glorious introduction. "And now you are here to see the Paramount King slain—"

"Aye, and risen again." The response was in Latin, and not Cymraeg. Motioning Cadfan to walk with him, Magus and the rest of the Nine made procession to the chapel. Being directed to see Mary's coffin, and having seen it, he gave the

Breton Bishop many accolades. "And the Cup, or the Ark of the Covenant? What of these?"

"The daughter of Meurig possesses, hides and enchants these lands that none can acquire them, lord. Her skill exceeds my skill, her magick greater than our shamans, her wit— "

"Your praise of her drips with respect, teems with affection." Magus's words changed from accolade to scorn.

Broken, bruised, exhausted, surely to die and then burn in some Christian concept of Hell for ransoming his soul to the Horned God, the dispirited priest was resigned to the fact that his hour of reckoning had come. *This cult will kill me anyhow; why lie?* "Affection, no. Respect, yes. She has outmaneuvered me for years! And now as I reflect, here at the consummation of your great work, she showed me mercy. A multitude of mercies."

Simon noted that the possessive pronoun had changed from *'our'* to *'your great work'*, and that his agent Cadfan had now become a meek, feverish risk. "Mercy?" Having been in *every situation*, the Masked Man remained calm, now evaluating every communication, mood and emotion. "How?"

"By not killing me, which she could have done with no further effort than a man squashes the roach. She probably preferred not to clean the squelch from her boot and thus let me alone."

"I appreciate your use of metaphor, Walles, and I concur. You *are* a crawling thing and no man, fearing a witch no taller than a schoolyard girl!"

"Is your dilution and delusion and deceit effectual with your Council, and your members scattered in orders and sects abroad?" Cadfan the

Bold emerged again, despite ill-health. "You know who Morgaine is, and I am certain your person, or at minimum your meddlings, had somewhat to do with the circumstances surrounding Mordred's birth and thus her selection for those cursed spring rites!"

"The bug has a big brain." Simon taunted his impetuous accomplice. "Is it your desire to leave our illumined brotherhood, Walles?" The Nine had compassed Cadfan. He noted that they uniformly advanced a step. Somewhere and somehow, candles had been lit within the sanctuary.

The bishop was barely robed, having neither sword nor dagger. Prey pacing in a snare, he speculated that his end was nigh. "I do!" Repentance reigned within the sorrowed Breton.

"Merlin left our order." Latin words, whispered in threatening overtures. "Strangled. Poisoned. Drowned. And before this beaten, bashed, gashed and bruised. The triple death awaits renowned criminals, as your own ancient customs."

"The Merlin lives," was Cadfan's retort.

The Nine advanced. Eight grey robes; each unnaturally tall, the hoods perversely long, concealing faces. Eight shadow ghouls, and one superior, clad from head to toe in crimson red.

"Should it surprise any that the child of the damned would not die as men do? Are you a Fae, that you too would roam the earth until the end of days as a wandering star?"

Cadfan ignored the question, knowing full well that he was but a man. A pathetic man. Instead he attempted redirection.

"I respect Morgaine. Yes, she has killed, she has erred, she has blasphemed the Church, she has brought shipwreck and calamity. I've seen her suffer failure and setback. And yet…" The more he reflected, the more he respected the king's sister. "She has a purpose."

"Tell me of the lass's purpose." The voice was more serpentine than of man, a hiss filled with words.

"Your great work is to build a kingdom, or conversely to delay a kingdom," Cadfan began.

"Immanentize or delay. You have grown in your understanding." The hiss was now garnished with parental pride.

"Her great work was to build, and sustain, a kingdom. The Summer Kingdom. In the Summer Kingdom the function of those who rule is to protect God-given rights and elsewise leave people alone! In this regard, the Summer Kingdom favored liberty over security, freedom over utopia, and privacy over Statism! The Summer Kingdom, filled with diverse beliefs and faiths of every sort; arguing, laughing, studying and above all, protecting one another's right TO EXIST!" Cadfan captured a glimpse of a shadow cast in the anteroom of the Church. He gave it little regard, pushing forward with what was sure to be his final sermon. "So obsessed became I with the imposition of my denomination that I never understood what Arthur, Dyfrig, Bedwini, Merlin, Vivien, and Lancelot labored to give us. Just in this very moment, I understand Camelot!"

"Your golden age is no more, Walles."

"Twenty years!" Cadfan immediately countered. "Fallen, sinful, corrupt man made it work for twenty years. This will inspire a thousand generations - and because of it, you will not win, should the Most High God tarry in sending His Son to avenge the Saints."

The red mask turned so slowly and with such

theatre that time seemed to still. "Corded rope." A short command given to one of his Adepts in Latin.

"You fear the Summer Kingdom." The bishop continued to verbally assail Satan's princes. "And Morgaine of the Faeries, second only to Arthur, is the champion and the heroine of the entire Matter of Britain. YOU FEAR HER!"

Another shift and flicker of a shadow.

Cadfan was right. Simon Magus did dread the ancient thing that indwelt Gwyar ferch Meurig. Her function was to resurrect Arthur as a false god. The unintended issue of the first rehearsal of the deed had brought forth an abomination: a monster for the god-king Arthur to slay. But she was unpredictable, too powerful, and filled with her own convictions and those unionized with her host. The Elven King, that ancient rascal who had ruled the Isles in the Sea ere Brutus colonized the shores, had owed different debts to the Morrigan, to the Council of Nine, and to Arddu himself. His charge had been to give Onbrawst a changeling, not put the Morrigan *in Gwyar*, keeping the best parts of both babe and goddess in one house of flesh.

This very ritual was intended for Judas Iscariot and Arthur. A fusion. Differing from possession in nature and essence. Morgaine the Changeling was to be taught this art by the king of the Tylwyth Teg. Instead he did unto the Nine in the person of Morgaine what they would do by Arthur. She needed no training, her powers greater than her Faerie Father – perhaps greater than the Father of Lies himself.

Morgaine could raise up Arthur as the Anti-Christ, fulfilling her designed purpose. Or she could avenge herself and slaughter the Nine. Her only limitation in using her craft was to determine the outcome of a battle. Should the God of gods break His own decrees, or make an exception in permitting her to do this, her powers might be without limit. She has fifty and six years in this incarnation, and yet has not fully actualized, not accessed all that she is.

Simon Magus believed that he could manipulate Morgaine to complete the rite. He trusted in his god, who was Satan, to aid him in doing the same. But the priest had exposed his sarcastic minimalizing. He DID fear Morgaine of the Faeries.

Suddenly, originating from a lower trajectory and another room, a voice attended the shadow Cadfan had glimpsed. And this voice *had no fear;* it was jovial in nature.

"Arthur, Dyfrig, Bedwini, Merlin, Vivien, and Lancelot? You forgot one!" The uneven thump of a walking stick. Instantly, the bard Taliesin stood between Cadfan and Simon Magus.

Each of the eight soulless, faceless hoods turned in concert, beholding what had been a hunchbacked toadstool before, now boldly in the center of their demonic, candlelit and dramatic circle. A small dog protecting a lame stag from a pack of wolves.

Simon, the Ninth of the Adepts, marveled, a curious grin behind his red mask. His eyes were patient, and searching to understand the reason for the visit, which was seemingly as spontaneous as his own.

Taliesin all but ignored the Nine; leaning his walking stick upon Cadfan's hip, the bard took each of the bishop's hands, looked him over thrice, and fixed upon the pierced foot.

"You are not well, old friend. Allow the druids to mend your foot, and chase away your fever with our herbs."

Cadfan's shame was as if Taliesin, in his

extreme kindness, had slowly ladled hot coals upon his head. "What judgment from above hath brought you here, showing tender kindness to your enemy?"

"My enemy is no man, for our foes are not carnal; rather, the spiritual forces behind men are with whom I war. *'For we wrestle not against flesh and blood…'*" The famous bard looked away from Cadfan, and at last acknowledged the presence of the Council, identifying them through the Scripture quote: "*'…But against principalities, against powers, against the rulers of the darkness of this world, against spiritual wickedness in high places,'* as says the Apostle Paul in his letter to the Ephesians." Taliesin resumed his focus on the friend of his youth, again ignoring the wolves. "Arthur gave me to Urien, who will join the campaign, and it was upon my heart to come and see how you do, seeing that you also are in the North."

Cadfan could not help but interject with a humorous inquiry. "Did not Maelgwn Gwynedd first give you to Arthur, and now you are passed around again?"

Taliesin ever appreciated a good jab, even if he was the object of it. He chuckled.

"You are discarded more than an old leather house slipper." Another jab.

Another chuckle. "I am not put to the circuit of many princes because I am a bad bard, old friend; rather because I am the best bard."

"Oh, Taliesin." Cadfan exhaled once, and his merriment turned to mourning. "What I have done to our kingdom, to the venerated offices of our Royal Clans, and to the king's own sister is treasonous, and worthy of death. My sins are unforgivable."

Simon's interests in the next words were keen;

he lifted his mask, though in a manner that the others did not see, that he could absorb every word.

"If even one sin cannot be forgiven, then did Christ die in vain. But the Good News exceeds this. For all men have already been forgiven their sins. Christ became your sin five hundred and thirty-seven years ago. The transgression of every man was put to His account. Simply trust this truth, and His righteousness will be imputed to your account, by grace."

"How can this be? 'Tis not what Religion teaches."

"The bonds of Religion were created by these fellows," Taliesin said.

The hooded Adepts closed the distance, offended inside their robes. Their masked leader paused them.

"If you stole a garment from the market and I, being full of mercy, arrested you not, but rather begged the shopkeeper apply the charge to my account, and being full of grace, paid the debt with my own gold, what then would your balance be?"

"But I have done wicked things."

"Your balance, Cadfan, please." Taliesin softly insisted that the Catholic priest see the logic and wondrous light of grace.

"My balance with the shopkeeper from whom I purloined would be at nil. The debt paid in full," he conceded.

"So it is that Christ paid the debt for every man. What if the thief were never baptized?" Taliesin tested.

"Debt still zero."

"And never crossed the archway of a church building?"

"Debt forgiven still, the being in church

having no relevance on what was paid in the sinner's stead." Cadfan answered true.

"God is already reconciled to you, Cadfan. Be thou reconciled to Him. And give your sword and your good foot to King Arthur Pendragon, who is surely the man of God."

"So." Magus hoped the Chief Bard of the Britons understood Latin. "You are the lad from Glamorgan who stole the world's finest wizard from me." He could discern that Taliesin did well understand him. "Are you not yourself the son of that famous witch Ceridwen? What is this marvel, that so many sorcerers and shamans turn to Christ in these bewildered Isles?"

"Our sect of the druids has ever waited for the Most High God to remove the scales and confusion, and reveal Himself to us. This He did by the preaching of the Apostle Paul."

Simon hated this name, the word a flaming arrow in his ears. The chief of sinners turned saint, spewing grace, begetting more sinners-turned-saints. It was repugnant and foul in the ears of Magus that he shared a room with a *real believer. For many were religious but most were lost, unwitting dupes and pawns of his master.*

"This Catholic bishop to whom you may or may not have brought the light of salvation today. I will miss him; he was a good agent and did much to bring about the end of days. I have but one question of him, then we will send him to meet God - yours or mine."

Cadfan remained bold, having no fear of death, full of deep contemplation and coursing with conviction over Taliesin's tidings. "Ask it, then happily I receive what is just recompense for my deeds in the flesh, knowing now where my soul goest."

"Does…" Simon paused, switching from Latin to Cymraeg. "Does Morgaine of the Faeries still have the cup? Is it now returned to its secret place within Yns Enlli?"

"That is two questions," Taliesin mused.

The conclusion was clear. The Council of Nine were wasting their time engaged in the current enterprise. The Bishop of Rome himself was at sea, making his way to address the confederacy and denounce Arthur, rousing the troops before the battle drums banged. Alan Fyrgan the Traitor's troops were positioned to defend against the first wave, and camped in the forests between Powys and Gwynedd, awaiting instructions on where to march. Cedric had assembled his men; likewise were the Picts standing ready. All was in order, and but two tasks remained for the Puppet-Master.

Have audience with the Whelp.

Find the Cup and use it to control Morgaine.

Sinister and knowing the Scriptures, commanding every word from Genesis to Revelation (for the Council must needs first know every Scripture in its proper context, that they might pervert and misuse it), he goaded the Christian bard. "Taliesin, son of Ceridwen, Grail Guardian of old, protector of the Mysteries and the relics. Pray you, give me the next verse, a continuation of the first you preached afore."

"Certain to oblige." Taliesin was bold. *"'Wherefore take unto you the whole armour of God, that ye may be able to withstand in the evil day, and having done all, to stand.'"*

"I see no armor, neither shield, nor sword – and yet the evil day is upon you! Kill them." He motioned.

"The verses are spiritual, not physical. Destroy

our flesh; Cadfan *has* withstood you, and the day. But…" Taliesin straightened his crooked back, beamed with a confidence that illuminated the room, took up his stick, still resting upon Cadfan, and tapped it thrice upon the floor.

Tap. A smile.

Tap. A wink.

"But what?" The accent was especially thick when readying to clutch at the prey.

"But I physically want to be here to see Arthur restored, Maelgwn restored, and you defeated. Therefore—"

"As I said: no armor, neither shield, nor sword." The order having already been given, eight swords with black blades were drawn, and already in flight.

"Therefore I brought the Tylwyth Teg with me. Though a Christian of Christians, I'm still a Briton, and we are a peculiar people."

Tap. A swift look to the chapel doors.

A blue, luminous, plasmatic *shield* surrounded Cadfan and the bard. Every sword shattered upon the enchanted shell, breaking into a thousand pieces, the steel becoming as sand.

The king of the Tylwyth Teg gazed long upon the coffin of Mary. "An elect Lady, of purest heart and bravest disposition. I remember you well, Mary. I see why men would have you as their goddess, though you would turn in your place of rest, protesting and railing against the same." Returning his attention to the mortal recipients of his assistance, the shield changed form, becoming a whirlwind or animated faerie ring, cycling up, down and round about the two.

Three and thirty-three thousand pixies swarmed the eight as so many little bees, each encased in their own bright star. Having no recourse but to wave frenzied hands and kick against the air, the Nine fled the church, cursing and crying, the Fair Folk giving chase.

Of the otherworldly rescuers, only the great Elf remained. "Retreat."

"The Lord Arddu has written a book wherein are described punishments as have never been imagined since the foundation of the Earth. The Creator God is a Being most boring, to think that a Lake of Fire is the most dreadful way to perpetually punish a man or an angel. My god has much darker designs than this! And *YOUR NAME* tops his ledger, being reserved for the most creative of these!"

"Better to fear the Creator than the creature." The Fae, who would typically have vanished in an impish fashion at this moment, remained to watch Magus depart, chasing after his retinue.

Knowing that the two men were secure, he approached Taliesin, giving dire warning. "Morgaine will do all to see that Mordred and her remaining sons besides come to no harm in the battle to come."

"It is my understanding that she cannot intervene, Lord of the Wood and Stream," Taliesin responded, showing careful respect of the Otherworldly Being conversing with him.

"Pray you are correct, Grail Guardian. I fear she has found a way. Even now Avalon is surrounded by a mist such as never before. She has pushed the Holy Isle into the realm of shadow with her fog and would wield the dragon's breath to shield her own."

"Can she be stopped?" Taliesin asked.

"None knows the resolve of the Sorceress Morgaine as I do," Cadfan quickly interjected. "No, she cannot. Once set about a task, the Lady will not be deterred, save perhaps by her brother."

"Then I will abandon my commissioning to Urien and to Arthur return."

"No, Taliesin, see to the battle lord of the North as bidden by *our king*. Let me do this thing, I beg you."

Though all men are forgiven, the repentant are still driven to do good deeds. Not for the purpose of being saved but, contrariwise, because they *are saved*, and thankful. Taliesin understood the importance of this quest, vain as it might turn out. Cadfan would warn Arthur of the Morgaine's mists. Meanwhile, Taliesin would pursue an additional scheme.

"Lord of the Wood and Stream, ere you leave again as you listeth, will you not walk with me, that we might speculate together?"

"I like you, bard, and will hear your scheme. Let your druids come and heal this *new man*, and into yonder circle behind the church, over there where the treeline changes, *we* will go. And there to hear your scheme and after release you, elsewise keep you in our court for five hundred years."

Praying they were but mischievous words of no weight, Taliesin the brave laughed with the Faerie King, and did go with him…

CHAPTER 16
Unarmed and Disappointed

June
AD 537

Where the Llyn Peninsula diminished into the sea resided a small village that the bards would later call *Aberdaron*. Waist-high grass of every green and moss-covered rocks garnished cliffs that framed a steep, natural border round the land's end. The drop from where homes resided and villagers dwelt, where the waters crashed upon the rocks, created the illusion that this region was as a magical realm, 'floating upon the sea'. Five walking minutes south of Aberdaron, a hidden harbor hid beneath the rocky overhang. The rather difficult but brief descent brought the traveler, so oft a pilgrim from Rome, else a druid or saint making their final sojourn, to a cove with smooth, flat rocks that appeared as a natural stone floor. The inlet, Porth Meudwy, seemed to be designed by God Himself for small vessels, which fitted perfectly here, and shoved off from the mainland.

To Avalon.

West on Llyn Pennisula, now further west but bending down the horn of the mainland, turn south, proceed to Aberdaron.

From Aberdaron, south to Porth Meudwy.

Board a barge or hired vessel at Porth Meudwy. By ancient decree only two sets of sons from two families were learned in navigating the *impossible waters*. These alone, or the boatmen of the Lady of Avalon herself, could bear a soul unto Avalon. Should the sons' sons refuse to sail (for they could read the weather, seeing beneath the currents what the untrained eye doth not see), then one could hire their own coracle and engage the trepid currents themselves - else swim. Many hundreds and scores of hundreds had done the same, and perished.

Avalon.

Ynys Enlli.

The place of healing. Of groves with apples that defied nature, growing under impossible conditions wrought of tempest and wind and climate. The resilient trees. Hew them down and leave one sprig or root and they returned, stronger than before. Better than before.

Avalon.

Ynys Enlli.

The little island of mysteries that harkened back to the antediluvian dispensations. Of all the islands that had broken away from the mother, and the mainland, this atoll, with one small mount that cast a shadow over the plain, hid the forests and concealed the founts, was coveted above all. The Romans coveted tin and the Hebrews lusted for gold; the Picts sought iron and the Saxons possessed an insatiable hunger for lands. Yet the sum of these material goods were as a farthing compared to the quest of all men to but touch the soil of Avalon. And now she was within the grasp of Simon Magus and the Council of Nine.

But Avalon was missing.

***

Two metal fingers and a steel thumb pinched two Roman coins, each debossed with the face of an emperor from old.

It was not that the boatman refused. It was that he was paralyzed, bewildered, frozen, and consumed with worry that his right senses had departed his mind.

A wall of fog rose nine hundred feet towards the heavens, and spanned three days' ride by horse, both east and west. The mist seemed *alive*, dancing and pulsating. *And disappearing.* At once it would dominate the landscape of the peninsula, an awe and a fright to the villagers (and these men and women, being neighbors to Avalon, saw supernatural and spiritual oddities each and every day), most of whom thought the fiery comet, or its kin, had returned to take up the work of removing the Cymry from the world of men; a moment later, clear skies.

Though the fog made the expert sailor a blind guide, it was the moments of clarity that caused him to refuse to launch.

Avalon disappeared.

The wall of fog would return, sometimes ascending from the deep, other times descending from the sky above - and whirlwinds and spins and cyclone shapes besides.

Avalon reappeared.

Returned, brimming with life and mirth. From Porth Meudwy an onlooker could see a dozen different kind of birds at play, flying in majestic dance patterns around the shore, then hastening to fly towards and over the zenith of the mountain, dissolving beyond the vanishing point of the horizon.

Avalon disappeared.

"A Sorcerer yonder experiments," the masked devil commented in Latin, still extending payment.

The seaman spoke only Cymraeg, but no matter; he emphatically refused employ.

There was a substance to the mist. It was heavy. Some of it broke from the rest and crawled to the mainland. When this happened, Magus could no longer see his own hand, let alone the obstinate fellow before him.

"None can sail in this, neither fight." He was angry, but wore no anger. Addressing his cult, he conceded: "We will not find the Grail on the Isle of Apples today, because we will not find the Isle of Apples. We must leave Morgaine of the Faeries to her own devices. Peradventure she will lead Arthur to this very place and facilitate our work, unknowingly. Whether this come to pass or no, let us to the House of Llew ap Cynfarch Oer, that privily we might have audience with the Son of the Pendragon."

***

Bishop Cadfan prostrated himself before King Arthur's court in the Round Table Hall, a broken and barely functional remainder standing in the shadowy ruins of the castle fortress Caermelyn above, that once-shining city upon the hill that the poets on the Continent referred to as *Camelot*. The city of freedom and the pulse of liberty that beats within the bosom of every man.

Merlin's great invention had been cleared away, the old wizard defiantly declaring daily that he would personally see it repaired to past glory. Instead, the Round Table Fellowship sat upon their ornate chairs, which were as thrones, in a great circle without the table.

With mourning and humiliation, Cadfan detailed his treachery; from the early days at the feet of Meirchion the Mad, whose progeny Mark the Cruel terrorized the Continent, to the plot to deify Mary, right through to the present unwelcomed visit by the Council of Nine during his moment of repentance and conversion. He shared all – all that he knew. Cadfan had not been in Simon's inner circle but had been of import nonetheless, perhaps two rungs outward from the same. Because of this, his gathered intelligence obtained, of the plans and aims of Maelgwn, Mordred, Caw, Llew, Cedric, Mark, Childebert and the diverse Pictist and Tribes of Eire, was of tremendous value to the Silures.

If the information was valid and not another act of conspiracy, lies and diversion.

"Merlin?" Arthur needed no expounding, having a living *truth-discerner* at his side.

The druid peered into the soul of Cadfan. A few whispers were exchanged, and two to three questions asked. The assembled knights and chieftains were silent, drawing a collective breath, unable to hear the Merlin, desperate to hear the outcome. The verdict was swift.

"Forgive him," Merlin declared. The exhale of the gathered was collective; a few jeers, but more showed grace than judgment, happy to see that rifts *could mend.* This was important for the morality of Arthur's core leaders, and would surely diffuse as an affirmative waterfall, splashing upon a hesitant, angry, and hungry army.

King Arthur, famed the world over for balancing mercy with justice, might well forgive

Cadfan, embracing him with a brotherly hug, seeing his wife and children succored, and showing him love as one loves his neighbor. He might then put him to death in a swift, civil and dignified way (the butchery and malice showed Gwen II being an aberration in the reign of Arthur). Conversely, he might prescribe restorative justice, including restitution or works meet for repentance.

Neither was the king a dictator. Cadfan's offenses were against the Sovereignty of Cymru, against the whole of the kingdom itself. Were it a matter of a local crime, or some regional intrigue, Arthur would exercise no jurisdiction, only giving his opinions and protests *as a man*, in every way equal to his kinsmen.

Where a matter did fall under the powers loaned the Round Table by the Tribes, Arthur carefully consulted his twelve, and Lancelot his twelve, until consensus was reached. In this way, power was checked, and cool heads designed to prevail.

Lancelot's chair as Champion of the Britons was vacant. Be it by reason of death, mission, exile or ambience, the twenty-four was no longer whole. Nevertheless, Arthur conferred with the remnant of the Round Table Fellowship. This he did, as ever, in the open of the day, before all. *Let no act of the Government be done in secret*, had taught Merlin, Meurig and a score of Silure chiefs for generations before Arthur had carried the precept forth, becoming a beacon of republican government in a tyrannical world.

And so the remorseful bishop stood at the base of the judgment seat, happy to die, having had his moment to declare his resurrected loyalty for Cymru. This council proved to be far exceeding in kindness, in humor, in war embrace, and in grace to that Council of Nine, the leader of which that he had but recently called Master.

After a short discourse, Bedwyr whispered in the king's ear, then said aloud, vociferously, "Our course with this rogue is as a clear as the surface of Llyn y Fan Fach, which is as a glass mirror!"

A man of great conviction and repentance can *say* he would rather die clean than live dirty, until the actual pronunciation of death is given. Cadfan, no less sorrowful, did fear the forthcoming words.

Bedwyr paused.

The pause continued.

No chair creaked, no boot shuffled. Silence encompassed the hall, and even the birds held their beaks. Bedwyr glared at Cadfan.

After some time, Arthur gave the Good Knight a look that communicated, *This is becoming uncomfortable for all, even me, and I'm High King!*

Bedwyr's fixed stare was unrelenting.

At last he rose, bidding by motion that each Round Table Knight draw his sword. This they did, each pointing his long weapon at the confessor.

Gwenhwyfar ferch Gwythyr was amongst the viewers, cleaving to her parents, watching the high drama unfold.

Seventeen swords formed a circle of death round the bishop. *And one of those the Sword of Power!* Excalibur's hum of victory was the only sound to be discerned, seemingly in the whole of the cosmos.

Bedwyr peered down his blade. *And then winked at Cadfan.*

The man could not swallow for fear, neither form spittle in his mouth, but he did manage a bewildered cock of the head.

"The surface of Llyn y Fan Fach is a mirror. What does a looking-glass do but expose the ugliness therein? A mirror shows us *our true selves.* Who amongst us, in these gray days, does not covet mercy? Who here has not committed some great error, or horrific war crime?" Bedwyr looked as though he suffered great physical pain in holding his cold, brooding expression, for now the entire assembly knew his silent stares were a yarn, his drama aimed to scare Cadfan with the love that simulates an older brother catching the younger stealing biscuits - often accompanied by judgmental lectures, soon followed by remembrances of when he did the same things. *Brotherly love is frightful, then warm.*

At last Bedwyr broke, the laughter as a rushing damn.

"Let this act here today remind us that, ruins and rubble or no, this *is yet* the Summer Kingdom!" Each sword was withdrawn, instantaneously sheathed. "Be thou restored, brother!"

Clapping and great laughter ensued, the witnesses seeing mercy motivated by and reminiscent of what they had fought to earn; what they fought for still.

"One further demand." The High King himself quieted the hall.

"My lord?"

"How far will they suffer us to advance? Where does Maelgwn make his stand?"

"My kinsmen Alain Fyrgan is positioned in the village near the chapel of Tydecho. There he will make a great name for himself abroad, delaying your passage whilst the Saxons surround you from the slopes above--"

Having been fostered nearby, having wrestled the Giant Itto not far from there, having supped with his Champion countless times not one hour north of the place, Arthur was thoroughly familiar with the favorite territory of Maelgwn Gwynedd. "Camlan," he interrupted, having his answer. "Lancelot would have a second Mynydd Baedan, save in his country, this time, instead of mine."

"He means to stall you in the wood, force you through the meadow, corral you on the farmland, then draw you to a low-ground position, causing a forced ascent up Craig Y Gamell," Cadfan continued in full cooperation, having truly changed allegiance.

The Bear of Glamorgan approached and then embraced the one whom he had pierced. "We will dress your foot; I apologize for wounding you." Herein was the greatness of the king on full display. Cadfan had in every measure shouldered much of the accountability for the ruin of Britain. And here *Arthur apologized to him!*

"I know the fighting dance of Vivien, having grown up in Brittany," Cadfan responded. "Let's not waste nursing but one wound." A pleading look. "Permit me to take the field with the Round Table Knights, and under the Pendragon banners run into a glorious death!"

"Rather, limp," Bedwyr offered. The assembled roared. The bishop blushed, feeling accepted and whole.

"A one-legged patriot is preferred to a two-legged fool. Join us," determined the king.

Some clamor and side-discussions erupted. Meanwhile, Gwenhwyfar negotiated the crowds, hoping to be near the king and announce her arrival in Cymru. Arthur had been at all hours training and planning. Hoel and Gwythyr notwithstanding, he had not greeted the flood of

Bretons who were suddenly under his command, and newly his neighbors.

But she was unable to get close enough to make eye contact with him.

The High King once more settled the crowds and ordered the circle. "Rest well this night, and the next. For the hour comes when we attack our foes, and our brothers. But prior to this..." Arthur looked again to Cadfan, a consolatory gaze, for the news would be hard. "The battle of Camlan starts today. Today." A hush fell. Fear. Anticipation. Confidence. Despair. "Cadog, Cai, Gareth, Bedwyr and I will be as thieves in the night and go ahead of the armies. We and nineteen bowmen will go ahead of the army. We will remove Alain's guards and watchmen, who will surely be stationed on the road that connects Powys to Gwynedd and terminates above Caer-gof.

"Giving neither signal nor warning, we will harass, discomfit and terrorize Alain where he waits. There is not a forest in Cymru that the Sons of Adam do not share with spirits and Fae and creeping things. Fright will destabilize their constitution, then arrows will fill their encampment as so many angry wasps, causing them to feel that, just as one is put to flight, three more replace it, more wrathful than the first. In this manner, twenty-four will slay nine hundred" – for three troops were now under Alain's lead – "and the woodland become a feast for the birds. Dead men cannot stall our advance, save to trip upon their corpses, and their design would fail."

Hearing this, Cadfan understood that there would be no place for surrender, for the tactic demanded stealth, and not engagement in an open field. The reality of war now pressed him:

Alain Fyrgan ap Hoel the Good will surely die, not many days hence.

"I will go as well." Being more *physically persistent* than the Lady of Lyonesse, Hoel (who was also a Round Table Knight) pushed his way to the center of the ring and stood next to Arthur, and before Cadfan. "It is not for you alone to bear the burden of battling your offspring."

Arthur could not refuse his demand, for he knew it had a double intention. Hoel would see his son for the final time and, if possible, save him. The Pendragon would not deny him this, and offered, "Should they abscond the scene and depart in a direction contrary from Mordred, we will not give chase. May the terror of the first few that fall warn the remainder, their lifeless eyes and cold bosoms beckoning them to abandon the vanity of their cause."

"And if they refuse to turn from their allegiance to madness, let the earth and the Underworld welcome them." Hoel had seen his gilded little kingdom fall, and would avenge it – even against his kinsmen, or his son.

Some discourse continued, the crowd dissipated, and Gwen found a valley of shoulders through which to sneak, pop up, and present herself to the king.

Her gown was dark blue, her jewels and plaits the same, for she knew that Arthur adored this hue, and would wear no other color if convenience permitted or if fashion did not forbid it. Usually her hair was kept not overly adorned but practical and modest, falling about her shoulders, else bound in simple ties. Here it was prepared to shimmer and shine, two maidens and three hours a protested testimony to the preparation time. This Gwenhwyfar's eyes were blue, matching those of the one she loved so dearly. Ever regal but never pretentious, the Lady of Lyonesse felt outside of her own skin, uncomfortable. In fancy apparel with painted lips and crimsoned cheeks that favored her high cheekbones and revealed a slight, adorable pointedness to her little nose, she did illuminate the shadowy hall. A splendor to be desired by any man, she was in one part Vivien's beauty and in another Morgaine's strength; at the same time she was not comparable by attribute or likeness to any, being wholly unique.

What mercy! What wisdom! Her inner voice complimented the one she pretended was already hers. A proud smile. *Lo, there he is – what shall I say?*

She was close enough now to grasp his hand, or to throw herself upon him with a passionate kiss. *Temperance; self-control.* Her mind chastised her heart.

The king did see her. He began to mouth a greeting, but his line of vision caught the tallest of Britons racing from left to right, and then behind him. Arthur turned at the torso so that his feet still faced the lady but his shoulders and head were in another direction. "Merlin!" he hollered.

The wizard stopped to talk, hearkening unto the beckoning of his lord.

"Where is Iddawg? Bring him hither, that I might dispatch formal message to Gildas ere I depart with the men." A natural, unassuming, normal request.

No secrets. Cover no sin, and disguise no error, for these things manifest and undo us. Merlin swallowed but once, then came out with it: "Iddawg has found himself in the snare of youth. Let us away, and we will discuss expediently."

Arthur adjusted his position. He did look upon

Gwen, and gave a friendly, yet disinterested and distracted nod, his every thought upon hastening to give Gildas final instructions before leaving, desperate not to delay his men. Altering his plans, he directed Cai: "Send three of our swiftest to Neath, and fetch me Gildas, that they may hasten to catch us, for we must talk as we ride."

Cai set about this charge.

And Gwenhwyfar set about hers.

She would not shed tear in public, nor make a spectacle of her emotions. Rather, she did sprint as a Greek competing in their games. Banishing her ladies (who were as sisters and no servants), she peeled her gown off and loosed her hair violently. Tears finally fell at the same time her locks lit on her shoulders.

I am a fool and a child! The man loves me not!

***

"Must you personally lead this advanced expedition? Surely we have thousands of stealthy young men who could make quick work of watchers, messengers and guards," Merlin protested, he, Meurig and Dyfrig joining Arthur for cider ere he departed for Gwynedd.

"I was fostered there; I know the area as I know Glamorgan and Gwent," he responded. "Besides, no one can disguise himself and navigate the secret roads and pathways like Arthur Pendragon." A comforting, confident smile to calm the older men.

"With this I cannot disagree." Meurig continued to glow as a proud 'new father', though well past the median of a man's years.

Arthur and Merlin articulated the battle schema several times, and when this was finished,

Dyfrig posed an important, thoughtful question.

"You have reported well your aims and where we are strong. It seems the veterans of the Saxon Wars are revitalized and the new soldiers ready to share in old glories, adding their own songs to bardic melodies and tavern lies." Dyfrig paused, waiting for the payment of laughter, and he was well compensated. "But tell me," he continued, "where do we have risk? Where are we weak?"

"Armor and smiths." Arthur did not hesitate. This issue concerned him the most. "The Red Dragon melted much and made ash of much more, and the generational skill of smithing and forging has been greatly damaged. The demand for arms and weaponry simply exceeds the supply." He was frustrated. "We are all uniformed in matching sigils, that we might discern friend from foe. But underneath some have leather, some have mail, some heavy armor, others a few salvaged sets of our specialty silver skin." Arthur shook his head, disgusted at the lack of equipment and uniformity. "Where armor fails there is space for error or thrusting amiss. We must be perfect. And this is our greatest risk."

CHAPTER 17
Embrace Your Abomination

June 19
AD 537

Creating a circumstance where Simon Magus could have private audience with Mordred was proving very difficult. Although Cedric had complete knowledge of the Council's aims, having received vast sums of gold and supplies for campaigns in times past, Arthur's other enemies were in league against the king on their own accord - and for their own motives.

Mordred would see in Arthur's death his true love avenged, and elsewise lived life day by day, his sole objective keeping his lungs filled with breath and his head attached to its neck; he took advantage where he could over the *cattle that is mankind* along the way.

His proposal to support Maelgwn as High King (thus avoiding ongoing strife amongst the confederacy's own ranks) in exchange for protecting his ascent to the rule of his ancestral lands of Glamorgan and Gwent was well received. The Northern Catholics would have their strongman in the brooding and unpredictable Maelgwn, who would likely be more hermit and less king, and they would have their puppet in the south. Should an assassin from Caerleon or Deheubarth, ashamed to have an abominable bastard ruling over him, put herb to drink or arrow to back some random early morn, it would be of no matter. Caw and Llew, having stabilized the kingdoms, would simply insert another of their own.

Mordred knew as much, but was content to tread forward where his lot had currently fallen. He had *a Cai-type figure* in Eda, a steward and protector who never left his side. And insomuch as a monster with no apathy can enter into friendship, he was fond of Eda, though he was no Amr. In Mordred's twisted morality, affection was a fixed sum, allowing him but one brother, and excusing his crimes and hatred for all others in the aftermath of his loss. Mordred had *loved* but two in his forty years, and Arthur had murdered them both.

And soon the Pendragon would come for him as well.

If the bards were not prejudiced and blind, they would record that all that Mordred did was in defense of himself against the tyrant Arthur. But Mordred will have no Songs.

As the sun rose two days before the solstice, 'twas this Eda pounding upon the door, beseeching Mordred to rise and dress.

Following curses, degradations and loud rants, curly locks as an unkempt curtain over one eye in the crevice at last appeared. "Eda! What?" the crevice barked.

"The Father summons you, lord Mordred."

"My father assumes that because he shares this rooftop with me he can call me at his whim, and command me as a slave!" The door closed, with a tantrum and belligerent words. "No wonder my brothers opted to live near Mother!"

Though Cai guarded brilliance and Eda protected a fool, they each shared the same attribute true to all stewards: patience.

"Not *your father" – and Llew is not your real father besides* – "rather THE Father. The Bishop of Rome."

Now the door opened.

"What hath the Religion of Rome to do with me?" Mordred wondered.

"Pope Silverius will address the gathered armies at noon on the solstice, blessing our campaign and condemning Arthur the Tyrant, and Illtud his false Prophet."

Realizing it would be of great political advantage to have the favor of the Potentate, Mordred would suffer his prayers, or sprinklings or bells and candles, entertaining his superstitions with a smile.

"With your own eyes see that it is true, and no assassin guised in vestments, Eda."

"This I have done, lord."

"Wait, then; I will dress. Then you will conduct me to him," said Mordred, offering no apology or courtesy after his rudeness against the mountain of muscle that shielded him.

Although the Round Table Fellowship had deprived Llew's grandfather, Meirchion the Mad, of land – especially in Corneu and the southeast of Cymru – his issue, who were of the ancient House of Coel, were allowed to maintain many of their holdings in the Old North. This had been done to safeguard the dignity of Urien and his siblings, but had had the unintentional result of leaving a wolf in the pen. Once again, past mercies caused present disadvantage, for the Northerners in league against Arthur enjoyed vast lands and large, well-defended fortresses in the *betwixt and between* lands above Gwynedd but below Alba.

It was in one of these, a walled, wooden fortress that housed two hundred residences (not including guards, stable-hands, smiths, those working the kitchens or governing the lead conduits, and networks for managing excrement and waste), where the chiefs and princes who were against Arthur lodged – save Maelgwn, who slept peacefully in a small hamlet called Dinas Maddwy, near to his farm at Maes-Y-Camlan.

The Saxon, Pict and Cymreig royals, including Mordred, were surrounded at all times by bowmen from above and mounted cavalry below. Maelgwn was guarded round about by the Dormarch: the hounds of hell Morgause had summonsed that he might avenge Gwenhwyfar II, giving Arthur an ironic death. Drest of the Picts, Cedric the Saxon and his Gewessi raiders, Llew and Hueil ap Caw, reposed in comfort, though it were daytime, using women and meat to feed their fear, knowing the battle was nigh.

Maelgwn, meanwhile, was tormented by *all seven of himself,* refusing to permit visitor, counselor, or strategist. None knew exactly what Lancelot would do, only that somehow he *and the Witch Morgaine* would decide the fate of Cymru.

It was during this opportune morning hour, and not during the cover of night, with distracted kings and Maelgwn riding through another fit of division, that the *two Popes* entered the fortress, and within the fortress, a small chapel in one of the nine palace courtyards. The Bishop of Rome was expected, along with his retinue, from Rome. None found it queer that he was a day early, and none questioned that one of his Cardinals was maimed, or the victim of some deformity, and lived behind a mask.

When Mordred was washed and shaven, and clad in simple black attire, he joined Eda in the courtyard. "Something feels amiss. You are certain that no ambush awaits?"

"It is the presence of the Pope himself that causes this unease. It is his office. His person. His celebrity. How many thousands of the faithful sleep the sleep of death, never having opportunity to wash his feet, or give oil for his hair?" Eda embodied all that was wrong with religionists: obsessed with theatre and ritual and stations of men, yet a rogue and a defiling cheater in his own private conduct. The type that believes the tithe or saying of loud prayers to capture onlooking eyes is license for misconduct and evil.

The illusion of religion had no impact on the Whelp. "You worship this man?"

"Nay." Eda was quick to deny idolatry, as are all idolaters. "You are nervous on account of his fame. I can think of no equivalent in our land... it would be like walking into a chapel and being spoken to by—" Eda snared himself, making an overtly embarrassing analogy.

"King Arthur." Mordred glared, flipping the latch, his stare never leaving his verbally disloyal steward as he wantonly entered the chapel.

***

In the chapel were twelve rows of paired pews, a processional pathway betwixt, facing a great pulpit and communal altar, which was situated in true-north within the fellowship hall.

Above the pulpit a large crucifix was fastened

with gargantuan cords to two rafters that rose and then bent to vault the ceiling. To look at the ceiling from the floor gave the parishioner, whose hereditary blood was still coursing with heathen traditions, the appearance and appeal of a grove; no detail of Catholic assimilation was spared.

The figure that was supposed to be the Son of God was of Catholic invention; pitiful, puny and pierced, fair-skinned, with hair like unto the Merovingian Kings who claimed him. The real Jesus had been as an ox, being a carpenter by trade; he had been olive-skinned like his kinsmen in the Near East, and had worn his hair and beard kept and well-groomed, fitting with his culture and the times. He had also been beaten beyond recognition, his lungs and organs exposed to the open air on account of Roman scourging. This Catholic "art" was insultingly contrary to the Biblical record.

Moreover, the real Jesus had not long remained on the Cross. It had been His shame to be there, but His passion to do the work of reconciliation for all mankind. Once done for all, He had ascended into the heavenly places and had no place in the sculptures made by blasphemous men perpetuating myths and imagery about the Savior being in a state of ongoing weakness - mocking Him.

Mordred fancied the blasphemy. But this particular cruciform he fancied threefold, and marveled. For the Cross, which was in height three times an average man, was upside down. Real blood, perhaps of some goat or child, streamed from the statue's eyes and wounded side, drizzling steadily upon the altar below.

There, kneeling, was a man, clearly a cleric, all in white. He wore a cap that gave the appearance of a fish's head and his cloak, also white with golden trimmings, was as a rolled carpet; a train of fabric with no end.

The Pope.

Kneeling beneath an inverted, Satanic Cross.

But he kneeled not before the altar or the dark relic; rather a second man. This one stood and faced the pews, as if he were preaching to an invisible congregation, his hands stretched out to further mock the Christian God.

His garb was black as night, and no flesh was revealed. *And he was masked.* This mask was made of lacquered porcelain, and the shaping was subtle but sure: he wore a face like unto a goat or hooved thing. Its expression was locked in permanent, freakish grin.

The black Pope.

The anti-Pope.

The False Prophet from the Book of Revelation.

Mordred was too immoral to fear what he ought to fear. Were this a ruse, five bowmen could have risen from behind the pews or baptismal font and filled him with a just death. He neither searched out the room nor performed basic measures to understand its composition; rather, with awed gawk, approached the two *Fathers.*

***

"Did you really slay this many Giants?"

"I take no pride in it. Something brought them from their slumber, causing them to think on nothing else but filling the countryside with perpetual violence." Arthur had been fond of many of the otherworldly beings that had met their demise by Excalibur or Rhon, wielded by the king's own hand.

Gildas, twenty years and one, continued to see Arthur as the god-king who had saved him from the Masked Devil as a lad. He faithfully did what the Pendragon bade; preparing histories, lists of kings, wedding registers; copying noteworthy land grants and church documents; collating the chronicles of the Cymru. These works were not songs, nor epic poetry - rather facts with minimal narrative and bereft of opinion or perspective.

Gildas ap Caw was objective, of temperate constitution, and possessed the memory of a bard coupled with the research skills of a schoolmaster.

The young man traveled with the small group of Round Table Heroes and their elite bowmen, who were preparing to pick a fight with nine hundred idle men, likely enjoying ale and harp presently, trusting in their soon-to-be-dead watchmen for warnings that would never come.

"I want you to record the battle census, and then to hasten and leave." A potentially final task issued by the king. "Though we adorn you as an emissary and accompany you with the white flag" - a custom started by the Roman Empire; from ancient times those waving such were not to be harmed, even by barbarous foes, the Saxons notwithstanding - "I cannot promise that the Saxons, or malefactors under Mark's employ, will not attack you, nor that Mordred will not murder you in order to hurt me."

"I understand the risk, my lord," Gildas said.

"Confer with your father; gather counts from Llew and from your brothers. The Pictish chieftains share our ancient codes and will not harm you. But tarry not amongst them. Count Cedric and Mark's lines from the ridge, then hasten away."

"Is Mark the Cruel amongst them?"

"Nay. He and Childebert close their fists around Brittany at present." Arthur closed his as he described theirs. "Derfel will lead his men, but we pray that upon seeing Cadfan turned, he will drop his spear, and abandon his post."

"It is rumored that Derfel is comparable in skill to Galahad."

"Yes. If he engages, many Silures will fall to his spear. He should be a Round Table Knight and, I hope, one day will be."

The king and his scribe enjoyed further conversation, then long silence, for the time was at hand that they must part ways. Gildas and a small company would travel the old road, built by Britons but claimed by Romans, in the light of day. Arthur required Gildas to dress as a Raven, and two bearers were constant with white banners; one on foot and one on horse. The Iron Bear did not need Gildas's count, for the army already had a sense of its opposition's forces. Rather, he wanted Gildas to record an accurate history, for truth's sake and no other motive.

Gildas would document the numbers and the notables and then leave. Unfortunately, the victor of the battle would be dictating the outcome of Camlan to the lad. The scene would be too dangerous for a man of letters with no sword. Arthur hoped that whomever sang the songs of Camlan would set aside embellishments and give Gildas a factual account. Too many foes had threatened to remove the Caermelyn's light from the world, and the Pendragon greatly feared that the histories would be altered or redrawn.

With proper timing and some good fortune, Gildas would have visited with his father, Arthur's great rival Caw, gathered his counts, conducted interviews and then hastened to the safety of Urien, who was ready to receive him, before news of the slaughter or surrender of Alain Fyrgan reached the Caw's ears. Elsewise, his son would be in grave danger, being accused of distracting the Northern armies, giving them cause to arrest or kill the brilliant young man - hurting the nation in doing so.

***

"So." The Goat relieved his hands from their crucified pose, folding his arms. "The Divine Child Mab stands before us, looking ferocious and virile. Truly blessed is the line of Meurig."

The use of flattery as a means of control is typically successful, but some great chasm was present in Mordred, preventing him from being flattered or uplifted. Magus searched the spirit of the troubled man and beseeched the spirits that he might know more of his inner-man. An audible answer was given. A high-pitched whisper that was from no place, and yet everywhere at once, the demon giving but one word: *"Fear."*

"Fear?" The Goat acted offended. "What should the son of a god fear?"

The secret and evil workings of the Church displayed in the open of the day did not frighten him, nor the dichotomy of the white and black popes peering at him, nor the spirits that made the chapel their comfortable home. Of a truth, nothing frightened the firstborn son of Arthur other than... Arthur.

Mordred made a brief attempt at changing the subject, endeavoring to absorb and make sense of the situation, and company, in which he found himself. "Are you the reason for all this death?" (The question arched back to the Saxon Wars, and before, for the Blessed Isles in the Sea were ever under covetous invasion.)

The Goat used *simple Latin, and spoke slowly, that each word was an hour.* "No. This is." An overly-long, gloved finger approached, and then poked, Mordred's bosom. "Man is the cause of death." The pace of speech increased. "Our college has simply had four thousand and five hundred years to develop a science, and art, of *helping you.*"

Mordred found himself in the presence of pure evil. And he favored it.

The Goat again demanded, "What do you fear, divine child?"

The Black Pope possessed an instant power over Mordred, as if Satan himself *wore the masked man as a mask.* The Whelp drooped his head, an adolescent boy receiving repeated scolding from an irritable parent.

"King Arthur," he confessed. "Spells, meditations, medications, incantations, mind sciences and more. I have done all to arrest my dread of my father. Yet I cannot."

"Only hate and arrogance conquers fear, and you are the sum of both. You are his shame, the dung on his unspotted cloak." Magus clutched Mordred by the hair, not violently, but authoritatively. "Is this what you think you are?"

Mordred was paralyzed. Hard truths fell from his numb mouth. "Yes."

"Does not the Scripture," for the Devil loves the Bible, and takes greatest pleasure in twisting and perverting or misusing its meaning, "teach 'AS MAN THINKETH, SO IS HE'?"

"I don't know this part of their book."

"No matter." Magus was now in Mordred's mind; molding it, reshaping it. "Men think you are an abomination. Good! Which of the great gods was not born of pure stock?" Simon the Teacher lectured. "Did Horus recluse himself in a cave; does Zeus hurl thunder shamefacedly? And of Tammuz son of Nimrod, our first pattern of the World Ruler - did he not take his own mother to wife, and beget demigods?"

"Even the Dynion Hysbys, the druids and pagans of every sort, recognize and reject such unnatural issue, and I AM unnatural issue."

"They are cattle, knowing not their own gods, or the Mysteries thereof." As Mordred viewed all men as livestock, the reference found its mark. "Boast in your uncleanliness, as did Caligula before you; rage against normalcy and the shackles of what conscience calls *right and good.* If it feels good, it *is* right and good. You are the son of the god-king Arthur and his sister, who is the Ancient of Days, even the goddess Morrigan. None save Lilith is more senior of her kind. The primal witch is IN YOU!"

For the very first time, ever, Mordred's drowning fear of Arthur began to assuage.

"And god-kings die that—"

"They may be reborn again in their sons," Mordred responded. "The Roman Church - She will never accept me."

"Has She not already pledged support for you in this Civil War? Her highest officer is before you."

"But the priests, the people—"

"Corrupt the priests with gold and feed the people, and they will cleave their own feet, and eat them." Simon loosed the Traitor's hair, freeing both hands for his dramatic preaching. "Those who fear the old gods will follow you, Son of Pendragon, provided the crops yield and the harvest is bountiful. We control the church. Leave fear of him in this *House of God* when you leave, for 'perfect hate casteth out all fear'; win this war and then DO AS YOU WILL! THIS SHALL BE THE WHOLE OF THE LAW IN YOUR NEW DARK CAMELOT!"

His mind melted, folded, hammered, then folded again by the Master Mind Smith, Mordred departed quickly, resolved that he would win the war and remarkably, not only survive decades of fornicating with the High King's wife, but *become High King.*

Eda could see and feel that Mordred was changed from the congress with Evil. He ordered his golden arm refashioned and took up a new weapon; a battle spike with rounded, fin-like blades along the front edge, which was both a hand-guard and additional killing option. Mordred's was longer than that of the Champion of Britain, being as a modified two-ended spear in appearance.

***

"We have elevated his confidence. He will engage Arthur upon the field rather than run as the field mouse."

"Still, Arthur will not be bested by this empty, pathetic man," the White Pope offered.

"Of course I agree, son," Simon Magus was well pleased with his work, "but his rage and hate may wound the king, or his courage might give Arthur a second of pause, allowing for a stroke to sneak through. We but need the Whelp to wound the Bear ere he meets his sure end."

Confident that the Popes would make calamity and chaos of Britain, and that one of their Anti-Christs would from the chaos rise,

Magus gave Silverius final instructions on how he might address the armies, soon fully gathered, at Camlan at sunrise on the summer solstice.

CAMLAN ACT I

CHAPTER 18
Alain's Cowardly Retreat and the First Day of the Dark Ages

Dusk
June 20
AD 537

Alain Fyrgan ap Hoel Dda commanded three troops, which is nine hundred souls, in the Battle of Camlan. A deserter from Arthur's kinsmen and renowned Breton ally, the chiefs of the Old North had offered the ambitious prince glory: the first wave of defense against the Silures, whose thousands of men would have to funnel through the winding valley and the thick, thorny wood, making their many numbers as though they were few. Alain would devote souls to the strategy of *delay,* empowering Cedric, with his Saxon, Gewessi and Lloegrian forces, to flank Arthur as his armies slowly emerged and fanned out in the fields and meadows of Camlan.

If he survived, Alain would be given the diadem over a small subdivision of Brittany, under the headship of Mark and Childebert, who would carve the country as if a pheasant.

Knowing that the attack would be soon, either

this week or the next – for the whole of the Island now noised about how Arthur would pursue Mordred and Lancelot up north – Alain was alert; but, trusting in his watchers and guards, who were stationed at beacons or on mounds and roads within a day's ride, he reposed and slept, though it were still day.

***

Snap – two pops – crackle.

It is but stags upon dried twigs.

Three more snaps, and close snaps.

Stags are not so large, nor deliberate in their gait. 'Tis men!

'Tis not men.

Screech and shadow, shadow and screech. Screeeech!

The brown owls; nothing more.

Owls cry not in the day!

Ohmmmm. Snap. Screech. Whistle. Ohmmm. Now distant. Now near.

That hum, as the chant of priests. Illtud's choirs, I say!

Worry not the men! All forests protest! We are nine hundred. Disquiet not the spirits!

Spirits! Thou sayest true! Spirits!

Silence.

Alain Fyrgan was disquieted. Fully awake, scrambling for his armor, yet slick as a buttered hen, unable to dress himself.

Snap – three pops – shuffle.

Wailings. Wailings. In Cymraeg, wailings. Haunting wailings!

Spirits!

Spirits, else men!

"Can a spirit drop a dead man from up there?" A young soldier pointed to the treetops where was perched a knight in light black armor, a kill impaled on three branches that had been modified with skill and haste to serve as a large fork. *The kill a warrior, one of Alain's own. One of the watchmen!*

The knight, who was Gareth, son of Morgaine of the Faeries, negotiated his kill off the fork and flung him below, the body splashing at the feet of Alain.

This occurred at the southern-most entrance of the Wood. Screams were heard in chorus from the north, the east, and the west as well. As quickly as he had appeared, Gareth was gone, leaving Alain's troops alone with their terror. Disorder erupted; infighting and clamor.

Then the arrows were loosed.

The Elves had given to the Cymry special knowledge of archery in the days of King Brutus of Troy. They immediately regretted that they had imparted this gift, for the men turned it against their hosts. This skill had been passed down from father to son, father to son (and daughters besides, who equaled men, and were often more accurate, having better dexterity of finger and thumb).

And those charged to chastise Alain were the most elect. These archers loosed two arrows every second; in ten seconds' time, twenty lay dead around Alain, who was unharmed. The missiles launched from every direction; many warriors ran upon a shaft in flight, the dart entering the face, bits of shaft and steel exiting the back of the head.

The Cymreig bowmen killed what they aimed to kill, and who they targeted not was safe as a newborn babe in his mother's arms.

Alain was as that newborn babe.

Shriek. Howl! Drums.

It is men AND ghosts. We are undone. Run!

Silence, save the sound of breathing, and running.

As the warriors scattered and fled, the arrows resumed. This time so many were loosed simultaneously, and then consecutively, that no sound separated them. *Whisp – whisp – whisp – whisp.*

The newborn babe shat himself, soiling his trousers and vomiting the whole content of his stomach at the same time. Frozen in terror as crimson pools rose to his ankles. Excrement, vomit and blood bathed the coward, who was no man of war.

The arrows stopped.

Dusk was but moments from giving way to full darkness. A hooded knight emerged, holding a lit torch in one hand and a shimmering blade in another. The last bit of sun touched on the hilt, and Alain knew of the script and markings, for every child born the world over had been told stories ere bed of the sword and the boy-king.

The light of the torch revealed the sandy hair beneath the hood.

"Aaa—" dry heaves - "Arrtth—"

The King of the Britons never withdrew his hood. He turned Excalibur a few times, that the glory of the blade might reflect light upon the disgraced visage of Alain.

It is not as the bards describe, and the poets do lie! I cannot move. And breath I have not; will he cleave me in twain, that I will die in my own shit?

King Arthur barely addressed Alain, speaking only to the ground, for the misguided fool did not deserve the address of the noble sovereign.

"I would not have your father, *my friend,* see his offspring as this. Take thee a blanket and run - *now.*" Arthur gave direction, pointing with Excalibur in the way where Alain would have safe passage from the scene.

Thus did Alain Fyrgan lift no arms against Arthur, instead emptying his bowels and making hasty flight from the Battle of Camlan.

And the Round Table Fellowship earned a victory in the first offensive of the woeful war.

CAMLAN ACT II

CHAPTER 19

The Ridge of the Saxons and the Fall of Cedric

As Hoel Dda, Gareth, Cadog, Arthur, and Cai guided their small company of archers to victory, a second wave, also few in number, had already been dispatched. These were led by old Gwynllyw, and Merlin was amongst them. Their task was imperative, but the performance thereof wretched.

To put every watchman, guard, messenger and any fighting-aged boy or girl that could relay report from the south into the midlands and up north into the enemy's ears to the sword. No exceptions.

Perfect stealth was not the objective, nor could it be. The movement of so many thousand souls by trains of wagons or by flat, hulking riverboats, and the galloping pound of hoof on Cymreig and Roman roads, could not be achieved covertly. Rather, the objective was to delay, even if but for half a day, the warning of *when* the armies would arrive. In this regard, by the time the scattered souls were tortured in the forest by the bowmen, or any other word came, the news would be confused, delayed, amiss and too late.

Having complete knowledge of every hilltop,

watchtower, and inn along the routes, the Silures executed an assassination operation. They met with great success, each kill breaking the heart of the knight who delivered the terminal strokes. The second wave equaled the triumph of the first, and Merlin arrived before sunrise, meeting with Arthur in the forest. He was readying for the next maneuver, wishing the match was gwyddbwyll and the stakes pints and boasting rights, and not the very soul of the Blessed Isles in the Sea.

***

Before Sunrise
June 21
AD 537

Caw wept uncontrollably, holding his son, who had now grown a full head taller than his father, with such intense emotion that none could look upon the embrace, lest the whole company sob.

"Your histories are *our history,* regardless of outcome. Arthur, though I loathe him, did well to choose my son, Gildas the Brilliant, to be chief of scribes in our time. Finish your counts and your interviews. You are safe. But then, as he commanded you, hasten to Rheged, where Urien will offer you protection and lodging." Bitter words given by Caw, but reason favored Arthur's aims for the lad.

Caw reckoned that, after at last ending the legend of lies that was the Round Table Fellowship, the Northern princes would have to then deal with Urien and Owain, perhaps adding to the chapters in the Civil War. Or perhaps negotiating terms, preventing further loss of life.

Regardless of outcome, Urien favored Gildas

(as did all Christian-oriented men, who promoted him and Dewi as the next generation of young Saints, philosophers, historians and wisemen to see the Church forward – should the Britons not annihilate themselves in this foolish, vain strife) and would bring him no harm, nor imprison him as hostage or make political intrigue of the situation.

The long embrace having ended, Gildas labored to finalize his census, which he collated and added to his Register of Neath. Knowing, lest some miracle prevent what was surely at hand, the losses would be immeasurable, the Scribe prepared the document in the past tense and affirmed what he had seen, having been with both sides, signing it with own hand:

'Recorded and attested before God and Man on the Summer Solstice morn, five hundred and thirty-seven years from the Lord.

'As sands of the sea, so were the occupants, both of Britannia and sundry strangers from abroad, gathered to wage this Civil War, principally between the North, by ancient and accepted borders and boundaries, and the South, by ancient and accepted borders and boundaries, at Maes-Y-Camlan, which is in the land of Maelgwn Gwynedd.

'Let those who would pilgrimage to honor their dead, or to rescue their effects, be informed of the sure location of bones; in the shadow of Craig Y Gamell; above the village of Mallwyd; by the chapel of Saint Tydecho; along the crook and wind of the Afon Dyfi; there look; there dig.

'Of the total number of souls, approximately three hundred and thirty-three troops, or one hundred thousand.

'And of the one hundred thousand, forty thousand lent their spear to Arthur, but twice thirty thousand gave their shields to Mordred and Maelgwn.

'And of the forty thousand that lent their spear to Arthur, half of these were of the tribe Silure. Rhun ap Maelgwn gave to Arthur two thirds of his own from Gwynedd, which was six thousand, and likewise Urien ap Cynfarch Oer did allot two thirds, also summing six thousand.

'Thus twelve thousand Ravens joined to the Round Table Fellowship, fighting their kin at Camlan, the remainder being eight thousand Bretons, who left one thousand of those exiled to rebuild Caerleon.

'God be witness and hearken ye the world over that not one Saxon, Angle, Jute or barbarian of Germania did with Arthur ally; neither would he conscript, employ or sup with them.

'But not so the Ravens, who have forgotten the Night of Long Knives, and abandoned reason.

'Of the sixty thousand conspired against the High King, half of these, or thrice ten thousand, were Ravens, excluding the elite Hosts of Lancelot, who numbered five hundred, the remnant of the twenty-four times twenty-four being reserved to preserve their kingdom should the Bloodhound Prince fall.

'Cedric's numbers were about thirty troops, or nine thousand Saxons.

'King Brychan gathered about three thousand from the South, and the Midlands.

'Alain turned from Hoel, causing nine hundred Bretons to fight for the North.

'King Drest brought down diverse painted Picts from every part of Alba, having ferocity

and great numbers, their census being one thousand times ten.

'The residue, numbering about six thousand and six hundred, hailed from Eire, else were confederates of Mark ap Meirchion.'

***

Simon Magus had departed, narrowly escaping the sweep performed by Gwynllyw and Merlin. The Black Pope, having ensured the White Pope was thoroughly rehearsed, would return again to Porth Madwy, examining again the accessibility of Avalon.

***

Maes-Y-Camlan was an open farmstead, a natural pitch, as if designed by God or the Devil to be repurposed as a battlefield. Flat enough here for mounted cavalry to safely execute their patterns, hills and short mounds there to make quick ditches and embankments for foot soldiers and archers to gain high-ground positions. The farm spread up, then terminated on the lower slopes of, the Craig Y Gamell. The mountain was one thousand three hundred eighty and nine feet tall and was the gateway to Dinas Maddwy. And Dinas Maddwy was the gateway to controlling the Northern kingdoms of Cymru.

Craig Y Gamell gave the appearance of the thighs and womb of a great goddess. There were two distinct slopes divided by a deep gulch, which was hewn straight and clean, then widened and fanned towards the navel of the mount; the zenith of the mount was curvy but flat. To be an eagle soaring above Craig Y Gamell would be to look at the mother of Cymru come into her fullness - about to be delivered of a new future for Cymru, be it for good or ill.

The Northern armies filled the mountainsides, looking as ants upon a log, except for the Saxons, whose camp was five miles east in a place the bards would later call Nant-y-Saeson, *the place of the Saxon.* But King Cedric and ten of his battle lords were present with the chieftains, lords, bards, scribes and renowned men assembled atop the westernmost slope of Craig Y Gamell. Drest the Pict, Caw, Huell, Llew, Mordred and many more were present, warming themselves with hands clasped around pewter mugs of scalding tea, waiting for the Pope to manifest and address the assembly.

Maelgwn was not amongst them. Rather he was a mounted statue residing alone on the eastern slope, at a slightly higher elevation than his tenuous allies. And they dared not trouble him, giving him space, knowing his blade would spill much blood, praying that it would be that of their enemy.

A red carpet, sewn with ornate designs of Ostrigoth, Visigoth and Italian origin, was carefully rolled out, then held to the rough surface by four large cherubic statues, made of onyx stone or gold, alternating in arrangement. A procession of priests and trumpeters with long brass cornets followed and at last Silverius, the Bishop of Rome, showed himself to the throngs of knights.

A servant of his own company (for the Cymru had neither slave nor servant, the lowliest of occupations treated with honor, respect, and compensation) placed a pillow at Silverius's feet. Although his vestments were simple, consistent with the fashions of the Church in Rome, he exuded arrogance, hubris, and dominion.

Kneeling slowly, his knees upon the pillow, he ritually rested upon both elbows, bending the whole of his upper torso, almost prostrate on the carpet, his position as a submissive dog. But this was a pretense; an empty rite. He slowly kissed the ground outside the boundary of the red carpet, quickly rising to his supreme posture thereafter.

Meanwhile, another procession had ascended the hill. The shock and fear of so many thousand soldiers froze them, for they had named their sons after him, and now here he was, riding with his wizard and his steward, three men against sixty thousand.

"When *his eminence* kisses the ground prostrate then erects himself again, that is his ritualistic announcement that the dirt now belongs to the Roman Church, and to HIM, its governor!"

A few veteran Saxon warriors, who were there with Cedric for the Papal Blessing, shuddered, having heard before this authoritative, hammering tone. In their ears he was more fearsome than Odin, more thunderous than Thor! *It was King Arthur himself, and lo, Excalibur!*

"You foolish brothers in the North. How many more times will we suffer you of Ynys Mon and Gwynedd, and the Old North, to invite the invader to our shores, and concede him our lands without even unsheathing his sword?" Arthur seethed. "What we just witnessed was an INVASION of Cymru."

"A rather aggressive opening statement for negotiations that precede the fight." Caw took the lead in addressing the confederacy's mighty foe. Meanwhile, young Gildas, snared by the curiosity of the procession from Rome, delayed his departure and was a hundred yards off, watching and listening to all.

Silverius was dumbfounded. Popes are not accustomed to disruption or reproof, even by princes. He ignored, or rather supplanted, Caw's attempt to engage discourse, and started to sermonize the masses.

"Yes, I have claimed Britannia for the Universal Church. But hearken unto me, and reason, brethren. Were not the powers to bind and loosen given unto Peter and succession – unto me? God would govern the earth and, as the Church are the People, the Government is therefore the People."

Arthur gave thunderous, interruptive laughter.

Merlin followed with the same. "Nay. Peter spake of a time when the Lord Himself would rule through the Twelve Apostles, through the Twelve Tribes, through Seventy Elders, over the Nations. I see not Jesus here, and you would twist what was written to Hebrews and make it your own—"

"Now is not the time for theological analysis, old friend." Arthur nudged the tall Briton in the side, his helm elevating just so due to his smile. "You sound like Dyfrig and Illtud, bantering about words during a time of war!"

Merlin blushed. "Never ought I to sound like them!" The Round Table Companions jested as if they were back in the library, and not in the center of the enemy's lair.

Before Silverius could recover control of the discourse, Arthur continued, and his rage returned. "The Government are NOT the People, and the People are NOT the Government. This is the trick of tyrants as old as fallen man himself – allowing you," Excalibur pointed at the Bishop of Rome; several mounted knights shifted, hollered protest, or drew their weapons, "to do whatever dark and manipulative deed you will, all in the name of the People. The Government is loaned power by the People, not the inverse. For the most part, the People ought to have the Government as I do; which is what best qualifies me to govern, as I desire ever and only to LEAVE THE PEOPLE ALONE!"

"Provided that they are Cymru." The Pope altered his game, seeking to make of Arthur a respecter of persons. "But God has made all men and women the same, each possessing of equal rights. Behold this assembly, Lord Arthur. Look how those of many nations now gather as one. This is the future of Britannia; that the Saxon, the Pict, the tribes of Eire, and the Britons might share these Isles. A brotherhood of Man under the Fatherhood of God. Your ways are dying, and before you is the New World Order."

"The utopian ramblings of a tyrant," came Arthur's retort. "When has the Saxon embraced nobility, or the Pict not traded a man's hide for a satchel of corn, or a horn of mead? You would put all men under one tent that you can crush him, not that you might make him free. God hath appointed the bounds of our habitation; let all men live free, WHERE He has appointed them."

The helm of the king then tilted towards the sky and turned east, his booming voice hurled in the direction of the other slope. "I offer the contest of Champions, a final plea that lives be saved. My sister did rework thy comely face, and the white hair suits you, Handsome. Come now; let us stand together and resolve our strife, Lancelot."

Whichever of the splinters sailing the shattered vessel that was Maelgwn Gwynedd, this one was not moved by the Silure's goading challenge. He moved not. *But Mordred moved.*

Newly filled with satanically-inspired assurance, the Traitor had taken up again the golden armor, underlined with black mail and cloak; he sprinted towards Arthur, then halted with the skid of raging bull, sizing up his kill ere the strike.

"Remove that," said Arthur.

"Remove yours," replied Mordred.

Arthur did. And Mordred did.

Mirrored, identical eyes, the only part or attribute passed from the loins of Arthur to the demonic shell that now confronted him.

You would have made me the cuckold, and taken my queen, and my throne.

You murdered my true love. She NEVER loved you. She loved me, or that brute atop that ridge at times, but never YOU.

You will be removed from the Earth.

YOU will be removed from the Earth.

The enemies never spake these things, and said nothing.

"A challenge of Champions to settle this war, only it will be Eda, and not Mordred." Llew voiced acceptance of the terms, and the other nobles agreed.

"Eda, Mordred, then Lancelot, followed by whomever else you would add to the list." Arthur continued to beg a fight. "However, there is one condition before we circle and celebrate peace ere the Sun reaches the height of his circuit."

"Present your terms," said Llew.

The Pendragon asked Merlin to speak.

"There will be no State Religion in these Isles," he began, "regardless of outcome; all Cymru will renounce the intrusion and invasion of this synagogue of Satan and the law of Caermelyn will be restored: namely that men worship whatever God they will, only that they don't kill their neighbors for it, or force him to do the same."

"We will not renounce the Church at Rome, nor the Holy Father. The primitive Church of the Britons once held some truth, but apostasy hath mined through her soul as a canker. Rome is the future, and is of no threat to the sovereignty of Cymru." Caw was resolved.

"They are kind unto the old gods," offered the Saxon king, Cedric.

Arthur calmly put his helmet on again and motioned the banner carriers to wave the flags, indicating the departure of chieftains or emissaries before the battle ensues. All civilized men honor such pre-war negotiations, and often suing for peace or mercy is successful.

Gwladys, the enterprising merchant, had fashioned a new ensign for Cymru. Working from the red dragon sigil flown by Arthur, by Meurig, and before them Tewdrig, and before him the Pendragons of old, she had added a thick stripe of green below, and white above.

"Have we not had enough of dragons?" Huell ap Caw, the cattle thief, raider and thorn of the Midlands and of the South, insulted and mocked: "Dragons of flesh, dragons dressed as Silure kings, and dragons from the sky; HAVE WE NOT HAD ENOUGH OF DRAGONS?"

"Ignorant and debased, you do shame your father, who is at least an honorable foe." Merlin's defense of the flag was swift. "The white is heaven about and the green the earth below. The dragon is no longer a symbol of the power of the king or supremacy of the warlord. Neither a veneration of worshiping a wise serpent."

"What then?" Huell was not interested,

shrugging his shoulders dismissively.

"The dragon is a symbol of what we have overcome. What we will ALWAYS overcome. Though heaven fall and the earth perish, the Cymru will survive. Though we falter and fail, though we stumble and fall.... We will get... back... up!" Merlin's words were rousing, and some of the Northmen cheered.

Arthur noted the time invested in the theatre and returned his attention to Cedric.

"Today, we conclude Baedan. Twenty years you've waited, and today you will make your stand against me." Arthur motioned to the Saxon's sheathed long-weapon. "Is it exercised and ready?"

"So Camlan starts today?" Cedric asked, a mixture of trembling and eagerness to at last slay the Pendragon that had defeated his people for an entire generation.

"Our troops will be in crimson silks and matching plume." Arthur made a full circle, communicating to all that might be able to hear, repeating himself two or three times. "The dead may not be removed during the battle; royals shall not be mutilated or defamed, neither their torques or rings purloined." These courtesies were basic, and all agreed.

"When do we commence?" Cedric pressed again.

Arthur waited a few more minutes, letting the intensity boil.

"King Cedric," the authority of God's voice again was selected, "is your steed swift?"

"Aye, Pendragon."

"Five miles. How fast could he bear you five miles... east of here?"

"Twenty minutes to negotiate these slopes,

and half an hour at most for the rest."

"Oh, he is faster than the Great Stag." Mocking words in *that tone of authority*, confusing all. Arthur turned and bade Merlin farewell; the wizard fearing none of the sixty thousand, he would go to Lancelot. "Give me one and a half hours, for I am aged, and my mare's knees trouble him, as do mine."

"Granted! In ninety minutes Camlan begins!"

"Begins?" Arthur calmly put Excalibur to sheath and turned his steed, and the small party began to retreat, the new Pendragon flags waving proudly, tossed to and fro by the morning mountain breezes. At just the right time, he turned, but did not stop. "Begins? In ninety minutes most of your men will be dead - for the battle began two hours ago."

"Trickery and ruse!" someone screamed.

"We are distracted, ambushed!" cried another.

The soldiers were not wrong. Arthur and Merlin had had but one objective with their bold entry into the heart of darkness: delay and distract.

Eda raised a spear and would loose it at the king, but Cedric beseeched him to lower the missile. "The Silures presently hack and chop at my men, my sons. I beseech you, let me have first chance. I beseech you!"

Mordred's *Cai* reluctantly withdrew, and Arthur's horse, contrary to his report, had perfect knees and was swift as the wind. The small retinue rapidly disappeared down into the farmland, then the thicket, and then were as small black dots on the trails below.

Gildas could not help but wonder, *Was I, too, a pawn? Bait tangled ere the trap wire yanked?* For the first time in his life, the young master had a pang of doubt about Arthur Pendragon. A pang that remained as he traveled further north to Rheged.

***

In addition to crafting brilliant new flags, Gwladys and her hired help had fitted the warriors with forty thousand red silks, and forty thousand red plumes. The production had been on a grand scale, her organizational gifts unsurpassed. Gwenhwyfar ferch Gwythyr had happily given hours of her own labor to the task, busying her hands that they might distract her disappointed, aching heart.

Each silk was fastened to the breastplate, creating uniformity and allowing for identification during the tempest of battle.

Gwladys's lovely chest pieces and plumes were where the uniformity ended. The shortage of armor, and the smiths to fashion it, had not been fully overcome by the Round Table Companions. Because of this, the quality, form and nature of leather, fabric, wooden or metal protection under the silks varied, creating risk.

Bedwyr. If there never had been an Arthur, a Galahad, a Gwalchmai or a Lancelot, he would have been known as the greatest knight that ever lived. In an age with a surplus of heroes, his Song was not sung frequently, nor loudly enough. It was the subtle, discreet things that separated him from the rest. His indomitable humor, his overcoming disabling wounds, and his empathy for others – these were the characteristics overlooked by damsels at tea, or minstrels in the tavern. These were also the characteristics that would cause all men everywhere, and for all ages, to measure what was good and just and right by the Cymry and their Round Table Fellows. And Bedwyr was the best of these.

As the Silures enjoyed their final rest for water and final adjustments, less than an hour's ride from Nant-Y-Saeson, Bedwyr noted a young warrior of similar proportion struggling with defective latches and cracked rivets. Bedwyr gifted the lad *his silver skin.* The countenance of the downtrodden, frightened boy immediately shifted, confident that he was surely invincible, wearing the actual armor designed by the Lady of the Lake and worn by a Round Table Knight!

The battle began at sunrise, at about the time when the Pope's procession began. The South, outnumbering the Saxon forces, and exceeding them in skill, tore through them as a starving dog tossed pheasant carcasses after a great banquet.

The Bretons rained arrows; the Britons swept through with mounted troops. The Saxons were on the defensive from the onset, and never recovered.

Merlin ordered that songs of victory referencing Baedan and the Twelve Battles be sung in Latin and in Cymreig. Drums drowned out screams, and horns muted death rattles.

It took the Cymry longer to move and stack bodies so that they might continue the slaughter than to perform the killing itself. Veterans were taken back to the days of invincibility, and new troops gained the confidence that comes only by earning the first kill. Then the first five kills. Then twenty.

Hoel and Cadog noticed *an absence.*

And that absence was Bedwyr.

No timely jests. No glorious speeches. No magical, infectious motivation.

Ogyrfan son of Gwyar was the first to find

him, slumped behind the debris of a broken supply cart.

Within the first thirty seconds of the battle, Bedwyr had felt a latch give way on the armor he had traded with the young warrior. Having but one hand, he had had to choose between *fiddle and fix or hack and whack*. Seeing his strait, a Saxon made a sloppy but somehow fortuitous swing with a double-headed battle-ax. The weapon was so sharp that Bedwyr did not feel the blow connect, nor did he suffer pain. Thinking he had either avoided the ax or absorbed the majority of the wound on the lower half of his chest plate, Bedwyr recoiled, reset his stance, and slew the Saxon with no difficulty. Then he collapsed.

King Cedric arrived, already filled with dread, seeing nigh the defeat of his divisive confederacy against the High King. The High King, meanwhile, had arrived moments earlier, and tasted the Golden Age again, fighting as a much younger man. Unlike tyrants and politicians who send others to die for their gain, the son of Meurig led his troops, ever willing to do that which he expected of his men. Even aged rulers of the Royal Clans were like-mannered. When their skills diminished, they would fight less, or battle only behind a ring of guards, but they were there, and not on some hill far away as a coward.

Arthur led by example. He led with his blade, not with his mouth.

And now his blade found Cedric.

Cai's club splattered grey matter on the Saxon king as two of his warlords fell upon his horse's front hooves, dead before they hit the dirt.

"Dismount!" Arthur challenged.

Cedric knew he was going to perish. He could

feel men falling all around him. Even if he did manage to defeat the Pendragon, ten Britons would run him through soon after. There was no escape, no secret route, no help from the shadowy Council of Nine.

He dismounted, hoping to earn victory in his final duel, and then hoping to die a brave death.

Arthur dismounted as well.

Cedric fought a defensive, slow match. He had no desire to rush upon Arthur, for the Cymreig warrior would counter any mistake; and all knew that counter-fighting was Arthur's special area of mastery. Moreover, the longer the match, the longer Cedric would draw breath and live.

Through the process of time, Cedric made minor errors, and suffered minor cuts. Spent, and bleeding from nine wounds, he withdrew, and removed his helmet.

"Will you suffer my sons to live?" he begged.

"You have become the unintentional founder of a nation. West Saxons and Lloegyr seem to be melding, and not many years hence shall be one nation. We do not attack other nations, and concern ourselves only with the defense of Cymru. Provided your sons at home *stay home*, they shall live, and - should this plague and calamity pass - prosper." Arthur offered kind, and true, words of solace, knowing in his heart that no Saxon ever *stays home*.

"Thank you, Pendragon. You are a just sovereign." Cedric engaged with his final reserve. And engaged amiss.

King Arthur ran Excalibur through the armor, through the heart, through the spine, and out of the back of Cedric. Twenty-one years after Mynydd Baedan, the third and last of the Germanic Chiefs was slain.

The rout had no ending and victory for the Round Table Knights was sure, each of them soaked head to toe in Saxon blood, giving shouts of praise and songs of triumph.

Bedwyr composed himself and stood aright, though his injury was grave.

CAMLAN ACT III

CHAPTER 20
Mist
The Misery of Morgaine

Arthur and his fabled companions had finished the Saxons prior to noonday on the twenty-first of June, five hundred and thirty-seven years from the Lord.

Though some of the younger warriors expected a reinforcing wave of Ravens to come, or to have to next deal with the pesky Picts, the more experienced knew that this would not be. So confident were they that the combat was finished for the day that they disarmed, washed in the river Dyfi, and set about erecting a small city of white tents, that they might have comfortable respite ere the next chapter of the Civil War.

The South was winning. Decisively.

The North's original strategy had been *slow them, flank them, make them climb*. However, the South had not been slowed in the woodland area below the farmland, and the force dedicated to flanking them lay in lakes of blood, piles of flesh. Although the scales were more balanced after the annihilation of Cedric, Arthur was still outnumbered by approximately ten thousand men. Therefore, the North would keep their backs to the slopes and their armies facing Maes-Y-Camlan, and simply wait for Arthur to cut back west from Nant-Y-Saeson and conduct the climatic final chapter on Maelgwn's farm itself.

Arthur's armies still had some risk of defeat, for fighting from a low-ground position is disadvantageous, and typically results in a resounding loss. Low-ground wars are only won through protracted, small skirmishes that bait those on the high ground to abandon their advantage, become overly aggressive, and leave a crease in the ranks that can be breached. Once some portion of Arthur's men were on the same level in the slopes, he could push the remainder of the Ravens down into the gulch, and then the farm, and have equitable chance of finishing them.

Moreover, Arthur planned to send scouts to cut supplies and to starve his foes, making the ridgetop a prison. Mordred's men could descend the opposite side of the hill and replenish themselves in Maddwy, thus conceding Craig-Y-Gamell to the Silures, or press down the mound for water, supplies and food, and in so doing, sacrifice position.

The scene was an inverse of Baedan, where Arthur had forced the Saxons to ascend; here he would cause his treacherous kinsmen to descend, else flee north, else starve.

The "waiting" part of war had come. Both sides knew as much, and rested.

***

June 22
AD 537

"Brother, wake with great haste!" Cai was pulling Arthur from his cot with the angst of a child tugging at its parent to rouse and give gifts at a harvest festival. "Get up!"

"I wasn't lying to those rogues about *my knees,*" Arthur jested, still in the drift of sleep, not alert enough to be startled. *After all, Cai's job is to over-worry and overthink.*

Cai found a tunic in Arthur's chest, and quickly unfolded linen trousers, almost dressing the king.

"But these don't even match - I will look awful before the men!" Arthur's mood was jovial, energetic, grand. Maelgwn had won the day at Llongborth, but the Pendragon had smashed his foes at Talgarth, in the Wood, and at Nant-Y-Saeson. *I am up two, old friend. Perhaps you will abandon this cause on this day or the next.*

"That's the problem, brother. The men WON'T see you - come!"

Arthur did the bidding of his well-meaning, overbearing foster-brother, giving two more jokes and one more protest, and was mid-sentence when he stepped from his pavilion. He stopped jesting. *Stopped speaking at all.*

A mist had enveloped the camp. The whole of the camp. Forty thousand souls: the fog so thick that none could see his fellow beyond the measure of six inches, unless they were in a tent or cave.

And the mist was enchanted, ethereal. It possessed substance and moisture, hues of yellow and green, flashes of blue.

Fear and confusion reigned. Clamor, debate, indecision, curses and sundry prayers that God or some god would remove the spell noised throughout. Cadfan found Arthur's forearm and identified himself, imploring his lord for audience. Arthur guided Cadfan within the folds of his tent and lit a candle, though it were morning time.

"'Tis Morgaine," the bishop informed him.

Before Arthur could respond, shouts of shock shook the tethers, the ground filled with stamping horses and bewildered knights.

The fog was gone. Though not all.

A swirl, a spinning cone of mist, concealed Gareth, Gaheris, Ogyrfan and, suddenly, King Arthur as well.

Five miles northwest, a mist shrouded Mordred as well.

Cadfan repeated, "'Tis Morgaine."

***

"I cannot control it; woe unto Cymru." The Sorceress's elbows rested upon the fount where she looked upon the results of her webs, and they were woven amiss. When causing pilgrims to lose their way, or priests to be befuddled, the mist was her servant. Where war was involved, it was as a wild brush fire, a hungry, slapdash dog.

Morgaine was undeterred. Thrice clockwise she motioned the green scrying waters; pause. Thrice clockwise once more. But the Vision did not improve. Her sons and brother were at once entombed in the protective cloudy cottons of the mist in one moment, the whole of Gwynedd the next, a mountaintop or gully bottom the following.

Her nine priestesses were grieved for the Lady of Avalon, and sorely worried for her. She neither ate nor slept, and was ever at her magickal workings. One maiden, called Thitis, who was patroness of stringed instruments, carefully laid Morgaine's head upon her lap (the Sorceress gave no protest) and strummed songs of soothing, melodies of mourning, refrains of rest.

"If the Christian God is truly the Most High" – she spoke as Gwyar – "then why will He not favor me for so long protecting the mother of His Son?" She wept. "I honored His Son, killed only His naughty priests…" Tears outlined a brief smile. "Why can He not spare the remainder of mine?"

"Men have bargained and bartered with the gods since the beginning, Mistress." Thitis continued to strum, for music was her method of communication. "I don't think even the gods can ultimately burglarize the free will of Man. And Man is a warring, killing sort."

Gwyar wept.

She was overcome with grief and introspection, grieving for not only the loss of her sons, which was imminent, but the passing of the Summer Kingdom.

"What makes me special, or differing from any other mother?" she judged herself. "The thick, fiery-haired, red-hot-tempered Pictish woman, hunting seals and making pelts in remote North – is her mourning and passion less than mine? In no way. The Jutish mom, whose young, yellow-haired boy is right now toiling in a foreign land, hearing songs and curses in unknown tongues, terrified as the Briton leaf snips his throat. Is her anguish and restlessness of no import whilst I moan over mine? The Raven. O, my sisters from Gwynedd and Ynys Mon! My mothers, my kinswomen! Is not each of their sons worthy of a bard's song? Why is Gwyar superior? Men, and women, ought not to think too highly of themselves. What hath my meddling wrought?" Here she called out to *the other noteworthy meddler.* "Merlin! What hath our meddling wrought?"

"A light of freedom against a darkness unimaginable when you and I are exiled, and Arthur sleeps." A direct, prophetic answer was given. The voice matched the wizard's, but whence it came, the weeping lady knew not.

But, through the blur of swollen eyes, a man did appear. A comely man. Youthful, virile, a heathen through and through, he seemingly stepped out of Britain's pagan past. But this druid was from Gaul, and had been apprenticed in these parts.

"Accolon," Thitis beckoned to the lad to approach and kneel near the fount where they lay, "bring it, that she may recover, for our Mistress is undone."

The young druid wore a giddy crest made of holly and went about without shirt, having only a single gold torque round his left arm as clothing above the waist. Only a simple plaid wrap below; and he was barefoot besides. Having a small dagger, he made five perfect slits in a plump pomegranate and opened it with careful, sensual skill, squeezing two wedges into a wooden goblet; giving Gwyar juice wherewith to drink, and fruit wherewith to eat.

Her attendants had not heard the voice of the wizard, but the words were at once painful and edifying, and the beautiful form before her reminded her that the Isles had heroes yet to come, futures worth defending. If a dark age was coming, she would fight it to the last, and not gently.

Gwyar had fallen. Morgaine of the Faeries rose.

"I like him," she commented to Thitis, with a

new voice. The other maidens giggled.

If there was a full and lasting fog, the armies might withdraw. Then she could assassinate individuals over time, sparing her loved ones, mitigating the loss of life. If an isolated, covering spiral of mist was about them, then they might escape, and live. *Broad or acute, only consistent!* Her resolve returned, for better or worse, and the Faerie did her spells cast, and her powers work, harder and harder still.

***

Lancelot and his Hosts camped atop the eastern ridge and remained, for the most part, inert. They hunted and prepared a well-organized camp, complete with a great log table, over which were spread parchments and maps. Merlin spied them out, but did not yet approach.

They watched the mists ebb and flow, come and go, swirl and vanish. None knew quite what to do; Lancelot calmly commanded them to take little food, to be vigilant, and to elsewise do nothing.

***

"Follow the sound of the crooked river, that we reach Camlan - let us at least do that much," commanded Arthur. The distance to be covered should have taken less than three hours, even for so many souls, carts, supplies and horses. Instead: twelve hours.

Darkness had settled over the field of Camlan, and approximately forty thousand soldiers were there. Cheerful for victory, baffled by the mists, which rested on nothing, as gargantuan clouds but inches from the ground. The moonlight, the mists, and the dark blue, starry night in Gwynedd. 'Twas a scene perfect for lovers and poets; not so for soldiers.

But Arthur would nonetheless have them initiate the next phase.

Organized skirmishes.

"Use the sound of the water and the position of the stars, and not the billows of white at your feet, and harass the southeastern tip of the hill," he ordered.

"How many?" asked Cadog, who was charged to lead the tussle.

"One troop, no more. Slash and withdraw, no volleys."

Cadog, an original Round Table Knight, had executed the scheme countless times. His role was to anger the enemy, draw him out, earn a short victory, and then capture the ground the enemy vacated. When this was repeated over and over again, the high-ground position would soon be a garble of friend and foe; then the Silures would rapidly reassemble and launch a level-to-level ground offensive by longbow, followed by horseback engagements.

Caw and Llew knew what the enemy would do, yet human nature made it impossible to prevent Arthur from doing to them exactly and precisely what he aimed to do. As brains were smashed with clubs, or kneecaps exploded all around the camp, those under assault would either flee - which they could not, having the gulch and the mountain terrain behind them - or draw anger and fury, and fight back, and chase.

They did the latter, riding, else sprinting, through the fog after ghosts in the night.

Cadog was victorious.

Likewise, Cador and his three hundred provoked the same response.

Four times this was repeated, each a battle within a battle.

Four thousand from the North were slain, else scattered.

Arthur could *feel* that their discipline would break on the morrow, and that the sum of Mordred and Llew's hordes would engage them on even ground on Maes-Y-Camlan.

"We have earned the ascent point of both ridges, lord. But the fog thickens, and is wet, causing our torches to fail," Hoel reported.

"Another day is ours," rejoiced Arthur. "Let us now rest and hope my sister's fog does tomorrow lift, that we might finish this."

"Whether it abates or no, I have an idea. Would you hear of it from me?"

"Would Merlin like it?" Arthur mused, inviting to Hoel to join him for cider and to tell the king his ambition.

CAMLAN ACT IV

CHAPTER 21
The Fateful Division of the Army and Derfel's Rout of the Silures and Bretons

Merlin would emphatically *not* like it...

Hoel favored a style of attack, which had been very successful over his long career, of dividing his troop cleanly, with perfect timing, to develop a flank - and then doing so once more. If the first flank was achieved, the second was easy, and the Bretons would simply meet in the middle, ceasing to hack and thrash when seeing their own sigils before them.

Merlin disliked this approach, favoring the 'widening V' method of war. His method featured a vanguard of elite troops forming the tip of an arrowhead formation, always wider at the base than at the front. This made *being flanked* impossible. The best warriors in front would wedge through the opponent with such ferocity and precision that the opponent would scatter and try to flank both sides of the 'arrowhead' at once. This never worked, and Arthur's Silures would simply pluck and kill the dross as they spilled from the side of his arrow formation.

These were the differing open-warfare, mounted-knight methods when engaged in a field. Both were successful, and there was no dogma where war was concerned. However, Merlin and Hoel, who were great friends, did argue over this much; especially when the pride that accompanies cider was over-consumed. Because of Hoel's love for 'divide and flank', he would, as all passionate and good leaders do, contend for his method – only, this time, he advocated dividing the army and sending one third of the men to the obverse side of Craig-Y-Gamell. If it was true, as assumed and evident, that Llew and Caw would empty the mountain into Camlan below, a divided section could earn the top of the western slope (opposite of Lancelot) and reverse positions, clipping the Ravens terminally from above.

Moreover, Hoel argued that by gaining some ascent, the troop commanders could negotiate the fog, all the more increasing the advantage.

There was reason in Hoel's presentation. But it also presented risk. Morgaine's mists made an apprised census impossible. If some of the allied armies of Mark, Llew, Drest, Caw and any remaining Saxons had shifted off the mount, they could gain advantage and ambush over Arthur.

The king found himself intrigued by the idea, and sought counsel from his Round Table Fellows, who were ironically, and equally, *divided over the division.*

Bedwyr ensured that he could not be found, lest he be engaged in a conference where he would be made to sit at a bench or table with the others. For the flow of red from his navel was constant. He borrowed a torch and, under the firelight, examined the severity of the wound.

A man should not see his own innards, yet Bedwyr did. Iron was scarce, so he withdrew the seax, or Saxon longknife, from the skull of a dead Briton, heated the blade until it was nearly molten, and then seared the wound. Bedwyr thanked the Lord for the thick fog, as it allowed discretion and preserved dignity, for he could wail and screech alone.

The proposal finding equal parts favor and opposition, Arthur was empowered and encouraged to decide.

Merlin would know what to do. But Merlin is not here.

"I will go to yonder chapel, and think, and pray. And restfully consider the matter. Let us convene ere the cock crows, friends." Arthur motioned for Cai, who bled from the forearm beneath his armor.

***

The chapel of Saint Tydecho, though located in Gwynedd, had friendly ties to both Arthur and Hoel. Tydecho was the son of Amwn Ddu, the Black Knight, and his mother was Anna of Gwent, daughter of Meurig. Thus Tydecho was nephew to Arthur and Hoel. His little church had been founded during the Golden Age, a few years after the Baedan, when liberty had reigned and a new church or school had been founded seemingly every week. Tydecho lived in the church, along with his fair sister Tegfedd, and both adored Arthur, though they worshipped God after the Roman Way.

The church was empty, for surely the siblings had taken refuge in the village of Mallwyd. It featured two bedchambers, a dedicated dining and study area for the brethren, a worship hall and baptistery. There was a soft, feminine décor and feel to the dwelling, and the Iron Bear felt soothed and calm as he pondered, prayed, and slept.

***

Sunrise
June 23
AD 537

Morgaine pleaded to Ogyrfan through her looking-glass. She brought her fists slamming down into the waters, hoping to reach through space, or bend time, with the might in her own tiny hands. Her mists had vanished and then reappeared around all whom she loved save Ogyrfan. He was exposed, and the hordes of Mark mixed with the Raiders of Eire, lured, angry and desperate, had spilled themselves into the field at the moment the fog had abated. *Or temporarily abated.*

"Run!" she screamed, the whole of the Castle on Ynys Enlli shaking to its foundation, its glass rafters protesting, sending dusty glass down onto the black marble floors. "Run!"

But Ogyrfan fell. Another red-silked Silure given to the soil of Cymru, who cried against the unwanted nourishment.

Lightning rained down, though the skies were clear and the morning light comely.

Seeing the field flooded with men, and gaining a brief, clear view that the Silures had gained equal ground on numerous patches of the mount above, Arthur directed Hoel to activate his plan. Instantly, and in unison, ten thousand red-silks turned their horses northwest, parading slowly to allow for spacing and proportion, and then *neigh, whinny, gallop, crackle* – and gone.

King Arthur's army was divided.

Hoel led the third that had departed, with many fabled knights joining him, Cadog, Cador, and Gwynlliw included. All were excited.

But in their excitement, an oversight.

Derfel!

The spear-wielding demigod of Brittany.

The new Lancelot.

Was he not his father's son?

'Twas he who loosed the men, giving appearance of full commitment to fighting upon the open field. And the moment the fog relented, he did dispatch ten thousand Picts to the obverse side of the mountain, where they would be waiting for Hoel, and have the double advantage of high ground and surprise over him.

Derfel would not see his brothers slain if he could prevent it, and the thought of his father's passing he put from his mind. But loyalty demanded sacrifice, and his loyalty had he sworn to Cadfan, who might also lead him to the Grail.

Seeing Arthur from afar the prior morn had filled the lad with awe, and his judgment haunted him. Therefore, Derfel deployed a tactic taught as part of those he had learned among Vivien's Martial Arts. Derfel would fight with a spear, which was longer than most and could not be used save for atop steed, allowing him to keep his distance. He would poke the upper thigh of his opponent's horse, then puncture the ankle of the rider.

Poke, puncture, on to the next. Poke, puncture, on to the next.

The new Lancelot loved animals and it vexed

him to harm them, but the two-step maneuver would create injured men instead of ghosts.

The mists returned, thicker, more blinding and debilitating than before.

What Derfel meant for kindness, his mates used for easy kills, finding wounded knights, making sport in torturing them. None of the one hundred and twenty-two men wounded by Derfel survived.

And here began the *longest day of the Civil War*. The warriors from both sides fought what felt like individual battles on account of the mist. One round of combat would conclude; they would peer through the billows and find another.

And the armor began to fail.

For the first two days the Silure had been dominant, and untested. Now blows of axe and sword were making minor wounds fatal or causing hastily-made buckles to give. There was more adjusting than fighting by legions of the red-silks, and the Ravens were at last earning casualties, in large numbers, of their own.

Meanwhile, none of those who had divided off from Arthur's ranks were ever heard from again.

The Picts, vicious and skilled, rained ten thousand thousand stones upon the noble knights, which were as wasps stinging them in a haze, and by volume, killing them. The slingshot - an ancient weapon as old as man - when mastered can penetrate thick armor and crush the thickest of bones and skulls. The flat stones of the slingshots incapacitated, and Pictish clubs and spikes completed the rout, the Silures suffering the greatest loss of life in a single military exercise in their kingdom's history.

Morgaine saw this as well and became white as a phantom. God or the gods had exposed

Ogyrfan purposefully, mocking her intervention. The remainder of her loved ones now fought in a blind haze, receiving no benefit of her ethereal sendings. Resigned to the fact that she could not arbitrate the wars of men, she began to do all to remove the mist, and let the free will of the Sons of Adam have its course.

CAMLAN ACT V

CHAPTER 22
Elvish Armor and War Dogs

Taliesin was conducted to the Good Court, where he was made to dance, revel, and oblige gifts to the Tylwyth Teg. This he happily did, and patiently. Every sinew of his being begged him to cry unto them to hasten and finish, but he could not. For the Fae are peculiar beings, and time for them is not as time is for the Sons of Adam. The Chief Bard continued to think on this, and not upon his kinsmen, whose battles were by now surely far advanced.

***

The Battle of Camlan was indeed far advanced.

Neither the North nor the South had established clear advantage. The first two days had been Arthur's, and this final day had thus belonged to Mordred the Traitor. He personally enjoyed kills, each of which were prepared and cleaned as freshly-caught fish by Eda.

Presently, Eda sought out Cai, that he might kill the Pendragon's lifelong companion, foster-brother, and steward.

And where Cai strove, there strove Arthur.

Lancelot the Statue peered through the fog, and was able to follow Mordred somewhat, on account of his golden skin and gold-clad horse. Even a mystical fog could not his arrogance hide.

It was at seeing Mordred's Champion draw near the king that Lancelot finally moved. At just the moment when his right hand, lifted high, was to make signal to his Hosts, the Merlin stood before him.

Lancelot paused, and dismounted.

***

"Name for me, Sir, the seven virtues of the Fae," the Elf King demanded, handing Taliesin a harp with one hand, a roasted turkey leg twice *the possible size* with the other.

Knowing that when the Fae offer, one should *take*, and do so with gratitude, Taliesin took, ate, and strummed. Seeing this pleased the Puck, Taliesin made an effort at friendly jest. "I have not eaten so well since December! May I please finish, and think upon thy riddle?"

The Prince of Pixies adored Taliesin, for he was powerful yet humble, mighty yet debased, foolish yet wise, and above all, a faithful keeper of the Mysteries. "Eat, Merlin II, eat!"

Taliesin searched his mind, filled with thirty years of bardic training. He could 'see' letters in his mind, and whole parchments could he recollect – with focus.

"Let me assist you, Taliesin; your mind seemeth too busy." If red eyes with no pupils could have a kind disposition, these did. "Are you contented with your meat?"

"Forgive me, Good King, I cannot eat another bite, but would not offend and will eat to the bursting; for it is scrumptious, and quite the delight."

"The answer of the knowledge I require of thee is already given in your responses. Ease thy mind." Other tall Faeries that had female forms took the scraps from Taliesin, tittered, and wiped his brow playfully. "With each virtue, strike one chord upon the harp. As you do this, I will draw one point of the Faerie Star, and we shall bring forth the knowledge and the wisdom already in you."

"Hospitality." *Strum.*

"Generosity." *Strum.*

"Yes, good! Go on!"

"Kindness." *Strum.*

"In our own impish way," he chortled.

"Compassion." *Strum.* "Courage!" Taliesin could see the lessons of his youth now, and finished with conviction. "Politeness and Adventuresomeness!" Not only did Taliesin pair each with a chord as directed, but he then played a lovely melody and stood in victory, having forgotten the power and truth paired in these rays, which were the seven rays of Faerie virtue, and the Law of the Good Court of the Fae.

"Yes!" cried the king, clapping and pleased. "Now harken, Merlin II, and note that I also am Lord of the Bad Court, which is the contrary pole of each of these." The septogram he had drawn comprised blinking white and gold dust on the one side; when he rotated it about, 'twas hot orange fire on the other. The lesson concluded, it diminished, falling to dust upon the ground.

"I understand." The Christian bard nodded.

Then the Faerie did something of stunning astonishment: he entered into a normal conversation with Taliesin.

"What would you have of us?" he opened.

"I understand, more than my fellows, why you cannot intervene in the all-out wars of men. That your kind will be loosed in the End of Days and battle against men is the subject of Prophecy, and easy to find in Scripture. Likewise, that you are forbidden from doing the same in this Grace dispensation is clearly detailed as well, knowing that we wrestle in the spiritual, and not the physical realm, during this time." Taliesin paused. "Easy to apprehend, impossible to comprehend." Not wanting to try the patience of his host, or the dozens of diverse creatures now gathered in what Taliesin felt was still the ring of stones (but of a certainty, he knew not), he made his questions direct. "Are there exceptions? And what happens if you try to intervene? For surely Morgaine has--"

"The exceptions are in accord with the will of the God of gods alone, in whom we believe, before whom we tremble, but whom most of us know not." First question answered. "An elect angel from above the firmament will come, and do battle with we Powers and Thrones, and could flick an unclean spirit like me into the Deep with no more effort than you would flick a fruit-fly from your breakfast." Question two answered. "Or the Most High Creator will, alternatively, intervene in some other unknown way, that His will be not usurped." Question two expounded. "Morgaine is more powerful than the whole of the Good Court and the Bad Court combined. She made as far as to change the weather for the final conflict, but could go no further."

"So she *did* intervene?" Taliesin asked.

"Somewhat, but methinks awry."

"Would God allow something, for the cause of

balance, in answer to her intervention? Nothing by way of spells that stung or dashed or harmed men, but rather" – Taliesin looked for the words – "protected him to make the fight fair?"

"He is your God and your Savior, Merlin II; why ask me these things and not Him?"

"Because I am no match for an angel if the answer is 'no'." The druid smiled, and gave a longing, desperate plea with his eyes.

"Oh, little bard, knowest thou not that God hath chosen the weak things of the world to confound the mighty? One day you will judge angels, and the disaster they created down here in God's garden of Men. I am one of those disasters. One day, you will judge me. Pray you remember this gift. Now go."

Taliesin knew better than to second-guess, or ask for further explanation. Before his boot touched the border of circle, the Lord of the Elves said unto him: "Know this; one of our own did beguile your Lancelot when he was sixteen. She vexed him, planting each of the seven virtues into the lad with dark, naughty magic, that each would be extreme – a person within a person, if you will."

"Lancelot is seven?" Taliesin reacted.

"Thou forgets so soon your lesson, after getting fat on my best bird!" The king was disappointed. But Taliesin rallied quickly.

"Polarity! Lancelot is FOURTEEN in one shell."

"Excellent, Merlin II! And she crossed them up and shook them as a jar of rocks and marbles, as a plaything for children."

"May Merlin the First balance and reconnect him, else we are all lost."

The Merlin Taliesin traversed the edge of the

stones and was back near the Chapel of Saint Mary in Ynys Mon, unsure of how much time had passed. Unsure, but thankful that the Tylwyth Teg would make effort to do *something* to counter Morgaine's meddling.

***

"What will you say at this last hour?" Lancelot at last broke his cold silence. The Wizard and the Greatest Warrior to Ever Live, again nostril to nostril, that spittle and spray was exchanged. These Titans had no fear one for the other.

"Nay." Merlin was brief.

"Will you cause me to relive the seven offenses, or the three blows that brought us to this precipice of hell on earth and devastation?"

"No."

"Or tell me how that I am mad?!" Lancelot took two giant steps backwards and roared, as a lion, "I saw your boy-king's eyes when Mordred was caught in the unspeakable act. I attempted to calm him - I saw madness, and for six months after I witnessed it increase. The Madness of Maelgwn is but a small thing to the lunacy of the Bear of Glamorgan! To slaughter his grandchildren and then goad that demon below to war—"

"He goaded him not, Lancelot," Merlin began. "'Twas I who recommended the use of shock, but to save lives, not to cause the end of more lives. The messenger Iddawg did change the message, activate the Just One in you, and cause Mordred to retaliate. The whole war is built upon—"

Lancelot found the intrigue interesting, but not overly. "The whole of the war is built upon 'I saw her first'." The two steps of retreat were retracted, the two rams' horns locked yet again.

"Would we have these discussions anew, with dealings to conduct below?"

"No." Again Merlin had no desire to look to the past; rather to the future, and the present. "Do you really want to be High King, Maelgwn? It is one thing to want Arthur *not* to rule, but would you do it in his stead? If he falls, the Picts, the Saxons, and whomever else Simon has waiting in line to invade, will be full of confidence knowing he is gone. This is not about the man Arthur; this is about the legend of King Arthur. YOU are King Arthur. I am King Arthur. Camelot must live, or we will all fall." Merlin now begged Lancelot. "Do not engage in this Civil War, or there can be no reconciliation."

"There can be no reconciliation." Cold words, bereft of emotion. "Look now below, Merlin Emerys, and see the end of King Arthur."

A flat, rocky surface jutted out from the slope, a natural platform on the incline of the slope. Arthur found himself there, unhorsed and surrounded, with Eda and ten men in pursuit. Ten versus three. And one of the three's insides were burst, held in place by the nub of Bedwyr. The scene was but five hundred feet below the ridge where stood Lancelot and Merlin.

"*Where are your war dogs?* Or do you use them only to hunt women and effeminate men, like your son?!"

Arthur's exhalations and pants were so heavy underneath his helmet that he did not hear the fullness of Lancelot's invectives. But he gathered their meaning when he saw what was loosed upon him, sprinting down the hill.

The Dormarch.

Arthur had seen four-armed Giants, questing beasts that were an abominable, unnatural mixing of various animals, flying things, witches and ghouls. Yet the reasonable part of him had still thought the Dormarch, or hounds of hell, only a fable to scare disobedient children into cleaning the crockeries or attending to their studies. Yet five descended upon him.

The alpha of the pack was most swift and leapt into the air, meaning to quickly smother and torture the Pendragon, but to leave him limbless and shamed with heart still beating, that Lancelot might tear it from his chest and show it to the king as he passed into the underworld.

Arthur quickly plunged Excalibur into the rock and took up Rhon, hoping to pierce the dog like unto the hooking of a great fish. Arthur's thrust went amiss, and the demon dog was atop him. Its jaws clinched on the king's armor.

But the armor was no longer armor fashioned by the hands of men…

Vivien had tried to replicate the metal skin of the Elves, but had never dared ask for *Elvish Armor.*

In the twinkling of an eye, EVERY RED-SILK that lived was adorned in the magical armor of the Elves. Nine blows required for every one blow that would breach the chainmail of man. So light that the warrior felt as though he were sparring or at play in the kitchen with his brothers. The pieces form-fitting to the shin, to the thigh, about the loins, and upon the chest and back, the arms in three pieces and the helms a shinier, stronger version of the Corinthian fashion. Moreover, the armor glowed and caused the fog to retreat wherever its wearer stood.

The dog's gnashings were of no effect and Bedwyr, who had freed Excalibur from the stone with his good hand, did stab the beast; the

Sword of Power caused it to vanish back to the underworld, leaving great pools of black bile in its stead.

Meanwhile, another factor was ebbing the tide of battle against the Round Table Knights.

Picts.

Having slaughtered Hoel and his retinue, they now poured down the mountain as locusts. Arthur, Bedwyr and Cai knew what their presence meant, and sorrowed as they readied to face them.

Derfel understood the same, not far off. Seeing the enchanted armor and the ongoing bravery of the middle-aged king continued to give the young hero pause.

Then pause turned to full repentance, for by chance Derfel caught a glimpse of Cadfan, bleeding out in an embankment.

"Cadfan!" Derfel galloped and leapt from his horse, tumbling twice in his desperation, losing his breath as he pounded upon the dirt. The Picts had pushed the whole of the conflict, save those scattered few below Lancelot's ridge, onto the open pitch of Camlan.

Recovering himself, Derfel attended to his kinsman, mentor and friend. "Red silk, Cadfan? A cunning disguise, brother?"

"My allegiance to the Council of Nine was my disguise, as was my dead Religion. I died today without my mask upon my brow, for my true self is loyal to freedom, and to—"

"Arthur of Caerleon."

Derfel held Cadfan, whose visage shone as the sun as he passed into the sleep of death, having perfect contentment about his countenance.

Derfel slowly and respectfully removed the red vest and fastened it upon his own black-lacquered, leather chest piece. The new Lancelot fought as had oft the former, with but a chest piece and leather gauntlets. A helmet slowed him down and impaired vision, and he was too quick of movement to be struck in the head besides. Knowing the battle was in balance, Derfel whispered, "I know you cherish this silk, and I promise to return it," and joined the fight – against the Picts.

***

Eda and Cai at last entered into single combat. Ten or more men were near, and all honored the clash. Bedwyr chased after Mordred, whilst Arthur toiled with the dogs.

After successive strikes, mirrored and blocked, Eda tackled Cai, shifting the duel to a grappling affair. Cai did well to lock one of Eda's wrists, breaking three small bones beneath the thumb. The rush of battle allowed Eda to ignore the wrist, which instantly swelled to thrice its size. Fortunately for Mordred's steward, it was his supporting hand; his strong hand still functioned well, and found a dagger stashed in his boot, which he plunged into Cai's side above twelve times.

Cai fought on, undeterred, and turned the match back into a standing contest. Cai regained advantage… until Eda the Coward kicked the Round Table Legend hard in the groin, underneath the frontal plate of his armor.

A man whose entire life, each and every day, from morning to night, had been lived with honor, was now incapacitated on account of dishonor. None can recover when kicked *there,* and there is no training to manage the pain thereof. Cai rolled upon the ground, paralyzed in pain, in vomit, in his own blood. His eyes found Arthur, and his final emotion was great disappointment in failing to be at his lord's side, vanquishing dogs and watching over the sandy-haired king. *I have failed to keep my vow, Meurig, forgive me--*

Eda raised the head of Cai high, vaingloriously boasting of his trophy.

***

"Which one of you steers the vessel, Lancelot? Who is in charge?" Merlin pressed. "You do not want to be High King. Your true love is lost, and yours she never was. You want to farm, and bed maidens, and study and live a quiet life. Do you not?"

Lancelot noted in his mind that Merlin was not wrong. He loathed politics and everything accompanied by a life devoted to it.

"Who is in charge?" Merlin reached for old magick, and sought to realign the circuits of the tormented man.

"Hospitality or unsociability?" And an ancient arrangement of words.

"Generosity or greed?

"Kindness or cruelty?" The spell continued.

"Compassion or a heart of stone?

"Courage or cowardice?" Merlin sought to tear the shards of Lancelot asunder, and reassemble him.

"Politeness or debasement?

"Adventuresomeness or recluse?" Seven multi-colored knights came forth from Lancelot, who did seize and convulse upon his steed. "Not you fellows" - Merlin charged, this time lightning and wonders discharging from his staff - "you!"

Seven more knights, void of color as shadowy

ghosts, emerged. Merlin then called upon the name of the Fallen One who had done this to Lancelot, knowing that there was more work to be done.

"Dragon, Giant, Water Spirit and Man; these are all part of you, and I cannot separate them from you, old friend. The foul things I have removed, but the former are part of your being. But henceforth, methinks you will be better." Merlin did curse the witch, an entity older than the Morrigan, that had bewitched Lancelot once more, but did not tarry about that, for the time was short. Instead, he brought Maelgwn back, fully back, to awareness, to consciousness.

The Bloodhound Prince mounted his horse, quickly.

Merlin asked but one question more of he who was yet the most powerful warrior in the land. "When it comes time to do that which you ought to do, what will you do?"

***

Arthur was taking wounds on his arms and calves, the mystical Elvish coverings saving his life - *but for how long?*

Eda continued to parade about with the head of Cai, singing aloud, "Camelot is fallen; fallen is Cam—"

A spear whistled through the air, flung from five hundred feet above. Flung by Arthur's Champion, Lancelot.

It pierced Eda between the shoulder and the heart, but was not fatal. He scurried from the scene, which was not difficult, given the erratic fog.

The surviving knights of old cried out. "Lancelot, Lancelot is with us! Fight, fight on!"

The Hosts of Maelgwn and Derfel were brilliant, noble, good, and restored.

But too late.

Lancelot personally slew King Drest, and Llew, and Arthur finished Caw, but the death count was so high that few souls remained as dusk fell; and many had fled hours earlier. Amongst these were Hueil ap Caw, and many of his brothers.

Gareth and Gaheris too were amongst the dead.

As was Gwynllyw ap Glywys, as was Cadog, as was Cador.

Arthur and Lancelot wanted to share words, but the loss of life was such that they could not speak.

The fog did diminish, beginning to recoil unto its source, which was Avalon.

And Arthur and Lancelot looked for Mordred the Whelp upon the field of Camlan.

CAMLAN ACT VI

CHAPTER 23
The Fog is Lifting
The Passing of Arthur

Some daylight remained. The sun was bright red, attempting to cut through the haze, as if helping the scant few surviving Round Table Fellows find the Traitor and finish their final stand together. The dead or dying numbered in the thousands, and the air was filled with final gasps, prayers uttered by desperate tongues.

Arthur began to panic, fearing that Mordred had fled the field and found a way, perhaps in league with the Council of Nine, to make the day for naught, bringing future devastation upon Cymru.

Morgaine of the Faeries was already upon the sea, cutting through the rough waters in a black barge, its bow fashioned as a swan. The Nine Maidens accompanied her, along with Accolon, and the boatman made twelve. The slight Faerie stood upon a platform that ran the width of the stern. Her spirit cried out to Arthur.

You are desperate, brother. But all is not lost.

"Gwyar?" Arthur ran this way and that. "Lancelot, did you hear her?"

"Nay, lord, I hear only death, and the consummation of our sins."

I was wrong, Arthur. Forgive me.

"Gwyar!" Still he could not locate the source of the voice.

The Swan Barge did not sail to Aberdaron, but rather cut directly east, making her way through the southernmost depths of the Ceredigion Bay. She would come ashore near Dolgellau, and then on to Camlan to fully restore her brother. *But I will help him ere I arrive.*

Forgive me, Arthur. Here at the end, we ALL align with you, for you are the Summer Kingdom, and the Summer Kingdom is you. Mordred shall not make the spires of Camelot to fall.

"MORGANA!!!!!" he cried, his voice hoarse, and his friends feared he was fevered, or mad.

***

Mordred hid beneath the corpses of three Ravens, fashioning a tent from their cloaks.

The mists themselves sang, a low, repetitious, brooding chant, then gave the sound of cymbals and shattered glass. Excalibur, still borne by Bedwyr, shone in response to the song, humming and vibrating, an effervescence of greens and blues. It caused the knight to point in the direction of the Whelp. The mist then fully retreated as Morgaine undid her spell and more, giving Arthur their son.

"The fog is lifting, Father." Mordred had no recourse, no way out. Drawing on the arrogance given him by the Black Pope, he slowly placed his golden helmet on, and the Divine Child approached the Pendragon.

"My lord, thy sword." Bedwyr offered Arthur his steel.

But Arthur declined. "He is not worthy to fall by Excalibur."

Arthur clasped Rhon, his fabled spear, and did the unexpected. *He attacked first.* The counter-fighter did not wait, nor plot, nor evade; rather, he attacked.

Mordred, surprised at this, fully expecting to test Arthur with the first two to three blows, was caught. And run through.

Rhon pushed through the golden armor and impaled Mordred, who gurgled, choking on an erupting fountain of his own blood. Knowing death was nigh, Mordred drew himself up on the spear, pulling it through him, drawing within striking rnge of the king.

This in turn surprised Arthur, who should have loosed the spear, stepped out of range, and then finished his son with dagger or, if needs be, by hand. Instead he froze and looked into *his own eyes*. Eyes that drew near, and nearer still.

Mordred swung his battle spike at the helmet of his father. It was a long weapon, and the flight time gave Arthur a half-second to recover from his startled state and avoid the strike.

Most of the strike.

The curvy-bladed hilt, fashioned to mimic Lancelot's, found Arthur's head, the force of the blow cracking the Elvish metal. The hinderside of Rhon impaled the ground behind Arthur, who would have fallen, but instead gave all of his weight to the mystical weapon. The leverage lifted Mordred from the ground, who dangled on the shaft like a freshly-speared fish, twitching, and then… lifeless.

Bedwyr ran to Arthur's side and caught him ere he fell with the full force of his weight to the ground. In the act of catching the Iron Bear, Bedwyr tore at the seam, but Derfel caught the man who caught the king.

Lancelot tended Arthur, signaling for cart and horse. Merlin was there as well.

On the field of Camlan Mordred and Arthur had fought, and Mordred had fallen.

A few moments later, the king's steely glove pulled first Lancelot, then Merlin close. The embattled lord whispered. Moments later, Britain's tallest Britons laughed in unison.

The other survivors demanded to know the meaning of such cruel blasphemy, but Merlin eased them. "Cider, lads. The old king wants cider."

"Conduct me to the chapel of my nephew," Arthur ordered, "that I might rest."

Arthur's head wound was not lethal, and the company rejoiced.

Night had fallen and Morgaine had to travel, by barge and by hired horse, eight hours more.

Bishop Tydecho returned from Mallwyd with Tegfedd. She was secretly a healer, hiding in plain sight of the Church. Arthur's niece could not heal Bedwyr, but she gave him a strong potion, that he might sleep free of pain. The company reckoned that the dearest of all Round Table Knights would pass, from blood loss or infection, in one to two days.

***

The night's rest did Arthur good, but his head wound brought nausea and early the following morning, being a discreet and private person, he walked outside, finding a place to vomit in the shade of a tree. The vomiting depleted and weakened Arthur above measure, and a hemorrhage occurred behind his eye, causing it to fill with blood and lose sight.

Derfel and Tegfedd (whose eyes had not unlocked from the moment of introduction the night before), being youthful, were first to find the king. Lancelot and Merlin slept.

"Niece and new friend" – Arthur struggled to speak – "sorrow not; I thirst."

Knowing the stream was near, Derfel bolted as a stag, leaping over brush and log, hurrying to fetch his lord water. The maiden Tegfedd was left alone with the legend, the Savior of the Cymru.

Ever looking to serve others, he attempted to ease *her* distress with light words, but she lovingly pre-empted him, wanting nothing of comedy during the tragic hour. "You shall have no cider, my lord. Only water, and herbs, and rest."

Tegfedd looked to the tree's branches, then to the sky to see what the weather might this day do; when she looked down, two thirds of a spear was in Arthur's left hand, the remainder buried deep into his loins.

Eda the Coward had thrown the spear from close range. He struck Tegfedd hard upon the jaw, that she might not spoil his stealth by screaming.

"Look how now the son hath become his father; for TWO lame kings now rule from Gwent!" Eda, himself laboring to outlast grave injuries, disappeared ere he, being unarmed, was slain.

"Merlin, Lancelot, Hosts of Gwynedd, Kernunnos, Bran, or Mabon, help me! Help me!" Derfel cried.

"Poison," the Merlin proclaimed. "A poisoned shaft hath found the loins of our king!"

Conversations with Meurig from forty and one years ago tried to invade the druid's mind, but he blocked them. The Tribes would never again accept King Arthur as Pendragon, but saving his life - not traditions or politics - was now paramount.

The cough, just a nuisance afore, now raged, and Arthur's each breath was contested. Every wound and hurt from a hundred wars worked in concert to remind the Titan of his mortality. He grabbed at his hand, clutching the scratch that Gwenhwyfar had but recently mended. Eyes rolled, and then returned only as pale slits beneath swollen flaps of burdened skin.

The hope of Britain lay nigh unto death…

CAMLAN ACT VII

CHAPTER 24
The Battle After the Battle is the Real Battle

Eda's poison was meant to render Arthur impotent, causing him to lose his office, and live out his days in shame - not to kill him. However, the head wound was causing swelling and pressure in the brainpan; in combination with the toxins, it was too much trauma for Arthur's chest and vital organs, and he began to die.

Merlin departed, hoping to find Morgaine along her way, and hasten her arrival.

Things always happen when Merlin is away.

This time, during the wizard's short absence, Arthur ordered Bedwyr take Excalibur and offer her to a still pool of water, that Arthur not die holding a false office.

Bedwyr could not receive these words - that any should reign save Arthur - but he obeyed, promising to return swiftly.

***

Dainty fingers shook the Bear's face, which had turned both ashen, and yet green.

"Brother, wake. A cart awaits, and my barge.

Come now to Avalon, where I will heal you of your grievous wounds." Morgaine softly kissed his forehead; *Sister, Lover, now Mother to whom she loved, of whom she was given charge.* She gathered his boots, found his belt, shook the dried mud from his cloak. Rhon was recovered, having rolled under Tydecho's bed.

"Brother." Morgaine was exasperated, and she could feel Merlin's impatience following her. "Where is your sword?!"

***

Morgaine the Healer was in full command, and all obeyed with ready minds her decrees.

"I am not going with you, Merlin."

The wizard was agape, bewildered at the change of course.

"Bear Arthur to Aberdaron; there let him rest for an evening in the chapel near the shore. Tomorrow morning, I will meet you on at Porth Maddwy. If I tarry, my Maidens will ferry you to Avalon's shores." She was resolute. *Maiden, Mother, Lover, Goddess.* "But I will not tarry."

She then turned to Lancelot. No words were exchanged - only an embrace and instructions that he hasten unto the Old North, there to reconcile with Urien and Owain. He obeyed the Lady, asking only that he might first run to Rhun, and hold him tight once more.

"Embrace him for me as well" - she smiled - "but do so as you travel, for our world is in chaos and lies of every sort will spread. I will save the king; you save the truth about the king." Here were Morgaine and Lancelot made whole.

"And WHERE do you go?" demanded the Merlin, overwhelmed by the swiftness with which events unfolded around him – showing signs at last of great age.

"To stop Bedwyr," she answered plainly. "The king will not be without his sword, and the land not without its king!"

***

"This dreadful end is not yet." Bedwyr. "Cannot, must not, do not cast it away!"

Vivien's outstretched hand withdrew, vanishing in the like manner to which it had appeared – instant and silent – back beneath the still of the Llyn Fawr.

"I failed you, fully and completely, my friend, my best friend," Bedwyr bewailed.

"Nay!" Morgaine called, now within thirty feet of the fading knight. "I AM the Lady of the Lake now! Cast Excalibur unto me, for Vivien and I are one."

Bedwyr could see the reason in this, and trusted that Morgaine would not entreat him falsely. The fabled sword shone in his hand, giving its own low, melancholy sound, bidding him, *Cast me away*. He whispered prayers to the sword, bidding farewell to the weapon in the stead of the king. And so Excalibur was cast, flipping twice, twirling thrice in the air, now stopping of its own accord, hovering in glory above the sacred lake.

The First Knight saw Excalibur float, contrary to nature, into Morgaine's own hands: choosing her, validating her, and releasing him, having completed his last quest.

"This is not your last quest," the Lady protested. "Look around you, Bedwyr; smudge and ash, blight and barren, and yet…" A pixie,

no greater than a butterfly in size, placed a dead flower upon Bedwyr's hand, which Morgaine had carefully opened, and stretched. "See how we do recover, for these are the Blessed Isles." Through her enchantment, the wilted petals were restored, and blossomed. "We need you to be our dry flower come to life again." She kissed his hand, closing it gently about the flower, and left him to the care of the Fair Folk, who promised to restore him, that the king would have his best friend upon his return.

Morgaine then gazed up to Craig-Y-Llyn, the shadowy asylum for Llyn Fawr and her sister lake, Llyn Fach. The holy mount was also a mammoth capstone for an antediluvian metropolis whose tunnels and conduits allowed those with knowledge of the Mysteries rapid passage unto sites both sacred and strategic.

And Avalon was both, being the most sacred and most strategic place in the whole of Britain.

The Sorceress made haste, arriving upon the shores of Aberdaron *before* Derfel, Tydecho, Tygfedd, the Merlin, Arthur, and their hosts from the Isle of Apples.

The king had had disruptive, intermittent sleep the prior night. His breathing patterns were irregular, his lungs filled with fluid. Morgaine and Accolon positioned him gently on the barge, situating his head upon her lap.

He spoke in broken, soft words, coughing. "Pray for my soul."

The contrary and ruthless currents about Ynys Enlli mourned and were still, the seas about the Blessed Isles themselves sorrowing over so great a loss.

Merlin noted Excalibur and did ask the Lady, "What moved you to risk losing our friend, that he might have *that* near at the end?"

"Excalibur and Arthur are One. And the Cup and I are One. And our union is One."

Her cryptic words befuddled the wizard, for he could make no interpretation of them.

But he will. And soon…

After reaching the shores of Avalon, Morgaine summonsed another mist – this one for protection against any survivors of the North that might have followed them. Accolon and Derfel bore the king into the Glass Castle, following careful instruction on where to lay their lord. Merlin stayed at the gates of the enchanted palace. His cap removed, he scratched his head, cocking his heard to the north, working Morgaine's puzzle.

The Sorceress attended them to the castle doors, bidding them exit and await her address, which she gave from a high tower, saying, "I and I alone can do what must next be done. You beloveds can proceed no further!"

She motioned with her hand, stopping Merlin, who had unraveled her hard words and began, too late, to desperately protest. "You left me to do this alone the first time; knowest thou not that what happened in the cave was but a rehearsal? We live life in reverse order, all, for yesterday ever is a cast shadow for what we must do today. Is not the entire Old Covenant in your Sacred Book filled with types and shadows of what Christ would later do?" She lowered her hand, looking into the druid's soul. "You are vindicated – you AND the Lady Vivien, lord Merlin. You put me through the Rite IN TIMES PAST that I might be prepared for the Rite TODAY. The trauma of that perversion did not ruin my life; it readied me to save his life."

A shadow fell upon the whole of the Isle, and

it was as midnight, though it were but newly morning-time.

"I am Gwyar ferch Onbrawst. I am Morgaine ferch Vivien. I am Morgana, daughter of the damned. Forbidden love captured my heart before the Flood, and by Lancelot did hopelessness yet again avenge my heart. I lost my children, again and again. But I will NOT lose my brother, my lover, my king!"

"She would perform the Sacred Rite! She is not laboring to save the king, but rather to resurrect him!" Merlin desperately tried every entrance, which were sealing and closing through sorcery before him. Though much of the Fortress itself was made of green glass, it was bewitched and impenetrable. *And her magick was greater than the Merlin's.*

When hope seemed lost, a bird appeared. *A merlin.* It appeared as if cast from the very high tower whence the witch had spoken; or, equally, as a gift fallen from heaven. Making a spiraling descent, the merlin landed on the Merlin. It plucked at his beard, then played with his ears, which were equally hairy, at last putting its pokey foot in Merlin's eye.

"What's this?" He swatted the bird away, dislodging a piece of parchment that had been tied to its twig-like leg. Scribbled in haste was but one word, a name, in the Cymreig alphabet: "Magus."

The coned hat refitted and snug, he clutched at his heart. Feigning defeat, he, the Nine Maidens, Accolon, and Derfel retreated deep into the forest, and further still, to the Sacred Grove. Still fearing demonic ears, the druid huddled the twelve beneath a sprawling apple tree – the kind of tree that had absorbed secrets for thousands of years; a mystery for each branch.

"An evil abides in the castle made of glass. The evil that has ignited the Fall of Britain, and before us, other gilded, advanced civilizations as well. She has a plan, a strategy. We can do naught but trust Morgaine."

***

"He will die unless you perform the Rite."

"He will die even IF I perform the Rite. You would have me open a gate into the Underworld and place Judas Iscariot, or some other vile spirit, into my brother."

"I would." Magus, like Morgaine, knew the king was expiring, and durst not delay with matches of wit. "What you must do to him… happened to you. You are still yourself, but you share yourself with another, and the twain in you are now one. This is what the angels from the world that was did, and taught to man on the other side of the Flood; the Sacred Rite!" Satan's Chief Minister relished in the abominable mocking of God that was, and was to be again. "It will be the same for Arthur. The Son of Meurig he will remain. If his will as host is stronger than the *other*, I will not be able to—"

"Activate him, as you did the Giants and monsters."

"Yes, my child." Magus clapped. "You truly are the more fascinating of the famed Walles siblings. Given that your brother is the Anti-Christ, that says much, yes?" His Italian, overly-accented, ghastly cackle followed.

Morgaine rapidly sought strategies, diversions, solutions… but time waged war on her. Frenzied, she determined what must be done.

"Seven candlesticks and four of my maidens, summon." If the Black Pope would have his Beast brought from the pit, he would take a subordinate role and assist the Witch in the performance of it.

"Mandrake, Vervain, Mercury, and Wolf's Bane," she next ordered.

"Do it, do it!" He chided the Damsel with his grotesque words, seeing her priestesses arrange the necessities of the craft, and smudge the air with pungent and curious smoke.

Arthur lay in Morgaine's own bed, around which Morgaine cast the circle, and lit the seven candles. She disrobed, then bravely confronted the Masked Man, fully nude. "I assume you have the marking sticks, and *our masks.*"

"This is the consummation of my life's work! Of course I do." More Italian snarls.

Four of the Nine Maidens were positioned at each corner of the bed: a large and comely iron frame, beautifully furnished with skins and throws and pillows of every sort (*Morgaine was a dark mistress, but a lass who loved pretty décor just the same)* representing the angelic Guardians of the Four Winds. They also did mark Morgaine as the Primal Witch, adorning her as that ancient goddess who had taken lovers from the sons of Adam and, worse, her own household, creating abominations that were more part god than man. Her mask represented the Moon, the fertile earth, the feminine Light that ruled the cosmic night.

Arthur they rendered as the Stag. The Solar light, the Hunter. That old Mighty One who would lie with wicked women and beget monsters. This Rite was not about welcoming the change of the season, or celebrating the gods of harvest, wheat, creek and stone. All these were benign practices of a people that knew not the Creator God, but were thankful for their grain, the sunshine, and the health and happiness wrought by a plentiful harvest.

No; the Sacred Rite was a Mystery to the uninitiated. It was a rehearsal, or a remembrance, of those vile angels who had polluted humanity and creature-kind, established their Religion, and provoked the Creator to clean the slate, and start over with a Flood.

And the Horned One was the chief sinner, practicing more than any other in this dark act.

Now Magus would tap into those dark powers from before the Flood to raise up his Anti-Christ.

In their youth the Stag, the Sun, had been made to enter the earth, below; and so did the clumsy boy Arthur atop his sister. As Arthur lay dying, the symbolism was inverted, for the sun was *down,* and the moon climbing atop him in turn; the lesser light giving power and new life to the greater.

Morgaine used the mixture, the potion, in an effort to wake Arthur, that he might be conscious and able to perform. In his delirium she was again his *nocturnal lover, his visitor, for he too had been rehearsing this very moment for the whole of his life.*

"I do dream; the night hag doth come for my loins again," he mumbled, overcome and confused; words so forced and weak that only she could hear him.

"Hush, brother, 'tis no dream. This is why you favor the mask; don it now and hide, and I will come for thee." She comforted him, and did embrace his cheek, softly kissing her brother.

She too fitted the mask to her face. The moon responded, sending ethereal beams of moonlight through the fortress of glass. The beams burned through the mask, marking her with a crescent moon between her eyes. *The burn of the moon was more fierce than that of her male counterpart.* She let out a gasp, but the pain of it quickly abated.

The Primal Witch did speak the words of the Rite. The candles, fixed as a Faerie Star, sent lines of fire, a crosswork of red-hot flame. The flames did overcome the bed, causing it to vanish; a circle of flame encompassed the scorching star besides. Morgaine and Arthur lay in coitus on an altar of flames where the bed had once been, yet burned not.

The Maidens, filled with terror, held their positions, and the four winds did come; the rush roared with such force and noise that the six actors were as gladiators in amphitheater, deafened by cheers, by trumpets, by gusts.

BUT MORGAINE DID NOT LET THE ABUSE OWN HER; SHE OWNED IT.

There would be no sacred fornication, no incest, no dark carnal magick. All Arthur had to do was call out for the goddess thrice, and all would be set aright.

The potion rendered Arthur erect. He was disoriented, mostly blind save to shadows and forms, and felt his life slipping. And yet he was aroused by remedies.

Knowing that Magus could not see their congress through the cyclone of wind, nor approach the flaming star, she instructed her dying brother in his ruse. "You will go down, and I will bring you up again… pretend." She rolled her hips upon him and whispered once more, "Call upon me. I am here. Call upon me."

Four winds.

Seven candles to make one star.

The moon.

The sun.

The earth.

The stag.

The sword and cup!

"Now, bring me the king's sword!"

Another priestess braved the crackle and tempest, and did hand the Lady of Avalon the Sword of Power.

Here did Simon know he was to see it not ten and five feet away. The Cup of Christ! *What evils he had been empowered to unleash with this idol!*

Call forth for it she did.

"You are the sword," she said unto her brother below, holding Excalibur high with her right hand, brandishing it thrice.

"Morgana," he called, confused as ever. Fourteen again, only then with spear and no magical sword.

"I am the cup!" she cried, and the Primal Witch filled her eyes with pitch and blackened the crescent upon her brow. The markings upon her naked form were as embers; black, now orange, now white-hot, now black again.

"Morgana!" Again, as loud as his failing voice could muster.

"You are the sword of truth, I am the cup of communion. And we are One. Forget me not in the hereafter, and above all, forget not who YOU are!"

"Morgaine!" The words escaped, then were doubled: "Morgana, Morgana, Morgaine!" And now the three times three did he make, crying, "Morgana, Morgana, Morgaine!"

The Primal Goddess fully manifested, a power above four thousand years old. It changed neither countenance nor image of Gwyar, except the shadow it cast, being unnaturally tall, for it *was Gwyar.*

At the king's final utterance, the candles

burst and the flames collapsed on themselves; the whirling tempest abated and the comely bed returned. In this moment, the Morrigan whispered words to the Pendragon in the tongue of luminaries.

And Arthur died, his soul falling into the Underworld.

"Good!" Simon was most pleased. "He went quickly; you did not even have to mount him much." He laughed and laughed, not knowing that Morgaine had shifted their bodies, and that no untoward act had occurred.

"Now, Walles, utter those ancient words and bring him back." The Masked Man corrected himself: "*Them*."

"You failed." 'Twas Gwyar, but the voice was that of a thousand rushing waters and ten thousand cymbals. The voice of a goddess.

"But the Rite! I saw—" Magus possessed no fear of the Witch.

"You saw with ambition and desperate hope to immanentize the End of Days. The ritual put him in the netherworld. He sleeps, but you… you die!"

The Morrigan rushed upon Magus, but an angel intervened.

Epilogue

The fleet of Prince Madoc ap Meurig discovered a new land.

A land of plenty.

The streams teemed with plump, girthy fish, speckled with every color of the rainbow. So plentiful were they that they leapt into the fisherman's net or basket, giving themselves to the grateful recipients. Eagles ruled regal skies of crystal blue and vibrant yellows and purples; so clean was the atmosphere that the sailors were awed, believing the sky to be a looking-glass.

The forests featured pools and springs filled with species of silver otters and spotted badgers of a kind unfamiliar to the Cymru. These frolicked and played, but also sang during their labor, building dams and appearing to work in union and collaboration with the native inhabitants.

There were alligators and lizards too.

Moreover, a peculiar bovine, much larger than a bull - possessing a powerful head, little horns, and a body with a singular large hump that was otherwise *all barrel and chest* - roamed free, giddy and unafraid.

So vast and majestic was this *undiscovered country* that Madoc's mind arrived at two possible conclusions:

We perished at sea and this is heaven, or…

We have reached the edge of the world and, having breached the firmament, come to the Otherworld beyond.

A feathered red man approached the prince, and offered him shelter, and wheat for bread…

Author Profile

Author Zane Newitt is an internationally-recognized Arthurian scholar, folklorist and historian born on September 3rd, 1975 in Glenwood Springs, Colorado, USA.

A prolific writer, Dr Newitt published Volume One of the epic seven-volume *Arthuriad* saga in 2017, with ongoing plans for short poems, spin-offs and a Morgaine Trilogy to follow.

Dr. Newitt is known for reviving the 'Bardic Method' - a writing style that combines epic poetry, Welsh Nationalism, folklore, theology and history in a uniquely "druidesque" blend that conceals more than it reveals, as well as containing something to inspire and offend anyone... Just as Merlin would do.

Rowanvale Books

Publisher Information

Rowanvale Books provides publishing services to independent authors, writers and poets all over the globe. We deliver a personal, honest and efficient service that allows authors to see their work published, while remaining in control of the process and retaining their creativity. By making publishing services available to authors in a cost-effective and ethical way, we at Rowanvale Books hope to ensure that the local, national and international community benefits from a steady stream of good quality literature.

For more information about us, our authors or our publications, please get in touch.

www.rowanvalebooks.com
info@rowanvalebooks.com